Pauline Bentley was b........................
as a legal secretary an.....................where
she dreamed of being .... indulging her
passion for historical d.....a. Her first novel was
published in 1987. As a dedicated author she is
meticulous in her research and enjoys visiting historical sites and houses. She now writes full time,
and lives with her husband and two teenage
children in Sussex. She is also the author of *Rogues
and Players*, which is available from Headline.

Also by Pauline Bentley

Rogues and Players

Fallen Angels

Pauline Bentley

KNIGHT

First published in 1993
by HEADLINE BOOK PUBLISHING PLC

First published in paperback in 1993
by HEADLINE BOOK PUBLISHING PLC

This edition published 1997 by
Knight an imprint of Brockhampton Press

10 9 8 7 6 5 4 3 2 1

ISBN 1 86019 6306

Printed and bound in Great Britain by
Mackays of Chatham PLC, Chatham, Kent

Brockhampton Press
20 Bloomsbury Street
London
WC1B 3QA

For Alison and Stuart

PART I

Chapter One

Chichester, 1642
'Angels by name, devils by nature!' A Puritan matron whispered to her companion as Laurence and Thomas Angel rode past. 'Decent folks aren't safe in their beds when those rogues are in the city.'

Angel Rowan heard the derogatory comment about her uncle and cousin, and tossed back her sable hair, her green eyes sparkling. At fifteen she had the colouring of her Celtic ancestors and the striking sensual features of the wild-blooded Angel kin. On this occasion she curbed the withering setdown which sprang to her lips. There was a more urgent need which brought her on to the streets of Chichester.

A chill grey mist shrouded the city. Angel Rowan gave a cry of alarm, and leapt into a shop doorway between two bay windows, seconds before a speeding carriage would have crushed her. A muttered curse was hurled at her from the driver.

Angel shook a fist at him. 'Drunken sot! You'll kill someone, if you don't break your neck first.' She was not as delicate as her tall, slender figure suggested. Her crimson silk gown proclaimed her the daughter of a respectable architect. There was a set to her chin and a dangerous light in her eyes which warned anyone rash enough to challenge it that she would be a formidable adversary. Only when the safety of those she loved became threatened was her confidence edged with vulnerability.

Her sense of panic grew. Where was young Firkin? Her brother, with his frail strength and crippled foot, could never get out of the way if a carriage rode him down.

'Firkin!' she heard her elder brother Alexander call from the next street.

3

It was typical of Firkin to sneak out of the church as soon as the baptism service for their nephew Julian was over. He was restless, impatient of his ill-health and the cosseting of his family. Yet the disease which ate into his lungs had begun to waste his body. He was only eleven but there was a proud courage in the way he hid the blood-stained linen which each coughing fit produced. In recent months there had been a desperation to his restlessness. Firkin knew he was slowly dying.

During the last week, Angel's elder sister Maressa had travelled from her home in Arundel for the baptism of her child. Maressa fussed over Firkin, insisting he rest more, and forego his morning ride. Angel sympathised with her brother. She would hate so much fuss.

She hurried past the row of gabled, timber-framed houses. Their overhanging upper storeys shadowed the streets, and high walls hid courtyards and gardens. Angel paused to scan the road ahead. Through the thinning mist she saw the crown-shaped market-cross where the four main roads met. Behind the cross the high-spired cathedral dominated the city. The imposing structure demanded reverence and piety from the inhabitants of its diocese, but the cross was the city's true heartbeat. Beneath its arches citizens gathered as a favoured meeting-place. Today there were no pedlars with performing monkeys or fiddlers to distract a young boy, and Angel turned towards the cathedral. She was certain Firkin was within its precincts, either loitering amongst woodcarvers and stone masons, or watching the training militia. Despite his infirmity, Firkin possessed the traits of most of her family. He was artistic, headstrong and fearless, with a hunger for adventure.

Entering the cathedral grounds, Angel saw the militia drilling on the green. The pikemen with their long staves were bunched, chanting as they pushed their way through an imaginary army. Musketeers practised loading and firing their cumbersome firearms. The cavalry fought duels on horseback. Many, to Angel's amusement, spent more time trying to control their mounts than striking any blow to their opponent. None were skilled warriors, but there was a desperate gravity in their faces to improve their mastery of both horse and weapons. Soon their lives could

4

depend upon that prowess. Daily rumours spread that Parliament was gathering an army to fight the King.

There was still no sign of Firkin and Angel crossed to some outbuildings, where the sound of hammering told her the masons were at work. At her entrance Abe Jessop put down his chisel. His eyes were red-rimmed, and his mouth a scarlet slash against the grey powder which covered him from head to foot, making him look older than his thirty years.

'Good day, Miss Rowan.' His eyes sparkled with appreciation as he regarded her elegant gown. 'No longer Miss Rowan, for 'tis a woman you've become.' He put a hand to his heart and bowed. 'Good day, Mistress Rowan,' he corrected. 'If it's your brother you want, he's in the woodcarver's hut. May I be so bold as to say that you rival your sister, the fair Maressa, in your beauty?'

'You may not be so bold, Mr Jessop,' she answered crisply, unwilling to encourage his attentions. The man was a known philanderer.

Angel found Firkin in the woodcarver's workroom. His fair head was bent over a carving of a rearing stallion as he chiselled the final grooves into its flying mane. He stood in the shaft of light from the window, his lashes forming shadowy crescents upon transparently pale cheeks. He had the face of a cherub, but his will was as tempestuous as her own. At his birth, the midwife had exclaimed at his fair beauty, so unusual in the new-born. Later, Angel had overheard the woman speaking in an undertone to the cook. 'That babe is fey and too beautiful to be long for this earth.'

'That's a wicked thing to say!' Angel accused. Fists clenched, she threw herself against the midwife's large body. 'You take it back. You evil old crone. He's fair and beautiful like Maressa. Like our mother.'

The midwife looked down at her sadly. 'There's nothing fey about you, little spitfire. With your black hair and dark skin, anyone would take you for a gypsy wench.'

''Tis my Celtic blood,' Angel answered, proud and defiant.

The memory brought a mistiness to Angel's eyes. She did not want to think of a life without Firkin. Forgetting to

5

rebuke him for running off, she said, 'That's a beautiful carving. You've captured the perfection of our Rowan horses.'

'Aye, the lad has a talent rare in one so young,' commented the gruff-voiced Master. He stopped his work on a large crucifix. 'The Bishop wants him to carve a lectern in the shape of an eagle.'

'You're honoured, Firkin,' Angel said with pride. 'A commission from the bishop, no less.'

Firkin shrugged aside the praise and studied his work with a critical eye. 'Do you think Grandpapa will like it?' he said with the single-mindedness of the young. 'I'm to have a gelding for my birthday this year.'

'So this gift is a tactful reminder. You'll not be twelve for another three months.' Angel laughed and clasped his shoulder.

Emrys Rowan, called Firkin by his brother and sisters for being the fourth born, jerked away from Angel's touch. 'Don't treat me like a child. This is for Grandpapa because he doesn't treat me like a sickly cripple.' His face lost its cherubic softness and his green eyes became fierce. 'I hate the way Maressa fusses over me. She's told Papa I mustn't ride. Why doesn't she nail me in my coffin now? I might as well be dead if I can't do any of the things I like.'

'Firkin, don't talk that way!' Her voice harshened with fear. 'Maressa loves you. You're not strong.'

He glowered rebelliously, but in his eyes she saw the stark fear which haunted him – to die without knowing what it was like to have truly lived. 'Wasn't Maressa ever young?'

Angel laughed, preferring to tease than to patronise him. 'Maressa was a perfect child. And when did Alex or I ever treat you as a cripple? Maressa fusses over me just as much as she does you. She sees it as her duty.'

Firkin sighed. 'She's only eighteen, just three years older than you, yet she acts like a middle-aged matron.'

'Perhaps that's what marriage does to you . . . Ages you before your time? Come, let's return to the house. You were supposed to help me find the stage props for when we perform Gabriellen's play.'

'Goodwife Bundy says we mustn't call her that. It must be Grandmama.'

6

'Not if Gabriellen says otherwise. She hates to be called Grandmama – says it makes her feel ancient.'

'Then I shall call her Gabriellen as well!' Firkin picked up a piece of sacking and carefully wrapped it around his finished carving.

'This is where you got to?' A deep voice came from behind them.

Alexander Rowan leaned against the open door, his tall figure dominating the room. Removing his hat, he bent his head to avoid contact with the low ceiling, his long waving black hair falling forward over the wide lace collar which emphasised his swarthy complexion. 'Uncle Laurence and cousin Thomas have just arrived, which has ruffled old Bundy's feathers. Gabriellen invited her brother down from London. You know how she disapproves of our black sheep.'

'Sometimes I think Goody Bundy disapproves of all of us, except for Papa and Maressa,' Angel sighed. 'Still, I suppose we've led her a merry dance since she became our house-keeper after Mama died.'

Alexander studied his sister. Four days ago he had returned to Chichester after a three year Grand Tour of the Continent. Every time he saw Angel, her dark beauty startled him. He still visualised her as the plump, over-boisterous girl he had left behind. She had changed in a way which both delighted and filled him with misgivings. At twenty-one he had known many beautiful women, selecting those of fire and passion to make his own. He had not expected to find his little sister blossomed into such an exotic creature. The plumpness and awkwardness had gone. Her oval face with its high cheekbones and green, almond-shaped eyes was bewitching. When her mouth curved into a smile, her full lips betrayed the sensuality of the woman she would soon become.

'Alex, you're looking at me strangely?' she queried. 'Have I done something wrong?'

'No,' he said, grinning at her innocence. When he did not elaborate, she lifted a dark-winged brow, her eyes sparkling with humour. Again, he was struck by the grace of her tall figure. Her beauty was commanding, almost pagan, enhancing the wildness of her spirit. Angel was one of those rare women that few would be able to resist. From an early age Angel had shown a headstrong nature and an uncanny ability

7

to take care of herself. He brushed some sawdust from the gold braid on his red doublet. The expanse of white lace falling back from his wrist showed skin darkened from hours spent in the open. 'Are you ready to leave?'

'How could I resist such a handsome escort?' Angel teased. She was still puzzled by Alexander's expression. Since his return there were haunted shadows in his eyes. Alex never spoke of his last year on the Continent, when he had fought as a mercenary for the King of Sweden, but she guessed it had left lasting scars upon his mind.

She linked arms with both her brothers. 'Let us return to the affray. For affray this week will be. Our family have gathered to celebrate the birth of Maressa's son Julian, the first born of a new generation, and any gathering of Rowans and Angels under one roof is bound to produce fireworks!'

The mist had lifted as the trio regained the street. A crowd had gathered around the market-cross. Men spilled out of the taverns and galleried inns, their voices harsh with expectancy as the Mayor, Robert Exton, approached on horseback. He dismounted at the cross as Angel and her brothers drew level with the assembly, opened a parchment roll and began to read. Angel was too far away to catch all the words, but it was a proclamation by the King against the ordinance in which Parliament had established its own army.

A rumble of angry voices greeted the proclamation and the atmosphere sparked with tension. A scuffle broke out between two apprentices. The crowd surged back, almost knocking Firkin off his feet, and several men joined the brawl, shouting insults against the King.

'Let's get away from here,' Alexander commanded.

Firkin was forced to break into an ungainly shuffle, his lame leg dragging as Alexander quickened their pace. They were jostled by several labourers brandishing staves and eager to join the fight.

'It's beginning,' Alexander said bleakly. 'Soon there'll be more than street brawls between supporters of Parliament and the King, unless sanity returns to this accursed country. God save us from this madness.'

The dining parlour glowed amber from the lighted chandeliers suspended above the long table. The gaiety faded from the eyes of the people and the atmosphere was loaded with emotion. During the meal the conversation had turned to Exton's speech at the cross, and the family harmony was broken. Men's voices were raised in dissent.

Angel studied her relatives. Across the table, her sister Maressa, her golden-haired beauty heightened by her pallor, clutched at the arm of her husband, Sir Henry Mortimer. Uncle Ambrose, her father's eldest brother, was seated beside her grandparents, Gabriellen and Mark Rowan. At the far end, Alexander argued with their cousin Thomas Angel, who was stabbing at the air with his table knife. Next to Thomas, Uncle Laurence tipped back his chair and, catching Angel's gaze, winked at her. Angel smiled. Rogue her uncle might be, but she refused to believe that he was as wicked as people proclaimed. Of all her uncles, Laurence – the most disreputable – was her favourite.

The conversation grew heated, until Laurence Angel banged down his wine goblet, pounding the table to emphasise each word. 'A man must follow the dictates of his conscience. I tell you it will come to war. When we left London three days ago, the citizens were digging trenches and placing chains and barricades across the streets to ensure King Charles does not re-enter the capital.' Pearls of sweat shone on the bald dome of Laurence's head as his agitation mounted, and he sat back, wiping a finger across his narrow grey moustache and pointed beard.

A charged silence following the heated words was broken by the rustle of the stiffening wind, which billowed the heavy tapestries, and caused the candles and oil cressets to flicker. A maidservant hurried to close the shutters over the windows.

Angel's stomach contracted with foreboding. There had been talk of the King's dispute with Parliament for months. Since his Majesty, accompanied by guards, had entered Parliament House to arrest five of its members on charges of treason, events had spread like a heathfire. Armed bands declared themselves in support of Parliament. Queen Henrietta departed for the Continent, ostensibly to attend her daughter's wedding to the Dutch Prince William, but many believed she had gone to pawn the crown jewels, in order to raise money for a Royalist army. Parliament responded by taking control of the trained bands of citizen militia and of forts and arsenals. The King and his court left the troubled capital for York.

Angel chewed her lower lip, concerned by the possibility of civil war. When her grandfather, Mark Rowan, leaned forward to speak, everyone's attention was turned upon him. Although his once black hair was white as ermine, his wiry figure, refined from long hours of training the famous Rowan strain of horses, bore little testament to his seventy-seven years. Fifty years ago he had been an agent in the service of Elizabeth Tudor and, as such, had prevented several assassination attempts on the Queen's life. His Roman nose, high brow and rugged features were handed down to all the male members of his family. The black eyes snapping across at his brother-in-law were bright with censure.

'I will hear no more talk of treason,' Mark pronounced with a scathing quietness, which retained the lilting cadence of his Welsh blood. 'When the King was refused entry into Hull, where the armoury had been assembled for war with the Scots, it was a direct act of hostility against the Crown. In Queen Elizabeth's day, it would have led to the governor being hanged from his own gatehouse.'

'With respect, sir,' Angel's father, Llewelyn interjected. 'The King will no longer listen to reason. The Queen incites him to rule by Divine Right without Parliament. The rights of the people are in jeopardy. For twelve years King Charles dissolved Parliament, and only recalled its members because of the threatened war with Scotland. Would you see that happen again? The treasury is empty. The Scots are pillaging along our borders. To appease his magnates the King has enclosed the common land. The fundamental rights of the people are abused by such tyranny.'

'Even so, Wyn, he is our sovereign,' Mark answered his youngest son.

Angel chaffed to voice her opinion. It was not the place of a fifteen-year-old girl to talk politics at the table. She hated injustice levied upon the common people. Though she believed that King Charles's faith in the Divine Right of the monarchy had been carried to the extreme, she remained fiercely loyal to her sovereign.

'The King is a tyrant!' Thomas Angel addressed them. He was a handsome man in his mid-twenties. He pushed a hand

10

through his long, fair hair. His wine-flushed cheeks and pale lashes made him look as uncompromising as the marauding Viking he resembled. 'By dissolving Parliament the King would put himself above the law,' Thomas continued. 'He's weak. If a man cannot govern his wife – who would make papists of us all – what chance has England? It's time the King was made to see reason.'

'Not by taking up arms against him.' Alexander leaned towards Thomas. It was rare that he allowed his temper to get the better of him. 'Civil war is evil,' he said contemptuously, strength of purpose evident in the set of his clean-shaven face. 'No one escapes it unscathed. It tears families apart, and plunders and ravishes the land we proclaim to revere. It brings out the darkest side of all men, corrupting and defiling everything it touches. Decency is forgotten as it generates hatred and persecution.'

Angel could no longer keep silent. 'King Charles has made mistakes, but our loyalty must be to him. Does Parliament rule by the will of the people? Or are they governed by their Puritan leaders?' She rounded on Thomas, her eyes flashing, discretion forgotten in her outrage that he should speak against the King. 'Have you not more than most to lose, Cousin? Has not Nell Lovegood's gaming house, owned by yourself, been closed by order of Parliament?'

There was a shocked gasp from Maressa, and what sounded like a hastily stifled snort of amusement from both Gabriellen and Laurence. But Angel was too incensed to be curbed. She jumped to her feet with such force her chair fell over. 'If you're against the King, Thomas, then I'll not sit at the same table as a traitor.'

Thomas stood to face her outrage, and at the amusement in his eyes, her anger rose. He threw back his head and gave a deep rumbling laugh. 'If it comes to a fight I'll come out for the King.' His eyes sparkled and, driven by the demon which possessed all of their name, he taunted, 'Nell Lovegood's was not closed. Since you mention the subject, Nell's has been in our family for generations. It was always more than a gaming house.'

'Thomas, this is not a subject to be discussed at table,' Laurence remonstrated.

'Why not? Does not our family pride itself on its lack of

hypocrisy? Nell's was your inheritance, Father. For many years Gabriellen ensured that its revenue was safeguarded for you. Our great-grandfather, Esmond Angel, was no saint. Whilst we glory in his acclaim as a great playwright, the money from Nell's kept him out of debtors' prison many a time. It's part of our family history.' He turned to Angel. 'The services Nell's provides are too popular with the bigots who govern for us to be closed down. They may shut the playhouses but not the bordellos.'

Mark Rowan interrupted. 'Good manners forbid such business is discussed before the ladies.'

Thomas shrugged. 'Angel, you defend your sovereign passionately. To aid our victory, do you intend to sit at home, hands clasped in pious prayer like all women? Surely not. You've a spirit which will not rest until you stand, sword raised against the King's enemies.'

He was deliberately goading her. Resting her knuckles on the table, Angel glared into Thomas's grinning face. 'I'll do whatever is in my power to aid the King's cause.'

He raised a goblet in salute to her and Angel's anger cooled. Thomas Angel had always intrigued her. She knew he had been imprisoned several times for brawling, even charged with murder once.

'And I'll be with the King, too,' Firkin piped up, his face glowing with excitement. 'I'll be a drummer boy, and the army will march to my beat.'

'Aye, lad, that's the spirit,' Thomas encouraged.

There was a cry of horror from Goodwife Bundy who was supervising the clearing of dishes from the table. Massive arms folded over a vast bosom, she faced Llewelyn. 'Mr Rowan, I've spent eight years in your household. My duty was clear, and I've spared nothing in the godly rearing of your children. I'll not stand by in silence whilst that man gives Emrys and Angel foolhardy ideas. Relative or not, such a man has no place in a decent household.'

'You forget your place, Goodwife,' Llewelyn said sharply. 'You have served my family well, but I'll not have a guest spoken to in that way.'

The rebuke drained the colour from Goodwife Bundy's face. She could be a tyrant when Llewelyn was from home, and his work as an architect often took him away for weeks at a time. She was a good woman, if narrow-minded. In recent years Angel suspected that Bundy was in love with Llewelyn. She was equally certain that her father had no amorous interest in the housekeeper. She doubted there was need. At a year less than forty, Llewelyn was still a handsome man. His dark eyes were always merry and that triangular face, with its black moustache and small beard worn in the style of their King, would be irresistible to many women. Though his hair had begun to thin at the temples there was only a speckling of grey amongst the long black locks.

Maressa rose and went to the housekeeper. Placing an arm around her shoulders, she glared at her cousin. 'Thomas, how could you be so mean-spirited? And Angel is just as bad. We're supposed to be celebrating Julian's birth. You've spoilt it with talk of war. Have you no sense of decency?'

Thomas bristled, but a frown from Laurence silenced him.

Gabriellen Rowan stood up to face her family. The height of an average man, her slender figure was a commanding sight. Despite her seventy-one years, the softening candlelight on her high cheekbones and full mouth gave her the appearance of a woman in her prime.

'Maressa is right. There'll be no more talk of war today.' Her green eyes flashed a warning that her family would be ill served to disobey her wishes. 'We are here to celebrate the birth of Maressa's first child. Four generations of the Rowan and Angel families are present in this house today. Could we not for once be united in peace and harmony?'

Maressa returned to her place, hiding her chagrin that it was Gabriellen and not Sir Henry who had reminded the family of their reason for celebration.

'Thank you, Grandmama,' Maressa said sweetly and signalled to a maid to replenish the wine flagons.

Gabriellen looked sternly at Laurence for introducing the subject of impending war. Maressa was surprised that her uncle flushed under her scrutiny. Somehow, she had expected a fierce retaliation from a man of his reputation. She shared Bundy's censure of Laurence and Thomas Angel. It was not often they joined the family gathering, and clearly, from Thomas's speech, they were both disreputable rogues.

The gaiety had gone from the feast, and Maressa was relieved when her father stood up and announced, 'We have a surprise for you, Mama.'

Uncle Ambrose rose, saying, 'In the tradition of our family, the entertainment is to be a play. The new Angel Players will perform Gabriellen's greatest play, *Boudicca*, for your pleasure.' Ambrose's long, grey-streaked tawny hair fell forward to curtain his face as he bowed to his mother.

'You do indeed pay me honour,' Gabriellen responded warmly, and she sat back in her chair as her family went to prepare for the play. As her gaze lifted to the low ceiling, Gabriellen frowned. The upper storey had not been there when she had lived here as a girl. This house had been her inheritance from her aunt and uncle. They had raised her whilst her father, Esmond Angel, travelled across England with his strolling players. She, in turn, had given it to Wyn when he married, and came south to pursue his fortune as an architect. Even though the notched and bolted timbers which supported the new upper floor had been salvaged from an old ship and carried the tang of the sea, she did not approve of the ceiling. She preferred the openness of the old parlour which had soared to the rafters.

When Ambrose returned to deliver the opening lines of the prologue, Gabriellen turned to her husband. Mark smiled and took her hand.

'Forty years we've been married,' he said. 'How quickly they've passed. Yet I still go cold when I remember how you faced imprisonment and I almost lost you. Those were dangerous days when the Queen took exception to this very play.'

Gabriellen smiled at the memory. 'Your eloquence saved me, when you spoke to Her Majesty in my defence. The years before our marriage were dangerous and turbulent.' Watching her family enact the words she had written so long ago, her expression became serious. 'There is uncertainty ahead. Soon Ambrose, Wyn and Alex will join the King's army. Maressa will always be level-headed, but as for Angel . . . I fear for her. The girl is headstrong and capable of doing something foolish.'

'Angel has your spirit, my dear.' Mark's dark eyes crinkled with affection. 'Like you, she will survive adversity. She's a fighter.'

Gabriellen watched Angel, who was throwing herself passionately into her role. Angel was a natural actress as Gabriellen had once been. Not that Gabriellen had been

14

allowed to take credit for her talent, either as an actress or as a playwright. She quelled the stab of frustration which still had the power to rankle. For years when her father's sight was failing she had managed the acting troupe, and had faced antagonism and prejudice with every command. Even the highly acclaimed plays she had written, some of them still popular, were all performed under her father's name. And prejudice against her sex had not changed. The playhouse remained the domain of men, and they guarded it jealously. The situation was changing on the Continent, where women were appearing on the French stage. Unfortunately, they were considered no better than trollops. Such injustice angered Gabriellen. Her younger years had been hampered by the constraints of her sex, and she hoped that lif*r* would be more tolerant towards the strong-willed Angel.

Whilst Angel's natural talent shone through with each line she spoke, Gabriellen noted that Maressa lacked the inner sparkle so endearing in her sister. There was a calculated precision in everything Maressa did. She was too eager to please, too concerned with being the perfect daughter and wife. At eighteen Maressa was an acknowledged beauty. Her skin was unblemished and smooth as the petals of a white rose. Her thick gold hair shone with reddish tints in the sunlight, and her graceful figure was full-bosomed and slender-waisted. More than a score of suitors had clamoured for her hand in marriage. All had been dallied with and left in eager anticipation until Sir Henry Mortimer paid court to her. The young baronet had inherited a title only. The estate had been sold by his father to pay his gambling debts, before he had shot himself, shamed by the disgrace.

Mortimer was too filled with his own self-importance, in Gabriellen's opinion. There was something about his manner which she did not trust. His charm was false and she suspected that he had a roving eye. How would Maressa regard his infidelity? Would the true character of her granddaughter surface and crack that saintly exterior?

Gabriellen suspected that it would. Occasionally, when Maressa thought herself unobserved, Gabriellen had caught an expression in her eyes which belied all that humility and sweetness.

There was a rustle of starched petticoats as Goodwife

Bundy came to stand behind Gabriellen's chair.

'Doesn't Maressa make a splendid Boudicca?' the house-keeper praised. 'Such a good and dutiful woman. Never a day's worry I've had over her.' She sighed, then frowned. 'I wish I could say the same for Angel. She insisted on taking the part of the captain of the guard, but look at her, wielding that sword against Alexander. And she's dressed in doublet and breeches. Such a hoyden. I've done my best to curb her wildness. Mr Rowan is too soft with her. A whipping is what the girl needs, but he'll not hear of it.'

'For that I'm grateful,' Gabriellen said emphatically. 'Angel knows right from wrong. That's what's important.'

The housekeeper sniffed her disapproval, but Gabriellen did not comment. She knew that Goodwife Bundy cared for Wyn's children, and her infatuation for Wyn was obvious, not that her son noticed. Neither a woman as strait-laced as Bundy, nor the beautiful but frivolous Marie, the mistress he had set up in a lace and ribbon shop near the market-cross, could tempt him into marriage. Why should it? Between Bundy and Marie, Wyn had provided himself with the perfect domestic arrangement.

Gabriellen raised an eyebrow at Angel's performance. Her granddaughter had added to her part in the play, and the new lines were the equal of any she could have written.

As the play continued Gabriellen remembered the days when she had lived with her father's players. So great had become Esmond Angel's fame that their patron, Lord Min-cham, had built a playhouse on Bankside for his troupe and named it "The Angel". The playhouse no longer existed. It had burned down whilst Esmond and his mistress Nan Woodruff were inside. Nan had been Laurence's mother, and Gabriellen had raised her half-brother, fifteen years her junior, along with her own children. That was before she had married Mark Rowan.

She looked across at her two sons. Ambrose sat on the side of the stage area, acting as bookholder and prompter. Wyn was playing the part of the Roman governor of Britain. Apart from her sons, she had also borne two daughters and it saddened her that they were not here. For many years before she married Mark, she had been the mistress of the buccaneer Sir Jack Stoneham. He had fathered her daughters.

16

Sadly, Jacquetta, the elder, had been drowned whilst on a voyage to visit Jack in the West Indies. He had made his home there after his part in the failed Earl of Essex rebellion. The younger, Sabine, now lived in France.

Gabriellen applauded as the scene ended. A chord was struck upon a guitar and Firkin limped on to the stage. He was dressed as a troubadour in striped parti-hose and sang a ballad of gallantry and daring. Mark went to stand by his grandson and joined in the song. When Mark returned to her side she addressed him by his full name, mimicking the lilt of Wales, 'Ah, Marcus Emrys Llewellyn, there's proud you must be of your grandson. He has the voice and a way with the music of his Welsh forefathers.'

Her hand was squeezed by her husband. After their marriage she had never missed the excitement of her life with the players, for living with Mark in the Vale of Clwyd had brought her love and fulfilment. From his beginnings as a stallion-man travelling to the country fairs, he had built up a bloodline of horses which were amongst the most sought-after in the country.

A shriek from the stage drew Gabriellen's attention back to the play. Maressa, as Boudicca, Queen of the Iceni, had played out the death scene and now lay prone upon the floor. Angel improvised yet another sword fight against Alexander, and Gabriellen was amused to see that he needed all his skill to keep his sister at bay. Angel was an accomplished swordswoman, her speed undermined only by her brother's superior strength.

Angel was forced into retreat. Her spurs caught in the hem of Maressa's gown, and she stumbled. Alexander's sword flashed, knocking Angel's weapon from her hand. Following this with a lunge, he supposedly impaled Angel with a stab through the heart. Angel sank to her knees and fell across the corpse of Boudicca. There was a stifled groan from Maressa.

'Sssh, don't make a fuss,' Angel hissed. 'You'll ruin the scene. I've got my spur caught in the lace of your gown.'

Ambrose returned to speak the epilogue. 'Boudicca is dead, but her spirit lives on. The spirit of a free Britain.'

As Angel lay on the floor, her heart stirred. If there was conflict between the King and Parliament, she would not shirk the fight. She would be another Boudicca – indomitable,

17

refusing to be cowed by the conventions laid down by men, a warrior whose sword was at the command of the King.

As she listened, Gabriellen felt her body grow cold. Memories haunted her. When the play had first been performed at Court, it had earned Queen Elizabeth's wrath. Her Majesty had seen those final words as incitement to insurrection on the eve of the Earl of Essex's rebellion. Now the words seemed pertinent to yet another rebellion pulsating through the hearts and minds of once loyal, honest Englishmen.

'A splendid performance and a wonderful surprise,' she said, dismissing her foreboding as the actors came forward to take their bows. Maressa was looking pale and strained. Since these celebrations were in her honour, Gabriellen embraced her first. 'You were superb as Boudicca, but I doubt that stoic warrior queen could match you in grace and beauty.'

She turned to Alexander, who was standing with his arm around Angel's shoulders. Bowing his head, he whispered in his sister's ear, and received a cuff on his shoulder for his pains.

'Alex, you brought my heart to my mouth with your fight scenes.' Gabriellen assumed a sterner expression. 'Though from the number of times Ambrose had to prompt you with your lines, you'll never make an actor.'

'Then 'tis as well I've no such yearnings,' Alexander returned.

Gabriellen looked at him expectantly. 'Has Ambrose spoken to you about your future?'

'Yes. I'm delighted to accept his proposal that I live at Rowan Hall and eventually take over the stud farm.'

Gabriellen embraced him warmly. 'Mark will be delighted. It means a lot to him that the Rowan strain continues. Ambrose vowed never to remarry after the death of his wife in childbirth. They had waited fifteen years for a child. The double loss devastated him.'

From the corner of her eye, she saw Angel watching her with an expectant look. Speaking softly, so as not to upset Maressa, she said, 'Many players would envy your natural talent. Unintentionally, you stole every scene from your sister. And the additional dialogue was equal to anything I,

18

or Esmond Angel, could have written.'

'You liked my speech!' Angel's eyes shone and her face was radiant in her excitement. 'Do you really think I have talent as a playwright?'

'Yes, but it's a profession which is frowned upon for a woman.'

There was a theatrical wince from Maressa as she limped to her husband's side.

'My dear, you're hurt.' Sir Henry Mortimer swept her up into his arms and carried her to the settle before the fireplace.

'Please, Henry, put me down,' Maressa implored with a light laugh. 'It's just a scratch – a trifling accident.'

Henry lowered Maressa on to the settle, his manner attentive and adoring. They made a striking couple. Henry with his corn-gold hair, aristocratic bearing and smooth classical looks, was saved from appearing too feminine in his features by his darker moustache and small beard.

'There's blood on your stocking,' he cried out.

Judith Bundy hurried to Maressa's side. 'You're hurt. There's a gash on your ankle. It must be tended to at once. This is all Angel's fault! She can be so thoughtless and awkward.'

'Angel was not to blame.' Maressa looked across at her sister, who had grown pale. 'She played her part perhaps a little too enthusiastically. Please, I want no fuss. 'Tis but a scratch.'

'Maressa, I'm sorry. Why must I be so clumsy?' Angel was contrite, though she could see the wound was not deep. 'It won't stop you from dancing tonight, will it?'

'Of course she cannot dance!' Judith rounded on Angel. 'You've nearly crippled her.'

Angel was hurt by the coldness of her tone.

'It was an accident,' Gabriellen said pointedly.

Maressa flushed becomingly. 'All this fuss over a scratch. Being unable to dance for one evening is not so terrible. My joy is all in Julian.' Her gaze went to the cradle by the fireplace, where her son slept. 'I insist no one curbs their own enjoyment.'

'Maressa puts us all to shame,' Judith declared. 'Was ever a woman more generous of spirit?'

Sir Henry Mortimer raised his wife's hand to his lips. 'I

shall sit by your side all evening. And perhaps if you're not overtired, you will sing to us. There's no sweeter voice in all England.'

'Of course I shall sing – but you must enjoy the dancing, Henry.' Maressa's eyes sparkled at her husband's praise. 'Since it's Angel's fault that I cannot dance, she must partner you.'

Sir Henry bowed to Angel, a speculative look flashing in his blue eyes.

'Then he had better look to his toes,' Alexander quipped.

Angel, ashamed of the carelessness which had injured her sister, walked away. She envied Maressa's tranquillity; her own temper and impetuousness were her greatest enemies, making her incautious and reckless. Her arm was taken by Alexander. Though Angel was a handspan taller than most women, at six foot Alexander still topped her by three inches.

'Don't look so downhearted,' he said. 'It was an accident, and not very serious at that.' He nodded to the settle where the family had formed an admiring circle around Maressa. 'Our sister may miss tonight's dancing, but she'll be assured of everyone's sympathy and attention. That will please her.'

'Alex, that's not fair,' Angel protested. 'Everybody adores Maressa. And not just because she's beautiful. She's the sweetest, kindest person I know. I wish I was more like her.'

Alexander tweaked one of her sable curls beneath her wide-brimmed hat. There was no guile in Angel's eyes and he had never known her to be other than honest. Within her steady, often disconcerting, gaze there was a strength of purpose. The intelligent brightness beneath those long shadowing lashes proclaimed an agility of wit and a craving to taste all life could offer. Yet an independent mind and spirit was thought unseemly in a woman. It had led to near disastrous misadventures for their grandmother.

As he looked down at Angel, her mouth parted in a taunting smile which was so often impossible for her to contain.

'Don't ever change, Dusty.' He used his pet name for her, earned in her childhood scrapes, when she was always covered in dust or grime. 'Sometimes Maressa is too good to be true. It can be somewhat wearing for us lesser mortals.' His grin broadened as his gaze flicked over her man's attire. 'Your charm is your unpredictability, Dusty.'

20

Angel's eyes sparkled at this unexpected compliment. Alexander saw her pleasure and could not resist adding, 'A pity about your temper, though. That's enough to try the patience of a saint.' He whirled away from her and strode across the hall.

With an outraged yelp Angel ran after him. She snatched her hat from her hair and whacked him across the shoulder. 'I don't have a temper, Alex. It's you! You're such a rat at times. You provoke me.'

He chuckled. 'And I succeed every time.' He frowned as he looked at her clothing. 'Confound it, Dusty, you're too old to dress as a lad. In that outfit every lecher in the country will be panting after you.'

'They'd feel the edge of my sword if they did!' she retorted fiercely. 'For a time in the stage-fight just now I had you on the defensive.'

'Nonsense.' His defiant tone told Angel she had spoken true. 'I was just humouring you.'

He drew his sword and before she could unsheath her own, dealt her a playful swipe across her behind with the flat of the blade. Then, ducking to avoid a second blow from her hat, he abandoned the dignity of his twenty-one years and ran laughing towards the stables. Angel pursued him, intent upon retribution.

Goodwife Bundy shuddered as she watched Angel's antics through the window. 'Why can't Angel be more like Maressa? The girl is a sore trial. I never know what mischief she'll get into next.'

'Don't judge Angel too harshly,' Gabriellen said from behind her. 'She's impetuous and less ladylike than you would wish, but she has a good heart.'

'That I don't dispute. Her heart is too generous.' Looking over her shoulder to ensure they were not overheard, Goodwife Bundy lowered her voice to an outraged whisper. 'I caught her kissing the stableboy last week. She's a born coquette. No good can come of such waywardness.'

'Angel is not wanton. She has a joy of life which makes her exuberant. Unfortunately, it's a family trait. It's the Angel blood. Bad blood, it was named once. I'd call it an independent mind and the will to survive, whatever the odds.'

21

Goodwife Bundy glared across to where Laurence was stroking the thigh of a serving maid while she filled his goblet with mulled wine, and clicked her tongue. 'Rogue's blood, that's what it is. Those Angel kinfolk bring shame to Mr Rowan's name. Twice Laurence has been imprisoned at Newgate.'

'And each time he left a free man, the charges against him withdrawn. It's not your place to spread gossip about your master's family.' Gabriellen defended her half-brother with unusual sternness. Her family name had been blackened by malicious gossip too often for her to let it pass unchallenged. Though, indeed, there was much within their background to substantiate those rumours, and Laurence made no secret of his links with the rogues and felons of the London Und rworld.

Gabriellen looked at Maressa. Angel had returned to stand behind her sister. To soften her reprimand, she added, 'The girls are a credit to you, and a perfect foil for each other. Maressa – petite, golden-haired and beautiful, full of grace and so sweet-tempered, whilst Angel . . . tall, exotic with her dark hair and olive skin, a vivacious firebrand, her joy of life is infectious.'

'Some would call it wanton,' Goodwife Bundy groaned. 'It's time she married.'

Gabriellen shook her head, her voice crisp with warning. 'Marriage is not the solution.'

'Of course the girl must marry,' the housekeeper declared. 'All the better if no romantic nonsense is involved. What Angel needs is a mature man. A man she can respect and who can provide her with a secure future. The silversmith Elias Johnson has spoken to Mr Rowan.'

'Not that old man who sat next to Angel in church this morning?'

'Mr Johnson is not old,' Judith protested. 'He's forty – scarcely older than Mr Rowan himself. A widower and eminently wealthy. He has a sober disposition which will bring Angel to heel.'

Gabriellen shook her head. 'Then you do not know your charge. If she's not allowed to wed where her heart wills, it will become a prison. Then I'd fear for the consequences.'

* * *

The dark solitude of the garden beckoned Angel. She ran away from the house as though a satyr pursued her. Through the open windows, candle-lights shone and the music carried to her from the courtyard. Sounds of laughter mocked her distress. Her heart was aching. Her conscience would give her no ease. She had never felt so wretched. And it had all happened so quickly – the events which had pitched her mind into turmoil.

She had been enjoying the dancing, then her life had changed. All it had taken was a squeeze of a hand, a warm caress of breath against her cheek. She had gazed into a man's admiring eyes. His look became heavy-lidded, beguiling, hungering – offering a forbidden promise . . .

Angel ran on. How could it have happened? She was in love, and its flames blazed through her like a comet. It seared her soul, tormenting her with anguish.

She had been dancing for two hours, her body flushed with pleasure, her witty comments making her partners hold their sides with laughter. Intoxicated by her success, she experienced the power of her womanhood for the first time, and the fascination it could wield over men. The sense of exhilaration was dangerous.

The exertions of the dancing had made her thirsty and she had drunk deeply of the wine – too deeply. During the next country reel her head seemed to float, and her laughter escaped her control. Vanity was not in Angel's nature. She had no illusions that she would ever be as beautiful as her sister. When donning her ruby velvet gown trimmed with silver lace that evening, she had studied her reflection before the long Venetian looking-glass. She had judged herself no more than attractive. Her cheekbones were high and prominent, her black hair drawn up and curled into ringlets each side of her face. Did not Grandpapa call her his 'gypsy vagabond'? And because she was too restless to be caged within the house, the sun had darkened her skin so that she could pass for a Spaniard. To her artistic mind her olive skin heightened the intensity of her green eyes. Grandpapa was right. She did look like a gypsy vagabond, and in her soul there was a wildness which sometimes made her feel like one.

Throughout the dancing she was unimpressed by the compliments paid to her, and laughingly turned them aside. She did not care that some of their guests frowned at her behaviour. When two of the matrons snubbed Thomas Angel, deriding him for a common rogue, her family loyalty made her seek out her cousin. For the next two dances she flirted with him outrageously. But it was not Tom who had captured her heart.

She danced on, unheeding of the opening jaws of a trap. The lure was there in the pressure of her partner's hand upon her waist. A smouldering look was all it had taken. Those treacherous jaws snapped shut, binding her fast. Her heart was stolen by a man forever denied her – her sister's husband, Sir Henry Mortimer.

Hᵉ had acknowledged her conquest with a wicked smile. The dance over, Angel had torn herself from his hold. Now she stumbled through the moonlit orchard to the rose arbour and flung herself down on a stone seat. She leaned her head against the flintstone wall.

Traitorously, her body ached for Henry to take her into his arms. She fought to master her emotions, cursing the indiscretion which had shown her the pleasure a man's touch could arouse. Until recently her only experience, even of a kiss, had been when Thomas Angel had caught her on the darkened stairs last Christmas and initiated her into its delights. Since then, curious to experiment further she had provoked Ben the groom into kissing her. Ben was twenty and darkly handsome. Angel came upon him early one morning when he was stripped to the waist and washing at the pump. Her gaze was drawn to the droplets of water running down his face on to his naked torso. The sight of his broad shoulders and defined muscles had stirred her strangely. For weeks she had been aware of the way Ben watched her. When she discovered the stableyard was deserted, she smiled at him before sauntering into the tackroom.

She was not surprised when Ben followed. Neither did she protest when he caught her in his arms. His hands had sought her breasts through the fabric of her high-necked morning gown, and her pulses had leapt to the thrill of his touch. When he bunched up her skirts to caress her thigh, she had been unable to stop a moan of pleasure. Her body tingled with a delicious urgency to experience more of the pleasure a man's touch could evoke, and she moved closer to his hard

24

frame. When she felt the evidence of his desire against her leg she felt no shock or fear. But, as exhilarating as his kisses were, she did not care for Ben in the way a woman should care for a man to allow him such liberties. The realisation was like a dousing of icy water over her senses. She broke free and stepped back. When he moved towards her, her hand came up, her voice cold.

'No, Ben. I was wrong to come in here. There can never be anything between us.'

''Taint right to tease a man that way,' he said gruffly.

She was appalled at what she had done. 'I didn't mean to tease you.'

He eyed her thoughtfully. ''Appen you didn't. You don't know the power behind the promise in your eyes. God knows you're a filly to tempt a man to lose his reason. If I didn't know you for a maid, 'twould be different.'

He leaned back against the wall and folded his arms across his chest. 'I've never needed to take a woman against her will. There's many would say you had it coming.' There was nothing menacing about his stance, but his words bit into her cruelly.

'Do you despise me for a wanton, Ben?' Shame heated her cheeks.

Unexpectedly he smiled. 'I've had women enough to know you're worth more than a quick tumble in the hay. And lucky the man you give your heart to.' He turned to go but paused by the door to look back at her. 'Passion isn't a game. Remember that.' He laughed. 'I never thought I'd hear myself give any woman a lecture on virtue. I'm too fond of robbing them of it.'

'I'm grateful, Ben.'

He inclined his head with a respect she no longer felt she deserved, then left. She was discomfited upon leaving the tackroom to discover that the cook was by the pump, talking to Goodwife Bundy. The two women watched her suspiciously. When questioned, Angel had denied everything. She disliked telling lies, but Ben's job would be in jeopardy if her father learned the truth. Goodwife Bundy had bristled, but nothing more had been said of the incident. Angel hoped that, with all the preparations for Julian's baptism, it had been forgotten.

A footfall on the gravel path made her swing round to

confront the approaching figure. The moonlight played over his blond lovelocks and silvered his small pointed beard and narrow moustache. Her heart pounded wildly.

'You should not have followed me, Henry.'

He laughed softly. 'How could I ignore the invitation in your eyes? You knew I'd follow you.'

She shook her head to deny his words, but in her heart she knew he spoke the truth. She had been aware of Henry's handsome looks from the first time he had visited this house to woo Maressa. Dazzled by her sister's beauty, Henry had no eyes for the thirteen-year-old Angel. But Sir Henry Mortimer had been too handsome, too accomplished in his charm, too dashing in his elegant clothes not to have stirred a young girl's heart. On the day that Henry and Maressa married, Angel resolved to banish Henry from her thoughts. But as her sensuality developed with the passing seasons, her dreams betrayed her. She imagined Henry declaring his love and kissing her. Awake she despised this weakness. In the last year she had battened down her pain, until eventually she believed that her infatuation for him was over.

'Go back to the house,' she pleaded with quiet desperation. 'Go back to your wife, Henry.'

'And deny what's between us?' He put his hands on her shoulders and drew her closer.

The touch destroyed her willpower. She trembled holding herself rigid in his arms. His blue eyes were dark and heavy-lidded with desire and he smiled with wicked enticement.

'There can be nothing between us, Henry.'

'Don't say that.' His kiss stopped her protest.

The heat of his mouth seared her lips. No kiss had devastated her senses as Henry's was doing now. She clung to him as she fought to cling to her sanity. His mouth was insistent, and his breathing became uneven. Then his fingers were pulling at the lacing of her bodice.

'No, Henry.' Appalled, she pushed away from him.

'Don't be a tease, Angel.' His lips were upon her neck, rousing sensations which flamed through her body. She tried to fight emotion with chilling reason. This was her sister's husband! It was a heinous betrayal to feel this way, to want him with a hunger which sapped all sense of honour.

'I want you, Angel. You drive me to madness with your sultry beauty.'

His embrace tightened, his whispered words echoed her dreams. The insistence of his mouth conjured emotions as exhilarating as they were alien. She swayed against him. But as her body yielded to her awakening passion, her mind clutched desperately at reality. She could not betray Maressa this way.

'No, Henry, I mean it. Stop!'

'My dove, there's nothing to fear. No one will come upon us.'

That he should deliberately misinterpret her denial triggered her anger. She pushed against his chest to break free. His arms became bonds, forcing her hands to her sides as he pulled her from the stone bench on to the grass. The pressure of his mouth on hers prevented her cries of outrage. When her struggles became frantic, he rolled across her, his weight crushing her attempts to escape.

'Don't fight me. I know you want me. All evening the invitation in your eyes has enticed me, your smile is bewitching.'

'But this is wrong.'

'My darling, I'll do nothing to hurt you. I love you, Angel.'

Although she was inexperienced his words were too glibly spoken, as though from practised seduction.

'Please, Henry, let me go.'

Above her, his face twisted with cruelty. 'Damn you for a tease! I shall have you.'

'No!' Her cry was cut off by the savage grinding of his mouth on hers. His strength overpowered her struggles, and his hand yanked her skirts and petticoats to her waist. Her mind screamed in protest. No! For the love of God. No! This was not love. This was a beast intent upon his own rutting – without tenderness, without decency. How could she have believed herself in love with this arrogant, selfish lecher? Where his hands touched her flesh it seemed to shrink on to her bones. He was intent only upon his own pleasure. Every twist of her body to escape his lust caused him to mutter obscenities in her ear. Horror at the violation Henry intended gave her a frenzied strength.

'No! Henry, stop! I beseech you!' She struggled to heave him aside and pull down her gown.

He grabbed her wrist and pinioned her arms above her head. She could smell his sweat as his lips drew back into a snarl. 'Your maidenly blushes are a lie. You're one of life's whores, Angel. And tonight you are mine.'

The passion which earlier had heated her blood now blazed into fury. The infatuation which had betrayed her honour was slaughtered by her disgust. Now she felt only loathing.

'Get off me! You filthy lecher. Your brains are in your balls if you think I'd betray my own sister.'

'Such spirit, such defiance.' Henry's chuckle was evil as his hand forced itself between her clenched thighs. 'I know you want me.'

Angel opened her mouth to scream but his other hand gagged her. Soil and grass fell into her mouth and threatened to choke her. She bit his fingers, drawing blood, but the pain she inflicted did not halt the attack. Wide-eyed with horror she stared into his face. It was no longer handsome but manic with lust. Her desperation to escape only enflamed him further.

'Damned hell-cat!' he grunted. 'You led me on. Such spirit and passion . . . a woman worthy to be loved. Unlike that frigid sow I married.'

The words were as defiling as his rape. The self-righteous rake blamed her for encouraging him.

She twisted her head to free her mouth from his hand, but the soil lodged in her throat made her cough. Her strength was failing. There was a ruthless cruelty in the way Henry prised her legs apart with his knees. A brief respite followed as he eased back to pull at the fastening of his breeches. Seizing her chance, Angel raised a knee to lever herself free. Lack of air to her lungs slowed her movements and left her weak, and a vicious slap slammed her head back on to the ground. A second blow left her gulping for breath. Henry positioned himself over her prostrate form, his mouth hard on hers, preventing her from crying out. In a last attempt to save herself, she dug in her heels and heaved upwards to overbalance him.

Disastrously, her frantic lunge aided rather than deterred his thrust for possession. Angel's body convulsed with pain as he rammed into her, careless of her virginity, mindless to every decency but his own need for release. With a final thrust, he shuddered and slumped over her.

Hatred gave her the strength to push him away and she

lay for a moment, gasping whilst air filled her tortured lungs. Then she eased herself shakily on to her elbow.

Henry looked up and grinned at her. 'You pleased me mightily. I'll insist you return with us to Arundel. Maressa has been melancholy since the birth of the child. You can keep her company during the day and at night . . . Ah, the nights shall be ours, my love.'

'You bastard! You selfish, degenerate bastard!' Angel scrambled to her feet, jerked down her skirts and stood swaying above him. Disgust twisted her lips. 'God have mercy on Maressa for being married to an unprincipled libertine.'

She staggered back from him as he fastened his breeches and stood up. On the point of fleeing against a further attack, her humiliation was complete as her body rebelled. She hunched over as her stomach contracted with nausea and she vomited on to the grass. When the spasm passed she straightened. Henry had left the garden.

Angel controlled the shaking in her hands to smooth out the creases in her gown. When she felt the stickiness of Henry's seed running down her inner thighs, she swallowed against rising bile. There was a feverish glitter in her eyes as she stared towards the house. Her first instinct was to make Henry pay for raping her. Both her father and Alexander would give him the whipping he deserved. But what of Maressa? To speak of her own defilement would bring ridicule upon her sister. Maressa would be devastated to learn that her husband was faithless.

She could not hurt her sister so cruelly. In her anger, she paced the rose arbour. She knew she could never speak of the shame of this night. Her body trembled so violently that she swayed. She sank on the stone bench and burst into tears. After a few minutes, she angrily wiped them away, and her eyes hardened with resolution. Henry would not escape without retribution, and it would be the sweeter by her own hand.

Tonight she had suffered the depravity of man. She had witnessed their falseness and selfish conceit. If that was the respectability assumed by marriage, she would have none of it. Tonight had also shown her the fickleness of love and how quickly it could change to hatred. By his actions Henry had dishonoured his wife as much as herself. So why marry? Better to remain unwed than be trapped in a meaningless alliance. She would be her own woman. She would defy convention and be true only to herself. She would demand respect and equality from any man she took as friend, or lover.

Maressa had seen Henry leave the courtyard. When he did not return she became uneasy. He had danced repeatedly with Angel, and she had not liked the way her sister had claimed his attention. Another survey of the dancers showed her that Angel was also absent.

Making her excuses, she limped into the house. Alone, she abandoned her pretence of being an invalid and ran up the stairs to search the upper rooms. From a landing window she looked down into the gardens and saw Henry walk out of the orchard. He was whistling. His expression of smug satisfaction was one she had come to dread.

She peered into the moonlit garden to discern his latest paramour, but she could see no one. Turning away from the window, she put a hand to her stomach, where she suspected another life was already growing. Her son was only two months old, and the difficult birth had left her weak. In the two years of her marriage she had miscarried twice before Julian's birth. Dr Goddard had cautioned that it would endanger her life to conceive another child before her strength fully returned. He had recommended a year's respite. Henry had sneered at the doctor's advice and flown into a rage at her pleading. He had not granted her even a night's grace after the bleeding from the birth had stopped.

She had endured, as a dutiful wife must endure. If she refused, he would seek out a servant, or the whore Peggy, from the tavern in Arundel. Henry cursed Maressa for being a cold and unresponsive bedfellow. He compared her inadequacies with the harlots he visited whenever her monthly flux denied him his rights. She had never enjoyed lovemaking finding it distasteful. Pride made her submit to her husband, since it kept him from those other women. But now her martyrdom at suffering his attentions – for it seemed like martyrdom – had been rewarded by having her womb immediately filled with another child. A pregnancy she did not want. The memory of her last protracted labour filled her with terror. Already the new babe was sapping her energy. She was rarely free from the queasiness which accompanied each pregnancy. She felt it rush to her throat now and hurried to her chamber.

When her stomach ceased its heaving she splashed her face with water and prepared to return to the celebrations. In front of her family she must appear the adoring wife, her pride would not allow otherwise. No one must guess her misery.

On leaving her chamber she came face to face with Angel. Her sister shot Maressa a guilty look and ran into her room, slamming the door. The creases and grass-stains on Angel's gown told their own story.

Chapter Two

Angel had never considered herself to be a coward. She would not shirk in her duty, no matter how unpleasant or dangerous the situation. On the morning following her ravishment she came to terms with her outrage. Her sleep had been filled by angry scenes, and when she awoke with cramping stomach pains and the familiar stickiness of warm blood between her thighs, her greatest fear was alleviated. There would be no child. Now she had to face Maressa. Somehow she had to look her sister in the eye and act as though the events of last night had never happened, a task which would need all her acting talents to accomplish. Nor would it be easy to act normally towards Sir Henry Mortimer before her family, but she must, lest someone questioned her hostility.

There was defiance in the tilt of her chin as Angel entered the parlour where the family were gathered to break their fast. Her step momentarily faltered when Maressa looked up and watched her approach. Henry was seated beside his wife, holding her hand and gazing adoringly at her. His blatant hypocrisy fuelled her contempt.

Gabriellen called to Angel. 'You join us in time to hear Maressa's news. She is again with child.'

'But it's too soon.' Angel spoke without thinking. 'She's barely recovered from—' She snapped off her words at seeing the colour drain from Maressa's face.

Henry's lips thinned with disapproval. Ignoring him, she went to her sister, speaking with warm affection. 'In everything you are the perfect wife. I'm sure Henry considers himself the most fortunate of men, and loves and reveres you above all women. He'd be a fool if he didn't.' She kissed Maressa's cheek and braced herself to suffer the expected rejection. To her surprise Maressa clasped her hand and smiled, though her lashes were lowered so that Angel could not read her thoughts.

'When you marry, I pray your husband will be as devoted to you,' Maressa said softly. 'You deserve no less.'

Angel blushed, aware of the irony behind those words. She forced a light laugh. 'I have no appetite for marriage.'

Goodwife Bundy was unlocking a wooden coffer to replace the unused silver goblets from the meal. The keys from the chatelaine about her waist fell against the side of the chest with a clatter. 'Upon my soul, I never heard such talk. Mr Rowan, I'm sure I don't know where she gets such notions.'

'Do not fret yourself, Goodwife,' Llewelyn replied, but the stare he fixed upon his younger daughter was daunting. 'Of course you'll marry. I've been remiss not to have pursued the matter before now.'

'Are my wishes of no regard?' Angel declared. 'With respect, Papa, I am resolved. I make this declaration before you all – I'll never marry. I intend to make my own way in the world and not be a burden upon my family.'

'You've bees in your head,' Alexander said sharply. 'How do you intend to achieve this independence?'

'There are ways. Since by my sex the stage is denied me, I could earn a living as a portrait painter. Everyone says I have talent.'

'For that you need a patron, or you will starve,' Llewelyn said sternly. 'No household will employ an unmarried woman for such a task. Who has ever heard of a woman artist? No one will take you seriously.'

'My work will be the only introduction I need.' Angel felt her temper slipping. 'It's time women stopped having their lives dictated by men. Gabriellen did it. She ran Lord Minchams's players for years, when her father's sight was failing. She was a woman ahead of her time. I hear women now perform upon the French stage. If I cannot make a living as a painter, I'll go to France and join a troupe of players. I may even become a playwright like Gabriellen. I've already started to write a play.'

Llewelyn glared at her. 'Angel, will you stop talking nonsense?'

'With respect, Papa. It is fact, not nonsense.'

Maressa coughed, but Angel caught a derisive smile

quickly hidden behind her handkerchief. As she dabbed at her lips, Maressa said in a honeyed voice, 'Papa is right. The sooner you are wed the better, Angel.'

'No. I will never marry!'

'All women must marry.' A steeliness entered her father's voice. 'The alternatives are unacceptable. You will have a say in the choice, of course.'

'What alternatives do you refer to?' Angel accused, her own voice harsh.

Unable to contain her indignation any longer, Goodwife Bundy burst out, 'I've never heard such wantonness! Without a husband no woman can support herself and still keep her reputation. You'll be considered easy game for any lecher.'

'Then I'd be an honest whore,' Angel pronounced. 'Would you rather I prostituted my body nightly to a man I couldn't love? My reputation would be safe, but in my own eyes I'd be no less of a whore – and a dishonest one at that!'

'Bravo, cousin!' Thomas Angel applauded. 'Well spoken.'

'Angel!' Llewelyn kicked back his chair and stood up. 'I'll not have such talk.' He glared at Thomas, who had raised his tankard to salute Angel. 'And you, Tom, should have more sense than to encourage the girl.'

Goodwife Bundy sank down on the coffer she had been about to open, her face flushed and the ruffles on her lace cap quivering with her vexation. 'I never thought to hear such talk from a charge of mine,' she wailed. 'Such language. Such disrespect. I brought her up to know better. I could die of shame.' She pulled a handkerchief from her sleeve and wiped her eyes.

Laurence Angel slapped the table with his hand. 'Nonsense, woman. The wench has the true *Angel* blood. You named her well, Wyn. I like her spirit. She'll make her mark in this world. What say you, Gabby?'

'Angel is not afraid to speak her mind,' Gabriellen's quiet but authoritative voice cut across the outraged mutterings. 'I admire her for that. Why should women be forced into marriage merely to stop being ostracised by society? It is hypocrisy. Angel is a gifted artist and a natural actress. From what I've read of her play, she shows a promising talent as a playwright. If she feels so strongly about marriage it would become a prison for her. You can't want that, Wyn?'

'You're twisting my words,' Llewelyn said stiffly.

'Papa is right.' Maressa added her own voice. 'It's every woman's duty to marry and have children.'

'I want to experience something of life first!' Angel no longer held her temper in check. 'I want to be free to lead the life I choose for myself.'

A stunned silence greeted her words. Goodwife Bundy groaned and looked as if she was about to faint. 'I've failed in my duty. I always knew the girl should have the wayward-ness beaten out of her.'

Llewelyn glared at Angel. 'Go to your room. And consider well the duties of a daughter.'

Angel stood her ground. 'Why is it so terrible that I should refuse to be shackled to a man's domination? Didn't you have your dreams once? You wanted to build beautiful houses which would be a memorial to you. I want to continue the legacy of Esmond and Gabriellen with my plays.' She spread her arms towards her grandparents. 'Mark began with Glendower, a single stallion, and from him came the blood-line of the Rowan strain. I don't come from ordinary stock and I'll not be consigned to an ordinary life.'

'There speaks a true *Angel*.' Thomas leapt from his seat and bowed to his cousin. 'I'm proud to call you kin.'

Gabriellen fixed her nephew with an accusing stare. 'Though a little more diplomacy would have been fitting, Thomas is right. I denied none of my children their chosen life, even though it took my two daughters far from me. Wyn, consider the consequences, should you deny Angel. She may be headstrong, but her pride will never let her be other than true to herself.'

Llewelyn held Angel's stare. 'It's your welfare I think of, my dear. I've no wish to see you face persecution and recrimination.'

'I know that, Papa. But even in my love and respect for you, I cannot live a lie.'

He sat down wearily. 'With the conflict between King and Parliament so unsettled, now is not the time to consider a marriage for you. For the moment we will leave it at that.'

An hour later, to avoid a meeting with Henry, Angel went to the stables and ordered her mare saddled. The groom who appeared was a stranger.

'You're new here,' she said. 'Where's Ben?'

The young man pulled his mousy forelock, but there was a sly look in his eyes as he regarded her. 'I've been here four days and b'aint seen no one called Ben. Were he the one who were dismissed – something about improper conduct? Heard tell he took work over Bosham way.'

Guilt assailed her. Ben had been dismissed after they had been seen in the tackroom together. The injustice of it shocked her. Mischief had prompted her to provoke Ben into kissing her. She was ashamed at her thoughtlessness. His livelihood had been sacrificed to her own selfish ends, no less than she had been sacrificed to Henry's lust. Never again would she allow her whims to prejudice someone less advantaged than herself.

As she took up the reins to ride out, Alexander appeared in the courtyard. 'I'll ride with you,' he offered.

'Not if you intend to give me a lecture. I meant every word I said.'

He regarded her seriously. 'I don't want to see you hurt.'

'Then you can help me by improving my skills with a sword, pistol and dagger. I intend to learn every means to defend my virtue.'

'It will come to war.' Thomas Angel stood with his back to the fire, his thumbs hooked over the dagger belt at his waist. His gaze studied the set faces of the six men in his family, seated in the winter parlour. 'In London, events move faster than here in the country. I know the mood of the people.'

Ambrose sucked on his long-stemmed pipe. He exhaled a slow breath, the blue smoke swirling around his head as he turned to his cousin. Laurence was in a surly mood, suffering from the effects of being put to bed gloriously drunk and singing at the top of his voice last night. His over-indulgence had brought on an attack of gout and he sat with one swollen, bandaged leg placed on a footstool. Pain had scored deep lines into his ruddy face, and there was an unhealthy sheen of sweat on his balding pate. Although only four years older than Ambrose's fifty-two years, Laurence looked a dozen years his senior.

Clearing his throat, Ambrose said, 'Laurence, are you of the same opinion as Tom?'

'Entirely. Were it not for this cursed gout I'd be riding to offer my sword to the King.'

Sir Henry Mortimer stood up and thrust an accusing arm at Laurence. 'Then you would support tyranny! For that's how England will be ruled without its Parliament. Parliament safeguards the good of the people.'

'By God!' Llewelyn shouted. 'Do you say you'd fight against the King? I'll tolerate no traitors under my roof.'

'Gentlemen!' Mark Rowan commanded the attention of his offspring. 'It may yet come that brother must face brother, and father confront son across a battlefield. But not today. Sir Henry is a Member of Parliament. We're here to rejoice in the birth of his son. Time enough later for each of us to examine our souls and decide how best to live with our conscience.'

Firkin's high voice piped out. 'I'm for the King! If Sir Henry is the King's enemy then I hope he chokes on the food he eats in this house.'

'Emrys, you will apologise to Sir Henry.' Llewelyn rounded on his son.

The boy stood in the doorway, white-faced and breathing heavily, his lips clamped defiantly shut.

'Emrys, apologise!' Llewelyn repeated. 'Or you'll spend the rest of Sir Henry's stay locked in your room.'

Firkin could feel his body beginning to tremble, but he remained silent. His father was furious. Grandpapa had raised a white brow, but there was an encouraging glitter in his eyes which strengthened his resolve. Alexander was looking at him with sympathetic understanding. Firkin knew his brother had little liking for Sir Henry. Yet under everyone's steady gaze, he was aware that he had been unforgivably rude to a guest. But he could not apologise, not upon so grave a matter.

Thomas crossed the room and put a hand around Firkin's shoulders. 'The boy speaks that which is upon all our minds.'

Scarlet colour ran into Sir Henry's face. 'Do you think I care what a useless cripple thinks?'

Alexander came up out of his chair, his fist smashing into Sir Henry's jaw. Mortimer's head snapped back and he reeled backwards, recovering himself as his body slammed into the wall.

Alexander warned, 'Don't ever speak that way about my brother again.'

'Strike me, would you?' Sir Henry's hand was on his sword.

'Hold!' Ambrose commanded, and placed himself between the two men.

Llewelyn grabbed Alexander's arms to stop him punching Sir Henry again, but Alexander broke free, his face dark with anger.

'That's enough!' Mark Rowan rapped out. 'I will not tolerate fighting between members of my family.'

'He deserved it,' Alexander raged, flexing his hand over his sword hilt. 'Only a cur would so insult Firkin.'

'Perhaps Sir Henry would like to insult me?' Thomas off:red, a menacing smile on his lips. 'My sentiments are the s:me as the boy's.' He looked down at Firkin, who was struggling to keep back tears. His expression softened and he tapped his sword. 'Tomorrow, before I leave, I'll buy you a sword of your own, lad. If you go round speaking your mind you'd better learn how to protect yourself.'

'What use is a sword to a cripple?' Firkin was stiff with affront, suspecting further ridicule.

'You can ride as well as any man,' Thomas stated. 'On horseback who will know you have a twisted foot?'

Firkin's expression brightened. 'The cavalry are the elite of the King's army.'

'Don't think upon it, Firkin,' Alexander warned. 'You're not old enough to fight.'

Sir Henry had shaken himself free of Ambrose's hold and stood, scowling. 'I'm leaving for London and Maressa will return to Arundel.' He marched to the door, shouting for servants to fetch his coach and horses from the inn.

Laurence drew a pack of cards from his doublet. 'We're well rid of the traitor. Let him go, and may he and his precious Parliament all rot from the pox. Who's for a game of primero?'

'Go to your room, Emrys,' Llewelyn commanded. 'And don't come out until you've learnt better manners.'

'Nay, Wyn,' Thomas intervened. 'You're too hard on the lad. I've no stomach to sit down and break bread with a traitor, even if you have.'

'To your room, Emrys,' Llewelyn insisted.

The excitement had started Firkin coughing, and soon his frail body was racked with spasms. Alexander saw him hide his handkerchief, but not before he had seen the speckling of blood amongst its folds. Firkin dragged his twisted foot as he turned to leave, and Alexander moved to his side.

'Hey, lad,' Thomas called. 'You're over-young for the cavalry, but a gentleman is never too young to learn the skills of pistol and sword.'

Firkin looked up at Alexander hopefully. 'Will you teach me to use a pistol?'

Alexander hid his misgivings, knowing how important it was for his brother to overcome his disabilities. 'Let's start with a dagger, shall we? Despite what Thomas says, you're too young to be handling a pistol.'

The words were drowned by another coughing fit and Alexander led Firkin from the room. Once outside, he lifted the boy into his arms and carried him to his bedchamber. He was shocked by the lightness of his brother's body. After laying Firkin on his bed, Alexander concealed his fears behind an encouraging smile.

'I'll send Goody Bundy up with a posset for you. Why not rest? If the weather is fine tomorrow, we'll steal away for a morning's fishing. Would you like that?'

Firkin nodded, but Alexander saw that the coughing fit had taken all his brother's strength. His pale blond hair was damp with sweat, his cheeks sunken and translucent. Alexander understood the boy's impatience to reach manhood and to prove his bravery.

'No one doubts your courage, Firkin. The brave way you cope with your illness makes me proud of you. Just don't overdo it. You need your strength to get well.'

'I'll never get well. I know that.' The words stabbed at Alexander's heart. 'But you mustn't worry. When you and Father ride off to fight for the King someone must stay to protect Angel and the servants.'

'They could not be in better hands.' Alexander had to force the words out through his tightened throat.

Angel was in the attic room which she used for her painting. Her favourite spaniel, Celeste, was curled on a cushion whilst Angel sketched her on to the canvas. A draught of cold air rushed through the room as someone opened the door, and Celeste growled. Angel turned. At seeing Sir Henry sliding the bolt into place, she leapt to her feet.

'I've no wish for your company, Henry,' she said coldly.

'But I have a wish for yours.' His face became flushed as he stepped towards her.

She backed away, putting the table containing her palette and paints between them.

'You're beautiful, Angel.' His voice was coercing. 'I can't get you out of my mind. The pain of wanting you is driving me wild.' He moved closer but as she edged away, he grinned and positioned himself so that she could not get past him to the door.

'Stay away from me,' she warned, touching the dagger hidden in the deep pocket of her gown.

Such cruelty, my love. You're angry because I've neglected you these last hours. We must take care, and there's so little time. I'm about to leave for London, but I couldn't go without making you mine again.'

His arrogance roused her temper. 'You disgust me! Have you no honour? Were it not for the shame it would bring to Maressa I'd rouse the house against you.'

'My darling, Angel. Why so coy? The role of tease ill suits you. Of course you'll not rouse the house. You want me as much as I want you.'

His ardent gaze turned to a leer which mentally stripped her of her clothing. It turned her blood to ice. 'Get out of here. Have you no decency? Maressa is in the room below.' Her fingers closed over the hilt of her dagger, determined not to be taken against her will a second time.

'Maressa is occupied with the child. Come, my love. Kiss me. There's little time.'

As he spoke he advanced towards her. Celeste began to growl, sensing the menace to her mistress. Angel edged sideways and darted to the door. Anticipating her move he was there before her. His hands caught her shoulders, his breathing laboured as his excitement mounted.

'It's because of me you will not marry.' He pressed a hand against her breast. 'You fear we could not be together. In a week or so you must find an excuse to visit Maressa at Arundel.'

Angel stood rigid in his arms, the dagger unsheathed and

clasped by her side. If she struggled now he would overpower her. Celeste began to bark.

'Shut that damned dog up,' Henry snapped. 'She'll have us discovered.'

Still barking, Celeste ran around Henry's feet and fastened her teeth into his stockinged leg. With a grunt of pain he kicked the dog, sending it sprawling across the floor. There was blood on Celeste's head and she whimpered but ran to attack Henry again.

Fearing Henry capable of killing the spaniel, Angel commanded, 'Down, girl. Be quiet.' For the moment Angel knew herself in no real danger from Henry. She wanted to deal with this her way and without interruption.

Henry laughed, his conceit goading her resolve. 'You're just as eager for it as I am.'

She tensed, no longer able to contain her loathing. 'You're a whoremonger with no concept of honour. It's not me you want. Any woman will do to ease the ache in your loins. Yes, it is because of you that I won't marry. You've shown me the falseness, the baseness I could expect from a husband. I will have none of it.'

Henry's hands tightened on Angel's shoulders. Clutching the dagger in her right hand, but keeping it hidden in her skirts, Angel allowed him to push her against the wall. She could feel how aroused he was as he pressed against her thigh.

'You don't fool me with your false virtue. I know you want me. You loved it last night.' His sweaty hand reached out, and she let him take her left hand and press it against his swollen member. 'That's it. Touch me. Stroke me. See how I need you.' He rubbed himself against her palm. 'That's good. So good . . .'

Angel swallowed against her revulsion. She was determined that Henry was going to be taught a lesson. She would show him that a woman was capable of exacting her own justice upon a rapist. He opened his breeches and clamped her hand over the hard tumescence and then guided her wrist in an urgent rhythm. Her fingers did not waver, holding him firmly. She remained calm, and slowly moved so that he was pinned against the wall. Her hand tightened around him and he groaned with pleasure as she increased her rhythm. His eyes closed.

Angel brought the point of the dagger against his testicles and her hand stilled. His eyes opened wide with shock as the steel caressed his shrinking flesh. 'Give me one good reason why I don't geld you now?' she asked.

His erection drooped. She could see the sweat breaking out on his brow.

'Don't move. One slip of the knife could be fatal.'

'Have you lost your wits, woman?' he squeaked.

'It's called justice, Henry. You took something I prized – my maidenhead. Would this not be fitting payment for your crime?'

He was sweating profusely now, his eyes bulging with horror.

'Are you afraid, Henry? You should be. Is this not apt punishment for what you did to me? You raped me, you bastard.'

'But I love you.' Henry had trouble forming the words, his eyes rolling with terror.

'You don't know the meaning of the word. You defiled me. You betrayed my sister. If I were to tell my brother, he'd kill you.'

She increased the pressure of the blade and he gave a high-pitched whine. 'For the love of God, Angel, spare me!'

'As you spared me?' she spat at him. 'When I take a lover he will be a real man. You sicken me. I pity Maressa.'

'But you drove me to it,' Henry pouted. 'You flirted with me all evening. You were begging me to make love to you.'

'Having some lust-crazed brute force themselves on you has nothing to do with love. It was base depravity for your own pleasure. You took advantage of my innocence. How many other women have you so abused?'

'I swear I love you,' he blubbered.

'You love only yourself. You're a pitiful excuse for a man.' She moved the blade, increasing the pressure just enough to draw a thin line of blood along his thigh. His bladder emptied from his fear, and she stepped back quickly, to avoid the splashing urine. His hands fumbled with his breeches as she unbolted the door. Celeste ran past Henry, giving a last snap at his ankle and making him jump back.

Angel paused in the doorway. 'If you ever try to lay a finger on me again I will kill you.'

She still felt sullied from Henry's violation. There was no

satisfaction in inflicting on him some of the terror he had forced on her last night. She had proved a woman could not be abused without retaliation. Perhaps now he would think twice before he again forced his attentions upon an unwilling woman?

Maressa refused to obey Henry and return to their house in Arundel. She declared her pregnancy made her too weak to travel, nor could she leave Firkin when he was so ill. Furious, Henry stormed off to London. It was unlikely he would return to Sussex for many weeks. Since Angel was leaving to stay with her grandparents in Wales, Maressa planned to remain at Chichester. Here she could forget the misery of her marriage and enjoy the adoration of her father and Goodwife Bundy.

In front of the departing guests, Maressa overcame her antagonism towards Angel and embraced her.

'God speed, Angel.' Her lips skimmed her sister's cheek. Drawing back, she counselled her in a way which she knew her father would approve. 'Whilst at Rowan Hall I beg you to consider your future. You'll be a social outcast if you don't marry. You're young and will meet a man you love . . .'

Maressa was startled at the anguish in her sister's forthright stare.

'I doubt not I'll fall in love – possibly several times. But I've little faith that such blissful euphoria will last. I'll not live a lie. I'll not bind myself for life to any one man.'

Alexander joined them. 'That's a cynical philosophy. So young and so disillusioned. What's brought this about?'

'If I'm to be a playwright, I must study life with honesty. We all have our ghosts, Alex. I've come to terms with mine. You've yet to lay yours.'

He tensed. When his lashes concealed the haunted look in his eyes, Angel regretted her outburst, and added, 'I'm glad you will be in Wales with us.'

'First I must call upon Bryan Penrose's widow and give her his possessions.' There was an edge to his voice which told her how deeply he mourned his friend.

Maressa heard it also, and felt excluded when Angel squeezed Alexander's hand. It was the first she had heard of his friend Penrose. Yet he had confided in Angel. Resentment

44

flared inside her. Alexander and Angel had always been close. Angel had been such a hoyden as a child, always trailing in Alexander's wake. They would leave the house at dawn to go shooting wildfowl on the watery plain leading to the sea, or go fishing. Alexander had even taught Angel how to use a sword. All unsuitable activities. Maressa shuddered with distaste. She was the closest in age to Alexander, and it was in her he should confide.

'Penrose was your friend?' she dutifully sympathised. 'A mercenary is a strange life for a married gentleman.'

'He was one of the best officers I served with.' Alexander patted the bundle tied to his saddle-roll. 'There's little enough here to provide for his wife.'

Maressa unpinned the smallest of three brooches worn on her bodice. It had been given her by Henry's mother before she died. It was old-fashioned and she had never cared for it, any more than she had cared for the woman who had given it to her.

'Give the widow this. Say it was a gift bought by her husband before he died.'

Alexander frowned, unappreciative of her gesture. 'That would be a lie.'

'If the woman loved her husband, she will treasure this keepsake.'

Alexander hesitated. With an impatient shrug, Maressa said, 'She can always sell it. You said there was little money.'

He pocketed the brooch. 'That is generous of you, Maressa.'

Maressa thought her brooch a small price to win her brother's approval, and suddenly she was frightened for him. 'With the King and Parliament gathering their armies, you'll not do anything reckless, will you?'

'I pray that the King and Parliament may yet come to terms. I've no heart for war.'

'But you'd fight for the King, if it came to it?' Angel demanded with passionate heat. 'I'd not hesitate if I were a man.'

Their grandparents had joined them, and Mark winked broadly at Angel. 'That's the spirit.'

Llewelyn overhearing the remark was not amused. 'Don't encourage the minx. Perhaps Angel would be better served by staying with Maressa in Arundel? I can rely on Maressa to instil some sense into her.'

Maressa, who had no wish to be thrown into Angel's company, was saved by Gabriellen.

'Wyn, would you deprive me of my granddaughter's company? I shall enjoy reminiscing of my days with my father's players.'

Maressa linked her arm through her father's and smiled provocatively at him. 'Angel will be happier in Wales. She'll come to her senses there, and I shall enjoy having you to myself for a few weeks. I've no wish to return to Arundel alone.'

'As always, your company will be appreciated,' Llewelyn replied.

Reassured by the love in her father's eyes, Maressa's fears that Angel had become his favourite were calmed. That would have been harder to bear than Henry's betrayal, for she loved her father with a passion she felt for no other man. Now she watched her departing family with mixed emotions. Gabriellen was saying her goodbyes to Laurence and Thomas. Maressa had distanced herself from her London kin, because she disapproved of their lifestyle, but Thomas had not been easy to ignore. He had constantly sought her company, and she had not realised how charming he could be. His compliments and admiration had soothed the pain of Henry's conduct. Thomas was handsome, and she had found it exciting to flirt with him.

While Laurence got into their coach Thomas grinned at Angel. 'If you grow weary with life in Wales, come to London. I'll show you our capital.'

'I may do that,' Angel replied.

Maressa compressed her lips. Angel was dishonoured, yet not once since that night had she seen her look penitent. Then, pride could make actresses of them all. Didn't she play the doting wife, when she had come to loathe the touch of her husband?

Perhaps Angel was right about marriage? Maressa envied her sister her freedom. What was it she had said about prostituting herself nightly to a man she did not love . . . ? Maressa flinched inwardly. She no longer loved Henry and was a prisoner in her marriage. Gone were the days when gallants flocked to pay court to her. How she had revelled in their adoration. Hailed as the 'Fair Maressa', men had brought her tokens of their devotion, becoming her adoring slaves when she had favoured them with no more than a smile. The realities of marriage had soon disillusioned her.

Her discontent returned again once she was devoid of all company except servants. She had never liked her own company, she needed to be surrounded by affection. Llewelyn had gone to a manor some miles away, to show the owner his design for a new wing, and Firkin had fallen asleep on the daybed in the parlour whilst she was reading to him. Maressa looked across to the settle where Gila the wet-nurse suckled Julian. Gila, with her large brown eyes and tight curling hair, was too pretty for Maressa's comfort. Because of Henry's roving eye she usually only employed plain women as her servants, but finding a suitable wet-nurse had not been easy. When Gila began to rock Julian in her arms and sing a lullaby, Maressa took the baby from her, resenting the way the girl was becoming so possessive with her charge. Julian wailed in protest. Maressa tried to comfort him, but he turned red in the face and screamed harder.

She handed him back to Gila, saying sharply, 'I have the headache. Take the child away.'

Motherhood was not the joy she had imagined either. And now there was another baby growing within her. That this new pregnancy fulfilled her role as wife gave her no satisfaction. She had thought, when she married Henry they would spend most of the year in London, his title giving them an entrée at Court. But since the dispute between the King and Parliament, the Court had moved to York. When creditors began to beat at the door of the London house, Henry had the place shut up, saying it was cheaper to live in Arundel. However thin their purse, Henry showed no sign of curbing his own extravagant lifestyle.

Her marriage may have brought her the title of Lady Mortimer, but it had given Maressa little other satisfaction. She forced herself to be a dutiful wife. Instead of winning Henry's devotion, he shamed her by seeking out harlots. She would not continue to be so humiliated. She had not expected Henry to seduce Angel. His depravity was without conscience. Angel was not innocent, either, and for that betrayal

Maressa vowed never to forgive her sister.

Since Henry could not be faithful of his own accord there must be ways of rendering him less able to fulfil his lechery. Surely, if there were love-potions to win a man's heart, there must be similar philtres to cool his ardour. Outside the city there was a cunning-woman, Meg Unwin, who was wise in such matters. She would visit her tomorrow and also procure something to ease the nausea brought on by her pregnancy.

The wind blew in from the sea, driving the rain against Maressa's back. Desperation had made her seek out the wise-woman in such atrocious weather. Unescorted and on foot, she pulled her hood low over her face and hurried to leave the city by the North Gate. Few citizens were in the streets at this early hour, but as the cathedral bell chimed and the gates were opened for the day, a vagrant, who had escaped the vigilance of the watch, crawled out from under a broken upturned cart. He shuffled towards Maressa, holding out a grimy, skeletal hand for alms. There was danger to any woman who walked the streets unattended and, frightened, she took two copper coins from her purse and threw them on to the ground behind him.

Increasing her pace, Maressa left the city and crossed Squitry Bridge over the River Lavant. Meg Unwin lived in a solitary cottage a quarter of a mile from Chichester. There was always a suspicion surrounding cunning-women. Although many people came to Meg for healing potions, in times of spreading sickness, poor harvest, or bad fish catches, others blamed her for their ill-fortune, and called her a witch. Rumour spread of the strange noises coming from the cottage at night. Maressa had no such suspicions. Meg was a pretty woman in her twenties, and lived with her young sister Hazel. Her popularity with the sailors who docked at Dell Quay probably accounted for the nightly revelry.

The track to the cottage was deserted, although the crushed grass and wild flowers showed a recent departure from the dwelling. Meg would rise early to pick her herbs. Maressa became uneasy. A loud bleating from some goats in the stable startled her. Neither the goats nor the chickens had been let out of their pens to forage. The hairs at the nape of Maressa's neck prickled, and when she noticed there was no smoke rising from the cottage chimney, her alarm increased.

A strong impulse to turn and run overcame her. She hesitated. The nausea was worse today. Her discomfort was making her fanciful, and the walk from the city had left her tired. She was not sure she had the strength to return without first taking a rest. Besides she had come this far – to go back without seeing Meg would be foolish.

The door to the cottage was ajar, and Maressa called out as she rapped upon it. There was no answer. She called again, pushing the door open to peer inside the dark interior. This time there was a rustle and what sounded like a sob. Then the thin figure of Hazel Unwin stumbled into sight. Her brown hair was matted and her gown was crumpled and ripped across the bodice, exposing her immature breasts. Both Meg and Hazel were always clean and neatly dressed. The girl's appearance shocked Maressa. There was a livid bruise on Hazel's cheek and her eyes were red and swollen from weeping. The expression on her white face was one of stunned terror.

'Hazel, what is it? What's wrong?' Maressa asked as she entered the cottage.

Hazel pointed towards the hearth, and Maressa stared at the twisted figure on the floor. Horror swamped her. She grabbed at the table to steady herself. Meg's skull had been smashed and a mass of flies were settled on the concealed blood. Unable to control the nausea rushing to her mouth, Maressa gagged. Shuddering, she turned away and vomited on to the floor. When her stomach had stopped heaving, she straightened to face Hazel.

'What happened?'

'The men went crazy.' Hazel began to tremble. 'Meg couldn't stop 'em. They'd come early and seen me. Meg always makes sure I stays hidden in the loft when the sailors come. There were two of 'em last night. The fat one said he'd never had a virgin and would pay double.' Hazel began to drag at her clothes, her eyes wild. Now she had started to speak of her ordeal the words spilled out like a burst dam. 'Meg refused. She didna want me to fall into that life. The fat sailor grabbed me . . . threw me on the floor. Meg tried to stop him . . . That's when he started to punch and kick 'er. The other one held me down. I couldna do nothing to

49

save Meg. We were both screaming. The fat bastard tore my clothes. Meg shouted . . . begged 'im to stop. The other one hit 'er with the poker, then Meg went quiet.'

Hazel sank down on to the floor, her arms hugged tight about her thin body. She stared at the corpse. Her voice cracked as she wrenched out between sobs, 'The fat one hurt me . . . they both did . . . and not just once . . . they were laughing . . . calling me dirty names. I kept shouting for Meg . . . only she weren't moving no more.'

Compassion overcome Maressa's horror and revulsion. She knew how awful it was to endure a man's base attentions. Taking the sobbing girl into her arms, she said, 'They've gone now. You're safe. The constable must be told. But I don't think you should stay here. Have you relatives nearby?'

Hazel shook her head.

'How old are you? Twelve – thirteen?' Maressa asked. 'Have you any money?'

'I be fourteen come autumn,' Hazel replied. Responding as though in a trance to the voice of authority, she crossed to a niche in the hearth. She picked up an earthen pot and emptied out three silver coins into her hand.

'You can't live on that.'

'Bain't the first time there's been no money.' Hazel lifted her head, her expression shuttered. 'I bain't the first woman to be raped. It's what Meg always feared.'

The girl's acceptance of her fate shocked Maressa. 'Those men must be found and brought to justice.'

'They be long gone. Who cares what 'appens to the likes of me? They'd say I had it coming, being sister to Meg. Where Meg went wrong was she should have 'ad a man to protect her – like the whores in the city. I won't make that mistake.'

'How can you talk that way?' Maressa backed away, disgusted.

'I gotta live, bain't I? Even Meg couldna survive on the money she made from her potions. Though she taught me all she knew.' Hazel started to sob.

On the point of leaving, Maressa paused. The set of Hazel's chin told her that life had given the girl many knocks. The poor lived on their wits, and grief had already left Hazel's eyes, to be replaced by calculation.

The girl held Maressa's stare. Then startled her by saying, 'Ye be with child. Aye, and something from thy look says the child's not wanted. There be potions can aid ye, if'n it's early enough. And there be potions to ensure ye never conceive again until ye wish.'

Maressa studied the girl for a long moment. 'Would you like to be my maidservant, Hazel?'

'What would a fine lady like ye be wanting with me fer a maid?'

Maressa smiled. In recent years she had performed many charitable works to enhance her reputation in both Chichester and Arundel. No one would question her rescuing Hazel from the fate of whoredom or the poorhouse.

'I think we would suit each other well enough. Though you'll have to lose your accent and speak as I do. Could you do that, Hazel?'

Hazel nodded. Her eyes were adoring as she gazed at her new mistress. 'For a chance to escape this life, I'd do anything. I'd be your slave.'

'Collect what possessions you need,' Maressa said. 'A servant will inform the constable of what has happened, and the goats and chickens can be sold in the market. From today you will be trained as my personal maidservant. I expect total loyalty from you, Hazel. And your skills as a cunning-woman are to remain our secret. But you will use them as I instruct you.'

A silent understanding passed between the two women.

Alexander parted from his family at the crossroads outside High Wycombe. They travelled on to Wales and he turned towards St Albans. Once alone, however, his mood became morose. Returning Bryan Penrose's possessions to his widow was not a duty he relished.

He rubbed his hand across his eyes, his thoughts bitter. He had been idealistic when he hired himself to fight for King Gustavus Adolphus of Sweden. That idealism had not lasted past the first battle. War was not a glorious adventure. It was a ruthless bloody business, inflicting suffering on thousands. He hoped never to endure the like again. Throughout the campaign he became adept at closing his mind to the horrors he witnessed daily.

Pride had made him risk his life in the cause he was paid as a mercenary to support. When he had been singled out for his valour and promoted to captain, he had been surprised. His troop captain had been killed in a skirmish. The leaderless men panicked into a disastrous retreat, which could have resulted in defeat for the army. Alexander had seen it as his duty to rally his comrades. His war-cries and commands restored their morale, and their ensuing charge had been the turning point of the fight. The incident had won him the notice of Prince Rupert, Count Palatine of the Rhine, a commander in the Swedish King's army. A year younger than the Prince, Alexander instantly liked the dashing soldier. He had been honoured that Prince Rupert, so often cool and remote, regularly sought his companionship. The Prince had shown interest in the Rowan horses, bred for their speed and stamina. The last he had heard of the Prince was a rumour that he was on his way to England to offer his sword to his uncle, King Charles.

There would be the very devil of a shake-up in the King's army when Rupert arrived. At twenty-two, Rupert was an accomplished commander who had already tasted victory. A fond memory of the warrior Prince and his equally warlike younger brother, Prince Maurice, made Alexander smile, but the smile did not reach his eyes. He'd seen too much of war to wish it upon his country.

Many images crowded his mind – not least the faces and the cries of the dying. One of those faces was Bryan Penrose. Bryan had screamed all night from the agony of a six-inch pike-wound to the gut. Only his hand clasped over his stomach prevented his intestines from spilling on to the grass. When finally the surgeon had attended to Bryan, his friend was barely conscious.

The doctor shook his head at Alex. 'All you can do is pray the end will be quick. I've seen them linger for days, going mad with pain and ripping out their own gut to be free of the agony.'

When the surgeon had passed out of earshot Bryan had lain a hand on Alexander's arm. He did not speak but the increasing pressure of his fingers and the silent demand in his stare were unmistakable. Alexander was appalled that his friend had heard his own death sentence. There was blood

52

around Bryan's mouth where he had bitten through his tongue to stop his screams. The plea in his eyes could not be ignored; even now it haunted Alexander.

He had shut his mind to the cries of his conscience as he leaned forward over his friend. 'God bless you, Bryan,' he said softly.

Hot tears splashed down over his hands as he positioned the point of his dagger over Bryan's heart, then he plunged the blade home. Bryan's body arched and gratitude flashed in his eyes before they began to glaze. Alexander withdrew the dagger, his eyes blurred by tears. He swayed as he rose to his feet and turned to discover Prince Rupert watching him from a few paces away.

'This man was your friend?' he demanded.

'Yes, Your Highness.' Alexander expected to be arrested for murder.

Instead Rupert put a hand on Alexander's shoulder. 'God grant that a friend would serve me in like manner, were I so wounded.'

That was the last time Alexander had seen the Prince. The next day he had resigned his commission and after a month of drunken forgetfulness in Paris, he had returned to England.

Swifts were darting across the late afternoon sky when he approached the village green where Bryan's house was situated. A young swineherd was bringing his pigs back from rummaging in the nearby wood, and Alexander called out to him, 'Which is the Penrose house?'

'That will be Oakfield Manor, sir. Over there,' the boy replied, pointing with his stick.

Alexander rode through an open gateway in a high stone wall. The house was larger than he had expected, its limestone walls golden and inviting in the sunlight. Ivy grew around the nine facing windows and willow trees swayed, graceful as dancing maidens, over an oval duckpond. There was an air of neglect about the place. It showed in the weeds in the overgrown flowerbeds and the grass sprouting between the cracks of the steps leading to the front door.

Dismounting, Alexander tethered his horse to a rail, and pulled the iron doorbell. To his surprise, it was not a servant who opened the door, but a narrow-faced man of less than middle height. He was dressed as soberly as a Puritan and there was a slyness about his eyes which Alexander instantly distrusted.

'Is this the house of the Widow Penrose?' Alexander asked.

'That is correct. But Mrs Penrose is not receiving visitors.'

The dislike he felt for the man increased. His gaze swept over the coarse russet hair which receded far back over the dome of his head, although the man appeared no more than in his late twenties. There was a blustering arrogance in his stance often apparent in men of short stature. His clothes were of good quality and, seeing the ingrained ink stains around his fingers, Alexander guessed him to be a lawyer.

'I believe Mrs Penrose will see me. I was with her husband when he died and bring his possessions. I am Captain Alexander Rowan. I did not catch your name, sir.'

'Fairburn,' the man rapped out, squaring his shoulders and reminding Alexander of a bantam cock. 'Mrs Penrose is my cousin. You've brought Penrose's goods, you say? Better come inside, Mr Rowan.'

Alexander was shown into a large parlour, the spartan austerity of its few furnishings out of place in so large a house. There were no portraits to relieve the severity of the oak-panelling, and the only furniture was a long table against one wall and two carved chairs. A rustle of a woman's gown trailing across the floor made Alexander turn. Removing his hat, he bowed to Beth Penrose. Her cousin stood at her elbow, his manner as fierce as a guarding sentinel.

Alexander had forgotten how young Bryan had said his wife was. She could not yet have reached seventeen, yet the pallor of her delicate heart-shaped face made her look even younger. Her pale blond hair was pulled back from her face and coiled in a knot, and the severity of the style accentuated her youthful beauty and the graceful lines of her long slender neck. She was dressed in black, a narrow band of white lace at her wrists and throat. Though her gown was of the finest linen, he saw that the hem had been turned and had already begun to fray at the edges.

'Good day, sir,' her soft voice trembled. 'Please be seated. I have to thank you for writing to inform me of Bryan's death.'

She indicated a chair by the fireplace and sat down opposite it. Fairburn took up a position directly behind her.

54

'Have you ridden far, Mr Rowan?' Beth Penrose enquired.

'From Sussex.'

'You will stay here tonight.'

Fairburn stiffened, but although his mouth thinned with censure, he made no comment.

'Thank you.' Alexander held out a bundle wrapped in Bryan's woollen cloak. 'There's not much I'm afraid. Soldiers travel light.'

Beth opened out the cloak. Her hand shook as it rested on the basketweave hilt of Bryan's sword, and then travelled to the pistol, dagger and gold timepiece. A tear rolled down her cheek as her fingers closed over the gold hoop Bryan wore in his ear. When her shoulders shook in a silent sob, she controlled it, her voice quivering. 'Forgive me.'

Fairburn placed a proprietary hand on her shoulder, in a way which antagonised Alexander. He seemed to watch over his cousin like a hawk hovering over a selected prey.

'Shouldn't you be lying down, Beth? You shouldn't be troubling yourself with visitors.'

Alexander stood up. 'Perhaps it would be better if I stayed at an inn. If you wish for any news I could give you of Bryan, I'd be happy to return in the morning.'

'No, please stay.'

Her beseeching tone touched deep within Alexander. She was so young and vulnerable in her grief, and, intuitively, he knew that something was not right within this house. He saw that she was nervous, her hands tight upon Bryan's pocket-watch.

'Did Bryan suffer?' she asked softly.

Alexander fidgeted with the black plume in his beige hat before answering. 'Bryan was my friend – there never was a better one. He died . . .' The words stuck in his throat, but he prised them out, aware of the young widow's pleading gaze. 'He died bravely. It was over quickly and at the end he did not suffer.'

A tremor passed through the silent figure and, when she raised her head, her blue eyes were filled with tears.

'We were married less than a year before he went away.' She sighed and looked around the hall. 'He did it to make his fortune, and to be worthy of me.' Her voice broke. 'As if that were not all nonsense. He was more than worthy! A

55

good, kind man. He went because of this house. It was my dowry – all that was left after my father's business failed. Bryan hated to see me selling the furniture so that we could live. I would have sold the house itself, only it's entailed. What an irony. I have a grand house, yet I face starvation because I cannot sell it, nor afford to live here.'

There was a snort of disapproval from Fairburn. 'Beth, Mr Rowan does not wish to be burdened with your problems. Especially since we have decided on the means by which to resolve them.'

Beth Penrose bowed her head. Alexander guessed at the bullying she had been subjected to by her cousin, but he held his opinion back. It was not his place to interfere in family matters, but he felt moved to help this woman. It was an impractical dream. For Beth Penrose to remain here she would have to remarry – and marry money. Strangely, since it was none of his affair, Alexander found the thought distasteful.

Beth picked up the brooch which Maressa had given him and was looking at it in puzzlement. Alexander said, 'Bryan bought that for you a few days before he died.'

To his alarm her eyes overflowed with tears. 'It's my fault he's dead. If only it weren't for this wretched house he'd still be alive. I hate the place. It's a millstone around my neck.'

'It's your security,' Fairburn said sharply.

There was a menace which Alexander did not understand in those words. Beth paled and flinched away from the touch of Fairburn's hand on her shoulder. Was she frightened of him? As a woman alone she would be at his mercy.

Alexander withdrew a pouch from inside his doublet. 'Mrs Penrose need not fear destitution. This is Bryan's army pay and the money he won at wagers. He had the devil's own luck at cards,' he explained, unwilling for her to guess that he had added another fifty pounds of his own money to the sum. He put the pouch into Beth's lap and was angered by the greedy way her cousin eyed it.

Fairburn sniffed. 'If it's invested wisely, I dare say it will bring you a modest income, Beth. But scarce enough to support you.'

Alexander hated to see an innocent manipulated to

another's will. He would await an opportunity to have a private word with Beth and learn the truth of her circumstances. 'I gave Bryan my word that I'd do anything in my power to help you, Mrs Penrose. He made no mention of a cousin.'

'Douglas is a distant cousin. And a lawyer. My father made him the executor of his will.'

Alexander saw her hands shaking and she gripped them tight, the whiteness of her knuckles revealing her tension.

'A woman cannot be expected to take charge of her own finances.' Fairburn answered too smoothly for Alexander's liking. 'As family, I have Mrs Penrose's best interests at heart. I could not expect you to undertake such tasks on my cousin's behalf.'

Alexander felt his temper rise at Fairburn's high-stomached manner, and he vowed to protect his friend's widow from the man's clutches.

All afternoon Douglas Fairburn remained at his cousin's side. It soon became apparent to Alexander from the occasions when Beth excused herself, returning with food or a flagon of home-brewed cider, that there were no servants at the house. When she left to prepare the evening meal, he went to tend to his horse which he had stabled earlier, in one of the four empty stalls at the back of the house. He returned by way of the kitchen and discovered Beth stirring a cauldron of potage over the kitchen fire. Two freshly baked loaves were cooling on the table.

Beth looked embarrassed. 'I had to let the servants go.'

'Is there anything I can do to help with the meal?'

'You are a guest, Mr Rowan.'

'I was Bryan's friend. I meant what I said about helping you – in any way I can.'

A look of distress crossed her lovely face and she glanced nervously over her shoulder. He owed it to Bryan to help his widow. Beth looked fragile, but Bryan had always spoken of her inner strength. Now she was at her most vulnerable and, like the carrion Fairburn was, he was using it to his advantage.

'Does Fairburn have some hold over you, Mrs Penrose?'

Startled, she dropped the ladle with a clatter on the stone

floor. 'He wants to marry me. He's always coveted the house and estate. There are two hundred acres behind the stables which belong to the property.'

'It would be a solution to your problems,' he said tersely, angered that Fairburn should press a widow into marriage so soon after her husband's death.

She shuddered. 'Have I any choice? I can't run the estate without servants, and I've no money to pay them.'

'There's always a choice. Some of the land could be rented to a tenant farmer – that would bring in an income. Your own produce could be grown. A few hens, a milk cow or two, some heifers to fatten – all these would give you food and money from the surplus.'

Hope flared briefly in her eyes then faded. 'To manage last winter I borrowed a hundred pounds from Douglas. If I don't wed him he's threatened to have me imprisoned for debt. He'll move in here and claim the house as his own.'

'He deserves horse-whipping,' Alexander snapped. 'Let me loan you the money to repay your cousin. You can repay me after the first harvest. To fulfil my promise to Bryan, to make sure you are safe and prospering, I'll visit whenever I can.'

Her blue eyes studied him and her look of gratitude roused a fierce need to protect this beautiful woman.

'I could not ask so much.'

Alexander held up a hand to stop her words. 'Bryan saved my life in battle. A small loan and a little of my time over a matter of such importance is yours for the asking.'

Beth relaxed and for the first time smiled at him. The warmth in its depths struck him as forcibly as a body-blow. A wave of heat spread through his body in the chill kitchen and his loins stirred with desire. He stood transfixed, knowing that this moment would be engraved on his heart forever. Ashamed of the desire which dishonoured his friendship with Bryan, he cleared his throat to conceal the thickness of his voice.

'You can achieve whatever you wish to achieve,' he said. 'Bryan said you had a determined will. Don't throw your happiness away by marrying Fairburn.'

Her gaze searched his and impulsively, like the child-woman she still was, she took his hands. The gesture was innocent and made in gratitude, but her touch struck like a

58

burning arrow straight at his heart.

'Mr Rowan, you've given me hope where I could see only despair. I'm grateful for your generous help. You're a loyal and good friend.'

He raised her fingers to his lips. 'Then, as friends, let there be no formality between us, Beth. If you wish it, I will engage the staff you need to manage the house and land before I leave. Also I would instruct a lawyer other than your cousin to find you a tenant farmer.'

She blushed, but did not rebuke him as she gently withdrew her hand from his. 'I shall value your friendship, Alexander.'

Maressa could not forgive Henry's betrayal. Neither did she now feel any affection towards him. The thought of him touching her and demanding his rights filled her with horror. Every morning the sickness from her pregnancy grew worse, and for three days now she had been too ill to rise from her bed. On the fourth morning she asked Hazel to bring her a looking-glass. The sight of her lank hair, her complexion dappled with red, flaking patches, and her dull, darkly-circled, sunken eyes made her cry out in despair. The nausea returned, leaving her weak. Hazel supported Maressa, and pressed a goblet containing herbs and wine to her lips, but the bitter brew made Maressa choke. She fell back on to the pillows, turning her head away. 'I know this child will be the death of me.'

'Ye mustn't talk so, milady. The first months are always the worst.'

The servant's hand was gripped and, using all her strength, Maressa pulled herself upwards to whisper hoarsely, 'This child is misbegotten. When I carried Julian I was never so ill. It will kill me, Hazel. Don't let me die.'

They stared into each other's eyes and Hazel nodded. 'We shall do what must be done when Goodwife Bundy visits her ailing friend this afternoon.'

Maressa sank back on the pillows. She had been right to make Hazel her maid. Once the child was aborted, Hazel's potions would give her new power over Henry. He would pay for every insult and abuse she had suffered at his hands.

Chapter Three

It was noon, though from the grey mist which swathed the border as the riders passed from England into Wales, it could have been dusk. In the hedgerow flocks of adolescent starlings, just beginning to show their adult plumage, feasted noisily on the abundance of red and black berries. Many of the wayside flowers had grown to the height of a man, their blossoms of yellow, white and pink brightening the gloominess of the lane. Ahead, Angel saw a colourful spread of flowers on the edge of a ditch. As they drew near she realised that it was not flowers which had caught her eye, but a figure wrapped in the strangest cloak she had ever seen. It was made from hundreds of small uneven patches of every colour and material imaginable: velvets of peacock, scarlet and emerald were mixed with colourful brocades, many of them threaded with silver and gold. There was something in the way the figure lay which alarmed her. Dismounting, she ran to kneel at his side.

'Good God, it's a man!' Ambrose exclaimed, joining her. 'What the devil is he wearing?'

'He's hurt.' Angel indicated the blood matted into the grey hair at the side of the man's head. She put a hand to his neck and felt a weak pulse. 'He's alive. Help me to turn him.'

They rolled him over and the figure groaned. There was a lump the size of an egg on his temple and a vicious cut behind one ear. The man's long face had an aquiline nose to rival an eagle's beak. His thick grey hair was streaked white from the temples and fell to his waist. Darker stubble shadowed his jaw but, despite his grey hair, his skin was unwrinkled. Angel opened his cloak and saw that his doublet was made of the same patchwork of materials and tied with coloured ribbons. Unfastening the bows, she eased back the doublet and pulled his shirt from the scarlet sash about his waist. A mass of bruises covered one side. When she ran her hands lightly across his chest, she suspected that three of his ribs were cracked, but fortunately not broken.

'He's been set upon by thieves, from the looks of him,' Ambrose said to Mark and Gabriellen who had joined them from the carriage. 'Though what they could find of value on him is beyond me.'

'There'd be more than enough to tempt thieves amongst his box of wares,' Mark announced. 'There's only one man I know who dresses like that. A pedlar known as Popinjay, on account of his attire. Usually he has a fiddle with him to draw the crowds to his wares.'

'There's no fiddle, or sign of his box of goods.' Ambrose looked along the hedgerow.

'We can't leave him here,' Gabriellen said. 'It's a two hour ride to Rowan Hall. Do you think he'll survive the journey, Angel?'

'If I bind his ribs and the coach does not hit too many ruts. At least while he's unconscious he's not in pain. Besides, where else can we take him? I doubt any wayside innkeeper would tend his wounds.'

Angel worked quickly over the injured pedlar. His body was cold and he must have been lying in the ditch for some hours. In this weather he would likely have contracted a lung fever which could endanger his recovery.

Ambrose picked Popinjay up. 'Let's pray he's stronger than he looks, or he'll be dead before we reach home.'

News of the conflict between the King and Parliament was the main topic of every conversation. It had dominated each night-stop on the journey to Wales. A week after arriving at Rowan Hall the growing threat of civil war marred the pleasure of Angel's stay with her grandparents.

This morning at breakfast, Ambrose had declared his intention to train and raise recruits for the King. The fervour with which Mark and Gabriellen had supported their son's decision fired Angel's loyalty to their sovereign. She sought out Ambrose who was training a colt on a leading rein in a paddock.

'It's at times like these I feel so useless being a woman,'

she declared. 'What I'd give to ride at your side and fight for my King!'

'And you would make a better show of it than most men.' Ambrose regarded her seriously. 'I've seen the way you handle a sword. But the King has no need of a petticoat army. There'll be work enough for you here. Have you thought of sewing a banner for my troop?' At her furious glare, he laughed. 'No. Somehow, I can't see either you or Gabriellen plying a needle. If a Roundhead puts one foot on to our land, Mama will take up a musket to defend it.' His expression sobered. 'It may come to that. You are needed here.'

It rankled to admit her uncle was right. Suddenly restless, Angel decided to walk to the far paddocks. She looked round to call to some of the dogs to accompany her. They were all with Mark who had gone with the gamekeeper to search Badgers Wood, where some poacher's snares had been found. The day was warm, and Angel was drawn to the river which meandered through the valley. She had spent the last week cooped in the house, tending to Popinjay as his fever rose. It had broken yesterday and, although he was still weak, this was the first time she felt she could leave his bedside. The pedlar intrigued her. His patchwork cloak and doublet, combined with his waist-length hair, made him a memorable figure. Mark had told her that his hair had turned grey a decade earlier, when he was in his early twenties. For two days he had been buried alive, after a landslide had crushed his family home. He was the only survivor. His wife, two children, parents and three brothers had all been killed. Her interest deepened further when in his delirium he had spoken fluently in several languages. Whoever Popinjay was she suspected he was not all he would appear.

Lost in thought, she had walked further than she intended. About to return to the house, she heard a whimper in the nearby hedgerow. She was surprised to see what looked like a sheep caught by its hind leg in a snare. There were no sheep on Rowan land. As she approached the animal a whistle sounded from the wood, and the creature leapt to its feet, blood streaming down its back leg as it struggled to be free. It was not a sheep but a breed of dog she had never seen before.

'Sit! Good dog.' The dog was distressed at being unable

to obey his master's whistle. 'Be still. Good boy. I'll not hurt you.' She sat on the grass and held out her palm for the dog to sniff whilst continuing to speak quietly. It growled, baring its fangs. 'Good boy.'

He eyed her warily, but as she spoke, its growl subsided, and he allowed her to examine the wounded leg. The wire of the snare had cut into the flesh, but she was in time to stop it cutting through the tendon. Angel worked quickly, heedless of the lacerations to her own fingers in her need to prevent the dog becoming crippled.

Another whistle, closer now, made the dog leap forward, and Angel cried out as the wire bit into three fingers, and her fawn gown was spattered with blood. A horse approached and it took all her strength to hold the dog down when the rider whistled again.

'Your dog is here,' she snapped. 'Don't call it. It's hurt.' She ignored the rider when she heard him dismount. The dog whimpered, edging forward on its belly towards his master. Her own pain sharpened her voice. 'If you care for this dog, tell it to be still. It's caught in a snare.'

There was a curse in what sounded like two different languages and a sharp command. 'Down boy!'

The dog lay as dead. Angel bent over him, breathing heavily, but her fingers slipped in the blood. 'I can't release it. The wire's too tight.'

The stranger squatted over the dog, his long brown hair falling forward to cover his profile as his tanned fingers prised the wire apart. The dog rose to his feet, wagging his fluffy tail, and holding the injured leg off the ground. The man ruffled its ears, his tall frame stooped as the dog licked his cheek.

'You saved his leg. I am indebted to you.'

When he straightened and turned to her, Angel found herself confronting dark, snapping eyes. Brown hair waved to his shoulders, accentuating lean cheekbones and a resolute jaw. His nose was long, thin and well formed, and over a mouth compressed into a stern arrogant line was a narrow moustache. He carried himself proudly, with the air of a professional soldier. Angel was unimpressed by either his scarlet cloak and sapphire-blue doublet or his noble hauteur.

'Are you aware that you trespass, sir?' she announced coldly.

The stranger took a silk kerchief from his doublet and knelt to bind the dog's leg. With an angry click of her tongue, she slapped his hand away.

'Permit me. A man will only bungle it.'

She thought he was about to protest. After a sharp intake of breath, he remained crouched at her side, his stare burrowing into her profile. She could feel anger vibrating through him.

The kerchief was tied, and when the dog licked her hand, she could not resist a taunt. 'The dog has better manners than its master. What an angry man you are. Are you always so disagreeable?' The shock on his face made her suppress a chuckle. Devilment prompted her to add, 'You're not used to having your attitude questioned, are you?' A smile softened her rebuke and her eyes sparkled with merriment. 'I doubt you are more than a year or two older than my brother Alexander. He has a way of affecting airs when it pleases him. Not that I take such nonsense from him. Nor will from any man.'

He eyed her speculatively. Then unexpectedly he laughed. It transformed his austere manner. 'I have a sister who is similarly unimpressed by my grand airs, as you call them.' He sprang to his feet. 'She also tells me I have the devil's own temper and the manners of a common trooper.'

'But you are no common trooper,' Angel stated, straightening up. He seemed to expect more from her and her brow lifted in question. There was a faintest trace of an accent in his voice which she could not place.

'I am the King's servant.' He swept his wide-brimmed hat from his head, its scarlet plumes knocking the heads from several buttercups as he bowed. 'Your servant, Madam. You saved my dog from crippling himself. For your pains you have ruined your gown.'

Angel shrugged. 'A necessary misfortune. Poachers have been setting those snares. It could have been one of our dogs hurt.' Angel looked down at her blood-smeared skirts. If it dried then the skirt would be ruined and it was one of her favourites. The river was close by. Since the stranger was again absorbed by his dog, she walked to the bank. Her hands throbbed painfully as she unlaced the ties at her waist and stepped out of the skirt. Kneeling in her petticoats, she soaked the skirt in the clear water which slowly turned pink.

As she held the garment under the cool flow, the pain eased in her hand. When the blood had soaked from the skirt, she sat back on her heels, staring down at her bleeding fingers.

'You're hurt.' The stranger had approached silently. He took her wrist and frowned down at her injury. 'Permit a bungling man to bind this for you.' He drew out another kerchief and skilfully bandaged her hand.

'I owe you an apology, sir. You were capable of tending your dog.'

'A soldier may owe his life to his knowledge of tending wounds.'

She smiled, but her answering quip was left unsaid. His enigmatic and unpredictable moods roused her curiosity. Without anger harshening his face, he was strikingly handsome. His height surprised her. He was four inches taller than Alexander's six foot, and when he moved, it was with the lethal grace of a predator. The elegance of his attire was deceptive. His attention was now centred upon the distant sight of Rowan Hall.

'Is this the estate of Mark Rowan, the horse-breeder?'

The man might dress with the flamboyance of a courtier, but he certainly did not possess the manners of one. His abruptness bordered upon rudeness.

'This is Rowan Hall, where we breed the most magnificent horses in all Wales and England, known as the Rowan strain,' she corrected. 'Mark Rowan is my grandfather. Have you business with him, sir?'

'The King's business.' He was walking to his black barbary gelding, the dog limping at his side. Lifting it in his arms, he placed it gently before the pommel of his saddle.

Intrigued, Angel snatched her gown from the water and, wringing it out, followed him. 'Grandpa is out hunting the poachers, but you will find my Uncle Ambrose at the house.'

The stranger swung into the saddle and, as he picked up the reins, he turned to her. 'You mentioned a brother, Alexander. Would it be Alexander Rowan? We fought together last year.'

'You know Alex? He's expected here tomorrow.' Her eyes lit with excitement. 'Are you one of the mercenaries who came to England with Prince Rupert?' She gave him no time to answer before ploughing excitedly on. 'Do you think the

Prince would take a woman in his troop? I can match Alex with my skill with a sword. And I can shoot as well as any man.'

'Women have no place in the field of battle,' he replied curtly, but there was a twist of amusement to his mouth.

She put her hands on her hips and regarded him severely. 'Damn you for your conceit, sir. I've the courage of a man – don't think I haven't! And if I ever see the Prince I shall tell him so.'

'He shares my opinion.'

'Does he, by God!' Angel's green eyes flashed with menace. 'Then should we meet, royal prince or no, I'll disabuse the arrogant knave of his conceit.'

The heavy eyelids lowered, masking the expression in his brown eyes. A muscle pumped along his jaw and she felt herself dismissed in a way that was disconcertingly regal. 'Shall I ask a servant to ride back with a mount for you? Your hands must be painful.'

'No. Please do not trouble them. The walk is not far.'

Again Angel found herself subjected to a searching stare. Then, with a curt nod, he touched his heels to the barbary's side and set off at a canter towards the Hall.

When Angel arrived twenty minutes later, she was surprised to find the place bustling with activity. Gabriellen met her in the doorway of the Baron's hall and, seeing her granddaughter striding through the house in her petticoats, a wet gown over her arm, stared at her aghast.

'Angel! What manner of dress is that? And now of all times! We have a guest. A most important guest.'

Angel shrugged. 'I know. I met him on the road.'

Gabriellen looked startled. 'I hope you were not in petticoats when you met Prince Rupert?'

'Prince Rupert!' Angel drew an unsteady breath. 'You jest, Gabriellen.'

'I do not.' Her grandmother gave her a reproving look which was mixed with curiosity.

Mortified, Angel groaned. 'I thought he was an acquaintance of Alex's.' Her discomfort increased as she saw the Prince striding towards her. Overcome with embarrassment, she sank into a curtsy.

'Do not be disheartened, Mistress Rowan.' Prince Rupert

sounded amused. 'Our meeting was most enlightening. I often travel the countryside incognito.'

Relieved that he had not taken offence, Angel's natural exuberance exerted itself. 'Your Highness, have I your leave to change?'

'Then dress appropriately, for I would bear witness to this remarkable skill you proclaim with a pistol.' Her hand was taken and he raised her up. Her gaze lingered upon his face. To her delight, his mouth curled into a hint of smile. When the pressure of his fingers tightened, her heart pumped erratically, a thrill of anticipation spreading through her as he raised her hand to his lips.

Brief though the touch of his mouth was, it left its imprint upon her skin. She was conscious of the power of his masculinity, the force of his will holding her enthralled. So great was its pull that she involuntarily swayed towards him, her eyes widening as she saw the veiled acknowledgement in his eyes. It was as potent as a gauntlet flung at her feet. In that moment she knew that her heart was lost – and this time to a man worthy of her love. She did not care that the only form that love could take would be an illicit one.

Alexander stayed with Beth Penrose for four days. The news he had heard at the market this morning meant he could no longer delay leaving for Wales. Rumours were rife. The navy had declared for Parliament and the Earl of Essex had been appointed by Parliament as Captain-General of their army. The King had raised his standard at Nottingham and been joined by Prince Rupert and his brother Prince Maurice. On hearing that Rupert was General of the King's horses, Alexander battled with his conscience. No matter his hatred for war, he would fight for the King.

Walking towards the tethered mare, he was satisfied with the day's business. The lawyer knew of a farmer willing to rent the Penrose land at a generous price. From the livestock market, four milk cows and eight heifers had been purchased; the latter to be fattened on the Penrose meadows and later sold at a profit. Also a dozen chickens and six ducks had been crated up and despatched to the house earlier that day. The only task he had not completed was to employ two servants to work in both the fields and the house. That morning the few servants for hire in the marketplace had all looked unsuitable.

'Mr Rowan?' A man waiting beside Alexander's horse came forward, and touched the brim of his felt slouch hat in greeting. 'I hear thou art looking to hire a steward.'

'I would not call the position as high as that. But it is one of trust and needs the right man.'

'Name's Dunnock. Elijah Dunnock. I'm in need of work and a place for my family to live.'

Alexander studied the man for some moments. There was no slyness in his round face and his eyes were honest. He was strongly built and in his mid-thirties, with short, light brown hair, growing in tight curls. He wore a plain leather jerkin, black breeches, and a clean shirt which had been neatly darned. A man who took care and pride in his appearance usually took pride and care in his work. Elijah Dunnock's level stare was reassuring, and there was a pleasant expression upon his face which Alexander liked.

'You'll be working for a widow.'

'No matter.'

'What experience have you?'

'I've worked as a steward, but I am willing to work on the land. Thou should know that we are the sect of the Children of Light. Thou may know us as Quakers. I was steward to Sir Peter Greyson. When I refused to join the militia he raised, he dismissed me.'

Alexander rubbed his chin. He knew little about this sect, but the few of its members he had met had been law-abiding and conscientious in their work. They usually lived quietly and, although they condemned frivolous amusements like dancing and the theatre, they were generally less fanatical than the Puritans. Alexander considered himself a good Protestant, but he hoped he was tolerant of all religions. He believed Beth Penrose would be the same.

'Your beliefs will be respected,' he assured Dunnock. 'You spoke of a family. How many children do you have.'

'Three. Two boys. The elder of which is fifteen and a good carpenter. The other is eleven and works well with the livestock. My daughter and wife are willing to do household chores.'

'Your family is a workforce on its own,' Alexander said

with a smile. 'But I fear Mrs Penrose is not wealthy. She wished only to employ a general workman and maid.'

Dunnock considered this. He shifted his feet, but his gaze remained unwavering. 'All we ask of thee is a roof over our heads and enough to feed us. We will all work for our keep.'

'There is one condition. The tolerance of religious belief must be on both sides. Mrs Penrose is a godfearing woman, but she cannot be expected to curb the pleasure which her faith permits because her servants do not approve.'

Dunnock nodded. 'We will not censure Mrs Penrose if she does not censure us.'

Alexander held out his hand. 'Then you are hired. When can you start?'

His hand was taken in a firm grasp, relief obvious on the Quaker's face. 'Now would be most convenient.' Dunnock nodded towards a cart loaded with furniture. His family was standing beside it.

Alexander nodded in agreement. 'With so many to feed, more vegetables must be planted and also a winter crop of wheat.' He counted out some coins and handed them to Dunnock. 'Buy what is needed for planting now, then report to Mrs Penrose.' He gave them directions to the village, and rode on ahead, wanting to be with Beth when the livestock arrived and she must face Fairburn's anger. After rubbing down and feeding his mare, he entered the house. The first thing he heard was Fairburn's fury directed at Beth.

'You'll obey me. I'm your guardian. This idea of Rowan's is folly – you'll starve before winter's out.'

'My mind is made up.'

'Is it, by God! Your head has been turned by Rowan's nonsense. Before he came everything was settled. You'll marry me, or I'll have you thrown into prison for debt.'

Alexander ran to the parlour, but Fairburn was too incensed to notice his presence. The lawyer held Beth's arm, and a clenched fist was thrust menacingly into her face. She was pale and shaking, clearly frightened by his bullying. When she twisted to escape his hold, the sleeve of her gown tore at the seam. It slid down her arm, exposing flesh turning dark with bruises.

'I'll never marry you,' Beth declared. 'Your loan will be repaid.'

'I suppose Rowan's lent the money to you. Damn him.'
Fairburn raised a hand to strike Beth.

Rage boiled up inside Alexander. 'You heard the lady's refusal.' He sprang at Fairburn, his fist slamming into the man's nose. There was a crack of broken bone and when Fairburn loosened his hold, Beth escaped his clutches. Blood ran from the lawyer's nose as he lashed out at Alexander. Ducking the blow, Alexander landed a punch which snapped back his opponent's head. A second blow knocked him spread-eagled on the floorboards. Drawing his sword, Alexander pressed it to Fairburn's throat.

'Mercy,' Fairburn whined. 'For the love of God, mercy!'

'You'd bully a woman but you haven't the guts to stand up to a man. Get out of here. And stay away. I've instructed a lawyer to look into your conduct over Beth's affairs. Your money will be repaid next week.'

There was a knock at the outer door and Beth went to answer it. Alexander eased back his sword. Fairburn scrambled to his feet, backing away to stand behind the settle.

'Beth, is it now – not Mrs Penrose?' his bluster returned. 'I know your type, Rowan. A damned fortune-hunter. You want to get your hands on her property.'

Hearing Dunnock's voice in the hallway, Alexander controlled his rage. 'Those are your motives, not mine.'

Fairburn dabbed at his bleeding nose with a kerchief, his expression malicious. 'As Beth's guardian she can do nothing without my permission.'

'I'll have you declared unfit to be the guardian of a flea on a dog's back,' Alexander warned. 'Beth has been provided with enough livestock to support her, and I've hired a family to help with the workload.'

Fairburn glanced towards the doorway where Dunnock stood, hat in hand, his family behind him.

'I know Dunnock,' he sneered. 'He's a Quaker. The country is about to be split by war. Do you think they'll be able to protect Beth, if soldiers are billeted in the village?'

In that matter Fairburn was right, Alexander realised. Beth would be at risk when two armies roamed freely across the land. Quakers were pacifists.

'No army makes war on widows and children,' he retorted. 'Beth will be safe enough. If any harm comes to her, I'll

71

know where the blame lies. And I'll hunt you down and kill you.'

He turned away from Fairburn in disgust, and the man sidled from the room.

Beth excused herself to the Dunnocks and came to Alexander's side, speaking softly. 'I've much to thank you for, my friend.'

The trust and warmth he saw in her eyes destroyed his composure. He wanted to pull her into his arms and taste the sweetness of her lips. He wanted to know what it was like to drown himself in the heat of her body. The impulse uncoiling like a viper in his mind, and he turned away, dragging a hand though his long hair. 'When I join the King's army, I shall be close by at Oxford. I'll visit you whenever I can, to assure myself that all is well here.' His tone was confident, masking his unease that Fairburn would not let matters rest.

Angel decided that the best way to show Prince Rupert that she had not exaggerated her skill with firearms was to ride out and hunt with him. When she appeared, dressed in a discarded doublet and breeches of Alexander's, the Prince looked amused. She already knew that he had expressed a wish to ride Caradoc, the Rowan stallion, and she chose the spirited chestnut mare, Morgan.

Caradoc, as though aware that a prince rode upon his back, tossed his chestnut mane and arched his neck. The white blaze on his nose was creamy in the sunlight. As temperamental as he was swift, Caradoc had thrown both Mark and Ambrose. Angel held her breath when she saw the stallion bunch his muscles. He reared up, pawing the air, and was superbly controlled by the Prince. Then with a snort, hot breath streaming from his nostrils, Caradoc bucked. He came down on all fours, and immediately launched himself upwards again, his back rounded and his head low. His hooves hit the ground with a bone-jarring force which should have unseated even the most experienced rider. Angel gasped, fearing the Prince would be thrown on to the cobbles, but he remained firmly in the saddle, his teeth gleaming white in a devilish smile. It reminded Angel of the nickname which his volatile temper and fearless courage had earned him in

Europe – *le Diable*, The Devil. Caradoc quietened, acknowledging the Prince as his master.

'A splendid horse, Rowan.' Rupert ran his hand over Caradoc's neck. He kept the stallion on a tight rein to control his prancing. There was a glaze of moisture on Rupert's narrow moustache from his exertions, but he was enjoying himself. 'For years I've heard the Rowan horses praised. I wanted to see them for myself. Their reputation was not exaggerated.'

As Angel rode to Rupert's side, her attention was caught by a movement at one of the upper windows. She stared up at the room given to the Prince and saw his dog, Boy, looking down at them through the diamond panes. They could hear his whines.

'Boy doesn't like you riding out without him,' she said.

Rupert followed her stare, his expression softening as he regarded the dog. 'Would that he could join us.' His voice was heavy. 'We had enough of confinement at Linz. But he must rest his leg to allow it to heal.'

Seeing Rupert's expression darken, Angel regretted her blunder. How could she have been so thoughtless as to remind him of those years when he had been a prisoner of the Catholic Emperor Ferdinand. Alexander had told her that Boy had been given to the Prince as a pet by Lord Arundel, the English Ambassador at Vienna. Rupert and his family were exiles from their own kingdom: his parents the Protestant Frederick V, Elector Palatine and Queen Elizabeth, sister of their own King Charles, were known as the Winter King and Queen. They had only ruled for a single year before being forced to flee from Prague by Ferdinand's army. Rupert was the only one of the Elector's children to be born during their brief reign. At nineteen, he had commanded the cavalry raised to restore his elder brother to their late father's throne, and drive the usurpers from the Palatine. When Rupert had been captured, he had been considered too important a hostage to be ransomed. He was held prisoner for nearly three years.

It explained the leashed ferocity of the energy in all the Prince's movements. He was rarely still for any length of time. The four household dogs which were to accompany them on the hunt were sniffing about the stableyard. Rupert was talking to Mark about the horses.

To dispel the chill aloofness which had returned to the Prince's manner, Angel dimpled provocatively and interrupted Rupert's questions.

'A wager, your Highness. If I beat you to the river ford a mile along the valley, do I earn a place in your troop?' Without waiting for his reply, she kicked Morgan into a gallop.

If any horse in their stables could outpace Caradoc it was Morgan. Angel raced past the paddocks, leaning low over her mount's neck. The wind blew back her hair, and she was forced to put a hand to her hat to hold it in place. Looking over her shoulder, she saw the Prince gaining ground.

'I never wager on certainties,' he said as their horses drew level.

'You think I will lose?' She raised her voice above the thundering hoofbeats. 'That's not my intent.'

She veered towards the paddocks furthest from the house, and Caradoc shot forward. Though now several lengths behind, Angel smiled to herself as the stallion approached the paddock holding two mares which had been separated from the rest. Caradoc lifted his head, his muzzle drawn back over his teeth as he scented the air. Chaffing at the bit, he emitted a shrill whinny, and careened towards the mares, intent upon leaping the fence. The mares had just come into season, and she laughed aloud as Rupert fought to bring the powerful stallion back under his control. Like a lightning bolt, Morgan sped past him and she could not resist a wave. She doubted even Rupert could control Caradoc once he had scented the mares. Victory would be hers, and with it a place to fight for her King. She was within sight of the ford when she heard hoofbeats closing on her. That Rupert had so expertly mastered Caradoc proved he was both a unique horseman and a man she could not afford to underestimate.

Exhilaration sped through Angel's veins as she urged Morgan faster. Her lighter weight should have been an advantage after such an extended gallop, but Caradoc pounded closer. A fallen tree lay across the track, its trunk as high as Morgan's nose. A cautious rider would skirt it, but Angel knew Morgan's capabilities. Without slackening her pace, she

74

urged the mare over it. Caradoc landed a length behind her. There were sixty strides to go before she won her wager.

'Come on, my beauty. Let's show the Prince what a Rowan horse can do.'

Angel exerted all her skill to win, short of using her whip and spurs, but Caradoc was now neck and neck with Morgan. As they galloped the last few yards, she knew Rupert was holding the stallion back so that they reached the ford together.

Angel slowed Morgan to a walk. She was breathing heavily and her face was flushed.

'A gallant gesture, Your Highness. The race is yours.'

'Where did you learn such devious tricks? This damned beast near unseated me in his lust to get at the mares.'

She smiled. 'But he did not unseat Your Highness. From your horsemanship in the stableyard I never thought he would. A woman would be a fool to rely upon strength and stamina alone in any contest against a man. We must use our wits to counter a man's superior strength.'

'Wit and wiles you have beyond measure.' Rupert surprised himself by his gallantry. He had never been one to indulge in light flirtation. He was amused by her trick to win the race. Such strategy would be an asset to any commander who served him. He had come to Rowan Hall to procure the finest steeds available for the King's cavalry, and dalliance had been furthest from his thoughts. A soldier before a gallant, his attention was now on the two horses, satisfied that neither was blown after its gallop.

Angel saw that this self-contained man had withdrawn from the intimacy of moments earlier. With a single-mindedness she found exasperating, she realised that his thoughts were again upon his purpose in coming here.

She looked across at him through lowered lashes. 'The horses have proved their mettle. Now I will prove mine. Over by those trees is a good place for us to stand whilst the dogs put up ducks from the reed bed.'

Tethering her horse, she took a brace of pistols from the scarlet sash tied about her waist, priming and cocking them in readiness. On command, the dogs dashed into the rushes. Immediately a mallard was put to flight, and Angel's swift reaction brought it down with her first shot. Rupert shot the next two which flew up, and a fourth plummeted to earth, decapitated by Angel's bullet. She turned to the Prince with a satisfied smile.

'No devious tricks there,' she said proudly.

'Diana the huntress could not rival you.' The admiration in his voice made her heart pound faster.

'Have I proved my worth to fight for the King?'

A flash of annoyance darkened his eyes. 'You're an exceptional horsewoman, and a superb shot – when bringing down a duck. But have you ever killed a man? Or faced a sword raised by an opponent whose only intent was to run it through your guts?'

'Of course not! But I'm the equal of Alex in a swordfight. What I lack in strength I make up for in agility.'

He raised a dark brow. There was a dangerous glitter in his eye which warned her that his temper was not far from surfacing. She lost control of her own first, refusing to be patronised, even by a prince.

'I'm no mouse to scurry for cover at the first sign of danger. Women are more resourceful than men give us credit. Any one of us will kill to defend her family or home. I'd not hesitate to kill to save the land we love from being governed by bigots. I'd not enjoy it, but it would be a necessary evil.'

She bent to snatch up the ducks retrieved by the dogs and Rupert's hand closed over hers.

'Such fire and vehemence. A veritable tigress.'

Angel stepped back, her eyes flashing with the force of her fury. 'Don't mock me. I'm serious.'

'Wars are not all won on the battlefield. If we do not break the Parliament force at once, the dissent will spread. Any estate known to support one side or the other will be at risk. With the men away, who do you think must protect the property? It's the women who'll keep the enemy from the door, or stop their home being put to the torch.'

She retaliated without thinking. 'Where's the glory in that?'

To her surprise, instead of becoming angry, he stripped off one of his gauntlets and tipped up her chin. 'There's valour and glory enough, Madame Warrior.'

His touch stole her breath, its warmth ignited a flame

76

within her blood, and the intensity of his dark eyes held her transfixed. The potency of his gaze was intoxicating, sending tingling spirals downward through her body, until her entire being glowed. It was unlike anything she had previously experienced. His gaze lingered upon her parted lips and he tossed the ducks back on to the ground. The arrogance was gone from his eyes, to be replaced by vibrant ardour.

They stood without moving, their gazes arrested, magnetised in the silent communication of sexual attraction. When his breath caressed her skin, exquisite sensations sped through her veins. Her lips became dry, longing for his kiss. Moistening them with the tip of her tongue, she was unaware of the sensual invitation of her action. His eyes were black with desire and with a predatory hunger.

For a moment she was assailed by the memory of Henry's rape. Her flesh went cold. Then a darker fear channelled through her terror. Had Henry mentally scarred her, left her crippled, unable to respond to a lover's touch? Her mind rebelled. No. Henry would not triumph.

Rupert saw the hesitation and questioned it with a frown. He was not forcing her as Henry had done. He was awaiting her consent. The knowledge stilled her panic. To combat a fear one must meet it head on.

She moved into his arms. When his hands slid down the length of her back to press her hips close against him, her fear was vanquished by the intoxication of his caress. As he lowered his head, her eyes closed in surrender. The heat of his lips possessing hers was tender. There was a thoroughness to his kiss which ravaged her senses; deepening and demanding, until a moan of pleasure rose from her throat.

He eased back. His heavy-lidded gaze was speculative. She had expected arrogant self-assurance from a man of such devastating good looks and royalty. Instead, she detected wariness and an icy control. Angel searched his eyes to guess his mood. Taking his hand from where it rested on her waist, she ran her fingers across its callused palm. Without lowering her gaze from his obsidian stare, she pressed his hand against the swell of her breast. Through his flesh she could feel the wild thudding of her heartbeat.

This time there was a fierceness to the possession of his mouth, but it was a fierceness which was echoed in her ardent response. In his arms she forgot he was a prince. He was the most exciting man she had ever met. It did not matter that he did not love her. There had been admiration in his eyes and she had glimpsed something more behind that enigmatic wariness, which set her heart racing. From the moment they met she had been drawn to him like a lodestone. Passion was shredding coherent thought. A detached thread of her mind warned that there could be no lasting future for them together. She did not care. Had she not foresworn a life of convention? This was the equality she sought in a liaison – the freedom to choose, the need to be true only to oneself.

She gave herself willingly to the caress of his hands, yielding to desire because she wanted to yield, more than life itself. She rose on to her toes, moulding their bodies closer, her fingers twining through his mane of hair. He unbuttoned her doublet, his hand slid inside. When his thumb grazed the hardened peak of her breast, her body became a furnace until her limbs turned molten.

Then abruptly she found herself released, and would have fallen had he not caught her hand to steady her. Her eyes opened, and it was only then that she heard the distant shout. It was Ambrose who hailed them. Quickly refastening her doublet, she cursed her fumbling awkwardness. When the Prince stepped back from her and adjusted the fall of lace at his throat, she saw his hand was also unsteady. They exchanged rueful glances.

'Over here, Uncle Ambrose,' Angel called, at seeing a chestnut horse moving through the nearby wood. She picked up the ducks and forced herself to appear composed.

'It appears we are to be chaperoned,' Rupert said thickly. 'Come to me tonight.'

She nodded, not trusting her voice.

Ambrose was within earshot. Drawing a steadying breath, Angel held up the ducks and smiled. Her skill as an actress enabled her to face him and treat the Prince in a circumspect manner. Rupert needed no such dissembling; his mind was already absorbed by his interest in the Rowan horses. He fired questions at Ambrose about their ancestry. Angel was surprised when he mentioned the stallion Glendower, who had established the bloodline. When he insisted on a detailed inspection of the paddocks, Angel excused herself to return to the house.

If she was to visit the Prince's room tonight, she wanted no one to suspect her intentions. As she swung into Morgan's saddle she saw that she was forgotten. A lesser woman would have been piqued, but Angel sensed the restlessness of the Prince's spirit. His enquiring mind had been too long starved of stimulation for her to take offence at his brusque manner . . . rather she saw it as a challenge.

'So you miscarried, madam!' Sir Henry Mortimer said in bitter greeting. He had just arrived from London and, finding his wife alone, glared down at Maressa who was seated in the parlour. 'A disappointment to be sure. As it is to find you here against my orders.'

'I'm too weak to travel,' Maressa protested.

'I think not. You neglect your duties at Arundel.'

Goodwife Bundy entered the parlour. 'Good day, Sir Henry. I hope it was not trouble which delayed you in London.'

He looked at the housekeeper as though she had lost her wits. 'The country is in a state of war. I was delayed because Parliament needs to raise an army and that takes a great deal of planning and expenditure.'

'You continue to support this insurrection against the King.' Llewelyn had just returned from surveying a house and had overheard Henry's remark. He came into the parlour, carrying rolls of house plans.

'I follow my conscience,' Henry answered haughtily. 'I'll not stand by and watch the rights of Parliament usurped by a tyrant.'

'Then you'll leave my house and be damned!' Llewelyn raged.

Henry rounded on Maressa. 'I'll return for you in an hour. Be packed and ready to leave.'

As he strode to the door Maressa stood up and swayed. Her hand went to her brow and she fell to the ground in a swoon. Henry's mouth curled into a sneer as he stared at his wife from the door. 'Your play acting won't serve you this time, Maressa. I meant what I said.'

'Bundy! Hazel!' Llewelyn shouted as he ran to his daughter

and lifted her into his arms. 'Can't you see she's ill? Had she not miscarried, that last pregnancy could have killed her!'

Henry shoved past Goodwife Bundy, throwing the housekeeper hard against the panelled wall.

'I will return in a month,' he declared. 'Maressa had better be ready to return to Arundel them, or she will rue the day she defies me.'

The evening at Rowan Hall passed in a fervour of anticipation for Angel. After the meal, the conversation touched upon Mark's interest in alchemy, and the Prince expressed a wish to see his laboratory.

'Will you accompany us, Angel?' Mark asked. 'Now that my joints are stiffening, you can mix the compounds with greater skill than I.'

'It will be my pleasure.' During her visits to Wales she had spent many hours helping Mark with his experiments. She worked now upon his direction and once, when the desired result of an experiment was not obtained, Prince Rupert made a suggestion which she hotly refuted.

'We tried that last summer. The compound is too volatile and caused a minor explosion.' She laughed at the memory and, seeing the Prince's puzzlement, explained, 'Our faces were blackened and our hair singed. Upon leaving the room we encountered a maid, and the poor woman fainted at the sight of us. We must have looked like two demons from hell!'

The interest in the Prince's eyes kindled as he studied Angel. 'Alchemy is an unusual occupation for a woman.'

Mark snorted. 'With respect, Your Highness, it would be a rash man who suggested to Angel that a woman's place is best suited to sewing or making preserves. She hotly disputes such notions.' He winked at Angel. 'At her own insistence she received an education to rival Alexander's. She was furious when her sex denied her following her brother to university. Apart from alchemy she has studied history, mathematics, astronomy, even astrology. And she is fluent in Greek, Latin, French and Spanish. As for her accomplishments as an artist . . .'

'Grandpa, you are embarrassing me.' Angel interrupted his praise.

80

'Your modesty becomes you, but you should take credit where it is due,' said Rupert, regarding her with intensity. 'Mr Rowan spoke of your interest in astronomy. Is there a telescope here?'

'Indeed, Your Highness,' Mark replied. 'It's in the turret room, two floors above this chamber. For the best view of the heavens it can be mounted upon the roof. The sky is clear tonight. Would you care to study the constellations?'

'I would, but the hour is late. I need little sleep, but I'd not keep you and your wife from your bed. If Angel is not too tired I'd enjoy an hour in her company, studying the heavens and comparing observations.' He whistled to Boy, who was curled asleep on the floor and, with the dog running ahead, strode out of the room. Clearly, he did not expect Mark to object to Angel being alone with him.

Mark studied Angel as he walked with her to the door. The concern on his face made her link her arm through his.

'For all Rupert's reputation as Le Diable, he is first a man of honour,' Mark said. 'Come the outbreak of hostilities between the King and Parliament, half the Royalist women will fancy themselves in love with so handsome and dashing a commander.'

'I'll not do anything I shall later regret,' she promised.

Discretion made her stay only half an hour on the tower parapet with the Prince. He had needed no guidance to find the telescope and when she walked out on to the roof, his long body was stooped over it, one eye to the lens. Without speaking, she stood, looking out across the paddocks below. Ignored by his master, Boy rubbed his nose against her knee, and she crouched beside him to ruffle his ears.

'He does not usually suffer women to touch him,' Rupert said drily.

'He knows I mean neither him nor his master any harm,' she replied straightening.

Rupert was studying her in a way which was disconcerting. His emotions were difficult to read. During his imprisonment he would have learned to guard them well. She had dressed with care this evening, in a gown of mulberry silk. The décolletage was the most daring she possessed, revealing the swell of her breasts, yet it would be considered modest compared to the fashions of the Court. Her hair was pinned high

81

on her head, a cluster of black ringlets falling over her ears. Two curls had escaped their pins during her work in the laboratory, and she could feel the breeze wafting them across her bare shoulders. Angel did not want to vie with empty-headed Court beauties. She wanted to be remembered by Rupert because she was different to those gilded lilies.

'You're a beautiful and fascinating woman,' Rupert said as he came to stand close beside her. 'But no seductive wiles will change my mind about you riding with the King's horse.'

'I'd not insult you by believing that they would,' she returned frostily. 'I've thought upon your words. Since Uncle Ambrose is to raise a troop for the King and leaves the day after tomorrow with the horses, my place is here. Should circumstances change and my sword better serve the King, I'd find a way to fulfil my duty.'

Her hauteur matched his and with a challenging stare, she curtsied and moved to the stairwell. His arm shot out to bar the doorway from her and she could feel his breath on the nape of her neck. Her throat dried and her heart pounded. 'Have I your permission to leave? My grandparents will not retire until I do.'

'You'll come to me later?'

'I think not. I'd not be accused of using my wiles to influence you.' Her sharp tone betrayed her anger at his brusque manner.

The moonlight showed the gleam in his eyes. Clearly, he was not used to a challenge. Angel leaned back against the door frame, her shoulder brushing his arm where it blocked her passage.

'It was not a command, but a request,' he added stiffly. 'I ask your pardon. I misjudged you. I'm a soldier, not a gallant.' Taking her hand, he raised it to his lips. 'I'd be honoured if you would come to me tonight.'

She capitulated with a smile. 'I'll come when the household is asleep. If it pleases Your Highness.'

His expression softened. 'It will please me greatly.'

He lowered his head to kiss her and she opened her mouth to his. Then, ducking under his arm, she sped down the stairs. On the landing below, she met her grandparents. Mark held up the candlestick he was carrying. The relief on his face stabbed at Angel's conscience.

'Good night. Do you think Alex will arrive before Prince Rupert leaves?' she said brightly. 'He'll be annoyed to have missed him.'

'You miss your brother,' Gabriellen observed wrily. 'I rarely hear you speak with such longing for your sister.'

'Men lead more exciting lives than women,' Angel returned, then added as an afterthought, 'but that need not always be the case.'

Before Angel went to her chamber she looked in upon Popinjay. The candle burning at his bedside showed her that he was asleep. She touched his temple to see if he was still free of the fever, and his eyes opened.

'My guardian, Angel.' His voice cracked with lack of use. When she picked up a goblet of buttermilk for him to drink, he pulled a face. 'I'd rather it were ale.'

'Tomorrow you shall have ale, when you are stronger.'

'I've missed your company today. Just as I get well enough to appreciate a beautiful woman at my bedside you desert me.'

'We have an important guest.'

He looked at her finery. 'You dress fit to entertain a king.'

'It is not the King, but Prince Rupert. He's here to buy horses for the cavalry.'

Popinjay's face became animated. 'The Prince is here?' He levered himself on to an elbow and began to push back the coverlet.

'You cannot get up,' Angel said. 'The night air is cool. Your fever could return.'

He shook his head and swung long thin legs to the floor, his nightgown rumpled over his bony knees. 'I must speak with the Prince . . . something I overheard.'

Angel put a hand on his chest to push him back on to the mattress, but Popinjay took her hand and looked into her face. 'His Highness' presence here proves where your loyalties lie. I must speak with him.' At her continued resistance, he said forcefully, 'He knows of me.'

Angel felt his strength ebbing as he tried to stand.

'Very well. Now lay back. I'll ask the Prince to visit you.'

She left the room, heading for the turret steps. The ring

of spurs on stone above her told of Rupert's approach. He ducked his head to avoid banging it on the low lintel of the archway and in the moonlight she saw his surprise at seeing her there.

'Your Highness,' she spoke softly, 'there's a pedlar in the house known as Popinjay. He wishes to speak to you.'

'Popinjay!' His frown deepened. 'How comes he to be here?'

'He was set upon by robbers and left to die in a ditch. We found him and brought him here to recover. He's still too weak to leave his bed.'

'Show me his chamber. I will speak with him alone.'

Angel led the way to Popinjay's room, then returned to her own chamber. Throughout her disrobing, Angel suffered her maid's excited chatter about the Prince. Gwen was a competent maid and always tended Angel when she stayed in Wales, but tonight Angel was in no mood for idle talk. She checked her impatience whilst Gwen removed the gown and petticoats, but when the girl began to unlace the corset which pinched in her mistress's waist, Angel drew a deep breath. 'Why do we torture ourselves merely to shape our figure?'

'Not that you be needing it,' Gwen said. 'You've a waist small enough for a man to span with his hands.'

Angel sighed. 'I've a figure like a youth. Why couldn't I have some of Maressa's curves?' She held her small breasts in her hand, lifting them so that they rose above the neckline of her shift. What if Rupert found her unattractive and skinny? Men so often seemed to prefer the fuller curves of an hourglass figure. Her hands fell to her sides. It would take more than the body of a goddess to hold Prince Rupert's interest. Taking the hairbrush from Gwen, she dismissed the maid and began to drag the brush through her thick curls with savage determination.

Listening for sound of Rupert returning to his room, she pulled off her nightshift, preferring to be naked beneath her scarlet satin robe. The cool touch of it against her skin was as sensual as it was provocative. It made her feel deliciously wicked. A fitting sentiment, since she was brazenly offering herself to a man who would never marry her. It shocked her that she should feel no shame. But why should she? It was the sordid attack by Henry which had shamed her. This was an honest response of a man and woman attracted to each other with no hypocrisy or pretence. As long as she was true to herself she could hold her head high with a clear conscience.

A footfall along the passage made her catch her breath. She heard a door open then voices. Her heart sank. Mark was speaking with Rupert. Would the conversation never end? At last the voices stopped and she heard the Prince's footsteps pass her room and his chamber door closing.

Angel leant against the wall. Her heart was racing so hard it threatened to stifle her, her whole being crying out to run into the Prince's arms. Caution stayed her impatience. She must wait half an hour to ensure that her grandfather was asleep.

It was the longest half hour of Angel's life. As she approached Rupert's room, she had a sudden attack of nerves. She hesitated. Her body was trembling and burning with anticipation. Breathing deeply, she ran her hands over her unbound hair which fell in raven black tresses to her waist. Then she tapped softly on his door. A scampering of claws on the wooden floor and a growl made her freeze. If Boy barked, the entire household would be roused. A low command silenced the dog and the door was opened.

Rupert stood back to allow her to enter. He had removed his doublet, his shirt was unfastened at the neck and the sleeves rolled back over his forearms. A candle burned on the table by the window, where the Prince had been writing. She saw a lifelike charcoal sketch of Caradoc's head. Prince Rupert was a talented artist.

'I have disturbed Your Highness,' she said, feeling foolish at the quiver in her voice.

In silence, she was drawn inside and the door closed behind her. Boy leapt up on to the bed, circling in preparation to sleep. A curt command ordered him off and into a corner. Then she was in Rupert's arms. Like tinder to a paper, his kisses set her blood afire, his mouth a living flame as it skimmed across her cheek and nuzzled the hollow of her neck. It travelled to her shoulders, her robe pushed aside to cling to the crests of her breasts. As the heat of his lips laid siege to her senses, her head rolled back. The scent of him was intoxicating, musky, a lingering trace of horses and leather, but above all essentially male.

She eased back to let the scarlet robe slide from her arms and fall to her feet. The harsh intake of his breath as he gazed at her nakedness was the sweetest accolade she had ever heard. When his lips left her mouth to kiss the pulse beating below her ear, a moan rose from her throat. Then his head moved lower and his tongue teased her breast, fanning a fire which seared her very soul. Passions flared. Senses were besieged. No quarter was given as a fervent ardour possessed them. His clothes discarded, they rolled across the mattress.

Beneath his caresses, sanity fled, her body moving in shameless pleasure. Fevered kisses were pressed over her ribs and down across her hips and stomach, until she was writhing from the pleasure they evoked. She cried out as his kisses gathered intensity, detonating into a white-hot blaze. His hands tilted her hips and as the thrusting heat of him entered and filled her, he guided her legs so that they locked about his waist. Angel matched his rhythm: gentleness displaced by a sensual frenzy until release exploded simultaneously between them, and Angel's cries of pleasure were smothered by lips both dominant and tender.

Angel moaned softly as her satiated body glowed from the force of her passion. Rupert's head was pressed into the curve of her throat. Smiling, she ran her hands over the muscles of his back and through his damp locks. Her love was all-encompassing and as powerful as a spiritual revelation.

The Prince leant back on his elbows to look down at her, his face in shadow. She erased her own uncertainty from her eyes. She regretted nothing. His pleasure had been as great as hers, and she could still feel his throbbing heat within her, loath to draw apart from that heavenly sanctuary. She heard him groan and with a twist of his body he brought her up astride him. As she bent her head to kiss him, his expression was as guarded and unreadable as ever. Except that the tension had gone from his face and there was a softening to the corners of his mouth. No words of affection had been spoken, nor had she expected them. But as she moved her hips, she felt the leap of his response within her and gloried in her power to bring pleasure and a degree of peace to this enigmatic man.

The night was young and she was an avid pupil. When their paths crossed again, she was determined that she would not be a forgotten face from an hour of sensual pleasure. She would make him remember her. That determination must sustain her through the empty nights ahead.

Angel, Mark and Gabriellen shadowed their eyes against the sun as they watched the riders pass the furthest paddock. Ambrose and Alexander rode at Rupert's side, taking with them eighteen recruits from the nearby villages, money enough to arm them, and thirty-five of the Rowan horses as mounts for the King's cavalry.

Angel fought against the pain of parting from Rupert. In two days, she had fallen hopelessly in love with him. She had visited his room on both the nights he slept at Rowan Hall. During the days it was obvious that his mind was upon his duties to the King and not dalliance. He had visited another estate fifteen miles away and brought back a dozen horses. When Alexander had arrived yesterday, the men had spent the evening closeted together, engrossed in talk of war and the first battle yet to come.

Now Mark stood with his arm around Gabriellen.

'I cannot believe it has come to this,' Gabriellen sighed. 'The paddocks look deserted.'

'We've kept a dozen mares which are in foal,' Mark replied. 'Next season I had a mind to buy new mares to strengthen the Rowan line. As long as we have Caradoc, the Rowan strain can have no rivals.'

Gabriellen grimaced, though her voice was teasing. 'Sometimes I think you think more of that stallion than you do me.'

Mark grinned. 'Let's be realistic, old girl. Caradoc is in his prime. You are past yours.'

Gabriellen cuffed him playfully on the arm, but her expression sobered as she saw the misery in Angel's eyes. 'You've not fallen for the Prince, Angel? It can only bring you unhappiness.'

'Where was it decreed that a woman gives her heart wisely?' Angel parried. 'I've no illusions. But I have my memories. And if fate is kind we'll meet again.'

'Do not tempt fate,' Gabriellen cautioned. 'It has a way of giving you what you wish for . . . but at a cost.'

Chapter Four

Any doubts Alexander maintained about joining the King's forces dispersed at meeting Prince Rupert in Wales. The Prince spoke passionately of the trouncing he would give Parliament, and of his need for experienced men. On Alexander's agreement to fight, Rupert promoted him to Major.

That was a month ago. Last night Alexander's scouting party had discovered the Earl of Essex's army encamped a few miles away at Kineton. By dawn on the twenty-third of October, Rupert's cavalry were positioned on Edgehill. They occupied the high ground, the steep scarp plunging down to the plain.

Alexander paced the hilltop, trying to bring some warmth to his chilled body. He took out a timepiece and studied it. It could be hours before the action began. He snapped the watchcase shut and ran his finger over its engraved surface. The watch was Bryan Penrose's. Beth had pressed it into his hands on the day he left the manor.

He could not get Beth out of his mind. Unable to return to ensure that Fairburn was not causing trouble, he was worried for her safety. What if the war was not resolved in a single battle, and the whole country was plunged into conflict? How would Beth, a young, beautiful widow, fare at the hands of either side? Elijah Dunnock and his family were good servants, and would ensure the prosperity of the estate, but their religion was against the use of violence.

Fearful for Beth's safety, he searched his heart. It was more than protection he wanted to offer Beth, but he had yet to come to terms with that deeper emotion. It touched perilously close to a betrayal of Bryan's friendship.

The distant beat of a drum tattoo drifted through the morning mist which obscured Red Horse Vale below him. Out of the gloom Essex's army appeared, lining up in formation, barricades hastily positioned as they prepared for combat. Alexander rubbed his red-rimmed eyes. There had been little sleep last night, and less food. Most of the army had gone supperless to their beds. It was still dark when he was beaten up from his quarters to take position on the escarpment.

Hours limped by. Flies buzzed around the horses; the growing tension making them toss their heads and stamp their hooves. Church bells rang out from the surrounding villages, reminding Alexander that this was a Sunday. The mist dispersed. The day was dry and windless. An autumn haze distorted the column of men spread across the field below. The terrain was rough, interspersed with ditches and hedges, some of it under plough. The rest was overgrown pasture, partly covered in scrub.

The heat shimmered, reflecting stars of light upon the cannon barrels, pike tips and armour. Except for the differing coloured sashes – red for the Royalists and orange for Parliament – there was little to tell the two armies apart. Armour and steel helmets from a bygone age had been taken down from the walls of manor houses to equip the men, and the infantry wore the dowdy garments of labourers. At the forefront of the column, pikemen massed to guard the musketmen and cannoneers. With dismay, Alexander saw that the Parliament army was better equipped and outnumbered the Royalists. Colourful banners marked the identity of each troop, lending spectacle to the grave occasion. Among both armies officers rode through the ranks, encouraging their men. Black-garbed preachers chanted prayers as they passed amongst the soldiers. There was one prayer that was taken up and spread through the ranks. Alexander bowed his head and repeated it.

'Dear Lord, you know how busy I must be this day. If I forget you, do not you forget me.'

Alexander stood at his horse's head, absently rubbing the white blaze on its nose as he stared towards the brow of the hill. There, beneath the royal standard, the King sat his horse. The twelve-year-old Prince of Wales and his brother James were with him. It was almost two in the afternoon. What was the King waiting for? Was he loath to join battle with his subjects?

Ambrose approached, leading his horse. 'How much longer must we wait?' he demanded. 'A dawn attack would have routed the enemy. We've delayed until they are gathered in force.'

Murmurings broke out around them and Alexander saw the King ride forward between the lines of troops, addressing them as he passed. 'Your King is your cause, your quarrel and your captain. God be with you this day.'

There was a cheer from the cavalry as Prince Rupert rode to the fore and spoke. 'When we charge, hold your fire until we are upon them. It's not our fire but the force of our charge which will break their ranks. A galloping horse is like a battering ram. It will mow down the enemy more power-fully than any sword. Mount up.'

Alexander swung into the saddle and brought Gawain, his Rowan chestnut gelding, under control. He removed his plumed hat and tied back his long hair to keep it from impairing his vision, then stood in the stirrups to test the girth. The two pistols were primed and ready in their saddle-holsters and his sword could be drawn easily from its scab-bard. The familiar routine quietened the icy fear kneading his gut. Yet there was a dryness in his throat and nervous sweat between his shoulders and on his gauntleted palms as he awaited the order for the charge.

He turned to Ambrose. Beneath a steel bonnet and face-guard, his uncle's expression was grim. Alexander had for-saken his own steel bonnet – a relic from the Tudor wars with Spain – finding it too heavy and cumbersome. Like Ambrose, he wore back-and breastplates.

'God be with you this day, Uncle.'

'With you too, Alex.'

Their gazes held. Alexander had always been fond of Ambrose and in the weeks since they had left Wales they had become even closer. Now, as they shared the pre-battle nerves, he felt a chill breath of fear from his uncle. Ambrose was by nature a gentle man and too heavy for a strenuous fight. There had been little time for training and although Ambrose possessed strength and courage, he had no great skill for combat. Courage was not always enough to survive.

A trumpet sounded and they began to advance down the hill. The Parliament cannons belched smoke, their shot thud-ding into the ground around them. The Royalist cannons answered, their roar deafening as they spewed dun-coloured smoke clouds across the field. Already several empty saddles appeared amongst the cavalry. Ahead of Alexander, Prince Rupert raised his sword, and trumpets sounded the charge as they raced onwards at full gallop.

A troop led by Sir Faithful Fortesque broke from the ranks of the enemy. They discharged their weapons into the ground and pulled off their orange sashes. This defection was greeted by a cheer from the Royalists. It unmanned the Parliamentary horse, who turned and fled under the whirlwind of the Royalist charge.

'At them, men!' Alexander yelled above the cannonade, his sword scything through any enemy within reach.

A cannon-ball exploded nearby, throwing up iron splinters and earth. In front of Alexander, a horse's forelegs crumpled. The rider was catapulted through the air, landing on his head and snapping his neck. Alexander veered to avoid trampling the fallen Cavalier. As he sped past he glimpsed the sightless staring eyes. Many times in the Swedish army he had witnessed that brutal moment between life and death. It still shocked him.

He clenched his jaw, thrusting the vision aside as he concentrated on controlling Gawain. They raced over rough terrain cluttered with bodies and fallen horses. The furious impetus of the charge never faltered. When they broke through the barricades, infantrymen scrambled to safety from the flying hooves. Using his knees, Alexander guided Gawain around obstacles and spurred him to jump an abandoned cannon.

Occasionally, he glimpsed Ambrose battling with an enemy. His uncle fought well, but without the fire and verve of a man who could deal death easily. From his own experience Alexander knew this was not something which was achieved in a single battle. It was acquired through a detachment of mind, mastered over many adversaries. Until you no longer saw the enemy as flesh and blood with families to mourn their passing, a soldier was always at risk. A moment's hesitancy, or a slipping of guard could mean death.

The charge took them through the Parliamentary flank and far along the road to Kineton. With relief, Alexander saw Ambrose amongst their numbers. Realising the futility of wild pursuit, he shouted, 'To me, men! Back to the field! We must support the infantry.'

His voice was lost in the tumult. It was useless. Only Ambrose and a dozen men answered his command. Fired by their victory, the Cavaliers sped on to Kineton to plunder Essex's baggage carts. Frustrated by the shambles of the charge, Alexander returned to the battle. He was too late. The Royalist foot were being driven back. Before his horrified gaze he saw Sir Edmund Verney, the King's standard bearer, killed, and the standard captured.

At the same moment a sword rang against Alexander's backplate with agonising force, pitching him forward on to the pommel of his saddle. He slashed backwards blindly, feeling his blade sink into the flesh of his assailant. Wheeling Gawain round, he parried a thrust to his neck. A swift sideways blow cleaved through his opponent's arm just above the elbow. Blood spurted over Alexander from the stump, and the sword with its gauntleted hand fell to the ground.

There was no time to recover his breath before the deadly point of a pike jabbed towards his face. He lashed out, his sword deflecting the pole before sweeping back to plunge into the pikeman's breast. Faces blurred as he turned from one defeated enemy to the next. His movements were spontaneous and detached, removing him from the bloody destruction he wrought. He was driven by the need to fight on, oblivious of the screams of the men he maimed, and the cries of the dying near his horse's hooves.

The heat of the day was fading and the air had sharpened with frost, but still the bombardment of cannon continued around them. The ground exploded to Alexander's right in a flash of orange. There was a stab of fire as a fragment of shot gouged into his cheek. But his wound was forgotten when he saw Ambrose's horse go down, mount and rider covered in blood. The steel bonnet had gone, shot away with the side of his uncle's face by a flying piece of shot. As the horse fell it rolled over its rider, crushing Ambrose beneath its weight. Horse and man were dead.

Alexander gagged and swallowed the bile rising to his throat. He slammed a door on his grief. The time for that would come later. There was no respite in the fight. A sword arced down towards his head and he parried the blade. Then, ducking low over the saddle, he attacked, fighting by instinct and reflex. Every muscle ached. His shoulders and back were bruised from sword blows, the hand holding the reins was numb. Glancing down, he was surprised to see his sleeve slashed and bloodied from a wound he could not remember receiving. Teeth clenched against weariness and pain, he fought on, knowing that if his strength failed he would die.

As night fell the two armies disengaged. Even if they could have seen to strike at the enemy in the falling dusk, their fury was drained by exhaustion. Retracing his passage across the battlefield, Alexander found Ambrose's body. He heaved the corpse over Gawain's saddle and trudged back to the Royalist camp.

After arrangements had been made to return his uncle's body to Rowan Hall for burial, and a friend had helped him to bind the gash on his arm, he slumped down by a camp fire. Exhaustion bowed his head and, resting it on his drawn-up knees, he closed his eyes. His companions were too tired to talk. They roused briefly when two camp women appeared. One offered a ladle of water to each man, the other passed out bread soaked in a greasy, unappetising gravy and a wedge of cooked meat.

The food revived him, but the night frost was too cold to allow sleep. As the numbness left his arm it began to throb like a beast gnawing at his flesh. Standing up, Alexander wrapped himself in his cloak. He walked between the fires to the ridge overlooking the battlefield and stared across at the bivouac fires of the opposing army. The moonlight was bright enough to show the dark shapes of the ghouls who appeared after every battle, moving amongst the corpses to strip them of their clothing and valuables.

A volley of German curses close by made him turn. The tall figure of Prince Rupert stood several yards away. At his feet, Boy sat, looking up at his master who slapped his gauntlets irritably against his thigh.

The Prince was in the blackest of tempers. Unwilling to become the brunt of it, Alexander backed away. A twig snapped under his foot and Rupert spun round, hand on sword hilt, ready to attack.

'I have disturbed Your Highness.' Alexander continued to retreat.

'The charge was a shambles,' Rupert raged, tension accentuating his German accent. He had been in the thick of the fighting, his fiery temperament making him reckless. 'The men must be trained to better discipline. You did well to rally those you could.'

Rupert scowled in the direction of a drunken chorus coming from Lord Wilmot's tent. 'That sot celebrates. Yet where was his troop on the field today? They did little fighting. There are not enough professional soldiers, or competent advisers to His Majesty.' He began to pace with long controlled strides across the frost-coated grass. 'The council claim that we have gained a victory today. We have gained nothing.'

The violence in that furious pacing amazed Alexander. He was bone weary from the battle and exasperated by the Prince's tireless energy.

Rupert's frustration exploded. 'Essex's army is still intact. The road to London lies open to us, yet will the council heed my advice? Will they seize the advantage and take the capital? No, damn their witless eyes! They hesitate like old women.' Rupert gave a bitter laugh, his breath visible in the night air. 'Why am I telling you this, Rowan?'

'I hope because you trust me, and know it will go no further.' Alexander studied his wild and often arrogant commander. The King's advisers were too set in their ways to know how to deal with this young firebrand with his new ideas on warfare. The Prince had no patience with those who urged caution. 'I fear your frank condemnation of the council has made you enemies, Your Highness.'

Rupert took a dagger from his belt and tested the sharpness of the blade with his thumb. Then he threw it at a woollen cap which had been blown from the campsite. The blade quivered as it pinioned the cap. Rupert snatched up his dagger with a tense angry movement. 'They cannot forgive my foreignness,' he spat out. 'Yet my mother is the King's sister. In my youth I spent many months in this country—' He broke off, a muscle pumping along his jaw.

It was the nearest Alexander had ever seen him come to losing control over his emotions. Despite Rupert's anger, Alexander knew that the Prince held King Charles in high regard.

Rupert went on, 'They accused me of firing London, should I take it ahead of the Royalist army.' A shudder of rage passed through his body as he remembered the insult. 'Would they stand and see the whole country under the sword? That will happen unless this rebellion is crushed now.'

Alexander nodded, the slight movement making him gasp. The throbbing in his arm felt like a hammer pounding hot metal. He cradled it beneath his cloak. The blood had seeped through his bandage and down his arm.

Rupert flicked aside Alexander's cloak. 'Get Captain Carver to tend that wound.'

"Tis nothing, Your Highness.'

'Neglect of such a wound has lost many a man his limb. You'd not so neglect one of your horses. Get it seen to. That's an order.'

Rupert disappeared into the night and Alexander stared down at his bloodied sleeve. His body was beginning to feel as though it did not quite belong to him. The surgeon and physician's tents had been erected at the rear of the camp, and Alexander trudged towards them. The ground surrounding them was covered with the wounded, and the camp women were moving amongst them, giving what aid they could. Outside the surgeon's tent men lay groaning, several with limbs so badly mangled that only amputation would save their lives. From within he heard the rasp of saw on bone and the guttural cry of a patient, muffled by the gag he was biting down on.

He paused outside the physician's tent. Seven hours after the battle a score of men still waited for their wounds to be tended. Most of the injured looked in greater need than himself. On the point of turning away, a spell of dizziness made him halt. He must have lost more blood than he had suspected and the frosty air ate into his bones. He sat on the ground near a fire to wait, his teeth chattering as he felt his body growing weaker. His eyelids drooped but he fought to stay awake, fearful lest if he slept now, he might never awake. Yet he must have dozed, for a hand shaking his shoulder made him start. Captain Carver was bending over him.

'Where are you wounded?' he asked.

When Alexander eased back his cloak, Carver glanced at the steel gorget round Alexander's neck, and then at the wound.

'Officers are treated first. What were you trying to do – see how much blood you have?'

Alexander responded to the Captain's humour with a dry laugh. ' I feel as weak as a babe.'

'You're lucky you didn't bleed to death. Can you walk?'

Captain Carver offered a hand to pull him up. Alexander swayed to his feet and was dismayed when his knees buckled.

'Lean on me,' Carver ordered, and he half dragged Alexander into his tent lit by four lanterns.

The physician worked quickly, peeling back the blood-soaked bandage. Where it had stuck to the wound, he paused to bathe the linen until it came away without pulling on the injury. Alexander peered over his shoulder at the handspan of sliced flesh and saw the glimmer of white bone.

'You were fortunate it is not broken, but it will have to be cauterised to stop the bleeding and prevent the rot setting in.' As Captain Carver spoke he continued to clean the wound, plucking out several threads of linen from the ragged flesh. Then he drew a knife from a small brazier of burning coals.

The blade glowed red. Alexander felt sweat break out along his upper lip and brow. He stared at Carver's face, seeing vivid blue eyes, darkly circled with fatigue. The physician's dark blond hair was tied back, the angular planes of his jaw as darkly stubbled as Alexander knew his own to be. What reserves of strength did Carver possess which he himself lacked? The Captain had been in the thick of the cavalry charge too. He knew Carver by reputation more than acquaintance. The man had spent some years studying in Padua and was credited to be the best physician in the army.

As Alexander braced himself against the searing touch of the blade, he noticed that Carver's face was peppered with pale freckles.

'Major Rowan, isn't it?' Carver said, gripping Alexander's arm and pressing the two edges of the wound together. 'You rode on the right of Rupert today. I saw how you tried to rally your men after the charge.'

'Untrained troops saw only the glory of robbing Essex of

97

his baggage carts, not the need to . . .' Alexander's words were cut off by a sharp oath as the blade was pressed on to his flesh and drawn swiftly along the length of the wound. The flesh sizzled as the two edges were sealed.

'Christ! You could have warned me!' he accused.

'And the pain would have been a dozen times worse.' Carver smeared a salve on to the puckered and scorched flesh and took up a fresh bandage. 'Keep that on for a couple of days. I'll take another look at it then.'

Carver straightened and rubbed a hand across his stubbled jaw. He followed Alexander to the tent entrance and sighed with relief that no more patients awaited him. He looked at Alexander, who could not stop shivering. 'You need plenty of rest to restore your blood.' He winked. 'And nothing will warm you quicker than the heat of a woman in your bed.'

'I'll settle for sleep,' Alexander muttered drily. Carver's reputation as a womaniser rivalled that of his skill as a physician.

'If Morpheus beckons you're fortunate. For me the God of sleep is not so kind. You can't spend three hours hacking down your King's enemies, then a further eight piecing together the wounded, and not despair of the stupidity of men. Were I a drinking man, I'd get roaring drunk. But I'd be a poor physician to indulge. Someone's life might depend upon me being sober. Instead I'll abandon myself to the pleasures of Venus and brief forgetfulness.'

Alexander saw a beautiful woman detach herself from the shadows as Carver sauntered by. She had been waiting to waylay him. What irresistible charm did Carver have? He was not more than an inch above average height and his freckled face was angular, with a cleft chin and prominent cheekbones. There was a scar across one eyebrow which gave him a cynical expression. Yet as soon as he smiled at a woman, they were ready to answer the slightest crook of his finger.

It was happening before his eyes now. Carver welcomed his paramour warmly and as he led her back to his tent, his expression was attentive. His success was simple. He loved women and it showed in his manner. He would take them and forget them, and they forgave him.

Until now, Alexander had dismissed Carver as just another

reprobate, but there was far more to the man than that. He had seen the physician on the battlefield, dealing death with the same expertise as he later saved lives. A soldier and healer were not easy bedfellows. He was a man of opposites, complex, a mixture of silk and steel. Carver had deliberately drawn him into conversation to take his mind from the burning blade. Few physicians were so considerate. If a man of Carver's capacity for caring sought forgetfulness in women, the ghost which haunted his sleepless nights must be something no ordinary man could bear.

Sir Henry Mortimer was in a foul mood as he confronted his wife on his return to Chichester. 'I've had enough of your excuses. You'll leave with me now. If you're not packed, a servant will collect your baggage tomorrow.'

Maressa nodded to Hazel, who was hovering by the door. 'Is that my medicine, Hazel? Bring some wine and saffron cakes for Sir Henry.'

Hazel returned, offering Henry the wine. He drank it in one draught and refilled his goblet. Maressa smiled at her maidservant as she left.

'Henry, can you not be reasonable? I am feeling stronger, but Firkin has had one of his attacks, and I hate to leave him.'

'Bundy fusses over him,' Henry snapped. 'The boy's in no danger.' He swung away from her and, as he did so, put both hands to his head.

Maressa cried out, 'My love, you look pale. Are you ill?'

Henry staggered against the dresser, his eyes glazing as he stared at his wife. 'I feel most odd. My head aches like the devil and I feel cold.'

'The ride from London is arduous. You are tired. Was there sickness where you lodged?'

'There's always pestilence of some kind in London,' he groaned.

'Then it's to bed with you.' Maressa took charge. 'I'll summon a doctor.'

Henry swayed and took three steps to the door, but was forced to stop and cling to her for support. 'I'll not stay in a Royalist house.'

'You're ill!' Maressa was all concern. 'I'll speak to Papa.

You can't ride to Arundel in this state. Hazel's herbal possets have helped Firkin. I don't know how I would have managed without her.'

There was no more devoted wife than Maressa as she hovered over her husband's sick-bed throughout the following weeks. The fever had lasted a fortnight, but the weakness remained, leaving him frail and shaking. It was impossible for them to journey to Arundel. Providing Henry remained in his rooms, Llewelyn tolerated him in the house. By the beginning of November, Henry was stronger but found himself incapable of making love to his wife.

'You've been ill,' Maressa consoled. 'Your vigour will soon return.'

'What would you know?' He was as sulky as a child at each failure. Pushing away the bedclothes, he grabbed her hand and pulled it down to rest on his inert member. 'If you were more of a wife, you'd bring life back to it. You're an insipid bedfellow. You do nothing to help me.'

Maressa withdrew her hand and averted her eyes from his naked flesh. 'I do not care for such talk, Henry. I'm your wife, not a common whore.'

'You're useless,' he spat. 'I won't be denied. Undress. Your body is beautiful. Make me want you.'

Maressa poured herself a goblet of wine and drank it down. Henry disgusted her. The only way she could bear to be in the same room alone with him was to have her senses blurred by wine. 'I will not play your sordid games.'

'You're my wife. You'll do as you are bidden.' He leered at her lasciviously. 'Or perhaps your maid will be more obliging? Why not? Summon the wench. Meg Unwin's sister, wasn't she? She must have learnt a trick or two from Meg. Now there was a wench who knew how to please a man.'

'As you would know well,' she returned with a shiver of distaste. 'I'll not be humiliated. Hazel is not for you, Henry.' She drank a second cup of wine and felt its warmth begin to numb the revulsion he roused in her.

'Then do your duty, wife.'

Maressa shuddered. She knew that whatever she did Henry would remain incapable of possessing her. The brew Hazel concocted each morning ensured that. But his inability had driven him to baser perversions which revolted her. If she did not comply he could become violent, and she was too ashamed to allow him to create a scene in her father's house.

'Undress,' he commanded. 'You know what I like you to do.'

'I cannot manage the laces.'

Henry made no attempt to cover his nakedness and folding his hands behind his head, he grinned, 'Why not summon your maid? You could undress each other.'

It was not the first time he had made the suggestion. Everything about him repelled her now. He was arrogant, selfish and ignorant of any emotion which did not gratify his own self-love.

Inside, she felt as if a part of her had died. Her need to be loved and adored burned as brightly as ever, but her innocence was gone, replaced by chilling insight. Her beauty had made her the Lady Maressa Mortimer. Her looks were her fortune and, until her marriage, they had given her power over her suitors. She had gloried in that power. Then she had been happy. Carnal love left her cold, it was the adoration and power she craved. To that end she had complied with Henry's commands and, by so doing, had enslaved him. She had lost her naïvety, and gained an insight into a greater power over men. Her smile might be forced and the light behind her eyes dimmed, but she was accomplished enough to play the part required of her.

When she turned her back on Henry, her voice was soft and beguiling. 'Undo my laces.'

His fingers were shaking and he fumbled with the fastenings of her gown and the corset beneath. Holding the bodice close to her breasts, Maressa drank more wine. It gave her the courage she needed to turn and face her husband. So that she would not have to see his leer, she closed her eyes.

Sex had never been pleasurable for her, it had been a necessity, to stop Henry visiting whores and humiliating her in public. Her gown slid to the floor and she gritted her teeth as her undergarments followed, but as her hands cupped her breasts she felt a quiver low in her stomach.

'You've the body of a goddess, Maressa,' Henry said in husky veneration, 'but a heart of ice. A man needs warmth and passion. If only you had that fire . . .'

Maressa regarded him through lowered eyelashes. There

was a sheen of perspiration on his face as he gazed at the movement of her hands across her body. So you want your wife to have the soul of a whore, she thought with cold calculation. Beauty may arouse a man, but fire enslaved them. Was she actress enough to hide her revulsion? If that fire was so important to a man, what power would it give to the woman who knew how to use it to her advantage?

For the first time since her marriage she knew she was in control. If men were fools to be so governed by the hunger in their loins, they deserved to be manipulated. Her hands stilled.

'Go on,' Henry rasped.

She was suddenly fearful that he would see through her ruse. His lecherous stare frightened her, and she drank another draught of wine. It dulled her fears. At least now there was no chance of her becoming pregnant, Hazel had the remedy for that.

'You want me, do you not?' Her voice was inviting as her hands caressed her breasts. 'Am I not more beautiful than your other women?'

He eyed her salaciously. 'The most beautiful.'

'Then tell me what I must do to make you happy.'

His instructions were explicit. It was strange that the touch of her own hands on her body did not repel her. Her stroking movements were inexperienced. Henry commanded her to lie on the bed and as her fingers worked between her thighs, stimulating new sensations, she gasped in delight. Her passion was fed by Henry's laboured breathing and the force of the power she now wielded over him. Her body glowed and began to come alive, to pulsate beneath her touch, delicious and exciting. Overwhelmed by the sensations, she arched her back and her own breathing changed.

'That's it,' Henry groaned. 'Now you want me. Tell me you want me.'

She ignored his demand, her body moving in wild response to this sensual initiation. As her body shuddered in a flooding relief, her eyes opened. Henry reared over her, hard and erect. When he entered her it no longer mattered that Hazel's potion had failed, or that his intrusion of her body gave her no joy. Henry's eyes were dark with desire and triumph, but Maressa knew that the triumph was all hers. She yielded to

102

his demands, played out the act of love until he cried out her name at the height of his passion. It no longer mattered that, as usual, Henry had failed to satisfy her. She would make herself indispensable to him. Never again would Henry leave her in Arundel whilst he enjoyed the pleasures of London. What use was a title if she could not flaunt it to win more power?

Angel stared at the messenger, her body frozen in shock. Gabriellen was also silent, then a sob rose to her throat and her body swayed. Jolted out of her stupor, Angel caught her grandmother in her arms, holding her as the violence of Gabriellen's sobs vibrated through her own body.

Mark, pale, and with tears unashamedly on his cheeks, carried Ambrose's broken body into the old hall and laid it on the long table. Gabriellen fell to her knees by the makeshift bier. When she reached out to remove the Royalist sash which covered her son's face, Mark stopped her.

'Don't look at his wounds. I will prepare him,' he said, in a voice raw with pain. 'The funeral will be today, as soon as the preacher can be summoned. It will be better that way.'

Angel stared at her grandparents bowed over the corpse and, though her own grief was acute, she left them to mourn in private.

The messenger who had brought the body was hovering awkwardly. He was Owain, one of the grooms who had ridden out with Ambrose.

'Go to the kitchens,' Angel said. 'Cook will give you wine and food. Later my grandparents will wish to hear the news of the battle. But first tell me . . . my brother, Major Rowan . . . he was not killed, or wounded?'

'It was Major Rowan who sent me. He was wounded in the arm, but not seriously. He was lucky. We both were.' Owain's composure slipped and his eyes were dark with remembered horrors. He pressed a grimy hand to his brow, adding wearily, 'Forty thousand men fought at Edgehill. They say six thousand died, and thousands more were wounded. And for what? It solved nothing. There was no victory and no defeat.'

A week after the funeral, though the atmosphere at the Hall was subdued, Gabriellen and Mark had not allowed their grief to cast a gloom over Angel's visit. There was always work to be done for the horses and those everyday tasks were their salvation. Angel finished mucking out the stables and was drawn to watch Mark grooming Caradoc. The stallion was skittish from lack of exercise. Mark's white head was pressed against the stallion's chestnut coat as he worked. Since Ambrose's death he no longer sang as he tended the horses.

Gabriellen put down her bucket after watering the mares and said, 'Why don't you ride Caradoc, Mark? He needs exercising.'

'I will later.' He glanced up at the milky clouds forming over the surrounding hills. 'There'll be rain before night, and a lot of it. With only ten mares there's room in the stables for them all this winter. Perhaps I should send to Llangollen for one of my nephews to come and help us?'

'Four of them rode with Ambrose,' Gabriellen reminded him.

Mark nodded. He laid a hand on Caradoc's back, his eyes crinkling as he grew thoughtful. Then he chuckled and looked at Angel. 'I doubt you remember my sister Aphra and her husband Saul. You met them when you were four. They both died before you came to Wales again. I spent a whole winter once, trying to persuade Aphra and Saul to continue to live here with us. We were partners in starting up the stud. But my sister was stubborn and so was her husband. They wanted land and property of their own.'

His eyes misted with remembrance, and then he laughed again. 'A sign of old age, my dear, when one's mind dwells more often upon the past than the future. It's not good for you, Angel, to spend so long in the company of we greyheads. I'll ask my nephew Davydd to send one of his daughters for companionship. It's time you saw more of your Welsh kin.'

Sadness returned to Gabriellen's face and she sighed. 'I still miss Saul and Aphra. How long is it since Aphra died? Seven years and Saul gone three before that. And now Ambrose . . .' her voice broke on a sob.

'Ellen, my love.' Mark took his wife into his arms.

'Gabriellen,' Angel spoke softly, hesitant to intrude upon their grief. 'Shall I write to Aunt Sabine? It's been three years since you visited her in Paris.'

Gabriellen drew back from Mark and wiped a tear from the corner of her eye. 'The winter gales will soon be upon us and my daughter gets terribly seasick. Remarkable, considering her father was a buccaneer. If the country is more settled by the spring we will all visit Paris.'

Angel recognised the effort Gabriellen was making to control her grief. She lifted her head and quoted softly:

' "*Do not weep for me when I am gone.*
For I am free of worldly persecutions.
Free of pain, free of this dark imprisonment of my soul.
I go to my God with glory in my heart, in honour and in triumph.
So do not weep when I am gone. Rather weep for those still living." '

'They are beautiful words,' Gabriellen said. 'Where did you hear them?'

'In my heart.' Angel smiled. 'They came to me just now. But wouldn't they make a splendid soliloquy in my play *The Tragic Queen*?' Lost to the former gravity of the moment, Angel clasped her hands to her breast, her expression rapt. 'The Queen would deliver them as she stands before the block in Fotheringhay Hall.'

The moment of levity lightened the atmosphere. Even Gabriellen smiled fondly. 'The blood of Esmond Angel is in her veins.'

'But 'tis the Welsh in her which brings poetry to her words,' Mark amended. 'I suspect a skill greater than Esmond's lies dormant. It equals yours, Ellen.'

'I think it surpasses mine. Her talent must not be wasted.'

Gabriellen buried her grief. Ambrose was beyond her help, but there still was much she could offer Angel. She hugged her granddaughter. 'Having you here is a great comfort, my dear. I look forward to seeing a play of yours performed upon the stage. And there's a man who will help you. Robin Flowerdew. He acted with Esmond's players. At the age of seventy he's formed a new company which he intends to take to France. He wrote to me, asking if he could have some of my comedies translated into French. Perhaps he'd welcome a new play to enhance their repertoire?'

Angel's eyes rounded with pleasure. 'Do you think Robin Flowerdew would perform work from my pen?'

'He's astute enough to know what will make his fortune. Besides, is not your name Angel bestowed on both sexes? I doubt he'll proclaim it was written by a woman. Yet if you've a mind to be a playwright, Paris is the place for you. I know Sabine would be delighted if you visited her. Let us use this winter to create a memorable play together. The French seem to prefer comedy to tragedy, so we will work on a humorous piece.'

'That would be wonderful.' Angel whirled away to spin round, unable to contain her pleasure. 'And perhaps in the spring we could visit Aunt Sabine in Paris. I shall never forget the glorious summer I spent with her three years ago.'

'So much energy,' Mark said with a laugh. 'What it is to be young! Now I must get these aged bones of mine down to the paddocks. The weather will not hold for long and I'd have the horses stabled by nightfall.'

'We will help,' Gabriellen insisted.

Mark lifted his hands in protest. 'There are few enough horses. I can manage, my love.' He kissed her cheek. 'Besides, there's a sparkle in your eyes from hearing that extract from Angel's play. That light has been absent too long. Go and help her create that masterpiece.'

Applause greeted the end of Angel's reading of her comedy play.

Gabriellen stood up. 'Bravo! I couldn't have written anything finer myself. You could be a great playwright if you're prepared to face the persecutions of our sex.'

Popinjay, who in the last week had been able to leave his bed and was gaining strength with each day, beamed his approval. 'I don't know when last I laughed more.'

'If you think I have talent, I'll face any persecution to have my work performed,' Angel said. 'If a woman has skill and a voice, it should be heard.'

'I'm proud of you, Angel,' Gabriellen said.

At the sound of several horses approaching at speed, Gabriellen went over to the window. 'Visitors!' She frowned. 'No, they look like soldiers. What can they want?'

Standing at Gabriellen's side, Angel saw Mark come out

of the stables, leading Caradoc, who was saddled ready for his daily ride. Mark tethered the stallion to the paddock rail and moved towards the horsemen. After a brief greeting the troop captain raised his voice in anger.

Gabriellen hastened towards the door. 'They wear the orange sash of Parliament. I'll see what they want. Stay here, Angel.'

'No. I'm coming too. And I'll bring Mark's sword.'

'Have you any other weapons?' Popinjay asked.

'There's not many since we equipped Ambrose's troop. Look in the gun room. There's an old matchlock pistol left and some rusty swords.'

'If it comes to running a man through,' Popinjay snorted, 'I'll not trouble myself that he'll get blood poisoning. Just as long as the blade's not been weakened.' He followed them, adding, 'I'll summon the servants. Best to be prepared. I don't trust those rebels.'

Whilst Gabriellen waited for Angel to collect Mark's sword, she loaded and primed his pistol. There had been menace in the heated exchange from outside. Mark would never aid any man who had taken up arms against the King. She looked across at Angel before they left the house. 'Hide the sword in the folds of your skirt. There's nothing to be gained by deliberately antagonising those men.'

As they approached the riders, Mark's angry voice carried to them. 'You'll not have the mares, Captain Pollett.' He stood between the soldiers and the stables. 'They're all in foal, and in no condition to be used as war-horses.'

'Those are the words of a Malignant,' the captain sneered. His voice rose several octaves, showing his lack of experience in command. 'I sequester them in the name of Parliament. Get out of my way, old man.'

Mark did not move. With fear in her heart, Angel knew that he would not allow them to take the last of the brood mares and bring an end to the Rowan strain. Mark would fight to his last breath to prevent a Rowan horse being ridden against the King.

Captain Pollett was young, about twenty, and his slight build was apparent beneath his buff coat and breastplate. And he was nervous . . . A dangerous combination. Obviously, Pollett needed to prove himself in front of his men.

His appearance was too immaculate, his blond hair too precisely curled, and his moustache too carefully trimmed. He looked like a pampered son of a wealthy merchant. But most disturbing of all was the frantic light in this eyes. The man was a coward.

Angel's fingers tightened on the sword hilt clasped to her side. 'Grandpapa, let the horses go!'

Even as she cried out, Pollett levelled his pistol at Mark. 'Stand aside! I'll not ask again.'

Tethered to the paddock fence, Caradoc pranced nervously.

'That's a splendid stallion.' Pollett eyed the horse greedily.

'He'll let no stranger near him,' Mark warned.

Embarrassed colour crimsoned the captain's face. There was a muffled titter from one of his men. Without warning, Pollett's pistol flared, and Angel stared in horror as Mark recoiled backwards for several paces. As he recovered his balance she saw blood streaming from his shoulder.

'God curse you!' Gabriellen screamed, running to her husband's side.

Mark waved her aside. 'Stay away, my love.' His face was as white as his hair. A scarlet stain was spreading across his green leather doublet. He stood, barring the way to the stables , his black eyes blazing his contempt. 'The mares are useless to you. They'll abort if ridden too hard. Go! There's nothing for you here.'

'And what of the other horses?' Jeremy Pollett demanded. He passed his pistol to the soldier beside him to reload. 'I was told there were at least forty in the paddocks here.'

'All gone. Taken by Prince Rupert some weeks ago.'

'Prince Robber, more like,' the captain sneered. 'The mares will have to do. Unless you want your house and land sequestered for hindering the just cause of your Parliament.'

'No court will uphold such blatant robbery,' Mark countered.

'There is no law which protects Malignants.' Scowling, Pollett jerked his head for his men to dismount. He retrieved his loaded pistol and laid it across his lap. 'Round up the mares. And you two get the stallion.'

'The stallion stays!' Mark shouted.

Caradoc's nostrils flared as he caught the scent of Mark's

blood. His eyes showing their whites, he reared pulling back on his rope tether.

'Is that a threat, Rowan?' Pollett sneered.

With a high whinny, Caradoc came down on all fours and lashed out with his back legs, catching a soldier on the hip. The man screamed in pain, and Mark sprang forward.

'No, Mark!' Gabriellen grabbed his uninjured arm. 'You can't take on an entire troop.'

'I've enough life in me to teach that milksop a lesson in manners.'

Two soldiers were circling Caradoc, avoiding his hooves as they tried to snatch at the rope. A third man appeared, holding a whip. When it was brought down on the stallion's muzzle, Mark tore himself from his wife's hold.

'Christ rot you!' He ran towards his horse. 'Leave him be! Don't you know a frightened stallion can kill a man!'

The soldier ignored Mark's outburst and brought the whip down a second time upon Caradoc's tender muzzle. The horse shied, his eyes rolling as he kicked out wildly. One shod hoof struck the soldier on the side of the head and the man went down beneath Caradoc's stamping hooves.

Gabriellen took Angel by the shoulder and tried to turn her way from the grisly sight, as the horse trampled the bloodied pulp that had once been a man. Angel wrenched herself away, her fears all for Mark and Caradoc. Mark pushed one trooper aside, but another crouched, trying to pull his comrade away from the lethal hooves.

'It's too late, man,' Mark yelled. 'He's dead.'

'That beast is a man-killer. He must die,' Captain Pollett raged. 'Shoot it, men!'

'No!' Mark shouted above the frantic screams of the terrified stallion. Caradoc was crazed by the smell of blood in his nostrils. Keeping a safe distance from the horse's hooves, Mark positioned himself between the soldiers and the stallion's head.

When the first of them raised his pistol to fire, Mark leapt at his arm to deflect the aim, but his wound and stiffened joints betrayed him. As the pistol sounded, Mark met the bullet full in the heart. He fell dead at Gabriellen's feet.

'Murderers!' Gabriellen pointed her pistol at Jeremy Pollett as she knelt on the cobbles by her husband's side. 'Get off my land. You've got what you came for.' Her voice was shrill like a soul in torment. 'Go before I kill you.'

There was a movement from behind the captain. A lantern-jawed veteran had drawn his pistol. They fired simultaneously.

Captain Pollett slumped over his saddle with a cry of agony, clutching his smashed kneecap. Gabriellen pitched sideways, a hole in the centre of her temple, where the bullet had entered her brain.

Angel saw it all with sickening horror. It was a nightmare. Dear God let her wake and find it had not happened! When Pollett primed his pistol to aim it at Caradoc, something in her mind snapped. Mark and Gabriellen had died to save the stallion – died so that the Rowan strain would continue through his bloodline.

A howl of fury scraped her throat raw as she raced across the intervening space. Raising her sword, she sliced through Caradoc's tether, and the stallion bolted from the yard. Angel whirled to face the soldiers, the sword held before her in deliberate challenge. Pollett remained slumped over his saddle, in too much pain to give a coherent order. Many of his troop were white-faced and appalled at the savageness of the events. The lantern-jawed veteran had been joined by a pock-marked comrade with a face as cruel as any villain hanged from Tyburn's gallows.

'Ain't she a spirited wench,' he jeered. 'Reckon she should be taught a lesson. Can't have 'er freeing a valuable 'orse like that.'

They advanced towards her. Angel backed away, the sword held like a talisman before her trembling figure. Her grandparents were dead. Her grief was so powerful it mazed her wits, bringing her close to hysteria. The soldiers approached her through a mist, but the lust in their eyes triggered Angel's instincts for survival.

Her attack was swift and unexpected. She lunged straight for the veteran's heart, but at the last minute he sidestepped and she felt the suction on her blade as it sank into his fleshy shoulder.

'The bitch! She's stuck me like a pig. Get 'er.'

Angel sprang away and, her sword raised on guard, she crouched awaiting the attack. It did not come. From behind the soldier, Popinjay appeared, carrying a brace of ancient matchlock pistols. The lighted tapers smouldered as they hung against each barrel. Both pistols were cocked and ready to fire. At his side, Owain held a sword; another groom and the cook were armed with a pitchfork and a meat cleaver, the gardener brandished a scythe, and Gwen the maid held out a rusty halberd.

'There's been enough killing and injustice here today,' Popinjay declared. His waist-length grey hair blew back from his figure like a mantle and his patchwork doublet was out of place in the gruesome setting. 'Take the horses and go. I can kill two more of you before you take me. Are you willing to risk others being killed by the servants?'

Jeremy Pollett pushed himself to a half-crouch. 'Get me out of here. I need a physician. The justices can deal with these Malignants later.'

Angel turned away from the soldiers and moved to her grandparents' corpses. Their blood had mingled on the flag-stones and in death their hands were touching. There was a roaring in her ears and the blur of tears blotted out the sight and sounds of the soldiers leaving with the mares.

'Caradoc. I must find Caradoc.' Her dazed mind veered away from the horror of her grandparents' death to centre upon a minor problem.

'The stallion will return to his stall,' Owain said, gently leading her away from the bodies.

She pulled back. 'I must see to them. Lay them out. Get the preacher . . .'

Popinjay put a hand on Angel's shoulder. 'I shall tend to all that. You should rest.'

Cook and Gwen were weeping hysterically and Angel stared at them numbly, then her gaze returned to Mark and Gabriellen. 'I'll not rest until they are avenged.'

She stumbled away, drawn to the peace of the hills. Moving in a trance she began to gather the few flowers untouched by the recent frost to place around her grand-parents' bier in the hall.

Everyone from the surrounding villages and hamlets came to the funeral. Angel had not spoken since she had walked away from the stableyard. Her eyes were dull throughout the

111

service, and afterwards she nodded absently as the congregation offered their condolences. She was vaguely aware that her cousin Davydd was insisting that she consider her future. Her eyes focused on his kindly face. He was almost bald and what little there was of his grey hair was cut short to his ears. Davydd was the eldest of Mark's nephews, but she did not want to listen to his words. She had wrapped herself in a world of silence to forget the horrors she had witnessed.

Still Davydd gave her no peace. When the guests had all gone and it was growing dark, he took her by the shoulders and shook her gently, his voice rough with concern.

'Angel, this silence is unnatural. Popinjay says you haven't cried. You can't keep your pain locked within you. You'll go mad.'

She did not respond. His voice droned on. Then what he was saying began to anger her.

'. . . go back to Chichester, Angel.'

She shook her head. 'They must be avenged. They must be avenged.' She began to chant the words over and over, her hysteria mounting as her hand balled into fists and she began to strike at her breast. Then one side of her face was on fire and her head snapped back. Davydd had slapped her. She stared at him, wide-eyed, then her face crumpled and tears flooded from her in hard, wrenching sobs.

'Cry all you need, Angel,' he soothed holding her tight as she poured out her grief.

It left her weak, but her resolve remained unchanged. 'For the moment the house will be shut up,' she said. 'Caradoc returned last night. His spirit seems to have broken, but he is still a fine horse. A horse who could serve Alexander well in battle. Caradoc is his now. I'm going to Alexander at Oxford. Later I may visit Aunt Sabine in Paris.'

'Return to Chichester,' Davydd insisted. 'Owain will escort you. He'll not go to Oxford. After Edgehill he has no wish to return to the fighting.'

'Then Popinjay will take me.' She looked across at the pedlar. His changed appearance startled her. He no longer wore his patchwork doublet, but was dressed in sober brown with a plain white falling band at his throat. His waist-length grey hair had been cut to his shoulders.

He nodded. 'I owe you that much for saving my life. I've

business in Oxford which I've delayed for too long. But I am no longer Popinjay. The times have passed when a brightly-dressed pedlar, who juggled and fiddled to draw the crowds to his wares, can pass unremarked through a village. Like as not the Puritans would stone me, thinking my simple sleight-of-hand tricks were the work of the devil. It's John Sparrow now – my real name, as it happens. Your servant, Angel, and the King's.'

'Angel, I wish you would reconsider,' Davydd protested.

A fervent glitter brightened Angel's eyes. 'I leave tomorrow.'

She did not add that she intended to don man's attire and fight for the King. She hated the Parliamentarians and everything they stood for; the deaths of her grandparents would be avenged.

Chapter Five

Llewelyn Rowan stormed out of the Old Priory, now used as the Town Hall. The air was damp with sea-mist, and the smell of malt and ale from the breweries and malthouses was oppressive as it hung over Chichester. He avoided the narrow streets leading off the main thoroughfare. After last night's rain the unpaved streets were ankle-deep in mud, and the runnels down their centre filled with stinking garbage. Seagulls, driven inland by the rough sea, circled the market-place with its penned cattle and sheep, their cries incessant as they swooped down to scavenge for food in the alleyways.

With each step Llewelyn's anger intensified. The meeting in the Town Hall had been called for the people to hear the city's plans to strengthen the fortifications. He had been uneasy since the trained band of militia had declared itself for Parliament, together with most of the town officials. Now, alarmed by the recent successes of the King's army, they had borrowed seven cannon from Portsmouth Castle to ensure the city did not fall into Royalist hands.

A sporadic burst of gunfire made him turn to investigate. Foreboding warned him that this was more than some hot-heads practising at arms. Until last week he had refrained from taking sides. He had recoiled from the havoc and destruction which civil war would wreak upon his country. Each day he had seen the hatred flaring between neighbours. Those he had once considered the most godly, he now saw as fanatics who would bring wholesale devastation to this land. Where was the godliness in that? Rather it was evil which triumphed, pervading the hearts and minds of law-abiding men. As an architect and builder, he abhorred war's destruction. He was by nature a diplomat, preferring logic and reason to mindless violence, but since the deaths of

115

Gabriellen and Mark he could no longer remain neutral. Despite the warning from the authorities, he had joined the minority of Royalist supporters within the city. Legislation had been passed to prevent the disturbance of the peace of the kingdom in an unnatural war raised by His Majesty against Parliament. The very wording of such a law roused Llewelyn's ire. It was now lawful to seize any Royalist's land, horse, arms, or money. It was a decree authorising pillage, and it had given an inexperienced officer the excuse to murder Gabriellen and Mark.

As he entered North Street, Llewelyn saw that the gunner at the North Gate was being attacked by Royalists. Drawing his sword, he ran to their aid. Tempers were high and in a rush of numbers the Royalists overthrew the gun from its carriage. A cheer went up and, with success pumping through their veins, they set upon the next enplacement. Again triumphant, they pressed on throughout the city until every cannon was in their hands.

'A watch must be set on these guns,' Llewelyn advised.

There were murmurs of agreement and the men looked at him for further orders. 'The streets must be patrolled,' he continued. 'There's bound to be trouble. Stop any attempt at looting.'

'Aye, and we should get the keys from the mayor,' someone shouted. 'Will you lead the deputation, Mr Rowan?'

'That I will.' Llewelyn did not hesitate. This was for Gabriellen and Mark as much as for the King. He would lose everything if he failed; not least his freedom, perhaps even his life. He raised his hand to summon the men to follow him. 'The keys must be kept for King Charles. And word must be sent to Sir Edward Ford of Uppark. As Sheriff he can order the trained bands to assemble here to defend the city against a Parliament retaliation.'

The next morning the Sheriff, accompanied by a small army, marched into the city. A Royal Proclamation of pardon was read to the assembled crowds.

Sir Edward Ford later addressed his men. 'Seize all arms hidden in the houses of Parliament supporters.'

'It's believed that several Parliamentarians have fled the city to get help,' Llewelyn spoke out.

'We must hold Chichester for His Majesty,' responded Sir Edward. 'Its coastal harbour will be a haven for any help sent from across the Channel and for maintaining trade. Holding Chichester is just the beginning. The county must be ours. Sussex and its iron industry can produce both cannon and shot. It must not fall to Parliament. To secure Sussex we must next take Lewes.'

In the first week of December Llewelyn rode out of Chichester with Ford's troops. When they encountered a Parliamentary force at Hayward's Heath they were completely routed. Too many of their number had been pressed into reluctant service, and they lost more men from desertion than in combat. Their confidence shaken, the Royalists fled back to Chichester to prepare against a siege. Within days, news reached them that Arundel, a few miles inland, had fallen to Sir William Waller. By the next day, Waller's army was encamped to the north of the city.

Maressa, like many others, stood on the city walls to watch and gauge the size of the army. What she saw filled her with alarm. Men and horses were spread across the heath and there was a great deal of activity amongst their troops. Tents for the commanders were erected and the colourful banners of each troop were dotted amongst their ranks. The baggage carts were drawn up at the rear, smoke rose from the cooking fires and barricades were being erected. Behind the barricades, Maressa saw cannon being mounted.

'There are so many,' she said to her father who stood at her side. 'Can we withstand a siege from such a number?'

'Word was sent to the King as soon as it was known that Waller approached. We must trust that Prince Rupert will relieve the city, but I fear the enemy within more than the one without.'

Maressa bowed her head and laid it against Llewelyn's shoulder. 'The enemy is indeed within and closer than you think. I must leave your house. Henry has declared for Parliament. Papa, I'm so ashamed. I'm married to a traitor. How can I honour a husband who would betray those I love?'

'I never did trust Mortimer,' Llewelyn said harshly. 'But you were besotted with the man. You were so set upon becoming the Lady Maressa Mortimer, I couldn't deny you. I'll have no traitor under my roof, but you . . .' He drew

117

his daughter close. 'How can I bear to lose you? But a woman's place is with her husband, and a dutiful wife must obey her husband in all things.'

'I made a terrible mistake. I don't love Henry. And now he has shamed me, humiliated me before my family.' She wanted to tell him about Henry's infidelities, of the obscene practices he indulged in. Pride made her keep silent. It was unthinkable to mention those depravities to her father. Instead she chose a safer ground for complaint. 'How can I revere Henry when he sets himself against my family and my King? What loyalty can I give to a man who supports the murderers of my grandparents?'

Grief contorted Llewelyn's face and Maressa slid her arm through his.

He patted her hand and said tiredly, 'They died defending what they held most dear. You will always be welcome in our house, but even a father should not come between husband and wife. Many families are split in their loyalties by this war. It's another burden we must endure. When it ends the breaches will be healed, for we are one nation – one family – even when divided.' He sighed and looked out across the encampment. 'Did you know Angel has gone to join Alex at Oxford? Of all the hare-brained antics . . . she intends to fight for the King.'

Maressa heard the note of pride mixed with anxiety in his voice and smothered her irritation. 'Angel always was a hoyden. You've said often enough she should have been born a boy.'

A trumpet sounded from Waller's camp. Under a flag of truce, a deputation rode towards the city gate and the terms of the city's surrender were read out. It demanded the delivery of the Sheriff and all Royalist delinquents.

Llewelyn looked grave as he led Maressa down from the ramparts. 'No man of honour could agree to those terms. God have mercy upon our city.'

When Maressa arrived back at the house she was startled to see Henry up and dressed. He was buckling on his sword as she entered their bedchamber. A more natural colour had come back to his cheeks and her glance darted to the bedside table where the cup of medicine had not been touched.

'It's good to see you out of bed, Henry. But are you sure

118

you're strong enough? You risk a relapse of the fever.'

'How can I lie abed when Waller is outside the walls? As a Member of Parliament it's my duty to rally men to our cause. We shall overcome the Royalists within the city and throw the gates open to Waller.'

She felt the same disgust at his treachery as she did for his depravity, and hid it beneath a false smile. 'I rejoice at your recovery. But you've not taken your medicine.' She picked up the cup and held it out to him. Hazel had made the brew stronger today, to ensure that Henry remained confined to his bed and could give no aid to Waller.

'Oddly, I feel better for not having taken it,' he eyed her narrowly.

She felt the smile freeze upon her lips. 'That's your imagination. This medicine helped you recover from the fever. Just because you're feeling stronger does not mean the fever will not return.' She pressed the cup into his hand. 'Take it for me, as a precaution.'

'You are very attentive to me of late.' His stare was suspicious.

She allayed it with a provocative look up at him through her lashes. 'Is that not a wife's duty? You were away for many weeks, and I missed you. I want to care for you, to cherish you . . . to learn how better to please you. I was so innocent when we married, I didn't understand the needs of a man. Please, Henry, drink your medicine.' She lifted the goblet. 'I'd not have you overtaxing your strength.'

He took the cup and drank, then pulled her towards him. 'Duty is onerous when it takes me from you. When I return I'll prove that my strength has not failed. We'll have a night of love.'

An hour later Henry was brought home on a litter, having suffered a relapse of his fever, and was again forced to his bed. It was not a serious attack, just enough to prevent him from aiding the besieging army.

Maressa was laying cloths upon Henry's hot brow when the bombardment began. At first the enemy fire overshot the city. As their aim improved, the houses around them began to reverberate from the impact of the cannonballs. Hazel screamed and dived under the four-poster bed to save herself.

Irritated by her maid's cowardice, Maressa ordered her

out. 'Get a hold upon yourself, girl. The noise of the bombardment is bad enough without you adding to it. Go and make a sedative for yourself and give some to Goodwife Bundy, I can hear her wailing downstairs.'

The next morning, Henry was lucid and started abruptly as the day's bombardment began. 'What the devil's that?'

'Waller is firing on the city,' Maressa said, laying a cool compress on his brow.

He lay back on the pillow. 'My head. It pounds. That feels good.' He took her wrist and held it against his stubbled cheek. 'I feel so weak again. Has the physician been?'

'He says you have the tertian fever. You must have caught it whilst in London. It will come and go. I warned you not to overtax your strength. The physician bled you, that is why you're so weak.'

'But the siege?'

Henry made to struggle up and was pushed down by Maressa. 'You can do nothing from your sickbed.'

'I won't stay in a Royalist house.' His blue eyes narrowed as they focused on her face with unnerving intensity.

'We will leave as soon as you're strong enough.' She hid her disquiet. She was worried about her father. Should Waller force the city to surrender it would go ill for their Royalist leaders. With Henry in residence, it gave them a foot in both camps. Maressa dismissed her lack of scruples. She had no patience with this war brought about by the stubbornness of men. It had disrupted her life and forced her to take sides against the family who adored her.

The siege continued over Christmas. The weather favoured the besieging army, remaining dry and free from frost as they camped in the open. Frequently, drunken revelry was heard in the streets as the citizens bolstered their courage. Soon there was dissent within beleaguered Chichester, and the Royalists feared betrayal as the bombardment continued.

Though Hazel ensured that Henry was intermittently free of the fever, he was never strong enough to leave the house. Throughout the siege he demanded Maressa remain with him, commanding her to sing to him. On his stronger days they played chess, or he would insist she lock the door and slowly disrobe in front of him. On days when the medicine kept him impotent he became more demanding in his appe-

120

tites. A fire was kept burning in the chamber and in the afternoons when Llewelyn was out of the house he insisted she tend him naked.

At first she was embarrassed by this, but gradually she found it exciting to hear Henry praising her body. She obeyed his commands and when he demanded that she stroke her breasts and thighs, she remained just out of his reach as he watched her. She used her newly learned sensuality to hold him captivated, prolonging her own pleasure and revelling in the power it gave her over him. When he wanted his hands and feet bound by silken cords to the bed-posts, she obeyed him. Had not her father said that a dutiful wife must obey her husband in all things?

She clung to that thought to salve her troubled conscience. At those times her power over Henry was supreme. He would beg for her favours, vow eternal devotion and plead with her to release him from his sexual torment. How sweet his pleas were to her ears. They assuaged her anger at his infidelities and soothed the humiliation of his betrayal. But most important of all they stopped him aiding Waller, she reasoned to justify her actions and ease her moral conscience.

It was some days before she realised that Henry seemed content to allow the fate of the city to be decided by Waller. He made no further attempts to leave his sickroom. Then she realised that, whichever side won, Henry could not lose. Whilst he was housed under a Royalist roof, he could easily declare his loyalty to the Crown. Since he had been carried away from the meeting on a stretcher, every Parliament supporter knew of his illness and inability to act.

Oxford lay in the valley below Angel. Outside the battlemented walls the steel-coloured river curved, overhung by willow trees. Beyond them the water-meadows were flooded in places and laced with twisting streams. Frost hung in the air, making the breath steam from Caradoc's nostrils, but Angel did not feel the cold. She felt anger, frustration and grief at the butchery of her grandparents. There was a wildness in her green eyes as she pushed her woollen cloak back over one shoulder. She was dressed in man's attire, a pistol and dagger in the red sash about her slender waist, and hanging from her grandfather's silver-studded baldric across

121

her chest was his sword. Upon it she had vowed to be avenged for her grandparents' deaths.

'There is Oxford,' John Sparrow said as he brought the Rowan gelding given them by Davvyd alongside Caradoc. 'Do you still intend to go ahead with your madcap plan?'

The stallion tossed his head and Angel kept him on a tight rein. 'The Roundheads must be defeated. England must be saved from their persecution before others like my grandparents are murdered.'

'Their deaths were tragic, but similar atrocities will occur on both sides.'

Angel removed her plumed hat and wiped a speck of dust from her eye. Her black hair had been trimmed to below her shoulders, and it framed her face in soft natural curls. Her face was grim with resolution. 'I'll not change my mind.'

She turned Caradoc towards the west gate. Frost silvered the roofs of the honey-coloured towers, turrets and spires behind the city walls, and the smoke which rose from the chimneys was sluggish in the approaching dusk. They joined a trail of wagons lined up to enter the city before curfew.

'What are your plans, John?' Angel realised the pedlar mentioned little of his past or his future.

He shrugged. 'I'll restock my wares and travel the countryside.'

'You must learn much information that way.'

'Pedlars are purveyors of gossip. It's what makes them so welcome in isolated villages and manors.'

'It would also make them invaluable as a spy.'

John Sparrow shook his grey head, but the look in his eyes was suddenly wary. She countered it with a wry smile. 'Mark recognised you. I'm sure you know he was Queen Elizabeth's spy. No ordinary pedlar would summon Prince Rupert to speak to him and be obeyed. You need not fear. Your secret is safe with me.'

'You have an active imagination, Mistress Rowan.'

Her smile broadened, certain she had guessed the truth. 'We all have our secrets. Am I not to be introduced in Oxford as Major Rowan's brother?'

A sharp blast on a trumpet warned of approaching riders. The wagons and riders ahead of Angel pulled to the side of the road. As Angel followed suit, she saw a troop of forty

Cavaliers cantering towards her. At their head rode Prince Rupert. Her gaze clung to his scarlet-cloaked figure and her heart contracted. As the Prince turned to stare at John Sparrow, her pulse raced. The Prince inclined his head in acknowledgement, recognising the pedlar, despite his changed appearance. Angel pulled her hat low over her eyes. If Rupert recognised her, she would not be allowed to fight. He frowned as his stare rested upon Caradoc as he rode by.

'Alex was not with the Prince,' she said, guiding Caradoc on to the road. 'If we follow the troop, someone must know where my brother is lodged.'

Once through the city gate, they rode up the winding cobbled street between tall gabled houses. The city was dominated by the high-walled buildings of the colleges, and through narrow alleyways and gatehouses she caught glimpses of gardens and paved courtyards. There were cheers from ahead as the Prince was recognised, and out of the houses children appeared to run after the troop. From one of the gardens came the sound of pipe music, and loud voices could be heard from the mullioned windows. The city was crowded: Cavaliers resplendent in bright brocades, velvet and expensive lace jostled with merchants in more sober attire. Boys ran yelling down the streets, wielding wooden swords, and dogs barked behind garden gates. To provision the army a constant stream of baggage carts poured into the city.

Ahead, Angel saw Prince Rupert ride into St John's College. When she reached the gateway she paused to stare into the courtyard, and saw Boy run out to leap, barking, around his master's feet. There was impatience in Rupert's long stride as he marched into the college. Angel sighed. Her love for him was as strong as ever, but she was realistic enough to accept that winning this war was more important than any woman. Although the Royalists were to winter in Oxford, Rupert had too much energy to remain cooped within its walls.

Three Cavaliers who had ridden with the Prince had dismounted before a tavern. Angel hailed them, deepening her voice to fit her masculine attire. 'Good sirs, I have just arrived in Oxford. Would you know where my brother, Major Alexander Rowan, is billeted?'

'Rowan? Never heard of him,' the burliest of the trio

grunted. 'Come, my friends, we waste good drinking time.'

Tired from her long ride and angered by the man's rudeness, Angel responded tartly. 'Go push yourself to the front of the trough. I would not inconvenience you further.'

The man swung about, his eyes narrowed and brutish at the insult. 'Would you care to repeat that?'

Angel realised her error. She had forgotten that she was disguised as a man and as such could expect little courtesy from a soldier. The stocky Cavalier was looking for a fight. From the quality of his clothes he was a gentleman, and from his girth, overfond of indulging his appetites. He was about thirty and beneath his waxed moustache was a small petulant mouth. This was a man who used his rank to bully his way through life, and her throat dried with sudden fear.

'My question was civil enough,' she said. 'I'll let you judge the manner in which you chose to answer it.'

'The young stripling called you a swine, Ned,' one of his companions needled. 'Time he learnt respect for his betters.'

'Name your seconds,' Ned demanded. 'You'll answer to that insult with your sword.'

'I'd name my brother, but I've yet to find him before he can perform such duties,' Angel returned, growing hot under her collar. She knew she was the equal to most men with a sword, but thought it a ridiculous way to settle a quarrel.

'The lad's scarce out of breeches, Ned,' the third man said. 'It'd be more fitting to give him the spanking he deserves.'

They guffawed loudly and one of them took a step towards Angel, as though to carry out his threat. Her pistol was out of its holster, cocked and aimed at the man before he could catch at Caradoc's bridle.

'Stay back,' she warned. 'If it's a duel you want, you shall have one. Though I'd have thought His Majesty had better use for our swords than turning them upon ourselves.'

'The youth's right.' A fourth figure joined them. He had been leaning against the wall of a half-timbered house, talking to two women. The richness of the ladies' gowns showed them to be the wives of courtiers, and they pouted with displeasure at the interruption. The steel gorget about the newcomer's throat told Angel that he was an officer.

'Duelling is forbidden.' His voice was husky and attractive. His blue eyes were not without humour, but there was censure in the set of his clean-shaven jaw. 'Apologise, lad. Your words were disrespectful. The matter will end there.'

Angel bit her lip, the apology sticking in her throat. Caradoc stamped impatiently and backed away, forcing her to control him. The Cavaliers gathered before the inn, silent and antagonistic as they awaited her response. Her green eyes flashed defiance as she held the officer's stare. There was a self-assurance about him which was unmarred by arrogance. In other circumstances he would have inspired confidence.

'I'll apologise if the gentleman does likewise. As a civilian I'm under no obligation to obey military orders.' The officer raised a dark blond brow indented with a white scar. There was a glint in his eyes which warned her against pushing her luck further. She turned to the Cavalier who had insulted her. The arrogant fool could be court-martialled for provoking a duel. 'I spoke in haste, sir. As I'm sure you did. I ask your pardon.'

The Cavalier grunted, but on receiving a frown from the officer, he cleared his throat and said ungraciously, 'Apology accepted. After a long day in the saddle a man can jump to the wrong conclusions. Your pardon, young sir.'

Angel's mouth tightened with disdain as the Cavalier stamped into the inn and called loudly for ale. 'Conceited ass,' she muttered as she wheeled Caradoc away.

'A moment, sir.'

The officer barred her passage and she again found herself staring into his upturned face. He had a high forehead, prominent cheekbones with a dusting of freckles and a broken nose, giving him a hawkish profile. His long hair was dark blond, streaked lighter by the sun. Darker brows and lashes defined his features in a rugged, but not unattractive way. It was a hard face. But as Angel stared into his vivid blue eyes she detected neither cruelty, conceit nor dishonesty.

'You were asking for the lodgings of Major Rowan,' he said. 'We both have rooms in Trinity College. I'll take you to him.'

'Thank you.' She looked askance at him for his name.

'Captain Nathan Carver, at your service.' He inclined his head in the briefest of bows, then turned to where his two female companions still waited. 'I bid you good day, ladies.'

His expression softened as he lifted their hands to his lips.

The way he regarded them told Angel that this was a man who enjoyed female company. From the fluttering of the women's eyelashes, it was obvious they had fallen prey to his charm.

'I thought Alex had only one brother,' Captain Carver said as he rejoined her. 'Firkin, who is twelve.'

'Firkin is everyone's darling,' Angel evaded. 'He's the youngest.' She turned to John Sparrow, who had kept at a distance throughout the encounter, and held out her hand. 'Thank you for accompanying me. I hope one day we'll meet in happier circumstances.'

The pedlar took her hand briefly, then he dismounted and passed the reins to Angel. 'I'll not be needing the gelding. I prefer to travel on foot. God be with you. I'll never forget the debt I owe you for saving my life.'

'Goodbye, my friend.' She watched him stride through the crowd his figure soon lost amongst the moving throng.

Captain Carver reached up to stroke Caradoc's muzzle. Her warning to take care was halted as she saw the stallion allow him to stroke him. After her grandparents' murder, the horse had become unpredictable and wary of strangers.

'This must be a Rowan horse. I've often admired your brother's gelding. This one surpasses Gawain.'

'So he should. He's Caradoc – the Rowan stallion. I've brought him to Alex. There's no point in keeping him in Wales without any mares.' The bitterness in her voice crackled and she knew herself to be close to tears. To cover her distress she dismounted, and led Caradoc through the press of people. Captain Carver led the gelding, Talisien.

'What happened to the horses?'

The concern in his husky voice almost destroyed her composure. 'Roundheads stole them,' she forced out. 'I'd rather not talk about it.'

'That will be sad news for Alex. He had great plans for those horses.'

The sympathy in his voice made her turn to study him. To her surprise she discovered that Captain Carver was not more than an inch or two taller than herself. Somehow she had gained the impression that he was a much taller man. He had a warmth of manner which made her feel as if she had known him a long time, and she decided she liked him.

Unwilling to speak of what had happened in Wales, she changed the subject.

'Does Alex often speak of his family?' Needing to know whether Alexander would allow her to stay in Oxford, or if her disguise would fail her, she asked, 'Does he mention his sisters?'

'Usually with exasperation,' Captain Carver said with a laugh. 'You know sisters – always a trial. I've three of my own, now all thankfully married and out of my hair. Alex is not so fortunate, I understand. He's still plagued by one of them. Bit of a hoyden, isn't she, your youngest sister? Alex despairs she'll never snare a husband and he'll be burdened with a spitfire spinster all his life.'

'Oh, I wouldn't say she was such a trial,' Angel said with asperity. She would certainly pay Alex back for that remark. 'My sister may be unconventional, but she's far too independent to be a burden on Alex. She's quite capable of running her own life.'

'Running it, or ruining it?' he rejoined. 'But she sounds an interesting minx. Unconventional women are always the most exciting. Remember that, lad, when you choose a mistress. Make sure they're already wed, or sooner or later they'll get that look in their eyes which means marriage is on their mind.'

'I take it that you're not married, Captain.'

He looked away. 'Life's too short to be bound to one woman.' His words were flippant but Angel heard an edge to his voice. Some woman in his past had caused that cynical note, she was sure.

They entered the courtyard of Trinity College and Captain Carver called a hovering servant to stable Caradoc and Talisien. As they continued across the courtyard, Angel was forced to lengthen her stride to keep up with his fast pace. He gave her a sideways glance, surprise entering his eyes as they encountered the fierceness of her expression. It was quickly concealed. Yet she could have sworn his lips had twitched with the beginnings of a grin. From the fine lines around his eyes and mouth, laughter was more common to him than a scowl. There was intelligence and strength of purpose in his features, together with assurance and confidence. He had the air of a man who succeeds in all he sets out to achieve.

127

They entered the college and Angel followed him up a flight of stairs and along a dim corridor. 'This is your brother's room.' He stopped before a door before retracing his steps to the stairs.

Angel rapped loudly on the door.

Alexander shouted a laughing, 'Go away!'

Grinning broadly in anticipation of the surprise Alexander would show at her arrival, Angel flung wide the door. 'Is that any way to greet . . . ?' Her words choked in her throat. The smile vanished as her face scorched with embarrassment.

Alexander was naked on the bed, as was the flame-haired woman who straddled him. The couple were laughing as the woman poured wine on Alex's chest and bent to lap it up with her tongue.

Staggering back, Angel stammered, 'I-I'll c-come back later.'

'Angel! Confound it, Dusty!' Alexander shouted, equally shocked. 'What the devil are you doing here?'

He pushed his companion away and grabbed at his discarded breeches as Angel fled the room. Fleeing blindly down the corridor she collided with a man. Strong hands saved her from tripping and she stared into Captain Carver's face. He was looking over her head to where her half-naked brother stood in his doorway, fastening his breeches.

'Damnation, Dusty!' Alexander snapped, pushing a hand through his black hair. 'I thought you'd more sense than to barge in upon a fellow.'

Angel was trembling and, conscious that Captain Carver was watching her, she drew a long breath. As the heat subsided from her cheeks, she stepped back from the officer and faced her brother.

Alexander held back his tart comment upon Angel's male attire. One look into her strained face told him that something was terribly wrong. Her cheeks had gone from scarlet to waxen.

'Gabriellen and Mark are dead,' she blurted out, her body beginning to tremble. 'Those Roundhead bastards murdered them for the horses.'

Before Alexander's stunned gaze, Angel's legs crumpled and, without Nathan Carver's quick reaction, she would have toppled down the stairs. He caught her and hoisted her unconscious figure over his shoulder.

'If you've a woman in there you'd best get her out,' he said.

Alexander disappeared into his room and bundled a protesting woman into her cloak. Nathan entered and, ignoring the woman, lowered Angel on to the bed whilst Alexander ushered his companion from his room.

Nathan felt Angel's pulse and lifted her eyelid. 'He's fainted. Combination of shock and exhaustion. A good night's rest is the best cure.'

'That's all it is? Shock and exhaustion, I mean.' Alexander looked at the physician who in the last weeks had become his friend.

Nathan nodded gravely. 'I'm sorry about your grandparents.'

Alexander put a hand to his temple, turning away as he struggled to master his grief. It took him several moments to compose himself. When he turned back, Nathan was seated on the edge of the mattress. The physician was frowning as he examined Angel's hand. He turned an amused gaze upon Alexander. 'This delicate hand belongs to a woman. Is she your sister?'

'Yes, that's Dusty – or rather Angel. God knows what possessed her to come here instead of returning to Chichester.'

'And I'm not going home.' A weak voice came from the bed. Angel levered herself on to her elbow, her eyes shining with determination. 'I want to fight, Alex. I want to avenge Gabriellen and Mark's deaths.'

'You said she had courage.' Nathan grinned. 'But you forgot to mention that her wits were addled.'

Angel moved with a speed surprising for someone who had just fainted. The point of her dagger pressed against the physician's throat. 'I can fight as well as any man.'

She saw his blue eyes darken to indigo, but not even an eyelash flickered to betray that the pressure of the blade alarmed him. He raised his scarred eyebrow with an amused admiration which exasperated Angel.

'What a bloodthirsty wench you are! This is the second time within the hour you've threatened an officer.'

'You're mistaken, Captain. This is no threat. Just proof

that I can take care of myself.' She lowered the dagger. 'Prince Rupert admitted that I'd not disgrace his regiment. I'm here not as man or woman, but as a loyal subject of His Majesty.'

'The Prince said that?' Nathan was clearly at pains to control his laughter. 'I despaired of Rupert ever making a gallant.'

'Don't mock me.' Angel pushed him so hard he overbalanced and slid off the bed on to the floor. She scrambled on to her knees to glare down into his face, her green eyes flashing. At the shocked surprise on his face, her good humour returned. 'Don't underestimate me either. I own no man my superior. Surprise tactics and cunning are my strongest weapons. I doubt any man could claim that they have planted your behind so unceremoniously upon the floor.' She grinned to take the sting from her words.

'They would answer to my sword.' He grimaced. 'I suppose as a woman you expect to escape retribution?'

Angel's glare was scathing. 'Nay, I don't fear the consequences of my actions, even though you provoked me by your mockery. It will be swords at dawn if you wish to satisfy your honour.' She swung her legs off the bed and stood up, offering him her hand. 'I'd rather we were friends than enemies, and that you thought of me as Alexander's brother not his sister.'

Her hand was taken as he rose to his feet. His gaze scanned her face, the twitch of his mouth revealing his amusement. When he lifted her hand to his lips, the pressure of his mouth lingered longer than was customary. 'Welcome to Oxford, Master Angel Rowan, or may I call you Dusty?'

She shrugged. 'As you please, Captain Carver.'

Alexander glared at his sister with displeasure. 'What am I supposed to do with you, Dusty? It's out of the question for you to stay here. And you can forget any notion you have of fighting Roundheads.'

'There are always wounded needing care,' Nathan offered.

'Dusty could help you.' Alexander seized upon the suggestion. 'She tended the sick and injured animals whilst at Rowan Hall. She even saved a pedlar from dying of the lung fever.'

'Women's work,' Angel glowered at her brother. 'Alex, I

can wield a sword as well as you. Do you doubt my courage?'

Alexander did not answer and in her frustration she turned to Nathan. He held up his hands in mock surrender.

'Don't involve me in a family dispute,' he said. 'But I'd value your assistance, especially since you have experience. The camp followers make poor helpers. You'd save the lives of many of our brave soldiers.'

'That's an unfair argument, Captain Carver.' As she spoke, her gaze rested upon the red scar on Alexander's arm and she felt her resistance ebbing. Had that wound not been properly treated, Alexander could have died of blood poisoning. Mark and Gabriellen had taught her how to treat fevers and common ailments and how to clean and dress many types of wounds.

'As my assistant there may be times when you have to engage the enemy,' Captain Carver said, brushing the dust from the seat of his breeches.

'I'll be no camp follower,' Angel told him. 'You'll safeguard my disguise as Alex's brother throughout this campaign?'

Nathan grinned. 'Indeed, for I'd not have my patients all falling in love with you.'

'Keep my secret and I'll help with the wounded. My hand on it.'

Her hand was taken in his firm grasp, but when he would have raised it to his lips again she pulled it away. 'Do you make a habit of kissing the hands of your male assistants?'

'The devil I don't!' Nathan almost choked in his outrage.

'Then in my guise as Dusty Rowan you'll not kiss mine.' She lifted a brow to regard him with the same amusement he had earlier directed at her.

'You're a most uncommonly perverse wench.'

'I protect my honour,' Angel countered, taking delight in turning his views on women back upon him. 'Neither would I wish to be a trial, or burden you with a spitfire spinster. Nor stifle your amours with the ladies. Life's too short, is it not, Captain?'

He had the grace to blush.

She turned to Alexander. 'Can I stay?'

His black eyes narrowed, studying her with unnerving intensity. 'Accommodation is scarce but there's an empty room along the corridor.' He sounded like a man who was acting against his better judgement. 'Its last occupant was killed in a skirmish yesterday. God knows how I'll explain this to our father, so you'd better be on your best behaviour.'

'You won't regret this, Alex,' she promised.

There was no relief for the Royalists of Chichester from Prince Rupert. Waller advanced on the outskirts of the city, burning the suburbs of St Pancras and St Bartholomew's at the East and West Gates. The bombardment was ceaseless. When reinforcements arrived for Waller, the city knew the situation was hopeless, and on the twenty-ninth of December Chichester surrendered.

When the conquering army entered the gates, many of the citizens who had deferred from taking sides now openly supported Parliament. It was only a matter of time before the Royalist leaders were arrested.

Llewelyn was prepared and, when the guards pounded on his door, he admitted them.

'You're to come with us, Rowan,' a bearded officer grunted.

'No,' Maressa cried, looking to her husband for help. 'Henry, stop them!'

'Maressa, spare me this,' Llewelyn said to her. 'I'm ready.'

'Where are you taking my father?' she demanded.

'He'll be held with the others for a day or so. Then all the Malignants are to be taken to London for trial.' The captain swaggered forward and prodded Llewelyn with his pistol.

'There's no need for such treatment, Captain,' Henry cut in sharply. 'I am Sir Henry Mortimer of Arundel and a Member of Parliament. I've been stricken with a tertian fever. Mr Rowan allowed me to stay here, even though he regarded me as his enemy.' He leaned against the wall to give greater effect to his words. 'I am far from recovered.'

Grateful for Henry's intervention, Maressa touched his arm, speaking with concern. 'You should rest, my dear.'

Henry moved towards the parlour but was halted when the Captain spoke.

'I've orders that this house is to be sequestered. It is now the property of Parliament. Everyone must leave by nightfall.' He shuffled uncomfortably. 'You may take a few personal items, that's all. At dusk a guard will be put on the house. Anyone remaining will be arrested.'

Henry started forward. 'Waller shall hear of this outrage.' Brusquely, he turned on his heel and walked into the parlour.

The soldiers surrounded Llewelyn and escorted him from the house. There was an outburst of weeping from Goodwife Bundy which Maressa ignored as she approached the officer who was the last to leave.

'Colonel? Will I be permitted to bring food to my father?'

'It is Captain, my lady.' He bowed stiffly. 'Captain Halroyd.'

She widened her eyes in feigned surprise as she studied the soldier. He was about thirty and of a similar height and build to her father. There were stale beer fumes on his breath, and from the way his gaze lingered upon her figure she guessed him to be a womaniser. His straight brown brows met on the bridge of his nose, and his mouth had a petulant droop. She summed him up as a man of great conceit and little imagination.

When she saw interest brighten in his eyes as he appraised her beauty, she smiled. A glance over her shoulder showed her that Goodwife Bundy had retreated to the kitchen, and she lowered her voice to an inviting whisper. 'Please forgive my husband for his rudeness. It's the effects of the fever. When may I be permitted to visit my father?'

'There will be no visitors without specific permission.'

Maressa tapped his arm with her finger. 'I'm sure a resourceful man of your position could arrange it for me. If I were to arrive at the gaol an hour after dark, surely you could provide the necessary escort for me to visit a prisoner? Naturally, I would not expect to be subjected to the common rabble when I visit my father. He'll be given a single cell. For such considerations I'd be extremely grateful.' Her smile suggested further intimacies.

He nodded. 'Until an hour after dusk, my lady.' The boldness of his stare told her that he was too conceited to see through her ruse.

Maressa hid her contempt at the man's gullibility. She was already devising a plan for her father's escape.

Once the soldiers had left the house, Maressa sent Hazel

to look for a breach in the city walls. Maressa then went to Firkin's chamber. Hazel had given him a sedative that morning to make him rest and Maressa found him asleep. Waking him, she told him of Llewelyn's arrest and the help she needed for his escape. He nodded eagerly.

'Your part is as important as mine,' she warned. 'Should anything go wrong, the consequences will be grave. Henry must know nothing of this.'

Leaving Firkin, she went to the chamber she shared with her husband. Peter, Henry's valet, was brushing the gold velvet doublet which Henry was about to put on.

'I'll help my husband. You may leave us, Peter.'

She waited until they were alone before she held out the doublet for Henry, and said, 'I'm glad you're feeling stronger.'

'I must speak with Waller to assure him of my allegiance.'

'But is that wise, my dear? I mean, to go abroad so soon?'

Henry paused in smoothing out the emerald ribbons on the shoulder of his doublet. 'I've no choice now your father has been arrested. I don't want my name linked with a Malignant.' He continued to worry a crumpled ribbon with his fingers. 'Rowan was a fool to give his support so openly. We'll leave for Arundel this afternoon. I've already instructed Peter to ride ahead and have the house made ready.'

Maressa held back a sharp retort in defence of her father. It was part of her plan to return to Arundel.

'Could you not send your compliments to Waller, expressing your regrets at your illness? Once we return to Arundel you'll soon recover.'

He looked at her doubtfully. Before he could protest she wound her arms around his neck and pressed her body against him. 'It's been so long since we enjoyed the privacy of our own home. There'll be little time for us to be together before you must return to your duties in London.' She smiled enticingly, circling her hips so that they rubbed against his thighs. 'And I want your vigour to return, my love. I hadn't realised how tired I'd become after my miscarriages and during the months I carried Julian.' She modestly lowered her eyes. 'Too tired to be a proper wife to you.'

Looking up at him through her lashes, she murmured, 'I've never felt comfortable making love under my father's roof. But at Arundel . . . ?' She kissed him passionately.

Henry chuckled, his humour restored. 'Why wait until tonight? And this is no longer your father's house.' He caught her waist and swung her round, pushing her down on to the bed. Without preliminaries he dragged her skirts to her hips and bore down upon her.

Maressa screwed her eyes shut, willing herself to relax and for her ordeal to be quickly over. She had misjudged his ardour. He was becoming too used to the medicine Hazel prepared for it to be effective. She endured, dutifully feigning pleasure until Henry rolled off her, and fell into an exhausted sleep.

Quickly, Maressa adjusted her skirts and went to the housekeeper's room. With her out of the way her task would be easier. The housekeeper's sobs had subsided and in answer to her knock Goodwife Bundy opened the door.

'The house has been sequestered,' Maressa said. 'Papa is to be tried in London, so Firkin must live with me at Arundel. Ask the servants to attend me in an hour. I'll give each one a written reference and wages until Easter. Their possessions must be packed and they must be ready to leave at once. Yourself included, I'm afraid, Judith.' She put an arm around the housekeeper's plump shoulders. 'It's poor reward for your loyalty, but we have no choice. Sir Henry has his own servants, but I'll ensure that you're well provided for. Have you somewhere to go?'

'Don't you worry about me. I've a sister at Amberley who I can stay with. It's the master I'm afeared for. Locked up like a criminal. It's unjust.' She sobbed loudly into her apron. 'Mr Rowan, how will he fare?'

'He'll fare better, knowing that his servants have been provided for.'

Judith Bundy sniffed and dabbed at her eyes. 'Very generous you've been, my lady. You always were a credit to your father.'

For the next hour Maressa curbed her impatience until all the servants had left. Then she began the next stage of her plan. Hazel had returned, and had found a suitable breach in the city walls.

'Tell the coachman to have the coach ready by three o'clock. But first prepare some wine for Sir Henry. Nothing too strong. Just something to make him too drowsy to be aware of what's happening. You'll dress in my clothes and take Julian with you in the coach. Firkin remains here. He'll guard the horses. He's to keep them hidden and quiet in your old stable. No one goes there since Meg's death. They think the place is haunted.'

From outside in the street came the noise of a door being smashed by an axe, followed by a scream and angry voices. Maressa looked out of the window. Several houses of known Royalists were being sacked. At least Henry's presence in the Rowan house had spared them that indignity. She shuddered as she saw a maidservant pushed into the street. The girl was surrounded by five coarse-looking Roundheads who manhandled her, one to another.

'Thank God you weren't molested, Hazel,' Maressa commented.

'I were too quick-footed for the drunken sots. Nowhere's safe, not even the Cathedral. They're ransacking the place. I saw soldiers running off with the silver-plate and vestments. They were laughing. They've hacked the saints' figures and rood screen to pieces.'

'Fiends! Despoilers! What hope has my father to be spared by such men?' Maressa fumed. 'God grant me success this night.'

''Tis a brave plan, my lady,' Hazel said. 'It won't be safe on the streets tonight with the soldiers drunk.'

Maressa quashed her fears, choosing instead to think of how proud her father would be of her. She'd prove she was as brave as Angel.

Later, the carriage was brought to the door as arranged. With Sir Henry drowsy from the effects of the drugged wine, it was easy to get him into the vehicle. Hazel held the sleeping Julian in her arms. She wore one of Maressa's gowns and held a nosegay pressed to her face as they travelled through the streets. The Mortimer coat of arms on the carriage would ensure they were not held up at the gate, and anyone who saw the vehicle would think that Sir Henry and Lady Mortimer were returning to Arundel.

Earlier, Firkin had taken two horses out of the city, on the pretext of getting them reshod at the farriers in the next village. The ruse had worked since all the farriers within

Chichester were busy working on the army horses.

Two hours after the carriage rolled away, Maressa came out of her hiding place in a neighbour's garden. She pulled the hood of her plain woollen cloak over her face. Underneath it she wore a grey gown and white linen cap, and in her basket was a bottle of drugged wine and some food. So far her plan had gone smoothly. What lay next was the greater test of her skill.

To any of the sentries who stopped her she passed herself off as a Rowan servant on an errand for Lady Mortimer. Maressa hoped that when Captain Halroyd was discovered tied up and her father escaped, that no suspicion would fall on herself as Henry's wife. Anyone who enquired would learn that Lady Mortimer had left the city two hours before curfew. Her reputation as a woman of virtue was unquestioned. No one would believe the protestations of a conceited captain who claimed she had seduced him. He would be a laughing stock, and Henry would escape being implicated in a Royalist escape – something Maressa knew he would never tolerate.

Maressa had never been out alone at night. The dark streets, lit by intermittent lanterns outside the larger houses, were menacing. She averted her eyes from her father's house. From within came the sound of looting. The moon was obscured by a veil of cloud but enough of its silvery light penetrated the narrow street, giving a bluish sheen to the dew-covered cobbles. Keeping to the shadows, she scanned the street. A cat hissed at her from a low wall, setting her heart racing.

As she passed shops and houses shuttered against the night, she concentrated on the task ahead. The urge to turn and flee was almost overpowering, but the need to prove to her father that she was as brave as Angel drove her on.

Her father would be a free man because of her courage. When had Angel ever done so much for him?

Before her, the pale stone of the market-cross was ghostly in the moonlight. Beneath its arches stood several figures and she heard the low drone of male voices. Her body chilled with fear. No respectable people gathered around the market-cross at night. These were thieves, vagabonds or common soldiers looking for any diversion to alleviate their boredom.

137

She had no intention of becoming their victim, but in her guise as a servant, she would be treated with little respect.

Flattening herself against the shadowed wall of a house, she studied the moonlit crossroads. From an inn came the sound of drunken laughter, and a bawdy ditty was sung in a slurred, off-key voice. Then along East Gate she saw a closed carriage approaching, glowing lanterns on each side of the coachman's platform. As it drew level with her it turned down North Street in the direction of Greyfriar's Priory, where her father was held prisoner. Using it as a shield Maressa hurried alongside.

With the cross behind her, she sped along a side street leading to the Priory gardens and a cluster of partly ruined buildings. Away from the town centre the muddy lanes were slippery with years of accumulated grime. When two bats swooped out of the trees and flapped around her head, she barely managed to stifle a scream. From the next street the stamp of heavy boots warned her that soldiers were patrolling the area. She froze in the dark shadows, holding her breath until they passed. Somewhere in the midst of the merchants' houses, the watchman rang his bell, his faint call drifting to her.

'Eight of the clock. Look to your locks. Guard well your lights and fires. God have mercy on us all.'

His voice faded as Maressa reached the Priory. A sentry stood at the entrance to the ruined gatehouse, his halberd extended to bar her way. She drew a steadying breath to calm her shaking legs.

'Captain Halroyd is expecting me,' she roughened her voice to sound like a servant.

'Aye, the cap'n mentioned a wench would be warming his bed this night,' the sentry sniggered. 'How about giving a little comfort to a lonely soldier first? What d'yer charge?'

He reached out to grab her, but Maressa sidestepped. 'I'm no two-penny whore, but a respectable widow. Captain Halroyd will hear of this.'

'Widow you may be . . . respectable, you ain't,' he sneered.

'Is that my guest at the gate?' Captain Halroyd called from out of the darkness. He appeared to stand between Maressa and the sentry. 'Was the man troubling you?'

'He was just doing his duty, Captain.' She hid her affront at the sentry's rudeness. 'It would not do for just anyone to walk in here.'

Halroyd took her arm. 'I began to despair you'd not come,' he whispered, his Sussex burr more noticeable in his agitation. 'Surely you didn't walk the streets alone?'

'Two servants lit my way as far as St Martin's Church. I dismissed them there, saying I intended to pray for my father's release. They'll return in two hours,' she lied. 'One cannot be too careful of one's reputation. Servants gossip. Did I presume too much? If the time is limited for my visit to my father, I shall have to place myself under your protection.'

'Dear lady, you honour me.'

She made her voice sound breathless as she laughed. The officer's breath reeked with brandy fumes and from the slight slurring of his words he was already far into his cups. It would make her task easier. She forced the smile to remain upon her lips as he led her inside a building.

'Where are the prisoners kept?'

'Some are in the underground storerooms, but Rowan has been put into an upper chamber. There's a guard in the anteroom.'

She remained silent as he led her to the stairs. The interior was dimly lit by candles dotted along the corridors which cast long shadows between them. Several soldiers were crouched beneath one sconce to play dice. Many of the doors were open and Maressa saw that the rooms were filled with Roundheads sprawled at their ease, in various stages of dress; some dozing, others gambling, eating or cleaning their weapons. Anyone who glanced up as Maressa passed with the captain, was quick to utter a ribald comment.

Twice Halroyd laughed and boasted, 'Bain't I the lucky one, lads?'

The comment made Maressa's blood simmer. How dare the braggart openly proclaim their liaison. He was a fool. She calmed her agitation. This was all to her fortune. Braggarts and fools were the easiest to dupe. They passed another open door and Maressa noticed several steel lobster-pot helmets. Further along the corridor Halroyd stopped before a closed door and rapped on it.

'Pickled herrings,' he said. 'Open up.'

The strangeness of his comment startled Maressa, then it dawned on her that it was the password for the night. The door was opened by a youthful soldier.

'Leave us,' Halroyd commanded. 'I'll stand guard. Don't return until you're summoned.' His wink made Maressa's stomach quake with revulsion.

When the door closed behind the soldier, Halroyd turned the iron key in its lock and drew Maressa into his arms. In the flickering light of a single candle, his eyes were dark with lust.

'Now, my beauty, time for you to show your gratitude.'

'You're bold, Captain.' Maressa leaned back from him, but he held her fast. There was a suspicious glint in his eyes which frightened her, and she chose her words with care. 'I like boldness in a man. But in its place. A woman doesn't like to be rushed.' Placing her basket on the table, she took out a bottle of Llewelyn's finest brandy. 'First, I'd see my father and assure myself that he's not suffering. Once my mind is at rest . . .' She smiled and ran a finger along his roughened cheek. 'Then you shall have all my attention as you deserve, my brave gallant.'

She offered him her hand and allowed him to press it to his lips. When he would have pulled her closer, she shook her head. 'Later, Captain. Relax with a drink whilst I visit my father. And then . . .' Her smile was full of invitation. 'I'll show my gratitude.'

'You'll not stay with him long.' He was impatient, his face already flushed with his growing ardour.

'Just long enough to ensure that all is well,' she promised, and moved purposefully towards the inner door.

Halroyd took a key from a hook and fitted it to the lock. She put a hand over his and spoke softly. 'Pray, sir, don't let anyone suspect that I had other motives in coming here tonight. If word of our meeting should reach my husband—' She put a hand to her breast and looked stricken. 'Sir Henry is jealous. He near-killed a man last summer in a duel. The man, a friend of our family, had done no more than speak with me in the street.'

The Captain paled. 'A duelling man, is he, Sir Henry?'

Maressa sighed. 'I fear so. I've never met a man so quick

140

to see a slight upon his honour. Two men at least have died when he challenged them after catching them cheating at cards. But that does not trouble you, does it, Captain Halroyd? It's in both our interests that Sir Henry learns nothing of tonight. I've taken pains that my reputation is safeguarded. The rest lies with your discretion.'

He relaxed and opened the door. 'Visitor for you, Rowan. Fifteen minutes, that's all you're allowed.'

As Maressa walked through the doorway she glanced back over her shoulder and saw Captain Halroyd pull the stopper from the brandy bottle and raise it to his mouth.

'Maressa! What are you doing here?' Llewelyn rose from the truckle-bed which was the only furniture in the room.

'I had to see that you were not suffering and were fed properly.' Putting a finger to her lips, she closed the door and whispered against her father's ear, 'I've come to get you out. The captain's been left with a bottle of drugged brandy. In ten minutes it will begin to work.'

'But I can't just walk out of here!'

'Sssh, Papa!' She looked towards the door, her nervousness growing with every minute. 'My plan is simple. But we must act naturally.'

Keeping her voice low she outlined her plans. On hearing a faint thud from the other room, she pressed her ear to the door. Just discernible was a ragged snore from the captain.

'Come, make haste!' She entered the outer room. Halroyd had slid down the wall and lay sprawled on the floor. Maressa began to undo his buff coat.

'Help me, Papa. Put on his uniform and we can walk out of here. They'll think you're Halroyd and I his doxy. I'll have the very devil to explain this to Henry if I'm caught. It's as important for me to get out of the city tonight as it is for you. Tomorrow must find me snug in my husband's bed before he awakes.'

'I suppose you also drugged him?'

'I did it for you, Papa.'

'And if he'd been but half the man you deserved to wed there'd never have been the need. I was wrong to permit the marriage.'

'Henry was my choice. You only wanted to see me happy.'

When the outer garments were stripped from Halroyd,

Llewelyn frowned at his daughter to look away, and carried the snoring captain into the inner room. He emerged several moments later, shrugging himself into the captain's buff coat. The sleeves were too short and the shoulders too narrow for her father's broader figure, but when Llewelyn drew the black cloak over his shoulders it covered him from shoulder to knee. He also wore Halroyd's swordbelt and pistol holster. Behind him Maressa saw Halroyd was trussed by ropes made from his own shirt. The man was naked and another torn strip from his undergarments had been used as a gag.

'Was it necessary to strip him?' she asked.

'Was it necessary for you to compromise your reputation by offering yourself as bait to his lechery?' Llewelyn looked at her sternly. 'Halroyd has been bragging all day of the fine lady who was to grace his bed this night. Little did I realise he meant you.'

'I've covered my tracks well. Lady and Sir Henry Mortimer were seen leaving Chichester this afternoon, hence my disguise as a serving maid.'

Llewelyn locked the doors of both rooms and kept the keys. 'They won't find Halroyd until we're far from here.' He surveyed the deserted corridor. 'I need a hat, or I'll be recognised by the first soldier we meet.'

'No, you won't.' Maressa ran into the empty room she had passed earlier, and emerged carrying a steel helmet.

'You've thought of everything,' he said, putting it on. The pride in his voice took the edge from Maressa's fear.

'The password for the night is "pickled herrings",' she informed him. 'There's a breach in the city walls not far from here, on the other side of the Priory orchard. Firkin's waiting with two horses in Meg Unwin's stables.'

Wonder, astonishment and, finally, admiration glowed in his eyes. 'That's a scheme worthy of Gabriellen herself in one of her plays. I'm proud of you. Very proud.'

Maressa was elated. All the danger had been worth it to rise over Angel and Alexander in her father's esteem. Three soldiers appeared from round a corner and Maressa snatched Llewelyn's arm, drawing him into a doorway.

'If they utter any bawdy comments,' she whispered, 'Halroyd always said, "Bain't I the lucky one, lads?" '

As the soldiers drew near, Maressa giggled and, putting

her arms around her father's neck, pulled him round so that his back was to the men.

'Is that you, Halroyd?' one man called out. 'Ain't you given her a taste of what she came for yet. Thought by now you'd be between her legs.'

She felt her father tense. With an effort he controlled his anger. 'And what would you know about how to treat a real lady?' He mimicked Halroyd's Sussex accent. 'We're off to a room in the best inn in town. Bain't I the lucky one, lads?'

Llewelyn put his arm around Maressa's shoulders and propelled her forward, down the steps and into the yard.

Once outside, she could not resist saying, 'Papa, one would think you often consorted with women of low virtue the way you handled that. And your accent was perfect.'

'You were brazen enough, yourself! I could have expected that from Angel,' he said as they hurried through the gardens and across the orchard, 'you surprise me, Maressa. And kindly remember, I may be your father, but I was young once! I didn't marry until I was thirty and I was certainly no monk. Now, where's this breach in the wall?'

Maressa was shocked by his outspokenness. She had always considered her father to be a staid and respectable man. It was from him Alexander and Angel had inherited the wildness of the Angel blood. Thank God it had escaped her, she thought with relief. She took after her genteel mother and she desired nothing more than to live a shameless and exemplary life.

The gap in the flintstone walls was directly ahead, but beside it were the orange flames of a sentry's fire.

Llewelyn groaned. 'They're taking no chances.'

'Don't worry about the sentry.' Maressa felt a tingle of excitement, and was surprised to find that she was enjoying this adventure. 'While I distract him, you creep up behind him and knock him out.'

Llewelyn stared at her and grinned. 'Maressa, there's hope for you yet – Angel blood will always out in the end.'

'Papa! You know I don't approve of our Angel kin.'

Even in the darkness, she had the uncomfortable feeling that he was amused by her indignation. When Llewelyn stepped deeper into the shadows, Maressa sauntered into the circle of light from the camp fire. The sentry, who was crouched and shivering by the warmth, started to attention.

'Who's there?'

'Looking for company, soldier?' she said, roughening her voice.

'Company!' the soldier squeaked and cleared his throat. He wore a steel helmet and a breastplate over his buff tunic. He was tall and heavily built and from his accent had probably worked in the fields before he joined the army. 'Bain't usual for a whore to work so far from the taverns. Not pox-ridden, are you? Come into the light.'

Maressa stepped closer. 'Ye be wantin' company, or not?' she drawled. 'It's too cold to stay where I'm not wanted.'

The soldier propped the musket against the wall and moved eagerly towards her. She giggled and side-stepped. 'Take off that old lobsterpot, man. They dig something terrible into a woman's flesh.'

He removed it showing a face raddled with pockmarks, and large ears which stuck out on each side of his close-cropped head. Llewelyn loomed behind him, bringing Halroyd's pistol butt down on his head. The soldier went down on his knees.

'Be quick, Maressa, lest we're discovered,' Llewelyn ordered.

Although in his fifties Llewelyn clambered agilely up the broken wall. He braced himself against the rubble and held out a hand to Maressa. She took it and scrambled over the pile of stones, stifling a cry as her ankle turned painfully. Then they were through, and paused briefly to listen. There was no sign of an alarm being raised from within. Maressa had just let out her breath in relief when a dog fox barked close by, and she jumped so violently that Llewelyn caught her to him.

He laughed softly. 'It's just a fox. Let's pray we reach the horses with similar ease.'

Maressa would not have described the last fifteen minutes as easy. They were the most nerve-racking of her life and ahead lay more danger. The smell of camp fires drifted towards them on the night breeze, and over by the heath, the sky was lit by their orange glow. Waller's army was so large that, although the city was crammed to overflowing, many soldiers were forced to bivouac outside the walls. Fortunately, Meg Unwin's cottage lay to the north of the encampment. Apart from a few heart-stopping scares as wild-life rustled in the undergrowth, they reached the horses safely.

Llewelyn hugged Firkin as he led the horses out. 'Well done, son. Were you scared?'

'No, sir,' Firkin answered swiftly, and mounted up behind Maressa.

An hour later they drew to a halt on the South Downs Way, which ran along the ridge of Sussex hills which over-looked the Arun valley. Below them, the river meandered through the watermeadows like a silver pennant in the moon-light. They could just make out the round Norman keep and battlements of Arundel Castle across the river.

'I must leave you both here,' Llewelyn sounded anxious. 'If Fate is with you, in another twenty minutes you'll be safe within your beds. Your courage tonight is something I'll always treasure. I'm proud of you both.'

'Oh, Papa. I love you so much,' Maressa replied. 'I can't bear to think that whilst the Parliament and King are at war we must be enemies. For that alone I hate Henry.'

'He's your husband,' he said heavily. 'Your duty is to him, but . . .' He paused before adding, 'These are uncertain times. Our family is scattered, but the ties between us are strong, even amongst the Angel kin. Thomas and Laurence would never fail one of the family, should they be in need.'

Maressa gasped. 'You frighten me with such talk. The war can't last long. You'll always be somewhere I can reach you should there be need.'

'War makes mortals of us all, Maressa.' He regarded his son. 'Firkin, you're to have my pistols, if Maressa brought them from the house. By your courage tonight, you've become a man. Protect your sister.'

'Let me ride with you,' Firkin pleaded.

Llewelyn shook his head. 'You're so weak from your recent illness you can barely stay in the saddle. Get well. Your sister may need you.'

'God be with you, Papa,' Firkin answered manfully. 'Thank you for the pistols. And you mustn't worry about Maressa. I'll look after her.'

Llewelyn turned his horse in the direction of Amberley.

He would be travelling through territory held by the Parliamentarians for most of his journey to join the King. Every mile would be threaded with danger.

Maressa urged her mare towards Arundel. Her body ached from the long ride but her head buzzed with excitement. Tonight she had cast aside her role of respectable matron. Though she had been scared she had felt more alive than ever before in her life.

What had conventionality ever earned her? The respect of people who bored her and a husband who treated her like a chattel. Tonight she had proved her mettle. Her blood had quickened with the thrill of a daring adventure and she had again used her wiles to hold a man in her power. And that power was intoxicating.

Chapter Six

Angel had been in Oxford for six weeks. Although she had seen Prince Rupert on several occasions, it was always from a distance, and usually as he was riding out on yet another foray. Oxford could not contain his restless spirit. During those weeks he had sped through the countryside like a heathfire, harrying Parliamentarian patrols, preventing their intrigues and relieving any Royalist town under attack.

These skirmishes with little loss of life had convinced the Royalists that the enemy would be crushed with the spring campaign. That was before Parliament's successes this week by Colonel Oliver Cromwell.

In her disguise as a man Angel was loath to mix with the roistering Cavaliers and felt equally uncomfortable in the company of women. She was becoming a recluse, shunning the company of both sexes. Her work as Nathan's assistant was rewarding, but there remained the driving need to fight and avenge her grandparents' deaths.

Alexander refused to let Angel accompany him when he rode with the Prince. Had it not been for Nathan's company, who remained to attend his patients, she would have been completely isolated. Even so, Nathan had his own life. Several times in the evenings she had gone to his room to spend an hour with him, and found it empty. Nathan was popular with women, and they frequently came uninvited to his room.

Her heart ached with love whenever she saw Rupert, but so many women gazed longingly after him that she was too proud to seek him out. Yet now she wanted him to notice her! Unable to banish her love, she lay sleepless in her lonely bed at nights. Often she would hear Nathan returning to his rooms in the small hours of the morning.

Early in February Angel was walking with Alexander and Nathan by the banks of the River Cherwell. Mist rolled along the river, making eerie spectres of the two herons foraging amongst the reeds. Angel stopped and, crouching on the dew-covered grass, quickly sketched the birds.

'Mr Rowan!'

Alexander turned as a page ran towards them. Her sketch finished, Angel stood up. Meanwhile, Nathan's conversation was caustic. He had learned that an officer was about to marry after falling in love with a woman he had met only a month before.

'What is this so-called affliction of the heart which we claim is love?' Nathan expounded. 'It's lust parading in moral guise, a trap to ensnare a man into the bondage of marriage.'

'When has love anything to do with marriage?' Angel returned, deriding his cynicism. 'Is that not a contract based upon the bartering of one's body for security, wealth or property? Love should never be fettered, for that will smother its fire. True love must have the foundations of trust and fidelity – bonds in themselves.'

'Therefore love is a contradiction of emotions,' Nathan proclaimed. 'It is inconsistent. Desire is an honest emotion, at least. Love is the word given to it by moral bigots.'

Angel shook her head, enjoying both the debate and teasing the physician. 'Desire is fleeting. Love is all-consuming. There's no greater pain than when its flame is extinguished, and passion is replaced by bitterness. But to truly love is to give oneself unselfishly.'

'So speaks a hopeless romantic,' Nathan declared. His gaze strayed to three women walking along the river path. Even on this cool morning, their cloaks were thrown back to reveal the low necklines of their gowns. He bowed to them, saying to Angel in an undertone, 'It is not love you speak of, but passion. Magnificent, fleeting, but once appeased soon doused by the boredom of familiarity.'

Angel laughed. 'So speaks a confirmed rake and bachelor. One day you'll venture too close to love's flames and be burned.'

'Not I.' His voice was frosty with contempt.

Alexander was chuckling as he pressed the paper to his nose and grinned. 'Such perfume – enough to heat any man's blood.' He held it out to Angel. 'It's meant for you and looks to be another *billet-doux*.'

Angel snatched the letter from him and broke the seal. She scanned the contents briefly, a blush turning her cheeks crimson as she screwed it into a ball. It was the seventh such note she had received from a lady of the Court.

'The devil!' Nathan laughed. 'Dusty makes more conquests than we.'

'It's no laughing matter.' Angel rounded on him. 'I knew it wouldn't be easy impersonating a man, but I'd not expected this . . . It's clearly the bad company I keep – your reputation as a libertine rebounds upon me.'

'I'm no libertine.' The vehemence in Nathan's voice startled her. 'It's the cool reserve you show the ladies which wins them. A woman can't resist a man who's something of a mystery.'

Alexander was also amused by his sister's discomfort. 'I did warn you, Dusty. It's still not too late to return with an escort to Chichester.'

'Never!' Angel glared at her two companions.

She was about to say more when her attention was drawn to a group of courtiers. In their lead strolled the small figure of the King, and towering over him was Prince Rupert. From the way he twice tossed his hair back over his shoulder and slapped the hat he carried against his thigh, it was obvious the Prince was angry and impatient for the audience to end.

Boy ran ahead of his master, sniffing along the river bank. The dog lifted its head and scented the air, then with a delighted yelp ran towards Angel. He jumped up at her, and as she bent to ruffle his ears, he licked her face. Barking excitedly, he leapt away, ran in a circle and bounded back to her to repeat the procedure.

Angel was laughing at his antics, aware that Alexander and Nathan were looking at her strangely. 'When His Highness came to Rowan Hall, I rescued Boy from a snare. You remember, Alex.'

'Aye.' His voice was taut and his expression suspicious. 'What was your real reason for coming to Oxford, Dusty?'

Angel held his stare, refusing to comment. Rupert was walking away from the King. He whistled to the dog and looked in their direction. Since Boy still barked around

Angel's legs, he marched towards them. Angel's heart hammered in her chest and she could feel her body flushing with heat.

She stepped back so that Alexander's figure partially obscured her from the Prince's gaze. After waiting so long for this moment, she felt tongue-tied and flustered. Rupert stopped a foot away from her and addressed Alexander and Nathan. She was ignored. Dressed as she was in breeches and doublet, she had not expected Rupert to recognise her, but that she should be completely invisible to him stabbed at her heart like a steel spike.

'Cromwell! Cromwell! I hear nothing but that man's name,' Rupert said without preamble. 'He's now fortifying Cambridge. Men are said to be flocking to his banner. Every day I learn of another skirmish where he has defeated our forces. My spies tell me his troops are well disciplined and that he instructs his men to trust in God. They say each of his men has sworn to lay down his life for the church and the state. Powerful motives.'

'He cares only for piety,' Alexander scoffed.

'Yet he gets results,' Rupert replied, glowering. 'It's time we showed him more of our mettle. Boots and Saddles will sound in an hour, gentlemen.'

He snapped his fingers at Boy who sat at Angel's feet, continuing to thrust his nose into her hand to gain her attention. As the dog trotted to his master's side, she tipped back her hat, and the Prince regarded her with a frown. Alexander and Nathan had moved several paces away, and Angel bowed her head in formal acknowledgement, aware that Rupert's mind was still on war. When he turned to leave, Angel was stung into retaliation.

'Boy has better manners than his master,' she challenged in a low voice. 'He does not ignore those who once served him.'

He whirled around, his dark eyes flashing with affront. Angel held his glare and lifted a brow as she removed her hat. The Prince's eyes widened in recognition and his gaze was amused as it took in the slender figure clad in breeches and doublet. Then his mouth set into a grim line.

'I warned you I wanted no petticoat army.'

'Alex has forbidden me to fight. I assist Captain Carver

with the injured. Here, I am known as Dusty Rowan, Alex's brother.'

Unexpectedly, he smiled. 'I'll be back in Oxford in four days. Attend me at St John's that evening.' He turned to leave.

Shocked by his abruptness, she retaliated without thinking. 'I'll not be summoned like a common doxy.'

Rupert retraced his steps, his brows drawn together and his eyes brittle with anger. 'You were willing enough at Rowan Hall.'

'On that occasion I was asked in an atmosphere of mutual attraction,' she said stiffly, conscious that Alex and Nathan were watching her. 'It's hardly flattering to be ordered like a trooper.'

'The devil—!' He looked astonished. 'You have an uncommon honesty about such matters – unlike most women.'

There was a gleam of battle in her eyes as she held his gaze. 'Many men see my independence as a threat. You could have any woman at Court.'

'Because I am a prince?'

She chewed her lip in contemplation, for his remark had not been a flippant one. 'Certainly not for your graciousness, or charm. But a woman would be a fool if she saw only the hero and the glitter of your title.'

Rupert strode away several paces, then walked back. 'Your wit and honesty attack with the speed of a swordthrust. Until my return, when I would like to renew your acquaintance.'

She answered with a smile and an inclination of her head. Again Rupert held her stare. The wariness left his eyes, and warmth kindled in their depths, striking like a flaming arrow to her heart. With a curt nod he marched away. When she turned, Alexander and Nathan were staring at her. Unwilling to face Alexander's questions, she walked towards the river and made a show of sketching some swans, though all she saw before her eyes was the image of Rupert.

On the afternoon that Rupert was due to return to Oxford, Angel retired early to her room. She had brought only two gowns with her, and she hung a scarlet and black striped skirt by the fire so that the creases would fall out. On a chair was a tight-fitting black bodice, its wide sleeves slashed with silver lace.

Her first setback was in discovering that her hairpins had disappeared. Unused to her short hair, she found it impossible to arrange in a fashionable style, and left it, falling in natural curls to her shoulders. Then she stepped into her skirt, secured its hooks, and tied the front lacing of her low-necked bodice.

With only a small hand-mirror to judge her appearance, she twisted and turned, surveying her reflection. Satisfied, she twirled around, enjoying the cool feel of the silk petticoats against her legs. For nearly two months she had worn breeches and it was good to feel like a woman again. It was dusk when she sat down to await the Prince's summons.

The candle burnt low and she replaced it. She kicked off her high-heeled shoes after her agitated pacing had rubbed a blister on one heel. Outside, a college clock struck midnight. He was not coming. Perhaps the troop had been delayed? She combatted the ache of disappointment and jerked at the lacing of her gown. She was a fool to feel so dejected. Rupert was the King's Commander of Horse. He had many duties. War was his mistress; women would always take second place. Angel did not mind that, she accepted it. But coming to terms with it was not easy. She was wide-awake and unable to sleep. A blank sheet of parchment on the table beckoned and she scanned the notes she had made for a new play. She wrote the title at the top of the page: *The Adventuress*. The first scene became vivid in her mind and she began to write, unaware of the passage of hours as the words flowed from her pen. When the candle finally guttered and died, she realised that it was almost dawn.

The next evening, again she wore the red and black gown. As soon as she was ready, she resumed her writing to fill the time until the Prince's summons arrived. Tonight the words were slower to form and her ear strained to catch the sound of a footfall on the stairs. Her meal lay uneaten, pushed to one side in nervous anticipation. Constantly she lifted her head and stared at the sands running through the hourglass. Twice she upended it to mark the passage of another hour, each time banging it down with greater vigour.

She knew the Prince's troop had returned to Oxford, for she had recognised several of Alex's friends in the town that afternoon, although there was no sign of her brother or

Nathan. That did not trouble her, for Alexander had spoken of visiting Beth Penrose. As for Nathan, she assumed that after four nights away from Oxford, he would be eager for the company of his latest paramour.

It was almost midnight. She threw down the quill and glowered at the shuttered window. Her eyes prickled with the tears she was too proud to shed. Rupert had forgotten her.

Impatient with her moping, she stood up and stretched, rapping her knuckles against the low beam of the ceiling. A knock at the door made her start and, her heart racing, she ran to answer it. So great was her excitement she forgot caution and opened the door wide. The candlelight was behind her, framing her in the doorway.

'Your pardon, ma'am. I've mistaken the room.' Nathan turned to go, then realising he had made no mistake, he stared at Angel. Giving a low whistle of appreciation, he stepped into the room. 'My God, but you're beautiful, Dusty. But why the gown?'

'When did you return?' she asked dully.

'Five hours ago. I have been at the hospital.'

'And the Prince?' She could not stop herself asking.

Nathan shot her an understanding look. 'So that's the way of it. Good God, Dusty! I thought you had more sense!'

'You're a fine one to lecture, Nathan.' She turned away, unwilling for him to see how deeply Rupert's neglect had hurt her.

'Rupert did return, but he rode out again almost immediately.' Nathan put his hand on her arm and turned her to face him. 'Did he make an assignation with you? It would not occur to him to send word.'

She lifted her head with proud defiance. 'Rupert was my lover in Wales. I know he can have any woman he wants, but I love him. I was tired of dressing as a man, and I wanted him to think I was beautiful.'

Nathan raised her chin with his finger. 'You're more beautiful than any of the bird-witted creatures who preen and saunter about the Court.'

She forced a smile. 'Flatterer.'

'It is not flattery, Dusty.' Nathan's face was serious.

A lock of dark blond hair had fallen over his brow and

the candlelight softened his angular face. There was an intensity in his blue eyes which eased the ache of Rupert's absence. His lips drew back into a smile, and when he spoke his voice was low and husky. 'What chance has a common physician with a royal prince as a rival?'

She refused to take him seriously. 'Rupert's royalty has nothing to do with it. I love him, not his rank. And you're not a common physician.'

He gave her a long silent look which surprised her for he was not usually at a loss for words. His expression was unreadable as he glanced at the untouched food. At seeing the sheets of closely packed writing he picked them up and scanned them. 'This is good. Did you write it?'

She shrugged. 'I want to be a playwright.'

His stare was admiring. 'You're a strange creature, Dusty. Just as I think I'm getting to know you, some new trait shows itself.'

'May the Good Lord spare me from becoming predictable.'

'I doubt you'll ever be that. That's your charm,' he responded, returning to his carefree manner. 'You've not eaten yet. Come and dine with me. Such finery should not be hidden away.'

'But my disguise . . .? If I dine in public I'll be recognised.'

'Wear a mask. I'll be the envy of every man in town. And you'll be a woman of mystery.'

'And become the butt of curiosity. That's exactly what I wish to avoid.'

'As Rupert's mistress you'll be notorious,' he said sharply.

Angel stiffened and her chin lifted. 'I don't intend that it should become public gossip.'

'You couldn't stop it! And what woman could resist being known as his mistress. It will not be without its rewards.'

Angel's eyes narrowed with a feral light and she pushed him towards the door. 'Get out! I'll never take a lover for the rewards it might bring me. I love Rupert! I know his faults – his foul temper, his obsession to win this war. I know the futility of my love, but none of that matters. He's the most exciting man I've ever met.'

Nathan grabbed her wrists, and stared into her face. Her eyes blazed with passion and he was touched by their fire.

Feeling his body stir in response, he ground out, 'This infatuation will bring you heartache.'

'That's inevitable,' she answered. 'But it's not infatuation. I'd rather love unwisely than live a lie.' Mischief glimmered in her eyes as she added, 'My love may have no future, but I'll have some scorching memories to warm me in my old age.' Her face became serious again. 'Does that shock you? Do you despise me? I hold loyalty and honour higher than any marriage contract. Dressing as a woman was a foolish fancy. How could I visit Rupert's rooms and not be noticed? However irksome, it's best that I maintain my disguise as a man.' Her voice quavered with uncertainty. 'But tell me truly, Nathan. Will Rupert think me ugly in my men's clothes?'

'Have you no idea how fetching they are?' Nathan said with a grin. 'We'll dine in style, but in my rooms so that you can wear your finery.'

Angel was tempted. She was hungry and wide-awake and the thought of spending another night alone held little appeal. 'I'd enjoy your company, but on one condition: you dine with Master Dusty Rowan. I'll understand if you'd prefer a more accommodating female companion.'

'You're determined to think me a libertine,' he said coolly.

'I've seen how women pursue you.'

'And upon that you'd condemn me?'

'I don't condemn you, Nathan. Enjoy the ladies, for they adore you. But I'll not be one of them. I'll never share a lover, no matter how much I love him. When Rupert's interest falls upon another, it will end between us.' She laughed to dispel the seriousness of the moment. 'You promised me a meal and I'm ravenous. I'll join you when I've changed into my breeches.'

There was regret in Nathan's regard. It prompted an impish response. Angel sank down into a deep curtsy. 'Are you waiting for me to take formal leave of you?' she quipped.

His gaze was drawn to the low neckline of her bodice, which displayed a generous view of her breasts. When he swallowed and his fingers tightened upon the door-latch, she put a hand to cover her décolletage.

'Devil take it! Angel!' His lack of composure showed in the use of her given name. 'How am I ever going to regard

155

Master Dusty Rowan in the same light again?'

'Restraint is good for the soul, Nathan,' she challenged.

'Heartless jade!' He gave a dry laugh and left.

'Alex, that's the second time I've put your king in check.'
Beth Penrose sat back from the chessboard, her expression
anxious. 'What's wrong?'

Alexander started, his eyes refocusing as he gazed upon
her face. The warmth and trust in her eyes almost destroyed
his control; her beauty was a torch to the desire he had
spent the afternoon fighting. He rose abruptly, knocking over
several chess pieces. 'Your pardon, I'm poor company. It's
time I returned to Oxford.'

'You're not going to stay?' Beth put a hand on his arm,
her eyes mirroring her disappointment. 'It's been five weeks
since your last visit.' She blushed. 'That sounds ungracious.
I meant only that I enjoy your company and . . .' Her gaze
dropped from his searching stare and she added, 'But I
understand. Your duty is at Oxford.'

'That isn't why I'm leaving . . . and I think it best if I
don't return.'

She looked up at him, fear bright in her eyes. 'Did I
displease you by writing to you at Oxford? Your replies gave
no intimation that my letters were unwelcome.'

'They were not unwelcome.' He groaned and put a hand
to the back of his head as he looked down into her face.
'Beth, you're the widow of my friend. What I feel—' He
broke off, at a loss to put his emotions into words. 'I treasure
your letters. They made me . . .'

Again the words froze in his throat. Honour and respect
for Bryan's memory battled inside him, together with the
need to protect this woman, to keep her safe – always. They
were ideals too powerful to be easily cast aside. There was a
fastidiousness about his nature which had stopped him from
casual dalliance. His mistresses were usually married and his
affairs with them would last for several months. None had
touched his heart. He could not use Beth that way, nor did
he want to.

Drawing an unsteady breath, he said, 'You know why I
must leave.'

'Yes,' she answered breathlessly. 'You're an honourable

man. But have you considered what I may want?'

He frowned and she took his hand and led him to the settle, pulling him down to sit beside her. She touched the brooch which Maressa had given to Alexander for her. 'Bryan did not buy this for me. Did you?'

Alexander said nothing. Beth's eyes were wide, their hazel depths flecked with specks of gold and the irises ringed by black. They were eyes a man could drown gazing into.

She sighed softly and smiled. 'You are loyal. That's what attracted me from the start. Bryan didn't love me. Our marriage was arranged. We were childhood friends. Bryan's father was parson of the village church, and he died three years before my own father's death. Bryan was here on a visit when my father suffered his last seizure. Papa begged Bryan to take care of me. The house and land was my dowry, but Bryan knew nothing about running an estate. The livestock died and the crops failed. He blamed himself for our poverty and returned to soldiering, as the only life he knew. He was good and kind and I was very fond of him, as I believe he was fond of me. But we were not in love. That's why I knew it was you who had bought the brooch.'

'It wasn't me,' Alexander hedged, knowing it would be cruel to tell her that his sister had given it to him. But he did not want to take the credit for something he had not done. 'Bryan spoke of you often. He was not one for speaking of his feelings. It was obvious that he cared for you.'

A tear rolled down her cheek and his restraint broke. He took her into his arms and held her close. He could feel her heartbeat against his own, the soft caress of her breath from her parted lips. When she held his gaze, her eyes were no longer tearful but luminous with yearning.

He kissed her. She closed her eyes in surrender and the scent of her skin set his blood on fire. He stared down into her rapt face. He wanted to kiss her again, but feared that his restraint would break beneath the promise of her lips.

'Do you know how happy you've made me? I love you, Beth.'

She wound her arms around his neck, her smile radiant. 'No happier than you've made me. I thought I was wicked to feel this way. I love you. It can't be wrong to feel as we do.'

157

She raised her lips to his, the ardour of her kiss stealing his reason, and he felt a tremor go through her body. He was exultant, happier in the realisation of his love than he had ever been. Then, as swiftly, he was wretched. Somehow he found the strength to draw back and put her from him. She was still Bryan's widow. He could not make love to her while she was still in mourning for her husband.

'I must leave,' he said heavily. 'In six months you'll be out of mourning and we can marry. Until then . . .' He kissed her passionately, then tore himself away, leaving the house before desire triumphed over honour.

On the night when Rupert finally returned to Oxford, Angel was busy in the converted storehouse where the hospital had been set up. She had been working for five hours without a break. Her hair was tied back and she was bent over the blackened face and neck of a musketeer, whose weapon had backfired, blinding him and burning his flesh. His eyes were already bound and she was smearing a soothing balm on to his cheeks to ease his pain.

Nathan worked with his back to her, treating a man whose ear had been hacked off by a sword. The room smelt of blood, sweat, and the sickly pungent stench of cauterised flesh.

She signalled for her next patient to come forward when a page bowed to her, saying, 'Prince Rupert's compliments, sir. He requests you attend him this evening at the hour of nine.'

'Thank you. I shall be there.'

Angel expected a teasing jibe from Nathan. Instead, his expression was grim and he turned away. He spoke gently to the Cavalier laid on the table then bent over him, to remove a bullet embedded in the man's shoulder. He nodded to another assistant to hold the Cavalier's arms. As Nathan gently probed the wound, he made conversation with his patient to distract the man from his pain.

Screams split the air from the far end of the building where the surgeon, Captain Pringle, was working. Angel looked up from cleansing the jagged edges of a sword cut which had sliced through the outer side of her patient's thigh. Once clean, she would cauterise it to seal the wound and prevent infection, as Nathan had taught her.

'No! Don't take off my arm!' a man cried out in panic. 'If I'm crippled my family will starve.'

The surgeon's gruff reply was too low to be heard, but the growing hysteria of his patient's screams chilled Angel's blood. She threw down her bloodied swab and saw Nathan's frown as he dropped the extracted bullet into a basin. Pringle ordered three men to hold down the screaming musketeer, and when the surgeon picked up his bloodied saw, the patient's eyes bulged in terror.

'I'd rather die than be a cripple,' he screamed.

'That's Sergeant Marshall!' Nathan ran across the room and snatched the saw from Pringle's hands.

'You're a bloody butcher,' he raged. Pushing the surgeon aside, he examined the patient by the light of the overhead lantern. There was a pile of severed arms and legs, partially hidden under a piece of sacking, and Nathan stared at them before he addressed the surgeon. 'I've yet to see you try and save a limb. Marshall has eight children. He's a tailor by trade. How can he provide for his family if you take off his arm? Oxford's streets are filled with men reduced to beggars because of such butchery.'

Angel could not hear Pringle's reply, but his stance was pompous. He was a short, stout man with a small beard and large bulbous eyes. Nathan grabbed him by the front of his doublet and the surgeon was forced up on to his toes. It was the first time Angel had seen Nathan lose his temper. He ordered the three assistants from the hall, and there was murder in his eyes as he turned back to the surgeon.

'Get out of here before I kick you out! You're not fit to practise. Marshall's arm is broken not fractured. It can be set in splints. All it needed was for you to take the time to clean the dirt and cloth from the wound to prevent infection setting in. But that's too much trouble for you! You'd rather condemn a man to life as a cripple and let his family starve.'

'I save their lives. Spare them gangrene which will send them to a screaming death,' Pringle spluttered.

'And how many die under your knife? Two yesterday, one today. I've warned you before, Pringle. This time I'll make sure you're dismissed.'

'You've got above yourself, Carver . . . Threatening a

fellow officer. You'll answer to the King.'

'As you'll answer to the Prince for crippling one of his men.'

'Rupert and his damned hotheads,' Pringle snorted his derision. 'He has more enemies than friends.'

Nathan turned his back on the surgeon and nodded to Angel to join him. Pringle stamped out of the hall muttering threats.

'Dusty, tilt the lantern over the wound so I can inspect the bone.'

Nathan looked at Marshall. 'Sword blow, was it? I'll clean the wound and, unless your arm is to be useless, I must sew the severed muscles together. It will hurt like the devil and I doubt you'll ever have the full use of it again.'

'At least you'd have done your best, Cap'n. God willing, I'll still have some use in it. For that, I thank you.'

The man's arm was already strapped to the table from the surgeon's preparations to amputate. Angel went to get the catgut and needle, and when she returned Nathan had pressed the two edges of bone together. Marshall had passed out. Angel stood by Nathan's side and he looked up at her. 'One of the others will help me. You'll be late for your meeting with Rupert.'

'Then I shall be late,' she said firmly. 'All the other helpers have left. At this moment Sergeant Marshall needs me.'

Nathan nodded. His attention was absorbed by his patient, but she noticed that the earlier tension had gone from his manner. Angel averted her eyes as the needle pricked the torn flesh. Marshall moved his head and, fearful that he was about to return to consciousness and start to fight, she spoke comfortingly to him. 'Be still, Sergeant. You'll not lose your arm, but you mustn't move until Captain Carver has finished.'

When Marshall began to twist and turn, she spoke again. 'Hold, man. Be still.' Marshall's eyes opened. His face was screwed up in pain and his jaw clenched as he bit down hard on the wood and cloth which gagged his mouth.

'Be brave. Don't move.' Tears pricked her eyes but she kept her voice soft and reassuring. 'I know it hurts. Dr Carver will save your arm.'

His fingers clung to her and she stifled a wince at their

crushing grip. A half hour later Nathan threw the bloody needle into a bowl. Marshall's body was drenched in sweat, but he hadn't made a sound. Ten minutes later he was asleep on one of the beds which lined the hospital dormitory. Nathan checked on each patient and then, pouring himself a small measure of watered wine, leant against the wall. He studied Angel as she collected up bloodied swabs and began to scour the operating table. She exasperated him, and he could not understand why she continued to dress as a man. Or why, knowing her secret as he did, other men did not realise she was a woman.

Beneath the padded doublet his discerning eye could see the fabric pulling over her breasts. Her figure was slender but there was nothing masculine about its form. Her delicate features were exquisitely lovely with none of the pampered softness of so many women he had known. She was earthy, sensual and complex. She appeared oblivious to the horrors of tending mutilated men. Even after hours in the hospital, she never left without a last circuit of the dormitory. He had seen her stay at a dying man's bedside all night to ease his passing, and to all she offered a cheery word of encouragement. In the weeks they had worked together, she had learned a great deal about medicine and healing.

He watched her rinse the suds from the table and straighten. As she rubbed the small of her back, revealing her fatigue, affection and admiration for Angel forcibly struck him. When she looked up and saw him watching her, he tipped his cup in salute.

Placing her hands on her hips, Angel regarded her friend, her gaze mocking. 'It's all very well for the great physician to stand there supping wine, like a lord of all he surveys. Some of us are still working and have a thirst fit to drain a well.'

Nathan laughed and offered her his cup. She took it and drained the contents. Handing it back to him she began to wash her hands. As she did so she swayed and put a hand to her temple.

'Dusty, are you all right? You must be worn out.'

'I drank the wine too quickly.' She smiled.

The shadow line of his beard accentuated the angular line of Nathan's jaw. He looked tired, and with his hair falling forward into damp curls over his brow, he looked younger and for once vulnerable.

'I admired the way you dealt with Pringle. Will he cause trouble?'

'If I save Marshall's arm, he'll have no case against me.'

There was a commotion by the door and a major strode in, accompanied by four guards. 'You're under arrest, Captain Carver, for attacking a fellow officer. You'll be placed under guard in your quarters until you appear before a disciplinary court tomorrow.'

'That's unjust!' Angel said hotly. 'A man's arm has been saved because of his action.'

The four guards surrounded Nathan, and Angel accompanied them to the college, continuing to berate the officer at the injustice of Nathan's arrest. As they entered the building, Nathan halted.

'May I speak a moment with my assistant?'

The officer grunted. 'Seems like the lad has more than enough to say for the both of you.'

'A loyal but over-enthusiastic youth,' Nathan responded.

The officer gestured for the guards to stand aside. Nathan took Angel's arm and drew her several paces away. 'I appreciate your defence, but you risk being arrested for obstructing an officer in his duty. Then how will you visit your Prince?'

'I can't be silent. It's infamous what Pringle has done. It's vindictive. It's petty and it's downright unfair.'

A smile lifted Nathan's mouth. 'I'm flattered by your concern. But my services are too valuable for them to keep me under guard. It will all have blown over by morning.'

'I don't think so. Pringle is a conceited braggart. He's a barber surgeon with little skill, and he's jealous of your expertise and popularity. I'll speak with Rupert. He'll have you released.'

Nathan's face darkened and his voice lost its warmth. 'I don't need any woman using her favours to help me.'

Her eyes glittered at the cruelty of his insult and her hands balled into fists. 'Damn you! I didn't deserve that!' She turned on her heel and ran up the stairs to her room, banging the door behind her.

Nathan sighed. It wasn't often that he felt ashamed of his actions, but some devil had goaded him to speak sharply to her. He had begun to feel protective towards Angel, and he didn't like the feeling. His present mode of life suited him. No ties. No regrets. And most importantly, no emotional involvements. A familiar ache returned to strike at his heart. He crushed the memories he had thought long-buried. Never again would he trust a woman. Once he had been capable of love. His eyes were bitter. He knew the folly of placing his trust in womankind.

'Conceited jackanapes!' Angel muttered fiercely as she slammed the door of her chamber behind her. 'Arrogant buffoon! Ass-witted churl!'

A chuckle came from the shadows of the room. The fire was burning brightly and a log settled deeper into the flames, sending up a fountain of sparks. Rupert uncoiled his long figure from the chair by the hearth and Boy lifted his head from his paws and thumped his tail on the floorboards.

'I trust it's not I who am the subject of your ire?' Rupert said, putting aside a piece of paper upon which he had been sketching some new type of cannon, with calculations and measurements worked out alongside it.

'Your Highness! I had not expected . . .' she floundered. 'I thought your summons was for me to attend upon you.'

'So it was – over an hour ago.' His voice was no longer amused.

'Didn't the messenger tell you I was in the hospital?' She could not see his face as he stood with his back to the fire.

'I have been given no peace this night,' he told her. 'A constant stream of petitioners beat their way to my rooms. To escape them I went for a walk and found myself by this college.'

'It wasn't my intent to keep Your Highness waiting,' she apologised. 'But the wounded needed my attention.'

She stared in dismay at her blood-splattered doublet and breeches. After hours in the hospital she was dirty and dishevelled. She paused in the shadows by the door, feeling unattractive. He was watching her, but he did not look displeased. She pulled the black ribbon from her hair and shook it loose.

'I'm not dressed as befits a meeting with Your Highness.'

'You are dressed appropriately for your role in Oxford. I

163

didn't intend this to be a formal meeting.' The lace at his wrists gleamed golden in the firelight as he held out a hand towards her.

She moved to take it and found herself pulled against him. When his mouth found hers, her lips parted, savouring the warmth and demand of their touch. His kiss deepened and his arms tightened urgently around her. She moved against him, burning with desire. Then with a choked sob she broke away from him, fighting to retain a hold upon her sanity.

The Prince tensed. Fearing she had angered him, she spoke quickly. 'I fear, before I allow passion to banish everything else from my mind, I must also play the supplicant.'

His straight brows drew together with suspicion.

'Not for myself,' she amended quickly. 'Captain Carver has been arrested. He stopped Captain Pringle from amputating Sergeant Marshall's arm. Nathan saved Marshall's arm, but Pringle has alleged that he attacked him and now Nathan is under guard.'

'He'll come to no harm there.' Rupert sounded impatient.

'No, but it's the injustice of his arrest! It's Pringle who should be answering for the limbs he's hacked off, because he's too incompetent to sew together tendons or set a broken bone.'

'I shall deal with the matter in the morning.'

There was an imperious edge to his voice which warned Angel that he would tolerate no more such talk. During her weeks in Oxford she had learned that women played a small part in Rupert's life. Alexander had told her that after long hours in the saddle, the Prince would often inspect the garrison, supervising improvements to their defences. Then he spent hours writing orders to his commanders, or planning new strategies. Often, he worked into the small hours of the morning until finally surrendering to an exhausted but all too brief sleep. He was a warrior and too short on patience to be a practised gallant.

He drew her into his arms. When his lips spoke of their hunger, Angel needed no honeyed words of love, nor a romantic courtship. She took the initiative. Removing his sword belt, her fingers were eager upon the laces of his doublet. Fevered hands discarded clothing. It was three months since she had lain with him in Wales. She wanted to ensure that tonight would be indelibly carved in his memory, as it would be in her own. From the weeks amongst the Cavaliers – when they had no suspicion she was a woman – she had heard much of their bawdy conversation, often quite graphically described.

She stepped back and removed her clothing, aware of his hungry stare upon her. Then she pushed aside his hands from his own clothing and slowly removed each garment, kissing his bare flesh as each article was thrown aside. When they were both naked, she returned his kisses with ardour, her breath hot and caressing, her hands sliding over the smooth muscles of his back and waist as she sank slowly to her knees. When her mouth closed over his erect manhood, his sharp moan of pleasure was the sweetest accolade she had ever heard. His body shuddered as her tongue and lips played over him, his fingers twining into her hair, binding her closer. Intuitively, she brought him to the brink of pleasure then sought to prolong it. He pulled the coverlet from the bed and flung it on the floor before the fire. Lying down, he pulled her on top of him.

Angel moved slowly, her breasts teased and tantalised, her hair cool, silken and erotic as it skimmed across his flesh. Through her lashes she saw sensual pleasure reflected on her lover's face. Before ecstasy could turn to painful torment, she pushed herself up and sat astride him, sheathing him deep within the heat of her. Until then she had remained in control. Now her restraint snapped and she was driven by a fervour which scattered sanity and reason. She lost awareness of her surroundings, enslaved by the building pleasure, the bitter-sweet torture craving release. The fury built within her, exploding and reforming each time to a higher magnitude, more profound and protracted than anything she had experienced before.

'I needed you,' he said hoarsely as he reared up to take her nipple into his mouth and she was pitched into another storm of passion.

Later, her body was replete, glowing and fulfilled. As her breathing became even she drew back to roll off her lover, but Rupert prevented her. He remained inside her as he placed a muscular arm across his eyes. When the arm was lowered, his dark eyes were serious.

He continued to regard her solemnly. 'It's good you've put aside your absurd notions to fight,' he said. 'The work you do here with Carver has saved many lives.'

'I've not abandoned my desire to fight. Captain Carver fought at Edgehill.' The firelight cast shadows over the Prince's handsome face, making his expression stern, and she rushed on. 'If I cannot fight in a battle, could I not ride with Alex in a scouting party?'

'You're safe here.'

Angel noted the irritation in his voice, but her smile undermined it. 'Safe but restrained like a prisoner. I don't begrudge my work in the hospital . . .' Her eyes glowed with fervour. 'I'm not afraid. I want to avenge my grandparents' deaths. Surely you understand that? Don't deny me my right to triumph over our enemies just because I'm a woman.'

Angel studied the terse lines of his face revealed by the firelight. There were shadows around his eyes, and the uncompromising lines at the sides of his mouth had not been there when they met in Wales.

All the frustration she felt from the weeks of being cooped up in Oxford suddenly burst out. She berated him as she would Alexander, forgetting in her anger that he was a prince. 'Do you think I'm such a miserable weakling?'

'You're about as weak as a tigress with claws extended for the kill,' he commented drily. 'But miserable you certainly are not. You're one of the few rays of light in this war. Though you're stubborn to the point of recklessness, and that displeases me.'

She detected a trace of menace in his words and her temper cooled. 'I'd never wittingly displease Your Highness, but I vowed always to be true to myself and to my conscience. Do I ask so much?'

He regarded her sardonically. 'I'll consider the matter. If Major Rowan does not disagree . . .'

She did not wait for him to finish but kissed him with growing passion. 'I shall not fail you.'

'I've not agreed,' he warned, but his expression had softened.

Suddenly fearful, she asked, 'Have I displeased you?'

Her obvious dismay wrung a clipped laugh from him, and his eyes sparkled with amusement. 'No, minx. You please me greatly.'

166

He shifted his hips and her eyes widened as she felt him harden within her. A husky breath sighed in her throat. She delighted in the pressure of his body and the warmth of his lips as he nuzzled the hollow of her throat. He arched his back and reached up to pull the pillows from the bed. Placing them behind him, he eased himself into a sitting position and hooked Angel's legs around his waist, so that they sat, locked intimately together. Angel gasped as her pelvic muscles throbbed from her own arousal.

Rupert's teeth glistened like pearls beneath his black moustache and his eyes held a devilish light. 'Perhaps I need more persuading?' he suggested.

Her answering laugh was smothered by his kiss. In each other's arms was peace, fulfilment and forgetfulness. The painful memories of war were banished. Angel abandoned herself to passion which would be all too fleeting. Soon he would leave her, and waiting and loneliness would again be her constant companions.

The morning after his arrest, Nathan was taken before the King and Captain Pringle's accusation read out against him. To his surprise, Prince Rupert, standing behind the King, spoke out before he could defend himself.

'Pringle does more for the Parliamentarian cause than an entire troop of Roundheads,' Rupert ground out as he paced the room in long terse strides. 'True, he saves many of the lives of the men he operates upon. But he leaves them crippled and useless. Invaluable men trained as soldiers are reduced to beggars. I've learned that two score men were unnecessarily mutilated by Pringle. Another dozen at least died under his surgery.'

A half hour later, Nathan left the chamber, not only freed, but with an unexpected promotion to Colonel. He now outranked any of the surgeons or physicians in the army and all had been placed under his command. He should have been elated at this chance to end the maiming done in ignorance and incompetence, but his triumph was clouded by the suspicion that Angel had been the instrument behind Rupert's intervention.

He confronted her at the hospital. Taking her arm, he marched her across a quadrangle into the privacy of an outbuilding which he used to write up his notes on the progress of patients and their treatment.

Angel wrenched her arm away and rounded on him as he closed the door.

'Devil take you, Nathan!' she raged. 'You act as though I betrayed your trust. All I did was speak out for a friend against injustice.'

'I don't need a woman speaking for me. I'll win my promotion on my own merit, not from any favours granted because you asked it of your paramour.'

She struck out at him surprising him by the violence of her attack. Her fists pounded against his chest, her green eyes sparking with fury.

'Damn you for an ingrate!'

The blows were painful but he did not retaliate. Despite his anger, he was fearful of hurting her. Instead he forced her hands down to her sides. 'That's enough, Angel.'

Immediately, the fight went out of her, but her expression remained wary and antagonistic. It was then he saw the pain behind the defiance in her eyes, and his anger cooled. They were both breathing heavily and he saw her blink rapidly to dispel tears forming in her eyes.

'You blind, stubborn, ass-headed clod.' Her voice crackled from the depth of her hurt. 'Of course your promotion was given on merit. Do you think Rupert would act on so important an issue because a woman asked it of him? You malign his integrity as a soldier if you do.'

She jerked away from his hold, turning her back and drawing several deep breaths to calm her anger. 'If I offended you then I ask your pardon. But you were promoted to Colonel because of your skill.'

There was no doubting the sincerity of her tone. Nathan gently turned her to face him. He had been wrong to judge her by the standards of another woman. Angel was nothing like that scheming bitch. Angrily, he thrust the memory of Sanchia Lorenzo aside. But, as always, any reminder of Sanchia, the beautiful but perfidious Venetian woman he had married, brought a bitter taste to his mouth. He deliberately banished Sanchia from his thoughts, as he had banished her from his life.

'Blind, stubborn, ass-headed clod, am I?' he said, grinning

168

at Angel. 'That's damned unflattering.'

For once she did not rise to his baiting. 'So was your accusation that I'd barter my body for favours. Since your opinion of me is so low, I'll leave the hospital. You won't have to work with a woman you despise.'

He shook his head. 'Dusty, where did you get that notion? You're like a cross hedgehog and just as prickly. I acted like a churl.'

Angel glared at him, her fingers drumming upon her hip. Nathan's face had whitened revealing the pale freckles across his nose. The sunlight lancing through a small window brightened his dark blond hair, making an auriel of light around his head. He regarded her in silence. Despite the cleft in his chin and the scar in his eyebrow, he was an extremely handsome man, and it surprised her to discover that she was not entirely immune to either his looks, or his charm. There was a warmth of affection she felt towards him which was disconcerting.

Too accomplished an actress to allow any of these emotions to show on her face, she folded her arms. 'Just what does a cross hedgehog look like? There's no chance of my head swelling from any compliments from you.'

'Do you forgive me?' he asked simply.

'Between friends there should be no need to ask forgiveness.'

For a long moment his gaze held hers with penetrating intensity. The clear sapphire depths were as enigmatic as they were silently challenging, and unexpectedly she felt an answering *frisson* of excitement. The darkening in Nathan's eyes warned her he was aware of that brief response.

Angel passed it off with a light laugh and they returned to the hospital in easy companionship.

Chapter Seven

Arundel garrisoned by Waller's troops was oppressive to Maressa. After a tiresome hour in the company of the town's matrons, she made her excuses and left. She wondered how she had ever found such meetings interesting. Since helping her father escape from Chichester she was restless and bored by charitable works. She smiled at the memory of rescuing Llewelyn. Fortunately there had been no repercussions.

It was now spring and she had heard no word from her father, Alexander or Angel. Resentment rose that they should be together in Oxford, where the King was in residence. How she would sparkle at his Court! But Henry's loyalty to Parliament had demolished those dreams, and isolated her from her family and the life at Court she craved.

Her mood blackened at discovering her sedan chair unattended. The two servants were lounging against the wall of the nearby tavern. She called to them sharply. Her cry drew the attention of several Roundheads taunting a vagabond in the stocks. Ignoring their coarse jeering and whistles, she looked past them down the incline of the street towards the river. Above the rooftops she could see the masts of two ships and there were a dozen sailors brawling outside the coaching inn.

She stepped into the sedan, bracing herself against its uncomfortable swaying. She disliked this mode of conveyance, but with so many soldiers billeted in the town, a decent woman was not safe walking the streets. Riding a horse was impractical because of the press of people, and the slope of the hill was too steep for carriages to pass with ease.

Sussex seemed far removed from the conflict which centred around Oxford and London. Were it not for the presence of the Roundhead soldiers in the castle there was little disruption to her everyday life.

Henry insisted that they live in Arundel. Creditors in London made it impossible for him to return to the capital until he had restored his finances. As a Member of Parliament he had visited many of the local gentry, and Maressa guessed that he was behind some of the sequestration of Royalist estates. Henry was unscrupulous and she suspected that he channelled money from those appropriated estates to himself. Her expression soured as they approached the parish church of St Nicholas where the Roundheads had stabled their horses. The beautiful stained-glass windows had been smashed in mindless destruction.

Alighting from the chair she entered the house with its views over the Arun valley. Hazel greeted her looking distracted.

'My lady, I'm worried about your brother Emrys. Sir Henry is with him in the garden, teaching him how to fire a pistol. But he's not strong enough to be taught such things.'

Hazel had changed a great deal under Maressa's tutelage. Her rough voice had modulated and she always dressed demurely, as befitted a lady's maid. Her skill with herbs was remarkable and without Hazel's dedication Firkin would not have survived last winter.

'Firkin is old enough to master firearms. Though I'd rather he didn't know of such matters with Waller's men in the town. He hates the Roundheads, and his head is full of fighting and war.'

Maressa entered the garden in time to see Firkin take aim with the pistol and fire at a piece of wood nailed on to a tree. The shot clipped the edge of the wood and he groaned in disappointment.

'One more shot. I'll load the pistol,' he yelled. The day was cold and he was not wearing a cloak. His cheeks were flushed, and in his excitement he began to cough. The hacking sound shook his slight figure.

Maressa snatched the pistol from her brother's hands. 'There'll be no more shooting today. You've tired yourself. You're supposed to be resting.'

'Stop treating me like a child, Maressa.' Firkin shocked her by his vehemence. His shout brought on another coughing fit, and Hazel ran out of the house to put a cloak about his shoulders.

'Come back inside,' the maid urged. 'Do you want to be ill again? You need your strength as much as you need skill with a firearm.'

'It's bad enough being a cripple, but to be an invalid as well is hell! I just want to be like Alex. I want to prove I'm a man!' The look he turned on Maressa was agonised. 'I'm nearly thirteen. You know as well as I, I'll never live to manhood.' Then another fit gripped his frail body and he allowed Hazel to lead him into the house.

Sir Henry chuckled. 'Tiresome brat.'

Maressa rounded on her husband. 'How could you teach him to use a pistol?'

'You cosset the boy too much,' Henry pouted. 'Besides, I was bored.'

'You'd endanger my brother's life because you're bored!' she sneered.

Henry eyed her sullenly. 'Well, I've the remedy to that. I leave for London tomorrow – alone. I've money enough to settle my debts there and I shall reopen the house in the Strand.' He glared at her coldly. 'I'll send for you once my business affairs are settled.'

Maressa was furious he was leaving without her. He had not taken a mistress in months and she thought her power over him was absolute. She checked her anger. London would not have the same excitement without the King at Whitehall, but Henry needed her if he wished to rise high in the new Government. She would follow him shortly. He would need to impress influential people, and who better than herself to charm even the staidest of Puritans? She had married Henry for wealth and position. She had not endured so much from her marriage to see the future she had planned thwarted by a weakling of a husband.

In the first months of the year Rupert had often been absent from Oxford. He had secured the countryside through Gloucestershire in the need to keep clear the King's communications with the Royalists commanded by Sir Ralph Hopton in the west. In March Rupert attempted to take Bristol, the second town to London in importance and a vital port. When he failed, he returned to Oxford in a bitter mood.

Later Birmingham fell to Rupert, but he was too late to

save the garrison at Reading. It went to the Roundheads. Now Oxford was exposed on that flank and under threat of attack.

Since Llewelyn had arrived in Oxford in January, Angel was determined that her affair with Rupert should not become common knowledge. In a place as crowded as Oxford it was not easy to escape gossip, but her disguise as Alexander's brother continued to work. When Alexander had first learned of her affair, he had been angry. But he was no hypocrite. Once he had seen how happy she was, he became her ally. As for Nathan, his moods could be variable and he was surprisingly protective of her.

At first, Llewelyn was appalled by Angel's disguise. He relented once he had seen the work she did in the hospital, and Nathan assured him that she was an invaluable assistant.

Earlier in the week Llewelyn had ridden out of Oxford on one of several raiding parties ordered by Rupert. The fine weather had made the Prince restless. Daily he quarrelled with the King and his councillors to begin the spring campaign in earnest. With each refusal, his mood became more irascible. Whenever he was in Oxford he turned to Angel for solace. Their time together was short, stolen from the constant pressure Rupert imposed upon himself to oversee everything possible and triumph in the war.

Rupert paced Angel's room. He had wrapped his long scarlet cloak around his naked body after making love to her. A scowl darkened his handsome face as he spilled out his venom that another manor had fallen to Colonel Cromwell.

Angel sat by the fire, wrapped in a coverlet from the bed and listening to his furious outpourings: his frustration at the delay imposed by the King's caution, and his contempt for his uncle's counsellors. With the coming of spring he was impatient for a decisive battle. She listened without interruption until the heat of his anger began to cool. With the abruptness of so many of his movements he turned on his heel, his knuckles resting on his hip as he regarded her.

'I've been raving on for an hour. Why didn't you stop me?'

She smiled and stood up. 'It was something you needed to get off your chest. A sympathetic ear is a great balm.'

He took her into his arms. 'You never judge me, and yet my talk must bore you.'

174

'No. I was brought up on tales of valour. I could listen to your plans for victory for hours. However, diplomacy is not your strong point. You've no patience. I'm flattered that you occasionally heed my words of caution. You have spared yourself nothing in your quest for success, and your victories outweigh your failures. I envy Alex for being able to share them with you.'

'You still have it in your head to fight?'

Hearing the note of warning and tiredness in his voice, she decided not to press the matter. Taking his hand she led him to the bed and lay down, her voice a seductive purr. 'I've it in my head to do many things tonight, but fighting is not one of them.'

'You're incorrigible,' he said, stretching out beside her and stroking the curve of her hip.

When his fingers traced the line of her cheek, she closed her eyes, awed that a hand which dealt death so skilfully with a sword could be so infinitely tender. His kiss burned her throat, his lips hungry as they moved up to take her mouth. Peeling away the cover from her body he caressed her breasts. The touch of his hands and the warmth of his body pitched her into a fever of longing. She yielded ardently, her lips trembling beneath his. She asked nothing of him but to share his joys and sorrows, to bring him peace and give him pleasure.

Later, their desire slaked, they lay, limbs entwined in a tumble of bedclothes. His dark head rested on her breast and she was aware of the tension which still corded the muscles of his body. When he sat up and swung his legs from the bed in preparation to leave, she snatched up a phial of perfumed oil. Kneeling on the bed behind him as he reached for his breeches, she nipped him lightly on the shoulder with her teeth. Her action startled him into glaring round at her.

'I have to go,' he said curtly. 'I've orders to dictate.'

'Will another half-hour make so much difference?'

His eyes blazed dangerously. Undeterred, she held up the phial. 'If you leave now you won't sleep. You're too tense. You'll pace your room for hours, bullying your exhausted scribes into penning some irate order to a far-flung garrison.' She grinned with devilment and dangled the phial closer to his face. 'Alternatively there is this.'

'I've no time for games, Angel. No matter how tempting.' He leaned forward to push a leg into his breeches.

She uncorked the phial. Spreading the oil into her palm, she ran her fingers across his shoulders and neck. He drew in his breath sharply.

'Angel, I have to go—'

She ignored the imperious order, gently kneading her fingers into the knotted muscles across his shoulders and neck. 'This will take just a short time. You'll feel better for it. Have I ever disappointed you?'

He hung his head, his long hair curtaining his face as her fingers began to work their magic upon the taut sinews of his neck. Gradually she felt the tension leave his body, but she continued with the massage, speaking in a low sensuous voice, relating amusing incidents which had happened since his last visit. When she began to mimic the most pompous courtiers, especially those whom she knew resented Rupert's influence on the King, he laughed. Rolling on to his side he clasped her to him. There was no sign now of the black fury which had eaten at him when he had arrived at her room. The tenderness in his eyes made her heart swell with love.

'That's the old dithering Earl to a whisker! I swear I'll never be able to listen to him babbling on about caution at a council meeting again without laughing. I'm stuck here in Oxford for at least a week, awaiting His Majesty's orders. Without you, Angel, I think I'd go mad.'

This was a side of Rupert that few people saw, and Angel knew that while she could chase the cares of the war from his mind, he would continue to visit her. He spoke no words of love and she did not expect them, but these tender moments formed a special bond between them.

Rupert wrapped her hair around his hand and gently drew her under him, his ardour rekindled. She could not resist taunting. 'I thought you were leaving, Your Highness?'

A less than playful nip on her ear was his reply. When Angel retaliated in kind, he swore in German. A mock wrestling match followed involving more tickling than caresses until, laughing so hard she could not catch her breath, Angel surrendered to his mastery.

Later, when she lay cradled in his arms, and Rupert showed no further intention of leaving, she ventured, 'Have

176

you been ordered to stay within Oxford? Or do you intend to lead a scouting party to learn the movements of this Cromwell who put you in such a taking earlier?'

His eyes had been closed but now they opened. He sat up. 'Cromwell's movements must be known. I daren't risk a troop, until I know his strength.' He placed a perfunctory kiss on her cheek. 'It's been some time since I rode out in disguise to play a trick on the Roundheads.'

'Then let me come with you. I'll adopt any disguise you wish. Let me do something to avenge my grandparents' deaths.'

It was obvious he was about to refuse until he caught the impassioned plea on her face and shrugged. 'You're so set on something like this, I doubt you'll give me rest until I consent. But Rowan and Carver must also agree. I can trust them to keep you safe if the need arises.'

They left Oxford the next morning. Rupert had discarded his flamboyant clothes and was dressed in black, as befitted a yeoman farmer travelling to visit relatives. In the role of his wife, Angel was dressed in a grey woollen dress and black cloak, her hair hidden beneath a plain linen cap. Nathan and Alexander wore brown breeches and leather jerkins, suitable attire for servants. Riding out of Oxford they passed pikemen drilling in the fields and a troop of Cavaliers with swords drawn who were practising at charging straw effigies. Rupert was in good humour as they ventured into Parliament-held lands. He rode ahead and Angel, excited by the escapade, was in high spirits joking with Nathan.

For the past hour it had been drizzling with rain and though it was only mid-morning the sky was ominously dark. By midday, when they had encountered no sign of Roundhead troops, Rupert's temper was on a short rein. An hour later the first boom of thunder sounded overhead and the rain became a drenching downpour. Ahead of them in a clearing was a deserted charcoal burner's cottage.

'We'll shelter here until the storm abates,' Rupert said gruffly.

Two hours later when the storm abated, it was too late to travel further. Rupert paced the single room of the hut too restless to settle.

'There's a village two miles from here,' he announced

impatiently. 'I'll ride to an inn and discover what I can of Parliament forces in the area.' He strode to the door.

'Shall I accompany you, Your Highness?' Alexander got to his feet. Nathan also rose expectantly, and the Prince eyed them both.

'Too many will attract attention,' he said. 'Rowan may come. Carver, you stay here and protect Angel.'

'I don't need to be protected,' Angel was indignant. 'I didn't ride with you to be kept safe in a deserted hut.'

'And I don't expect to have my orders questioned,' Rupert rapped out.

Angel clenched her teeth and held back her retort. As his mistress she must expect no special treatment. Though he might enjoy her teasing in the intimacy of her chamber, outside she must never forget her place. She inclined her head.

'As Your Highness wishes.' She spoke to empty space. He had already left.

There was no furniture in the hut. Angel spread her cloak on the earth floor before the fire they had lit in the hearth. Sitting down, she drew up her knees and she stared into the flames. Nathan stretched out, propping himself on one elbow and respecting her silence.

Eventually she turned to him, her voice showing her frustration. 'I doubt you relish the role of nursemaid. Wouldn't you rather be with Rupert?'

'Given the choice of riding in the rain, then spending an hour in a dirty, flea-infested inn, or sitting by a fire with a beautiful woman, which do you think I'd choose?'

With a laugh, she struck him lightly on the arm. 'You always know how to cheer me. But I wanted so much more from this day. I had hoped to achieve something.'

'You have achieved something remarkable getting Rupert to allow you to join us. We aren't back in Oxford yet. Who knows what tomorrow will bring?'

He lay on his back with his hands behind his head and stared up at the ceiling. He was always so relaxed. Did nothing ruffle him? she wondered.

'What made you become a physician?' Angel asked, curious that Nathan rarely spoke about his past life.

His stare did not waver from the ceiling and he did not

178

immediately answer. When he spoke, his voice was distant, as though all emotion had been carefully erased from it. 'I was always interested in medicine. My father was an apothecary. I helped him in his work when I was home from the grammar school. When I was fifteen my father was run down by a coach. A child had stepped out in its path, and he tried to save it.' His eyes narrowed with pain as he stared at the struts of the thatched roof. 'He was crushed, and lingered for months in agony before he died. There was nothing any physician could do to ease his suffering. My mother died when I was a child. I was their only son; my half-sisters by a previous marriage of Father's were long married. On his death I sold the shop and with the money I travelled to Padua in Italy, to the college of healing there. I studied for four years and, in no hurry to return to England, spent another year travelling on the Continent. In Venice I met a Moor, a gifted physician. I worked with him for two years, learning all he could teach me. The Moors are far more advanced in their knowledge of healing than we are. When I learned of the King's quarrel with Parliament I decided to return to my homeland and offer my sword in his service.'

'What is Venice like? Is it strange to live in a city built on water?'

'It's the maritime trading centre of the world. A place of great art and learning, but most of all, it's a city of pleasure. I can think of no finer place for a man to dissolutely squander his youth.' There was an edge of bitterness in his tone. 'The courtesans are reputedly the most beautiful in Europe, and the most callous and ambitious.'

'And the woman you fell in love with in Venice, was she beautiful but callous and ambitious?' She guessed at why he always spoke so scathingly of love.

He turned a glacial stare upon her. 'Sanchia was all of that and treacherous into the bargain. Love is only for the young and idealistic.'

The harshness of his voice told her that whatever had befallen him in Venice had left scars, as yet unhealed. What treachery could so have hardened his heart?

Nathan stood up and lifted the shutter of the unglazed window to stare out at the night. His body was tense, the tendons in his neck corded. Angel stifled an impulse to go to him. She had revived painful memories for him and she regretted her curiosity. After stoking the fire, she continued to stare into the flames, uneasy at the tension which lay between them.

His voice was mocking when he eventually spoke. 'Run out of questions? Aren't you going to ask me who she was, or what terrible deed she committed? Women always want to know everything.'

'If you want to tell me, you will.' She looked over her shoulder at him. 'You've travelled and seen much of the world. Your life seemed so interesting and your comment prompted me to draw a conclusion. I didn't mean to pry.'

Nathan was drawn by the sincerity in Angel's gaze. For a moment he felt his resistance waver. It pulled him up short. It was a small warning, but a warning all the same. Too often for his peace of mind, Angel could get beneath his guard. He would have to keep a tighter rein on his attraction to her, but she was not an easy woman to ignore. Her charms were more subtle, her personality unlike other women of her station. She had a distinctive beauty of which she seemed unaware. Her manner was as direct as a man's, while her natural femininity remained unblemished by self-interest. What drew him was more charismatic than the normal attraction of a man to a beautiful woman. He admired her honesty and courage, and it made him wary.

The intensity of Nathan's stare was so profound that Angel thought he was about to tell her more of Sanchia and her betrayal. Then he turned his head back to the window and stared out at the clearing. She heard the sound of wagon wheels approaching. Putting a finger to his lips to caution her to silence, Nathan retrieved his pistol from his saddle-roll.

Aware of possible danger, Angel lifted her skirts to her knees and drew out the dagger which she had taken the precaution of strapping to her thigh. She caught Nathan's look of astonishment as she turned away to scatter the twigs on the fire and stamp out the flames with her boots.

Gripping the dagger, she moved to the door and put an eye to a crack in the rotted wood. The rain had stopped but there was no moonlight. A lantern hung on the side of a covered wagon. It gave off enough light to show an ancient nag driven by a man in a battered slouch hat and draped in a cloak as he sat hunched over the reins. The wagon halted by the hut and when the man did not move Nathan went outside. The brim of the driver's hat was low over his face.

'Put 'ee shooter away, man,' the driver said in a thick country accent. 'I don' mean 'ee no 'arm. Poor pedlar I be.'

'You're far from a town and trade, pedlar,' Nathan challenged. 'How do we know you're not a Royalist spy? Cromwell's troops are spread throughout the county.'

There was a cackle from the driver. 'Do 'ee think I've the looks of a Cavalier, with they roistering ways an' velvets an' lace an' the like?'

Nathan kept his pistol raised. 'Go on your way. This hut is overcrowded as it is.'

His command was greeted by a crack of familiar laughter from the wagon. The pedlar removed his hat and a tall figure leapt to the ground.

'Your Highness!' Nathan voiced his astonishment. 'Had you no thought that we could have shot you?'

From out of the back of the wagon another figure emerged and Alexander joined in Rupert's laughter.

The lantern illuminated Rupert's saturnine face and he looked more pleased with himself than he had done in weeks. He mimicked Nathan's tone: 'How do we know you're not a Royalist spy? That was rich, Carver.'

He was still laughing as he entered the hut. 'Tomorrow we shall go to Cambridge and learn what we can, right under Cromwell's nose.'

'How did you come by the pedlar's wagon?' Angel asked.

'I borrowed it from someone you know,' Rupert replied. 'Popinjay, or rather, John Sparrow, as he calls himself now. He was passing through the village. Gave me some interesting information about the defences of some of the towns. He was on his way back to Oxford to report his findings.'

'He's not with you?' Angel was disappointed at missing a reunion with her old friend.

'No. Our meeting was doubly fortuitous,' Rupert told her. 'Sparrow had taken a chill and was near to collapse with the fever. He made his report to me, and I ordered him to take to his bed.'

'I'll examine him when we return the wagon,' Nathan offered.

They entered Cambridge the next morning and set up their

wagon in the market-place. While Angel and Alexander sold John Sparrow's wares, the Prince and Nathan went their separate ways, visiting taverns to discover what information they could.

Trade was brisk, and Angel enjoyed bartering with her customers as she kept an eye on Rupert's and Nathan's movements as they went from one tavern to another. In the mid-afternoon a troop of Roundheads rode across the square and tethered their horses outside the inn which Rupert had just entered. Alarmed, Angel turned to Alexander.

'What can we do?' she whispered as her brother finished selling an iron pot. 'The Prince may be recognised. It's not easy to disguise his height.'

Alexander nodded towards his four customers rummaging through the goods. 'Make your choices, good people. I'm about to finish for the day. It'll be dark in a hour and I must be away from here before curfew.'

Unfortunately, two women were disposed to linger, and one began to haggle with Alexander, but Angel was too anxious about Rupert to delay longer.

Her voice sharp, she exclaimed, 'Where's my lazy sot of a husband? In the tavern drinking our profits, I'll warrant!' She rolled her eyes in exasperation and snatched up a hazel broom before getting down off the tailboard of the wagon.

'Give the drunken wretch a taste of that broom,' a stout matron advised.

The woman's companion nodded. 'Men! Every quarter day I daren't let my Harold out of sight until my hands are on his wages. He'd spend the lot on drink and dicing. Not a penny I'd get to feed our six mites!'

Angel waved the broom with menacing intent. 'Just wait till I get my hands on him.'

'That's the spirit!' the first woman called after her as she strode towards the tavern.

'Where's my husband?' Angel bawled, pushing past a soldier who lounged in the doorway. Her stance that of an outraged wife, her voice boomed out into the smoky fug of the dingy taproom. 'Where's the lazy scoundrel? Has anyone seen the pedlar who came in here?'

She saw Rupert sitting in a dark corner, his hat pulled down over his eyes as though he slept. Brandishing the broom with such malevolence that a path opened before her, Angel advanced across the taproom. Aware that several soldiers had turned to watch her, she dared not temper her role. Fear cast caution aside and working herself into a fury, she played the harridan to perfection. The broom came down upon Rupert's hunched shoulders.

'Asleep!' she screeched. 'Drunken sot! That's the second time this week you've drunk our profits!' The broom descended again. She caught the glint of warning in Rupert's eye as she subjected him to this indignity, but she did not balk. 'Get up, you lazy sot. Call yourself a man? You're a disgrace.' The third time the broom came down across his shoulders, Rupert rose to a crouching position, using his long cloak to conceal his height.

'A plague on 'ee, woman,' he answered in the peasant's accent he had used the previous night. ''Ee be a damned shrew! Mind yer blathering.'

There were several guffaws of laughter from the soldiers and Angel warmed to her part. In her enthusiasm, she planted the broom upon the Prince's buttocks as he made to duck away from her tirade. 'Shrew, am I? I'll give you shrew. Lazy bag of bones!'

Putting up a hand to stave off the blows, Rupert shuffled forward. 'Yewoow!' He let out a piercing whine like a scalded cat and hurried towards the door. 'Ger off wi' 'ee, damned vixen.'

Angel swung the broom from side to side with such gusto that no one attempted to halt them. The soldiers stepped back, enjoying the spectacle her screams of abuse provided. Rupert played his part of shrew-cowed husband as if born to it. The taproom erupted into laughter at their antics. Angel rounded on a skinny customer whose face was red with mirth. She waved the broom in his face. 'Think it's funny, do you? Perhaps you'd like a taste of my broom?'

The man went pale and choked on his ale. The laughter increased around her and she saw with relief that Rupert was almost at the door. When the sergeant put a hand on Rupert's shoulder, Angel watched in horror. Would he be recognised?

'Let me pass,' Rupert yelled. 'The damned shrew will have my hide.'

The sergeant laughed so hard that tears ran down his

cheeks. 'Your wife's in need of a scold's bridle to silence her tongue.'

'Don't think I haven't 'ad her up in the courts and tried it,' Rupert groaned, keeping his head down as the shadow of the broom waved above him. Many of the soldiers were now incapable of stopping them as they held their sides and laughed. 'But when it's off, she nags twice as bad.'

'I'll give you scold's bridle!' Angel jabbed at him with her broom.

Giving a loud yell, Rupert shoved past the sergeant with such a show of terror that the jeers and laughter in the tavern was deafening. Angel pursued him, the sound of the laughter following her as the broom again struck the Prince's back and he kept up his unholy racket. Across the market-square Alexander and Nathan were already in the wagon, waiting, their expressions incredulous as she chased Rupert's shuffling figure. For the benefit of any curious eyes she brought the broom down once more on to the Prince's shoulders before he scrambled into the back of the wagon. Red-faced from her exertions she heaved herself up beside him.

Immediately Alexander set the wagon in motion and Angel collapsed on her knees at Rupert's side, her head hanging down as she recovered her breath. All at once, Angel realised the enormity of what she had done and growing pale lifted her face to regard the Prince. He sat on the floor of the wagon with his knees drawn up. His face was taut, a muscle pumping along his jaw, and his dark eyes snapping with fury.

'Madam, one does not accost a Royal Prince with a broom upon his breeches with impunity. One has a whipping-boy expressly for that purpose.'

She swallowed appalled at the insult she had unintentionally dealt him. She had acted spontaneously thinking only of creating a diversion. She had not stopped to consider the consequences.

'Was I to leave you there to be recognised and arrested?' she demanded.

Aware of the fiercer side of his temperament, she felt an inner quaking. Propaganda pamphlets issued by Parliament reviled him as 'The Bloody Foreigner Prince', 'Prince Robber' and 'The Devil Prince' and they were the kinder epithets. He was fearless in battle, his courage equalled only by a temper, which when roused was blistering in its fury. She saw it blazing furnace-bright in his eyes, and faced it without flinching.

Rupert snarled, 'Is that all you have to say for the humiliation you have subjected upon my person?'

'I'd do it again if I thought it would save you from arrest.' Tilting her chin a notch higher. 'Though God knows why! You're a graceless, ungallant fiend at times.'

Surprise widened his eyes and thinned his lips. Meeting that haughty glare, Angel's flesh prickled. This time she had gone too far! Rupert would never forgive her. Still her incensed gaze did not falter from his anger and condemnation. The atmosphere in the wagon crackled like static before a storm, and Angel steeled herself to hear his dismissal.

Abruptly, Rupert's mood changed. He threw back his head and laughed. 'Devil take you for a hand-maiden!'

'Oh, I think he has "le Diable",' she countered with a relieved grin.

His laughter rumbled deeper. 'No one else would dare to use such disrespectful tactics, even to save my hide.'

'Disrespect was never intended. I was terrified they'd take you.' She knew her love for him shone bright in her eyes. She had always tried to shield it before; now she was too distraught to care. A tear welled on to her lashes and overspilled on to her cheek. 'I feared they'd put you on trial for your life.'

He crooked a finger to brush the tears away, the tenderness of his gaze making her heart ache. 'I'm undeserving of your loyalty. I owe you my freedom,' he admitted with dry irony.

She smiled ruefully. 'There are times when I wonder why you trouble yourself with me. You have so little patience with women.'

He leaned back on his elbow, his gaze gentle but uncompromising. 'You bring me peace. A rare commodity in the midst of war. You're a refuge who brings light to my darkest hours. And most importantly . . .' The pause was significant. 'You never ask or expect more of me than I am prepared to give.'

The warning was clear. It laid the boundaries of their

185

association. Though she had always hoped to win his love, she must content herself with the proof of his need for her. Proof which she saw in the way he looked at her when they were alone – in the softer inflection of his voice and the urgency of his touch.

He took off his battered slouch hat and absently scratched his head, his eyes narrowing. His thoughts were far away from her, dwelling upon the information he had learned today and the use to which it could be put.

A discreet cough from the front of the wagon warned them they approached the city gate. Rupert jammed his hat on his head and buckled on his sword belt which had been hidden in the wagon, but they passed unmolested by the sentries.

When he relaxed, Angel asked, 'Did you learn anything of importance?'

He nodded with satisfaction. 'Much of the Roundheads' strength, and the fact that Colonel Cromwell has introduced a stricter form of drill and discipline amongst his troops. It will be interesting to see how they fare against our next charge.'

They returned to the charcoal burner's hut to collect their horses, then pressed on to the village to return John Sparrow's wagon. At the inn Rupert warned Angel that her visit must be brief and he and Alexander went to collect their horses from the stables.

Angel was relieved to find her friend sitting by the fire in the taproom. Even in his sober brown attire and his grey hair cropped to just below his ears, she still thought of him as Popinjay. He looked flushed but his face had filled out in recent months and he did not seem to be suffering from another attack of the lung fever. As she walked across the taproom, she saw this was a very different Popinjay to the man she had befriended in Wales. Now he was acting the buffoon, appearing to be slow-witted and deceiving everyone. He was playing tricks on his audience, using a sleight of hand to make it look as though he had drawn a penny out of a farmer's ear. His companions roared with laughter at the farmer's gasp of disbelief. John looked up and, seeing Angel, said something to the men which made them laugh and turn to look at her with amusement. As he came to meet her, she kept her eyes downcast and shuffled awkwardly,

186

pretending to be a simple servant. Nathan's presence just behind her prevented any man accosting her. He followed as Popinjay led Angel to a bench in a deserted corner of the taproom.

'I was worried when I heard you were ill,' she said. 'The life you lead is hard, and your lungs have weakened.'

'I'm much better.' He regarded her affectionately.

'I'm a physician,' Nathan said. 'If there's anything I can do?'

Popinjay shook his head. 'Another day's rest and I'll be able to travel.'

Nathan touched Popinjay's forehead and, apparently satisfied he had no fever, ordered two beers and sat back. His nearness protective of Angel but unintrusive upon her conversation.

'How was the market in Cambridge?' Popinjay asked.

'Informative, but hair-raising. Though, as you see, we're all safe.'

'You risk your life,' he said with fatherly concern.

'For my King and to avenge the deaths of Gabriellen and Mark.' She looked at his sober attire. 'I did so like your patchwork doublet and cloak. Now you look like the sparrow of your name.'

His grey eyes crinkled at the corners. 'Dull and inconspicuous. A buffoon . . .' He deliberately knocked over his tankard as he spoke, and there was a titter from the men he had been entertaining earlier.

'Not dull,' Angel amended, realising that she had missed his company. The events in Wales had forged an affectionate bond between them which could never be broken.

A movement by the door caught her attention and Alexander beckoned to her. She stood up. 'Take care, John Sparrow. To me you will always be Popinjay.'

He tapped his long hooked nose with a bony finger. 'Popinjay will return – when the King again sits in Whitehall. God speed, Angel.' He put both his hands over hers.

Parting from Popinjay saddened Angel. She could not help fearing for his safety. If he was caught as a Royalist spy he would be hanged, but then, whose life was safe in war-blighted England?

Two hours later they were almost out of Parliament-held

territory and beginning to relax. A beech tree had blown down, blocking the road, and Rupert hauled his mount around to jump over the hedgerow. The others followed suit, and found themselves facing a startled patrol of six Roundhead scouts lounging on the grass, their horses tethered nearby.

Unsheathing his sword, Rupert raised it high. 'At them, men!'

Angel cursed that her woman's dress had prevented her from wearing a sword. She drew the dagger from her thigh as Nathan and Alexander positioned themselves on either side of her. They bore down on the soldiers. The Roundheads hastily donned their steel helmets and ran to mount their horses. Alexander struck one on the shoulder with a blow from his sword and as the man sagged to his knees, Alexander swept down from his saddle and yanked the soldier's sword free from his baldric. Swinging upright, Alexander handed the sword to Angel. She thrust the dagger back into its sheath and at the same moment saw a sword arcing down towards her. Instinctively, she parried the blade, but the impact sent a pain shooting the length of her arm. As her opponent's horse carried him past her, she swung round and smashed the basketweave hilt against the side of his unfastened helmet, knocking it from his head. Her opponent was fast. He turned his horse and there was bloodlust on his contorted, ginger-bearded face as he attacked. Angel had never fought on horseback before. Her agile fencing skills were useless and she was disadvantaged by the man's superior strength. All she could do was fight on grimly, using her knees to guide Talisien.

The Roundhead bared his teeth, and spittle sprayed from his mouth. His blood-shot eyes were murderous, and he attacked with a stroke which would have decapitated her had she not thrown herself low over Talisien's neck. Recovering quickly, Angel turned her mount, attacking with speed. Her blade was blocked inches from his throat, parried with a force that sent a bolt of fire through her body. Her teeth clenched against pain as she countered the mesmerising flashing of his blade.

Around her she could hear the clash of steel and she absently noted two wounded Roundheads on the ground.

Concentrating on surviving the next vicious lunge of her opponent's sword, her own blade twisted and turned as she attempted to get beneath his guard. With each jarring parry, numbness spread in her sword arm. She was breathing heavily, cold sweat drenched her spine, and each stroke sapped the strength from her body. Again their swords locked at the hilts, and Angel was forced back in the saddle, every blood vessel and muscle straining against being pushed to the ground. Dimly, she heard Alexander cry out her name.

A red haze of exhaustion had formed before her eyes, and she laboured to drag breath into her tortured lungs. Her strength was almost gone. With a last, superhuman effort, she heaved with all her might against the sword locked with hers. The weapons disengaged. Then searing pain shot through her shoulder from a lunge she had not seen. She countered instinctively, fear that she was about to die giving her the strength for one last blow. Through a mist of pain she stabbed at her opponent in an unconventional attack. There was a scrape of steel upon bone as it glanced off his hip. She pushed her weight against him and felt the resistance against the blade give, then heard a soft sucking noise as its point was embedded in his gut.

Screaming in agony, the Roundhead fell back, clutching his stomach as he toppled to the ground. Slumped over her saddle, Angel focused slowly on the fallen soldier, and bile rushed to her throat as she saw blood bubbling through the fingers of his gauntlets. She swallowed it down and, close to swooning from the pain in her shoulder, pushed herself upright in the saddle. All the Roundheads lay wounded. Rupert stood over one, his sword at the man's throat as he questioned him about troop movements and numbers.

Angel struggled to remain conscious, but her vision blurred. The trees and skyline began to revolve around her, and she slumped forward into enshrouding blackness.

She returned to consciousness to find Nathan bending over her, and Alexander squatted at his side. The lacings of her bodice had been loosened and Nathan had drawn it down so that it just covered her breasts and he could inspect her wound. His hands were smeared with her blood.

'You were lucky,' he said. 'The sword did not pass right through. The shoulder blade is undamaged, but you've lost

189

a great deal of blood.' He took a bandage from his saddle-roll and placing a wad of cotton over the wound bound it tightly, adding as he did so, 'The bleeding has ensured that the wound is clean. The wound is a thumb's length long. It will have to be sewn together as soon as we reach the hospital.'

Alexander eased her bodice back over her shoulders and laced it. 'Can you ride on your own?' he asked. 'Or would you rather ride with me?'

'I can ride.'

He lifted her into the saddle and, though his expression was strained, he managed a smile. 'You fought bravely. The Roundhead was no mean swordsman.'

'I had a good teacher.'

Rupert replaced Alexander at her side and his dark eyes were sombre as they lingered upon her bloodstained bodice. 'You fought well. But it would displease me to have your life so imperilled again.'

It was the closest he had ever come to expressing his feelings for her, and she could not stop a fiery blush heating her cheeks. She smiled into her Prince's eyes and spoke very softly. 'Does that mean I am forgiven for attacking Your Highness' breeches?'

He did not deign to answer but self-mockery gleamed in his eyes, setting her heart racing with pleasure.

May Day in London was a bitter disappointment to Maressa. She had arrived from Arundel the previous week to take up residence in Mortimer House, in the Strand. To once again live in the magnificent house with its gardens running down to the river delighted her. Not so the changed atmosphere of London. With the maypoles cut down by decree of Parliament, as instruments encouraging licentiousness and depravity, the capital was no longer joyful and carefree. Merrie England of old had been crushed beneath the wrath and censure of fanatics.

Maressa considered herself a devout Protestant and God-fearing Christian, but each week it seemed a new religious sect such as Anabaptists and Congregationalists emerged alongside the Puritans. These frowned upon laughter or any form of pleasure. Twice she had been reviled in the streets for wearing gowns of sapphire brocade and emerald silk. She, a respectable, titled woman, married to a prominent Member of Parliament, had been called a harlot for dressing in the devil's clothes.

What appalled her most was that yesterday she had seen a woman of the Rantist sect parading naked through Cheapside, and screaming a mixture of preaching and obscenities. That foul-mouthed creature had been taken seriously, and such fanatics fuelled the rebellion against the King! Last Sunday Henry had taken her to hear the sermon preached from St Paul's Cross. Until recently, the fanatics' cry had been to abolish bishops and other popish figureheads within the church; now many preached to bring an end to the monarchy as well.

Whenever Maressa ventured into the streets now she wore sober grey. She still refused to wear black, declaring it made her delicate pink and white complexion look sallow and her shining golden hair as dull as tarnished gilt. Within the privacy of her home she continued to wear the bright colours she adored.

The city streets were noticeably less populated than before the King's break with Parliament. All loyal citizens in Parliament-held London were expected to work on the ring of twenty-six forts which were being built around the city, and which spread from Lambeth to Whitehall. Many ladies of quality worked amongst the common people to safeguard the capital from attack by its King. Maressa would not. Her refusal angered Henry, who saw it as a slight upon his reputation. When he insisted she had stood her ground, declaring that she had no intention of straining her back or breaking her nails to work against her sovereign. When her absence was noted and reported upon, she had been ostracised by several eminent citizens' wives.

Often, after an afternoon spent visiting the shops at the Royal Exchange, she returned home to discover Henry absent. Nightly she dined alone and then, bored with her own company, retired early. She had thought that life in London would be exciting, and that her presence would curb Henry's whoring and gambling. Instead, his bad habits had increased. In public, he dressed soberly in black and paraded his self-righteousness in Parliament. Yet every night he attended private parties, returning home in the early morning, drunk and reeking of a whore's sickly perfume. From the number of creditors who presented themselves at their door, it was obvious that he was also gambling and losing heavily.

A door banged shut downstairs and she heard Henry shouting for his valet. He sounded only slightly drunk and in high spirits. Maressa got into bed, deciding to feign sleep if he should come to her room. Not that sleep would stop him if he was capable of mounting her, but increasingly of late there had been no need for Hazel to drug his wine. Henry's appetites were taking their toll, and he was often incapable of making love unless perversely titillated. Maressa had learned that her power was greater over her husband if she complied. She shut her mind to the humiliation of those experiences, refusing to acknowledge that the only sexual pleasure she gained was by her own hand – a practice which Henry delighted in watching.

There was a soft tap on her bedroom door and Hazel slid quietly into the room. 'Sir Henry intends to come to you tonight, my lady. I just heard him talking to his valet, Peter. Sir Henry is in an excitable mood. Shall I fetch the physic to be put in his wine?'

Maressa sighed. In recent weeks Henry had been complaining about her dressmaker's bills and threatened to send her back to Arundel if she did not curb them. This afternoon she had visited a shoemaker's and ordered five pairs of shoes, two with diamond studs; and on passing a milliner's shop she had been unable to resist a jewelled, feathered hat. The bills would arrive at the end of the week, and Henry would be furious. She chewed her lip. A night with her husband was a small price to pay for the hat and the shoes.

'No, Hazel. I suppose I had better receive him.'

'My lady, thee canna risk that!' Hazel forgot her speech training and lapsed back into her Sussex brogue in her agitation. 'Peter says His Lordship has a dose of the clap.'

Maressa's knuckles showed whitely as she gripped the lace-edged sheets to control her shudder of disgust. 'Sir Henry will not be visiting my chamber tonight, nor any other night whilst he's riddled with the pox. As if I'm not humiliated enough without that depraved beast infecting me!'

She locked the door behind Hazel and had just lain down in bed when she heard Henry's step outside her door.

When he found it locked he bellowed, 'Open this door! Or I'll take a damned axe to it.'

'I'll do nothing of the kind,' Maressa shouted back. 'You're not fit to be a husband. You're diseased.'

'Diseased, am I? It's you who are diseased. In the mind. You've never been a natural wife to me. What man doesn't get a dose of the clap from time to time. At least my inclinations are natural.' His snort of laughter chilled her. 'You're no better than a highly paid whore – very highly paid. Time you danced to the piper's tune. Now open this door.'

'When you're cured you may return to my bed. Not before.'

He hiccoughed and his next words were inaudible. Maressa sat, clutching the sheet to her chin. When she heard his footsteps retreating she relaxed, but her unease remained. Henry was becoming more violent in his habits. If she played his sordid games she could dominate him in his perversion, but several times he had actually struck her in anger.

Maressa tried to compose herself for sleep, but footsteps outside in the corridor made her sit up with a start. She held her breath, praying that he would pass by her door. A loud thud shook the door and in the candlelight she saw a crack appear in the wood. The second thud split the door and the edge of an axe was embedded in it. The third stroke splintered the panel and Henry thrust his arm through and unlocked the door. His face glistened with sweat, and breathing heavily he lumbered towards the bed, still carrying the axe. Convinced that he meant to murder her, Maressa screamed. He tossed the axe aside and, gripping the front of her robe, pushed her down on to the bed.

'Don't ever bar your door to me again.' He slapped her twice across both cheeks, then stood back to glower down at her. 'You sicken me. For all your sister fought me tooth and claw, she was a true woman, capable of passion. But you're my wife and I'm stuck with the bargain.'

He reached out, his fingers cruel as they pinched hard on her nipple. The pain made her gasp, tears forming in her eyes. His gaze moved over her cringing figure, then his fingers hooked over the neckline of her nightrobe and with a brutal jerk, he ripped the garment to her waist.

'So beautiful, so perfect in form, yet so cold and disappointing between the sheets,' he sneered. 'You'd better think about mending your ways, Wife. Be grateful for your good looks, or I'd cast you out on to the streets.' He opened the jewellery casket by her bed and, picking up a handful of precious gems, shook them in her face. 'It's time you did something to earn the pampered lifestyle I provide for you. You're quick enough to spend my money. Now the time has come to pay your debts.'

'And just how do you intend to make me do that?' She forced the words out from a throat dry with fear.

'Men are susceptible to beautiful women. I won't play the jealous husband when I expect you to use those charms upon an influential guest.'

'I've never failed you in the role of hostess,' she responded haughtily. 'But I will not whore for you, Henry.'

'Will you not, dear Maressa? Everyone has their price.'

Kneeling on the bed, he grabbed her wrists and forced her hands over her head. 'You've been shopping today. That means more bills for me to settle. What do I get in return?'

'But you have the pox, Henry,' she said frantically. 'I was wrong to lock my door against you, but what use would I be to your sordid schemes if I am infected too?'

He was breathing heavily and his eyes glittered like the points of twin daggers. A shudder passed through his body and then to her relief he eased back. He stood up and bowed to her, but his malevolent smile froze her to the core of her soul.

In July, an air of expectancy filled Oxford. After months abroad, Queen Henrietta had landed in Bridlington with a consignment of arms. She was now on her way south to join the King. Rupert was ordered to meet her with an escort, and he took Alexander and Llewelyn with him. Nathan remained in Oxford because there had been an outbreak of measles, and a score of soldiers had been admitted to the hospital with the childhood disease. They were kept in an isolation ward to prevent it spreading. Both Angel and Nathan had had the disease as children, and Nathan was certain that this had left them with a resistance to it, and that it was safe for them to treat the afflicted. Angel's wound had healed, though her shoulder was still stiff. Nevertheless, she visited the hospital each day.

During the hot summer days it was good to take an hour's break from the hospital and walk along the river, or sketch in the shade of a willow tree. Whenever she was able she rode Talisien out of the city. Angel was restless, with Rupert away. Because of her injury the Prince had refused to allow her to ride with him again. She knew her work at the hospital was important, but it was not enough. Even her playwriting could not replace the excitement she craved.

Today Nathan accompanied Angel and they sauntered towards the Magadalen Bridge as two covered wagons were rattling across it. Angel cried out in surprise, 'Robin Flowerdew!' She waved to the elderly actor sitting on the front of the wagon. 'Robin was with Esmond Angel's players,' she explained to Nathan. 'He knew my grandmother, Gabriellen.'

Nathan smiled. 'I saw Flowerdew perform some years ago in Windsor, where my father had his apothecary's shop.'

Angel could not suppress her excitement. 'This could be my chance to act at last, and maybe have my plays performed.'

Once formed, the idea burned like molten metal in her mind, and she ran to greet Robin Flowerdew. He was staring at her in puzzlement, though clearly intrigued and delighted that he had been recognised.

'Mr Flowerdew,' Angel said, breathless after her run. 'I doubt if you remember me. I'm Angel Rowan – Gabriellen Angel was my grandmother.'

'I have great respect for Gabriellen's work. I was distraught at learning of her death.' His clear blue eyes were sorrowful. He was a short man and though seventy still had a shock of grey hair.

'Could we talk, Mr Flowerdew? Gabriellen said you were interested in having her plays translated into French. I have them here with me.'

The actor's eyes lit up with interest. He climbed down out of the wagon and gestured for his companions to drive on.

'I saw you in Ben Jonson's *Volpone* at Windsor,' Nathan said warmly. 'You were superb, Mr Flowerdew.'

Robin laughed and preened his moustache. 'That was long ago when I was in my prime.' He turned to Angel. 'These plays you speak of – *The Widow Went a-Wooing* and *The*

Imprudent Rascal – would be a great success here in Oxford –' he broke off and frowned. 'But there's little time to rehearse. Not for myself, for I remember the plays well, but for my company.'

'There would be a condition upon my allowing you to perform the plays.'

Robin Flowerdew stiffened. 'A condition? I, Robin Flowerdew, most famous of players, do not bow to conditions. Rather I honour any playwright whose work I deign to perform.'

'A pity you won't consider my proposal.' Angel turned to leave. 'I thought you wished to take Gabriellen's plays to France.'

'Perhaps I was over-hasty.' Robin Flowerdew's eyes were wary. 'What is your condition?' He was staring at her with a frown. 'Angel Rowan,' he said softly. 'Now I remember. But you're Gabriellen's granddaughter! What are you doing dressed as a man?'

'I'm known in Oxford as Master Dusty Rowan. This guise is to protect my reputation. I want to act in one of the plays. Of course, I'd maintain my disguise as a man. I'd not scandalise the Court.'

Robin blew out his cheeks, his face becoming so red she feared he would suffer an apoplexy. 'I do not perform with women.'

'Then you will not perform Gabriellen's plays.'

Robin glowered at her. 'What you ask is preposterous!'

'No one will know that I'm a woman.' Somehow she had to convince him. 'I've been in Oxford for six months and my secret hasn't been discovered yet. Gabriellen said I was a natural actress. Is my request so outrageous? Women are now appearing on the French stage. If you go there, you must have women in your troupe.'

'You drive a hard bargain,' Robin muttered, considering the matter. '*The Widow Went a-Wooing* is the ideal play to perform before the King and Queen. But this is not France. If I agree, your true identity must be our secret.'

Joy radiated from Angel's face. 'Yes! If I were not dressed as a man, I would kiss you for your generosity, Mr Flowerdew.'

'You're as wild and impetuous as your grandmother.' The

rebuke sounded like a reluctant compliment. 'Rehearsals will start tomorrow. We have less than a week before we perform at the Queen's welcoming banquet. But first you must prove that you are accomplished enough for the part.'

Robin paused and smiled. 'I could tell you some tales about Esmond Angel. Though most of them are not fitting for such tender ears. Aye, Esmond would be proud to know that his great-granddaughter has the same love for the play as he did.'

Chapter Eight

Robin Flowerdew sent word to Angel that they were rehearsing in the stableyard used by Rupert's Life Guards, who were still out of the city, and for her to attend at nine the next morning.

She was there ten minutes early. She had been up since dawn to ensure that she was word-perfect in her lines. The stables were empty, and would remain so until Rupert and his men returned. On entering the yard, Angel looked round for Robin and found her way barred by a stout, short man of middle years. He was dressed in orange satin, his short cloak of kingfisher-blue velvet thrown back over one shoulder to display its cloth of silver lining. The man's buttercup-yellow hair was elaborately curled and there was carmine on his fleshy cheeks and lips.

'Is this Master Rowan come to grace our honourable troupe?' he cooed in a high-pitched voice. He walked around Angel with short mincing steps. Limpid honey-coloured eyes took in every detail of her appearance. The player rubbed his clean-shaven chin, then turned to the other players gathered behind him and waved a dismissive hand in Angel's direction.

'Why, Master Rowan's cheeks are smooth as down and he looks scarcely out of long skirts. Is it to this stripling that the great Orlando Fortemaine must be relegated to a role fit only for an apprentice?'

He pirouetted on his high-heels and flounced away. One hand rested on his hip, while the other held a lace handkerchief which reeked of a sickly rose perfume. His voice lifted another octave. 'I'll not be put aside by this upstart! What do we need with Esmond Angel's plays? Is our repertoire not sufficient?' he sneered as he joined a group of players on the far side of the yard. 'If Master Rowan is so fine an actor, why does he need to barter Esmond Angel's plays to get a part?'

There were several murmurs of agreement and Angel sensed the troupe's hostility. In response, she bowed to the players. 'My ability will speak for itself. As will the worthiness of the play.' Her hand went to her sword. 'Does anyone dispute my right to be here?'

At that moment, Robin Flowerdew entered the stableyard, his voice strident. 'Master Rowan is here on his merits as an actor, which I have witnessed for myself. You were each given your copied parts last evening. So let us begin.'

Angel handed Robin the playbook of *The Widow Went a-Wooing*. Robin read the prologue and Angel, in the role of a lecherous earl bent upon seducing the widow, began the opening lines. From the moment Orlando Fortemaine, who had been relegated to the part of the widow, came into the scene he deliberately disrupted the play.

First, he cut Angel's cue. He proceeded to fling himself from one side of the stage area to another, giving a performance which bordered upon dementia. Several times Angel found herself addressing a vacant space, where Fortemaine should have been standing. Whenever he tried to make her appear foolish, Angel improvised, her quick wits making sure that she took command of the scene. Twice Fortemaine made a premature exit to confuse her, and Angel responded with extemporised soliloquies which ridiculed the player. Fortemaine returned, his colour dangerously high. The other players sniggered at his futile attempts to oust her, and cheered when Angel delivered another verbal *coup de grâce*. Finally, Fortemaine burst into a tantrum of incoherent rage. Angel turned her back on the players and regarded Robin, who had been watching the proceedings wearily. She was puzzled that he had not interrupted the shambles the play had fast degenerated into.

Robin took out a dagger and cleaned the nails on one hand before addressing his players. 'Now that the preliminary antics are done with, may we perform the play as Esmond Angel intended?'

Angel realised that Robin had been testing her.

A brown-haired player stepped forward. From the way the

other actors parted for his passage, it was obvious he was a man of importance within the troupe.

'Some of the new lines are most witty and pertinent to the politics of today, rather than when Queen Bess ruled.' The actor had a French accent. He was of medium height and in his late twenties, several years younger than Fortemaine. His complexion was sallow but a flamboyant upturned moustache and a small beard gave him a distinguished appearance. He bowed to Angel. 'I am Etienne de Luc. Your skill, Mr Rowan, is exceptional, but I feel . . .' He sighed and spread his hands wide. 'I feel that, superbly as you play this part, with your smooth cheeks you'd be better suited for the part of the widow.'

There was a shout of agreement from Fortemaine. De Luc rounded on him and lifted a hand in a dramatic gesture for silence. 'As I say, Mr Rowan would make an admirable widow. With such wit, the part should be extended.'

Angel was flattered at his suggestion, and immediately began to imagine new scenes to extend the widow's role. Suddenly she burned to play the part of the widow, but she was also aware that it could destroy her disguise as a man. That would cause a scandal throughout Oxford which she would rather avoid. Uncertainly, she looked at Robin for advice.

He said, 'I admit Rowan has all the qualities needed for the part of the widow. Yet it takes great skill for one sex to adequately portray another.' A glint of mirth flashed in Robin's eyes as he added, 'Perhaps Dusty has no wish to appear before the Court in the guise of a woman.'

It was a challenge Angel could not resist. To accept meant her skills would be stretched. She must play the part as a man acting the role of a woman and ensure her costume did not betray her real female form. 'I will not fail you, Mr Flowerdew, nor you, Monsieur de Luc.'

'Pray call me Etienne, *mon ami*.' His hazel eyes were heavy-lidded with appraisal.

Angel realised it was not because of her acting skill that he suggested she play the widow. There were several amorous scenes in the play and his part was that of the widow's lover. Clearly de Luc desired her, or rather, desired the young man he believed her to be. This was an unforseen complication.

She turned to Robin for help, but found him studiously reading the script. Without looking up, he said, 'Can you produce the extra lines by tomorrow, Rowan? Other changes will also be needed. Fortemaine will play the devil and I shall take the part of the earl.'

'Yes,' she said curtly, angry that Robin knew of de Luc's preferences, and was making it difficult for her. Crossing to him, she hissed in his ear, 'Sir, that was a scurvy trick!'

There was no malice in his answering gaze. 'I'd do nothing to endanger the reputation of my players,' he answered drawing her out of hearing of the others. 'Do you not relish being the first woman to perform before royalty on the English stage? After the performance you could reveal your identity. If you ever decide to pursue your career in France, think of the acclaim that will precede you. You will be famous.'

'I think infamous might be more accurate,' she said wrily. If it was known that Dusty Rowan was a woman, her reputation would be lost. And the association she had with Rupert was so special, she did not want it spoilt by notoriety. 'Deception and suspension of belief is a player's greatest craft. I prefer to keep my disguise as a man.'

Robin regarded her with greater respect. 'Gabriellen never sought notoriety. All she wanted was recognition for her talent. I hope you achieve that. If you've one half of your grandmother's ability you deserve acclaim, and I've a feeling you will be Gabriellen's equal.' He clapped his hands for the rehearsal to continue.

Dressed in her man's attire, Angel found it easy to maintain the ruse. The play was one of her favourites, a tragicomedy. The widow is forced by her aged husband on his deathbed to make a scared vow of chastity, or be struck from his will. Terrified of being penniless, she agrees. After his death and wealthy beyond her dreams, she soon resents the unnatural life she must now lead. Her beauty attracts several suitors. Tempted by the devil who appears to her in dreams, the widow surrenders her inheritance to marry a lecherous earl. Then she falls in love with his illegitimate son, played by de Luc. They become lovers. Tragedy ensues. The earl discovers their affair and blinds the son. In remorse, he then suffers a seizure and dies. The widow is cast from her home by the earl's legitimate heir. Soon the widow and her blind lover are reduced to vagabonds. The devil comes to them again with a scheme to murder the earl's heir. The widow repents of her past life, and they scorn the devil. When they are on the point of starvation, a lawyer tracks down the widow and claims that her first husband's will was invalid. With no other kin to make a claim against the estate she is again a wealthy woman. She marries her blinded lover.

It was an exacting role, the expertise of the comedy lifting the darker side of the plot. It showed many sides of the heroine's character: subservience, avarice, temptation, wit, lust, and eventually remorse and salvation. Angel revelled in the chance to prove her talent. Twice during the rehearsal she played the part in too manly a fashion so that Robin could admonish her.

During the following days of rehearsal, when the actors each had to adapt their parts to fit Angel's extended lines, she discovered that Fortemaine's resentment went far deeper than she had thought. From his spiteful glares, she suspected that he was de Luc's lover. Unfortunately, the more Angel discouraged de Luc, the greater his interest in her became. She was careful to ensure that she was never alone with him.

When Queen Henrietta rode into Oxford escorted by Rupert's troop, the players lost their rehearsal yard. While Robin scoured the city for somewhere else, Angel went into the street to watch the procession. It had been three weeks since she had last seen Rupert and she was eager for sight of her lover. In the press of the crowd Rupert did not notice her. He was at the Queen's side and from the blackness of his expression was barely holding his temper in check. When Rupert visited England some years ago he had been a great favourite with Henrietta. Since his return, their affection for one another had cooled. Each resented the other's influence over the King. Their policies for winning the war were too different for Rupert to accept what he considered to be his aunt's interference.

Disappointed that Rupert had not noticed her, Angel returned to her room. The play was to be presented tomorrow evening before the Court and she still had some work to do on her costumes. The troupe employed no seamstress and each of the gowns had to be altered to fit her. She wore a specially padded undershift over her bound breasts. As she was sewing the last seam, one of the actor apprentices arrived with a message. A full dress rehearsal was to take place in the refectory of one of the colleges in an hour. There were two costume changes. A single room had been put aside for the actors, and Robin apologised that Angel would have no privacy. She decided that she would arrive in her first costume, her figure already hidden by the specially padded shift and her petticoats. As a further precaution, all her bodices were front-fastening, so that she could change costumes without assistance.

Her arrival in costume prompted a sarcastic comment from Fortemaine.

'I'd only just finished the alterations,' she countered and saw Robin wink at her.

Apart from the usual last-minute setbacks, the rehearsal went smoothly enough. De Luc as the young lover twice improvised, manipulating her into an embrace and forcing his tongue into her mouth in a passionate kiss. Nor had de Luc stopped at kisses. At each rehearsal his attentions became more blatant, his hands constantly straying to her buttocks. Only her nimbleness prevented him from thrusting a questing hand between her thighs.

When the rehearsal was over she saw de Luc lingering in the corner where her clothes and costumes hung. The costume she was wearing was extravagantly ragged, depicting the widow and her blind lover in their poverty. It was impossible to avoid changing. If she walked through the streets in the costume she would be arrested as a vagabond. She waited by the stage, hoping that de Luc would leave, and to avoid making herself conspicuous, she spoke to Robin about the performance.

'Is de Luc becoming a problem?' Robin queried.

Angel shrugged. 'Nothing I cannot deal with.'

'I hope so. He'll not act with a woman. He's always made that clear. If he leaves the troupe, so will Fortemaine, and I'll have to abandon my plans to work in France.' Robin looked over to Angel's dressing-corner and his expression relaxed. 'He's gone.'

When Robin left, Angel pulled off her bodice and skirt. She was in her shirt about to step into her breeches, when there was a laugh from behind her. De Luc had returned so stealthily she had not heard him approach.

'Alone, *mon ami*?'

There was a thickness to his voice which alarmed Angel. She backed away and hastily pulled on her breeches.

'Ah, you blush,' de Luc taunted as he moved closer. 'You do not mix much with the players. And always you have our patron or Colonel Carver so close. What is it you fear?'

'What should I fear?' she said, pushing her arm into her doublet and inwardly cursing her fumbling fingers as she tied the fastenings.

De Luc chuckled. 'How old are you, *mon ami*? Fifteen? Sixteen? Too young yet for a beard to grow. Perhaps too young to have bedded a woman? Or is it that you do not care for them?'

'I like women very much,' Angel parried. She picked up her dagger and felt less vulnerable.

'You cannot trust women,' de Luc pursued. 'They will toy with a handsome youth. This concerns me. I'd not like to see you hurt. You're a good lad.' He edged closer and, putting one hand against the oak panelling, trapped her in the corner. His smile was coercing as he brought his face inches to within her own. 'You've a natural acting talent, *mon ami*. With expert coaching you could rival any of the great leading players.' His hand slid down the wall on to her shoulder. 'Friendship is important within a troupe. Do you think of me as a friend, Dusty?'

She placed her hands between them as he leaned closer. The dagger was poised just below his chin as she answered, 'Respect and admiration is also important.' She smiled apologetically, and turned the blade so that the light reflected along its length. 'If you would stand back I could put this away. I would not like there to be an accident, *Monsieur*.'

Annoyance darkened his eyes. 'Etienne,' he insisted.

'Etienne.' She eyed him levelly. She dared not offend him, for her position in Oxford was too vulnerable. Instead, she hoped to play upon his worldliness and avoid his attentions without wounding his pride. 'I do not know you well enough to think of you as a friend.'

He twirled the ends of his moustache. 'That's soon remedied.'

The words carried an ominous challenge. Too uneasy to

sheathe her dagger, she kept it in her hand and made to pick up her skirt which had fallen on the floor. As she bent over, de Luc's hand touched the curve of her hip and moved down towards her inner thigh. Her body jerked upright, the palm clutching her dagger slippery with sweat.

'Why so coy, *mon ami?* A handsome youth should not be shy with his friends.' De Luc was unperturbed. If anything, her reaction seemed to amuse him. His smile was confident. 'I like innocence. It's so rare. I think we'll become close friends, *mon ami.*'

'De Luc! Rowan!' Robin Flowerdew called from the doorway. 'What are you still doing here?'

'I'm just leaving, Mr Flowerdew,' Angel said, throwing her costumes over her arm and striding towards the door.

'Good,' Robin replied. 'Your father is asking for you.'

As Angel hurried past de Luc, he winked at her. She had an uncomfortable feeling that de Luc was going to be a problem for her in the future.

Maressa was enjoying another visit to the Royal Exchange. Hazel walked a respectful pace behind her, carrying the parcels already purchased. The Exchange remained a popular meeting place, though with the Puritan influence so strong in the city, few of the shops now sold the beautiful lace, materials and accessories which had been abundant before the King's departure. Maressa's mind was upon her unhappiness, not on her purchases. Henry had recovered from his dose of the pox. Since the night he had taken an axe to her bedroom door he had insisted that she was more accommodating towards certain of his guests. Whilst she was happy to flirt with them, she had no intention of taking any of them as her lover, so they would cancel Henry's gambling debts. Last night after she had ignored Henry's hints to encourage the Earl of Northcliffe, her husband had flown into a violent rage, beating her until she begged for mercy. Then he had raped her and left her sobbing on the floor. Today she was forced to wear a vizard to cover the cuts and bruises on her cheek and brow. It was small revenge to know that Hazel had drugged Henry's morning ale with a strong laxative and he was too ill to leave his room.

Maressa wandered aimlessly past the stalls and shops. Her

body ached from the beating, but she had no wish to return to the house. Her marriage had become a waking nightmare. There were times when she thought she could control Henry but his moods were so unpredictable that Hazel could not always judge them in time to drug his wine. Just then, a man, busy talking to two companions, barged into her and she cried out as she was knocked off-balance. Her arms were gripped and she was caught before she could fall.

'The deuce on it!' The man voiced his irritation.

'Your pardon, sir,' said Maressa. Surprise widened her eyes. 'Thomas!'

He frowned, trying to discern her features behind the mask. 'Good God! Is it Maressa? Are you all right? You look pale.'

'I was foolish enough to leave the house without having eaten this morning.'

'That's easily remedied. The Nag's Head is close by. They serve the finest Scotch collops and syllabub in London. Or are you too proud to accept your disreputable cousin's invitation?'

She was so relieved to see a friendly face that she forgot her usual antagonism towards him. 'Thomas, we are family. How can you think that?'

'That's a comment I'd expect from Angel, not you,' Thomas said, with a grin. 'How is Angel? Last I heard of the minx she was in Oxford. What a woman!'

The admiration in Thomas's voice annoyed Maressa. Her cousin had always shown his preference for Angel, and after the way Henry had treated her last night, Maressa needed warmth and affection from someone. And Thomas was family. Why should she not accept his invitation? Hazel was here as chaperon. It would be amusing to flatter Thomas and supplant Angel in his regard.

'I really should return home,' she sighed regretfully.

'That would not be very cousinly,' Thomas replied. 'Besides I just prevented a cut-purse stealing your purse.' Holding up her purse he pushed it into her hand. His eyes sparkled with mischief and within their grey depths Maressa saw the warmth and admiration she craved.

She put her purse back into the hidden pocket within her cloak, suspecting that Thomas had cut the gold chain which tied it around her waist. 'It's been months since I've seen any of my family. I'll be happy to dine with you.'

As they entered the Nag's Head, she asked, 'But what are you doing in London? I thought . . .'

He silenced her with a glare. 'Take care of what you speak. There are spies everywhere,' he whispered. 'The King has need of loyal subjects in London. I can raise two hundred men when His Majesty would secure his capital.'

Thomas wore a long black cloak, beneath which was a doublet and breeches of gold-braided emerald velvet. There was as much lace at his throat and wrists as worn by any Cavalier. It was satisfying to be in the company of a man who did not fear to dress as he pleased.

Thomas insisted on a private parlour and Hazel sat on a stool on the far side of the room. Throughout the meal he was charming and lavish with his compliments. Maressa flirted with him, enjoying his admiration. At last she gathered her gloves together and stood up.

'I fear I've kept you from your business too long.'

Thomas took her hand and raised it to his lips. 'Nonsense, dear coz. A most enjoyable meal. This is the first time we've really spoken to each other. I always had the impression that you never approved of me.'

'I always thought you favoured Angel, not myself.'

'Given the opportunity I would disabuse you of that opinion.' He smiled.

It was impossible not to respond to the charm of that smile. This was the light-hearted flirtation Maressa enjoyed, and she pouted in regret as she answered, 'I doubt my husband would approve.'

A look of hatred crossed Thomas's features. 'You made a poor choice for a husband, Lady Mortimer.'

Taken aback, her gaze dropped from his. Had he guessed how she suffered at Henry's hands? A tear formed on her lashes, but pride made her blink it away. Thomas tilted her chin and looked into her eyes. What she saw in his gaze sent a shiver through her. His grey eyes which could glitter with the hardness of steel, and be so merciless towards a victim, were now smoky with affection. Those handsome roguish features represented everything that was disreputable and scandalous. Hadn't Angel often described him as having the

208

looks and ruthlessness of a rampaging Viking?

He frowned at the mask she had refused to remove. With a speed which took her unawares, he whisked it from her face. Her cry of alarm froze at the anger on his face as he saw her bruises.

'Did Mortimer do that?' he rapped out. 'He'll answer to my sword should our paths ever cross.'

'No, Thomas.' Her hand covered his in entreaty. 'Henry was drunk and I provoked him in a quarrel.'

She was too proud to let Thomas know how miserable her marriage was. Again he tipped her face up to meet his gaze. 'If ever you're in trouble I can always be reached at Nell Lovegood's.' He shrugged apologetically. 'Not a very suitable establishment, but I'd not fail you, sweet coz. I'd like to see you again.'

She was moved by his sincerity. 'I think not. Henry would not approve.'

'I shall dine here at the same time next week. Join me, dearest coz.'

There was nothing cousinly in his bold appraisal and Maressa put a hand over her heart, willing it to still its erratic beating. 'Perhaps,' she answered softly, startling herself by her compliance.

Of course, she had no intention of pursuing her kinship with a rogue and bordello owner, however charming and fascinating Thomas Angel might be.

From the moment Angel walked on-stage in Oxford she experienced an exultation which changed her life. When Robin delivered the prologue there had been little lull in the noise from the courtiers. Gallants flirted with the Queen's ladies-in-waiting. The war seemed far away, banished by light-hearted chatter which all but drowned out the opening words of the play.

Angel was determined to capture her audience's attention, and played with a verve which soon began to steal everyone's attention. In the first scene, when her dying husband condemned her to a life of chastity, she portrayed the part with such poignancy that all conversation was stilled. When a nobleman made a remark which was met by sniggering, Angel responded. Holding out a hand in appeal, she stood at the front of the stage, and improvised.

'Am I not condemned to a living hell? Must my body forever be denied the comfort of a loving embrace? This heart . . .' She clutched both hands to her breast . . . 'will never quicken from the pleasure of a lover's kiss. My lips will turn to frigid stone. Was ever a woman so tormented? Or so cruelly abused? To be denied love is to be denied the breath of life.' As she staggered back to the death-bed, she heard a woman in the audience utter, 'It is too cruel.' Several others murmured assent. And when a man raised his voice to flippant response, he was silenced by a chorus of angry hisses.

The play progressed and all present were now hanging upon every word. The atmosphere in the hall was palpable. This was the life Angel wanted, a life denied her in England. If she wanted a future as a player, she must travel to France. It was part of her destiny, too strong to be denied.

After a costume change she stood to one side of the stage backdrop, awaiting her next cue, and looked out at the courtiers. The King and Queen were enthroned at the centre of the front row of seats. But Angel's gaze was drawn to Prince Rupert who sat behind the King. She had not seen him since his return. Now her heart leapt with joy. He lounged back in his chair one arm linked over the high back. Twice she saw him speak to one of the Queen's ladies seated beside him. There was a look of such rapt attention on his face that jealousy twisted her heart. The woman was beautiful, everything about her softly feminine.

Angel clenched her fists and expelled a jagged breath. She looked down at her gown. It was an unflattering garment, padded and sewn to conceal her womanly form. Rupert had never seen her in Oxford wearing a dress. It was obvious that he was attracted to the beautiful woman in her silk gown.

She closed her eyes and swallowed against the cramping ache in her throat. A sharp dig in the ribs from Orlando Fortemaine brought her rudely to her senses. De Luc was speaking her cue. A light dimmed behind her eyes. Squaring her shoulders and holding her chin high, she swept on to the stage. To cover the pain in her heart she acted as though her life depended on it, and there was an expectant lull from the audience as the play reached its climax. Now she hid behind her role, as she had hidden behind her man's attire. Each word and movement was eloquent, poignant and fraught with passion. She was the wronged widow: the desperate, tortured soul craving love, but needing to forsake her true nature in self-denial. When she became a creature possessed by Satan's promises an awed silence descended on the audience, as they saw the widow turn seductress to charm her chosen lord. Then she became the embodiment of passion as she regarded her young lover, and finally a creature wrecked by desire's bitter vengeance. The ladies in the audience dabbed at the tears streaming down their cheeks; the men were entranced. The force of the widow's passion held everyone in thrall.

When the players took their final bow the applause was deafening. Both Robin Flowerdew and Etienne de Luc took Angel's hand and led her to the front. Then, acknowledging her success, they stepped back to allow her to stand alone. The audience were a blur to Angel. Tears of joy mingled with those of disillusion, heartache and euphoria. She bowed to the King and Queen and turned a long look upon Prince Rupert. For a moment, their gaze held. He inclined his head in tribute to her skill, but she could tell, even across the distance which separated them, that a special light had gone from his eyes. When his companion spoke his attention was all for her.

Angel knew that it was over between them. Somehow, though her heart was splintering, she kept her smile bright and her chin high until the applause died and she could leave the stage.

'*Magnifique!*' She was pulled into a smothering embrace by de Luc. 'They loved you, *mon ami*.' Orlando Fortemaine's scowls were in their own way, a tribute to her acting skills. Robin was beaming with pleasure as he approached. De Luc kept an arm across her shoulders, and to disengage the unwelcome hold, Angel moved towards Robin.

The player-manager applauded. 'Dusty Rowan, you're a true Angel – acting is in your soul. Esmond would have been proud of you.'

'If I decided to go to France, would there be a place within your company for me?'

'But can you speak French?' Robin queried.

'Fluently. I spent a summer there with my aunt and uncle.'

Robin looked thoughtful but de Luc intervened before he could speak.

'You can't refuse, Flowerdew. The boy held the audience in his hand. Never have I seen a woman's part played with such perfection.' His lascivious gaze rested upon the line of Angel's slim hips outlined by the ragged gown. 'How well Dusty suits the female lead. I insist he join our troupe. All the female parts must be his. Dusty's talent speaks for itself.'

Robin nodded. 'Dusty has talent. I trust you'll not forget that it was upon your insistence that he joins our troupe.'

A smile on his wrinkled face, Robin took Angel's arm and drew her to one side. 'The matter seems to be settled, if you wish it. But surely your life is here in England?'

'Not if I want to be a player or write plays,' Angel answered. 'Besides, I would be myself. I'm weary of parading as a man, and I want to prove there's a place for women on the stage.' She struggled to master her emotion as her throat tightened, before adding, 'There's nothing to keep me in England now.'

Over Robin's shoulder she saw Alexander and Nathan approaching.

'You outshone them all, Dusty,' Alexander grinned, but cast a puzzled eye over her padded clothing. 'What have you done to yourself? You're an uncommonly odd shape.'

'Am I not supposed to be a man dressed as a woman?' A new determination came into her voice. 'Tonight I end the folly of my disguise.' She spread her skirts and curtsied. 'Dusty Rowan is no more – Angel Rowan, at your service, gentlemen. All I need now is a partner to escort me to the dancing later.'

Nathan bowed to her. 'It would be an honour.'

'I will need an hour to rid myself of my stage make-up and to change.'

Nathan was studying her closely and she knew that she had failed to hide her pain at Rupert's defection.

He said, 'I'll come to your room in an hour.'

Angel nodded. Then, seeing Llewelyn appear, she whispered quickly, 'Please don't mention this to my father.'

'What are you up to, Dusty?' Alexander asked, frowning.

'Nothing. Just for one night I want to be myself. Everyone in Oxford knows me as Dusty Rowan – tonight I shall be Angel.'

She turned to Llewelyn as he approached.

'I'd be a poor father if I approved of you performing on the stage, but I'm also Gabriellen's son,' he said. 'She would have been proud of you. As I am proud.' He held out his hands to her.

Angel no longer cared if the other actors saw through her disguise. She hugged Llewelyn. 'Papa, I'm so glad you understand. The play is in my blood. I can't help it.'

Angel saw de Luc watching her with a frown, but she did not care. She was tired of the subterfuge. She felt only one regret. If she went to France she would miss her family. To dispel her mood she smiled at Llewelyn. 'Is it true that the King has spoken to you about designs for modernising the Palace at Whitehall?'

'His Majesty spoke of the subject,' Llewelyn said modestly. 'But first we must win this war. He liked my ideas and has asked me to submit plans once he is again residing at Whitehall.'

'That's wonderful, Papa! A royal architect. Isn't that what you've always worked for?'

He laughed. 'It's certainly an honour. What man does not want posterity by leaving a building which people will marvel at long after he is dead?'

Alexander was signalling for her to follow him and, intrigued, Angel excused herself to the others.

'There's someone I want you to meet,' Alexander said, leading her out through the courtyard and into a secluded garden.

On a seat sat a young, dark-haired woman, her fingers nervously twisting in her lap. At their approach she stood up. Her smile was strained, but her eyes were filled with adoration as they gazed at Alexander.

'May I present Beth Penrose,' Alexander said. 'Beth, this is my sister, Angel.'

The two were so obviously in love that Angel could not help smiling. 'At last we meet, Beth. I'd begun to suspect that it was more than duty which took Alex so regularly from Oxford.'

213

'Beth and I are to wed. Her year of mourning is over now.'

'Then marry before I leave England. I want to dance at your wedding, Alex.' She kissed Beth's cheek. 'I wish you happiness. Alex is a fortunate man. But look at me! You do not meet me at my best. I must look like a trollop, wearing all this stage make-up.'

'You were wonderful,' Beth said with awe. 'I was shocked when Alex said you were to perform in a play. But he explained about Gabriellen and how she worked with her father's players. I admire your courage, to stand out for what you want. Why should women not perform? You outshone everyone today. No wonder men so jealously guard their domain – they can't bear rivalry.'

'I can see we will get on well,' Angel said, chuckling.

She left them and hurried to her rooms. The excitement of the play, her father and Alexander's news had lifted her spirits. But as she climbed the stairs to her chamber, the heaviness which had seeped into her heart, returned with greater intensity. She walked the last steps to her room weighted down by unhappiness. As she opened her door, an arm scooped her round the waist and pushed her inside. The door was slammed behind her and de Luc laughed with delight. He held up a flagon of wine.

'This is to celebrate, *mon ami*. You were a success. The way you extemporised to get the attention of the groundlings was sheer genius. You're a born actor. One day you'll be as great an actor as myself.'

'You're very kind, de Luc,' Angel said stiffly, wanting only to get him out of the room.

From the glint in his eyes, he had more than praise on his mind. He waved the flagon of wine expansively. 'I've decided that I shall nurture your talent. With my guidance you will have the groundlings revering you as a god – as indeed they revere me, in my own country.' His expression changed as he noticed the anger in her face. He placed the wine on the table, his tone impatient. 'But you do not revere me, do you, Dusty? You are cruel.'

'I think you had better leave, de Luc,' she said, sidling around the table to put a safer distance between them.

He threw up his hands in dismay. 'De Luc, is it now? Was it not decided I am Etienne? Why so cold, Dusty?'

214

He surprised her by vaulting the table, and he caught her in his arms before she could escape. He held her fast. Hot lips brushed her cheek, as she twisted her head away.

'Don't be cruel. I'll be gentle.' He was breathing heavily and his hand was forcing down between them to grab between her legs.

'Get your hands off me, you lecherous ape!' Angel raged, trying to wrench his probing hand away.

As his fingers encountered her pubic bone, she felt them jerk in a spasm. He let out a cry of utter horror and leapt back, staring at his hand as though it had been bitten by a snake.

'*Mon Dieu!* You are a woman! Ugh!' A shudder went through him and he turned deathly pale.

'*C'est impossible!* What unnatural fiend are you? No woman can perform the way you did.'

'There's nothing unnatural about me, *Monsieur*. And I thank you for your praise.'

De Luc groaned and put a shaking hand to his head murmuring, '*Une femme! C'est impossible!* I'll denounce you. You'll be reviled as a harlot. The people of Oxford will stone you from the town.'

'I think not. This is 1643. Women are taking up arms and defending their houses against marauding troops. Besides, women perform in France.'

'It is why I left.' Disgust twisted his features. 'They bring dishonour to our profession.'

'Perhaps you're afraid they will rival your talent?'

He glared at her. 'Never.'

'Then what are you afraid of?'

He swept back his dark hair, his head tilted in a dramatic pose. 'De Luc is afraid of nothing.'

'Then we should work very well together. It was at your own insistence that Robin engaged me in his troupe.'

He broke into rapid French which cast a colourful but unflattering slur upon her parentage and stormed from the room. Angel closed the door behind him and laid her forehead against it. She felt drained. This would be a day she would certainly remember and it was not yet over.

An hour later she had arranged her black hair in a cascade of ringlets and donned the scarlet and black gown. For a long time she had frowned over her reflection in the looking-glass. The wound on her shoulder had left a long red scar which was visible above the low neckline. It was unsightly and must be covered. Her glance fell upon a wide black satin ribbon. Taking up her nail scissors, she studied the ribbon for a long moment before cutting into it. A few minutes later she had cut out the silhouette of a winged angel. Taking the glue which the actors used for fixing false beards and moustaches in place, she placed the silhouette over the scar and considered the effect in the looking-glass. The black satin emphasised the creaminess of her skin, while the angel hid the scar and drew the eye to the curves of her breasts. It made her feel rather wicked. At a rap on her door, she eased the neckline of her gown lower over her shoulders with a defiant tug.

Nathan's whistle of appreciation heartened her. 'It's a crime for you to dress as a man. You're a very beautiful woman. And that black Angel . . .' He placed her cloak around her shoulders and pressed a kiss on the nape of her neck. 'There won't be a hot-blooded man there tonight who'll not want to kiss the pulse that beats so irresistibly above it.'

'And all will be disappointed,' she countered.

He was dressed in doublet and breeches of midnight-blue velvet trimmed in silver braid. His freshly washed hair was shot through with golden lights and fell in waves to his shoulders. Unlike most of the Cavaliers, Nathan wore no earring and his long delicate fingers were free of rings. She had often supposed his lack of jewellery was because of his work as a physician, but for an occasion such as tonight it was considered part of court dress. From the richness of his clothing it was obvious that he could afford such jewels if he chose. Yet he needed no outward display to prove his worth.

As they left the college, he said sharply, 'Have you abandoned your disguise to please the Prince?'

'That is over.' Angel took his arm as they walked together. She tried to keep her voice light, but heard the quiver in its depths. 'Who was the noblewoman Rupert was sitting next to? He seemed very enamoured.'

'So you noticed. Nothing will come of it, Dusty, if that's what you fear. She's the Duchess of Richmond. The Duke of Richmond has long been Rupert's friend.'

Angel considered this. 'It changes nothing. I saw the look in Rupert's eyes as he spoke to her. While his heart remained unattached I knew that what we had was special to him. There were other, casual mistresses of course, but they were unimportant. I'll not share any man, even Rupert.'

'You no longer love him?' he said ingenuously.

They were approaching the ballroom now and the orchestra could be heard above the clamour of voices and laughter.

'I did not say that,' Angel replied. 'But this way there will always be good memories and no regrets. Tonight I'll tell the Prince that I'm leaving Oxford. For that is my intent. I grow weary of my masquerade. I want to be a woman again.'

'After tonight, half the garrison will declare their love for you.' There was an edge in his voice, but his expression revealed nothing of his thoughts and his blue eyes were carefully guarded.

'I'll be no camp follower,' she declared. 'Enough of this talk – Tonight I want to dance and enjoy myself. Tomorrow can take care of itself.'

Two columns of dancers greeted their entrance into the ballroom. The mood was merry and the dress of the courtiers dazzling. Jewels glittered on the necks and arms of the women and Angel was conscious that her only adornment was the black silk patch above her neckline. In a moment of doubt she covered it with her hand.

Nathan took her fingers and pulled them away from her scar. 'You look ravishing. You need no jewels to enhance your beauty, and that patch is more alluring than the cold glitter of diamonds. By tomorrow every woman here will be copying it.'

The dance ended, and when the next one began Nathan led her on to the floor. Angel saw several curious gazes fixed on her, some from women who had sought Nathan at the hospital or in his rooms. Their glances were brittle with antagonism. The men, aware of Nathan's reputation as a rake, were admiringly speculative as they watched her take her place. The dance was a stately procession, where one's partners constantly changed, and soon Angel's head was ringing with the whispered invitations from Cavaliers.

With a smile, she parried all their questions, unaware that by so doing she increased the mystery building around her.

After several dances the enthusiasm to claim her attention was overwhelming. Each time she partnered Nathan he seemed amused by her popularity, but his gaze rarely left her when the dance took them apart.

She took comfort in his watchful protection. When he brought her a glass of wine, she refused all offers to dance and remained at his side to drink it. They were standing with Alexander and Beth, but the couple only had eyes for each other.

'Another good man lost to the world,' Nathan said with a shake of his head. 'I hope Alex's love-sick look is not contagious. With the Queen's ladies returned from France, I don't need an influx of dreamy-eyed, heartsore gallants filling my hospital.'

Angel stiffened at his flippant words. She glanced at Rupert on the far side of the room; he was listening attentively to the Duchess of Richmond.

'I'm sorry.' Nathan looked contrite. 'My words were thoughtless and in poor jest.'

She shrugged, trying to appear unconcerned. Two Cavaliers passed them and turned to subject Angel to appraising glances.

'Did I not say you would be the toast of the court?' Nathan returned to his usual banter.

'Has not your own reputation something to do with their interest?' she countered. 'You are renowned for the number of women who have been unable to resist your charm.'

'You flatter me.'

She lifted a teasing brow. 'I've seen how woman waylay you in the streets, at the hospital, and they come to your rooms.'

She was whisked on to the dance floor by Alexander before Nathan could respond, but found herself only listening absently to her brother's comments. He was full of praise for Beth and though his joy in love reminded her of what she herself had lost, she was happy for him.

All evening, despite her smiles and teasing, she had been aware of the tall figure who stood at the far end of the room. Rupert was not dancing, and was surrounded by his brother Maurice and several companions. Twice, she had seen him talking with the Duchess of Richmond. There was a tension in his stance, and his expression was dark and brooding. He had made no attempt to speak with Angel, and she needed all her skill as an actress to hide the pain cutting into her heart.

When Alexander left her to partner Beth, Llewelyn claimed her, then she danced with two Cavaliers. Nathan did not dance and often their glances found each other. It was kind of Nathan to ignore the invitations of the women who flirted with him, and to be so concerned for her welfare. Unwilling to cause her friend worry, Angel made more effort to appear carefree.

At the end of one dance, he appeared at her side. Tucking her hand firmly into the fold of his arm, he led her purposely towards Rupert. Angel's first instinct was to protest, but too many curious gazes were watching them. Besides she wanted to speak with Rupert, to make it clear that she understood how matters had changed between them.

'Your Highness,' Nathan said, attracting Rupert's gaze. It flickered over Angel, and she saw wariness in his dark eyes. 'May I present Mistress Angel Rowan, the sister of Major Alexander Rowan.' He played up to the new role which Angel would present to the court. 'She's recently arrived in Oxford and after Major Rowan's wedding is to visit France.'

Rupert had not been expecting that. 'A sudden decision, Mistress Rowan, this desire to visit France?'

'One I had decided upon some time ago, Your Highness. The time now seems right to me to pursue my wishes.'

Rupert held her stare and she saw his suspicion mellow to a familiar warmth. Then, as quickly as it appeared, it was gone. The Duchess of Richmond had appeared at his side. Her gaze was cool as she stared haughtily at Angel.

She said, 'Why, you bear a remarkable likeness to the actor who took the part of the widow this afternoon.'

'That was Mistress Rowan's brother,' Rupert defended curtly. 'They are the great-grandchildren of the playwright, Esmond Angel.'

'Ah!' The Duchess said absently, her possessive gaze resting on Rupert.

Angel watched them. She had heard that the Duke and Duchess of Richmond were very much in love with each other. Had the Duchess been dazzled by Rupert? What woman could fail to be moved by his handsome looks? She certainly took pains to seek his company.

As for the Prince . . . his expression was unreadable. He was not relaxed in the Duchess's company. Perhaps his friendship with her husband troubled him? It looked as though Angel would not get to speak with Rupert in private, and she spread her skirts in a deferential curtsy, unwilling to prolong the meeting. To her surprise, Rupert held her forthright stare and his lips curved into a smile.

Aware that many courtiers' eyes were upon them, she said softly, 'Both Major Rowan and Dusty have been honoured in serving Your Highness.' She hoped it was enough to convey that she had no regrets or recriminations.

His gaze held a trace of amusement. 'Dusty gave a superb performance. He brought something quite unique to the role.'

She smiled. 'Timing. It's a player's greatest asset . . . to know when to make an entrance and a graceful exit.'

For an instant his eyes kindled with warmth. His gaze lowered to the black silk angel on her shoulder and a flicker of regret shadowed his eyes. 'Alexander and Dusty have served me with courage and loyalty. I could ask no more of any man. I bid you fair wind to France.'

Several courtiers were looking curiously at them and Angel knew that, with so many ears straining to overhear, it was Rupert's way of saying goodbye.

With a terse inclination of his head, he strode across the floor to join the King's party, leaving the Duchess to gasp at the abruptness of his departure. That was something to which the pretty creature would have to grow accustomed, Angel reflected. Rupert was first and last his own man. And it was better this way – to part amicably, before the flames of desire turned cold and were doused by bitterness.

Nevertheless, her smile was strained as she turned back to Nathan, and he squeezed her arm reassuringly. Then all at once a ring of courtiers surrounded them. Foremost amongst them was the Prince of Wales. His stare was openly admiring and she sensed the shyness of adolescence which made him tongue-tied. He was already as tall as Nathan and though his swarthy looks and dark melancholy eyes were not considered handsome, they were arresting. Vulnerable to raw emotion herself at this moment, she warmed to the young Charles and found it easy to respond to his shyness.

Ignoring the courtiers whose trivial compliments bored her, Angel sank into a reverent curtsy. She had met Prince Charles on several occasions in her role as Dusty Rowan, for he avidly sought Rupert's company, clearly idolising his warrior cousin. He had not been shy then, believing her to be a man. She found his shyness now painful to watch and trusting that she would be forgiven, she broke the formal etiquette of the Court by speaking first in his presence. 'Did Your Highness enjoy the play?'

'It was the most exciting performance I've seen.' He shed his shyness in his enthusiasm. His dark eyes glowed with interest and she glimpsed the ripening sensuality of the man he would soon become. He added, 'There's a remarkable resemblance in both your looks and voice to your brother Dusty.'

'Not so remarkable, Your Highness.'

He smiled and she knew that he had guessed the truth. He lowered his voice so that only she could hear. 'I'd like to see more women on the stage. Is that why you're going to France?'

'One of the reasons.' She did not trouble to deny it.

Prince Charles glanced towards Rupert. Had he guessed about that also? 'When our playhouses re-open I hope you'll return to England. One day I shall be the patron of my own group of players.'

'And will there be a place for women in your company?' Angel enquired. 'How fortunate the woman to be the first to perform on the English stage.'

He leaned closer and his black hair brushed against her cheek. 'Surely you have achieved that already?' His voice was admiring.

She tapped his arm with her fan. 'That must remain our secret. And since it does not shock you, I'll tell you another outrageous secret. The play performed under Esmond Angel's name was actually written by my grandmother forty years ago. Today's performance was adapted by myself.'

Angel saw that he was taken aback, but something had prompted her to be honest with him. One day he would be King. What better way for women to win acceptance on the

221

stage than by the approval of their monarch?

The Prince of Wales was being beckoned by his brother James. As Charles left their party a Cavalier raised his voice to attract Angel's attention.

'Colonel Carver, do you intend to keep this ravishing creature to yourself all evening?'

'That is for Mistress Rowan to decide.'

'I'd not be so callous as to abandon a friend,' Angel responded. The strain of hiding her heartache took all the pleasure from the evening. Her head was beginning to throb from the noise of the music, the laughter and the loud talk amongst the press of people in the hall. The King and Queen had retired and the hour was growing late. Unwilling to spoil Nathan's pleasure, she smiled at him. 'But I must not be selfish. I've seen how certain women have resented Colonel Carver's lack of attention. I'd not deprive him of their admiring company.'

'Do I look deprived?' Nathan raised her hand to his lips.

'Have a care, Mistress Rowan,' warned a tall blond courtier with several ribbons tied in his curling lovelocks. 'Colonel Carver loves and leaves his paramours with frequent ease. But I would be your devoted slave.'

Angel felt Nathan stiffen at the insult. She recognised the Cavalier as one of the most dissolute in Oxford. 'You mistake my friendship with Colonel Carver,' she said. 'He's a friend of our family and a man of impeccable honour. I've never heard him besmirch any man's reputation merely to win the favours of a woman.'

The Cavalier flushed, his eyes narrowing with affront as he marched away. One of his companions went after him, the other one paused to say, 'Carver, if I didn't know better, I'd think you smitten of this virago.'

Nathan's hand went to his sword-hilt, but Angel put her own hand over his. His face was pale and taut as he replied, 'If that were the case, I would think myself a most fortunate man.'

Dismissing the Cavalier, Nathan smiled at her. 'They are taking their places for the next dance.'

'Would you mind very much if we found Alex, or my father? One of them will take me back to my room.'

'I would certainly mind. Am I not your escort this evening?'

'But I've kept you from your friends too long. I've no wish to spoil your pleasure.'

He held her hands against his chest. 'I thought we were friends, Angel.'

Her gaze searched his, but their blue depths were deliberately shuttered. 'We are, but I'm poor company tonight.'

He slipped her arm through his and led her from the room in silence. They did not speak as they walked through the streets. Outside her door, Nathan said, 'Do you truly intend to sail to France?'

'Yes.'

'What of your work in the hospital here?'

'I'm not indispensable.'

'And if I said that you were?'

'That would not be true.'

He put his hands on her shoulders and drew her into the torchlight. 'What if I said that I wanted you to stay, Dusty?' His voice was husky, and there was such intensity in his gaze, that she felt her heartbeat slow. He was a handsome man, and in the months they had worked together she had become extremely fond of him, more than she was prepared to admit.

'I shall miss you, Nathan.'

'Then stay.'

His arms were around her drawing her against his body. The seductive scent of the sandalwood he always used filled her senses, and before she could protest, his lips took hers in a deep and tender kiss. His mouth moved over hers with accomplished persuasion and she felt a stir of pleasure in her loins. With a strangled gasp she pulled back.

'No, Nathan!' She was startled at how difficult it was for her to form the words. Her heart ached with love for Rupert, yet her body had responded to Nathan's kiss. The regret in his eyes was sincere. She pressed his hand to her lips, her eyes closing at a renewed sense of loss.

Nathan could feel the heat of her reaching out to him. All evening he had been aware of the sensual grace of her body, and it had made him burn to possess her.

'I adore you, Angel.' He drew her closer, his lips brushing her hair. He swallowed and felt his pulse begin to race. He knew he should suppress the desire sweeping through him, that he should turn it aside with a banal remark. But he was like a man seized by dizziness on the edge of an abyss. 'Angel, I want you. More than that, my darling, I . . .'

She put a finger to his lips, her lovely face lifted to his. Her eyes were shadowed by pain. 'If you came to my bed now it would destroy something I hold very special – our friendship.'

'It would not be like that with us.'

'It would be worse, for there's a bond between us. I'll not sleep with you to ease the pain of parting with Rupert.'

'And you'll not stay in Oxford?' He ran a finger along her jaw. 'We would have been good together, Angel.'

Until now he had never regretted his reputation as a rake, which was grossly exaggerated. The evenings when Angel believed him to be involved with women, he was in reality shut in the room behind the hospital. There, he copied out his notes on the treatment and cures of his patients, or dissected dismembered limbs to study the movement of muscle and tendons. He had encouraged his reputation as a lover as the only way to win the privacy he needed for his studies. If he was not in his own room, friends assumed that he was closeted with a woman and did not seek him out. Now was not the time to dispute it.

He was shocked to discover how close he had come to losing control. Had he not vowed that his emotions would never again be engaged by a woman? He wanted none of their treachery and deceit. But Angel was not Sanchia. Neither was she ready to give her heart . . . Nathan cauterised his emotions. Women had always been attracted to him because he remained aloof, giving only so much of himself. That was the way he liked it, the way he intended to control his life.

He felt her hands on his chest, as she drew away from him, her voice heavy with sadness. 'This way we shall remain friends. And I know that our lives will cross again . . . in happier times.'

Nathan let her go. He remained outside her room as the door closed, staring at it. He had made love to many beautiful and promiscuous women, but he had never wanted any of them as he wanted Angel. What was it about her? Her smile? Her sincerity? Her touch that set his heart thudding like a callow youth in love? He frowned and made his way slowly to his room. Nay, not love. Angel was right in that. Love was not for him. He was immune to love . . . And yet Angel affected him deeply.

The thought of her having denied him became a growing torment. It flared into anger. She was no innocent, though he never doubted that she loved Rupert. He had felt her response to his kiss; it had fired his own need. There was a sultry promise which emanated like a sexual aura around her and he had lived too long in its thrall.

He shook his head to clear his anger. He could still smell her perfume in the air. He told himself that what he felt was deflated pride and the ache of frustrated desire. It had nothing to do with love. So what right had he to feel angry?

Chapter Nine

Paris

Angel fell in love with it immediately. As the hired carriage drove through the streets, the atmosphere of gaiety, now so lacking in England, was entrancing. The streets were narrow, muddy and dingy, the houses so steeply gabled that only a slender band of sky was visible above the rooftops. As for the noise and frenzy of gabbling voices, it was deafening after the tranquillity of the open countryside.

The streets were so overcrowded that their carriage was forced to slow almost to a halt. Angel stared out of the window. From doorways, shopkeepers' apprentices shouted the excellence of their masters' goods. Pedlars and street-vendors praised their wares, vying with each other to attract customers. Sedan-bearers demanded passageway. Shouted curses from coachmen rose over the steady rumble of wheels, and competed with the footmen who ran in front of carriages, crying, 'Make way.'

Not only noise but smells invaded the carriage. The mouth-watering aroma of baked pies and spiced cakes mingled with the pungent odour of a cartload of cabbages, and the steaming piles of horse dung, abuzz with flies, which littered the road.

The noise and stench increased the deeper they drove into the city. Angel shared the cramped space with the three other members of the company, the only members of Robin's troupe who spoke French fluently enough for them to perform in France. Since Etienne de Luc had discovered Angel was a woman, he'd acted as though she did not exist. When forced to address her, he spoke in clipped monosyllables. Orlando Fortemaine smirked at every snub. Throughout the journey the two actors had made it no secret that they were lovers. That did not trouble Angel, but it pained her that they resented her presence in the troupe. So far all her overtures at friendship had been rejected.

At least Robin Flowerdew enjoyed her company. He sat at her side, dozing, his head on his chest. He had been ill during the sea-crossing and looked pale and drawn. Angel worried about him. Seventy was no age to return to the hard life of a strolling player. She had learned that, despite Robin's appearance of prosperity, he'd been forced to sell his home to pay off his debts. He could not afford to hire the plays from Angel. Instead, he promised her a quarter-share in the profits as both actress and owner of her grandfather's plays. When de Luc had learned that Angel held a higher percentage of the shares in the company than himself, he had been furious. Angel suspected that de Luc was escaping from his own debts in England.

They were all escaping from something by leaving England. Angel had stayed another month, until Alexander had married Beth Penrose. Each time she saw Rupert, she pined for what had been between them. She did not believe he was the Duchess of Richmond's lover, but his interest in the Duchess was the speculation of the Royalist headquarters. Even for Rupert, Angel would not accept second place, but pride made a lonely bedfellow. The wild passion she had felt for him would fade with time, but she would never forget him. Paris could not banish him from her thoughts, but it was the beginning of a new life. There was no room for regrets.

At last the carriage entered the Rue St Honoré, where Angel's Aunt Sabine lived. It drew up before a three-storeyed, half timbered, gabled house with large diamond-paned windows. Stepping down on to the street, Angel was forced to hold her travelling bag close to her chest in the crush of people. She wished she had worn wooden pattens over her fine leather shoes. Even in this wealthy quarter of the city the street was ankle-deep in rotting debris.

She stared into the ground-floor window of her Uncle François' perfume shop. Two customers were talking to a dark-haired man in a grey and silver-braided doublet and breeches. Angel hesitated. She had sent a rider ahead, warning her aunt of her arrival.

The carriage carrying the other actors moved away, taking

228

hem to the inn near the Pont Neuf where they were to stay.
Angel avoided the perfume shop and pulled the iron bell-
ever to the private entrance. A maid in a grey gown and
arge white apron opened the door. She was black-haired and
aer oval face, which must once have been pretty, was dis-
igured by smallpox marks.

'I am Angel Rowan.' She spoke in French. 'My aunt is
expecting me.'

'But, of course! Enter, Mademoiselle. Madame Toulon is
delighted that you visit. We did not expect you for another
day. I am Hortense.'

She led Angel up a flight of stairs to a large salon at the
ront of the house. There Hortense halted, and placed her
inger to her lips in a gesture of silence. A tester bed with
gold hangings stood in one corner, and in the centre of the
oom was a gilt-carved settle covered in the same material.
Angel's gaze was drawn to a mahogany and gilt desk by the
window. Here sat a statuesque woman, her honey-coloured
aead bent over a ledger and the tip of her tongue caught in
concentration between her teeth. She looked too young to be
aer aunt, who Angel knew had recently celebrated her forty-
eighth birthday.

On hearing the footsteps, the woman held up her hand as
he continued to run her quill down the column of figures.
Angel felt her doubts returning. Had she been foolish to
come?

The quill was thrown down with a satisfied sigh and Sabine
Toulon glanced up. She looked startled at seeing Angel.
Then, with a sweeping glance that took in everything about
aer niece, she leapt to her feet.

'Angel! How you've grown! But I'd have recognised you
anywhere. Except for your Celtic colouring you're the image
of Gabriellen. Such a shoddy welcome. La! I'm ashamed I
eft you standing there like that.' Sabine enfolded Angel in
aer arms. 'My dear niece. Welcome to Paris and to our
aome.'

Angel was held at arm's length and subjected to an assess-
ng stare. 'There's much of my mother in you. You've the
ame strength of purpose in the tilt of your chin. And you
aave Llewelyn's smile.'

'You do not mind that I have come?'

'Mind? La! The baggage says do I mind?' Sabine kissed her on both cheeks. 'My dear, if you knew how I miss my family. Of course, François is the most adorable of husbands and I have my darling, Lucrèce. She'll be distraught that she's visiting a friend and has missed your arrival. You and Lucrèce will be wonderful company for each other; she's only a year older than you.'

'I'm looking forward to meeting her again.'

At that moment there was the sound of a man's tread taking the stairs two at a time. 'Sabine! Hortense says our niece has arrived. Is this true?' A man of medium height entered the room, his clean-shaven face already showing the blue-tinge of his beard line.

'This delectable and ravishing creature cannot be our little Angel?' he said, grinning. 'I do not believe it.'

'François, you'll embarrass the girl,' Sabine laughed. 'Pay no mind to him, Angel. He's a tease. And, like all Frenchmen, an outrageous flirt.'

At the sincerity and warmth of her aunt's welcome, Angel knew she would enjoy her visit. This opinion lasted for two hours until her Cousin Lucrèce returned. One look at the petite, beautiful woman who was wearing too much jewellery for good taste, made Angel's heart sink. Lucrèce stood poised in the doorway, her nose tipped disdainfully high, her hazel eyes hostile.

'Is that what passes as fashionable in England?' She spoke slowly, to be certain that Angel understood her French, and in a tone that suggested she addressed a simpleton. 'It's a style we've not worn in Paris for two years. And your hair! La! Is that another peculiarity of England? To wear it short like a man?'

'Lucrèce!' Sabine said sharply. 'That's no way to greet Angel. There's war in England. Angel cut her hair to disguise herself as a man. She wanted to fight for her King.'

Lucrèce shuddered. 'How unladylike. Mama, since when do we permit common camp followers into our home?'

'Apologise to your cousin,' Sabine ordered. 'You've been unforgivably rude.'

'It doesn't matter.' Angel smiled as she spoke, her French fluent and perfectly accented. Lucrèce was a spoilt only child, jealous of anyone else claiming her parents' attention. 'Lucrèce has been protected from the horrors which England

230

faces. She's not seen the heartbreak of a King forced to fight his own people, or witnessed an uncle's battle-scarred body brought home for burial. Had she been present at the murder of her grandparents, her heart would need to be cast in bronze not to cry out for vengeance and justice.'

Sabine paled, but Lucrèce remained unmoved. A sneer twisted her Cupid's bow mouth. 'I would have stayed with my family to give them the support they needed.'

Or rather have them protect you, Angel thought, despising her cousin's self-centredness.

Lucrèce fingered a curl of her wine-gold hair which she wore in ringlets high on her head. 'I understand you'll not be staying with us for long, as you intend to join a troupe of players here. Any woman who acts upon the stage is a whore.'

Angel's temper erupted. 'You forget that your grandmother ran her father's acting troupe. They were a famous and respected company. How dare you revile them! Gabriellen was a remarkable and talented woman. You should be proud to be her granddaughter.'

'Papa!' Lucrèce wailed and threw herself on to her father's chest. 'That creature insults me. She flaunts her English blood in my face. Does she not know that my French grandfather was one of the King's most trusted advisers? And that my grandmother was the daughter of a count? I'll not have her in this house. She's rude and . . .'

'There's nothing at fault with your cousin's manners,' François said sharply, disengaging Lucrèce's arms from his neck. The shocked expression on her face told Angel that he had never spoken to her so coldly before. 'You've insulted your Mama. Apologise at once. And then to Angel.'

Stricken, Lucrèce stared at Sabine and mumbled an apology, but as she turned to Angel her eyes flashed with venom. 'I'll not apologise to that creature.' With a rustle of silk, she ran sobbing from the room.

'I apologise for my daughter's behaviour,' François said stiffly.

'Perhaps it would be better if I didn't stay?' Angel suggested.

'La! I'll not hear of your leaving.' Sabine's voice quivered. 'We are your family.'

Tears spilled down her aunt's cheeks. It was more than

Lucrèce's rudeness which had upset Sabine. Contrite, Angel knelt at her feet.

'Forgive me. I shouldn't have blurted out about Gabriellen's death. She died bravely. They both did. They wanted to save the horses Mark had spent a lifetime breeding. They didn't suffer.' Angel's own face was wet with tears as the horror of that day in Wales returned. 'Gabriellen encouraged me to write . . . we were working on a play when she died. Robin Flowerdew has brought Gabriellen's plays to France, and I'm to translate any which will appeal to a French audience. Does that make me so bad? I know Gabriellen would have approved.'

Sabine put a hand on the top of Angel's head. 'Your grandparents would be so proud of you. Lucrèce does not understand. She's all French. There's none of the Angel wildness in her. That wildness has not always served our family well. Do you remember my sister Jacquetta? Like me, she was the daughter of Gabriellen and her lover the buccaneer Sir Jack Stoneham, before Gabriellen married Mark. Jacquetta visited our father who then sailed the Spanish Main. She sailed with him for two years, risking death for adventure at his side. Fate was cruel, and she was drowned when the ship bringing her home to England was sunk in a storm. You also have the Angel courage and determination, my dear. But be wary of the wildness of our blood. La! I'll hear no more talk of you leaving.'

François Toulon put a hand on Angel's elbow and raised her to her feet. 'I admired Gabriellen. You must stay. I'll talk with Lucrèce. It's my fault she's so spoilt. She's the only one of our seven children to have survived infancy, and so has been denied nothing.'

Overcome with emotion, Angel kissed her uncle's cheek and watched fondly as he left the room. Unlike Lucrèce, who foolishly despised her English ancestry, Angel felt an empathy with the country where her great-grandmother, Sabine Toulon, had been born. That first Sabine had fled France after the Huguenot massacre on St Bartholomew's Day in 1572. She had married Esmond Angel; Gabriellen was their daughter. Years later in 1625, François Toulon, a distant relative of the first Sabine, came to England with his father who was an emissary of King Louis at Charles I's Court. Whilst his father was engaged at Whitehall, François tried to locate his Huguenot relatives. By a stroke of fortune he saw the graves of Gabriellen's parents in St Ethelburga's churchyard. Recognising the name of the famous playwright, François had learnt through his father's connections at Court of Gabriellen's existence and her residence in Wales. He visited Rowan Hall and within two months was married to Sabine.

Seeing that her aunt and uncle still appeared very much in love, after twenty years of marriage, brought back the pain of Angel's own broken affair with Prince Rupert, with searing intensity. Despite her resolution never to marry, she acknowledged that at heart she was a romantic. She wanted adventure, but she could not live without love.

'Don't look so worried, Angel,' Sabine said. 'Lucrèce does not like to share her father's love, not even with me. She saw how François admired you and was jealous. Now tell me of our family. Is Llewelyn fighting with the King? And Alexander? They've not been wounded, have they? How is Maressa? And Firkin? Is baby Julian crawling yet?'

The questions were fired at her with such speed, Angel laughed, her humour restored as she related the news of her family.

At last the questions ebbed and Sabine said proudly, 'If you intend to put Gabriellen's plays on to the French stage the first one must be a comedy. That is what the people here prefer. We shall visit the Hôtel de Bourgogne to see the Italian comedy players and also the Théâtre du Marais. There is also the L'Illustre-Théâtre, which has been recently formed. La! One of the founders was born in this street. He is Jean-Baptiste Poquelin, though he has changed his name to Molière. His father's an upholsterer and I've known the family for years. Jean-Baptiste is a pleasant young man, just a few years older than yourself. He will help you to select a play. Perhaps his company may wish to perform it.'

Alexander had not seen his new bride for two months since their wedding. Beth had returned to Oakfield Manor, anxious not to leave the estate unattended now that it was becoming profitable. The Dunnock family had served her well, and the livestock and crops were producing a surplus to be sold in the local market.

As Alexander approached the village, several people

stopped to greet him. Jonathon Gideon, the village priest, came out of the vicarage and held up a hand to halt him.

'Good day, father,' Alexander greeted the thin, ruddy-faced priest.

'God be with you, Major Rowan.' The priest's normally tranquil face looked worried. 'I must speak with you about young Isaac Dunnock. He's taken to preaching in the villages and is gaining a following. It worries me. Isaac has none of Elijah Dunnock's moderation. Several times he's disrupted my own services. He's been abusive and aggressive, demanding religious and social reforms.'

'I'll talk to Elijah and Isaac,' Alexander promised. The news dimmed his pleasure in the day, stolen from army duties. He respected Elijah Dunnock but, though Isaac declared himself neutral in this war, he had no sympathy with the Royalist cause. That meant his loyalty could not be trusted.

Beth was in the stableyard when Alexander rode in, and he leapt from his horse and gathered her into his arms. The perfume of her hair and skin and the touch of her body as he kissed her ignited his desire. Aware of curious gazes from the servants, his kiss was brief and he led Caradoc into a stall. The stallion attempted to nip Alexander's shoulder, in protest at the unaccustomed impatience with which his master dragged off his saddle and blanket. Caradoc was too unpredictable to be trusted not to kick or bite a groom and Alexander always tended to the stallion himself. As he worked now, Beth leaned against the stall, chatting of inconsequentials.

When Caradoc was settled, Alexander took her once more in his arms, his voice taut as he whispered against her hair, 'I've missed you, my darling. And I've only got a few hours here. I leave at dawn to join my troop at Abingdon.'

'Are you hungry?'

'Ravenous,' he kissed her with deepening passion. 'But not for food.'

'But, Alex, it's midday . . .' A blush darkened Beth's cheeks.

'And your husband has not seen you for eight weeks.' His grin was irrepressible as he propelled her towards the house.

Beth kept her head lowered as she was hurried through

234

the kitchen, aware of Prudence Dunnock's knowing smile. Alexander's passion both delighted and disconcerted Beth. Her first husband, Bryan, had never been demonstrative, his passion only apparent when they retired for the night. To make love during the day still seemed indecent to Beth, but when Alexander kissed her, her inhibitions fled and her desire matched his own.

An hour later Beth lifted her head from her husband's chest. The languor following his lovemaking was still with her, but she was conscious of the time they had spent behind the locked door. Sunshine streamed through the window, filling the chamber with a golden light. Remembered caresses and murmured endearments added to her contentment. Gazing at Alexander laying with his eyes closed, her love for him overwhelmed her. His black hair was spread across the pillow, and his handsome, swarthy face no longer showed the strain which she had noticed earlier.

A blush heated her cheeks as she recalled that they lay abed in the middle of the day. How could she look Elijah and Prudence in the eye? There was a meal to prepare. Guiltily, she eased to the edge of the mattress, unwilling to disturb her husband's sleep. At her movement Alexander stirred. His eyes opened. There was such tenderness in their dark depths that her heart felt it would burst with love for him.

'Are you abandoning me so soon?' he teased. His arms slid around her waist and he pulled her to him, his lips seeking her throat. She gasped as his hand moved down across her stomach to her thighs. The sheet had slipped away from her body and with a squeal she tried to recover it, but he caught her hand and pressed it into the pillow above her head.

'Don't hide yourself from me.'

'Alex, please!' she began to protest.

'Since you ask so politely, how can I deny you?' His lips moved across her shoulder to her breast and his tongue teased its rosy peak. As his hands stroked the curve of her spine, she felt her blood answering in eager response, until she was consumed with a need that matched his own.

Later, fulfilled, she lay propped on her elbows, smiling down at him. He reached up to touch her unbound hair. 'Have you any idea how precious you are to me? I hate leaving you here. Especially now. Father Gideon tells me Isaac has been causing trouble. He'll have to leave.'

'Elijah and Prudence will not like that.'

'Isaac is old enough to go his own way. From his preachings and demands for social reform it's obvious he's against the King. Reform is needed, but it must be achieved within the law. I'd be happier if you lived at Rowan Hall. This house is too close to Roundhead-held territory.'

'But it's easier for you to visit me here. In Wales I'd never see you,' she protested. 'I've friends here in the village to protect me and, besides, the estate is beginning to prosper. You'll need the money to re-establish the Rowan strain when you return to Wales. Don't banish me to a strange estate.'

Alexander could not argue with her reasoning. During the summer months he would be away from Oxford often, as Rupert answered the call to relieve any Royalist town or castle under siege from Parliament troops.

Once dressed, he summoned Elijah to attend him in the small parlour. The Quaker stood before him, ill at ease.

'I've no complaint about your work,' Alexander began. 'The estate is well run and profitable. But I've heard disquieting news about Isaac.'

Elijah looked downcast, his thickset body sagging. 'There are many such as he within our sect. Our movement is growing, spread by the unrest and the people's need for reform. The young become idealistic in their beliefs.'

'I didn't condemn your beliefs when you came here,' Alexander returned. 'There was only one condition to your employment – religious tolerance. Isaac must leave. There's no place for him in this village. I'm not dismissing the rest of your family, for I value your work, Elijah.'

The Quaker's eyes creased with pain. 'It grieves me to turn my son away. But I cannot sacrifice my little ones for him. Thou art a good master. Isaac has chosen his path. Christ guides him differently from the way He guides me.'

Isaac left the house within the hour. He was angry at his dismissal. No man should be at the mercy of another, as his family were to Major Rowan. He spat on the ground as he trudged over the hill away from the village. Neither did he approve of frivolous Beth Rowan. Before her marriage

236

he had tried to make her see the error of her ways. She had scorned him. And he knew her now for the devil's hand-maiden. She was a harlot, unashamed by her husband's lech-ery. He had seen them kissing and fondling during the day. Beth Rowan was a wanton. Had not her beauty tempted him to impure thoughts? He would wake sweating in the night, visions of her naked beneath him torturing his dreams. His member would be hard and aching with lust. As his hand closed upon it, working furiously to seek release, he had reviled her for the cause of his shame.

Isaac strode on. Christ worked within him, giving him the vision of a better England. He would not shirk his call. Cromwell's men were steadily advancing towards Oxford. Oakfield Manor lay in their path. Many within the village agreed with his views on reform. The steeplehouse was a place of idolatry and Jonathon Gideon was the King's man and practised near-popery. The people needed to be saved from the devil's influence, and to be shown that salvation and the light of Christ was within them all.

He had heard that Douglas Fairburn was captain of a troop serving under Colonel Cromwell. Isaac's calling was clear. Not to fight, but to serve as their preacher. Fairburn had no love for Royalists or Major Rowan.

Isaac sank down on to the ground and prayed. He had been called by God to preach. The monarchy was corrupt. The landowners enclosed and stole the common land from the people. Everywhere there was godlessness and sin. If the King won this war godlessness would rule in England, wan-tons and degenerates would be their masters.

Isaac raised his arms to heaven. Christ was within him and he had heard His calling. The people were rising up against the King and his idolatry. England was another Gomorrah and must be brought back to God's favour.

Maressa gazed out of the salon window of her house in the Strand and scowled to discover a thick fog over the city. The fog obscured the church spires and the masts of the ships anchored in the Thames. It was mid-September but it had been days since the sun had shone. She hated London when it was foggy, which was often. The clear air and sunshine of Arundel beckoned, but at Arundel life was dull. She gave a bitter laugh. Not that life in Puritan London was much fun. She rarely saw Henry, his days were supposedly spent in Parliament. From his drunken singing when he returned in the early hours of the morning, his evenings were spent gambling and wenching.

Twice she had met Cousin Thomas to alleviate her boredom, and each time she had enjoyed his company. His compliments had been effusive when last they met. Hurt by her husband's neglect, Maressa had flirted with Thomas. She played the coquette, promising much, but in reality giving him little, so that his interest became heightened.

At their last meeting Thomas had taken her to the Spring Gardens near Charing Cross. They had strolled amongst the trees, accompanied by birdsong. The Gardens were a popular place for assignations, with seats set in the privacy of secluded hedges. There, Thomas had declared his passion and she allowed him to kiss her. One kiss she was prepared to permit, but when his lips became more demanding, she tensed. His passion alarmed her. The touch of his hands sliding along her legs had been frightening.

Frantic, she had pushed against his chest. 'No, Thomas. I'm married.'

He laughed. 'What difference does that make?'

'But this is a public place!' She feared that to deny him outright would rouse that dangerous side of his nature she did not trust.

'I'll take a room. Will you come to me there?'

'Thomas, you go too fast. I enjoy your company but . . .'

'You're a damned tease.' The hard light in his eyes added to her fear. 'A prudish Mistress Goody-goody. If there was but one-quarter of your sister's fiery blood in your veins, you'd be all a man dreamed of in a woman.' He pushed his cocked hat back over his blond hair, his clean-shaven cheeks taut with frustration. 'Do you think Sir Henry prizes your virtue? He'd pimp for you if he thought it would clear his gambling debts.'

Maressa blenched. That was precisely what Henry had suggested. Yet Thomas's unflattering comparison of her and Angel had struck a deeper wound. How dare he judge her so unfavourably? He was her only friend in London, and she did not want to lose him.

Blinking rapidly to force tears into her eyes, she said, 'Thomas, how can you think so ill of me? You know I care for you. It's not easy for me to overcome my morals. I'm attracted to you, but . . .' She looked down at her hands in her lap, feigning embarrassment. 'Please be patient with me.'

She looked up at him through the thick fringe of her lashes and met his piercing grey stare. Inwardly she shivered. There was something ruthless in that controlled, steely gaze. But Thomas could be an important ally. She reached out to touch his hand.

'If you care for me, then give me more time?' she entreated. 'This is only our third meeting. I'd forgotten what it was like to feel young and carefree. To be happy.'

'I'm not a patient man.' There was a warning in his voice which sent a shiver of fear through her. 'I'll not wait forever. Or be toyed with.'

He stood up and when he tucked her arm through his, she could feel the tension in his body. Thomas was not a man to cross. And he would expect a return for any favour given. As they approached the edge of Spring Gardens, where it opened out on to the spacious walks of St James's Park, she flirted with him, trying to draw him out of his dark humour. She wished she had Angel's quick wit, but she knew how to use her looks to keep a man interested. By the time they returned to the Strand Thomas was again smiling and even found it amusing when she did not ask him into the house.

Maressa was uncertain of how to keep Thomas's friendship without having to succumb to his attentions. Obviously the ties of kinship were not enough to keep him at her side. The problem was never far from her thoughts and when Hazel entered the salon she was not paying attention to her maid.

'Did you say a gentleman caller, Hazel?' Maressa's heart leapt. Had Thomas been reckless enough to visit?

'A man, my lady. Says he has a letter for you from your brother, but he insists on seeing you personally.'

'Then send him in, but stay yourself.'

Maressa was excited at the prospect of a letter from Alexander. Since he and her father had joined the King at Oxford she had heard nothing from them. A tall, thin man with grey hair entered. He wore an unfashionably long, cassock-style coat of dull brown, and his large feet in the buckled shoes made his skinny ankles look too fragile to support him.

'I am Sparrow.' From within his threadbare coat he drew out a sealed letter. 'It was written some weeks ago when Major Rowan knew I was travelling to Sussex. You were not at Arundel, and I had business to attend before I could continue to London.'

Aware of the difficulties of delivering letters in these times, Maressa did not comment on the delay. Before she opened it, she asked, 'Will you be returning to Oxford, Mr Sparrow?'

The man looked at her blankly. 'I'm a pedlar. But even a pedlar is not always free to go where he would wish. I may be travelling north soon, if you wish to reply. If I can't deliver your letter a shilling will pay another to carry it for you.'

She did not question him further. The opportunity to communicate with her family was too good to miss. 'I'll pay you to ensure that a reply reaches Major Rowan. Wait in the kitchen. Cook will give you refreshment.'

He bowed and stepped back to leave. Then he cleared his throat. 'My lady, perhaps you should know that I had to call three times at the house in Arundel before I got a reply. The maidservant was obviously in her cups. I'd not mention it except for the coughing I heard from an upstairs room. Major Rowan said that his brother was not strong. When I enquired of your brother's health, the door was slammed in my face. The maid's loud abuse then turned upon whoever was cough-ing inside the house. If your brother is ill, I fear that woman will be the cause of his death.'

Appalled, Maressa stared at the messenger. Firkin should be at grammar school, not in Arundel. Who was the drunken slattern? Maressa was particular about the servants she employed, but Henry was always talking of economies. Had he refused to pay her brother's school fees and hired cheaper servants?

'How long was it since you were at Arundel, Mr Sparrow?'

'Ten days.'

Maressa sank down on to a chair. When Firkin had his attacks he needed special care. She must go to Arundel. God willing, she would not be too late. Immediately she ordered Hazel to pack her bags and for the coach to leave in two hours' time. Julian and his nurse would stay in London. The journey would be too arduous for her son and she intended to return to the capital with her brother before autumn rains turned the roads into a quagmire.

Only when her plans were made did she pause to read Alexander's letter. It told her of his marriage and was full of news of Angel tending the wounded, writing a play, performing before the King dressed as a boy, and how she had been wounded in a skirmish when she had accompanied Prince Rupert on a scouting party. Now Angel was in France. Maressa's eyes narrowed. Angel was having all the fun and attention. Every word echoed Alexander's pride in his younger sister.

Maressa was furious at having missed his wedding, and resented the way he lavished praise upon Angel. He said nothing of missing her. His mention of Llewelyn sending his love seemed to have been added as an afterthought.

A glower spoilt her beauty as she stared out of the window at the fog-shrouded city. She did not want to be in London. Duty must now take her to Arundel, and she did not want to be there either. She wanted to be in Oxford. She wanted to be praised by her father for performing a daring feat to aid the Royalist cause. She wanted to sing before the King. Above all, she wanted to be admired and fêted for her beauty. London was dull, but Arundel would be worse. Maressa sighed. She would not shirk her duty. She saw herself now as a dutiful daughter dashing on an errand of mercy to save the life of her brother.

Life in Paris was never dull for Angel. Today, accompanied by Sabine, she was enjoying the sights on the Pont Neuf bridge over the River Seine. They were drawn to a booth by the piercing notes of a trumpet. Angel winced as she watched a toothpuller struggling with his tongs as he bent over a man tied to a wooden chair. With a grunt of triumph, the man held aloft a bloody molar for the inspection of the crowd.

'Behold the cause of all his misery!' the brawny toothpuller proclaimed. 'He suffers no more. Come forth, good citizens. Who's next? Jean-Pierre is the gentlest, most painless toothpuller in all Paris.'

There was a barrage of hooting as the patient, a large-boned man, was helped by the toothpuller's wife from the chair. His step was uncertain and his knees buckled, rousing a jeer from the delighted onlookers.

'About as painless as having a foot crushed under a cartwheel,' shouted a bearded spectator with a swollen jaw.

'Only a coward feels the pain,' Jean-Pierre countered as he eyed his next victim. 'Now a strong man like yourself . . . a brave man of undisputed courage, you'll not feel a thing. You have the toothache I can see, from the swelling of your jaw. Will you show yourself to be a coward before your friends? Let me put you out of your pain.'

'I'd as lief face the Inquisition,' the man grunted, edging away.

'You're a coward then!' the toothpuller jeered.

The man's swollen face suffused with colour. 'No one calls Gaston Le Brun a coward!'

The toothpuller beamed effusively and with a bow gestured to the chair. Le Brun's companions began to cheer and push him towards the booth. The crowd shouted, enjoying the diversion. Angel turned away unable to watch as the man, tricked by his own bravado, was subjected to those brutal tongs. She was drawn to a crowd around a mountebank, and she paused to listen to the charlatan who held up a phial of amber liquid.

'Buy my wonder elixirs! This cures the plague, pestilence and all manner of fevers.' He held another phial up which contained a reddish liquid. 'This, good people, cures all sexual ills. Impotency will trouble you no more. Barrenness becomes a thing of the past. As for birth-pains – it will banish them. And should the joys of Venus visit the pox upon you, this is the cure.'

'How can they buy such potions?' Angel said, amazed at the number of people clamouring to purchase the useless philtres. 'The man's a rogue, playing upon their fears and superstition.'

'It gives them hope,' Sabine said with a shrug. 'Some of them are such pitiful, desperate creatures. Would you deny them that ray of hope?'

A man in front of Angel let out a yell as his high-crowned hat with a large ruby brooch holding a feather in place was hoisted up into the air. Looking up at the houses which lined the bridge, Angel saw an urchin hanging out of a window. He held a pole, and the hat was fixed firmly on its hook. The boy pulled a face at his victim, then ducked out of sight.

'The scoundrel!' Sabine said. 'He'll be away over the roofs before his prey has reached the first floor. Guard well your purse and valuables, Angel.'

Angel noticed another crowd around a thin man wearing an eye-patch, who was bent over an upturned barrel. Closer to, she saw that he was shaking dice in his fist and encouraging bets. Then, with a flick of his wrist, he rolled the dice. A groan went up from the gamesters and the sharpster raked in his hoard of livres and silver ecus. Whilst the crowd was distracted, another cut-purse darted away with a bulging prize.

Above the noise of the people a persistent drum tattoo set Angel's blood racing. The crowd parted for the drummer who was dressed in gaudy finery. Behind him a Harlequin followed, capering and announcing the play to be performed by his company that afternoon. Ragged children ran around the Harlequin, taunting him to perform tricks and antics. The play they were announcing was for Molière's troupe.

'Can we visit the theatre this afternoon, Aunt?' Angel asked, her eyes glowing with excitement. 'Robin Flowerdew will accompany us. It's important that he meets Monsieur Molière.'

'If François can join us, we will go. The playgoers can be rowdy and boisterous. A pity that today's play is a tragedy, but it is what Molière prefers. La! That's why he's so poor. Comedies are more popular.'

There was a disturbance in the crowd, as a swaggering braggart in an emerald green cloak pushed forward. 'A plague on Molière and his pauper troupe,' he announced. 'If you want to see the best performance in Paris, come see Montfleury grace the boards at the Hôtel de Bourgogne.'

'Montfleury is a buffoon!' a loud voice answered.

The crowd fell back to reveal a menacing figure in russet doublet and a wide-brimmed hat pushing through their midst. The man's hand was on the sword-hilt which hung from a leather baldric across his chest, and his face was flushed in anger.

'Montfleury is a murderer. He strangles the poetic muse

243

with his pretentious conceit,' the newcomer shouted. 'Molière is my friend. I defy anyone to insult his troupe.'

An expectant hush had fallen upon the crowd as the angry man paced before them. He was like a caged lion and clearly spoiling for a fight. From his arrogant bearing and the way he prowled, hungry for his sword to feed upon a victim, Angel guessed him to be a soldier.

'Come away, Angel,' Sabine urged. 'There'll be trouble. There always is when Cyrano de Bergerac's blood is up. His brawls are the talk of the city. He once fought a hundred opponents in a single fight. Or so he boasts.'

Angel was intrigued and held back. Once started, there seemed no end to the swordsman's rhetoric.

'Montfleury is a clod. An ass!' de Bergerac declared. 'Because this preening fop . . . this posturing rascal is so stout that one cannot beat him all round in one day, he gives himself airs.'

Angel grinned. 'The man has wit.'

Sabine sighed. 'A wit as sharp as his blade and just as deadly. He scribbles at plays and books, but he lives by his sword. Cyrano de Bergerac was an officer in a guards regiment until he was wounded during the taking of Arras from the Spanish a few years ago. He's the most quarrelsome man in Paris. Come away.'

Reluctantly, Angel obeyed, but she could not resist looking back as Cyrano de Bergerac circled the crowd, his sword half-drawn. No one accepted his challenge and Angel saw the swaggering braggart who had reviled Molière scampering like a frightened hare through the jeering throng.

'Monsieur de Bergerac is loyal to his friends.'

'He has few friends – too many men fear his sword.'

'I liked his wit.'

'Then it's as well he's ugly,' Sabine stated. 'Any adventurer with a silken tongue is the enemy of all women's virtue. Cyrano de Bergerac is one of Molière's acquaintances I'd prefer you not to meet.'

The Toulon party arrived at the playhouse half an hour before the performance was due to begin, and joined the disorderly queue pushing through the single door to pay their entrance fee. Once inside, Angel saw that the theatre was not what she had expected. Situated on the city's ramparts, it had once been a tennis court before it was converted by the players. Unlike the circular, open-roofed London play-houses, this covered building was rectangular, with two tiers of partitioned galleries which ran along three sides. At one end was the stage, with a curtain for the actors to pass through. There was not even a painted canvas as stage decoration.

The noise within the playhouse was deafening as they made their way to their seats in the gallery by the stage. The air was stale with sweat and unwashed bodies. Burning candle-wax from the lights along the front of the stage and hanging from the ceiling added to the stench. The partitioned boxes of the gallery were occupied by the wealthier people who moved freely from one box to the next, renewing acquaint-ances or calling across several partitions to attract the atten-tion of friends.

Angel took her seat between her uncle and Robin. The smells did not bother her, nor the noise. She loved the atmosphere and excitedly studied her surroundings. The stage was a raised platform, with two ladders on either side which led down to the pit. From beneath the stage the musicians struck up, the flute, drum and violin barely audible above the din rising from the audience. The central space was filled with the groundlings who stood to watch the per-formance. They pushed and jostled for the best positions, some even squatted on the floor rolling dice. Others called to the wenches selling wine and fruit who moved amongst them. The girls' laughter was shrill, and Angel suspected that they were selling more than their wares as they made assignations.

A fanfare blasted and the curtain on the stage was pulled aside to let a dozen actors file out – four of whom were women. Dressed in their finery, they climbed down into the pit to parade amongst the audience, stopping to converse with any important or wealthy person who caught their eye.

François Toulon leaned forward and waved in acknow-ledgement to a young man of medium height with long, brown, unruly locks and a stocky figure. The player approached their box.

'Monsieur Toulon,' he said in a deep resonant voice. 'You and your lovely wife honour our humble company.'

He bowed and turned to Angel who found herself appraised by dark, alert eyes. There was an underlying melancholy to the set of his mouth and soulful gaze. His face with its straight brows and narrow moustache was attractive, but too saturnine to be truly handsome.

François said, 'Monsieur Molière, may I present my niece, Angel Rowan. She's visiting us from England. And this gentleman is the renowned English actor, Robin Flowerdew.'

The Frenchman's eyes lit with interest. 'Mademoiselle Rowan is then a descendant of Esmond Angel, the playwright. I've heard much of his work from Madame Toulon.' He turned to Robin and held out his hand. 'It's a pleasure to meet an actor of such repute. Madame Toulon has also spoken of you. Were you not for many years with Esmond Angel's players?'

'With them I performed some of my finest roles. Mr Angel was a gifted playwright,' Robin said with unusual modesty. 'Mistress Rowan has the plays in her possession, and we are considering translating them into French.'

Molière lifted a brow, but before he could reply three sharp blasts on a trumpet announced that the play was about to begin. The other players were already disappearing behind the stage curtain.

Molière bowed to them. 'An interesting idea. One which I would like to discuss with you.'

'Perhaps then, Jean-Baptiste,' Sabine said quickly, 'you will join us for our evening meal?'

'It would be my pleasure,' he said, and hurried to the stage, calling out in a bantering tone to the restless groundlings who were chanting for the play to start. He paused to speak to an elegantly dressed gentleman sitting with several companions on seats placed on the side of the stage. Then he disappeared behind the curtain and a fiddler and piper struck up a tune.

When Molière stepped out into the light of the stage candles to recite the prologue in thunderous tones, there was little abatement to the buzz of conversation. The gentlemen seated on the stage were men of fashion: there to be seen and renew acquaintances, rather than to enjoy the spectacle of the play. They greeted late arrivals effusively, unconcerned that their conversation was as loud as the actors'. At times, they even stood up, blocking the view of the performance from the groundlings, who erupted in a roar of protest.

The play was a tragedy of indifferent quality. The best moments for Angel were when Molière or Madeleine Béjart, his red-haired leading lady, entered into raillery with the audience. These sallies were greeted with cheers which encouraged Madeleine to hone her wit at the groundlings' expense. At each response, she blew kisses to the audience.

'Bravo, Madeleine,' a voice shouted from the gallery above. 'You shine tonight whilst these *canaille* can only bay at the moon.'

Angel recognised the voice of Cyrano de Bergerac. Instantly, everyone's attention was drawn from the stage to the gallery opposite, and the voices stilled.

'At last a fitting quiet to hear the poetry and sweetness of Béjart's voice,' de Bergerac declared. 'Let there be silence whilst Madeleine enthralls us with the magic of her words.'

'I'd rather she did a dance and showed us her legs,' a burly man from the pit shouted.

There was an expectant hush as de Bergerac leapt on to the rail of the gallery and climbed down to the stage.

'Who spoke?' he demanded. 'Let the knave answer with his sword.'

Four gentlemen rose from their seats on the stage. Their satin and velvet doublets and breeches were beribboned at shoulder and knees, their long hair curled over lace falling bands. One of them spoke: 'We did not come here to listen to your bluster.'

Cyrano de Bergerac drew his sword and a gasp rippled through the audience. 'There is but one way to silence me.'

'Do you hear the braggart? He's but one and we are four,' another of the gentlemen on stage jeered.

'Fighting talk,' de Bergerac responded. 'Who'll be the first? Whose name will be engraved on their tombstone?'

The four men who had challenged him hesitated. With a wicked gleam in his eye, de Bergerac swung round to confront the groundlings. The men nearest to him fell back trembling.

'Come, heroes,' he taunted. 'I cry silence. Do I have to slit your gullets, or skewer your tongues upon my sword?'

No one took up his challenge. Angel watched, fascinated

by his recklessness as he turned to face the four gallants.

'Posturing apes!' he shouted. 'Beribboned milksops! Is there not a man among you? You defame our poetic muse by chittering like monkeys. Sons of she-asses – fight!'

At this, the four gallants drew their swords and advanced. Uproar broke out amongst the playgoers as they jostled for a better view. Angel held her breath, mesmerised by the skill of de Bergerac's blade. It danced like quicksilver in his hand, swiftly disarming three of his opponents. The fourth, forced into retreat, was brought up short by the rail of Angel's box.

'Mercy,' the man cried as de Bergerac's sword rested against his neck. Over the man's shoulder Angel saw the feral glitter in de Bergerac's eyes, his face hard and unattractive, his lips curled into a sneer beneath an aquiline beak. He lowered his sword.

'Get out,' he snarled. Putting his boot to the young man's buttocks, he sent him sprawling into the arms of a bawd. They fell to the floor, the man struggling in a tangle of the woman's petticoats to get to his feet.

'What's your hurry? Ninon's a tasty piece,' someone shouted. 'Give her one for me. I've been trying to get between her legs for weeks.'

Ribald shouts greeted his efforts to rise and the woman giggled, wrapping her legs about the gallant's waist to hamper his escape. 'Oh, he's a vigorous one,' she moaned in fake ecstasy. 'He ruts like a raging bull. Oh, I die, I die!'

Red-faced and furious, the gallant extricated himself from Ninon's clasp. Angel ignored his departure, but could not help a smile. Cyrano de Bergerac had been more diverting than the play. Suddenly she found her gaze held by his. The swordsman was not smiling.

'Do you mock me, Madame? I take no mockery – not even from a woman.'

'Would I mock the greatest swordsman in France?' she countered, holding his stare. 'Mock a man with a rapier wit! Rather, I would mock the moon for shining less brightly than the sun. I never mock courage. But your talents are wasted, Monsieur de Bergerac. You should be on the stage. I've seen no actor in England who can extemporise with such verve and panache. When you spoke the groundlings were silenced.'

'It was fear of my sword not my tongue.' Cyrano regarded her belligerently. 'But you have spirit and beauty. I concede to you.'

A cheer went up from the crowd as they pushed forward to hear this new diversion.

'Never concede to beauty,' Angel admonished, 'only to wit.'

'Is that a challenge, Madame? You have the benefit of knowing my name whilst I do not know yours.'

'I am Angel Rowan.'

'A celestial beauty, with a devilish way with words.'

Angel held his stare, but did not reply. His eyes narrowed with interest. With a curt bow, he turned on his heel and strode to the stage to address the assembled cast.

'Molière, you have the silence I requested. Proceed, my friend. Would you keep your audience waiting?'

The play continued, but Sabine and François remained uneasy throughout the performance. As the actors took their final bow, Angel asked, 'Have I offended you by speaking out?'

'Cyrano de Bergerac is not a man to trifle with. He has the devil's own temper and a worse reputation.'

'I've no intention of encouraging the man. I liked his wit. But his courage would be better served in a more worthy cause than vented spleen. My interest is in Molière's troupe. The play was poor, compared to Esmond Angel's work, or that of Shakespeare and Ben Jonson. Though the players were accomplished. I would have thought the audience would be larger.'

'I hear the company is struggling against debt,' Sabine explained. 'The Béjarts are a volatile family. Apart from Madeleine, her sister Catherine and brother Joseph are also in the troupe. For many years Madeleine Béjart has been the mistress of the Chamberlain to Monsieur the King's brother. One would have thought he could have given the company more financial support. However, like so many actresses, Madeleine is renowned for her wantonness. She is also Molière's mistress.'

'Sabine,' François admonished gently. 'You should not be talking of such matters to your niece.'

Sabine shrugged. 'I doubt I've shocked Angel. She should

know the situation within the company if Molière is to dine with us tonight.'

François frowned. 'You seem set upon indulging our niece.' He looked anxiously at Angel. 'I wish you'd reconsider. Sabine says nothing because she sees no wrong in the way Gabriellen worked with her father's players for many years. She remembers the visits to the play as a child and the excitement of the rehearsals. I fear it's an uncertain profession, little above vagabondage.'

'Only if one is not successful. And I intend to succeed,' Angel responded. 'If not as an actress, then as a playwright like Gabriellen. The playhouses will not always be closed in England, and there's much I can learn in France. I want to meet all the great writers. When the playhouses of England reopen I'll return to London, and make my name as the foremost woman of the stage.'

Chapter Ten

'Mademoiselle Rowan, that's the finest play I've heard in months,' Jean-Baptiste Molière said with warmth.

He looked from Angel to Robin Flowerdew, who sat holding the book containing the French translation of the first act of *The Widow Went a-Wooing*, which they had read out to the family after the evening meal.

'Bravo!' Molière continued, his dark eyes flashing with admiration. 'But before it's performed here I'd suggest one or two minor amendments. It should reflect the French culture rather than the English.'

'I expected as much, Monsieur Molière,' Angel returned with a smile. 'But I've just arrived in France. How can I learn?'

Molière smiled and spread his hands. 'I will help you.'

'But you're busy with your troupe.'

Molière regarded Angel and rubbed a finger across his narrow moustache. 'To perform that play I'd do much more. You must meet other poets. I shall introduce you to Paul Scarron. A most amusing wit, though sadly crippled by a debilitating illness which makes him a prisoner in his rooms. He will delight in meeting you.'

There was a look of annoyance on Robin Flowerdew's face as he handed the book to Angel and addressed Molière. 'Let there be no misunderstandings concerning this play. It is to be performed by my players. Angel will play the widow, de Luc the lover, Fortemaine the devil and myself the earl. Other players will be hired as they are needed.'

Molière's stocky figure tensed. He pushed back his long hair and eyed Robin with the antagonism of a terrier about to bait a bull. 'I was under the impression that it was the play which was for hire, not the entire troupe.' Molière

251

bowed stiffly to Angel and then to Sabine and François. 'A charming meal, Madame Toulon, but I must leave. Should my troupe agree to perform this play, it will be under my direction. I shall say who performs which role.'

'The devil you will!' Robin thrust his head forward aggressively.

Molière shrugged and turned to Angel. 'Those are my terms. With respect, Mademoiselle, you're an accomplished enough actress, but inexperienced. Madeleine Béjart would take the part of the widow. As for Fortemaine and de Luc, I know nothing of their skills. I like well the role of lover for myself.'

'What do you know of troupe management?' Robin scoffed. He puffed out his chest and adopted an imperious stance. 'Your company is in debt. I've spent fifty years perfecting my expertise. I'm one of the most acclaimed actors in England.'

'Precisely,' Molière retorted. 'In England! And that was many years ago. You retired, did you not? Here in France you're not known.'

'Gentlemen!' Angel interceded. 'Let's not quarrel. The translation of the play isn't finished yet. If need be, I can adapt it so that actors from both troupes have adequate parts.'

'You will adapt it?' Molière subjected her to a look of keen interest.

She regarded him levelly. 'It was my grandmother's play, although it was performed under Esmond Angel's name – as were many of her works. I learnt all she could teach me. You'll not be disappointed, Monsieur Molière. Especially as you've offered to advise me on the finer points of French humour and culture.'

Molière held her stare with his melancholy gaze and lifted a brow. 'I was not aware that I had agreed to do so much.' Then he smiled, taking the sting from his words. 'But it's a worthy challenge, is it not?'

He turned to Robin. 'Very well. Until I see the finished play I promise nothing. If Mademoiselle Rowan can write parts for everyone . . . and I approve them, it will benefit both our companies to work together.'

Seeing Robin's obstinate glare, Angel feared he would object. She hastily placated. 'I'm sure Monsieur Molière will appreciate so seasoned an actor in his troupe. And you did

252

say all the best actors are already employed in established companies. Of course, Robin will receive an equal share with Monsieur Molière, is that not so?' She looked pointedly at Molière, the tilt of her chin warning him that this was one condition upon which she would not back down.

Molière nodded. When Angel smiled in appreciation, he mellowed towards the older actor. 'Mr Flowerdew, I'd be honoured to have so eminent a player in my troupe.'

Angel held her breath as Robin studied Molière. To her relief, he bowed his head in acceptance. She clasped her hands together, her eyes alight with pleasure. 'You'll not regret your decision, Monsieur Molière. In three days the translation will be finished. We will work on it from there.'

'If we're to work together, please call me Jean-Baptiste.' He took her hand and, pressing her fingers to his lips, stared into her eyes. It was impossible not to respond to the admiration in their dark, soulful depths. For the first time since she had left Oxford, Angel's spirit lightened. She had come to Paris to build a new future, not to dwell upon the past. She still loved Rupert, and would always carry a flame for him lighting the deepest recesses of her heart. But she refused to pine over a lost love forever.

'Jean-Baptiste, I'll enjoy visiting Monsieur Scarron. I've a feeling we are going to work well together.'

He lifted her hand to his lips. 'The pleasure will be all mine.'

Two days later, Molière escorted Angel on a visit to Paul Scarron. As the hired carriage moved slowly through the crowded streets Molière grew quiet. Sensing that something was troubling him, Angel put a hand on his arm to ask, 'Is aught amiss, Jean-Baptiste?'

His eyes were grave. 'I must warn you that Scarron's illness has hideously distorted his body. Though he suffers acute pain, it hasn't affected his sense of humour. I believe you're too sensitive of another's feelings to show shock or repugnance, but it's best to be forewarned. However, you'll be delighted by his wit,' Molière said more enthusiastically. 'And you'll bring a burst of sunshine into his life. Scarron is very susceptible to a beautiful woman.'

'Aunt Sabine warned me that in his youth he was a hell-raiser and a libertine. She said no woman was safe from him, for all he had been ordained as an abbé.'

Molière leaned back against the cracked leather upholstery of the hired carriage. 'Scarron must have been the Church's greatest misfit. As the younger son of a distinguished family he was thrust into it by his stepmother . . . and with disastrous consequences.' Molière fell silent, looking out of the window at the rooftops and church spires thrusting upwards against a clear blue sky.

'Aren't you going to tell me why the church was so bad for him?' Angel could not contain her curiosity.

Amusement sparkled in Molière's eyes when he faced her. 'The matter is rather indelicate. I would spare your blushes.'

'You'll do no such thing – I'm burning to know what happened.'

He laughed. 'Would you have me repeat unfounded gossip? Scarron has never admitted the truth of the story.'

Angel looked grave. 'I would not encourage idle rumours.'

'You wouldn't?' Molière responded in surprise.

'Never,' Angel said firmly, 'but since I would know the nature of the man I'm about to visit . . .' She could no longer sustain the feigned piety which had left her companion nonplussed. 'I declare I'm eaten up with curiosity. I'll burst if you don't tell me!'

Molière's eyes crinkled with amusement, though his voice was grave. 'Whether true or not, the tale depicts the spirit in which Scarron lived. He was a prankster with tremendous *joie de vivre*. From a window in his monastery in Le Mans, Scarron was watching a carnival winding its way through the town. Imagine the laughter, the music, the joyous dancing he witnessed, whilst he was cooped up in dreary pious surroundings. His high spirits rebelled. He ripped open a mattress, smeared his naked body with honey and rolled about in the feathers. Once covered, he ran out into the street and joined in the carnival. There he played the fool – somersaulting, dancing, rushing up to terrified women, chirping and flapping his arms. During these antics his feathers began to fall off. Inevitably, he was recognised. A cry went up, that he was a disgrace to the Church. The outraged people turned on him, plucking off his feathers. Some scandalised matrons beat him with their brooms. Scarron fled. To escape his tormentors he plunged into the freezing waters of the river and was forced to hide in the bullrushes until dark.'

Angel put a hand to her mouth, her body shaking with laughter.

'Soon afterwards,' Molière went on, in a sobering voice, 'Scarron contracted a paralytic fever which left him a cripple. The progressive swelling of his joints transformed this once wild and fun-loving man into a deformed dwarf bound to his bed or chair.'

Angel's body chilled with horror at the tragedy. 'Poor man.'

'He'll not want your pity,' Molière said sternly. 'Despite his deformity his spirit is uncrushed. In acknowledgement to his literary skills he has been granted a royal pension, but it's pitifully inadequate for his needs.'

When the carriage halted before a shabby building Molière drew a wicker basket from under his seat. 'It's the custom of Scarron's friends to bring food when they visit him.'

Hardly knowing what to expect, Angel followed Molière through the gloomy corridor of the house. From what she had read of Scarron's work she had been captivated by his caricatures and cutting satire. His fiction parodied the adventures of rogues, which delighted her, and his love songs brought a tear to her eye and a poignant ache to her breast.

The room they entered was dingy and crowded with half a dozen other visitors. Two richly dressed gallants stood behind a seated woman of outstanding beauty. The three other men, from their ink-stained fingers and threadbare jackets, were probably poets.

'Molière!' a crisp voice called. 'I'd thought you'd abandoned me for that wretched theatre of yours.'

'I begin to suspect that Paris has no wish for another theatre,' Molière said sardonically. 'Takings are poor, my friend. But soon I hope to change that, with the help of my charming visitor.'

As Molière introduced Angel the man in front of her moved aside. A hazy beam of sunlight filled with dancing dust motes cast its light upon a shrunken figure. Scarron's head lolled forward, his chin resting on his chest and his thin, wasted legs twisted back beneath him. Angel avoided staring at the gnarled joints of his fingers which were folded together, her gaze drawn to the piercing and intelligent gaze focused upon her. Grateful that Molière had prepared her, Angel's warm smile was genuine. She took the distorted hand extended towards her and covered it lightly with her own, careful not to cause further pain to the swollen joints.

'Monsieur Scarron, it's an honour to meet you. I've read much of your work and enjoyed it immensely.'

'Kind of you to say so, my dear.' Scarron's stare was wary.

'I spoke not out of kindness.' She regarded him with wry humour. 'For there was little kindness in some of your caricatures. You have the most devilishly barbed wit. No one equals your skilful thrusts at pomposity.'

Scarron relaxed, satisfied at her honesty.

The woman laughed with delight. 'Mademoiselle Rowan has the measure of you, Paul.' She nodded in polite acknowledgement to Angel. 'I am Marion de l'Orme.'

'I'm enchanted to meet you,' Angel said, instantly liking Marion. The woman's reputation preceded her. She was unmarried and notorious, having numbered Cardinal Richelieu amongst her numerous lovers.

Caught off-guard, Angel spoke impulsively. 'What was Richelieu like as a lover? His portraits make him look so imposing and remote.' As soon as she had spoken she could have bitten her tongue. 'Oh, your pardon. How could I have asked that?'

Marion was holding her side and dabbing at her eyes with a lace handkerchief, her mirth was so great. 'Molière, you've found a rare treasure. She's a delight. Every woman I meet burns to ask me that. Yet she's the only one with the courage to do so.' The older woman leaned forward to whisper, 'A cardinal is nothing special without his red hat and scarlet robe.'

Angel laughed. 'Perhaps he should have worn his tall mitre to encourage his flagging member! In England a cardinal's red mitre is often painted on the signs above bordellos.'

Her remark brought a guffaw from the men and again Marion de l'Orme held her side with laughter. Scarron touched Angel's hand, his lips drawn back into a grimace of a smile. 'A beautiful woman is always a joy to entertain. But a beautiful woman with a wicked wit will become the toast of Paris. Come, sit on the footstool by my side, Mademoiselle Rowan. Tell me about these plays of which Molière sets such store.'

'Your grandmother wrote plays which were performed on the English stage?' Scarron said incredulously, when Angel had explained her history.

'Only under Esmond's name. Our sex is prejudiced against in such matters,' Angel retorted.

'These translations I must see,' Scarron insisted. 'A woman playwright! How many years ago was this?'

'Fifty.'

There was a murmur of disbelief from the poets. Angel's eyes flashed. 'Don't you think a woman capable of writing a play? In France you have accepted women on the stage. Why should not a woman be acknowledged for her intellect as well as for her talents as an actress?' She cast a challenging stare at both Molière and Scarron. 'It's time you men looked to your laurels.'

'There speaks a woman with true spirit.' Scarron cut across a snigger from one of the gallants.

Marion de l'Orme slapped her fan down on her companion's arm. 'Jacques, I had thought better of you than to deride the worth of any woman.' She stood up to take her leave, and, bending unceremoniously over Scarron, kissed him on the mouth.

'You treat your old friends abominably when you discover a new beautiful woman.' Marion's teasing tone took the sting from her words. 'You're still an incorrigible libertine.'

'Ah, were Fate so kind,' Scarron quipped and his eyes twinkled wickedly. 'I live on memories now. But such vivid and sensual memories . . . there wasn't a woman in Paris safe from me in my youth. You were the most memorable, Marion.'

'Still no woman is safe from you,' Marion chuckled. 'You woo us all and steal our hearts with your poetry and flattery.' She turned to Angel. 'I visit Paul often. I look forward to meeting you again, Mademoiselle Rowan.'

Once Marion de l'Orme's party had left, the three other men also made their farewells. Molière stood up, saying, 'We would not tire you.'

'Please stay. I want to hear more of these plays and of your plans for them, Molière.'

They stayed an hour, and within that time Angel fell beneath Scarron's spell. In his presence she forgot the dinginess of the room and she no longer saw his suffering figure.

His words and wit entranced her. Finally, when another group of visitors arrived, they made their excuses and left, but not before Scarron made Angel promise to visit him again, to read one of her plays.

Angel was alone in the salon of her aunt's house, finishing the translation of *The Widow Went a-Wooing*. Tomorrow she would begin work on the revision with Molière, in time for it to be staged before Christmas. There was a clatter of high heels along the passage and a swish of silk as Lucrèce burst in.

'Because of you I've just been snubbed by Madame Verrault and her son. Gaston was my most handsome beau,' Lucrèce raged, sweeping the copied parts of the play from the desk in her fury. 'I hate you! Why did you come here? You've brought shame to us. Our house has become a haunt for coarse, common players. How will I ever hold my head up in the street again?'

'If you continue to indulge in self-pity, never,' Angel answered, stooping to pick up the scattered papers. 'You only think of yourself. Sabine enjoys the company of players.'

'You've dragged Mama down to the gutter. She's laughed at for opening her house to rogues and vagabonds. And I'm being laughed at too.'

Angel eyed her cousin with contempt, and strove to keep her temper in check. 'No true friend of your mother would laugh at her. They would delight in her pleasure. What you can't abide is that when the players visit, it's Sabine they want to see. Your pretty looks don't interest them.' Angel continued to pick up the papers, her voice scathing. 'Until you learn to see the finer qualities in others, you'll never obtain those qualities yourself.'

Lucrèce stamped her foot, trampling on the pages, tearing and muddying them. Angered by her cousin's tantrum, Angel's hand shot out. She grabbed Lucrèce's foot and, with a heave, overbalanced her cousin. Lucrèce yelped as she landed with a hard bump on the floor, her petticoats frothing around her knees. Angel picked up the ruined pages and began to put them in order. Lucrece made no attempt to rise. Instead, she started to scream and drum her heels on the floor. Her pale oval face became mottled and red, her mouth gaped, showing teeth already beginning to blacken from her over-indulgence in sweetmeats.

'There's no one to hear your tantrum, you silly child,' Angel snapped. 'Sabine is visiting a sick neighbour and your father is attending his duties at Court.'

The screaming stopped abruptly, and Lucrèce scrambled to her feet, her body shaking as she straightened the skirts of her gold silk gown. 'You think you're so clever! So heroic because you dressed as a man and cavorted about England with Prince Rupert,' she screeched. 'Well, you're not! No decent woman would parade in breeches. You shame our family. I hate you! It's time you paid for your wantonness.'

Hortense appeared at the door, looking startled by Lucrèce's outburst. She recovered herself to announce, 'Monsieur Molière is here. Are you receiving visitors, Mademoiselle Rowan?'

Angel was grateful for the diversion. 'Please admit Monsieur Molière.'

'I'll not stay in the same room as you and a common player,' Lucrèce screeched. 'It's the third time this week Molière has called. There's gossip that you're his mistress. Have you no care for your reputation, Cousin?'

'Molière is working with me on the play.' Angel glared at Lucrèce, certain that she was the one spreading rumours. 'The envious often spread gossip, but vicious tongues and evil minds reap their own reward.'

Lucrèce cringed before her cousin's formidable green stare, then stamped out of the room, ignoring Molière when she met him in the corridor. Her hatred burned like a brand in her breast. Ever since Angel had come to this house she had been ignored. Their visitors hung upon Angel's wit, praising her beauty and paying her compliments. It wasn't fair! Angel was not as pretty as herself. The Englishwoman was brazen in her manners and her outspokenness was unladylike. The bold way she stared a man straight in the eyes as she spoke to him was shockingly wanton. Yet everyone fawned over Angel as though she was something special . . . even her own Papa.

Tears stung Lucrèce's eyes. Papa's defection was the hardest of all to bear. Her lips thinned maliciously. It was time people stopped treating Angel as though she were special;

Lucrèce knew otherwise. Angel mixed with the greatest libertines of Paris. Everyone knew that actors had no morals. Yesterday she had seen Angel on the Pont Neuf, talking with the notorious Cyrano de Bergerac. He had made no secret of his interest in her cousin.

'Forgive Lucrèce's rudeness, my friend,' Angel said. 'I never thought I'd say it of a member of our family, but she's a narrow-minded prude.'

Molière laughed. 'Your cousin is a pretty, spoilt child, whilst you're a vivacious and fascinating woman.'

Overhearing the conversation, Lucrèce clenched her hands in rage. 'You'll pay for this, Angel Rowan.'

A hoar frost covered the Sussex landscape, and in the November sunshine the hills of the Arun valley seemed to be veiled in diamonds. Maressa huddled inside her fur-lined cloak. Her hands were thrust into a sable muff and her feet placed on a cooling hot-stone on the carriage floor. The vehicle jarred her bones as it lurched over the frozen rutted track, but without the frost the journey would have been impossible. For weeks at a time in winter the roads were quagmires, with carts sinking wheel high in the sodden mud.

As the carriage halted before her house, she waited impatiently for the coachman to get an answer to his knock. She had sent no warning of her arrival. If the housekeeper was neglectful of her duties Maressa wanted to catch her out. It took twenty minutes before the front door was opened. The dirty, slatternly figure with mousy hair hanging loose and matted about her shoulders bore little relation to the soberly dressed woman Maressa had employed last summer. As Maressa stepped out of the carriage with Hazel, the housekeeper's mouth gaped open in alarm. Maressa pushed past the woman, and caught the strong smell of ale on her breath.

'Pack your bags,' Maressa ordered. 'Hazel, don't let her out of your sight. I don't want to find half the silver missing when she leaves.'

Maressa went straight to Firkin's chamber. No fire had been lit, and her brother lay motionless under his bedcovers, his eyes closed.

'Firkin!' She hurried to the bed. The greyness of his face alarmed her. Was she too late? Then the blue-veined lids flickered and his eyes opened slowly.

'Maressa!' he croaked. 'Am I dying, Maressa? I feel so tired – so cold.'

She pulled off her cloak and threw it over his coverlet. Taking his hands, she gently rubbed them to get some warmth back into his body. 'No, Firkin. You'll get well. I came as soon as I heard you were ill. I've dismissed the housekeeper and Hazel is with me. Her medicines will cure you.' She smiled to hearten him, but she had never seen him look so ill. 'Once the fire is lit and you've taken some broth, you'll feel better.'

He tried to sit up and began to cough. When she put an arm around his shoulders to steady him, she was appalled at his thinness. She could feel his lungs vibrating as he coughed up blood.

'Lie back and rest,' she said shakily. 'Everything will be all right.'

Maressa dismissed all the servants. None of them had given Firkin the attention he needed and not even a doctor had been called. The cook, sour-faced and bitter at her dismissal, spat on the floor as she waddled from the kitchen.

'There's death writ all over 'im. I knows. I lost two sisters with the wasting sickness. No point in bothering no doctor. Nothing he can do.'

Maressa slapped the woman's face. 'You evil slut! Firkin won't die. With careful tending he always gets better. Get out of here before I have you whipped for your neglect!'

The day after her arrival, creditors began to call, and she was shocked to learn that no bills had been paid for nearly a year. So that they would continue to supply her she paid each of them something on account. Since she had brought little money from London, she was forced to sell several pieces of jewellery to ensure that they had ample wood, coal and food within the house. As if her problems were not great enough, a letter arrived from Henry. He was furious with her for leaving London. He had arranged a card party for the evening she had departed, and had expected her to be there to entertain his guests. His letter condemned her failings as a wife and held a warning that in future she must be more accommodating towards Lord Northcliffe. Several times

Northcliffe had suggested she become his mistress. How dare Henry suggest that she comply in order to settle his gambling debts? The letter ended in a torrent of curses. To punish her he ordered her to remain in Arundel until the spring. Also he demanded the return of the carriage and all the jewels he had given her since their marriage. The rough-looking messenger who had brought the letter was to convey the jewels to London. Her first instinct was to refuse. Her jewellery was small compensation for the nightly degradation to which Henry subjected her. But one glance at the messenger's brutish face told Maressa that he would not hesitate to use violence to carry out Henry's orders. When he had gone, taking the jewels with him, she flew into a temper and angrily consigned Henry's letter to the flames.

Life in Arundel was preferable to a winter in London, where she would be prey to both Henry's and Lord Northcliffe's demands. The loss of her jewels fuelled Maressa's hatred for her husband – one day he would pay for the way he abused their marriage vows.

With little money the winter would be hard, and she could not now afford to hire servants. Under Hazel's care, Firkin was regaining his strength and his coughing fits were less frequent. Already he could leave his bed for an hour or two each day, and Maressa was hopeful that by Christmas he would be strong again.

There was heartening news the following week. It was rumoured that Lord Hopton with his Royalist army had taken Petersfield and was advancing into Sussex. The Roundhead garrison in Arundel Castle was small. Sir William Waller had relied on the Sussex mud to protect him from the Royalists and was presently in London, negotiating the refit of his army with Parliament. The frost which had aided Maressa's journey from London was now assisting the Royalist advance from the west. The news was both exciting and disturbing. Arundel could shortly be under siege.

It was dusk when Molière and Angel sat back in their chairs, the revisions to the play complete.

'It will be our greatest triumph,' Molière pronounced. 'In three weeks, the Christmas revels commence. Time enough for us to rehearse. Our fortunes are assured.'

262

Angel saw the strain in the young actor's face and guessed that his troupe were deep in debt. 'I couldn't have done it without your help,' she said.

Her hand was taken and raised to Molière's lips. 'I've enjoyed every moment. You're an exceptional woman, Angel.'

There was reverence in his expression. A single candle burned on the table between them. Its amber flame was reflected in his eyes and the golden light sent a shiver of expectancy through her. She had become fond of Molière during their frequent meetings. His dark eyes, heavy-lidded and melancholic, reminded her of Rupert, and in his company her pulses often quickened when he looked at her a certain way. When he brushed a tendril of hair from her cheek neither one spoke. His eyes conveyed a silent declaration which made the breath catch in her throat. The space between them closed. His gaze focused upon her parted lips and then his mouth was warm and sweet on hers. Her fingers curled through his long hair and he raised her from her seat, holding her in a fierce embrace.

Angel's head rolled back as he kissed her neck. She gasped. Her heartbeat quickened as fiery tentacles unfurled through her veins, and a tremor of longing possessed her slender body. It was a shock to realise that she could respond so ardently to a man she did not even love. Easing back, she placed one hand against his chest and felt the rapid thudding of his heart.

'Don't deny me, Angel,' he whispered against her ear before his lips again took her mouth. His passionate kiss was intoxicating and for a moment sensuality overrode sanity. She returned his kiss with ardour and he gripped her waist lifting her on to the table. As his kiss deepened with passion he pushed his body between her knees, his hands scooping up skirts and moving over the bare flesh of her thigh.

'No!' Angel tore her mouth away from his lips. 'Jean-Baptiste, you go too fast.' She gripped his hand preventing him raising her skirts higher.

'I adore you.' He ignored her protest and kissed her again.

Her hand was on his shoulder to push him away when an outraged screech from behind them broke them apart.

'Do you see her wantonness?' Lucrèce screeched. 'This

creature has tricked my parents into taking her in. She shames us all.'

Angel turned to regard her cousin by the door and was appalled to discover two matrons with her, their expressions shocked and hostile.

Molière lifted Angel from the table, his tone angry. 'You wrong Mademoiselle Rowan.'

'Disgusting behaviour,' one matron sneered, her stout figure bristling. 'Shameful and lewd! What else can one expect from a woman who mixes with players?'

Her companion, equally fat, eyed them with haughty censure. 'Poor Sabine's trust has been betrayed.'

'No one has been betrayed,' Angel responded sharply.

'She's not even repentant.' The first woman's face was cruel as she vented her disgust. 'The brazen harlot! I'll not remain in this depraved house. Poor Sabine. I warned her no good would come of allowing players into her home.'

Angel kept her head high as the two women left the salon with a hiss of taffeta and silk. Lucrèce smiled malevolently at her cousin and left the room.

'*Mon dieu!*' Molière swore. 'That was Madame D'Oubray. The woman has the most vicious tongue in Paris. I fear, *ma chérie*, your reputation is ruined.'

Angel's eyes gleamed with a dangerous light. 'Damn their malicious spite. I doubt that shrivelled-up vine ever felt the sap of love in her loins. Let's look on the bright side – as an infamous actress I'll draw greater audiences to the play.'

She twisted her head away from him to hide the hurt behind her defiance. Gently Molière turned her back to face him. Holding her close, his expression became grave. 'Madame D'Oubray sees herself as a guardian of the city's morals. She'll make trouble. Since we're to work together, why not join my troupe and live with us?'

'And what of Madeleine Béjart?' Angel reminded him.

Molière dropped his gaze from hers.

'She is your mistress, then?'

'Madeleine has other lovers.' He tightened his hold around her, but Angel drew back with a shake of her head.

'This afternoon's passion was a delicious madness, born of affection and the spontaneity of the moment. Rivalry sparks too easily between players and lovers. I'd not be the cause of it. Love and work cannot mix, *mon ami*.'

'There speaks an ice-blooded Englishwoman. I thought you were different, but you are soulless and unromantic.'

'I am not,' she said with a grin. 'You speak as a Frenchman. I cannot love where the heart is not involved. And recently I loved too well.'

'He must have been mad to have abandoned you.'

She sighed, her voice growing sad. 'He had a war to win. Love was not what drove him. I left England before our feelings for each other could turn sour . . . It was a matter of pride.'

The regret in his eyes changed to admiration. 'Few women would be so wise. Although your lover put war and duty before your love, he'll never forget you.'

'I intended that he would not.' Her smile was mischievous.

During the next week, Angel became aware that women were crossing the street to avoid her. Upon encountering a group of them, they stared at her, their lips curling in disgust, their conversation hushed. Angel ignored them, walking past with her head held high. When she realised that few customers now visited the Toulons' shop, she went into the laboratory behind the shop, where François was busy over his glass containers, blending a perfume.

'You were always in here when you first arrived,' François chided gently. 'Since you befriended Molière I've seen little of you. I'm creating a new perfume. What do you think?'

Angel smelt the cloth dabbed with the perfume. 'Heavenly! Any woman wearing it will be a temptress to all men.'

François laughed. 'I'm delighted you like it. I've named it *Sultry Angel* in honour of you.'

She embraced him warmly. 'You make what I have to say more difficult. I love you and Aunt Sabine dearly, but I've decided to live with the players.'

'Your aunt will be upset.'

'Scandal about me spreads, and it's harming your business.'

'I've heard this scandal and disputed it.' François Toulon signalled to his assistant to take over, and led her out into the garden.

'The play opens in a week,' she said, kissing his cheek.

'I've been happy here, but if I'm to become an actress, I must live with the players.'

'But you will stay in touch,' François insisted. 'You're like a daughter to Sabine and me.'

Angel nodded, but knew that she must leave. Lucrèce's jealousy was beginning to distress her parents.

A thunderous banging on the front door jolted Maressa awake. Her heart thudded against her breastbone. It was pitch dark. Who would rouse the house so loudly at this hour? No one with good intent. The insistent knocking was impossible to ignore. Perhaps it was Henry?

Pulling on her velvet nightrobe, she went to the window and opened it to look out. A frosty blast burned the breath in her throat. A man's muffled figure stood in the bright moonlight, his horse tied to the gatepost. He stood back from the door and looked up at her window.

'Thomas! What are you doing here?' Maressa said in astonishment.

'Let me in, Cousin. I'm freezing.'

'Take your horse round to the stable,' she ordered.

Shutting the window again, she turned to find Hazel at her bedroom door holding a lighted candle. Her face was pale with fear.

'Who is it, my lady? Not the watch come to arrest you for debt? They came to my sister Meg once in the middle of the night. Only she knew how to pay to keep them sweet.'

'It's my cousin, Thomas.'

Maressa looked past Hazel as Firkin appeared in the doorway, a blanket wrapped over his nightgown. He was holding a pistol, and she felt a stab of pride that he wished to defend her.

'It's all right, Firkin. Go back to bed. It's Cousin Thomas. Though what he's doing in Arundel I've no idea.' She put a hand to her mouth in horror. 'You don't think it's news of Father or Alex? Let him in. There may have been a battle we know nothing about.'

They hurried to the kitchen. Hazel stoked up the fire and hung a kettle on the chain over the flames while Firkin, still clutching his pistol, unbolted the kitchen door. Thomas stamped in, beating his arms about his body to bring some

266

warmth to his limbs. His cocked hat was low over his face and he was swathed in a long black cloak. When he pulled off his leather gauntlet his fingers were blue with cold.

'Is it bad news which brings you here, Thomas?' Maressa asked.

He unwound the muffler from about his face and put his hands out to the warmth of the fire.

'It's not my father? Or Alex?' Maressa burst out, unable to contain her fear. 'They're not dead?'

'No, it's nothing like that. Just give me a chance to warm myself. Some mulled wine would help.'

Hazel poured wine into a goblet and sprinkled in some herbs. Taking the poker, she held it in the fire until it began to glow red, then she wiped it with a cloth and thrust it into the goblet. The wine sizzled, filling the room with the pungent smell of cloves and herbs. Thomas sipped it. As a more natural colour returned to his face, he removed his cloak and smiled at Maressa.

'Not much of a welcome for a man who's been riding for two days to see you.'

'I don't understand!' Maressa exclaimed.

He looked at her significantly and leaned forward so only she could hear. 'Would you have preferred Lord Northcliffe?'

At her horrified expression, he reassured her. 'I came to help you. Henry was at Nell Lovegood's last week. He's losing heavily to a degenerate crowd of gamesters. Not that I'm one to moralise, but we are kin. And we did have a rendezvous in the Spring Gardens which you didn't keep. I was concerned. I saw Henry paying off a debt to Northcliffe with the necklace you wore at your son's baptism. Later when he was in his cups he cursed you, saying he'd banished you to the country to teach you a lesson in gratitude. I wanted to reassure myself that you were safe.'

'I came to Arundel because Firkin was ill.' Her brother was watching Thomas suspiciously, and shivering beneath the blanket. 'Firkin, you should be in bed. Hazel will bring you up some mulled wine. You can speak with Thomas in the morning.'

'No. I want to hear what Tom has to say,' he said stiffly. 'Stop treating me like a child.'

Thomas grinned across at the boy. 'Do as your sister says.

I'll see you tomorrow.' He nodded at the pistol and winked his approval. 'You can show me how good you are with that.'

Firkin remained antagonistic. 'It is not right that you visit my sister in the middle of the night.'

Maressa stared at her brother in astonishment. She was about to protest when Thomas, instead of taking offence, turned to Firkin with understanding. 'Don't mistake my intentions, lad. I hold Maressa in the greatest regard. With Llewelyn and Alexander in Oxford I feared that Sir Henry was unjustly punishing her. I thought you were away at school.'

'I can protect my family.' Firkin remained stubborn.

'I can see that. But there's nothing to fear from me. And you do look ill. Why not do as Maressa says and return to your bed?' He picked up his muffler and gauntlets. 'I'll take a room at an inn for the night.'

'I'll not hear of it, Thomas,' Maressa interceded. 'Our family has never refused hospitality to our kin.'

Hazel put an arm around Firkin's shoulders. 'Back to bed with you. I'll bring up that mulled wine before I make up the spare bed in your room.' She looked back at Thomas. 'Mr Angel, you don't object to sharing with Firkin? I could make up the bed in the green chamber, but there's no fire lit.'

'I'm happy to share with Firkin.'

When Hazel and Firkin left the kitchen, Thomas came to Maressa's side. 'Have you no kiss for the weary traveller?'

She stepped back, her hand clutching the edges of her robe together. 'Thomas, behave yourself.'

'That's a bitter greeting,' he said sharply.

He caught her arms and pulled her to him. When she began to struggle his expression hardened. 'Damn it, Maressa. All I want is a kiss. Is that too much to expect after I've ridden so far on your behalf?'

She held herself stiffly, straining away from him. 'Perhaps you had better leave, Thomas. My reputation . . .'

'Is that all you care about? I'm your cousin. You've a maid and brother as chaperon. Did you know that Hopton's only a day's march from Arundel? Do you want to face a siege unprotected? There could be half a dozen rough soldiers billeted here tomorrow.'

Her hand went to her throat. 'You're trying to frighten me.'

He shook his head. The candle burning on the table cast a mellow light around him. 'Don't you know I care for you, Maressa?' His gaze was tender. After the angry words Henry had written reviling her, she was warmed by his admiration. She stopped struggling but remained tense in his hold.

'Henry does not deserve you for a wife,' Thomas said huskily. He stroked her hair, but made no further move to kiss her.

Though still suspicious of his motives, she began to relax. If Hopton's troops were to be billeted in the town, would she be safe within her own house? How much better if Thomas were here to protect her! He was smiling at her in a roguish fashion which, despite her reserve, she found appealing.

Thomas said, 'I admit my motives were less than honourable when I learned that Henry would not be here this winter. I want you, Maressa. But I'll not force you. At least let me stay until we know what Hopton's forces are planning.'

'You'll respect my wishes and not force your attentions upon me?'

'You drive a cruel bargain.'

The ease with which he agreed did not deceive her. He would be more difficult than most of her admirers to keep at bay, but she believed him when he said he would not force her. Seduction was his ploy and in that she suspected he was an expert. She must be careful.

The evening before the play was to open, Angel entered the inn where she lived with the members of the L'Illustre-Théâtre. The players were huddled miserably around a table in the back parlour. Molière was not with them.

'What's wrong?'

Robin Flowerdew rose stiffly from his stool. 'It's Molière. He's been arrested for debt. The theatre is closed.'

'Can't the money be raised to pay his debt?' Angel asked.

Madeleine Béjart rose from her seat and, with hands on hips, tossed back her red hair and sauntered towards Angel. 'Our money is gone. Molière has neglected his duties. Had he spent more time these last weeks drumming up custom for our present plays, instead of escorting you to his poet friends, he might have escaped imprisonment. You're not welcome here, Mademoiselle Rowan, and neither are your plays.'

Angel ignored the actress. Madeleine resented the attention Molière showed to her. The atmosphere in the room was tense with suspicion, and the other players regarded Angel with equal animosity.

'How much does Molière owe?' Angel asked Robin.

'A few hundred livres,' Robin answered. 'It's not the first time he's been imprisoned for debt, and I doubt it will be the last.'

'I will pay it. I owe him that much for all the help he has given me. But for that I would become a sharer in the company.'

'No!' Madeleine threw herself at Angel, her hands clawing at her hair.

Angel side-stepped and, flicking up her skirts, drew the dagger from where it was strapped to her thigh. The weapon extended, she threatened the actress. 'I will not brawl like a strumpet. Molière is my friend. Do you hate me so much that you would prefer he rotted in prison, rather than accept my offer?'

Joseph Béjart pulled his sister away. 'She's right.'

Furious, Madeleine rounded on him. 'Would you see me displaced? She'll give the orders. She'll insist her plays are performed.'

'The plays are good,' Joseph reasoned. 'Do you want to be poor all your life? Or do you think to be rescued by one of your wealthy lovers?'

Madeleine slapped her brother's face. He returned the blow, sending her staggering back. As Madeleine held her cheek which was fast turning scarlet, he snarled, 'We can't afford for Molière to be shut in prison. He's our friend. I say let Angel become a sharer.'

'You'd act against your own sister?' Madeleine raged. Her eyes were wild as she stormed towards the door. 'Then I will leave the troupe.'

Angel lowered her dagger and stepped in front of the door to prevent Madeleine leaving. 'You're our most talented actress,' she soothed. 'Please do not leave because of this. I've an idea for a new play and the lead is perfect for you.

You're too talented to resent my presence here. I can write the lines which will make all Paris worship at your feet. Would you break up the troupe? We all need you. Molière needs you.'

Madeleine stopped pouting and eyed Angel more benevolently, but her tone remained suspicious. 'You don't want to steal the lead from me?'

'No, but I would learn from you. I enjoy acting, but my greatest pleasure comes from writing plays. We're not rivals, Madeleine.'

The French girl nodded grudgingly. 'Then go rescue that worthless rascal Molière with your money. And this new play had better be all you promise, or you will have to answer to me.'

Molière was swiftly released, and in the next few weeks new premises were found for L'Illustre-Théâtre, in a converted tennis court called the Croix-Noire. Life with the players was always volatile, but gradually they accepted Angel amongst them. In repayment, she began to adapt the play she had started writing in Oxford – *The Adventuress* – taking care that Madeleine Béjart had the wittiest lines.

'Still writing?' Robin Flowerdew addressed Angel as he entered the deserted parlour of the inn. The other players had gone out to celebrate the success of the opening performance of *The Widow Went a-Wooing*.

'Jean-Baptiste wants *The Adventuress* completed so that we can begin rehearsals next week.'

'You'll ruin your eyes working so late into the night,' Robin said. 'I'd hate to see you lose your sight as Esmond Angel did.'

'My eyes are strong, and a new play will keep the creditors away.'

Robin rubbed a hand across his grey beard. 'I'm not so sure Paris can support another theatre. The Hôtel de Bourgogne has a loyal following and the Théâtre du Marais is also very popular. Our audiences remain small. Molière is beginning to talk of touring the provinces. I'm too old for that.'

'I'm not sure I'd relish such hardship either,' Angel replied truthfully. 'Let us hope that Paris can support three playhouses.'

Chapter Eleven

Within days of Thomas Angel's arrival at Arundel in early December, Sir Ralph Hopton's Royalist forces attacked the town. Their advance was aided by the morning mist which covered the surrounding hills and dulled the sounds of their approach. Parliament troops retreated into the Castle. Their leader, Sir William Waller, was still in London. Hopton had seized his opportunity to make his winter headquarters at Arundel, in preparation for an assault on London in the spring. Three days later the garrison surrendered to Hopton and Royalist rule.

Maressa was delighted. Three Cavalier officers had been billeted in her house. At first, they had been surly on learning that she was married to a Parliamentarian. Only Thomas' presence had saved the house from being looted. He had declared himself for the King, explaining that Maressa was his cousin, and that her father and brother were in Oxford. Maressa told the officers that she was estranged from her husband because of his allegiance to Parliament. They believed the story and Maressa and her property remained unmolested.

However, Thomas resented the Cavaliers' presence. He confronted Maressa one morning as she came out of her bedchamber. He stood legs planted apart, preventing her from passing. His flaxen hair heightened the angry colour in his cheeks. Seeing his bloodshot eyes, Maressa was disapproving.

'You look awful, Thomas. If you retired earlier and lived soberly—'

'By the bowels of Christ!' he cut in. 'You've an unsympathetic tongue, woman. Have you no idea why I was drinking until three this morning with those officers here?'

'Kindly moderate your language in my house.' She made to move past him, but his arm shot out, and he pushed her against the wood panelling of the hallway.

'Don't take that tone with me,' he raged. 'Do you know what a temptation you are? Especially when you flirt with those officers. They've laid wagers on which one will be the first to win your favours!'

'How dare they!' Maressa whitened with indignation. 'The base knaves. I've not encouraged any of them, just been polite.'

Thomas stared at her incredulously. 'You're so naïve! You flirt outrageously with them. It's a dangerous game. Why do you think they stay here every evening, instead of joining their fellow officers in a tavern?'

'Men have always sought my company,' she answered pertly. 'Before I married Henry I had a host of suitors clamouring for my hand.'

'Good God, woman!' His voice rose to a bellow and Maressa became alarmed. She was alone in the house. Hazel was buying food in the market and Firkin had recovered sufficiently to take a short morning ride. 'It's not your hand they want! It's to get between your sheets. You're a beautiful woman who's announced that she's estranged from her husband. They see you as ripe game. Confound you, Maressa! You must be the ultimate tease. Don't you realise they expect you to take at least one of them as your lover?'

Maressa was shocked. 'But they're always so courteous.'

'Because I take care that I'm always in the room with you. I know what a torment you can be to a man.'

'That's not fair, Thomas. I told you I'll not dishonour my marriage vows. I didn't ask you to come to Arundel.'

Snatching his hat from a peg on the wall, he marched towards the door. 'Perhaps I should return to London and leave you to enjoy your admirers?'

'No!' She was distraught, realising that Thomas was her greatest protection. 'I don't mean to be a tease. Not to you. I do need you here. But . . .'

'There can be no buts.' His stare was cold and uncompromising. 'I'm not cut out to be a monk. I've been patient long enough.'

'You'd leave me at their mercy?' she cried.

'Firkin knows how to use a pistol and he's stronger now.

If you're worried, move in with a neighbour.'

'And leave my house to be ransacked and despoiled!'

He raised his fist and for a moment she thought he was going to strike her. Then it slammed down on to a table, sending a large porcelain bowl filled with dried scented flowers crashing to the floor. 'Which do you care for most? Your virtue or your damned possessions?'

'That's unjust,' she blazed back at him.

To her consternation, Thomas threw back his head and laughed harshly. 'There's more Angel blood in you than I gave you credit for. But you're a hypocrite – and don't flutter those innocent eyes at me. You use men. God, you'd be happy to make eunuchs of us all!'

Her head came up. She was scared that Thomas meant to abandon her. 'I do like men. And I like you more than any other man. But I can't stand to be mauled, or subjected to their disgusting habits in the bedchamber.' Tears flowed from her eyes as she held Thomas's astonished stare. 'I'm frightened, Thomas. What will I do if you leave me?'

He took her into his arms, and let out a sharp rush of breath against her hair. 'Mortimer has a lot to answer for. The love between a man and woman should be a joyous experience for them both. My poor darling, let me show you that the touch of a man can be wonderful.'

She tensed. 'You want what they all want. Your tricks and threats are more subtle than Henry's, that's all. I'd not expect a man who runs a brothel to understand why I hold morality and respectability so high.'

'Then tell me.' His voice had a dangerous edge but he no longer frightened her. From Henry she had learned how to manipulate men and how to play for time. Coyness would not work with Thomas. He respected defiance.

'I've spent years trying to live down my Angel blood. The matrons of the town respect me as they never respected Gabriellen. They look to me as an example to their wayward daughters.'

'Fine sentiments!' Thomas scoffed. 'And all false. If that Angel blood of yours could win you acclaim you'd flaunt it to the heavens. I know you better than you think, Maressa. You believe piety is the way to win popularity. You're wrong. And one day I'll prove it.'

She lifted her hand to slap the insolence from his face. It

was caught and twisted behind her back, and the pain as he jerked her body against him made her gasp. When his mouth closed over hers, she was surprised at the tenderness of his kiss. Warm and firm, his lips moved persuasively. She did not respond – neither did she resist. There was reverence as well as desire in that passionate demand. The reverence quickened her heartbeat.

'Dear heart, say you'll be mine.' His voice was thick with ardour. 'And anything you wish for will be yours.'

He was again under her spell and the sense of power exhilarated her.

The front door banged shut and there was a jingle of spurs on the wooden floors. One of the officers had returned, and Firkin was with him talking excitedly.

Releasing her, Thomas stepped back, his voice taunting. 'You deny yourself, if you deny your Angel blood.'

Firkin limped into the room, his face flushed with excitement. 'Lieutenant-Colonel Elliot says I can be his cornet!'

Maressa looked over her brother's head to the sandy-haired officer who lodged with them. He was in his late twenties, with a ruddy, kindly face, bulbous eyes and yellowing, protruding teeth. Of the three officers in the house, he was the most amiable, and he regarded Firkin's eagerness to fight with a brotherly interest.

Elliot refused to hold Maressa's angry glare. 'The lad will give me no rest. I had to agree. You shouldn't mother the boy so, Lady Mortimer. He's fifteen, though a mite small for his age.'

'He's just turned thirteen,' Maressa corrected sharply.

Firkin looked at Thomas for support. To Maressa's dismay her cousin winked at him.

'You cosset the boy,' he said. 'Thirteen is a man, not a child.'

She knew he was paying her back for not submitting to his advances and was disquietened. Thomas was a dangerous man to thwart.

'I suppose so.' She stifled her misgivings and put a hand on her brother's frail shoulder. 'I'm proud of you, as Father and Alexander will be. At least they're not afeared to fight for the King.' She glared at Thomas condemning him for his neutrality.

Lieutenant-Colonel Elliot followed her gaze, but Thomas returned the accusing stare with bland insolence. He pushed his hat hard on his head and whistling a bawdy ditty sauntered from the house.

The next week was the most exciting of Firkin's life. He rode the Rowan mare, Red Dawn, given to him by his grandfather, and not only was he a cornet, but Lieutenant-Colonel Elliot trusted him to carry orders to other commanders. He rode from the castle to the outlying entrenchments which Hopton was reinforcing, proud of his new status. Hopton had left two hundred men to garrison Arundel whilst he marched to defend Winchester.

Though Firkin's legs were often raw from a day in the saddle, he never complained; for the first time in his life he was away from the fussing of women. Last night Thomas had taken him to a room behind an inn and paid Betsy, a young doxy, to initiate him into the pleasures of the flesh. An hour later, Firkin had emerged, red-faced, but glowing with a new worldliness. At last childhood was behind him.

All the excitement brought a return of his coughing. He hid away his bloodied linen and took from the kitchen a bottle of the medicine which Hazel always gave him. It eased the cough and gave him the strength to continue. Eventually the cough would take its toll on his health, he knew, but he refused to dwell upon the consequences. He had dreamed of this moment. At last he was a Cavalier; his cornet and pistol served his King.

The Royalists' euphoria at the capture of Arundel was soon doused. Within days, Royalist refugees began to arrive from Petworth. The Parliament army was on the march, recapturing garrisons which the Royalists had recently taken. On the 19th December Firkin was on the outer bank of the entrenchments when his sharp ears caught an odd muffled sound. The morning mist lingered in the air, distorting vision and hearing.

'Stop digging!' he shouted above the noise of shovels thwacking against frozen earth.

Several soldiers jeered, but needing little excuse to cease their toil, they rested on their shovels. Firkin stood up in the stirrups, his eyes straining into the grey mist. The noise was clearer now. It was the distant rumble of wheels and stamp of marching feet.

'There's an army out there,' he warned, and raking his feet along the side of Red Dawn, galloped over the uneven ground to the officer on duty. 'Soldiers! I can hear soldiers!'

The officer's face hardened. 'Good lad. Back to the castle and report this to Colonel Ford. It must be Waller's men.'

Firkin guided Red Dawn through the press of soldiery, his heart nearly bursting at the thought of action. At last he would get his chance to fight. The alarm was raised, and as soon as his duties were over, he went to his sister's house to warn her of a possible attack.

He walked straight into an argument between Maressa and Thomas. He had never seen his sister so furious, nor heard her voice sound so shrewish.

'You can't desert me!' She jabbed a finger accusingly at their cousin. 'You've sat on the fence this long, why fight now? I've heard Waller has six thousand men. That's six times the number of Royalists.'

'All the more reason for me to add to their number,' Thomas said curtly. The coldness in his eyes and set to his mouth would have done justice to an executioner. As Firkin watched, Thomas gripped Maressa's shoulders. 'I won't be governed by a woman. No matter what I feel for her.'

'You're cruel and heartless.' Maressa began to cry. 'You'd abandon me. Leave me to the mercy of Waller's men!'

'Why should they harm you?' Thomas fumed. 'You're Lady Mortimer. Your husband is a Member of Parliament.'

'A woman alone is never safe.'

Maressa began to strike Thomas's chest with her fists and, to Firkin's surprise, his cousin did not try and restrain her. When at last Maressa tired, he gently took her hands and looked down into her tearful face.

'Whoever is billeted here, you will charm them to your will.' He lifted a brow in tender mockery. 'And if they get unruly, I'm sure Hazel can slip something into their wine to stop them becoming troublesome. You're a survivor, Maressa. That's what I like about you.'

Maressa held herself stiffly away from him, her voice cold. 'If you leave me now, I never want to see you again.'

'Don't threaten me.' Thomas put his arms around her and kissed her, but Maressa stood rigid in his embrace.

Firkin limped forward. Thomas was his hero, but he could

not stand by and see his sister so used. 'Cousin, you overstep your welcome here.'

Thomas released Maressa and faced the boy. There was a smile on his lips, but no mockery in his expression. 'Look after your sister. I'm off to report to Colonel Ford.' He turned to Maressa. 'Don't let anger make you turn your back on me. There may be a time when you'll need my help.'

'I need it now,' she pouted, her face sullen.

'You're in no danger here. You can always take refuge in the church.'

The next morning the house was deserted except for Hazel. The three officers, Thomas and Firkin had all left after an urgent summons from the castle. There was sporadic musket fire from Waller's snipers, the sound echoing around the encircling hills. Maressa was angry with both Thomas and her brother, but that anger was overlaid by her concern. Neither of them had eaten any breakfast, and she had heard that provisions were low within the castle. The day was bitterly cold and it was not right for a man to fight on an empty stomach. Putting some ham, fresh bread, and cheese in a basket, she left the house. Already the street was crowded with townspeople carrying their most precious possessions, their faces drawn with fear. They were either fleeing into the country, or taking refuge in the Church of St Nicholas. As she climbed the hill towards the main entrance of the castle, she was forced to flatten herself against its battlement wall as a troop of pikemen marched out to the entrenchments. At the drawbridge a sentry stopped her.

'I've brought food for my brother and cousin. Here, sir, take some bread and a slice of ham for yourself.' It was snatched from her hands and with a jerk of his head he allowed her to pass into the castle precincts.

'I'm looking for Cornet Rowan,' she repeatedly asked.

No one had seen him. A woman with straggling red hair and a round, smallpox-raddled face waved to her. 'He the young lad with the twisted foot? He's in the old keep.'

Maressa thanked the woman and climbed the stone steps on to the parapet, which led to the oldest part of the castle built on a high earth mound. She passed several women, also carrying food and ale to the soldiers on duty on the walls. The bawdy jests directed by the women at the soldiers brought a blush to Maressa's cheeks. With a prim gesture she drew her cloak tighter about her figure and lifted her head higher. Many of the soldiers sprawled on the ground, some playing at dice, two fighting over a whore. They were unruly and undisciplined. She was shocked that some were already the worse for drink, and that others were red-eyed, their faces grey from the excesses of the previous night. One musketeer doubled over and vomited in front of her, and she quickly flicked her skirts away from the splattering bile. Another man stumbled to his position, tripping over the cumbersome pronged musket-rest and dropping his five-foot long weapon.

'Can't the officers control them?' she asked Firkin with disgust when she found him on the parapet.

He turned from studying the plain below. Taking a piece of cheese and biting into a thick crust of bread, he swallowed before replying. 'They're just letting off steam before the battle.'

His apparent worldliness was another shock for Maressa. He had changed in the last days and there was a new confidence about his manner.

'You will take care, won't you? I mean, if there's a lot of shooting?'

The look of derision he gave her reminded her so much of Alexander that her heart contracted. 'It's time I stopped hiding behind your skirts, Maressa,' he said. 'Go back to the house, or take shelter somewhere. It won't be long before the shooting starts in earnest.'

A wave of fear engulfed her. She looked out across the plain. The mist was beginning to thin and she was horrified to see the mass of Waller's army camped below. Even from this distance the line of cannon trained on the ramparts looked vicious. The coloured banners of the different regiments flapped idly in the light breeze. There was a great deal of activity within the camp. Distant, shouted orders were unintelligible, but loaded with menace. The army was spread out in the green valley like a huge spider, waiting to seize and devour its prey.

A cry went up from inside the castle and a trumpet blasted. There was a cheer from the battlements as a troop of cavalry rode out. To her alarm, Maressa saw Thomas in their midst. A contingent rode out from behind Waller's guns to meet them. Then the two companies merged, swirling together as they fought in close combat. As valiantly as the Royalists fought, they were slowly beaten back towards the castle.

Firkin grabbed Maressa's arm and began pushing her towards the parapet steps. 'Get out of the castle while you can. If the Roundheads take the town you'll be safe as Mortimer's wife.'

'But what about you?'

Firkin looked suddenly much older than his years. 'My place is here.' His outburst started him coughing and his frail figure hunched over.

'Come with me, Firkin. You're in no state to fight.'

His green eyes were haggard as they turned upon her. 'Better to die like a man, than rot away in my bed without having lived.'

Tears scalded her eyes, and she blinked them aside. Firkin would despise her pity. The over-brightness in his eyes told her that he was fighting against his illness, and she did not know how he found the strength to keep going. Hazel had warned her that Firkin's last attack had been so severe that his lungs were permanently damaged. The look in his eyes forbade her to speak of his disease. She did not agree with his actions, but she was proud of him.

'God be with you, Firkin,' she said affectionately, and left him.

The Royalists were beaten back through the first gate. If she did not hurry she would never get through the postern gate before the castle was sealed against the Roundheads.

The ear-splitting crackle of gunfire accompanied her flight. Officers yelled orders which were lost amongst the great boom and crash of cannon fire. A man fell off the parapet into her path. His dead body was twisted by the fall, his chest a gaping hole of bloody tissue. Swallowing against her rising nausea, Maressa ran on. A cannonball whistled overhead. When it gouged into a tower, she was splattered by falling flintstones.

The postern gate was barred, and it took the last of her money to bribe the sentry to let her through. Outside, the town was in chaos. Clouds of cannon-smoke drifted across the streets. Its acrid stench clawed at her throat and lungs. A black-frocked preacher strode through the smoke. His cropped grey hair greasy and his eyes wild as he raised his Bible to the sky.

'Repent thy sins,' he shouted. 'The Lord is with our government. Repent!'

The sight of him filled Maressa with rage. Because of such men, her grandparents and uncle were dead, her family was scattered and constantly in danger, and she was forced to live under the shadow of enemy fire.

'Stupid old fool!' she screamed in his face.

Startled, he backed away. Then he saw her saffron gown. 'Repent, my child. Vanity is sin. Wickedness abounds. The Day of Judgement is upon us. Right is on the side of the godly.'

Decorum deserted Maressa. The Angel temper so rigorously suppressed erupted in all its fury. 'Bigot!' she screamed. She shoved him in the chest and he fell, sprawling in the muddy gutter. Maressa bent over him, waving a fist in his ashen face. 'What would you know of godliness, you sanctimonious bigot? All you bring is death and destruction to our country. It's the devil's words you speak, not God's.'

Sixteen days later the Royalists within Arundel Castle were still being battered by enemy guns. Firkin was weak from continual coughing and leant against a turret wall on the battlements. His face was blackened by powder from his musket. Pistols were useless at firing at the enemy from this range and he was still awkward and slow in reloading the unwieldly weapon. Across his chest hung a bandolier with its twelve leather cartridges of powder known as the apostles. There was a pouch at his waist which held wadding and bullets, and a flask of powder to be used when priming the firing pan. If all these accoutrements were not fiddly enough to cope with, there was the long musket-rest which seemed determined to trip his shuffling gait at every step. The most troublesome piece was the match-cord, which was put across the firing pan to ignite the powder. This had to be kept lit at all times and, to avoid scorching his clothes, or inadvertently igniting his powder, had to be carried in his hand.

Firkin cursed his ill luck in being on duty in the rain. There was no use in complaining. Each day reinforcements arrived to swell Waller's army which now numbered ten thousand. None arrived to help the Royalists, and their numbers had dwindled from casualties and daily desertions. Many of the townspeople had gone over to the enemy when the town was taken. Those who were loyal had taken refuge in St Nicholas' Church, where they had been smoked out until they surrendered. The small Royalist stronghold was doomed. The man sent to summon Royalist aid had been caught and hanged from the bridge over the river, in full sight of the garrison.

He closed his eyes and sighed, huddling closer to the turret wall for protection against the fierce wind. In the last days the weather had broken. There was no satisfaction in knowing that the besieging army camped in the meadows suffered more from the weather than those within the castle. The rain increased and he pulled his hat down over his face. It was a problem to keep the match-cord soaked in saltpetre dry in this weather. Without the match-cord his musket was useless. He shifted his weight on his crippled foot and tried to ignore the stabbing pains in his diseased lungs. Somehow in the last two days he had drawn upon reserves of strength he did not know he possessed. That was the action of a man. A child would have given in to his weakness and taken to his bed.

A firm hand on Firkin's shoulder jerked his eyes open. Thomas was looking at him with concern.

'You shouldn't be out in this rain with that cough,' he said.

'I'll take my turn of duty the same as everyone else.'

'You know we can't hold out much longer,' Thomas said, staring out at the bivouac fires of Waller's army. 'The water's all gone since those bastards turned the course of the stream feeding the main well. Now the other well is fouled. A dead ox was found in its stream. The men weakened by thirst are deserting in droves and being taken prisoner. That's not for me. I'm going over the wall tonight and taking a boat up the river. No one's been caught yet.'

'You'd desert the King's cause?' Firkin's faith in Thomas was shaken.

'I'm no use to him as a prisoner. Are you coming with me?'

Firkin slapped his crippled leg. 'This would be the death of us both. I can't run and I won't slow you down.'

There was a volley of fire from the two small field guns which Waller had mounted in the tower of St Nicholas' Church.

A musketeer shouted, 'Take cover! Those bastards are—' His words were cut off. The glow from his match-cord had made him an easy target in the gathering gloom. Decapitated by a cannonball the musketeer fell to the ground, blood spurting from his severed neck. There was another explosion further along the line of soldiers and a burst of yellow flame showed the stark silhouette of a musketeer, as he fell screaming to his knees. Emrys looked away. He had seen that happen before. In a careless moment the man had put his lighted match-cord into the powder pouch at his side, blowing off his own hand.

'When are you going over the wall?' Firkin asked, his voice cracked with anguish at the horrors he had seen.

'As soon as it's dark.'

Firkin nodded. 'I'll come to the riverside wall with you and cover your descent.'

A half hour later Firkin pulled back the rope which Thomas had used to climb down the castle walls. There was no moon, but Thomas had paid handsomely for a fisherman to have an oxhide boat waiting to take him along the river. As Firkin pulled the rope back over the crenellated wall he leaned against a round tower. He could just faintly hear the splash of oars in the water. Thomas was on his way to freedom.

Even though it was dark, the cannon-fire from Waller's army had not stopped. They had their range and they were systematically destroying the castle walls. The pain in Firkin's chest stabbed cruelly and he had trouble getting his breath. He hated the thought of surrender. Colonel Ford and his counsellors were even now discussing the possibility in a meeting.

No surrender! His mind screamed rebellion. The siege had not been the glorious battle he had hoped for, but he had proved his courage. He had seen several Roundheads shot down by his own hand and, in his way, he had avenged his grandparents' death. His crippled leg ached from the cold and he leaned against the tower. He coughed again, and before he could lift his linen to his mouth, blood sprayed his hand and dotted the flagstones of the parapet. When the spasm passed Firkin straightened. He knew he was dying. The pain returned like an iron hook, tearing and ripping into his lungs. To master it, he forced himself to think about Betsy. Three times he had visited the prostitute at the inn. She had shown him that a cripple could still be a man. He relived the heady pleasure of his passion and for a few moments forgot his raging thirst and the pain in his lungs and leg.

No surrender, he repeated to himself. If he was to die, let him die avenging the wrongs to his King and the deaths of his grandparents. Dimly, his tired mind registered the whine of approaching cannonballs. There was a terrific crash overhead. The stonework beneath his feet shifted and the wall of the tower shuddered against his back. An ominous tearing and cracking filled his ears. He spun round awkwardly, hampered by his twisted foot, and took the first step to hobble away. A shower of stones pelted down on his shoulder.

'No surrender!' he shouted above the rumble of falling masonry. Then his brain exploded into fire as the crumbling turret crushed him. He was dead before his body was buried under the rubble.

The winter of 1643 was a bitter one for Angel. It was obvious that the L'Illustre-Théâtre was failing. Their two greatest successes were Gabriellen's play with Angel's revisions, *A Widow Went a-Wooing* and her own play, *The Adventuress*, but still they could not win the audiences from the two established playhouses in Paris. When it became obvious that Molière was infatuated with Angel, the Béjart sisters refused to act in the two plays. They were backed by de Luc and Fortemaine. Angel was livid; Molière was not her lover. Since it was a rule of their company that any play performed must be voted for by the sharers, her plays were dropped from the repertoire. Angel controlled her disappointment. She had already begun work on a third play about an aging miser who falls hopelessly in love with a courtesan. Molière had promised that it would be staged in the spring.

The Béjart sisters were a constant barb in Angel's side. They were jealous of her friendship with Molière, fearing that she would oust them from the leading female roles, but

Angel was content with minor parts. For her, the greatest thrill came from her writing. In her enthusiasm, she would often extemporise during a performance, and the groundlings would go wild, cheering her wit and beauty.

After one such incident Angel returned to the inn to find Molière sitting pale and drawn in a corner, holding his head. Madeleine and Catherine Béjart were screaming at him.

'The English crow will not be happy until she steals all the applause,' Madeleine was storming.

'She makes fun of us,' Catherine wailed. 'My part was in shreds and only received titters after the last outburst from that bitch.'

'Ladies, please,' Molière groaned. 'Our takings are increasing. Angel has a natural talent. She does not seek to steal your popularity. She cannot help it when wit inspires her to speak.'

'You defend her because you want her in your bed.' Madeleine stamped her foot and began to hit Molière on the head.

He stood up, his handsome face dark with fury. 'Enough! Your jealousy is ill founded. I'm tired of this squabbling.'

Pushing the actress aside, he strode to the door. His expression did not change even when he came face to face with Angel. 'Women! I can understand why England forbids them the stage. All they do is cause trouble.' The door slammed behind him.

Angel turned to Madeleine. 'I didn't mean to outshine you. The words just came to me. The groundlings loved them. Surely, winning an audience is the most important thing.'

'You want all the glory,' Madeleine raged. 'Molière loves you.'

'He's not my lover. It is you he cares for, Madeleine.'

Madeleine's eyes glittered with venom. 'I don't want your cast-offs. I have lovers enough. Do you think it bothers me who Molière sleeps with? He can do it with a sheep for all I care! I'm sick of your virtue. Do you think yourself better than us? You tease and play with the audience but you give nothing of yourself. Why so pure? What are you waiting for? A prince to carry you off, like in a romantic play? There are no princes – just men with hot pricks. Molière knows how to cool his. He's with some whore now. If you gave in to him now and again, his temper would improve.'

Madeleine picked up a scarlet velvet cloak and wrapped it about herself. 'Molière and I have an understanding. He knows I can't resist a wealthy lover. His interest in you will soon pass once he's had you. Then perhaps this troupe can get back to how it was.' Madeleine swept past Angel, followed by her sister.

Joseph Béjart had been sitting in the corner, watching the scene with amusement. 'Pay them no mind, Angel. They're just jealous of your talent.'

Angel sat down at the table and stared at her clenched hands. 'All I want is to learn from the French stage. Their talent is much greater than mine. Why are they so jealous?'

Joseph grinned at her. 'Our audience adores you. The actresses are jealous. Perhaps they would accept you better if you took a lover,' he said with a laugh. 'They cannot abide someone setting them a good example.'

Angel smiled. 'I'll not take a lover to please anyone but myself.'

'Women. I shall never understand them.' Joseph sighed heavily. 'You adore Molière, why make him so miserable?'

'I do not love him. And he has other paramours.'

Joseph shrugged. 'It is not in a man's nature to be faithful. If you expect that you will never find happiness.'

'Neither will I settle for second best.'

Throughout the winter Angel regularly visited the poet Scarron, and often Marion de l'Orme was there. A friendship grew between the two women. Twice, Angel visited Marion's home, where the greatest wits of the day were encouraged. Angel was popular, but quickly realised that the men believed that all actresses were willing bedfellows. Her pride rebelled. She wanted freedom to love as she chose. For all her wish for independence, she was not naturally promiscuous. The men who pursued her were witty, handsome, but with reputations as libertines, which left her cold. Her aloofness, the novelty of an actress who was not available to a generous protector, spurred them to woo her with greater fervour. Cyrano de Bergerac, who was often in the tiring house where the players gathered after the performance, dubbed her 'the Crystal Angel'.

'Is Angel so transparent?' Molière chided him, displeased.

'To a seer, the crystal unlocks the secret of many mysteries.'

De Bergerac bowed to Angel. 'A mysterious woman is a potent aphrodisiac.'

'There you wrong me. I'm not at all mysterious.'

'Are you not?' he challenged. 'There's unhappiness in your past which you never speak of. You act the celibate, but a tender love poem will bring a mistiness to your eyes. On the stage you show a passion which cannot be feigned. I believe you have known an exceptional love.'

'You mock me,' she said sternly.

He held up his hands in reproof. 'Never. You play a Madonna but have the heart of Eve. Hold a cut crystal to the light and your eyes are dazzled by its radiance. Look into its heart and behold all the colours of the spectrum – from chill indigo through to a vibrant and passionate violet.'

There was a slow clapping from Madeleine Béjart. 'Fine sentiments, Cyrano. If I didn't know you better I'd think you enamoured.'

'Since I have known you better, and the pleasure cost me but a meal and a flagon of wine, that is nothing to your credit,' Cyrano sneered.

There was an outbreak of coarse laughter at Madeleine's expense. Hands on hips Madeleine regarded the gathering. Her red hair glowed fiery in the candlelight and her eyes flashed with a salacious gleam. She sauntered to Molière's chair and rubbed her breasts against his cheek. 'When was that, Cyrano?' Her voice oozed venom. 'Were your prick as agile as your sword, perhaps I would have remembered the occasion?'

Cyrano started forward, his eyes narrowing dangerously. Madeleine laughed softly, her stare malicious as it turned upon Angel.

'The gallants prowl round as though the bitch is on heat,' she sneered. 'My money is on the man who makes the highest offer.'

'Then your money is lost,' Angel countered. 'And I thank you not to judge me by your own standards.'

With a screech Madeleine flew at her, her fingers snatching at Angel's gown. Angel sidestepped and moved behind Cyrano, her fingers closing over his sword-hilt. 'I would borrow your sword, Monsieur,' she said, drawing it from its scabbard.

Angel swished the blade twice through the air in a dramatic gesture to test its flexibility and weight. 'Stay back, Madeleine. I'll not brawl on the floor for the amusement of men who would see us rip each other's clothes to shreds.' The sword and the dangerous light in Angel's eyes made the actress back off. 'You are wise,' Angel went on. 'I know how to use this weapon. In the service of my King I've felt its steel sink into a man's gizzards and rob him of life.' She swivelled slowly on her heel, keeping the sword poised, and regarded the men. She eyed them stonily. 'Messieurs, I am not a prize to be won, purchased, or conquered. If any of you think I am, answer to me now with your sword.'

The men looked away, and she returned the sword to Cyrano. He was grinning. 'You tempt me to put you to the test, just for the hell of it.'

'I'm no match for you, Cyrano – just ordinary men.'

Angel left the room. The incident had left her with a bitter taste in her mouth. She did not prize her virtue. There was a deep void in her life. There were nights when she dreamed of England and of the bliss to be found in a lover's arms. She would wake, her body throbbing with frustration. She had been attracted by several admirers, but their kisses had not stirred her heart, and sex without emotion was an impossibility for her. As the months had passed, Rupert's image had blurred in her memory. The mention of his name could still make her heart flutter, but she conquered her yearning. Gradually, her thoughts turned to her homeland. She missed her family and friends.

Easter in London was as bleak as Christmas had been in Arundel. When the Royalists surrendered in January, Maressa had wept to see the prisoners marched out of the town. As soon as the roads permitted it, Henry had sent the carriage to Arundel and ordered her return to London. The Puritan yoke constrained Maressa in a way she had not thought possible. Restless and discontented, she paced her bedchamber in the Strand house. She missed Thomas, but stubbornly refused to see him during the three weeks she had been back in London. Two days after her arrival a messenger had delivered a letter from him, asking her to meet him in the Spring Gardens. The scoundrel must have put a watch on Mortimer House to discover her return. Secretly, that pleased her. While she was relieved that Thomas had escaped imprisonment, she was still piqued by the way he had deserted her. Life had been intolerable when Waller's troops recaptured Arundel. The officer billeted in her house was a Bible-canting pompous prig – which had not stopped him trying to get into her bed. One of Hazel's potions had curbed his lust, and threats of Sir Henry Mortimer avenging his wife's honour in a duel had kept the officer at bay.

There had been no affection or forgiveness in Henry's greeting, and Maressa had the uncomfortable feeling that she had been brought back to London for a purpose. All her instincts told her it would be an unpleasant one.

On her arrival, Maressa had gone straight to the nursery to visit her son. Gila, the nursemaid, had changed out of recognition. The woman was wearing one of Maressa's gowns and her hair was curled beneath a lace cap. As Maressa paused in astonishment, she had given her mistress a sly, insolent smile. It was obvious that she had been Henry's whore during Maressa's absence, and Maressa immediately dismissed her. When she confronted her husband, he merely shrugged.

'You did right to dismiss the wench,' he said, as calmly as though he was discussing the weather. 'She was beginning to get above herself. Engage another nursemaid.'

Since then, Maressa had taken a closer look at all the servants. Two young maids who were pretty enough to catch Henry's eye were also dismissed. The replacements were not due to arrive until tomorrow. Hazel doted on Julian, now almost two, and was happy to tend him herself.

Maressa stopped pacing, got into bed and willed herself to sleep. However abhorrent Henry's motives proved, nothing he did could touch her as Firkin's death had done. Tears ran down her cheeks as her grief overwhelmed her. How many more of her family would this cursed war kill?

Outside in the street she heard the slow tread of the watchman and his plaintive cry announcing two of the clock. She turned over and thumped her feather pillow. From the parlour below drifted the sound of men's voices, their laughter high-spirited with drunkenness. Every night since her return

Henry had brought his gambling friends to the house. Amongst them was Lord Northcliffe, a gross barrel of a man with slack lips and sweaty palms who was always trying to paw at Maressa behind her husband's back. His reputation as a womaniser was the scandal of the city. From the way Henry had refused to meet her eye this week, it was obvious that he was heavily losing money they could ill afford.

She closed her eyes and prayed that Henry's luck would change. The sound of the latch on her door clicking open made her start upright. Through the gap in the bedhangings she saw Henry, and her stomach clenched in sudden alarm. Lord Northcliffe was with him. Both men carried lighted candles. The hairs at the nape of her neck prickled and with her heart thudding wildly, Maressa clutched the bedclothes to her chin, striving to keep her voice calm.

'Henry, what is the meaning of this intrusion?'

'Good. You are awake, my dear.' He placed the silver candlestick on a coffer by the door, but his manner was ill at ease. 'Northcliffe . . .' He cleared his throat, giving Maressa the chance to voice her anger.

'You graceless fop! Are you cup-shot, Henry? His Lordship has no business in my bedchamber.'

Henry gave a nervous laugh. 'You are wrong. At the moment, his Lordship has every right.' With brutal force, Henry jerked the covers from Maressa's hand, whipping them back from her figure. Fear stopped her heart. He meant to use her to pay off his debts.

'In the name of God . . . !' she cried out.

Her hair was a shining golden mass spilling over her shoulders to her waist, and her silk nightgown clung to the contours of her body. She could feel Northcliffe's eyes burning into her flesh. Her throat dried. Henry, looking smug, refused to meet her gaze. It was the smugness of his expression which finally brought her paralysed senses to life. She leapt from the bed and, snatching up her nightrobe from where it lay across the cover, pulled it around her.

'You said the lady would be willing,' Northcliffe said gruffly.

'She'll do as she's told,' Henry growled. His drunken laugh chilled Maressa. 'Come now, man. You don't expect a wife to act with shameful willingness when her husband is present! I'll leave you to enjoy her.'

'Henry!' Her voice was a shrill plea as he moved to the door.

He turned, smiling spitefully. 'Don't be coy, my dear. You sold yourself to me for a title. A night with Northcliffe will release me from my gambling debts.'

'Then take my jewels,' she gasped. 'Sell them! But, I pray you, Henry, spare me this!'

'What jewels? Those baubles are worthless. The real ones were sold and replaced with paste replicas months ago. You should be honoured, my dear. For your favours Northcliffe has waived one thousand pounds in debts.' The door was slammed shut behind him.

She could feel hysteria rising in her. Whilst her attention had been upon Henry, Lord Northcliffe had put his candle down on the bedside table. He now stood at the foot of the four-poster bed, barring her escape.

'Tonight the fairest woman in all London is mine!'

Through eyes wide with horror, she stared at his fat figure. He was still in his twenties, but debauchery and overindulgence in every vice and gratification had ravaged his face and bloated his body. His small eyes were almost hidden by folds of flesh. The thought of his swollen hands on her made her break out in a cold sweat.

'I'll not be bartered for like a whore.' She backed away until she was stopped by a tapestry-hung wall. 'Have you no chivalry, my lord?'

Northcliffe shrugged. 'Why should I concern myself with that, when your husband clearly had none?' He came towards her. 'Your protests are seemly, but misplaced. It will be better for you if you don't fight me. I've no wish to hurt you.'

Before she had time to retaliate, her waist was encircled in a flabby arm. She was twisted around and pushed towards the bed. As he forced her down on to the mattress she struck out at him, but his strength was immense. Her fists pounding his chest made no more impression than a leaf battered against a window pane in a storm. His weight crushed the breath from her lungs and stripped the power from her screams. It was like being pressed to death under torture.

His hands were merciless as they tore her robe and silk nightshift. When his mouth clamped down upon hers in a brutal kiss, she gagged; his breath was foul from his rotted teeth.

Frantically, she pushed her hands against his shoulders. It was disgusting to be kissed like this – humiliated and used as a strumpet. Shuddering with revulsion, and keeping her teeth clenched, she thrashed her head from side to side to avoid the bruising ravishment of her mouth. The silk shift was ripped to her waist and he cruelly kneaded her breasts.

'Stop fighting, damn you!' he spat, spraying her with his saliva.

A vicious pinch on her nipple made her cry out. The sound was stifled as he plunged his tongue between her teeth. Repellent as a striking snake, it thrust inside, filling her mouth. When his sweaty palm found her naked thigh, her body jerked rigid. Lord Northcliffe swore profanely in his frustration.

'The time for coyness is past. Stop being so stubborn and enjoy the pleasure I'm giving you.'

Pleasure! There was no pleasure in his loathsome mauling. The disillusion of her marriage was complete. She had dreamed of being a titled lady, accomplished, fêted and admired. Instead, she had been sold into whoredom. Maressa's mind and body rebelled against the vileness of all men. Tears streamed from her eyes, and her soul screamed against this violation.

'God damn you! Open your legs!' He struck her across the face and she tasted blood from her cut lip. 'When I say pleasure me, you will pleasure me. Or find yourself and your pathetic husband marched off to the Clink, to moulder in the Debtor's Ward. You'll fall on your back fast enough then to get the shackles removed from your pretty ankles and a bowl of greasy gruel inside your belly. Damn you, spread your legs!'

'You're hurting me,' she sobbed. He was outlined above her in the flickering candlelight, his heavy jowls quivering in his lust. A vision of the devil himself, bent upon defiling her.

A brutal tug on her pubic hair made her back arch from the pain, and he thrust a knee between her thighs, his fingers questing. His nails scraped against her tender dry flesh. Desperate to be free from the nightmare, Maressa pushed against his hips, but it was useless. Then her hand brushed against the dagger he wore at his waist.

Her mind cleared, clarity bringing with it the need for caution. She could not fight this fiend in a contest of strength and win. However repulsive his touch, she must lure him into a sense of false security. A man driven by the sexual urge was mindless to anything else but his own fulfilment. She forced herself to relax.

'That's it, my fair one. I said you'd enjoy it.'

He pulled her thighs apart and she sensed his perverse pleasure in her resistance as he pressed his mouth against her womanhood. She clenched her teeth to stop her cry of outrage when his tongue probed the sacred recess of her body. Inwardly, she was screaming. He moaned in anticipation as he pulled at the points lacing his breeches. She could feel his hard member pressing against her thigh. His breathing loud and laboured, he lifted his head and with a grunt of satisfaction positioned himself over her, his eyes screwed shut in an agony of lust.

Maressa snatched the dagger from its sheath, at the same time she twisted and slashed at his throat. His eyes bulged with shock. When a spurt of hot blood pumped from the wound over her breasts, something in her brain snapped. Withdrawing the blade, she plunged it a second, third and fourth time into his repulsive body, until her arm ached. The blade sank into his fat paunch like a knife slicing bacon, and with each strike her voice rose on a higher scream.

Suddenly the door was thrown wide and she saw Henry's horrified face. He turned Northcliffe over and the nobleman flopped back on to the pillows, his eyes sightless, blood trickling from his mouth.

'You stupid bitch!' Henry shouted, his face twisting with fear. He staggered back from Northcliffe's corpse. His eyes crazed with fury, he hit her across the mouth with such force that her head cracked back against the bedpost. Maressa screamed. Another punch slammed into her stomach whilst Henry yelled obscenities at her. Her head was reeling from the blows, her stomach felt on fire. When her hair was grabbed and her head yanked back, red hot nails hammered into her scalp and her eyes were blinded by tears of pain.

'Henry, stop! I didn't mean to kill him! He was so repulsive!' Even through her blurred vision she saw murder in Henry's eyes. He was going to kill her.

She wriggled away, but he dragged her back and she saw his fist raised to smash into her stomach. The blow never came. Henry's eyes started, huge as trenchers. His mouth gaped like a red open wound, then he fell sideways to the floor.

Hazel stood by the bed, holding the heavy silver candlestick. Its base was scarlet with blood. The two women stared at each other and with a sob Hazel dropped the candlestick on the floor.

'I've done for him, my lady. As you did for his Lordship. What're we to do? There'll be a hue and cry out for us now. We'll hang for sure.'

Maressa rolled to the edge of the mattress, fighting to control the shaking which gripped her body. She rose from the bed, her eyes darting wildly around the room. Her mind raced to find a solution. Apart from Peter, Henry's valet, Hazel was now the only servant who slept in the house. Thank God, the new servants did not arrive until the morning.

'Where's Peter?' she asked as she began to pull petticoats from a coffer.

'It's his night off. He visits a doxy at the Mermaid tavern.'

Maressa nodded in satisfaction. 'Good. Get dressed. Make sure Julian is wrapped up warmly. There's no time to pack more than a spare dress. We must be far away from here before all is discovered.'

'But the bodies, my lady? Surely suspicion will fall on you?'

'That will be dealt with. Do as I ask and be quick.'

Fifteen minutes later Maressa was dressed and had packed a small valise with a fresh gown and the few jewels given to her by her father. She needed money. She braced herself to look at Henry's prone figure, and with shaking fingers went through his pockets. They were empty. He had gambled his money away. She glanced at Northcliffe. Overcoming her disgust, she went through his pockets and discovered more than two hundred pounds.

When Hazel returned, she carried a valise. Julian nestled against her shoulder, sound asleep. Maressa was at the window, peering through the partially closed shutters down into the street. She stepped back out of sight as she saw a lantern appear at the street corner and heard the cry of the watchman.

'Wait for me by the garden door, Hazel.'

'What are you going to do, my lady?'

'Destroy the evidence.' Holding her valise in one hand and a flickering candle in the other, Maressa moved to the bedhangings with deliberate intent. As the flame whiplashed upwards she touched it to the opposite hanging, and then ignited a large tapestry on the wall. After dragging the coverlet from the bed, she placed it halfway down the stairs beneath another tapestry and set light to that. As the smoke collected in the house, she began to cough. The orange flames were spreading quickly, and black smoke was curling along the white plasterwork ceiling.

Satisfied that within minutes the entire house would be ablaze, she touched the candleflame to a final tapestry in the hall and, with a handkerchief pressed to her nose and mouth, ran through to the back of the house. Once outside she locked the door and threw the key into some shrubs. She paused long enough to pass Hazel a black silk mask and secure one in place for herself, then she led the way across the lawn to the alleyway which led down to the Thames. Five minutes later they were on the river steps.

'Boatman!' she called.

A man started from his doze and rowed his wherry towards them. They stepped aboard.

'To Blackfriars, man.'

'That's not a district a lady should be visiting at such an hour. It's the haunt of rogues and criminals.'

'Wot makes yer think I'm such a lady?' Maressa disguised her voice. ''Tis Nell Lovegood's I be wanting. I work fer Thomas Angel. Bin visitin' a fine gentry mort.'

'With a child in tow?' The boatman was disbelieving.

'The child is Flo's,' Maressa explained, indicating Hazel. 'Lucky I found her. Walking the streets she were – thrown out by her drunken sot of an 'usband. I don't reckon Thomas Angel will turn away a pretty piece the likes of 'er.'

'If it's Nell's yer be wanting yer can afford to pay double the price. Unless we can swap trade fer trade,' he chuckled in anticipation.

'Mr Angel don't take kindly to us giving us favours to jes' anyone. He 'as his reputation to consider. And he knows 'ow to guard that reputation . . . if yer get me meaning.'

'Aye, 'appen so,' the boatman grunted. 'I'd not like to cross 'im.'

Relieved that Thomas's name carried so much weight, Maressa decided to press her advantage. She had no idea where Nell Lovegood's establishment was, except that it was near Blackfriars. 'Yer'll get a silver shilling if'n yer take us ter Blackfriars and rouse us a linkboy to light our way.'

'Agreed!'

As the wherry pulled away, Maressa glanced back at the house. Just visible through the closed shutters of the upper windows was a yellow chink of light. By the time they reached the curve of the river at the Temple, there was an orange glow on the skyline.

When they stepped ashore at Blackfriars, Maressa was at once aware of shadows detaching themselves from the nearby buildings, and her nostrils were filled with the stench of unwashed flesh and rancid clothing. Two linkboys were hired by the boatman. The mention of Thomas Angel's name was enough to keep the rougher inhabitants of the district at bay.

Nell Lovegood's was an imposing four-storey red-brick building, and torchlights burned on each side of a portico door. Maressa's knock was answered by a giant of a man in scarlet and gold livery. He showed no surprise that two women should appear at the door in the early hours of the morning.

'Mr Thomas Angel is not available,' he said gruffly.

'I'll speak with my uncle Laurence Angel,' Maressa insisted.

'Mr Laurence Angel has retired for the night.'

'Even so, you will inform one of them that I am here.'

The haughty command prompted the footman to allow them to enter. It crossed Maressa's mind that she was in a den of depravity. But where else could she go?

From behind closed doors came the sound of women's laughter. The entrance hall was not what Maressa would have expected of a bordello and gaming house. It was panelled in light oak and lit by a row of double gilt candle-sconces. The floor was black and white marble, and plinths on each side of the main staircase held life-sized Italian marble statues of male nudes standing over subjugated naked women.

'Wait in here,' the footman said, opening a door at the back of the entrance hall. 'Mr Thomas Angel is entertaining a private party.'

The room was not what she expected either. It was dominated by a large walnut desk. A marble fireplace was set in one wall and above that hung a portrait of Esmond Angel, Maressa's great-grandfather. The room held many treasures. On one table was a huge silver-gilt salt cellar, fashioned into the shape of St Michael slaying the dragon. There was a large gold-chased Venetian crystal bowl standing on a solid gold base. Three tapestries, woven from the richest silks and gold thread, hung on the walls. They were of a quality which one would expect to see in the house of a grand nobleman, though their subject – that of naked nymphs and satyrs, was more appropriate to its setting. Maressa had not realised that Thomas and Laurence were so wealthy.

The door opened and she stared at Thomas's unwelcoming face. Pushing back her hood, she removed her mask.

'Thomas, I'm desperate. I need help.'

He looked at the bags by Hazel's feet. A blond eyebrow was raised as he saw Julian asleep in her arms. 'Desperate indeed, for you to come here and at such an hour.'

The tension she had been under for the last hour sapped her strength and she began to tremble uncontrollably. As Thomas caught her in his arms, Maressa spilled out her tale.

His face was impassive when she finished. 'So Northcliffe and Mortimer are dead,' he said. 'You did well to set fire to the house. You ask for help. What if the price I ask is too high?'

'Price? But we are kin!' she said, appalled.

Thomas's stare was piercing. 'And you've kept me dangling after your favours too long. If I were to offer you my protection – it would be in the fullest sense of the word.'

She stared at him in horror. 'I trusted you.'

'And you did right. Who else could save you from the hangman? Come now, Maressa. After what happened this night you can't be that naïve. You'll not find me ungenerous.'

She looked around the treasure-filled room and then back to her cousin. 'I'd be solely under your protection?'

'I don't intend to share you, Maressa.' His voice had an ominous ring.

'Promise me that my father never learns of this. I couldn't bear the shame.'

Thomas smiled and filled two gold goblets with wine from a flagon. Handing one of them to Maressa, he lifted his in a toast, his grey eyes glittering. 'To us, my dear. My protection will save you from arrest, persecution and almost certain death. Whilst you live here you . . .'

'But I thought you would set me up in a house of my own?' she interrupted. 'I do have a few jewels and two hundred pounds.'

'How long do you think that will last? Even if you escape the authorities you'll be condemned to a life of poverty – unless you sell your body for what pitiful rewards a common man could offer you. You will have to pay dearly for people's silence. I suspect there'll be a price on your head.'

Grim amusement lightened his eyes. 'Here, I can protect you from the law. No constable who values his life ventures into my domain. You will be kept in luxury and provided with the finest jewels and clothes. My word is law. There is no escape unless I will it. And to thwart my will would mean your death.'

Chapter Twelve

Angel's homesickness increased when Robin Flowerdew died suddenly. He collapsed from a seizure during a performance and was carried to a trestle bed in the tiring room. Angel knelt at his side, holding his hand and willing the elderly actor to live.

He opened his eyes which were sunken with pain. 'Keep writing, Angel.'

As she bent over him she smelt death on his breath. 'Don't speak, Robin. Save your strength. A physician has been summoned.'

'Would you deny me my final soliloquy?' he forced out. 'Heed me. Keep writing. You have talent. Esmond and Gabriellen's plays will not succeed in France. Write your own. Comedy is your forte, but your humour is English not French. One day England will sing your praises.'

She took his hand, tears running down her cheeks. His pallor alarmed her and his lips were turning blue. 'Robin, you'll be fine. Rest now.'

'No.' His voice was a thread of its stentorian stage roar. 'I'll not see this night through. Promise me – keep writing!'

She nodded, too choked with her grief to speak. An hour later Robin died.

With his death, Angel began to pine for England, and on Palm Sunday Molière took her to the last day of the Fair of St Germain to cheer her spirits. As they strolled past the booths, the cries of fortune-tellers vied with stall-holders proclaiming the wonders of their marionettes, two-headed calves, or the world's fattest man or bearded lady. Gradually, Molière's caustic wit dispelled Angel's melancholy. The smell of roasting meats and spiced cakes tempted their palates. Here was every exotic wonder: scented Marseilles soaps,

Siamese bonnets, Brussels lace, Venetian glassware, Greek and Italian wines, Chinese silks and brocades. Goods from every country, but what Angel suddenly longed for was a glimpse of good English pewter, or sight of the Morris dancers with their hobby horses or representing the legend of Robin Hood. She missed Alexander and her father. She even missed the English fog.

As they paused by a booth selling carved wooden toys, Angel picked one up, thinking of her nephew Julian. Then she heard her name called and saw Sabine and François approaching. She embraced them warmly.

'My dear, you would think you had not seen us for a year,' François said with a laugh. 'Yet you visited us only last Friday.'

Sabine studied Angel's face. 'You look tired. I wish you would return to the Rue St Honoré. If Llewelyn saw you now he would tell me I'm a bad aunt for allowing his daughter to grow so thin.'

'I'm missing Father and Alex,' Angel admitted. 'I feel I should be in England. The war drags on. If I cannot fight maybe I can help the injured.'

'Llewelyn would not want you in danger,' Sabine advised.

'I didn't come to France to live in safety. I came to follow a dream and to forget a man who is impossible to forget. I was selfish. I never thought the war would last so long. I can continue my life as a player later. Now I should be tending Royalists wounded in battle. I leave for England next week.'

'We shall miss you, my dear,' Sabine sighed. 'You'll visit us before you leave? I've a letter for Llewelyn and a gift for young Julian.'

'Of course.' Angel drew apart. 'I'll come on Wednesday.'

'You cannot leave France,' Molière said with unusual agitation as they moved away through the booths.

'I must.' She linked her arm through his. 'I won't forget my time here. Nor you, my dear friend.'

Molière fell silent, and remained withdrawn until they had reached their lodgings. All the players were out. Disturbed by Molière's quietness, Angel sought to ease the tension between them.

'When I return to France, will there be a place for me in your troupe?'

'Always.' His voice was thick as he took her into his arms. 'Angel, I adore you. I've kept my distance out of respect, knowing that your heart was held by another. But now you speak of leaving . . .' His hands moved to her face, his thumbs drawing lazy circles over her skin as he gently eased her head back. 'Angel, I want you – I've wanted you for so long.'

His embrace tightened. He kissed her eyelids and the tip of her nose. She trembled at the touch of his lips, yearning to ease the loneliness and heartache which had settled over her in recent weeks. Closing her eyes, she returned his kiss, then with a sob broke free.

'I'm sorry, Jean-Baptiste – truly I am. But we cannot be lovers.'

The city church bells began to ring the angelus and from the corridor outside came the murmur of voices. The other actors had returned. Angel whispered, 'It is better this way. Madeleine regards you as her property and I'd not have you suffer her shrewish tongue because of me.'

'It would be worth it,' Molière persisted with a rueful grin.

Angel shook her head, but felt a pang of regret that she was leaving this charming Frenchman.

Maressa slept badly. With a jolt she started awake, ill at ease in the strange bedchamber. She had killed a man to preserve her honour. The truth stuck her with awesome finality. Murder was a hanging offence, no matter that she had been goaded beyond all endurance, beyond decency. Panic welled up in her throat and stifled her breath. She gasped, fighting for air.

Terror filled her! She was a murderess! Her soul was imperilled. She looked at her outspread hands, surprised that they were not stained with blood. Her eyes wild, she clutched the bedclothes to her body and rocked back and forth. She thrust her hand to her mouth, her teeth drawing blood as she bit into the knuckles. And what of her bargain with Thomas Angel? What had possessed her to agree to become his mistress? His mistress! The thought revolted her. It was immoral. Yet where had morality got her? To the very shadow of the gallows – that's where!

Her mind revolved in a crazy spiral. She had sought

sanctuary here. She should have known that her cousin would have demanded more from her than the ties of kinship. She should have known better than to trust a man.

Maressa looked around the room. The bedhangings were of scarlet brocade woven with gold thread. Two bacchanalian tapestries covered the walls and, though the subject was lewd, they were made from the finest silks. Opposite the bed was a Venetian looking-glass, its gilt border carved with cherubs. Her gaze was drawn to the table of toiletries. A beam of morning sunlight played over its contents, sparkling upon gems set into the lids of gold cosmetic pots and perfume phials. She had never seen such extravagance and wealth. Drawn to the beautiful objects, she arose from the bed. As her fingers traced the delicate pattern on a gold-backed hairbrush, they tingled with a new and awakening thrill. An intense longing to possess such beauty and wealth consumed her, more powerful than anything she had ever felt sexually.

She smiled knowingly. So Thomas wanted her for his mistress, did he? Lord Northcliffe had shown her that men were prepared to pay high prices to win her favours. Her widowhood had released her from a loathsome marriage, but she had little money to support herself and her son. A life of poverty appalled her. Especially when the wealth displayed here proved that Thomas could afford to pay highly for the privilege of her favours . . . very highly.

'My lady,' Hazel said softly as she entered, carrying a tray of spiced wine and saffron cakes. 'Would you like a bath brought up? Master Thomas sends his regrets. He's been called away on a business matter and doesn't expect to return for two days. Master Laurence bids you remain here as his guest. He's bed-ridden with gout and too ill to see you today.'

'It looks like I've won a reprieve,' Maressa sighed with relief. 'Have you recovered from our ordeal, Hazel?'

The girl looked pale and nervous. 'It brought back fearsome dreams of Meg's death!' she replied. 'Master Thomas said we were safe here, my lady. Is that true?'

'There's no safer haven in England. No constable will venture in here.'

'But it's a bordello, my lady!'

'Of a most prestigious kind, I believe,' Maressa said with conviction. 'As my maid, you'll not be part of such trade.

304

Fate has dealt us a blow, but we need not be the victims of circumstances.'

Fate conspired against Angel's departure from France. François Toulon was struck down with the palsy, the attack so paralysing they feared he would not survive the week. Angel visited her uncle's bedside to find Sabine hollow-eyed as she held her husband's hand, and Lucrèce sobbing loudly into her handkerchief by the window. As she entered the room Angel heard the physician order Lucrèce to leave; her sobbing was destroying the peace that was necessary for his patient to recover. Lucrèce wailed louder, almost colliding with Angel as she ran from the room. She stopped at recognising her cousin, her face red and swollen from weeping.

'How dare you come here?' she screeched. 'It's your fault Papa was struck down. You've brought shame upon us. You're wicked! Evil! You did this!'

Angel reeled back, shocked by the virulent outburst. She looked towards the figure of her uncle lying, eyes closed and unmoving, on the bed. One side of his face was pulled down in an odd distortion.

'I'd do nothing to harm François,' she said brokenly.

'Go to your room, Lucrèce,' Sabine said quietly. 'Your Papa needs peace, not this caterwauling. Angel is not responsible for his illness.'

Lucrèce screwed up her face as a fresh tide of sobs broke from her. 'You always defend her. You love her more than me. Just because she writes stupid plays you think she's special! It's not fair! Papa loves me and because of her he's dying. I hate you! I hate you both!'

She fled to her bedroom, banging its door shut.

Sabine looked haggard. All the vitality had gone from her face and her eyes were bleak with fear. 'Lucrèce is upset. It's been a shock. François collapsed last night after our meal. He's lain without moving all day.'

Her voice broke and Angel took her aunt into her arms. 'You must not give up hope,' she said. 'I saw a similar case in Oxford. The man gradually recovered over a period of weeks. Nathan said that the healing can be slow but the paralysis need not be permanent. We must wait and pray.'

'You will stay with me?' Sabine beseeched.

'Of course, I'd not abandon you in your time of need.' Angel put aside her plan to return to England, for she knew that Lucrèce would provide no support for her mother.

After three days in Nell Lovegood's, Maressa was summoned to see her uncle. Laurence Angel sat before a roaring fire in a private salon on the second floor of the house, his bandaged leg propped up on a footstool.

'Maressa, welcome to my home,' he said. 'It's a pleasure to see you, albeit in such sad circumstances.' His stare was uncomfortably forthright. 'But were the circumstances not so dire, would you have given any thought to your Uncle Laurence?'

'It is not my habit to visit bordellos, Uncle,' she countered.

Unexpectedly, he laughed. 'So there is some spirit in you! I'm glad to see it. Shows you have Angel blood in your veins after all.' Again his assessing stare fixed on her. She smiled, but he did not return it. Her stomach knotted with dread. Her beauty did not move him, neither did the tenuous link of kinship. 'What do you expect from me, niece?'

'From you, nothing. Thomas is my friend. I had thought . . .'

'You thought that after you kept Tom dangling for your favours in Arundel, he would house, feed and clothe you. Not to mention use his influence to protect you from the law.'

'I don't expect charity,' Maressa defended herself. She knelt by her uncle's chair, her eyes wide and pleading in an expression which she knew few men could resist.

Laurence fingered his small grey beard, but his expression remained hard. 'Kin or no, everyone here earns their keep.'

Maressa gasped. 'You do not mean for me to become one of your whores?'

''Tis an honest enough trade.'

Maressa hung her head, fighting back tears of disappointment. 'The rumours about you are true,' she blurted out as her anger rose. 'You're a rogue with no sense of decency. Thomas was kinder. At least he only suggested that I became his mistress, but you'd have me serve any lecherous sot with gold in his pocket.'

'Only the most innovative of the women here receive gold.' He studied her as though she were a mare for sale at a fair.

'It's a hard life and a short one. I keep no one over the age of three-and-twenty. You are nearly twenty and I doubt have had the necessary training.'

'Most certainly not.' Maressa stood up, outraged. Hands on her hips, she spat out her contempt. 'You're a blackguard, Laurence Angel.' She jabbed an accusing finger into his chest. 'I killed a man to save my honour from defilement. I refused to let my husband use my body as a means to settle his debts, and I'll not submit to your tyranny either!' She spun on her heel and, with her skirts swishing angrily around her, strode to the door.

'Niece!'

There was such lethal intent in the command that she halted, but her eyes remained bright and defiant as she glared back at him. To her astonishment, he was smiling.

'You have the Angel temper and spirit, despite your prim, demure manner. What a pious act you've shown to the world these last ten years! I had despaired of you, Maressa. Come here.'

Keeping her head high, she moved slowly forward. His gaze was appreciative as it moved over her figure. 'You're beautiful. Today you have shown spirit. I'd never expect a niece of mine to work here. But I've a proposition to put to you.'

He lifted a handbell and rang it. A liveried footman answered. 'Is my son at home?'

'Yes, Mr Angel.'

'Ask him to attend me at once.'

Laurence indicated for Maressa to sit on the highbacked chair opposite him. 'We will wait until Thomas arrives.'

He turned away to pick up a pipe, filling it with tobacco from an ivory casket on the table beside him. He leaned back and puffed out a cloud of blue smoke. When Thomas appeared, he sat forward.

'Maressa informs me that you expect her to become your mistress as reward for helping her,' Laurence stated without preamble. 'Is that right?'

Thomas threw a suspicious glance at Maressa. 'I'd not have put it quite so baldly.'

'But those were your terms for protecting her from the law?'

Thomas shrugged. 'Yes.'

307

'Then you shame our name. Good God, Thomas, she's your cousin!'

Maressa hid her surprise at her uncle's words. Thomas's face had darkened with anger, but he made an effort to control it. Folding his arms across his chest, he said insolently, 'Cousin twice-removed at the very least. So why the fuss.'

'Because she's an Angel by blood,' Laurence snapped.

Thomas stared at his father as though the old man had lost his wits. 'Have you gone moralist on me? The arrangement is to our mutual benefit. You made the rules: no one lives under our protection without paying.'

'I'll not have you turning your cousin into a whore!' Laurence shouted.

'Then what will be her role – kitchenmaid?' Thomas glared at Maressa sitting stiffly in her chair. 'A lamentable waste of her talents. Or perhaps you've an eye on her as a bedwarmer for yourself.'

'I've mind for you to marry her, you insolent cub.'

'Marry!' Thomas spluttered.

'Marry!' Maressa gulped, her face draining of all colour.

'Yes, marry!' Laurence stabbed the air with his pipe. 'You're six-and-twenty, Thomas, and I'm not getting any younger. I want to see my grandson before I die. I want to know that the name of Angel lives on. Maressa will be an ideal wife. I want a grandson with fire in his blood. She's already proved she can breed.'

'The terms are unacceptable,' Maressa protested. 'I've been a widow but three days.'

Laurence grunted. 'Don't insult my intelligence by telling me you loved that lecherous oaf. Good God, woman, he seduced your own sister!'

Maressa put a trembling hand to her mouth, her eyes wide. 'How did you know that?'

Laurence ignored her and glared at his son. 'You will marry her. If you refuse I'll change my will and you'll get nothing.'

'You'd never let Nell Lovegood's go out of the family!' Thomas jeered.

'I want a grandson. You've shown little inclination to settle down and provide me with one. Remember Nell's daughter,

Thomas? She's eighteen and has been trained by her mother in the business. For five generations Nell Lovegood has been a figurehead of this establishment, the name and responsibility handed down from mother to daughter. Young Nell bore me a son last winter. A lusty lad, young Esmond is proving to be. Marry Maressa or I'll change my will in Nell and Esmond's favour.'

Maressa cleared her throat. 'You've forgotten one important fact . . . my agreement. I've no wish to remarry.'

Laurence's expression was cold. 'Perhaps you prefer to moulder in Newgate whilst you await the hangman? Refuse and I'll have you handed over to the constables within the hour.'

Maressa slumped back into her chair. Laurence had won.

Thomas paced the room, his glare murderous as he regarded his father. 'You know my views on marriage. I want a wife of some status. Damn it, if it hadn't been for this war I'd have eloped with the Earl of Wivenfield's daughter, but he bundled her off to France as one of the Queen's ladies before I had the chance. I'd be one of the richest men in England with such a wife.'

'Your fortune matches most of the nobility in England. Confound it, most of them have squandered their money on our whores and gaming-tables! Their blood is weak. I want my grandson to be strong. I want my grandson to have true Angel blood! I've two, three years at the most left to me. Long enough to see him born. Then all I possess is yours.'

Laurence turned to Maressa. 'Fail at your peril, niece. If I die without a grandson I shall leave instructions for your arrest. That way at least Thomas will not be burdened with an unfruitful and useless wife.'

Thomas looked at Maressa, his expression far from that of a tender lover. 'Do you agree to this madness?'

She smiled tautly and looked at Laurence. She knew his threats were not idle. But he had claimed he was proud of her Angel blood; in which case, he could pay for it. 'And what would be my allowance as your son's wife? I presume you'd not keep me penniless.'

'No allowance. I'm not giving you money so you can run out on our bargain. Besides, to attempt it would be foolish. My spies are everywhere. I'll pay your dressmaker's bills and everything you need for your comfort to the cost of one thousand pounds a year. When a healthy boy is born you'll get five thousand pounds.'

'And if my first child is a daughter?'

'Then you had better ensure you produce my grandson the following year. Only a son can carry on the legacy I leave to Thomas. Do you agree?'

Maressa was trapped. 'Yes.'

'Good!' Laurence nodded in satisfaction. 'I'll make the arrangements.'

Thomas bowed to Maressa and, offering his arm, escorted her from the room. Once outside he turned to her, his expression masked.

'I'm sorry it has come to this, Thomas,' Maressa said quietly.

He chewed at his lower lip for a long moment, his gaze steady and unrelenting. 'Give me a son and you'll be a wealthy woman, sweet Coz.'

She smiled. Misfortune had placed her at the mercy of Laurence and Thomas. She had little liking for the bargain, but for five thousand pounds she would give Laurence his grandson. Her future security lay in financial independence. Where had honesty and fidelity got her so far? Only a short step removed from the gutter. Never again, she vowed.

Throughout the early summer Angel helped Sabine tend François. He had recovered consciousness the day after Angel's arrival, but his speech was slow and difficult, and he constantly had to be reminded as to who people were. It was heartbreaking to witness. Angel showed Sabine how to massage her husband's palsied arm and leg with a herb unguent which stimulated the flow of blood, and gradually, his movements became stronger. His memory returned too, and by the end of the month he was able to walk slowly, dragging his right leg. When François was first stricken, Angel wrote to Nathan for advice, not knowing whether he would receive her letter, or when a reply would reach her.

It arrived after several weeks. The letter covered four pages of closely packed writing. It explained the best treatment for the patient, and also gave her news of her family and events in England. Nathan had written it two days after the battle at Marston Moor. He had been without sleep since the fight. The casualties were high but neither he, Llewellyn, nor Alexander were injured. But their army had been routed. It was the first major Royalist defeat. Rupert had taken it badly. Another sad note was that Rupert's dog, Boy, had been killed during the battle.

This news sent a chill of foreboding through Angel. Boy had been Rupert's talisman. Sermons had been preached against the Devil Prince's dog. Now the Wizard Prince was without his familiar – and the battle had been lost. Parliament would rejoice at the dog's death. Rupert had lost his demonic reputation. He was reduced to a mere mortal. No longer was the Cavaliers' whirlwind charge invincible. With the defeat at Marston Moor the whole of the North was lost to the King. Nathan now believed a turning point had been reached. He was no longer convinced of the King's inevitable success. There was no bitterness in his letter, just grim acceptance. Tears filled Angel's eyes at the misery and devastation inflicted upon her countrymen.

Loyalty tore her in two directions. She owed her aunt so much, and did not want to leave her whilst François still needed care. Yet England was suffering. The Royalist cause might be doomed, but it was not yet lost. How many more battles must there be before the killing stopped? She should be there, healing those brave warriors. What if Alexander or her father died through want of care? She would never forgive herself.

Her step was heavy as she rejoined her aunt in the salon, where she was reading to her husband.

'You look worried,' Sabine said. 'Is the news from England bad?'

Angel nodded and passed her the letter.

After reading it, Sabine looked up at her niece. 'Then you must return. This Lieutenant-Colonel Cromwell whom Colonel Carver mentions . . . he sounds formidable.'

'It appears so. Alexander wrote some months back that skirmishes were being lost because of Cromwell's Ironsides – as they call Parliament's New Model Army. Oliver Cromwell is emerging as a respected commander, more popular than Essex and Fairfax. It's said that his disciplined troops are more than a match for Prince Rupert.'

Sabine shook her head sadly. 'Colonel Carver writes that Cromwell's disciplined cavalry won the day at Marston Moor. In my heart I'm still English. This news saddens me. La! Is it possible that King Charles might lose the war?'

Angel shuddered. 'That's unthinkable.'

'Then we must keep our faith. You've done so much to aid François' recovery, and I will follow Colonel Carver's instructions. Go back to your family, Angel. Go back to your Colonel Carver. Was he the one you came here to forget? It's clear he cares for you.'

Angel smiled. 'Nathan was not my lover. We are friends, no more.'

'La! You speak of him as often as you mention Alex – I thought . . .'

'You've lived in France too long, Aunt. You have become a romantic. Nathan is a friend – a special friend – and I've missed him. Though why, I don't know. He's a womaniser. I suspect that I'm a challenge to him because I haven't succumbed to his charm. Neither will I. It would ruin our friendship.'

'There's not a rake alive who cannot be tamed by the right woman.'

'Too many have believed that and rued the day.'

Sabine looked at her niece with concern. 'And what of Molière? You see much of him. He's very fond of you. I'd wish a more stable life for you than marriage to a player.'

'I've no wish to marry Molière. Or any man.'

'But you should marry, Angel,' François said with painful slowness.

'Yes.' Sabine took up her husband's advice. 'You need a strong man. A special man who will tame you.'

Angel knelt at her uncle's feet. 'You're special, François. But you're already spoken for.'

He patted her hand, slowly forming his words. 'You are like a daughter to me.'

There was a rustle of silk and Angel turned to see Lucrèce standing white-faced by the door. There was a flash of venom in her eyes before she whirled and ran from the room. Moments later the front door slammed.

Angel sighed. It was time she returned to England. Her uncle was improving by the day. She would make her final round of visits to say farewell to her French friends and leave for England at the end of the week.

An hour later Angel left her aunt's house to return to her lodgings with the actors. The June evening was overcast, making the narrow street with its overhanging houses gloomy. Angel paid little heed to the people around her. Her mind was filled with plans for her departure.

'There she is – the Rowan whore!' a harsh female voice shouted.

Angel started in surprise, her blood running cold. Ahead of her were several of the city's matrons, stern-faced and well fleshed. She knew their type – pious, plain, usually with unfaithful husbands. They were harridans, unlovely and unloved and spiteful to the core.

'That's her.' Another woman waved a menacing fist. 'English bitch! Whore!'

'Strumpet!' A third lisped through missing front teeth. 'Bringing shame to a respectable household . . . ruining a God-fearing man.'

The women were standing in the street, barring her passage. Others were gathering, their expressions greedy for a diversion. Angel glanced around. There was an alley to her right and she ran to it. As she approached, two brawny men detached themselves from the shadows. Leering at her, they blocked her path.

'Whore!' The women took up the chant. 'English vermin! We don't want your type here.'

The crowd closed around her as Angel desperately sought an escape. There was none. She refused to show her fear. Standing tall, she stared at the woman who appeared to be their leader and recognised the harsh face of Madame D'Oubray.

'Seize her!' Madame D'Oubray screamed. 'Show the English whore how we deal with trollops who would seduce our husbands.'

The two men lunged at Angel, catching her arms and dragging them behind her back. Pain, merciless as red-hot pincers, shot through her body, bringing a prickle of tears to her eyes. Yet she refused to cry out. She kicked at their shins, but was hampered by her skirts. 'Let me go! I've done nothing.'

'I saw your disgusting behaviour with Molière!' Madame D'Oubray shouted. 'Everyone knows his reputation. You visit the poet Scarron, where all the city's libertines gather. You've the morals of an alley-cat. You've shamed the Toulons who are respectable citizens! I spit on you!'

The globule of saliva was cool upon Angel's burning cheeks. It slid down to her jaw. Molière had told her that Madam D'Oubray's husband, a known profligate, had died last month whilst being treated with mercury to cure the syphilis he had contracted from the city's brothels.

'You're filth,' Madame D'Oubray shouted. 'You wallow in the gutter in your depravity. See how she dresses – flaunting her breasts like a whore?'

Fat fingers grasped the neckline of Angel's sapphire-blue silk gown. The neckline was modest enough but the men held her so that the bodice gaped revealingly. Her neck was jarred forward as the woman ripped the silk to Angel's waist. The air struck cold on her hot skin, and her shoulders felt as if they were being wrenched from their sockets. The men holding her were panting. She could smell the garlic and stale beer on their breath. One was rubbing his groin against her hip, his arousal sickeningly obvious.

'Shame her as she has shamed our city,' a woman demanded.

'I'm no whore!' Angel shouted.

'Any decent woman is married by her age,' Madame D'Oubray retorted.

'Whore! Whore!' The crowd began to chant.

Angel continued to struggle, frightened by the menace of the people around her. Then she was grabbed and thrown to the cobbles. Nails scratched her flesh as her clothes were ripped from her in a frenzy.

'No!' Angel screamed. 'Stop!'

Her frantic struggles met with kicks and punches which battered her body. The pain dazed her consciousness. Faces bent over her. Men leered. Women screamed abuse. Terror spun out the scene in horrific slowness as her shoes, stockings, tatters of gown and petticoats were claimed as prizes. She was held down spreadeagled, a man gripping each wrist and ankle. Still Angel fought like a trapped wildcat, her body twisting and heaving as she tried to shake off the hands which shackled her. The pain from their punches slowed her movements, her voice hoarse as she screamed, 'No! No! Stop!'

She was left with only her corset and silk chemise which had been ripped to expose her breasts and barely covered her hips.

Angel cried out, 'Have you women no decency to expose another thus?'

She strained to draw her knees together but her ankles were jerked apart, and the last of the chemise ripped away, lewdly exposing her to the men's lust-crazed stares.

'Whores deserve no better,' Madame D'Oubray wheezed. The fat matron held a pair of scissors in her hands. 'Hold her while I shear her hair. She'll not look so tempting then to lure our husbands.'

Angel's head was banged down on to the cobblestones and, though she twisted and squirmed, her raven tresses were clawed free of their pins and hacked off short. Some locks even yanked out by the roots, so vicious was the women's attack. Dazed by pain, Angel stared up at them as they chanted obscenities. Then the scissors flashed before her glazed eyes and she felt the tightness about her ribs give as her corset's laces were cut. Her eyes screwed shut as she was hauled naked to her feet, but her legs could not support her.

The pain in Angel's abused body was agonising. Her head throbbed, her mouth was bleeding and one eye was swollen and shut. A man had grabbed her breasts, pretending to hold her upright. At this further outrage, her eyes opened and, sucking the last of the saliva from her throat, she spat in the oaf's grinning face.

Her voice was raw as she screeched, 'Bastards! I've never harmed any of you.'

'You corrupt our society,' Madame D'Oubray declared. 'May you be an example to all whores that decent women will not tolerate them.'

The women had stepped back, but in their places came ragged urchins, laughing and jeering as they held out their laden hands towards her. Then the stench hit her and her flesh cringed as the still-warm horse excrement was plastered over her body and hair. The older boys were the cruellest. Their hands pinched and squeezed her breasts, buttocks and inner thighs. All around her she could hear the obscene chanting, then it became fainter as consciousness slipped away.

She passed out, but it must have only been for a few moments, for she saw that the watch had arrived and were pushing back the crowds. Yet they did nothing to aid Angel, intent only on dispersing the rabble. Shocked into paralysis, Angel remained motionless. She stared at the blood and horse dung which formed a foul crust over her body. Though many of the crowd had gone, nearby one woman stood laughing. Through the mists of pain, she saw Lucrèce, laughter gushing from her gaping mouth.

'Not so angelic now! Devil's daughter! Maman and Papa will turn away in horror when they see you.'

'Your cloak, Lucrèce,' Angel croaked. 'Have pity!'

'I'd as lief give it to a leper. The gutter is where you belong, with the filth of your sins upon you.'

Lucrèce walked away. Slowly, Angel levered herself up on to one elbow. Pain made her giddy and she fought to overcome it. It was growing dark and the street was deserted. She wanted to crawl into a black corner and hide her degradation. There was a low wall twenty yards ahead . . . she would crawl there and recover her strength. Every movement was torture. Her knees were bleeding and as the dung dried, it caked and fell from her body. Where could she go? To return to her aunt's house was impossible. Sabine would be devastated to learn that her daughter had instigated such an abomination. Would Scarron help her? He too had suffered at the hands of the mob . . . but he lived too far away for her to reach in this condition.

Footsteps echoed on the cobbles. A black-frocked priest was approaching, and she held out a hand in supplication.

'Help me, Abbé. Something, I beg of you, to cover my shame.'

His eyes rolled with horror as he regarded her. Hastily, he made the sign of the cross and muttered a prayer to protect him from the insane. He crossed the road and hurried on his way. More footsteps followed and Angel saw several men coming towards her. From their dress they were respectable citizens.

'Messieurs . . . A cloak . . . I've been attacked . . . Abused.'

'*Mon Dieu!* A lunatic and naked at that,' one man chortled. 'And beneath all that filth not a bad figure. What say you we take her somewhere, clean up the loon and have some sport?'

Laughing, they approached her. Angel screamed, her mind reeling at the prospect of yet another humiliation. She had heard appalling tales about the hapless women who lived on the streets – most of whom, the pious matrons declared – brought their fate upon themselves.

She kicked out at her new tormentors. 'Help! Someone, for the love of God, save me!' she shouted in French and English as two of the men hauled her to her feet.

She clenched her teeth against her pain and, summoning what was left of her strength, hit out at her assailants. Dimly, above her screams, she heard the sound of pounding feet. There was an angry shout and a sword scraping from its scabbard. Two men ran off, but Angel was still held by her arms, her terror pumping the blood through her veins in a desperate renewal of strength.

'Help me!'

'Pigs! Go rut in the stews,' a familiar angry voice challenged. 'Leave the loon in peace.'

'We'll share her,' her captor grunted. 'She's English. Never had no English whore afore.'

'Cyrano – it's Angel. Help me!' As she cried out she twisted and brought up her knee, ramming it into the groin of one of her captors. The man howled in agony and sank to his knees.

'*Sacré coeur!*' Cyrano de Bergerac raged. 'That's no whore. Sons of bitches, leave her be.'

Steel clashed upon steel with ferocious energy.

'It's de Bergerac,' one man wailed. 'I'm off. No whore's worth getting killed over.'

Angel was flung aside with such force that she fell to the ground. Two of her assailants hauled the man still holding his groin to his feet and dragged him away. Another was duelling with Cyrano. Angel scrambled backwards, crouching in the dark shadows of a house to hide her nakedness. As she watched, Cyrano ran his sword through his opponent's shoulder.

'Mercy! Don't kill me!' the man cried out, his eyes starting with terror.

'You make me ashamed to be a man,' Cyrano growled. 'There's bawds aplenty to be had for five sous. Why should I spare you? Would you have spared her?'

'Don't kill him,' Angel said. 'He's not the one who did this. There's been injustice enough this day, Cyrano.'

'You would have me spare a cur who'd rape you?'

She could not see his expression in the last rays of a crimson sunset.

'You saved me from that fate,' she said. She was shivering with reaction and cold. Her body hurt from the beating and abuse, and her mind was dazed with terror. Yet she did not want the man to die. Her voice was a hoarse rasp of entreaty. 'Take me somewhere safe. I cannot bear this shame . . .'

'You're fortunate that the lady has a gentle heart, whoremonger.' Cyrano stepped back. Before his opponent could move Cyrano's sword slashed three times and in the fading light Angel saw the man's breeches fall in tatters around his ankles. As he bent down to gather them up, Cyrano laid the flat of his sword against the man's bare buttocks, and, yelping with pain, he shuffled away.

A cloak was thrown over Angel's trembling figure and she was raised to her feet.

'Can you stand?'

'Yes.' She lifted her face to regard her rescuer. 'Your cloak will be ruined,' she apologised. 'I owe you a great debt. I can't return to my aunt's house like this. Neither would I be the jest of the players. Could you take me somewhere I can make myself clean? And if word is sent to Molière, he could bring my clothes from the inn.'

'Come back to my lodgings. I'll send for Molière and a physician. Who did this? I'll run the bastards through.'

Her knees buckled as her strength failed her, and he caught her in his arms.

'It was the pious women of the city,' she said. 'They were encouraged by the lies spread by my cousin. It's better if the matter is forgotten. Thanks to you, I escaped the final degradation.'

'Your cousin cannot be allowed to get away with such actions.'

'I'll do nothing to hurt my aunt and uncle,' Angel said thickly. Shock was causing her to shake violently, and she turned away abruptly and vomited into the gutter. Then she began to cry. The sobs were wrenched from her, impossible to halt.

'*Mon dieu!* Those bitches deserve to die for what they've done to you,' Cyrano raged. 'It's over, Angel. You're safe now.' He lifted her in his arms and she clung to him as he carried her through the streets. At the corner he hailed a hire carriage.

'Wait. What's that stink?' the coachman shouted. 'Get yourself another carriage. I'm not having mine reeking for a week.'

Cyrano placed Angel gently inside the carriage, then leapt on to the carriage wheel and hauled the driver from his seat and threw him to the ground. 'Your carriage will be left at the Place de Greve.' Cyrano cracked the whip and the horses plunged forward.

Angel hugged the cloak about her, closing her eyes as she fought to control her tears. She was too wretched to pay heed to their journey. When the carriage stopped, Angel opened her eyes and saw several flambeaux lighting the Hotel de Ville. The carriage door opened.

'The street is too narrow for the carriage. I'll carry you.'

'I can walk,' Angel insisted. 'Please don't let anyone see me like this.'

'They won't. The streets are deserted.'

He put an arm about her shoulders as they turned away from the Place de Greve. They walked through several side streets and up a dark alleyway to the back of a tavern.

'I've a room here,' Cyrano explained.

A woman called out as the garden door shut behind them. 'Who's there?'

'Bring a tub and hot water to my rooms,' Cyrano ordered.

'But you bathed last month, Cyrano. Have you a new mistress you wish to impress?' A bright laugh preceded a plump figure in a white cap and huge apron over her grey gown. 'Who's this?'

Angel hid her face against Cyrano's chest as the landlady's face showed her horror and contempt.

'Holy Mother of God! The wench stinks like a midden. I thought you had better taste, Cyrano. There's pot-girls enough here for your needs. I want no gutter harlot in my inn.'

'The wench is no harlot,' Cyrano snapped. 'She was set

319

on by the mob. She's an Englishwoman ill used by our countrymen. Have a bath prepared and brandy brought to my room. Will you tend her, Etta? And no questions.'

'Trouble and scandal! It's always the same with you, Cyrano. I don't know why I don't throw you out.'

'Because your bark is worse than your bite.' Gently he pushed Angel ahead of him up a flight of stairs and into a dingy room. She stumbled to a chair in a darkened corner. When he lit a candle and bent over her to examine a cut on her cheek, she turned her head away.

'Don't look upon my shame. Apart from a few bruises I'm unhurt. I just want to rid myself of this filth.'

'The mob can be cruel and unjust. Don't let them break you, Angel.'

'It would take more than a jealous woman and a few sanctimonious bigots to do that.' She tried to smile but her lips were trembling too violently. She put a shaking hand to her head, but her eyes were bright with resolve. 'To hell with them all, Cyrano. I was warned I'd be persecuted and reviled. It makes me all the more determined to succeed as a playwright.'

Moments later he pressed a goblet of brandy into Angel's hands. 'It will warm you and give you strength.'

She thanked him, but could not look at him. She was embarrassed that anyone should see her so degraded and humiliated. When the bath was ready de Bergerac left her.

'I'm going to Molière. I'll return in an hour with your clothes.'

'Please bring all my possessions from the inn. I shall sail for England as soon as I can.'

'Because of this?' Cyrano sounded angry.

'No. I had already decided to leave. My father and brother are fighting for the King, and the war is going badly. I can care for the wounded.'

He stared at her from the door. 'Etta will have a room prepared for you. You'll need a few days' rest before you travel.'

Maressa and Thomas were married in the porch of St Bride's near to Ludgate Hill. The ceremony was brief. Few people had been invited to the service, for Laurence feared Maressa might be recognised. There was an uneasy moment when a procession filled the street, bringing their coach to a standstill. Maressa glimpsed a bare-chested man, his neck and hands locked in a wooden yoke, being whipped whilst the crowd jeered and reviled him for a blasphemer.

At Nell Lovegood's they were greeted with revelry. The place was crowded with guests, mainly the rogues, thieves and scoundrels who worked for Laurence. Several men were dressed in finery: wealthy profligates who were regular patrons of the bordello; professional gamesters who posed as young noblemen, and the Upright Men who ruled adjoining districts. Laurence and Thomas walked amongst them all like princes.

The air was sweetened by perfumed candles and the floors were strewn with rose-petals. Thomas was lifted on to two men's shoulders and, to her dismay, Maressa suffered the same fate. They were carried to a saloon laid with a lavish banquet. While Maressa detected a false note in the laughter of the whores who disliked her, Thomas was fawned over by the women. It was obvious that many of them had been his mistress. Fortunately, the suite of rooms she would share with Thomas were on the second floor of the house and isolated from the activities of the bordello.

Now, as she sat by Thomas's side, Maressa hid her resentment at again finding herself married to a lecher. At least Thomas was wealthy and would keep her in the manner to which she aspired. She did not love him. The marriage was a business arrangement – nothing more.

Thomas leaned towards her, his gaze upon the low neckline of her gown.

'Mine at last, Maressa. And legally bound. There was never a more beautiful bride.' He lifted the loving cup they shared and drank, then passed the goblet to her. She took a small sip. There could be no secret possets slipped into Thomas's wine. He must perform as was expected of a husband. And the sooner he got her with child – the sooner the unpleasant business would be over.

As the meal progressed the guests became drunk on the free-flowing wine. Very soon Maressa found it hard to avert her gaze from the women being dragged down upon men's laps. Garters and stockings were thrown over shoulders and bosoms exposed as the whores giggled in delight. In drunken rapture, the men sucked and fondled their breasts and the bawds encouraged them to greater depravity. Maressa's sensitivity was outraged at seeing a woman lift her skirts to her waist and sit astride a man's sprawling figure on a table. She yanked his breeches down over his knees and, to a chorus of cheers, impaled herself on his swollen member. Two naked women lay on the floor amidst a litter of goblets, caressing each other and writhing in pleasure. When they turned head to toe and began kissing each other between their thighs Maressa felt her face flame and her breath dry in her throat. Yet her gaze remained on the two women and though shocked, she found it impossible to look away from such debauched abandon. She jumped violently when Thomas laid his hand over hers.

'Things are getting rather wild,' he said. 'It's time we retired. But first a toast: to us, sweet wife. May our union be blessed.' He raised the loving cup and pressed it to her lips, giving her no option but to drink deeply. The mulled wine trickled from her mouth.

'I'd make a run for the stairs if I were you,' Thomas warned. 'Drunk as they are, they'll have both of us naked before we reach our chamber.'

'Thomas, no!' Maressa protested in horror.

He grinned. 'Just a little fun, my dear. Go on, make a run for it.'

Maressa picked up her skirts and fled. Immediately the women closed around her, their faces flushed and exultant, boisterously pushing her forward, their fingers picking the bows sewn as wedding favours from her gown as tokens of good luck. She stumbled on the stairs as she felt them start to pull on the lacings of her bodice and sleeves. A triumphant cheer greeted the first sleeve of slashed velvet as it was stripped from her arm and tossed to the revellers. As the second sleeve followed there was a sharp command from Laurence:

'My new daughter will be treated with respect.'

There was an angry muttering from the whores nearest Maressa. Nell Lovegood came to her side, her painted face thrust close as she winked at the bride.

'Jus' you run ahead. Tom would have my hide if any of those lechers got a glimpse of what is strictly his for the viewing.'

Maressa didn't wait to be told twice. As she ran up the second flight of stairs towards her chamber, she risked a glance back at the wedding guests. Denied their sport with Maressa, they had turned their attention to Thomas. He was already stripped down to his breeches and she saw Nell Lovegood's daughter reach eagerly for the points fastening them. Maressa's face burned with embarrassment and she ran into her chamber, where Hazel was waiting.

'Quick, my lady. Out of those clothes and under the covers.' As she spoke, Hazel jammed a chair under the latch of the door to give them a few moments longer to preserve Maressa's modesty. Maressa was standing in her stockings, garters and chemise as the wedding guests banged on the door.

'Open up for the groom!' a man yelled out. 'Young Nell's made good and sure Tom's all ready for you.'

Maressa darted for the bed. She dived under the covers and pulled the sheets up to her chin just as the guests burst into the room.

Thomas was flushed and at least two of the whores were caressing him. Young Nell's head was bent over Thomas's stomach and as she looked up, Maressa could not believe what she had seen her sucking upon. In all her married life, Maressa had never kissed Henry there. She turned away in disgust, her hands tight on the bedcovers. The women shrieked and seemed intent on snatching the covers from her. The room was a nightmare of leering, laughing faces and Maressa felt a violent trembling seize her body. Thomas, completely naked, was laid on the bed beside her. The ribald comments on his readiness to consummate the marriage and the suggestions as to how it would be best done turned her flesh to stone.

As Thomas slid under the bedclothes, the good humour left his face. 'Enough merriment, my friends. You've had your fun, now leave me to my bride.'

'A kiss. A kiss,' the guests chanted. 'The groom must kiss his bride.'

Smiling, Thomas put an arm around Maressa's shoulders. His eyes widened questioningly as he felt her trembling and saw the strain on her ashen face. Tears were glittering behind her lashes as they kissed.

'Now show us what married life is all about, Tom,' one rake shouted.

'I'll be doing that most readily – but not before an audience. Out!'

Laurence raised his voice. 'Leave them. The wine and girls are all free this night. Nell has planned an erotic tableau in the main salon with our six most accomplished girls. No man will be disappointed, I promise. Enjoy yourselves, my friends. The bride and groom would be alone.' He ushered the guests from the chamber and, when the last one had left, turned to face the couple in the bed. 'May this night be fruitful – as I'm sure it will be a delightful pleasure to you both.'

When he had gone, Maressa bowed her head and put a shaking hand to her temple.

'I'm sorry their comments were so coarse, my dear.' Thomas lifted her hair back from her shoulders and kissed her skin. It was like kissing marble – cold and unyielding. 'It was harmless fun,' he added, his lips moving across her icy flesh to the nape of her neck. 'You took it well and I'm proud of you.'

'It was terrible,' Maressa answered, flinching away from his touch.

When Thomas put his arms around her, she sat in frigid stillness, staring blankly at a gold tassel on the bedhangings.

'Don't be frightened, sweeting. I'm not Lord Northcliffe, nor Mortimer. I've had reports from the women about his inadequacies. Two-minute-Henry, they called him, because he spilled his load so fast.'

'You mean it takes you longer?' Maressa could not keep the dismay from her voice.

'Pleasure is never to be rushed, sweeting. But you're cold. Drink some of the mulled wine Hazel has prepared for us. It will warm and relax you.'

He filled two goblets from the flagon placed by the bed. When she would have refused he put the goblet to her lips, forcing her to drink. Then he drew her head against his shoulder and gently stroked her hair, removing the last of the pins. Outside in the corridor, a minstrel strummed his guitar and began to sing a love song.

'Is that not better?' Thomas spoke against her hair. 'Relax,

I'll not rush you. But you're no innocent maid, and I mean to have my rights. Let them be in as pleasant manner as possible. Pleasurable to us both.'

As he spoke he ran his fingers lightly down her spine. She shivered and clenched her teeth against his unwanted touch. 'The light, Thomas. Please snuff the candle.'

'I want to see you.' He drew the sheet down to her waist, his hand knocking aside her fingers as she held them over her breasts. He slid the straps of her chemise from her shoulders and Maressa closed her eyes as he peeled the silk away from her breasts.

'You're too beautiful to hide your charms in darkness,' he murmured.

Thomas was a connoisseur of women, but he had known few to rival his wife in beauty. The candlelight bathed her breasts in a golden glow and the dark nipples stood erect. Not from passion, for she was stiff as a corpse, but from the cool of the night air. Her whole body seemed coated in ice. He doubted Mortimer had given her much pleasure between the sheets. He did not want to force her – but the bargain made by his father rankled. At five thousand pounds for producing a son, she was the highest paid brood-whore in the country. And whore she was, for it was the money which had brought her to his bed. But a whore was paid to give pleasure, not lie like a martyr put to the torture.

When she shuddered as he caressed her breasts, the sensualist in him demanded that she respond. Her beauty aroused him, but he stifled his own needs, although the ache in his swollen manhood pressed against the silken skin of her thigh was almost unbearable. There were faint bruises like shadows marring the perfection of her breasts, caused by Lord Northcliffe's lust-crazed attack. Was it any wonder that she was tense after the horror of that night. Thomas forced himself to be patient. The wine he had given her had been drugged with an aphrodisiac.

'You're more lovely than Venus herself,' he said, knowing Maressa's weakness for praise. 'Relax, I'll not hurt you.' He reached for a gold phial beside the candle on the bedside table. 'You are cold. Let me rub this oil into your skin. It will relax you.'

Maressa kept her eyes closed as Thomas began to rub

the musk-scented oil over her shoulders. Beneath his skilful fingertips it spread a langorous heat and as his palms circled her breasts, a warm tingling spread through her body. She moaned and sank lower on the pillow. His fingertips skimmed over her body, and with each stroke, he praised her beauty and perfection, something Henry had never done. He was seducing her with words as well as with his touch – and a touch so sensual . . . it was like nothing she had ever experienced before.

When his hands returned to her breasts she gasped. Her body was undulating to the rhythm of his sensuous message. When his hands moved lower to seek the moist warmth between her thighs, she cried out aloud in her pleasure. But she kept her eyes closed. She preferred the touch of the disembodied man than the sight of the man himself. Her legs spread without her conscious volition. Sighing, she rolled her head from side to side, her hips moving to heighten the rhythm of his hand. Her fingers clawed his shoulders as he brought her to release and a moan rose from her throat. Before the last of the sensations ceased, he made the craving begin again, building to a ferocity which made her gasp with pleasure. Then, as she was again on the precipice of surrender, he covered her body with his own and entered her. Her body tensed even as he brought his arms beneath her thighs and lifted them around his waist. She lay still as he thrust into her, feeling his sweat dripping down on to her rapidly cooling flesh. Then with a shudder he gave a harsh groan and slumped over her.

Three more times he took her that night, his experienced touch bringing her to a pleasure that Henry had been incapable of. Yet each time he entered her, she was repelled by his invasion of her body.

Angel spent a week saying her farewells to her friends. Both Scarron and Marion de l'Orme made her promise to return to Paris. She waited until she knew Lucrèce would be out before calling on her aunt and uncle.

Sabine's welcoming smile became concerned as soon as she saw her niece. 'You look pale. What has possessed you to hide your lovely hair under a lace cap and high-crowned hat? Though I must say the style becomes you.'

'Who knows? I may start a new fashion in England,' Angel said brightly. It would take a year at least for her hair to grow back to a respectable length.

'For that you must be at Court.' Sabine was smiling broadly.

'And where else would I go but to visit Father and Alex in Oxford? Aunt, you look like a starving child given a basket of bread.'

'With every reason. I've not been idle since you said you were leaving for England.' Her face aglow with pleasure, Sabine opened a leather and brass-bound coffer on her desk. It was filled with a score of leather pouches. Sabine picked one up and tossed it to Angel.

She caught it with a gasp, startled by the weight and the unmistakable chink of coins. Opening it, Angel stared amazed at the gold louis within.

'I visited every family I know with connections in England. There's a thousand pounds for His Majesty's cause. You'll be our emissary, and two trustworthy men have been hired to escort you and guard the money.'

A storm at sea delayed Angel's departure from Calais. A second storm once they set sail blew them miles off course. Then, to Angel's frustration, they were becalmed for another week. It was August before she arrived in England, where she was shocked by the change in her countrymen. All sense of gaiety had vanished. Whoever she spoke to mentioned a member of their family who had died in the conflict. As she travelled through the southern counties she was alarmed by the number of people now wearing sober grey and black. Even when she travelled north into Royalist country, though the clothes were brighter, any gaiety seemed false. People's faces showed the strain of divided communities. There were more preachers in the streets, sermonising on the sins of the flesh and the tyranny of man. And everywhere there was suspicion.

After the defeat of the King at Marston Moor, York had fallen to Parliament. One name was foremost on everyone's lips, either spoken of with reverence or spat out in hostility: Lieutenant-General Oliver Cromwell and his trained band of Ironsides.

Since Marston Moor, Queen Henrietta had returned to

France to raise further money. Rupert was in Wales, seeking recruits to train a new army. On her arrival in Oxford, Angel found only a small garrison there. The King was on the march. At learning Alexander was garrisoned at Banbury, Angel went to meet him. He had received a shoulder wound after Marston Moor, and she found him with his arm still in a sling, supervising the training of a hundred men and horses in cavalry skills.

The horses were skittish and their riders inexperienced. Alexander sat astride Caradoc, who stood solid as a rock, his chestnut coat gleaming in the sunshine. Her brother's voice was impatient as he ordered the recruits to repeat the last exercise. Then a dozen men with swords raised charged a line of wooden effigies with straw heads and decapitated them. As a second row formed for their charge, two horses reared, dislodging their riders. Angel started to smile, and when three horses took off after the charge, galloping across the field to unseat their riders into a hedge, she had to stifle a laugh. The sound made Alexander swing round in the saddle, his expression thunderous.

She waved. 'Alex, don't you recognise me?'

His long black hair had blown across his eyes and as he brushed it aside, his swarthy face lit with a smile. Wheeling Caradoc around, he trotted towards her, shouting an order for his men to repeat the exercise. He leapt from the saddle and with his good arm swung her round and kissed her cheek. There was a chorus of whistles from the recruits and several ribald remarks.

'Get back to your training. It's my sister,' Alex said, grinning. 'What's with the lace cap and hat, Angel? France must have tamed you. You look very demure and twice as beautiful.'

'Would you have me remain a hoyden all my life? I was seventeen last month – a veritable matron.'

Alex raised a black brow. 'You've not lost your agile tongue. Where are you staying?'

'In the village, but I intend to join the King and help with the wounded. How is your arm?'

'It heals.'

'And Father, is he well?'

'He's with the King. Not far from here, actually.'

'Have you heard from Maressa? I wrote to her twice from France, but received no reply.'

Alexander looked grave. 'Mortimer House burned down in London. We've heard nothing from her or Mortimer since.'

'No! I cannot believe that Maressa is dead.' Angel bowed her head in shock, and was taken into Alexander's arms.

'From the report I received only one body was recovered.' Alexander held her away from him to stare down into her worried face. 'Maressa never was much of one for letters. Perhaps Henry took her abroad. That way he'd be preserving his own skin should the Royalists win.'

'Let us hope so,' Angel said, determined not to be morbid. 'How's Beth?'

Alexander's expression brightened at once. 'Adorable as ever. We have a son, named Mark after Grandpapa. She's still at the Manor and I see her as often as I can. We'll not live at Rowan Hall until the war is over. But you must visit her. She would like that.'

'So would I.' Angel smiled warmly. 'And what of Nathan? Is he still with Rupert?'

Alexander's eyes narrowed. 'Have you returned because of the Prince?'

'That's over, Alex.'

'I'm glad. Nathan is with the King. God willing, I join him at the end of the month once this arm heals. That's if I can get these clodpates trained in time.'

'I must leave tomorrow for an audience with His Majesty. I bring funds from France, raised by Aunt Sabine.'

'Would that I could come with you.' Alexander voiced his frustration.

'We will meet again soon,' Angel said. 'I've decided to offer my services to Nathan.'

'Perhaps that will stop him brooding.'

Angel looked at Alexander in amazement. 'Nathan never broods!'

'Well, he has done since you left. He's poor company – spends hours locked away in that secret room of his, working on his notes.'

'That doesn't sound like the Nathan I know,' she laughed. 'There's always his women to cheer him.' She frowned. 'And what secret room?'

329

Alexander was studying his sister intently and there was amusement in his dark eyes. 'The one behind the hospital. Didn't you know? That's where he spends most of his nights – always has done, apparently. I discovered it quite by chance. He'd fooled me like he'd fooled everyone else. I had him down for a confirmed reprobate. Seems he encouraged the rumour just so he could sneak off to get some peace for his studies.'

Angel was about to dispute this with her brother when she realised that he was serious. Nathan was not the reprobate she had always believed. Her spirit lightened, and she felt more carefree than she had done since the outset of the war.

Chapter Thirteen

Angel discovered the King at a small manor house, some miles from Banbury. After waiting for three hours in an antechamber, she was led into his presence in the long gallery at the top of the house. The Chamberlain announced her, but the King appeared not to hear. He stood by the mullioned window embrasure, staring down into the courtyard. His short figure was wreathed in the sunlight which sparkled on the diamond garter star on his breast and whitened the grey streaks in his long brown hair. One hand rested on the stonework, his expression soul-weary and tragic.

Outside Angel heard the sound of tired and dispirited voices. Horses whinnied, their harnesses jangling as they shook their heads and stamped their feet on the cobblestones. A lacklustre voice shouted an order for the scouts to ride out. From the disgruntled murmuring Angel sensed apathy. Defeat had permeated their morale. Rupert had shown that he was not invincible, and that had struck at the heart of the Cavaliers. Victory was no longer a certainty, and, while the King evaded a final and conclusive battle, it slid further from their grasp.

Angel sank into a curtsy, and the rustle of her silk skirts finally drew the King's attention. He sloughed off his melancholy as he beckoned her to rise.

'You are the young gentlewoman recently returned from France?' He spoke slowly and carefully, to overcome a life-long stutter.

There was a barrier of aloofness about him, an hauteur which was intimidating. Several inches taller than the King, Angel found it disconcerting to look down upon his figure. For so small a man, he had immense dignity, yet there was something about his manner which left Angel unmoved.

Because of his implacable belief in the Divine Right of Kingship, this man had brought his country to war. He had overriden Parliament and sought to put himself above the law of the land. Not even a King had that right. Yet, she remembered, throughout the conflict he had been reluctant to fight his own people and avoided battle whenever possible. That was not the act of a despot. It was the act of a man sensitive towards the people he was born to govern. In war sensitivity was a weakness that could cost him his crown. But despite her misgivings, he was their King. Her allegiance would always be to him.

'I bring money from France,' she said, indicating the coffer which a liveried footman had placed on a table. 'A thousand pounds, raised from the English community in Paris and from Frenchmen who have relations here.'

'A goodly sum. Their loyalty is much appreciated.' Some of the lines of strain softened around his mouth, but the sadness remained in his eyes. 'Though even that will not go far when I must provision and arm so vast an army.' He regarded her with keener interest. 'You must have faced danger on the road with such a sum to transport.'

'I was provided with sufficient escort. It was an honour to be able to serve Your Majesty even in so small a capacity.'

'I would like to reward your loyalty, but alas, I cannot give you a place among the Queen's waiting-women, for she is not at Court. Present yourself when the Queen returns. There will be a place for you then.'

There was a beat of a rod on the floorboards and the Chamberlain announced Lord Digby. An imperious wave of the King's hand dismissed Angel. Lord Digby strode past her without acknowledging her presence, and before she left the Long Gallery she heard his harsh voice lambasting Prince Rupert.

'Has His Highness forgotten the purpose of his campaign in the West? I hear he's at Bristol . . . apparently succumbing to the delights of the fleshpots in the lowest quarter of the town.' Digby's voice was loud with scorn. 'His Highness is so lost in his pleasures, his men have become disheartened by his excesses. Should any try to curb him, Rupert flies into the blackest passion. He's not fit to command and should be relieved.'

Angel was appalled. Rupert had once told her that there was no love lost between himself and Digby. But she could not believe Rupert would sink so low. What demon was driving him? Was it despair that he had failed the King? A pain clutched at her heart that he should be so demoralised. That ferocious wildness which spurred him to purge England of his uncle's enemies, sparing himself no hardship in the process, had now turned its destructive force upon himself. Something must be done.

It was a disappointment for Angel to find neither her father nor Nathan with the King. Llewelyn was escorting a baggage train of arms and ammunition to a Royalist garrison. Nathan had left for Bristol where, it was reported, the pestilence had broken out.

Angel rejoined Alexander in his training camp. He had been ordered to take his recruits to join Rupert in Bristol. He argued against her plan to travel west with him, but finally agreed. They entered Bristol at the beginning of September. Dispirited soldiers lounged outside taverns, many reeling drunk, even at midday.

'It's worse than I feared,' Angel groaned.

'The men are bored from this inactivity.' A muscle jumped along Alexander's jaw. 'What is Rupert about, allowing his men to drink their time away?'

He asked the same question of Nathan when they had tracked him down at a hospital set up in a disused warehouse.

'Rupert will listen to no one. A devil rides him. He spends his nights in the taverns, mixing with rough seamen and vagabonds. He, who always was so abstemious in his habits, now debases himself with drink and low slatterns.'

Nathan looked hard at Angel. Their reunion had been restrained. When she would have hugged him in welcome he drew back, his manner that of a stranger. His attitude hurt Angel. She had not realised how much she had missed his companionship until she had seen him walking towards them – and he had snubbed her.

'Rupert's rages are terrible. They're exacerbated by his drinking,' Nathan went on. 'I tried to speak with him and got a tongue-lashing for my pains. He blames himself for the defeat at Marston Moor. He knows it was the turning point of the war. There are times when I fear for his sanity.'

'Then some means must be found to rouse him,' Angel protested.

'He won't listen to me, nor any man. He avoids his officers. Letters, even those from the King, are torn up unread.'

It was not a state of affairs Angel was prepared to allow to continue. Rupert must be made to see sense, even if she had to do it herself. 'I vow he will hear my words,' she said crisply. 'They'll have to clap me in irons and gag me before I halt them. Where will we find him?'

Nathan's manner remained cold as he answered her. 'Not in his lodgings – the waterfront taverns, most like, and they're no place for a woman. By this time of day he'll be in no condition to listen to anyone.'

Angel refused to be discouraged. 'Then it must be early tomorrow.'

The next morning, dressed in the guise of a maidservant, Angel entered the Prince's rooms, carrying a bowl of water. Placing the bowl on a table she opened the shutters. There was a curse from the bed, the violence and profanity of which chilled even Angel's intrepid spirit. Rupert was sprawled across the coverlet, still in his boots and clothes after returning from a night of debauchery.

'Your Highness! Most noble commander of His Majesty's cavalry,' she said scornfully. 'Is this the Devil Prince? You're hardly a sight to strike terror into the hearts of Cromwell's Ironsides!'

A red-rimmed eye opened to glare at her with murderous intent.

Angel sauntered to the foot of the bed and with her hands on her hips regarded him sternly. 'You can glower all you like, but you don't impress me with your ill-humours. When did wenching and carousing win any war? The noble and valiant warrior has become a sot.'

'The devil!' he roared, rolling from the bed, to be brought up short. With a groan, he clutched his aching head. Rupert had not shaved in days and his handsome face was haggard. His clothes were crumpled and stained. Angrily, he dragged a hand smeared with grime through his tangled dark hair, then drawing his lips back in a snarl, he rounded on her. 'Get out, wench, before I have you horsewhipped for your insolence!'

'Your foul temper does not impress me.' Angel stood her ground. 'Your Highness, you are so more worthy than to live like this.'

Iron hands locked about her throat. Stale fumes of rum hung heavy on his breath as he glowered down at her without recognition. When she stared into his eyes, fear coated her spine. She was gazing into the soul of a man wandering in the deepest pit of hell.

'Rupert! It's Angel Rowan,' she gasped out before the pressure on her windpipe robbed her of speech.

His expression cleared as he glared at her and his fingers slackened their hold, but he did not release her. 'How did you get in here?'

'With the aid of friends.'

'You forget whom you address, wench.' His tone was murderous.

'As you forget your duty, Your Highness.'

He pushed her away from him. 'Get out! I need no lectures.'

Angel remained where she was. She folded her arms, her expression disdainful. 'Self-pity ill becomes you.'

He shot her a withering glare. Then, with a groan so heartfelt it struck like a sword through her heart, Rupert sank down on to the bed and put his head into his hands. 'Boy is dead.'

'I heard. I'm sorry.'

'I failed the King.' His frustration broke forth.

'You failed no one. This upstart Cromwell beat you in one battle! He can win a dozen battles and he's still a rebel. The King has but to win one great victory and he will be undisputed monarch.' She kept her tone stern, and went on more forcefully. 'A few old women posing as the King's counsellors bewail that the war is lost. What would they know? Your Highness, you're the Royalists' hero. They look to you for example. When did wenching and drunkenness ever succeed?'

'You go too far!' His voice crackled like musket fire as he rose to glare at her. 'Go, before you provoke me further.'

He grabbed her arm and propelled her towards the door, but she turned and threw herself against the portal. 'No, you will hear me out. Haven't I always been honest with you?'

She was breathing heavily as she outfaced the demonic fury in his black eyes. 'So you met your match in Cromwell! The unthinkable happened . . . You lost a battle! Yet recruits still flock to your banner. Your voice alone urges the King to more decisive action. I never thought you a defeatist.'

She flung the last words at him in challenge. For a moment she saw her death written on his face. His tall frame shuddered as he spun abruptly away from her, to fling himself down on a chair. He glared at her with blazing eyes, his long fingers clenching and unclenching as he battled against his fury.

'I don't want to hurt you, Angel. You've said your piece, now go!'

Given the choice most men would regard twenty lashes as the lesser punishment than being subject to his blistering glare. Angel drew a shaky breath and plunged on before her courage failed her.

'I speak out of respect, not insolence. I'll not stand by and see a man whom I admire destroy himself. Your enemies are using your behaviour to turn the King against you. Digby says you're no longer fit to command.'

Rupert picked at a piece of torn silver lace at his wrist, his mouth compressed into a murderous line. When he finally looked up at her, she saw the anger had left his face.

'You've the devil's way with words, Angel. They cut a man to the core.'

She lifted an eyebrow, and studied his dishevelled appearance. 'You expect flattery in your present condition?' She smiled, and, kneeling by his chair, placed one hand on his arm. 'You've been tireless in your efforts to win this war. Your energy is drained. No one deserves rest and relaxation more than you. But this is self-destructive. You are the King's champion – the most noble and worthiest of his commanders.'

'I'm no chivalrous knight in gleaming armour.'

Her laugh was sardonic. 'You are far from that – especially reeking of cheap perfume and rum.'

She made to rise but he caught her wrist. 'Stay! I would retrieve from all this bitterness a few blessed hours of sweetness.'

It was not what she had intended in coming here, but her

heart betrayed her. She saw his vulnerability for the first time and it pierced the guard she had resolved to keep upon her emotions. She had gone to France to forget him. Now she knew how lamentably that ploy had failed. She loved him as passionately as ever. Her body was already beginning to respond to his touch. Why deny him? Why deny herself?

Her smile was enticing as she sat back on her heels. 'First I shall order a bath for you. While you soak I shall shave you.'

He rubbed his hand across his stubbled jaw, his humour restored. 'And then . . . ?'

'Am I not your humble servant, Your Highness?'

'Never humble and much too high-spirited to be servile.' He drew her on to his lap. 'My captains tremble before my rages. Not you. I had forgotten you were so stubborn.' His hand trailed along her cheek. 'I had forgotten also how beautiful you are. A true Angel come to wrest me from Satan's coils.'

A brothel was no place for a prude to live. At first shocked by the women walking around with their breasts exposed and the sight of men in various stages of undress lolling on couches, Maressa gradually became immune. She tried to avoid the lower floors of the house but it was not always possible. Bedroom doors were often left ajar in a customer's haste to bed his companion. Were there really so many variations to the sexual act? Maressa marvelled as she quickly hurried past. If she witnessed any of the more perverted pleasures, physically she felt sick.

She had been married to Thomas for three months. He was a very different lover from Henry, and always considerate of her needs. No matter how long it took him, his hands could always bring her to pleasure. When she cried out at the height of her ecstasy, she would open her eyes and see him studying her with a strange expression on his face.

'There'll be few men knowing what it takes to make you sing that sweet song, dear wife.' He always sounded insufferably pleased with himself.

'You have done your duty well, husband,' she replied, stung into coldness by that expression which she did not understand. 'I am with child, Thomas. There's no longer a

337

need for you to come to my bed.'

'I'll not bed where I'm not wanted.' His tone was nasty as he abruptly swung his legs to the floor. 'Better pray it's a boy, or you'll be obliged to play the martyr once more if you're still greedy for my father's promised riches.' He walked out of their bedchamber, and Maressa smiled as she sank back on to the pillows. Unaccountably, she was ruffled at the ease with which he had accepted her dismissal. She placed a hand across her waist. Within her womb was her security for the future. She prayed her child would be a boy. Then she would never have to suffer a man's touch again.

The next morning Maressa informed Laurence of her news.

'I knew you'd not fail me,' he chuckled with pleasure.

He crossed the room to unlock a large gold and enamelled casket on a table. There was a glitter of precious jewels spread over his hands. When he held up a rope of perfectly matched pearls, Maressa gasped with pleasure.

He fastened it around her neck and stepped back. 'If it's a boy, this will be a bauble to the jewels I shall give you.'

'I don't want jewels, Uncle Laurence. I want a house, an establishment of my own. Your grandson may one day own Nell Lovegood's, but that does not mean his childhood should be spent surrounded by whores and rogues. He should be brought up as a gentleman.'

'Like Thomas you mean,' Laurence laughed. 'His mother was a real lady – she wasn't one of the girls here, you know. She was the Lady Margaret Ferris from the county of Buckinghamshire. When I met her she was being forced against her will to wed a friend of her father's. We were introduced at a country ball when I was staying with a young lord in the same county. She was very susceptible to my charms and, to avoid a marriage she dreaded, she eloped with me. The shock killed her father. Died of a seizure the day he learned she'd wed me. Most fortunate as it turned out. The old clutchfist intended to disinherit her, but he died before he could change the will. Margaret was his only child. Those pearls were hers.'

'I did not know you had an estate in the country.'

'I sold it after Margaret died giving birth to Thomas. My life has always been in London. I don't care for country ways. Unlike my father Esmond Angel, I've never gambled my savings away. I leave that to the gullible coves who come here. Nell Lovegood's has always been the most prestigious establishment of its kind, but I own several similar establishments in the city. So if it's a house you want, my dear, it shall be your reward for giving birth to my grandson. Though I warn you, the constables are still looking for you in connection with the fire at Mortimer House. You're safe here, Maressa. I may not be able to protect you, should you venture outside my domain.'

The brutal reminder of why she was a prisoner within these walls made Maressa's heart race with alarm. She had hoped that the hue and cry would have died down by now. It seemed she was still a wanted woman, under suspicion for the deaths of both Henry and Lord Northcliffe. What use were riches and luxury when she must remain a prisoner to escape the gallows?

Maressa screamed. She had been screaming for three hours to push the child into the world and as the tiny bundle was laid naked at her side, she screamed again. This time in vexation.

'It's a girl! All that travail for a girl!' She turned her head away. She had endured her husband's lechery, her figure becoming gross and bloated – and all for a girl.

She screamed again in frustration. A boy would have given her a house of her own, and an income fit for a duchess for the rest of her days. She put a hand over her face as the child began to cry. 'Take it away. I don't want to see it.'

'You're an unnatural mother,' Thomas mocked her from the foot of the bed.

She opened her eyes. 'A son was required of me. I've produced a daughter,' she muttered bitterly.

Thomas moved to the squalling bundle wrapped in a linen towel and lifted it into his arms. As he stared down at the infant, the anger on his face drained away. He held the child awkwardly as though it would break and to Maressa's surprise his eyes brightened with tears.

'She's ugly!' Thomas chuckled. 'Her face is all screwed up. She's bald and her skin's all red.' He peeled back the linen wrap. 'And she's as scrawny as a skinned rabbit. But she is my daughter.'

The pride in his voice stung Maressa. 'I'd have thought you'd fathered a host of bastards on your whores not to make such a fuss over this one.'

'A whore's child does not count.'

As he spoke, the babe stopped crying and squinted open its eyes as though regarding him. Thomas chuckled again. 'That's more like it. Not so ugly, after all. I expect she'll be a beauty. We shall name her Thomasine.'

Maressa shrugged. 'She's yours to do with as you will. A wet-nurse must be engaged. I've no intention of suckling the babe.'

'She shall have the best.' Thomas smiled down at his daughter. Then he pulled a startled face as a spread of dampness seeped on to the sleeve of his doublet. 'Is that any way for a daughter to greet her father?' He grinned and handed Thomasine to Hazel, then, reaching into his doublet, he took out a jewel case.

'For you, dear wife, in gratitude.'

Curious, Maressa painfully propped herself on to one elbow and opened the case. Her eyes rounded with joy as she picked up a diamond bracelet, then she flopped back on to the pillow with a sigh. 'What use is finery when I go nowhere to wear it? I'm a virtual prisoner here.'

Thomas eyed her speculatively. 'You have a hunger for wealth, jewels and a place amongst the highest in the land. That's why you married Mortimer, wasn't it? For his title?'

'Little good it did me.'

'Because you didn't know how to handle him. You won him with your beauty. A man would have to be cast from iron to be immune to it.'

Maressa sniffed. 'Men can be such fools at times.'

'You don't like men much, do you?'

'How can you say that? I adore my father.' Maressa did not like his sardonic tone. 'And Alexander . . . I still grieve for Firkin.'

'I didn't mean family,' Thomas returned.

Maressa shrugged. 'I know little of other men. Henry claimed to love me, but would have bartered my body to pay his debts. To Laurence I'm little more than a brood-mare, to provide him with a grandson. To you, Thomas, I am . . .' She stared at him. 'What am I, Thomas? A means to your father's fortune?'

Thomas guarded his expression. It would never do to let Maressa know he loved her. She was as beautiful as a goddess, but her heart was pure steel. She would be ruthless if she knew how he felt. Maressa was as ambitious as himself, but she was vain. She thrived upon being adored and petted.

He sat on the edge of the bed. 'I've tried to make you happy, Maressa. I make no excuses for how I live and I've no complaints in you as a wife. We suit each other well, my dear. We have the same aims. You and Thomasine will want for nothing. I'll see my daughter a countess at least.'

The pride and tenderness in his voice as he spoke of Thomasine unexpectedly touched Maressa. He never used that tone with her. And what of her? What of her dreams? The title of countess was dazzling, but she did not want it for her daughter. She wanted for it herself.

'You aim high for a child born in a brothel,' she said waspishly.

'My daughter will not spend her childhood here. I will buy a house in a fashionable quarter of the city.'

Maressa gave a mocking laugh. 'For your daughter to be accepted in society, her background must be impeccable. I'm a murderess and you're an Upright Man, leader of the low criminals who haunt London.'

'I can be anything I choose to be, dear wife.' Thomas's smile was provoking. 'As Lady Mortimer you once moved within the circle I would infiltrate. Is not the blood of both rogues and players in our blood?'

Maressa caught his enthusiasm and returned his smile. She really was quite fond of Thomas. He was handsome and totally unscrupulous, but he also had the charm of a true rogue and could captivate all who came within his circle. His plans echoed Maressa's dream. Together they could not fail.

'You are wealthy by many people's standards, Thomas. Yet what you propose will take a King's ransom.'

'It shall be done.' His gaze held hers, compelling and challenging. 'With your beauty and my cunning, in five years I vow that all I have promised will be within our grasp.'

'You aim high, Thomas.'

'It's the only way.'

Eleven months after Angel's reunion with Rupert, she again returned to Bristol. There was despair in her heart, and it was echoed within the hearts of all Royalist forces. Naseby was on everyone's mind. The swift and bloody defeat and the ignominious flight of the Royalists had demoralised them all. Few believed that the war could now be won. But Bristol was strategic to the West and Rupert had vowed to hold it for his uncle.

The Prince rode out in frequent skirmishes against the advancing troops of Fairfax's and Cromwell's armies. He was no longer Angel's lover. She had saved him from the pit, but Rupert was ashamed of his lapse. His parting gift was a rope of incomparable pearls. He had put it and her part in redeeming him behind him. She accepted it, though for many months her heart ached with emptiness. Any chance encounter, as she watched him ride at the head of his men, was always acknowledged by a slight inclination of Rupert's head. His desire had waned, and her only comfort was that she was not forgotten.

But a woman who had been loved so thoroughly by the hero of the Royalist cause, could not replace such a lover with ease. In the following months few men met her exacting standards, and their kisses left her cold. August came and went, and still Angel did not take another lover.

Her work with the wounded kept her too busy for romantic attachments. She no longer needed a man's disguise while she was Nathan's assistant. She was a woman doing a man's work and determined to be acknowledged as such. Indeed, her patients adored her. They hotly defended her name and reputation to any who dared to suggest that she was no better than the usual slatterns and whores who helped with the wounded.

When she told Nathan how Cyrano de Bergerac had dubbed her the 'Crystal Angel', he had laughed, calling it apt. Within a week others had begun to call her by it – not with derision, but with respect.

In the months since her return from France, Angel had stayed with the Royalist army, and her work was exacting. Twice, at Alexander's insistence, she had taken a few days' rest to stay with Beth. It was a welcome respite and their friendship grew with each meeting. A week before they rode to Bristol, they heard news that Beth was expecting Alexander's second child.

Bristol was preparing for a siege, and each returning patrol brought more wounded. Angel was now adept at setting broken limbs, cauterising or sewing up sword cuts, treating festering grapeshot, bullet wounds and fevers. It was rare to find the hospital free of new casualties, but when Angel arrived one morning, only four men were confined to their beds. As she walked in, Nathan looked up from rebandaging a young man's eyes.

The patient turned towards Angel. 'Can't Mistress Rowan finish my bandage? She's got gentler hands than you, Colonel Carver.'

'How did you know it was me, Jamie?' she said with a laugh, coming to stand at the soldier's bedside.

'I can tell by the way your skirts rustle. There's not a woman in all Bristol who walks like that.'

'Like what?' Angel laughed. 'Do I approach like a galleon, gunports belching fire and sails full-blown?'

'Good Lord, no, Mistress Rowan,' Jamie assured her, a blush staining his smooth cheeks. 'More like a siren's whisper drifting on a summer breeze.'

'You are a poet, Jamie, and a flatterer.'

'Do I lie, Colonel Carver?' the Cavalier protested.

Nathan stood back and regarded Angel for a long moment before he answered in a lazy drawl, 'You do not lie, Jamie.'

It was the first time in weeks that Nathan had complimented Angel, or even looked at her as though she was an attractive woman. It brought a rush of heat to her cheeks, and suddenly she found herself unable to hold his appraising stare. Her gaze slid away and she busied herself by straightening the cover of Jamie's pallet.

'Have I offended you, Mistress Rowan?' Jamie asked. 'You're very quiet.'

'No. I'm not offended.' Her voice sounded strained to her ears, and she was disconcerted to find that Nathan continued to watch her.

Nathan rolled down his shirtsleeves and Angel's gaze was drawn to the fine blond hairs on his tanned forearm. There was something so masculine in the strength of that arm that Angel's heartbeat quickened. She looked quickly away. There were times when Nathan was too attractive for her peace of mind. He came to stand in front of her. He had hooked his

343

maroon doublet over one shoulder, for the late August morning was already hot. His gaze held hers and she noticed how very blue his eyes were, something she had not been aware of before. Their intensity increased as he smiled.

'The patients have all been tended. Bassett is on duty to see to any of their needs. I've a mind to ride for an hour. In a day or so, Fairfax and Cromwell will have us under siege, unless our numbers are reinforced. Will you join me, Angel? You've spent too many days cooped up here. I'd not have my most able assistant sickening.'

'I'd love to ride with you. Could we take the route Father will be returning by? He should have arrived back in Bristol yesterday evening.' Her voice was heavy with her worry for his safety. 'He was on patrol to escort food carts to reprovision the city against a siege.'

'You worry about your family too much,' Nathan admonished fondly. 'Llewelyn is a good soldier and an expert horseman.'

She sighed. 'I can't help worrying when Father or Alex are overdue.'

'Then we will ride out a mile or so to meet Llewelyn if it will put your mind at rest.' He smiled in understanding. 'But we should go no further without an armed escort and must keep to the hills overlooking the road. With the Roundheads advancing there is always a chance of encountering a scouting party. I don't want you in danger.'

Angel paled, her stomach contracting with foreboding. 'Then Father could be in danger?'

At the fear clouding her eyes, Nathan took her hands, surprised to find them trembling. 'There should be no danger. But it is wise to be careful.'

Once outside the city walls they raced to the Downs and along the ridge. The sun was warm on their faces and Angel pushed aside her concern for her father, determined to enjoy this respite from the pressures enforced by the war. Nathan was at his wittiest and it was impossible not to respond to his banter. When he challenged her to a race, she touched her heels to Talisien's sides and sped ahead. His horse was a magnificent grey but was no match for the Rowan gelding. Laughing and exhilarated from the gallop Angel slowed her horse to a walk.

'I don't think we should venture further,' Nathan warned.

She nodded, accepting his advice. They halted atop a ridge which looked across the Severn River to the distant purple hills of Wales. Angel dismounted and tethering Talisien to a gorse bush, she tipped back her head allowing the warm sunshine to play over her face and neck.

'You'll get freckles,' Nathan teased as he joined her.

'Then it's as well I'm not vain of my looks.' She stretched her arms and twirled round. 'It's a wonderful morning! I'd forgotten what it was like to be carefree.' Rising on to her toes she spun round again, but her heel caught in a tussock of grass and she stumbled.

Nathan caught her. At the same moment their gazes met and Angel's heart gave an unexpected flutter. Nathan did not move, repressed sexuality almost tangible in his stillness. There were tiny lines around his eyes from squinting against the summer's sun which gave strength and depth to his ruggedly handsome face. His blue eyes burned into hers. His hand seemed to pulsate with life, sending shock waves through Angel's palm. Her lips parted and she moistened their sudden dryness with the tip of her tongue.

Without being aware that Nathan had moved, she found herself in his arms. His lips took hers in an all too brief caress before he drew back, his eyes dark with passion, to study her intently. Then he kissed her again, kindling her blood to fire. Angel responded with passion. It had been so long since she had been cherished in a man's tender embrace, or felt the singing in her blood as desire surged through her veins. Her fingers slid over his broad shoulders and she clung to him, trembling.

'Oh, Nathan, this is madness,' she whispered, desperately hanging on to a last thread of sanity.

His mouth moved to the soft flesh of her ear. 'You are so beautiful,' he murmured. 'Ever since you left for France I've been fighting against my need for you.'

'Oh, Nathan, I thought you despised me,' she said breathlessly. 'You were so cold and remote when I again took Rupert as my lover. Yet you knew I loved him.'

Holding her in the circle of his arms, he stared deep into her eyes. 'I was jealous. How can a physician compete with a prince?'

'But you are my dearest friend.'

'It is no longer enough,' he said as he lowered his head to kiss her.

Her lips parted to deny him, but no sound was uttered as his mouth took hers. It was a kiss so poignant, so reverent, so filled with sensual promise that she found herself melting against him, her senses scattered in a storm of unexpected desire. The scent of his skin was a potent aphrodisiac. It was ten months since she had parted from Rupert and beneath the onslaught of Nathan's passion her memories of her royal lover were banished. The attraction which had always been between them, blazed into something more profound. It was madcap, impetuous, an abandoned sensual action, but impossible to halt or deny.

He caught her hair in one hand, slowly drawing her head back so that he could kiss the sensitive hollow of her throat. He spoke her name like a caress as his kisses seared from her throat to her cheeks, then back to her mouth which yielded, all resistance conquered.

'Oh, Nathan, this is not what I ever intended,' she managed to gasp raggedly. 'I want to forget this terrible war and the ache of loneliness. Help me to forget, Nathan.'

'Angel . . .' His voice was hoarse with emotion. Then abruptly he stiffened. 'Good God, what was that! Did you hear pistol fire?'

He looked down into the valley below. Several pistols echoed in the distance, stilling all birdsong. Angel clutched his arm in alarm and saw a single rider appear, galloping towards Bristol. Her heart jolted. The passion of moments earlier was doused as she recognised a chestnut horse from the Rowan strain. Something was wrong. The rider kept looking over his shoulder. Two more Cavaliers appeared on bay horses, crouched low over their saddles. They were riding for their lives. Moments later the cause of their flight was obvious. A troop of buff-coated and steel-breastplated Roundheads were in pursuit. Several more shots were fired. Angel cried out and clung to Nathan in her horror as the two trailing riders fell from their mounts. Only the man on the Rowan horse remained. It was closer now, and she saw the horse's white-stockinged legs and the wide blaze on its nose.

'That's Caedwalla . . . Father's horse,' her voice rose in

alarm. 'Nathan, we must help him!'

'We can do nothing. He's too far away.' He put an arm about her shoulders. 'Llewelyn will get away.' He sounded confident. 'They'll never catch him on that horse.'

Angel chewed on her thumbnail as she saw her father glance behind him, then flatten himself along the chestnut's neck, urging the horse to greater speed. Caedwalla responded, his tail streaming behind him as the space widened between the pursuers. She held her breath. Caedwalla was carrying Llewelyn out of danger.

'Go on, Papa,' she urged. 'Just to the other side of that copse. Then you'll be in sight of the city's cannon. They'll cover you.'

Llewelyn was almost at the wood. Suddenly, from out of the grass a hare leapt up and ran out in Caedwalla's path. Startled, the gelding reared, shying away so violently that her father lost his footing and fell.

'No!' Angel screamed.

Caedwalla heaved himself up and continued running. But he was without his rider. Then to Angel's horror, she saw that her father was being dragged along the ground, one of his legs caught in the stirrup. At first she thought he was unconscious, but his head lifted and an arm stretched out towards his boot. The ground in the valley was rough. Llewelyn's body was bumped over the terrain, his figure tossed like a straw bale as the gelding raced on.

Out of the wood came a score of riders, alerted by the pistol shots. At their head rode Rupert, in scarlet and silver. One Cavalier broke away and brought Caedwalla to a halt.

Angel ran to her horse and swung into the saddle. As she turned the mare down the hill, she saw Rupert in pursuit of the now fleeing Roundheads. She dug in her heels, urging her mare faster, heedless of her own safety. All her attention was centred on the still figure on the ground and the Cavalier bending over it.

Her vision blurred with tears as she saw Llewelyn's bloodied body hoisted up and laid over his saddle. Nathan was ahead of her as she leapt from Talisien's back and ran to her father's side. A glance from the Cavalier made Nathan catch Angel in his arms and prevent her from reaching Llewelyn.

'Don't look, Angel. He's dead.'

'No!' She tore herself free and put her hand on her father's back as he hung, face down. His doublet was ripped to shreds and covered in blood.

'Papa,' she said, touching his long dark hair. 'Papa!' Her voice broke as she saw the indented bloodied pulp at the base of his skull. His head must have been smashed against a boulder, killing him instantly.

'Oh, Papa! Not you also! How many of my family must I bury in this cursed war?' Grief-stricken, she bowed her head and rested it against her father's body.

Nathan gently drew her away. 'I'm so very sorry, Angel. He was a brave and respected soldier.'

Llewelyn was buried the next morning in the city. With the country now held so strongly by Parliament, taking his body to Chichester or Wales was impossible.

It seemed to Angel that the bells of all the churches now tolled night and day for the dead. Plague had also entered the city. The people were hostile and terrified as it spread in the summer heat, and their loyalty to the crown wavered as deprivation and sickness spread. Though the Cavaliers appeared to control their fear and despair, it was there – a dark insidious flame deep within their eyes.

Rupert ordered the bells to be silenced, but nothing could halt the fear sweeping through the city. Fairfax's troops surrounded the walls and no food could be brought in. Hunger added to the misery of the inhabitants under siege. The city was doomed. The Royalists were outnumbered and the Roundheads' cannonfire was remorseless. Everyone prayed for Royalist reinforcements. If they did not arrive soon, then the city would fall, and with it the last hopes of Charles Stuart.

So many wounded were brought to the hospital that Angel had no time to grieve properly for her father. She worked late into the night, grateful that she fell exhausted on to her bed.

Rupert did not surrender the city without a bitter fight. The Royalist defence inflicted severe losses on the Roundheads. When Fairfax's cannon broke through the city walls, Bristol's heroic defenders were massacred. Fires broke out as the thatched roofs were ignited by sparks. Smoke hung like a funeral pyre over the city. The screams of the dying and wounded were accompanied by the thundering of cannon and gunfire. There was no respite and no word of reinforcements from the King. The city surrendered.

The Cavaliers rode out in disgrace, but not without dignity. Rupert was impressive, mounted on a fine black Barbary horse, dressed in scarlet with silver lace at his throat and wrists.

'Give him no quarter!' The beleaguered citizens shrieked their hatred for the foreign stranger prince, blaming him for their troubles. But Fairfax was a man of honour. The enraged citizens were pushed back with pikes and swords and the cavalcade rode on. Rupert's swarthy face was expressionless. He sat, stiff-backed and tall in the saddle, looking straight ahead as he rode. Nothing showed of the pain and humiliation of defeat which lacerated his fierce pride.

Angel rode between Alexander and Nathan. She had again donned male attire to avoid the abuse hurled upon any woman following the King's army. Even before they reached Oxford, word reached them that the King viewed the surrender as an act of betrayal by his nephew. Now the threat of ignoble exile awaited Rupert.

Fairfax's army wintered in the West of England. Captain Douglas Fairburn fared better than most, quartered in the comfort of Exeter. The wind howled down the tavern chimney, sending puffs of smoke back into the taproom, while the shutters barred over the windows against the rising storm shut out the fading afternoon light. The taproom was thick with wood-smoke and the blue haze from the soldiers' clay pipes. Since the taking of Bristol the Parliament army had been jubilant. The Royalists were crushed but not yet beaten. With Rupert, the Devil Prince, disgraced and stripped of command, there were only Hopton's forces to defeat in the West. Fairburn like his companions fretted at the delay caused by the winter. Many were tired of the harsh life imposed by the war. They sensed victory was in sight and wanted to crush Charles Stuart, to end his tyranny for good.

Fairburn scowled at his cards and at the stack of silver coins on the table between the four players. He threw down his losing hand and glared across at the winner.

'You've the luck of the devil, Major Pollett. That's the fifth hand you've won in a row.'

Jeremy Pollett grinned and stretched out his wooden leg to massage the sore stump where it had been cut off above the knee. When the December winds blew from the East his wound ached like the devil. As a sharp pain shot up his thigh, he went white about the mouth.

'A curse on all the damned Rowan brood. I should have had the whole family hanged in Wales as Malignants.'

'Rowan?' Fairburn leaned forward with keen interest. 'What Rowan family is this?'

He was not the only one interested in Pollett's answer. A young man crouched by the fire, his head bent over his Bible, turned towards the gamesters. Fairburn saw the movement and ignored the Quaker. An hour earlier the preacher had been calling down hell and damnation upon all the ungodly and ranting about the sins of the flesh. Four tankards of ale had mellowed him and he had quietened to peer blearily at his Bible, his mutterings growing more incoherent.

Major Pollett's narrow face with its weak chin and pale eyes was set with hatred. 'No one you know. Come from Wales. Horse-breeders. Did this to my leg. Two of them were killed. I shouldn't have spared the girl. The family are Malignants. There's a brother too, somewhere.'

'Major Alexander Rowan?' Fairburn suggested, his stomach tightening with anticipation. 'Owns Rowan Hall in the Vale of Clwyd. He's a horse-breeder. Or was. I heard he'd lost the last of his brood mares at the same time his grandparents were killed.'

'Rowan Hall. That's the place,' Major Pollet snarled. 'Don't know the brother's name.'

'But you've no liking for the man.'

'Liking!' Pollett spat out. 'I've vowed to see them all hang. There's not a day goes by I'm not racked by pain and vow vengeance upon all who bear their name.'

Fairburn studied the Major for a long moment before adding, 'Major Alexander Rowan is married to a woman who lives at Oakfield Manor not far from Banbury.'

'Oakfield!' The preacher leapt to his feet, his eyes wild. 'Who speaks of that Satan's den? That lair of wantonness and debauchery?'

Fairburn turned his interest upon the Quaker. The man was a fanatic. He had wanted to join Fairburn's troop. He had turned the man away, disliking the fervent gleam in his eyes.

'What do you know of Oakfield Manor?' Fairburn asked.

'I know enough to have them all hanged as Malignants,' Isaac Dunnock answered.

Fairburn looked across at Pollett. 'I've no love for Major Rowan. Nothing would please me more than to see him brought to justice.' He turned from Pollett to the preacher. The man was clothed in rags, his bare toes showing through the slashed toes of ill-fitting boots. Boots no doubt stolen from the dead of a battlefield.

There was an expectant hush as the three men looked from one to another and each gave an almost imperceptible nod of acknowledgement.

'Can't do anything until the spring campaign is over,' Fairburn said. 'Come the King's defeat, all Royalist property will be sequestered if it is owned by proven Malignants. And why should that property not be given to a loyal supporter of Parliament?'

'You can have the property with joy,' Pollett stated. 'I want Rowan.'

'The woman must be made to see the errors of wantonness,' Isaac Dunnock declared.

Douglas Fairburn saw the desire in the preacher's eyes and shrugged. His cousin had defied him. She was the cause of Rowan humiliating him.

'The woman is yours if that's your price,' Fairburn pronounced. 'But I shall need evidence against her and her husband that will stand up in Court.'

'I'm like a prisoner here. We never go anywhere.' Maressa's lovely face was white and set with fury. Her lilac silk skirts rustled behind her as she swung about and continued to pace her saloon above Nell Lovegood's bordello.

'It's for your own good, Maressa,' Thomas said stiffly. 'I've received reports that a man is asking after a woman of your description. He's offering a hundred pounds for information.'

'What man?' She glared at her husband.

'I can't find out. He's working through hired spies. Those

351

I have questioned could tell me nothing. Lord Northcliffe died without naming an heir, and there are three claimants to his estate. It could be one of them.'

He did not tell Maressa that only one body had been discovered in the ruins of Mortimer House – a body burnt beyond recognition. He had also kept the news from Laurence. If Henry Mortimer had somehow escaped, then Maressa was bigamously married, and Laurence might carry out his threat to disinherit himself. And now there was Thomasine to consider. Thomas loved his daughter too well for her to carry the stigma of bastardy. Thomas had employed his own spies to search out the truth, but so far, whoever was seeking Maressa had concealed his identity well.

Maressa sank down into a chair and put her head into her hands. 'Thomas, you don't know what's it like being shut away for weeks on end.'

'Here at least you have comfort. Would you prefer the squalor of Newgate while you await the hangman's pleasure?'

The cruelty of his words lashed into her and she burst into tears. Thomas took her into his arms and drew her up against him. 'Here you're safe.'

'You're using that as an excuse. You're too busy with those printing presses you've set up here which print pamphlets against Parliament! I thought you a better businessman, Thomas. Where's the profit in that?'

'An England run by Puritans will never make me rich. The hypocrites may permit the brothels to stay open, but I've lost a third of my income through the closure of the playhouses. Where do you think pickpockets, cutpurses and whores did their best trade? Royalists know how to enjoy life, Puritans are against gambling. I'm losing a fortune every week they keep the pleasure-loving Cavaliers out of London.' He tipped back her chin and wiped the tears from her cheeks. 'If you want more excitement, then come downstairs of an evening. Wear an auburn wig and a spangled mask and sing to our customers. You've a voice like a nightingale. Word will soon get round and men will flock to hear you. Our profits will soar and you would receive a fair proportion of them.'

Interest flickered in her eyes.

'Your voice will captivate our customers, and even behind

a mask your beauty will beguile them.' Thomas saw the calculation in her eyes and knew exactly the right course to hook her with his bait. 'They are the very men who make you a prisoner here. What sweet revenge to rob them of their fortunes to provide the security for your future. It is justice.'

Two years ago Maressa would have been shocked by such a proposal, but now she could see the advantages. Her voice had always won her acclaim. To have men sigh their devotion to her was a powerful attraction.

'If I agree, I must have no connection with the baser activities in this establishment. No whores will attend my performance.'

'You will give a private audience to a few select customers who are prepared to pay for the privilege of watching you. To aid your disguise you will be introduced as an Italian contessa, abandoned by her faithless husband and driven by necessity to sing for men of refinement and discernment.' His smile broadened. 'You shall have several new gowns sewn with jewels, as befits your rank of contessa, although no one will be permitted to see your face. You must perfect an Italian accent in order to disguise your voice. I know an Italian beggar who will teach you. With such a disguise no one will recognise you.'

Maressa visualised herself as the most fêted woman in all London. The beautiful, mysterious Italian contessa, whose golden voice could enslave men. The lure of such power was irresistible.

There was little celebration in the hearts of the Royalists over the Christmas of 1645. Angel still mourned the death of her father. So many of her family had given their lives for the King's cause: Uncle Ambrose, Gabriellen, Mark, Firkin and Llewelyn. And there was still a mystery as to whether or not Maressa had survived the fire at Mortimer House. Angel feared the worst. If Maressa lived, surely she would have written. From a chance meeting with Popinjay in Chester last month, Angel had learned that a reward had been offered for information about Lady Maressa Mortimer, in connection with the fire. Obviously, Maressa's body had not been recovered.

Since the surrender of Bristol Angel had seen little of

Alexander. At present he was convalescing at Oakfield Manor. Caradoc had been shot from under him in a skirmish and as the stallion went down, Alexander had been thrown and had landed awkwardly in a ditch, breaking his leg. Nathan had set it with splints and Alexander was still hobbling about on crutches.

They had despaired of the stallion's life. He was the last of the Rowan stallions and without him the strain of horses bred by their grandfather would die out. The bullet which brought Caradoc down had entered the muscle of his chest. After a plea from both Alexander and Angel, Nathan had operated on the horse and removed the bullet. Caradoc had survived, and Alexander's spirits had lifted further when it was discovered that the Rowan mare Morgan found riderless by Alexander after the battle of Naseby was in foal.

Angel missed her brother. He had invited her to spend the winter at Oakfield Manor, but he and Beth had spent so little of their married life together she did not want to intrude on their privacy. She had stayed in Chester where Nathan had set up another hospital. It was always full, if not with wounded, then with patients stricken by the bloody flux and other diseases that follow an army on the move.

Llewelyn's death hit Angel hard and though she tried not to show it, depression settled like a leaden cloak about her shoulders. Without Nathan she did not know how she could have coped. He refused to allow her to give into her melancholy. Often in the evening he would take her to listen to musicians or ballad singers. But he had not become her lover.

Angel was haunted too by the memory of the passionate response of her body to his kiss on the hillside. A look from him could steal her breath and rob her legs of power. Her mind became a battleground of conflicting emotions. She wanted him, but a stubborn part of her held back. Still the memories gave her no peace. She was plagued by whispering echoes of the rapture she had tasted in his kiss and the passion which his touch had ignited. There was no denying the pleasure that Nathan could give a woman. If that was all she wanted – a tender, innovative and skilful lover, he would have no equal. Once that had been her ideal of the perfect lover. But her ideals had changed. Now she needed more than a frenzied coupling which engaged the body and mind, but not the heart. Her self-respect demanded more.

Angel, who had sought freedom from the constraints of her sex, now found herself bound by her own imagination, her creativity, her fantasies. She wanted the impossible dream of the legends of romance and chivalry. The euphoria of the myth, that two star-blessed lovers are destined to love until all eternity. She knew too well Nathan's scorn of love.

She laughed mirthlessly as she acknowledged the absurdity of her reasoning. The bathwater in which she was soaking had become unpleasantly cool. She glanced at the window and was startled to discover from the fading light that it was later than she had thought. Nathan would arrive at any moment to escort her to dine.

There was no answer when Nathan tapped on Angel's door, but when he heard her bitter laughter, he entered the room. He halted in mid-stride at the sight which greeted him. He had wanted her for so long, it seemed that he had been denied her forever. She had driven him almost to the brink of distraction by refusing to become his mistress. Each nerve in his body was aware of her sensuality: she was untamed, passionate, a woman of fire whom every man dreamed of possessing.

She had been hurt by Rupert, and he knew Angel would never now give herself to a man whom she did not love and who would not love her in return. Even to Angel he would not lie and speak words of love which were meaningless to him. But Angel could never be a fleeting paramour. She was his torment. Her body spoke invitation with every graceful movement, but a will of unbending iron continued to deny him.

Angel was staring into space, unaware of his presence. Her expression was soft and dreamy. Was she thinking of Rupert? Nathan wondered. The thought roused a jealousy he had never known before. He could not drag his gaze from the vision of her loveliness displayed so temptingly. With her wet black hair sleeked back from her forehead and now grown long enough to reach her shoulders, there was sensual earthiness in the contours of her oval face. He studied the fine line of her brow, the proud elegance of her high cheekbones and the delicacy of her slender neck and curving shoulders. Even the scar from the bullet wound added to the pagan splendour of her beauty. His gaze followed a droplet of water as it coursed down her throat towards the swelling of her breasts, and he felt his body respond.

When she glanced towards the window and stretched her arms languorously above her head, her breasts rose out of the water, their rosy peaks uptilted and beckoning. She was still unaware of his presence and Nathan did not trouble to conceal the longing in his eyes. Desire became a physical torment. Unwittingly, a sound must have risen to his throat for she turned swiftly to discover him watching her. Her arms shot down to cover her breasts and she slid beneath the soapy water with such violence that it spilled over the side of the tub, splashing his boots.

'How dare you enter my room without knocking!' Her voice shook with rage, but to his surprise a blush spread across her cheeks.

She looked so desirable that he could not resist taunting her. 'I did knock, but you were daydreaming – and from the look on your face your thoughts were all for a lover. Was it Rupert?'

'My thoughts are my own affair,' she snapped. 'I'm sure you've seen plenty of naked women before, so if you've finished gawping at me, kindly remember you're supposed to be a gentleman and leave.'

The torment of wanting her was almost more than he could stand. 'You've tempted me beyond reason.'

'Nathan, say one more word . . .' she warned, her eyes flashing dangerously '. . . dare to take one more step closer and I vow our friendship is at an end.'

'Is that a threat, Angel?'

Immediately, she saw her error. She had not meant it to sound like a challenge. She had no idea how long Nathan had been watching her. His breathing was low and dangerously uneven. Alarmed, she snatched up the towel and, holding it against her, stepped out of the tub.

'Nathan, this has gone beyond a jest.' Her eyes glittered with warning. 'Get out!'

He laughed and advanced towards her. Angel's throat dried. His gaze was focused upon her figure moulded so revealingly against the damp towel and the ardour in his midnight-blue gaze was like a flame to her senses. He was so handsome. His long honey-coloured hair curled over his lace collar emphasising his broad shoulders, and the scarlet sash at his waist added no bulk to his slender figure. She swallowed and took a step backwards. The smile on his lips was assured of a willing conquest.

Stubbornly she refused to surrender to the call of her blood. When she moved sideways, he countered, and countered again as she darted back.

Nathan laughed softly. What had begun as teasing turned to something more, and his body throbbed finally to possess her. He moved quickly, his gaze so intent that he did not see the bar of soap until it was too late. The heel of his boot skidded from under him and he landed with a thud on the uneven wooden floorboards. When his sword-hilt dug painfully into his hip he let out a startled grunt.

'Your lechery and conceit are your own downfall,' Angel said as she darted away. She scooped up a satin robe and threw it around her shoulders.

'Mock a fallen soldier, would you?' Nathan stood up, grinning.

'Just stay away from me,' Angel warned, her fingers shaking as she fumbled to tie the sash at her waist.

Even then Nathan knew that he could have conquered his desire and laughed aside their encounter. Fate conspired otherwise. The sash slid from her fingers and the robe fell open. There was a rush of blood to his temples. He moved without conscious thought, capturing her in a fierce embrace, his kisses ardent upon her lips, forestalling her protests.

The moment Angel felt his arms about her, her naked body caught against the hard pressure of his manhood, her passion exploded into fire. The attraction between them had been denied for too long. Her lips parted. Her body became a flame as it moved against his and desire ravaged her senses.

Lifting her into his arms, Nathan carried her to the bed and laid her on the edge of the mattress. He knelt beside her and holding her tight against him, he kissed her throat. The heat of his lips made Angel lose touch with reality. There was only the feel and taste of him which filled her soul, the sweet urgency of his kisses as she was consumed in the violent storm of his passion. When his mouth moved to circle her breasts, kissing each in turn until they hardened, swelling firm and proud, Angel gasped in pleasure. Her moans deepened to an ecstatic sigh as his mouth moved down over her ribs. His blond locks were cool and sensually arousing against her creamy skin. His tongue teased across the taut skin of her stomach until he reached the dark curls below.

When he pressed his mouth against her softness, her neck craned back and her fingers laced through his hair. She abandoned herself to the waves of pleasure that scalded through her, expanding, mounting, and finally pulsating into release. As her body shuddered with the force of her passion, her eyes opened to encounter his gaze, dark with his own need. So powerful was her desire to return the pleasure he had given her that she found her hands were shaking as she helped him remove his clothing. When he was naked, she spread her hands across his chest with its hard sculpting of muscles and light sprinkling of hair. His erection drew her gaze – and then her hands. When he stretched out beside her on the mattress, she pressed her lips to his stomach. Then her mouth closed over him, her tongue tantalising, licking, teasing until, with a groan, his hands lifted her face, his eyes naked with a need which was echoed in her own.

He took control, turning her on to her back and she raised her hips to accommodate him. He penetrated her slowly and held the moment as their gasps of pleasure mingled. With masterly precision he moved within her and with each thrust, their rhythm matched in ardour. Their passion was all-consuming, building to a pinnacle which was as bitter-sweet as it was ecstatic, until the moment of release.

Angel stirred and opened her eyes to find Nathan staring down at her with concern. With a start, she realised that she had swooned. She had never fainted before after making love, nor had she believed that it was possible to lose consciousness at such a peak of ecstasy. But the pulse still throbbing deep within her told her that it was possible – that she had reached a summit of rapture unequalled with any other man. Why did it have to be with Nathan, who, by his own admission, despised the ideal of love and constancy?

Nathan stared in wonder at Angel. He was still held within the warmth of her, and felt a rare peace as he gazed into her eyes. As she stared up at him, something within the smokey-green depths of her eyes changed and a single tear formed on her lashes.

He kissed it away. 'A tear? What brings that to your eyes, my darling?'

For a long moment she did not answer, but he saw the slender column of her neck tighten as she swallowed with some difficulty. 'I've spoilt everything. I valued your friendship above all others, but when friends become lovers that friendship must suffer.'

'It will never be like that between us.'

'I don't want to take the risk.'

He eased away from her, to lie on his side, studying her. 'I don't understand you, Angel. Our friendship is special. You are special to me. Desire can only heighten what we have. Have you so little faith in me? I've wanted you for so long. But your heart was held by your Prince. I've waited, discovering a patience I did not believe I possessed.' Even as he spoke he could feel her tension, tinged with sadness and regret.

'As you say, our *friendship* is special,' she said heavily. 'What happened today will not be repeated. It was wonderful and I shall treasure the memory.'

'My darling, what is this nonsense?' He took her into his arms again, to smooth the sable tendrils of her hair back from her neck and cheeks. When he lowered his head to kiss her mouth, her hand came between them and the kiss was taken in her palm. The brightness in her eyes had increased to a luminous intensity.

'It would be all too easy to fall in love with you, Nathan,' she murmured hoarsely. 'And that would be foolish, would it not?'

Nathan felt a hollow sensation in the pit of his stomach. For over two years he had been tormented by Angel's elusiveness. She fascinated him and intrigued him. She had become an obsession. The triumph he had felt at finally conquering her had been equalled by the pleasure she had given him. Women who gave themselves easily to his attentions quickly bored him. Always, he shied away from commitment, yet Angel's rejection struck at his heart. Cynically, he tried to ignore the protective need she roused in him. It had been a dozen years since a woman had touched that chord in him.

The memory brought a return of bitterness he had thought long dead. It was an experience he had vowed never to repeat.

'Your silence says more than words, my dear friend.' Angel drew the sheet around her and rose from the bed. 'They say it's just a matter of time before the King gives into the demands of Parliament. I must visit London to try and find out what happened to Maressa. Then I'll return to France.'

'How can you consider that after the way you were treated there?' He came to her, naked and unashamed, taking her into his arms and tenderly running his fingers through her hair. 'Angel, my darling, why throw what we have away?'

Her eyes were dark with torment. As she stared up at him, she took in every detail of his handsome face: the way his long honey-blond hair fell forward in tousled curls over his forehead, the dusting of pale freckles, the slant of his arched brows – one with its roguish scar, and the smouldering promise in his blue eyes. His full lips parted in a heart-stealing smile and Angel felt her courage wavering.

'What we have is too special to deny, Angel,' he murmured huskily.

'Perhaps too special.' Her voice broke as she pulled away from him.

Then her shoulders were caught and he drew her back to the bed. He held her in his arms, turning her to face him. Desire was there in his vivid blue gaze, and something more, so profound that it held her spellbound. Neither spoke. Angel's throat was too tight from an aching need not to snatch back her words or sacrifice pride and self-respect by surrendering to the silent demand in his eyes.

'I don't want to lose you, Angel,' he said finally. 'You know I despise the ideals of what romantics call love. What I feel for you is—' he broke off, obviously having difficulty in putting his feelings into words. 'I am never more content than when we are together. You make me forget this accursed war. I admire and respect you above any woman I've known. Is that not enough?'

'It is something I will always treasure,' she said softly. 'I, who thought myself so free-thinking that I could change the role of women, find myself trapped by my own nature. The thought of drifting through life from one empty affair to another frightens me. For me there will always be the ideal. Not only must I love, but I must be loved equally in return. Anything less is unacceptable. Even from you, my very dear friend.'

Nathan lay still. Each word she had spoken rammed into him like a musket shot. He shifted his weight and, leaning over Angel, pressed her down on to the mattress. Her black hair spread like midnight silk across the pillow and her green eyes were large and misty with regret. They mirrored his own sense of impending loss.

'Angel, I won't say words of love which are meaningless to me, just to keep you at my side. You deserve better than that. But I will tell you what I've never told anyone else. When I was seventeen I had those same ideals. They lasted all through my studying at Padua, then I went to live in Venice. There's no other place like it for a young unattached man. The courtesans are the most—' he broke off and grinned wryly. 'I shall spare your blushes. Suffice to say they are extremely accomplished, beautiful and exotic. They are also the most decadent and amoral. They thrive on duplicity and deception. And not only the courtesans . . .' his voice hardened. 'I met a woman one year younger than myself. I had tended her father when he had suffered a seizure of the heart. I visited the house daily whilst the old man was an invalid. He knew his heart was not strong and was worried for his daughter's future, so he thrust me into her company. She was beautiful and appeared so shy and innocent that I fell in love with her. I expected the old man to bar me from the house. Instead he welcomed me. It was he who suggested our marriage and because of his ill-health wanted it settled without delay. I adored Sanchia. I so respected her innocence that I never laid a hand on her throughout our courtship. When we married I discovered she was four months gone with child . . . her lover was her own brother. He had conveniently stayed away during our courtship. When he returned, my wife made it clear that she wanted him in her bed, not me.'

Nathan paused to stare vacantly at the wall for several moments. Angel reached out to put a hand on his arm and he looked down at it, covering it with his own before continuing. 'To cut a long story short: I walked out of the house in

361

disgust. The next night I was set upon by the brother and three of his friends. I heard Sanchia laughing as they beat me senseless and, thinking me dead, threw me into the Grand Canal. The cold water revived me and I managed to swim to a landing-stage and crawl out. When I recovered from my beating I challenged the brother to a duel and killed him. By then Sanchia's father was dead. My wife is now, I believe, the most highly priced whore in Venice . . . Now you know why I've no faith in that which you call love.'

All the colour had left Angel's face. 'Nathan, I had no idea. I understand your cynicism, but it changes nothing between us.' She rolled away from him and sat on the edge of the mattress to look back over her shoulder. 'Hold this day in your memory and let us return to the friendship which we both hold dear.'

'Angel, you mistake me. I've no wish to lie with other women if I am your lover.' He kissed her bare shoulder before pulling on his shirt.

Angel lay, silently watching him as he dressed. It took all her willpower not to give in to the persuasion of his words.

He paused at the door. 'Do you really think we are meant to live apart?' He blew a kiss to her and left.

Angel rolled from the bed and paced the room trying to come to terms with her emotions. Nathan's charm was his ability to make any woman in his company feel that she was the only one important to him. Her body still glowed from his lovemaking, but still she fought against the impulse to run to the door and call him back. She closed her eyes, feeling the hot path of tears coursing down her cheeks. Why had she allowed her stupid pride to send him away? Her arms had never felt so empty, nor her heart so wretched. She was as foolish as all the other women who had fallen prey to his charms.

Chapter Fourteen

In the spring of 1645, Maressa left London with Thomas. She was his accomplice in a ruse which would make a fortune during their travels. Thomas had planned their route, first circling through the Kent countryside, then into Surrey and across into Berkshire. They were to remain firmly within Parliament-held territory, visiting isolated areas. All their victims would be chosen with care and Maressa, who had always despised the wilder members of her family, was excited at the thrill of outwitting the gullible.

Maressa was ambitious. Throughout her life, she adopted the role that most suited her ends: to hold her father's adoration she had feigned sweetness, morality and obedience. To snare Henry into marriage, she had employed her beauty and her refusal to yield to his advances. Henry had been a mistake. After living in Nell Lovegood's she was no longer so naïve. Having mixed with the bigots and hypocrites who used the King's dispute with Parliament to advance their own fortunes, she was no longer burdened with a conscience. Now, for the first time since Henry's death, it was believed safe for her to leave Nell Lovegood's. She was twenty-one years old, and intelligent, her beauty irresistible. The world seemed ready to fall at her feet.

Success intoxicated her. As the contessa she had learned how to play the temptress, using her body and eyes to beguile a man. The life of an adventuress on the road also appealed to her vanity. She and Thomas travelled in style, in a coach upholstered with velvet and pulled by four matching bays. Besides the coachman, the groom, and Hazel, a valet was engaged to attend Thomas's needs, and an armed guard rode postern to protect their valuables, ostensibly Maressa's jewel casket. They travelled in the guise of Sir Thomas and Lady

Mary Fanshawe returning to their country estate. At a distance of a mile or two behind them rode four horsemen, Thomas's henchmen.

Their plan was simple and on five occasions in Kent and Sussex had already proved successful. They were now in Surrey, travelling west, and their groom – known as Ferret to his Underworld accomplices, but now using the alias of Sam Black – travelled ahead of them to the next district. There he would spend a day, heavily disguised with wig and whiskers, visiting the local taverns to discover which of the local gentry were most susceptible to Thomas's scheme. Their prey must be wealthy and living alone in a secluded manor house, employing few servants. Whether widow or widower did not matter. Thomas was as capable at charming a lone woman as Maressa was of beguiling a man. Having resumed his role as groom, Ferret would approach the house in the early evening. He would declare that Sir Thomas and Lady Mary's coach had broken a wheel close by and that Lady Mary had suffered an injury to her side and was badly shaken. The laws of hospitality demanded that any respectable traveller was given accommodation for the night.

From the moment Maressa was carried into the presence of Geoffrey Latchmore Esquire, she set out to charm her host.

'Mr Latchmore, it's kind of you to allow us into your home. And such a lovely house it is, with a warm and welcoming atmosphere.'

'It's made the brighter by your presence, dear lady.' Geoffrey Latchmore bowed over the hand she held out to him. He was in his fifties, portly from good living, bald-headed, with a round, pleasant face. He had been a widower for twenty years and it was rumoured in the village that Annie, a young servingmaid, was his mistress.

Maressa dramatically held her side as she walked slowly into the main hall of the manor. She looked sidelong across her shoulder and smiled at her victim. 'Such a delightful hall! I trust we're not inconveniencing you, sir.' She winced and clutched at her side.

'Lady Fanshawe, I will have Annie prepare your room at once. You will wish to retire in order to recover from your ordeal.'

'How considerate you are, sir. But the pain is bearable now that I am in such comfortable surroundings. Travelling from London to one's estate is always a feat of endurance. Do you not find it so?'

'I've only visited London once, my lady.'

Thomas intervened, his expression concerned. 'Are you sure that you would not prefer to dine in your room, my love? You are looking pale.'

Maressa shook her head. 'I know you will take me for a foolish woman, Mr Latchmore, but you've made me feel so welcome that I feel I've come to the house of an old friend.'

Latchmore beamed, his brown eyes already adoring as he followed Maressa's progress across the room. She spread her skirts and seated herself on a covered settle. 'Please sit beside me, sir. That is, if I'm not taking you away from important work. Tell me something of this lovely house. Has it been in your family for many years?'

Within an hour she had learned his family history, and over the evening meal, she ensured that Latchmore was captivated by her charm and beauty. She had been delighted when Latchmore appeared at the table in a brown periwig and elegant jacket of gold brocade. After the meal she crossed to the spinet which stood near the mullioned windows. The ruby curtains were drawn and three silver candlesticks threw a soft intimate light over the room. She struck a note and turned in delight to her host. 'The instrument is in tune.'

'The spinet was my wife's. She loved to play,' Geoffrey Latchmore explained. 'It's regularly tuned, though sadly no longer played.'

'Would it rouse too many painful memories of your dear wife if I were to play for you?' Maressa asked sweetly.

Thomas was sitting in the far corner of the room, careful to act the bored husband.

'It would be an honour, Lady Fanshawe.'

As Maressa played she sang a tender love song, and her gaze remained upon Geoffrey Latchmore. The squire's eyes were dark with desire. He was unable to take his eyes from the rise and fall of her breasts as she drew each deep breath. After two songs, she leaned forward over the keyboard, her hand on her ribs, and gasped.

Latchmore came to her side, but Thomas was there before

him, his tone stern. 'My dear, you've overtired yourself. You're in pain and must rest.'

As she allowed Thomas to lead her to their chamber, she smiled over her shoulder at their host. 'It has been a most pleasant evening, Mr Latchmore.'

'The pleasure has been all mine, Lady Fanshawe,' he replied.

The next morning Thomas left the house early to check the repairs to the carriage at the local wheelwright. He returned as Maressa was seated at breakfast in the dining-room with Latchmore. He hid a smile to see the squire again wearing his long wig and sporting a jacket of scarlet velvet.

'The carriage will be ready for us to leave by noon,' Thomas announced.

'So soon?' Geoffrey Latchmore voiced his dismay. 'I hoped you'd stay for another day or so. I see so few visitors.'

'We could not presume upon your generosity any longer,' Maressa said.

'Nonsense, it's my pleasure. I insist.'

Thomas bowed to their host. 'Then I will accept your offer. My wife is still in pain.'

Maressa looked round the hall at the row of family portraits and the display of silver on the dresser. 'This house is Elizabethan in style, is it not? Have you a long gallery?'

'Would you like to see the rest of the house?' Latchmore smiled in pleasure. 'Or perhaps you would prefer to rest.'

She put her hand on his arm. 'I should be delighted to see your home.'

'You're so uncomplaining, Lady Fanshawe. Brave as well as beautiful.'

Maressa flirted with her host as he escorted her over the house, and in each room she noted the items of value. When Latchmore pulled her into his arms in one of the bed-chambers Maressa clutched her ribs in pain. She winced as she pushed herself away.

'I fear I've walked too far. So foolish of me, but I was enjoying your company, Geoffrey.' She smiled to show that she was not displeased at his boldness. As she left the room Maressa noted the expensive gold and enamel clock on the mantelpiece and a set of a dozen gold toilette boxes on a walnut table. She left Latchmore at her chamber door, promising to rejoin him later.

At dusk, Ferret slipped out of the house to contact Thomas's men and give them Maressa's report. On his return he made certain that a window was left open on the ground floor. Once the house was in darkness Thomas's men silently entered and stripped it of its valuables, even taking Maressa's jewel casket to deflect any blame from them.

The house was roused at first light by Hazel's screams. 'Lady Fanshawe's jewels are gone! We are robbed! Thieves! Thieves!'

Maressa appeared on the landing in her nightrail. Thomas burst from the room, declaring that his pearl-handled pistols and purse had also been stolen. Servants appeared, babbling in alarm, then Geoffrey Latchmore stumbled out, his night-cap askew on his bald head.

'Search the house! Find out how the thieves entered.' Latchmore's face worked with fury. 'Line up the staff for questioning. Did no one hear anything? This house has never been robbed before.'

'My jewels!' Maressa wailed, working herself to near hysteria. 'Those thieves stole my jewels! And I heard nothing!'

The maid who had served at table on the previous evening wrung her hands and sobbed, 'The silver's all gone.'

'And the master's gold snuff-box and watch.' An elderly valet added his voice to the clamour.

'And Mrs Latchmore's clock and gold toilet set,' Annie said sullenly, her coppery hair hanging loose over a green woollen robe.

'Your dear wife's possessions, as well! How cruel,' Maressa wailed. 'Oh, the shame of it.'

Latchmore rushed into several rooms, his face ashen as he returned to the landing. 'They've taken everything of value.'

Thomas, clad in shirt and breeches, his sword in his hand, ran down the stairs shouting, 'We're all robbed! I thought this a respectable house. The authorities must be alerted. Od's blood, I'll not stand here whilst the villains escape! Summon my servants. I'll scour the countryside for these rogues. Do you join me, Latchmore?'

Their host nodded, overwhelmed by Thomas's commanding tone.

Thomas said, 'My men will search the area to the east and north. Your servants take the roads west and south, alerting the authorities.'

A half hour later Latchmore and his servants left the house. Apart from the cook and Annie the house was deserted. Hazel ensured that the two women were drugged and Maressa gathered her possessions together. As soon as Hazel informed her that both women were snoring in the kitchen, Maressa left the house. Ferret and the coachman had already returned and were harnessing the horses. An hour later they were out of the district, and Maressa began to breathe easier as they sped towards the meeting-place arranged with Thomas.

Maressa ran into her husband's arms as he paced the parlour of the isolated inn. 'Tom, we cannot fail,' she laughed as he held her tight. 'How much did we make from Latchmore?'

'It was a good haul,' he returned her laughter.

'Where do we strike next?'

Thomas released her and sat down on a stool by the table to regard her with amusement. 'You're too impatient. The plans must be carefully laid and the ploy cannot be repeated too often or the authorities will be on the alert. I'll not chance the same ruse within thirty miles. And next time you'll wear a different wig, in case any descriptions have been circulated. Greed has been many a rogue's downfall. During the summer we should make several such hauls. Does that satisfy you?'

She stood behind him and put her arms around his shoulders and kissed his cheek. 'We will live like Lords! Have you decided yet where we shall buy our country estate? And of course there must be a house in a fashionable part of London.'

'What you ask will take years.' He swung round and, putting an arm about her waist, drew her down on his lap. 'Give me a son, Maressa, and Father's fortune will be ours.'

She stiffened. 'I've not denied your rights as my husband, Thomas.'

'You've done little to encourage my attentions. Devil take it, Maressa! A man needs to know that his wife finds his attentions pleasurable.'

'That's unjust.'

'Is it?' His stare was cold. 'You give nothing of yourself. I had my first whore when I was twelve. I know when you withdraw from me. It's unnatural and unmanning.' He reached for her hair and wrenched back her head. Maressa gasped at the pain. She knew he was capable of brutality,

368

for she had seen him deal without mercy to anyone who dared to cross him. 'Our marriage bargain was for you to give me a son. I suggest you take note of the whores, for they at least simulate their pleasure.' He released her hair and stalked from the room.

Shaken, Maressa gripped the table for support. She had begun to believe that Tom had a fondness for her, that she could use her wiles upon him as she had used them on Henry. His mood today had frightened her. She had thought it enough just to submit . . . clearly a man demanded more. It was not a mistake she would make again.

The summer of 1646 saw the last of the Royalist army defeated. Sir Ralph Hopton surrendered the western forces in March and the Prince of Wales fled to the Scilly Isles. The remaining Royalist force around Oxford was routed a week later by Cromwell's Ironsides. Cromwell had watched the defeated Cavaliers and their baggage train ride over Magdalen Bridge. Though still plotting with the French, King Charles surrendered to the Scots at Newark and was taken North, despite the horrified protests of Parliament at Westminster. The King's supporters had been defeated but not destroyed. Although the King was a prisoner, the Prince of Wales was in France, and around him Royalists gathered; new plots were devised to continue the fight.

It was not a resolution which Oliver Cromwell found to his liking. There was now disaffection between Parliament over the King. Some people were demanding Charles Stuart's head; Cromwell wanted moderation . . . though he did not trust the King. In his hands were letters written between Charles and Henrietta during the last few years. These showed that despite the King's apparent efforts to reach a settlement with Parliament, he had also been trying to bring Irish rebels and foreign mercenaries into England. Clearly, he had no intention of submitting to a compromise.

When Cromwell returned to his duties in Parliament he was regarded by many as the most formidable figure in England. It was not an accolade he openly sought. Born in Huntingdon he was descended from a nephew of Thomas Cromwell, minister of Henry VIII. He had studied law at Cambridge before he married, content in his life as a country squire. As a Member of Parliament for Cambridge his voice had been behind the reforms demanded of the King before Parliament had been dissolved. With the outbreak of civil war he had joined the army as a captain and secured East Anglia for Parliament. Raising a troop of God-fearing men, he had conceived the idea of loyalist enthusiasm with Puritan zeal and strict discipline. His force was so efficient that soon the whole army was remodelled on the same lines, and his Ironsides had brought victory at both Marston Moor and Naseby. Not that the war had been without its personal tragedy; having already lost his eldest son Robert, his second son Oliver had died of the smallpox during the campaign. Both his other sons Richard and Henry also served in the army. He took comfort in his religion and never fought without some text of scripture to support him. His victories he believed were by the hand of God and though his faith guided him in the path of his duty, his nature was not oppressive. He was merciful to vanquished enemies and mixed familiarly with his men which won their loyalty. Even rough-horseplay was not beneath him and his jests and free speech had scandalised the stricter Puritans.

Yet he remained a man of ideals. With the war seemingly at an end, he feared that victory would not be used to the people's advantage. While he was kept busy dealing with the problems of the army and the interests of his men, he feared that Parliament would disband the army. Not that he wished for military tyranny. His greatest dread was anarchy. Even an imperfect Parliament must be the centre of government. He had spoken in the House, declaring, 'In the presence of Almighty God, before whom I stand, I know the army will lay down their arms at your door whenever you will command them.'

His words had disappointed the extremists who had looked to him to lead a revolution. Gradually, in the following months, he became disillusioned and his health suffered. Still, he had a vision of a greater England and his faith in English Law to resolve the *impasse* between the King and his Parliament remained strong.

Angel was contemplating returning to France, and it was proving a difficult decision to make. Despite her resolve not to be Nathan's mistress, she had found it impossible to resist his ardour and had deferred her journey to the Continent.

They had come to Oakfield Manor to visit Alexander and Beth. Beth had just given birth to Bryan, Alexander's second son, and their third child. All afternoon Angel had been making sketches of her brother's family, for she had promised to paint their portraits before she left for France. The sketches done, she had spent an hour nursing Bryan before withdrawing to freshen herself before the evening meal. Nathan followed her into her room.

'You make a doting aunt,' he teased. 'Seeing Bryan has not made you want a child of your own, has it?'

Angel sighed. 'Bryan has the look of Firkin about him, though, thank God, he's a lusty child. I hadn't realised how good it felt to hold a baby in one's arms. Perhaps I'm a little broody. Though I'm long past the age when most women have borne a child, I've no wish to bear a bastard.' She remained thoughtful and when Nathan put a hand on her shoulder, she turned to look at him, her expression concerned.

'Nathan, do you think I'm barren?'

'A midwife knows more of such matters than I.'

'It would be for the best since I've no wish to marry, but . . .' She shrugged and, dropping her gaze from his face, put her hand over his as it rested on her shoulder. 'I'm being foolish. It would be irresponsible for me to have a child.'

Nathan's fingers curled around hers. 'I know you well enough to realise that your fluxes are less frequent than most women. It does not mean you are barren, but that your chances of conceiving are less.'

'Then it's as well. I'll not produce any embarrassing by-blows.' She spun away from him and stared vacantly across the room.

'I'd not find it an embarrassment if you bore my child. I'd be proud.'

The sincerity in his voice brought a lump to Angel's throat. She despatched it with levity.

'The war has made us old before our time,' she said. 'We're two vagabonds at heart. You've spoken of continuing your studies of medicine abroad. And I . . .' She swept her arms wide in a dramatic gesture. 'I'd thought to return to

France, to write and appear on the stage.'

'That is still your dream?' Nathan was watching her closely.

Angel felt her heart contract. Constantly, she spoke of her return to France because it covered her vulnerability. She was becoming too dependent on Nathan for her own happiness. The aftermath of those last bitter months of the war had left her feeling cast adrift, and it had been easy to surrender to the pleasure Nathan gave her as a lover. But her future was in the playhouse. That was her destiny. Nathan's destiny was to be a great physician and he wanted to travel and improve his knowledge.

She kept her voice light. 'When I finish the portrait for Alexander I'll go to London to visit my Cousin Thomas. If anyone knows what happened to Maressa and her child after the fire, he will. So many lives have been wrecked by this war. It's time we did something worthwhile.'

'You're right.' Nathan picked up a book on anatomy and idly thumbed through the pages. After a pause he added, 'But must you go to Paris? Why not the Hague? I've lost everything in my support of the King's cause. I need a patron to provide me with the means to study medicine.'

There was a tension in his manner which Angel did not understand. Was he so eager to be rid of her and continue his studies?

'I can help you there,' she said. 'My father's lawyer saved our house in Chichester from sequestration. When the fines on Rowan Hall rose too high Alex sold the Chichester house to pay them. From the money left over he settled an annuity on me to replace my marriage portion. Let me loan you the money you need.'

'I'll not take your money, Angel. Though I know the gesture is kindly meant. I may never be able to repay you. My work will be with the common people, not the wealthy. I want to find a cure for the diseases which ravage our country – the pestilence, the plague, the smallpox, the sweating sickness, the wasting sickness. There are so many.' He took her into his arms and stared down at her. 'You say we're both vagabonds. Then travel at my side.'

'For that I must give up my dream of being a playwright.' She held him close and laid her head on his chest. 'We're both driven to succeed. Your cause is worthier than mine, for you seek the knowledge of healing. But I too am driven. Our months together have been glorious. I'll never forget them and I'll never forget you, but we will destroy each other if we stay together.'

She felt his sharp intake of breath and his hands were tender as he stroked her hair. 'I don't want to lose you, Angel.'

'You won't. There's a bond between us which is special and can never be broken. We'll seek our destinies and if Fate is kind, our paths will cross again in better days.'

She kept her head bowed so that he would not see the tears of regret forming in her eyes. Nathan's arms tightened around her. Then his lips were on her hair, his kisses growing more fervent as he unfastened the lacings of her bodice. A gong sounded in the lower part of the house announcing that the meal was about to be served. It was ignored. As Nathan caressed Angel's breasts and dipped his head to kiss each nipple, the desire that exploded through her was so fierce that she cried out. Nathan lifted her skirt to her waist and drew her down on to the window seat. As he entered her, Angel locked her legs tight around his waist and began to rock her body in time to each hard thrust.

Outside in the corridor she could hear Beth calling to Alexander, telling him to warn his sister that the meal was ready. Angel bit her lip to contain her moans as their rhythm built to its height. There was a loud rapping on the door and Alexander called out.

'Angel? We are ready to eat.'

Angel was in the throes of her climax. She bowed her head and was forced to bite into Nathan's shoulder to stop her cries. At once she felt Nathan shudder and then the hot surge of his release.

'We're coming, Alex,' Nathan answered in a strained voice. 'We're both coming.'

Angel collapsed against Nathan, her body shaking with laughter. 'Did you have to proclaim it to the world?'

'Roguery is in your blood, Maressa Angel.' Laurence chuckled, gazing at the precious gems spread on the coverlet over his knees. 'You've done well.'

373

Maressa acknowledged his words with a shrug of her slender shoulders. 'I am glad you're pleased, Laurence. And there's more news – I'm again with child. That's why we returned to London. Thomas would not risk my health on the roads.'

Tears formed in Laurence's rheumy eyes. 'That's good news. This time it must be a boy.'

Maressa gripped her fingers together until she felt her nails draw blood. Was that all Laurence cared about? A male grandchild? He picked up a pair of ruby eardrops and handed them to her. 'For you, my dear, in appreciation. The rest will be disposed of in the usual manner. Another three or four seasons of equal success will make you and Thomas a very wealthy couple. I always knew that prim act of yours was a sham. You're quite without scruples.'

As Maressa left Laurence's chambers, she heard a sudden disturbance from the lower floor of the hall, then Thomas gave a shout of pleasure. Curious, she moved to the head of the stairs and froze in disbelief. Her husband was locked in a fierce embrace with a woman in a scarlet cloak and was kissing her. The woman was laughing and kissing him in return. When they finally broke apart, the woman still held Thomas's hand as she stared up at him. A movement of her head made the hood of the cloak fall away and Maressa saw a cascade of black curls.

Her blood ran cold. It was happening again. Wasn't it enough that her wanton sister had thrown herself at Henry Mortimer? Must she now seek to steal Thomas's affections? Maressa's eyes narrowed as she recalled the humiliation of Henry's infatuation for Angel. Then she remembered seeing Thomas and Angel kissing under the mistletoe one Christmas. Had it stopped there? Thomas had always admired Angel's wild spirit. Jealousy skewered her and with it a need to be avenged on her wayward sister. Maressa concealed her fury. She could afford to pick her time, for revenge was only sweet when exacted in full.

She fixed a smile upon her face and called, 'Angel! Is that you? Is it really my little sister?'

Angel broke away from Thomas, her face more beautiful than Maressa found comfortable to acknowledge. Picking up her skirts, Angel ran towards her. 'Maressa, we've been out

374

of wits with worry. Why didn't you send word that you had survived the fire?'

Maressa was enfolded in an ardent embrace, and stood stiffly while Angel pressed a kiss against each cheek. There were tears in her sister's eyes as she stepped back to regard her. That Angel was so visibly moved by the reunion eased Maressa's initial mistrust.

'I couldn't believe it when Tom said you were here.' Angel hugged Maressa in her excitement. 'I came to Tom, hoping that his associates in London might know what had happened. We heard of the fire whilst in Oxford, but when there was no word from you we feared the worst.'

'I didn't want Father to know I was here,' Maressa said crisply.

'Father!' Angel choked on the word. 'Then you don't know – Father's dead. He was killed just before we lost Bristol.'

Maressa paled and shook her head. 'No. It cannot be. Not Papa! Not my dear, loving, Papa!' When Angel would have comforted her, Maressa stepped back. 'I suppose you were there.'

'I saw it happen. He was thrown from Caedwalla.'

Thomas stepped forward and, with his arms around the shoulders of both sisters, led them into the salon. Realising that Maressa needed time to accept Llewelyn's death, Angel continued to bombard Thomas with questions. Each one was parried by Thomas. He wanted to know everything about Angel's adventures since last they had met. After an hour, Maressa cut in sharply.

'So much talk and so many questions! I declare you quite tire me, Angel.' Maressa needed all her control to stop her smile slipping. She had seen how rapt Thomas had been, listening to Angel's stories. 'It seems that Thomas has neglected to tell you that we are married.' She shot her husband an accusing glare. 'We also have a daughter, and another child is expected at the end of the year.'

'That's wonderful news,' Angel said, smiling mischievously at Thomas. She turned to Maressa. 'There's so much to tell you. Alexander, of course, sends his love. He has two boys and a girl now.'

'Is it Angel?' Laurence demanded, coming into the room. 'Come to me, my dear niece. Are the rumours about you true? Your name was linked with Prince Rupert! What other scandals have you created?' There was no censure in his voice, only pleasure.

Maressa's resentment towards her sister grew. She was not about to have all she had worked for here undermined by her sister.

Alexander bent over the mare Morgan, his expert hand running along her swollen side. He felt the muscles contract and the horse tossed her head as though to shake off the pain. By nightfall she would have foaled and the first of the new strain of Rowan horses would be born. He looked up as young Peter Dunnock came running into the stable. The ten-year-old son of their steward was breathless, his eyes wild.

'Roundheads! Mistress Beth says come at once. They're riding up to the house.'

'How many?'

'A dozen, sir.'

Alexander hurried out, still in his shirtsleeves. He reached the hall to see Prudence Dunnock pushed roughly aside as she opened the front door. A stout officer in breastplate and helmet marched into the house.

'Are you Major Rowan?'

'What business have you with Major Rowan?' Alexander challenged.

'Government business about the non-payment of fines imposed upon all Malignants.'

'I paid the taxes.'

'Not the new ones due last month,' the captain snarled.

Alexander clenched his fist and struggled to calm his rising anger. The new taxes upon anyone who had supported the King were forcing many to abandon their homes. Already, Alexander had been forced to sell the house in Chichester. Was Oakfield Manor to be next?

'Your name, sir?' he demanded.

His question was ignored and the thickset captain thrust out a document towards Alexander. 'We've come for payment.'

Rage boiled in Alexander's gut. It was an extortionate sum. He couldn't raise that much in a year! 'I don't have that amount of money here. This is robbery!'

The officer gave a bitter laugh, his thin lips drawing back over blackening teeth. 'Justice. Simply justice. I've no love for Royalists.' He hawked and spat on the polished floor-boards. 'I lost two brothers at Marston Moor and Naseby. My wife and sister were raped by a drunken band of Rupert's bluecoats.'

He spat again, and this time the globule of saliva landed on Alexander's boot. Then the officer leered at Beth, holding her sleeping daughter Lizbet in her arms. Alexander put an arm around his wife's waist and drew her closer.

The captain rapped out, 'You have a week to pay, or this property will be taken as payment. Be content that they're allowing you to keep the property in Wales . . . for the moment. An example is to be made of all Malignants. Charles Stuart plots to re-establish his army.'

'These terms are impossible,' Alexander flared.

'I will return in a week. If the fines are not paid, you and your family will be turned out into the street. To resist will mean imprisonment.'

'I cannot believe that justice in England could be so corrupt,' Alexander raged. His hand went to his hip but he wore no sword.

The officer saw the gesture and grinned. 'It's as well you're unarmed. My men are ordered to shoot anyone who refuses to pay. One week, Rowan.'

As the officer marched out of the house, Alexander swung round and slammed his fist into the oak panelling. He stared down at the document in impotent fury. He could never meet those fines. When he studied the signature at the bottom of the letter a frown creased his brow. Pollett. The name made his gorge rise. He turned it to the light to study the signature closer. Major Jeremy Pollett. Was it more than a coincidence that the name was the same as the man who had murdered Gabriellen and Mark?

Alexander's first instinct was to fight to keep Oakfield Manor. He applied to the High Sheriff of the county, but the Sheriff was in London and his deputy hated all Royalists. If he raised the money from usurers he had no means of paying it back, and next year there would be further fines and taxes. Unless the King escaped the Scots and raised another army.

'We'll leave,' Beth insisted. 'There's nothing we can do.'

'This is your family home.'

'Your life is more important to me than bricks and mortar.' Beth went into his arms and looked up into her husband's face. Deep lines scored either side of his black moustache and his eyes were bloodshot from a week of sleepless nights. 'I don't want to lose you, Alex. We can fight this action in the courts if we have to. You have Caradoc and the mare Morgan, and now her foal, Guenevere. We'll start a new life in Wales and re-establish the Rowan strain of horses.'

Alexander kissed her hair and clasped her to his breast. 'Would it were that easy. I've no wish to breed horses as fodder for the battlefield. The King's cause is broken, but not defeated.'

'When the King is again in power all that was stolen from his loyal subjects will be returned by a grateful sovereign,' Beth insisted. 'We cannot afford the taxes and upkeep of two estates. We have Rowan Hall and are lucky to have kept that. Many of the King's supporters have lost everything. It will be safer for us in Wales, if war should break out again.'

Alexander hid his misgivings. Wales had not been safe for Gabriellen and Mark. But they had died defending Rowan Hall and the horses. Rowan Hall must be saved or their deaths would have been in vain.

'It seems we have little choice,' he said at last.

'What of the servants?' Beth asked, concerned. 'The Dunnocks have been loyal and hardworking.'

'I'd not turn them out, but their religion may make them unacceptable to the new owner of the Manor. If they wish to accompany us to Wales they may. There'll be work aplenty for them there. The estate has been neglected in recent years.'

A week later, two covered wagons were in the courtyard. The Dunnocks were seated in one wagon, and behind the Rowans' wagon, Caradoc, Caedwalla and Morgan were tied, the foal left to trot beside its mother on the journey. Halfway down the driveway they were halted by approaching riders. A man in brown with a high-crowned hat accompanied them, and Alexander heard Beth draw in a sharp breath.

'I should have guessed my cousin Douglas was behind this.'

Alexander's sword was half drawn, but Beth stopped him.

'No, Alex,' she said. 'At any sign of resistance they'll arrest you. I can bear to lose my home but not you. Please, Alex, swallow your pride. Ignore them.'

Alexander flicked the reins and the horses started forward. He kept his eyes straight ahead when the Roundheads began to jeer, but he could feel Beth trembling as her hand rested on his knee. Douglas Fairburn took off his hat and bowed to his cousin, his ruddy face malicious with triumph.

'I said the Manor would be mine.' He laughed cruelly.

Beth leaned forward and grabbing the whip from Alexander's hands, struck her cousin across his face. 'Take the Manor with my blessing. May you never find peace in it. If there's any justice it will be your tomb not your home.'

Holding his bleeding cheek, Douglas Fairburn hurled abuse at them. As they approached the gateway, a rider appeared, blocking their passage. Forced to halt, Alexander studied the man ahead of him. He wore black with the sleeves of his doublet banded in gold braid. There was a look of hatred on his almost chinless face.

'Halt!' the man ordered and as he turned his horse towards them, Alexander saw that one of his legs ended at the knee.

'Where is the Malignant, Angel Rowan?' Jeremy Pollett demanded. 'She's charged with spying for the Royalists. It's alleged she was also the Devil Prince's whore and parades in the ungodly guise as a man.'

'My sister is in France.' Alexander hoped Angel was already out of England and safe from persecution.

'And a nestbed of Royalists that country is becoming,' Pollett sneered.

'Just watch your step, Rowan,' he added. Parliament governs England now. Known Malignants risk imprisonment if they intrigue against the State.'

'Drive on, Alex,' Beth urged. 'They're spoiling for a fight.'

As the wagons passed out of the village, a preacher stopped haranguing a group of young villagers on the evils of licentiousness. Seeing the procession, he clutched his Bible under one arm and ran towards the Manor.

'You let them go!' he shouted at Pollett. 'Fairburn got what he wanted from our bargain – The Manor. You promised me the woman! The wanton must be made to see the error of her ways.'

'We have the property. That is a start,' Pollett answered. 'Your family goes with the Rowans. I want you to keep in contact with them. I want to know the whereabouts of Angel Rowan – a whore and traitress who will be brought to justice. I want that family destroyed.'

Nell Lovegood's intrigued Angel. She had none of her sister's disgust for the women working there and soon made friends with them all. It was the squalor and hardship some of the women had endured before working at Nell's which appalled her. Many had been raped or were victims of incest and drunken brutality. Others had been abandoned by faithless lovers. A few of them despised men; making love to each other both for payment in a staged tableau, or in private for their own pleasure. From the backgrounds most of them came from, Angel would have expected many of them to be bitter about their fates. But the women working for Laurence and Thomas were content. None were ever abused by their customers. The price of injuring one of Nell's girls was death. Twice it had happened in the last decade and the man's body had been found castrated floating in the Thames.

One whore summed up their lives with a saucy wink. 'Well, luv, it's better than starving in a gutter and giving it away for a couple of pence, like me ol' mother did. Here we're well fed, looked after proper so we don't get the pox, or an unwanted brat. And we aren't mistreated. The coves who can't get it up without a bit of violence use Coriander and Mace.' The whore gave a throaty laugh. 'Spicy names for spicy goings-on. Coriander was used by her father and four brothers from the age of ten. Says a whipping's nothing compared to wot those sods did to her. And she earns triple what we do. Then she has a day or two's rest afterwards. Thomas don't allow her to get too badly beaten, neither. There's always a watch put on her room. And Mace likes to have a go with the whip herself. Lawd, but she hates men, that one.'

Not all of Nell's girls came from poor homes. Bethsheba was the daughter of a wealthy silk-merchant. She was here because she could not get enough sex.

If the women intrigued Angel, what happened in the cellars totally absorbed her. Here, Thomas had set up the printing press for the pamphlets which reviled the Government. She began to haunt the place. It was from her pen that the most scurrilous condemnation was written about Cromwell, Fairfax and anyone she could ridicule for the persecution of Charles Stuart. Her caricature drawings which were reproduced were cruelly witty in depicting the worst in her subjects.

Thomas was constantly at her side. He had always been her favourite cousin and she enjoyed the outrageous stories he told about the inhabitants of the criminal Underworld he ruled. Often, as they sat drinking and laughing, he would put an arm affectionately about her waist and was not above stealing an innocent kiss or two. When Maressa came upon them in such an embrace, it was obvious from her outraged scream that she did not think so.

Angel drew back from her cousin. Thomas had done no more than kiss her lightly on the lips as they leaned their foreheads together, laughing at one of his anecdotes. Maressa stood at the top of the stairs watching them, her hand on her swollen stomach.

'My sister betrays me again,' she screamed.

'Maressa, you are wrong.' Angel hurried to her sister's side. 'Tom and I were just joking together.'

Maressa's voice cracked like splintered ice. 'You want him, as you wanted Henry! Get out of my house!'

'Tom and I are not lovers.'

'I won't listen to your lies.'

'I'd never betray you. Please, we've spent so many years apart, we mustn't quarrel now. There's only you and Alexander left, and I don't want to lose you because of a misunderstanding. Tom and I have always been close and I was just flirting with him. Tom loves you.' Angel took her sister's cold hands. 'And I love you, Maressa. You're so good. I know it can't be easy for you living here, but you'll soon have the grand house you deserve. You're lucky to have a husband who adores you, and two healthy children. You have so much more than I. I envy you.'

Maressa bent her head, her lowered eyelids hiding the expression in her eyes. But to Angel's relief her voice was warmer as she spoke.

'You're right. We should not quarrel. It's my condition. It makes me over-fanciful. I'm fat and ugly. Is it any wonder that Thomas flirts with a prettier woman?'

Thomas stood beside them. 'Maressa, you're more beautiful than ever.'

Maressa lifted her head, her smile beguiling as she studied her husband. When she tilted her cheek for Thomas to kiss, Angel saw that her sister's eyes glittered – not with love, but with anger.

'I'm leaving for Dover in the morning,' Angel said.

'Lucky Colonel Carver.' Thomas winked at her. 'I suppose you're off to join him at the Hague. You speak of him often.'

It was a shock to Angel to realise that Thomas spoke the truth. She did miss Nathan's company, but they had agreed that their futures lay apart. 'I'm returning to France,' she said, emphatically. 'Nathan is devoted to medicine and my future is within the playhouse.'

Maressa hugged her sister. Now that Angel was leaving she was prepared to appear forgiving. It would not do for Thomas to think her petty-minded. She accepted Angel's words of devotion and envy as her due, but she also remembered old scores still unsettled. Thomas had betrayed her marriage by his open admiration of Angel, no less than Henry when he had violated her sister. The pain and humiliation of that still cut deep, and one day Angel would learn what it was to feel such betrayal by a sister's hand.

PART II

Chapter Fifteen

France, Spring 1648

A ride in the countryside around St Germain became routine
for Angel. Here she met exiled Royalists who gathered
around the court, plotting their return to England and reviv-
ing the King's cause. During the two years she had been in
France His Majesty had become a prisoner of Parliament at
Carisbroke Castle on the Isle of Wight. News from England
was gloomy. A new force of Parliamentary fanatics known as
Levellers was strong within the Government, and demanded
radical reform, believing power should be in the hands of
the common people. Oliver Cromwell was now one of the
strongest voices in England. He wanted to retain the monarchy, but to ensure that the sovereign's powers were cur-
tailed and the country was governed by Parliament. Charles
Stuart refused to become a puppet-King and an *impasse* was
reached.

On Angel's arrival in Paris she had discovered that
François and Sabine had sold their business and moved to
the Loire Valley, where Lucrèce lived with her new husband.
After the way Lucrèce had treated her, Angel knew they
could not meet easily, and it grieved her that she could not
visit Sabine and François. She was also disappointed to learn
that Molière was no longer in Paris. His theatre had failed
and, to escape his debts, his troupe had taken to the roads
to make their living as strolling players. Other old acquaint-
ances, like Scarron and Marion de l'Orme, welcomed her and
introduced her to their friends.

Her popularity swept her into a whirlwind of pleasure, but
life could not be all enjoyment. She had promised Alexander
that she would seek out any mares descended from the Rowan
horses which had been sent to France in the earlier years

of Sabine and François Toulon's marriage. Leaving the gaiety of Paris behind her, Angel resumed her male disguise to travel through France. Eventually, she tracked down eight young mares with the distinctive markings and rich chestnut colour of the Rowan strain. Alexander had met her at Boulogne and shipped them back to England.

Tracing the Rowan mares took three months and when she returned to Paris a letter from Nathan awaited her. He had gone to Italy to spend several months researching contagious diseases and over the following months they continued to correspond. She missed Nathan but refused to brood over their parting. It had been a memorable interlude and had even deepened their friendship and not destroyed it as she had once feared.

In the meantime new friends claimed her time. Marion de l'Orme frequently invited her to her salon where she mixed with the most celebrated poets and libertines in Paris. As Marion's protégée Angel soon rivalled the notorious Ninon de Lanclos as the most sought-after beauty in Paris. Ninon was beautiful and voluptuous in spirit and sensuality. But unlike Ninon who reputedly never kept a lover for longer than three months, Angel flirted outrageously with her admirers, but admitted none to her bed. Once Ninon saw that Angel was no threat to her own affairs they became friends.

With her usual candour, Ninon declared, 'Love is but a fleeting whim, a caprice, insubstantial and without substance, delicious whilst it lasts but best abandoned before it loses its piquancy.'

Angel shook her head in dispute. 'How like a dear friend of mine you sound. Those are his sentiments on love. But they are not mine.'

'Is he in France? I must meet him,' Ninon declared. 'Such men make perfect lovers. But first we must find the right lover for you. For shame, Angel. What use is freedom to you, if you do not exploit the pleasure it can bring? Here tonight are a score of the most witty and handsome men in all Paris.'

Angel put a hand to her breast below the silk Angel patch which covered the sword scar. 'Alas, I'm a hopeless romantic.

Besides,' Angel laughed, 'I don't need a man in my life to make me feel complete. I can wait until the right one comes along.'

Across the room a handsome count of military bearing was trying to attract Angel's attention. Ignoring him, she turned away to take up a wine goblet from a passing servant.

Ninon fluttered her fan and raised an eyebrow as she turned her gaze upon the count. 'How can you be so cruel as to ignore Arnaud? I will make it my duty to seduce and console him. He's just got back from patrolling the Spanish borders. Tomorrow I'll tell you how great was your sacrifice to virtue – or not . . .' She snapped her fan shut and tapped it against her nose. 'Valour does not always win acclaim beneath the sheets. Our gallant soldiers are not all aware that it takes a hundred times more skill to make love, than to command an army.'

Angel hid her laughter behind her fan. Ninon was incorrigible. As Angel watched her friend captivate the count, she reflected upon her reluctance to take another lover. Chastity was not a state she deliberately chose, or even enjoyed, but she had not met anyone who matched up to Rupert and Nathan. When she gave herself it would be completely: with body, mind and soul which rose above lust and desire.

Had she been foolish not to accompany Nathan to the Hague? She curbed the thought. She was in France now and had planned to visit Italy later to study the play. The Continental stage was far advanced in scenery and props, and Angel wanted to see the new machinery which could propel sea monsters across the stage, or draw chariots through the air to add spectacle to the drama. It was unfortunate that the Paris playhouses were closed because of the street riots against the French Queen's lover Cardinal Mazarin.

Whenever Angel visited St Germain she found her company eagerly sought by the English Royalists, and often she saw the Prince of Wales. Her heart went out to his tall, slender figure, cooped up here when he longed to be fighting for his father's cause. At seventeen, Prince Charles was rather shy and ill at ease in the role of a penniless Royal Prince. Even the small allowance granted him by the French Court was seized by his mother. Henrietta-Maria declared that as a Prince of England it was an insult for him to take a French pension, whereas she, as a daughter of France, was entitled to it.

On Queen Henrietta's instructions the Prince was ordered to pay court to the Grande Mademoiselle, Ann-Marie Louise, daughter of the Duc d'Orléans and reputedly the richest heiress in Europe. Charles obeyed his mother, but stubbornly refused to speak the French language. The Grande Mademoiselle was haughty and made the Prince dance attendance on her, then ridiculed him as a destitute prince. This angered Angel. Pauper or not, Prince Charles was heir to the English throne.

Angel had first met the Prince at Oxford when he was fourteen. She had been delighted that he remembered her when they met again at St Germain. Since then, she had made a point of using subterfuge to press a pouch of coins into his hands whenever possible. At first he was embarrassed by her action, but with repetition it became a silent jest between them. She wanted no reward; the brightening of his sombre eyes was sufficient.

Now, as she rode through the trees in the park surrounding the palace, she saw a dozen riders returning from hawking. She slowed her Rowan mare to a walk as they approached and smiled upon recognising Prince Rupert and the Prince of Wales amongst the party.

It was the first time she had seen Rupert since leaving Bristol. When he arrived in France he had been made Mareschal de camp. He commanded the English troops in the service of Louis XIV who was engaged in a war with Spain. She had heard rumours that, after four years of battle in England, and emerging unscathed, he had been wounded, and had left his command to return to St Germain. Expecting him to ride past with only a brief nod, her eyes lit with pleasure when he halted.

'Good day, Mistress Rowan,' Rupert greeted her warmly. 'What brings you to France? Rowan Hall was not sequestered by Parliament, I trust.'

A glow spread through her. Rupert was as handsome as ever, but the warmth she felt for him was not that of desire. It was pleasure in their reunion and the knowledge that Rupert had not forgotten her.

'Alexander paid the fines. He intends to re-establish the

Rowan strain. In my grandfather's time, some of the mares were sent over here. I located several of their offspring and shipped them back to England.'

'You're riding one now.' Rupert's experienced eye studied the chestnut mare with its broad white blaze, arched neck and tail held proudly high. 'They're unmistakable. The finest breed in England.'

When he swept his plumed hat from his dark head, Angel was shocked to see the livid red crease made by a bullet across his skull. Rupert's face was unusually pale and his eyes shadowed with pain. A strenuous morning in the hunting field would have caused a lesser man to be reeling in the saddle with agony.

Rupert turned to Prince Charles, who had remained at his side whilst the rest of their party rode on. Charles was watching Angel with interest, and she smiled and bowed her head.

'Your Highness, I'm doubly honoured by your company.'

'The pleasure is ours, Mistress Rowan,' Charles said, answering her smile. He was not strikingly handsome, for his face was too dark and swarthy, his heavy-lidded eyes too soulful and his mouth too full. But there was nothing youthful about his appreciative gaze. From those large somnolent eyes emanated a light which held her transfixed. There was interest, admiration, and something so blatantly sexual in his eyes that Angel felt a flush rise to her cheeks. He was seventeen, not much younger than herself. And in that look she glimpsed the sensual lover which he would become – a man who adored and revered women.

Rupert had also noticed the Prince's interest and withdrew several feet while Charles edged his mount closer to Angel.

'There is a masked ball at the palace tomorrow night. Will you attend as my guest?'

'I would be honoured, Your Highness. But aren't you supposed to be escorting the Grand Mademoiselle?'

Devilry brightened his dark eyes. 'It's your company I desire. Though I cannot openly snub the Grand Mademoiselle, I'll send a carriage and a suitable escort for you. Where do you live?'

She told him and was surprised at how breathless she sounded. He smiled and held out his hand for her to take.

As Charles held her gauntleted fingers, he pulled off her glove and raised her hand to his lips. The simple gesture sent a lightning bolt of fire through her body and her mouth dried. She could not believe the response from her body towards him. Still, his dark stare held hers. This was the future King of England. Beneath a suave but melancholy exterior, he was tortured by fear for the safety of his father. Sensitive to the hidden anguish of others, Angel felt his frustration at being unable to fight for his father's cause. The admiration in his gaze with its mixture of melancholy affected her deeply.

The spell was not broken until Charles smiled in farewell and rode away. Rupert swung about and drew his mount level with hers.

'This Court is a bed of vipers,' he clipped out. 'Charles has need of a friend. Someone he can trust. Someone who will understand his pain.'

Angel stared after him as he rode off after his cousin. Rupert had just suggested that she become Charles's mistress. She should be outraged. Yet, coming from Rupert, it was probably the greatest compliment he could give her. She stifled a laugh. But nothing could halt the quickening pace of her heartbeat as she contemplated her next meeting with Charles Stuart.

The bright candlelight in the ballroom at St Germain hurt Angel's eyes. The room was hot from the press of bodies. She had arrived an hour ago in the company of Henry Jermyn, companion to the Prince, and at once her presence had caused a stir. Her graceful figure in a gown of mulberry silk, with the black silk angel patch covering the scar on her shoulder, drew the speculative gaze of the courtiers. She danced constantly, but only once with Prince Charles.

'I wish I could carry you off into the gardens and enjoy your company in private,' he whispered as the dance brought them close together. 'Sadly, too many eyes are upon us.'

'The night is young, Your Highness,' Angel answered with a smile.

Behind his dark lashes his eyes glittered appreciatively. 'In an hour I will fidget with the lace at my cuff, like so.' He grinned conspiratorially. 'Go into the gardens and I will follow discreetly.'

Angel's pulse quickened with anticipation. She was aware of curious glances upon her, not least from Queen Henrietta, who frowned at her son for dancing with a woman other than the Grande Mademoiselle.

The next hour passed in a blur. Every courtier Angel danced with asked for an assignation. She refused them all. When Jermyn claimed her for a third dance he was intercepted by his friend George Villiers, the Duke of Buckingham. At twenty, the handsome duke already had a reputation as a rake, but there was something about the petulant droop of his mouth which Angel distrusted. When she refused to go outside with him there was a brittleness in his glare which warned her that he would make a dangerous enemy. With relief, she saw the Prince of Wales flicking the lace at his wrist, and she turned to Buckingham with a smile.

'My lord, forgive me, but I must decline your generous offer to escort me back to my rooms. I am otherwise engaged this evening.'

'Madame, no man has claimed your attention more than myself . . .' his tone was affronted.

Harry Jermyn laid a hand on his arm and, with a nod in the direction of Prince Charles, gave a discreet cough. When Buckingham scowled as he realised his error, Angel smiled apologetically.

Leaving the ballroom, she walked into the gardens. A footstep made her turn expectantly, and she found herself gazing up into the Prince's saturnine face.

'I feel like a wayward child who has just escaped a governess,' Angel said with a soft laugh. 'It must have been harder for you. The Grande Mademoiselle kept you close to her side.'

'Her pet, pauper, puppet prince,' Charles answered drily.

'The woman is an arrogant fool. You are no woman's pet. France should be privileged to play host to England's heir.'

'You're a loyal subject,' Charles said, and giving the first carefree laugh she had heard from him all evening, drew her into the shadows.

In the pale moonlight his sensual features were darkly handsome, and she knew that the desire in his eyes was mirrored unashamedly in her own. He kissed her ardently, but with the impatience of youthful passion. When he bunched up her skirts to caress her thigh, she pulled back, and her soft laugh was full of promise.

'No, I pray you, not here. If all you wished was a hasty tumble on the grass, then I fear you have misjudged me, Your Highness. Is there nowhere within the palace where we can be alone?'

There was a slight stiffening to his figure at her presumption. Her heart lurched, fearing that she had slighted him. But slighted or not, even for a Royal Prince she would not be tumbled like a common doxy.

There was a low rumble of laughter in his chest. 'Can you blame a man for his ardour when he's bewitched by your beauty?'

Warily, she looked up at him. Her lips parted as her senses were dominated by his nearness. He dipped his head as he cupped her chin so that her mouth slanted beneath his. The tip of his tongue explored the softness of her lips before he moulded her mouth to his. When he raised his head and looked down into her eyes, his smile filled her with elation. Taking her hand, he led her to a palace entrance far from the ballroom. At the sound of someone approaching, Angel was pulled into a recess, where Charles seized the opportunity to kiss her with deepening intensity, his hands caressing her breasts through the silk of her gown. They were both breathing heavily when they broke apart and hurried through the corridors, seeking the privacy of a secluded room.

An exchanged glance showed them both controlling their laughter. The excitement of the furtive flight through the palace added to the piquancy of the occasion. From behind an open door darkness beckoned and Angel was drawn inside. The moonlight streaming through the window revealed a cushioned day-bed and a writing desk. There was a click as the Prince turned the key in the lock.

'At last I have you to myself,' he said, drawing her down on to the couch. When he again lifted her skirts she drew back.

'Love should be savoured slowly,' she whispered. 'Undress me.'

She guided his fingers to the lacings of her gown. As her bodice slid down he kissed her shoulder, his hands again impatient as they reached for her breasts.

'Slower, Your Highness. I promise you will not be disappointed.'

She moved to stand in a ray of moonlight and stepped out of her gown. Untying the ribbons which held her petticoats in place, her gaze unwavering upon the Prince, she slowly slid each petticoat over her hips. Charles sprawled back on the couch, watching her in captivation. Angel kicked the petticoats aside and, placing her stockinged foot beside him on the couch, she leaned forward. The stiffened corset pushed her breasts high as she leaned forward and slowly removed her garter and stocking. Then Charles pushed her hand aside and removed the second garter himself, his mouth seeking the soft flesh of her inner thigh. When he would have pulled her down to him she spun away, smiling. Remaining just out of reach, she began to unfasten the front lacing of her corset. He watched her spellbound as the garment was tossed aside. Beneath it she wore only a transparently thin silk chemise and the silhouette of her figure was provocatively outlined by the moonlight shining through the window behind her. Still holding his gaze, she pulled the pins from her hair and shook the raven tresses free to tumble down to her shoulders. Only then did she begin to slide the chemise down over her breasts and let it fall at her feet revealing her naked body.

When his hands pulled at his own clothes Angel halted him. 'Let this pleasure be mine,' she whispered throatily and drew him to his feet.

His breathing became heavy as she removed his jacket and then his shirt. She took her time trailing slow kisses over his flesh, his quick snatches of breath telling her of the pleasure she gave him. Her kisses were light upon his chest, her tongue teasing his nipples, her teeth gently nipping the taut flesh of his ribcage as she crouched on the floor before him. Then she was unfastening his breeches, her breath caressing his aroused member, before her tongue teased its tip and her lips drew it into her mouth.

'Angel, you give me such sweet torture,' he gasped. 'Never has the pain of wanting been so blissful. You are all temptress.' He crushed her against him.

'Patience,' Angel counselled. 'There is more.'

'I am your willing pupil,' he laughed, lifting her into his

arms and carrying her to the day-bed.

As they caressed, she subtly instructed, giving of herself slowly, guiding him in the art of restraint. Her skill enhanced both their pleasure until the eager pupil became the master.

Twice they coupled. Before Angel's heartbeat had returned to normal his lips, now tasting of her juices, again sought hers. Just as she thought herself replete, his caresses made her body burn for more. Their sighs mingled in the darkness, their rapture fiery, volcanic. Finally, locked in each other's arms, they dozed.

The distant strains of music faded and as dawn crimsoned the sky, their roles were reversed. Charles kissed Angel to wakefulness. She was now the supplicant to his mastery. He was poised above her, unhurried and in control. He kissed her eyes and lips; whispered words of endearment as sensual as his caresses were murmured against her ear. Then his mouth moved over her breasts, and his tongue explored a tingling circle around each crest, his lips tugging gently as he took them into his mouth. Angel moved sinuously, exulting in his skilful lovemaking and her own overwhelming passion. Hungry for his possession she answered his demands, initiating new delights, prolonging and savouring the exquisite tension. Imaginatively she fulfilled his needs, their kisses smothered moans of passion, until both of them were drained and incapable of any movement other than holding each other close.

Angel sighed and Charles pushed aside a tendril of her tousled hair and kissed her again.

'I've no more strength,' she pleaded with a shaky laugh.

'A mercy on that, for neither have I.' He leant on one hand, looking down at her. 'I've never known a woman as exciting as you. Never felt this much contentment and pleasure.'

She was humbled that the man who would one day be her King should speak so. 'It's been an unforgettable night.' She looked to the window and the crimson sunrise. 'And now I must leave.'

'Nay, my sweet Angel. You have pleased me too well to leave so soon.'

'The palace is beginning to stir. I can hear the servants tending the fires.' The door rattled and there was a disgruntled voice outside. 'Really, I should leave before we are discovered.'

Charles rose from the bed and stretched. 'I want to see you again. I'll take a room for you in a inn close by. Will you stay there? Dearest Angel, you've shown me that life away from England can finally be bearable.'

He kissed her swiftly and as he felt her mouth trembling beneath his lips, he knew that he loved his captivating new mistress. She was loving, erotic, tender, intelligent and amusing – a woman of earthy passion, without guile or self-seeking ambition.

Soon the whole Court was speculating upon the Prince's latest mistress, glimpsed occasionally at St Germain. Angel moved to rooms in a secluded inn a mile from the palace and Charles rarely allowed a day to pass when he did not come to her.

'Only with you, my love,' he repeated often, 'can I forget the wretchedness of my father's plight.'

'The King's cause is not forgotten. He will regain his throne.' She would kiss him, weaving her own spell to make him forget his anguish and pain. 'Remember, everything is possible. Keep faith.'

Each meeting left her in no doubt of his deep affection. Though she did not love Charles with the same intensity which had governed her affair with Rupert, he had a very special place in her heart. And it was not only sex which kept them closeted together for hours upon end. In a second room within the inn, Charles had set up a small laboratory where he indulged his love of science. Angel showed him the experiments in alchemy which she had worked on with her grandfather in Wales, and together they began to improve on these. In Charles's company she often forgot that he was her prince, for he enjoyed her teasing, and never displayed the pompous hauteur of so many exiled noblemen.

Throughout the spring their passion remained undiminished. One morning, after a night when he had not visited her, Angel heard Charles's voice in the courtyard. She ran to the window and saw the yard filled with mounted men. Charles's tall figure was stooped as he ducked his head to enter the inn. A premonition clutched at her heart. She waited in the doorway of her room as Charles bounded up the stairs two at a time. His face was flushed with excitement as he took her into his arms.

'I leave at once for The Hague. The English navy is rebelling against Parliament. Now is the time to strike. God willing, my father will soon be sitting in his rightful place at Whitehall.'

'God be with you, Your Highness. And with His Majesty's cause.' There was nothing else she could say. He had come to say farewell before he rode to aid his father and that meant a great deal.

His kiss held a trace of regret, even though he was impatient to leave and support his father's cause. 'Join me at The Hague.'

For a moment she was tempted. But in her heart she knew that Charles's infatuation with her would not last. Better to end it now, then perhaps he would always remember her with kindness.

Sensing his impatience to leave, she said softly, 'You have a great destiny ahead of you. I am not part of it. But I shall always be Your Highness's most devoted servant. God be with you.'

Sadness shadowed his eyes before he broke away. 'And with you, Angel. Nothing less than this would drag me from your loving arms.'

She forced a bright smile. 'Then do not delay. Your men are restless. Remember always *tout est possible* – everything is possible.'

He kissed her swiftly and then was gone. From the window she watched him ride to the head of the column of men, and her eyes were so misted with tears she could scarcely discern his tall figure in the saddle. Their affair was over. It had been wonderful, and all too brief. But there would be many beautiful and accomplished women at The Hague, and his roving eye would take pleasure in them all.

She regretted nothing. In time, she knew, the ache in her heart would fade. The old restlessness consumed her. It was time to leave France. There was much to be learnt from the Italian theatre. There were great cities to visit throughout the vast Continent and she meant to learn from them all before she returned to England.

* * *

No one who lived with the Underworld fraternity could look upon the scaffold and not feel the spectre of death standing at his own shoulder. Thomas Angel shuddered. The morning of 30th January 1649 was bitingly cold. The wind cut through his fur-lined cloak, but the greater chill he felt came from within as he stared at the black-draped scaffold outside the Banqueting House at Whitehall. He had never thought it would come to this – that the King of England would lose his head.

The press of people was immense. Even the rooftops were crowded, men and boys perched like vultures over an expected feast. Every window was jammed with people elbowing each other aside for a better view. There had never been such a public spectacle before. Many people in the crowd were silent, and pale-faced with disbelief that this day should come to pass. Others derided the monarch who had split the nation in war. A troop of pikemen in buff coats and breastplates surrounded the scaffold, their weapons held rigidly upright, their faces impassive beneath their steel helmets.

Thomas dragged his eyes from the sight of the block, his stare hard as it scanned the crowd. A pie-seller was doing a brisk trade, as were the man with his brazier of roasting chestnuts and the drab selling mulled wine to the crowd eager to combat the cold. Several times Thomas saw a cutpurse or pickpocket lift a valuable prize and disappear undetected into the gathering. They were his men, but for once the sight gave him no satisfaction.

Earlier, the King had been brought from St James's Palace where he had spent his last night. With colours flying and drums beating, a regiment of foot marched both before and behind him. The King walked briskly until the shrill yapping of a dog brought a hesitancy to his step. His Majesty turned and saw one of his dogs running after him, dragging the chain from which he had broken free. When a soldier caught the dog and took it away a look of concern crossed the King's face before he continued on his way.

Thomas had been struck by that look. A strange complexity in a man whose stubborn belief in the Divine Right of his Kingship had brought thousands of his subjects to untimely deaths on the battlefield.

A hush fell over the crowd when the King appeared at a window of the Banqueting House and stepped through it on to the scaffold. He looked small and fragile against the black-garbed men who had been his accusers and the two uncouth, masked executioners. Short in stature His Majesty might be, but his stance was regal. He showed no fear. Charles Stuart would die as he had lived, with dignity and pride.

Maressa moved restlessly at Thomas's side. Her feet were frozen and the silver charcoal warmer which she clutched in her hands had lost its heat inside her muff. She wished she hadn't come. The crowd jostled against her and she winced as another heel ground down on her frozen toes. When the King began his speech, she heard only snatches of his words. She heard him pray for his enemies to be pardoned and that his country should be freed from the tyranny of the sword. As she watched the King secure his long hair under a white satin cap and expose his neck her stomach tightened.

The King knelt before the block and spent a moment in prayer. The headsman took up his axe and when Charles Stuart stretched out his hands the awesome weapon was raised. Maressa gasped in horror as it swung downwards in a swift arc. There was a sickening thud, then a moment of utter silence. It was broken as a cry rose from the crowd. Several women screamed. Someone in front of Maressa fainted at the sight of the jet of blood pumping from the severed neck, staining the straw around the block.

'So die all traitors!' the executioner shouted, holding up the King's head.

The crowd surged forward and began to dip their handkerchiefs in the King's blood. Shouts broke out as the King's hair was shorn and his locks sold for keepsakes. As the body was lifted into a plain wooden coffin Maressa felt Thomas shudder. With a groan, he turned his head away.

'God save King Charles the Second!' he murmured beneath his breath.

'Thomas! How can you say that?' Maressa glanced over her shoulder fearing lest he had been overheard. The look on his face made the hairs on her neck prickle with alarm.

'That England should come to this,' he said softly.

'It's rather late in the day to sympathise with Charles Stuart.' Her voice was sharp. 'Except for the siege at Arundel, you've sat on the fence throughout the conflict. You've made a fortune whilst those Royalist fools have bankrupted themselves for a lost cause.'

'My pamphlets have always supported the King. There was no profit in them. But it was not enough . . .' his voice cracked. His face had lost all colour, and there was a bleakness in his eyes which Maressa had never seen before. 'People fought for what they believed was right,' Thomas went on. 'Whilst I . . .' His expression showed his self-contempt.

She had never seen Thomas like this and it frightened her. 'You were the sensible one. Stubborn pride brought the King to this end. We must all bend to survive and adapt to the circumstances which Fate throws at us.'

'Like you have adapted, Maressa?' Thomas kept his voice low but there was an edge to it which made her heart contract. Despite the chill of the day, perspiration broke out on her forehead. He spoke as though he hated her, blamed her for what had passed.

'I've no regrets,' she said. 'And we shall make the best of life under the Commonwealth. When have we failed?'

There had been one or two setbacks in the last two years. When her son Richard had been born Laurence had prevaricated over the money he had promised her. Rogue and blackguard to the end he had manipulated and cheated her. When he had died three months later – his heart giving out whilst he was making love to one of his women – Maressa had been appalled to learn that his entire fortune had been thrown away on the King's cause.

She stared at the scaffold as the corpse was carried away in its plain coffin. She had no sympathy for lost causes. Laurence had blackmailed her into giving him a grandson and cheated her out of the inheritance. She had been furious when Thomas had laughed aside his father's trickery.

Thomas had toasted his father's memory: 'He lived a rogue and died a rogue.'

Maressa did not remain cross with Thomas for long. During the past two years, when they had continued their adventures on the road, she had become fond of her husband. Until now, she had always believed that they had the same interests at heart – themselves.

As the crowd began to disperse, Thomas took her arm and

pushed a way through to their carriage. Once settled inside, she tried to reason with him. 'You cannot mean to become embroiled with the new King's cause. It's already swallowed up the fortune which should have been ours. And for that, I blame Angel. She spent hours closeted with Laurence when she was in London. She always was an idealistic fool.'

Thomas's expression was fierce. 'Angel's courage to stand by her beliefs only adds to my shame. But the cause is not lost. We still have a King. Do you think I could stomach life under a Puritan yoke? The young King Charles is not like his father. He'll bend to circumstances. Did he not send Parliament a *carte blanche*, a piece of paper with only his signature on, so that they could state their own terms, providing they spared his father's life. There's many in England appalled by today's events. When King Charles II raises an army to reclaim his throne, I'll not fail him.'

Marissa sat back in the carriage, her face devoid of emotion. Inwardly she seethed. Angel was somehow behind Thomas's change of heart. She had inveigled her way into their household, dazzling Laurence and Thomas in a way that Maressa could never forgive. Yet again, her sister had brought havoc to her life. She closed her eyes to hide the feral glitter in their depths, her thoughts upon revenge.

Chapter Sixteen

Wales; Summer 1651

The Vale of Clwyd was masked in early morning mist. The purple shadowed hills rose up to the milky sky, and in the distance could be seen the mellow-stoned gables of Rowan Hall. It was the first time Angel had returned there since her grandparents were murdered. The image of that scene flashed into her mind and brought tears to her eyes. She blinked them aside. Rowan Hall had always been a place of peace and happiness; it would be so again.

The French mares had already foaled and were now grazing in the paddocks. On a leading rein behind her were another four Rowan mares discovered in France. These she had purchased as a surprise for Alexander.

During the three years of her travels Angel had learnt a great deal about drama. Two of her plays had been performed in France, and she had appeared on the stage in four other countries. The occasional lovers she had taken had never matched the happiness she had experienced with Rupert, Charles or Nathan. Yet in her dreams it was the physician who haunted her sleep, not the princes. She had heard nothing from Nathan for two years, their travels too diverse even for their letters to have found each other.

As she urged her mare to a canter, she saw Alexander come out of the house. He still had a slight limp from when his leg had been broken. He waved as he watched her approach. His hair was long and curling to his shoulders, but there were flecks of grey at his temples. Angel leapt from the saddle and ran into her brother's arms. She was lifted up and swung round as he kissed her cheek and hugged her close. When he set her feet back on the ground, he held her at arm's length, his black eyes regarding her with amusement.

'Still a hoyden and dressing as a man, I see! At four-and-twenty, isn't it time you learnt some decorum?'

'I have it when the needs arises.' She laughed. 'I've missed you. But now I'm back and I intend to stay. I'm done with my wandering.'

'From your letters you covered most of Europe.'

Angel shrugged. 'I wanted to forget that my country had beheaded its King, so I decided on a Grand Tour. A dozen different countries with so much to learn from their cultures.'

'And a broken heart left behind in each place?'

A shadow passed across her face and her smile faded. 'Not so many.'

'Do you still pine for your Prince? That was an ill-fated affair.'

The mischief returned to Angel's eyes. 'Which Prince was that? I've known two. Neither affair was ill fated but very special. Then there was the Spanish grandee – very arrogant but an exciting lover – a Viennese count, a German general, and a French and Tuscan player or two. Not to mention my impoverished Florentine artist.'

Alexander was unimpressed. 'Your imagination always was exceptional, but you forget how well I know you. The impoverished artist I can believe was your lover. Rumour linked your name with the Prince of Wales before he went to The Hague and met Lucy Walter. Europe was scandalized when she bore him a son.' He raised his brows sardonically. 'Were you to blame for leading our young Monarch astray? They say the Scots are horrified at his dissolute ways.'

Angel grinned. 'Fortunate are the women who win His Majesty's favours.'

Alexander studied her. 'You never mentioned Nathan in your letters.'

'Our paths never crossed. I didn't come here to be quizzed over my lovers,' Angel chided. 'What do you think of the mares? They're to improve the stock. My present to you, for being such an understanding brother. Many would disown me for the life I lead.'

'Have you been happy, Angel?'

'I've not been unhappy and I have no regrets. I've seen the great cities of Europe which I dreamed of visiting, learned new languages and met many new challenges. My playwriting will be the richer for it.'

Alexander appraised each mare, running his hands over their backs and legs and examining their teeth. His pleasure was obvious in his grin. 'I could not have chosen better myself. And with so many mares I need a dedicated assistant. After the excitement of Europe's grandest cities, could you bear to make your home here?'

'I will stay while you have need of me, at least until the mares are settled. But much as I like Beth, two women in the same household must eventually clash.'

Alexander put an arm about her shoulders and led her into the house. 'You still have no plans to enter the wedded state?'

'Am I not a fallen woman? And brazen enough to regret nothing of my life. Who would have me?'

'Beauty and wit will entrap the most wary. If that fails, there's always the village simpleton who'd never notice your faults.'

Hands on hips, she rounded on him. 'You weren't supposed to agree with me! If I'm such a trial I can always visit Thomas and Maressa in London.'

He caught her finger as she jabbed it against his chest. 'Home just a few minutes and already you talk of abandoning us.' His expression sobered. 'Actually, I do have need of you. We have another visitor. An old friend of yours – John Sparrow. He comes to raise an army for Charles Stuart.'

Upon entering the old hall Angel was embraced by Beth, who introduced her to her four children, Marcus, Lizbet, Bryan and the youngest, Wyn, born six months ago. To Angel's surprise, Maressa's three children were also present: Julian, now nine, Thomasine, who was seven, and five-year-old Richard.

'Marissa did not want them brought up in London,' Alexander explained.

After Angel had greeted the children, she saw John Sparrow come forward. His face was tanned and his tall figure had filled out. When he bowed stiffly, she laughed and rose on tiptoe to kiss his leathery cheek.

'Let there be no formality between us. It's been a long time, my friend. You look well.' She stood back to study him and wrinkled her nose at his plain brown suit. 'I miss the extravagance of the old Popinjay. That patchwork cloak suited you.'

'Peacock plumage is for less troubled days.'

'It seems that I've returned in time to aid my King.'

The pedlar frowned and looked over her shoulder at Alexander. 'Not this time, Angel,' he said forcefully.

As she opened her mouth to protest, Alexander interceded. 'Sparrow is right. I want you here. How can I ride out leaving Rowan Hall unprotected? I trust your sword and skill as I would few men. Beth and the children need you. I need you to protect all we have salvaged of Grandfather's work.'

'But the wounded?' she protested. 'Even if I don't fight, they need me.'

'Who knows what form this rising will take,' Alexander said wearily.

John Sparrow looked worried. 'The response from the people is not what the King hoped for. Many Royalists are hesitant to risk further losses. The first battle could be all-decisive. If His Majesty is the victor, many will flock to his banner when he rides towards London, but if he loses . . .'

'Please, Angel, don't forsake us,' Beth pleaded. 'I can use a pistol and I don't fear the enemy, but I don't want to face it alone.'

Against such pleas and reasoning Angel could not refuse.

Six weeks later Alexander defied the ban on any Royalist travelling more than five miles from his home. He rode out to join King Charles's army, determined to help his sovereign regain the throne. On the second day of his journey he learned that Charles Stuart had entered Worcester, and had there been proclaimed King.

Alexander approached Worcester with caution. Cromwell's troops were in the area and he had no wish to be shot as a Parliament spy before he could declare his allegiance. Through the thinning trees he could see the city ahead of him, the sun gleaming like a gold thread on the River Teme. Behind the city walls rose the gables of timber-beamed houses silvered with age, and dominating these was the pink-stoned cathedral with its high tower. The Royalists looked set to defend the city. Trenches were being dug, and construction work had begun on the new Fort Royal outside the Sidbury Gate. Within sight of the city walls, Alexander drew from his saddlebags the scarlet sash which he had worn in every battle since Edgehill and wound it around his waist. Then he also fixed his officer's steel gorget around his neck.

This was not the first time he had been at Worcester – the

'Faithful City' as it had been dubbed. He had been here with Prince Rupert in 1642. Whilst out on a patrol they had stopped to rest the horses in the hot summer sun by Powick Bridge, some three miles distant. They had been surprised by a troop of Roundheads. Rupert's call to arms had been swift and the victory brutal. It had been the first encounter between Royalist and Roundhead, and then the Parliamentarians had been routed. Alexander hoped that now, nine years later, the same would prove to be the case.

His practised eye scanned the city walls, pitted with musket and cannon shot from battles in the late King's struggle for power. They looked strong enough to hold.

He was informed that His Majesty was at the Commandery, which had been turned into the Royalists' headquarters. Alexander rode through the streets filled with carts hauling ammunition to the defence of the city walls, or stones for the new fort. In every available space new recruits were being put through their paces. Soldiers sat on the ground, cleaning their muskets, repairing harnesses or polishing their armour. In the grounds of the Commandery pikemen drilled, whilst in the orchard, men practised their swordplay. Everywhere was the shout of commands, the sound of marching feet and the air was filled with tangible expectancy.

Stopped by a guard, Alexander gave his name and was ushered through to an inner room, where King Charles was seated around a table with his counsellors. At the announcement of Alexander's name, the King looked up. It was five years since Alexander had last seen him. Then, Charles had been an eager youth, courageously riding by his father's side. Since then the soft lines of youth had vanished from his swarthy face. At one-and-twenty there were lines of cynicism at his mouth and eyes, which told of his years of humiliation as a supplicant and exile. Alexander marched to his sovereign's chair. Bending one knee, he knelt and held out his hands in homage. His hands were clasped in firm brown fingers.

'Major Rowan, we welcome you. Did you bring recruits? Our numbers are not as great as we would wish.'

'Fifty men pledged to follow me. So far only a dozen have arrived in the city. We had to separate when pursued by the Ironsides.'

'You did well to evade them,' the King said sombrely.

'Cromwell is even now building boat bridges across the river to besiege us.'

A burst of fire from Cromwell's cannon outside the walls drew the conversation to a halt. Everyone looked strained with anxiety and tired after the enforced march from Scotland. The Royalists were vastly outnumbered and they knew it. From the tension within the city there was dissent among the Scots and the English. Neither trusted the other, and that did not bode well for the forthcoming battle.

Following the King's execution Maressa had been helpless to stop the squandering of Thomas's fortune as he became obsessed with restoring Charles II to the throne. Though Nell Lovegood's remained opened, all other forms of entertainment were banned by the Puritan majority Parliament, singing, dancing, even ribbons adorning gowns were frowned upon. Although Maressa knew that many of the people like herself hated these restrictions, she had little faith in the revival of the Stuart cause. And now Thomas had left London to join the Royalist army.

Their last year together had been one of constant quarrels and she was surprised to find how much she missed her husband. Despite Thomas's promises, he had not purchased a separate house of their own. He had warned her that renewed interest had sprung up about the fire at Mortimer House and the death of Lord Northcliffe. Should she be recognised as Lady Mortimer, she would be called for questioning and her activities in the last years scrutinised.

At first she had thought he had said that merely to frighten her. After all, it was seven years since they had married. But recently when she had ventured out, with an armed servant in attendance, she had a feeling that she was being watched. It was absurd. Yet without Thomas to reassure her, her unease increased. In seven years none of the dreams they had planned had materialised. Now Thomas was squandering their hard-won fortune on another lost cause. Her fists clenched and she beat her hand against her hip. Had Thomas tricked her as Laurence had done? Her frustration mounted. She was scarcely better off than when she first married him. She chose to disregard that she possessed a casket of jewels worth a king's ransom, and had forty expensive gowns to her name.

Maressa ran her hands over her figure. It was still full-bosomed and round-hipped, her stomach flat, even after bearing three children. With her face hidden behind a mask whenever she appeared in the gaming rooms or in the street, her luxuriant hair and shapely figure still attracted admirers. But she was not getting any younger. She picked up a hand-mirror and, moving to the harsher light of the window, scrutinised her skin. The creams which Hazel prepared left Maressa's face smooth and as unlined as a maiden of sixteen. She twisted her head from side to side. There was only the faintest tracery of lines at her eyes, and her neck was as smooth and slender as ever. She smiled. She was eight-and-twenty, but in the softer glow of candlelight would pass for a woman a decade younger.

Satisfied that at least her looks had not betrayed her, Maressa continued her pacing. She was tired of living under the shadow of the Underworld. Had Thomas not squandered his fortune they could be living in a grand house in the country! She clenched her fists. Damn Angel for coming here with her high ideals.

Maressa halted in her pacing. Angel was to blame for this. And where was her sister now . . . ? Returned from her scandalous life roaming Europe and living in peace and security at Rowan Hall. Maressa's eyes narrowed. At her last visit to her children in Wales, Alexander had not stopped praising Angel. A low snarl rose from Maressa's throat. 'My sister is a whore and Alexander idolises her.'

Were the rumours true which Thomas had laughingly reported? Had Angel been the mistress of the young King? First Prince Rupert and then the King. It was too much. Did she have no shame? Yet, even as she reviled Angel's wantonness, Maressa was beset with jealousy. What power could there be for the woman who took a King to her bed? Not that Angel had profited by it! Now if that had been her . . . Maressa smiled in contemplation of the riches such a position could demand. She stamped her foot in sudden temper. Angel was feted by princes, and she was stuck here. There was no justice!

Maressa picked up a perfume phial and smashed it on the floor. Angel was the cause of all her misery. First she had stolen Henry's love – for that was how Maressa saw that affair now. Then, not content with destroying her first marriage, Angel had filled Thomas's head with idealism. Because of Angel she did not have the grand house she deserved. In London she was a prisoner. Why should she tolerate it? The weather grew hotter and more unpleasant by the day. She'd go to Rowan Hall to see her children. A visit that was long overdue.

She picked up the handbell and rang for Hazel. When her maid appeared she announced, 'We leave for Wales tomorrow. Order the coach and horses for ten.' Her head was beginning to ache with tension. 'Have a bath sent up for me, Hazel. And then I would have you tend me. I am too tense to sleep. You have such a tender hand when you rub my body with oils. I do not know how I would cope without you.'

Unable to sleep, Alexander was up at first light and standing on the city walls. He had not found suitable quarters within the overcrowded city and had made do with a bed of hay in the loft over some stables. He soon met up with several old comrades, and to his delight was reunited with Nathan Carver.

'I thought you were studying with some Moorish doctor in Granada?' Alexander said, holding out his hand to his friend.

Nathan clasped his hand. 'I went from Granada to Venice then to Florence on some unfinished business. There I heard that His Majesty had been crowned in Scotland. I hadn't been through all the other battles to miss the last one. So here I am.'

'What do you think of our chances?'

'Would that Prince Rupert was here to lead us.'

'But he's now Admiral of the Fleet and being harried by Blake somewhere in the Mediterranean.' Alexander looked out across the fields to the river and gripped the wall's crenellated parapet with his hands. 'It's a wonder Rupert has kept the fleet together. He's short of money to pay the sailors. If he hadn't such verve as a buccaneer, seizing and plundering enemy vessels to the discomfort of the English Government, we'd have lost both ships and men. Unfortunately, there's no port the King can claim as his own, and so, to keep the fleet together, Rupert is forced to roam the seas.'

Nathan rubbed his arms to bring some warmth back to

his chilled body. 'To think that a month ago I was basking in the Venetian sunshine.' He looked up at the overcast sky. 'England and its blessed weather. There'll be a storm before the day's out.'

The morning mist was thinning and from the far side of the river the bivouac fires of Cromwell's army glowed like wolves' eyes in the gloom. Their numbers were daunting. Alexander sighed wearily. Was it possible for so few Royalists to triumph over so many?

'Angel's back from her travels too,' Alexander said wrily.

Nathan was studying the enemy encampment, but Alexander saw his friend's throat cord with tension. His voice was gruff as he asked, 'How is she?'

'Madcap as ever and still unwed. I despair of her.' His expression became serious. 'I thought for a time you'd make an honest woman of her. But then you're not the marrying kind.'

Nathan's expression didn't change. 'Well, you're wrong on that score. Didn't Angel tell you, I've been married for years.'

Dumbstruck, Alexander opened his mouth to speak, when the day's bombardment began with a belching of dun-coloured smoke from Cromwell's cannon. The walls shook as cannonshot thudded against them and the air was filled with the whine of musket-balls. A sentry to their right was struck in the throat and with a sickening gurgle he tumbled over the wall.

The two friends ran to take up their position amongst the King's Lifeguards. Shortly they must ride out to attack those guns. Cannonballs were striking within the city, making houses vibrate and windows crack. The streets were filled with shrieks from terrified women and children hurrying to safety. Unseasoned recruits hid their fear behind overloud bluster, whilst citizens scurried about their business, hollow-eyed and pinched-faced. A bugle call summoned the cavalry to boots and saddles. Alexander found his groom waiting with the assembled troops. There was just time to buckle on his steel back- and breastplates before they rode out to face Cromwell's cannon.

Since Cromwell's appointment over Fairfax the previous year to Captain-General and Commander-in-Chief of all the forces, news had reached London of Charles Stuart landing in Scotland. Last summer Cromwell had marched North to defeat the Scots at Dunbar. He held the lowlands but the Royalists in the North remained defiant and, on 1st January 1651, Charles Stuart had been crowned at Scone. Ill-health had thwarted Cromwell's plans to finally bring the Royalists to heel. In February he had fallen ill to an old malady, the ague and, more than once, he was close to death. It had taken until the summer for him to recover his strength.

Throughout his sickness he chaffed at the delay of routing the Royalists. He had some consolation knowing their fleet would not be a problem. Spain had finally recognised the Commonwealth and France showed no sign of supporting Charles Stuart. Eventually Rupert with no port had turned pirate and had sailed for the Atlantic, bound for the West Indies.

When Cromwell returned to duty, he intended to rout the enemy. A summer of cat and mouse tactics ended with the Royalists holed up in Worcester. Now, as he viewed their defences, Cromwell knew his foe to be outnumbered. But they were desperate men, and desperation should never be underestimated. He was resolved that it should end here – England had suffered enough. Trade was crippled by piracies and the hostility of foreign powers. The drawn-out conflict had reduced thousands of honest citizens to beggars. The highways were rife with homeless vagrants, and the prisons filled with debtors. It could not continue. This must be the last bloody fight. The Royalist cause must be crushed.

By the afternoon Alexander ached in every muscle. His breastplate was dented, the lace at his neck and wrists tattered and blood-stained. Sweat slicked down his long hair and stuck his shirt to his bruised and aching torso. Exhaustion and a crushing sense of failure added to his pain. The Royalist army were being beaten back. Earlier the King had left his vantage site on the top of the cathedral tower to lead his men into the thick of the fighting. His presence had roused his troops to fight on though the battle was going against them. Success would have been theirs if the Scots had not refused to support the infantry.

Inside the city was chaos. It was the worst carnage Alexander had witnessed and he was no stranger to bloody battles. He licked dry lips, tasting the acrid grit of gunpowder where earlier he had pulled the stop from his powder flask with his teeth to reload his pistol. His ammunition had long ago been spent.

'What's happening, Major?' an infantryman shouted.

'Do you think Cromwell sent me his compliments and a detail of his plans?' Alexander snapped. 'How do I know what the bastards are up to? Just hold your ground.'

Alexander's mare streamed urine on to the cobbles and the soldier jumped back, cursing. 'Bloody cavalry! Ain't I got enough troubles today without being sprayed with horse-piss.'

At Alexander's side he heard Nathan grunt in pain. A glance showed him the ashen face of his friend. Nathan's right hand was hooked through his officer's sash as he switched his sword to his left hand and continued to fight for their survival.

An urgent shout was followed by the ring of galloping hooves upon the cobblestones. Alexander hauled his mount aside as the King approached.

His Majesty's face was haggard. The saturnine features were streaked with sweat and grime, and there was pain and uncertainty in his dark eyes. It was obvious the battle was lost. The cries of dying men surrounded them and the hoarse shouts and staccato musket-fire of the pursuing Ironsides was drawing closer. The King had shown his courage today. Now his stare looked into the bowels of hell, his heartache naked at witnessing so many dead in his cause. For a moment Alexander thought the King meant to turn and continue the fight.

'Ride, Your Majesty,' Alexander urged. 'You must save yourself.'

The King hesitated. 'I have a brother to continue the Stuart cause. I must fight. Men have given their lives for me this day. I will not run.'

'Save yourself,' Alexander shouted. 'They gave their lives willingly for your cause. Would you let their deaths be in vain? No one doubts your courage. You have fought as hard as any man.'

'Your Majesty must not delay.' Nathan added his own voice. His eyes were red-rimmed with fatigue. 'Go, Your Majesty. We'll hold the street.'

The King bowed his head in defeat and sped off. There

was no respite for those who chose to stand their ground. Broken carts were dragged to barricade the street as the Royalists were forced into retreat. Each minute they held the enemy off gave the young King a greater chance of escape, but the cost was high.

Their horses were shying away from fallen bodies. The bombardment smashed into houses, sending bricks, plaster and shards of window-glass showering over them. Still, the Royalists fought on. Half-blinded by the sweat running down into his eyes, Alexander raised his sword towards a hazy opponent whose sword was raised towards him. Only a shout halted his lunge.

'Damn it, Alex, it's Angel! Tom Angel! Would you slice up your own cousin?'

Belatedly recognising the blackened and grinning face of Thomas, Alexander forced out between laboured breaths, 'Been tempted many a time to run your black-heart through – but not in this fight, coz.'

Thomas spiked a crop-haired Roundhead in the gut with his sword. 'Fort Royal has fallen,' he announced. 'The defenders killed. The bastard Ironsides are showing no mercy.'

Side by side they fought. Nerves coiled with apprehension drove them on. When several Roundheads fell to their swords, fear was checked by the elation of danger. The need to survive revived their exhausted bodies, until they were beaten back relentlessly towards the city gate. Their hearts weighted with despair. The battle was lost. Prisoners would be shown no mercy. Capture meant transportation if not the noose. Desperation pumped through their veins, their sword-strokes blurred. Pain was ignored. One thought drove them. Escape.

Gunsmoke hung like a thick fog in the narrow streets. The acrid clouds choked agonised throats and lungs as the staggering and exhausted Royalists retreated. All around them were the high-pitched whinnies of injured horses and the screams of the wounded. Their horses jostled together in the narrow space of the street. A musket ball grazed Alexander's neck and, as he reeled in the saddle, he found himself staring down at a young soldier on the ground, the broken shaft of a pike embedded in his chest. Death was everywhere. Defeat mocked the battle-dazed survivors.

Alexander straightened and surveyed the Parliament troops advancing through the city, their figures distorted by the drifting gunsmoke. Behind them the road was barely open and within minutes the gate by which the King had escaped could be closed.

'If we're to escape, we must go now,' he yelled.

'I can't leave. I must tend to the wounded.' Nathan swayed in the saddle.

'You're wounded yourself and in no state to tend anyone,' Alexander shouted, appalled at the amount of blood on Nathan's buff coat where he cradled his injured arm.

Thomas was already pushing his horse through the foot soldiers. Many of them had dropped their weapons and, bloodied and wounded, were stumbling towards the city gate, desperate to avoid capture. Nathan slumped unconscious over his horse's neck, and a pool of scarlet spread across the shoulder of the bay gelding Nathan was riding. Alexander grabbed the bridle and, digging in his heels, urged his own horse to push a passage through the fleeing Royalists. Ahead he saw the city gate still open. At a groan from Nathan he pulled a brandy flask from his doublet and pressed it against his friend's lips.

'Drink, man. It will revive you. You've lost a lot of blood. We must get out of Worcester.'

Nathan swallowed and pushed himself upright. His face was grey with exhaustion, his bloodshot eyes darkly circled.

'Leave me and save yourself,' he croaked.

'You're coming to Wales with me.'

Worcester lay several miles behind them, when Alexander at last called a halt to their flight. It was almost dusk and their route had taken them along little-used farm tracks into the Malvern Hills. He would have liked to travel further, but Nathan had lost too much blood. A delapidated shepherd's hut would give them shelter for the night. Once out of Worcester, Alexander had taken Nathan up before him on his horse and Thomas had led the bay. For most of the ride Nathan had been unconscious.

Thomas did not dismount. 'I'm riding for London. The countryside will soon be a-swarm with Roundheads. They'll be searching for the King and others like us. I've no intention

413

of rotting in gaol for choosing the wrong side.'

Alexander eyed him cynically. 'You would see it that way.'

'It was a costly gamble. Maressa had her heart set on a life at Court.' Thomas shrugged. 'Once a rogue, always a rogue. I'll recoup my fortune, given time. Providing the hangman doesn't make me pay my dues first. Maressa must learn patience.'

'Give Maressa my love. She knows she's always welcome at the Hall. God go with you, Tom. You're undoubtedly more talented as a rogue than a martyr.'

Despite his tiredness, Thomas's answering grin was wicked. 'Our Parliamentary brethren are not all as pious as they would have us believe. Therein lays the means to recoup my fortune.'

'Then reap it well.'

As Thomas rode away, Alexander dragged Nathan's unconscious figure into the barn. Inside, in the fading light, he cut the tattered gauntlet from Nathan's injured hand with his dagger. What he saw filled him with dismay.

Nathan shuddered, groaning as his eyes opened and focused. When he lifted his right hand to his face, his voice was harsh with bitterness. 'Sweet Jesu, could they have not dealt me any wound but that.'

There were no words of comfort Alexander could offer. The most accomplished and gifted physician in the country was missing his index and middle finger.

When Alexander left Rowan Hall, Angel had feared that Parliament troops would seek reprisals and use his absence as an excuse to sequester the horses. Ten mares were in foal and these were herded to a paddock in a remote part of the valley, where Elijah Dunnock and his son Peter tended them. Angel left the household chores to Beth and Prudence Dunnock, whilst she and Ruth Dunnock, now seventeen, managed the dozen horses left in the stables. Ruth was a pleasant girl with light brown hair and a dimple in her chin. Much to the consternation of her parents, who did not approve of Angel's lifestyle, she followed Angel everywhere, asking about her life abroad and the people she had met.

Angel had no wish to encourage the Quaker girl against her parents' wishes, and was careful to keep her answers circumspect. Even so, Ruth's blue eyes sparkled with admiration. She began to emulate the graceful and sensuous way Angel moved and when working with Angel, away from her parents' censure, wore a scarlet ribbon in her hair. She spoke incessantly of falling in love and openly scorned the dour Quaker gentleman Elijah wished her to marry.

Two days ago a Roundhead patrol had searched the house, looking for Alexander. They had also questioned all the servants as to whether they had seen a black-haired stranger who stood two yards high. Then later a Wanted poster was pinned up, offering one thousand pounds for information leading to the capture of the fugitive Charles Stuart. To Angel's horror, Ruth had boldly eyed one of the young Roundheads and during the last two evenings had taken to walking in the woods for an hour or more. A careful watch would have to be placed on the girl, any connection with Roundheads was dangerous for a Royalist household.

Threats had been made in Alexander's absence. It was impossible to convince the authorities that he had not joined the King, and this time Angel feared that Alexander would pay for his loyalty by imprisonment. That was unless he had fled to France, but she could not see her brother leaving Beth and the children to fend for themselves. If the Royalists had been defeated then, God forbid, they might lose the Rowan estate.

From the open window of the solar she heard the sound of a harpsichord and Maressa's voice. Ten days after Alexander had ridden out, Maressa had arrived in Wales. For a month she had played the grand lady, lying abed until noon, refusing to work, though allowing Hazel to help in the kitchen. Completely overawed by Maressa's proud airs, Beth would hear nothing said against her behaviour.

When working with the horses Angel invariably wore a plain russet skirt, the back hem of which she hitched up between her knees and tucked into the waistband. Her hair was tied back with a saffon satin ribbon.

Apart from Alexander, Angel was the only one who could control Caradoc. Returning from Caradoc's morning ride, she tethered the stallion to the paddock fence, removed his saddle and began to rub him down.

'You look like a gypsy wench in that brown skirt,' Maressa

415

sneered. 'And all hitched up like that, it's indecent. If Father were alive I don't know what he'd say.'

Without halting in her rhythm, Angel looked over her shoulder. Maressa was dressed in a crimson gown more appropriate for an afternoon idling away the hours in London.

'He'd not condemn me,' Angel replied. 'I've done nothing I'm ashamed of. I dress to suit the work in hand. And there's work aplenty to be done here.'

'You always were a hoyden. Circumstances may have forced me to live as we do in London, but I insist on maintaining certain standards.'

Angel straightened, her green eyes glittering dangerously. 'What standards are those, sister? You married Henry for his title and Thomas for his fortune.'

'How dare you judge me?' Maressa seethed through bloodless lips.

'I'm your sister. I know you for what you are.' Angel pulled some chestnut hairs from the horse-brush before adding, 'I don't condemn you. I've never judged Tom for what he does. He's always been honest about admitting he's a rogue. I lead the life I choose. Providing I hurt no one, I've no reason to be ashamed.'

'I suppose you're proud of being Prince Rupert's whore! Yet where did it get you? Nowhere. Where are the fine jewels and gold he should have given you?'

Angel's head came up, her stare defiant and amused. 'That's where we differ. I loved Rupert. I wanted nothing from him but his time. My memories are more precious to me than jewels.'

'Do they put food in your belly? A roof over your head? And that episode with the young King – if it's to be believed,' Maressa scornfully tapped her fingers on her hip. 'Beth tells me you actually gave him money!'

Angel smiled in remembrance. 'He had none, and I could afford to live comfortably. I didn't take him as my lover just because he was the heir to the throne. I was very fond of Charles. He loved me.'

'You're a fool,' Maressa scoffed. 'You call yourself a free woman – yet all you do is let men use you.'

'Only one man used me,' Angel said darkly. 'And I doubt

416

he served you any better for all his title.'

Maressa started as though Angel had struck her at the reminder of Henry's betrayal.

'Henry certainly had you figured out for an easy tumble,' she retorted savagely. Then she turned and flounced back into the house.

Angel stared at her sister, staggered by the depth of loathing in her voice. A moment or two later she heard a dog barking by the end paddock. A rider was crossing the ford in the river, leading a second horse. The ginger horse could only be from the Rowan stock.

'Alexander's returned!' she shouted. Then she leapt on to Caradoc's bare back and galloped out to meet her brother. Halfway to him, she saw that there were two men on the horse. Alexander's head was drooped with exhaustion and the second man was slumped over the gelding's neck, apparently unconscious.

When she halted at his side, her eyes widened with alarm at the blood smeared on Alexander's buff coat. 'Alex? Are you hurt?'

He lifted his head. A week's growth of beard blackened his cheeks and his eyes were sunken and bloodshot. 'We were routed,' he croaked. 'The bastards were all over us like maggots in a corpse. Got a scratch or two, nothing serious. Unlike . . .' his voice broke as he stared down at his companion. 'It's Nathan, Angel. Poor sod's lost two fingers. Reckon he'd rather have lost a leg. He's taken it hard. Says his life's work is over. He's been unconscious for the last hour. Never thought I'd get him here alive.'

Angel stared mutely at the slumped figure. The honey-gold hair, blackened by gunpowder, hung in tendrils soaked with sweat. A grimy blood-soaked bandage covered the hand which swung limply. Such an overwhelming rush of pain filled Angel, that she swayed in the saddle.

'Is there no justice? Not his hands!' she said, as tears streamed down her cheeks. 'But he'll not die, I won't let him.'

When they arrived at the house Alexander slid wearily from the saddle, and Beth ran weeping into her husband's arms. He hugged her briefly. 'Have a room made ready for our guest.'

417

'No. Put him in my bed,' Angel insisted. 'I will tend him night and day until he regains consciousness.'

Maressa came forward and put a hand on Alexander's arm as he made to lift Nathan down.

'You've come to the Hall in unhappy times, Maressa. But you look well. I left Thomas three days ago. He was returning to London.'

Maressa pouted. 'Your companion is wounded. A sword cut, is it?'

'A common enough battle wound,' Alexander answered tersely.

'Then you're a fool to bring him into the house!' Maressa exclaimed. 'Twice, Roundhead patrols have been here in your absence. Each time the house was searched. If they come and find a wounded man you'll be imprisoned.'

Beth cried out in anguish, her gaze fixed on her husband's face.

'This man is my friend,' Alexander said sharply. 'I'll not leave him to die in a ditch.'

Angel stood at Nathan's side. When she touched his brow she was relieved to find it was not feverish, but the chill flesh was equally alarming. His sleeve, leg and horse's back were dark with blood.

'Maressa is right,' Angel said. 'We must try to cover your tracks. If Nathan is found . . .' She held Alexander's questioning glare. 'You could lose everything. I'll take Nathan to the old woodcutter's hut in the next valley and tend him. The hut is isolated. We shall be safe there, and, God willing, Rowan Hall will be spared.'

'We've journeyed far enough.' Alexander was on the point of collapsing. 'Tomorrow will suffice.'

With a glance over her shoulder to ensure that none of the servants were close by to overhear Angel whispered, 'I think not, Alex. Ruth has become friendly with a Roundhead billeted in Llangollen. She steals out to meet him secretly. What if she betrays us? Let me take Nathan now. Owain the groom can be trusted. Send him over with food and blankets.' She turned to her sister. 'Will you ask Hazel to give Owain the necessary physic to combat his infection and aid his recovery?'

Maressa eyed Angel sullenly. 'Is that man important to

you? You risk much to save his life.'

Angel's hand rested tenderly on Nathan's damp hair. 'He's a special friend. One of England's finest physicians.'

Maressa avoided Angel's stare as she answered. 'Hazel will prepare what's necessary. I think Alexander should take to his bed with an assumed fever. That will be his excuse for not being here when the patrol searched the house. If they return he must say he was visiting his mistress, but that discretion forbids him revealing her name.'

Alexander glared at Maressa. 'I'd not shame Beth with such a lie.'

'Then you may lose Rowan Hall, if not your freedom,' Maressa warned.

Angel mounted Alexander's tired gelding, unwilling to risk transferring Nathan to another mount since their journey would be a short one. Sitting behind him she eased his unconscious figure back against her body. With her arms around him, she picked up the reins and turned the gelding away from the house. Her voice carried back to her brother. 'Our King is a fugitive. For now his cause is lost. Save yourself, Alex. Save Rowan Hall.'

All that night and throughout the following day, Angel forced infusions of herbs between Nathan's cracked lips. As soon as he was settled on a truckle bed in the woodcutter's hut she stripped the bandage from his hand. The mutilation appalled her. Not because of its gory sight, but for what it meant to Nathan's future. What worried her most was the amount of dirt around the wound from the grime of battle. First tying Nathan down so that he could not throw his arm about, she cleaned the wound. Both fingers were severed at the lowest joint – a freak wound received as Nathan's hand somehow lost its grip beneath the protective sword hilt. The stumps had bled profusely and as soon as she touched them, began to bleed again. At least the blood had cleansed the dirt inside the wound and had probably saved him from infection. But the bleeding must be stopped. Loss of blood was the cause of his unconsciousness. If he lost much more he would die. She must cauterise the wounds. Heating the blade of her dagger in the fire, Angel waited until it glowed red and then pressed it against each stump, gagging at the stench of charred flesh. Nathan jerked in his bonds and cried out, his lips bloodless. She lifted one of his eyelids and saw the whites rolled back into his head. Alarmed, she felt his pulse. It was faint. She worked quickly, smearing a pain-soothing salve over the scorched flesh, then rebandaged his hand.

At the sound of a horse approaching, Angel tensed and took up the primed flintlock musket which she had earlier propped against the wall. Tucking the butt against her shoulder, she moved to the shuttered window and, through a knothole, saw a rider approaching. To her surprise, it was Maressa. Laying aside the musket Angel opened the door.

Maressa swept into the hut, her exotic perfume and sapphire-blue velvet riding habit out of place in the humble surroundings. Her blonde hair was dressed in ringlets which fell to her shoulders beneath a high-crowned hat trimmed with white plumes. Pressing a nosegay to her face, she inhaled its perfume.

'How can you abide staying in this hovel?' she jeered.

'To save Nathan's life I'd willingly live in a cave.' Angel ignored her sister's jibe. 'What are you doing here? Owain brought us food to last a week. It's dangerous to draw attention to the hut with so many Roundheads in the area.'

Maressa looked around the cottage. The only furniture was a three-legged stool and the truckle bed. She placed a leather bag on the hard mud floor. 'That's a fine greeting for my trouble,' she said waspishly. 'Hazel prepared a special tisane to strengthen the invalid and Alex put a change of clothing in the bag. This Nathan Carver must be very special for you both to risk so much.'

'He's an exceptional man.'

Maressa moved to the foot of the bed and studied Nathan's unconscious figure. 'I suppose beneath that stubble he's handsome enough. Beth says he was your lover.' Maressa sniffed disdainfully. 'Have you no pride? The princes I can understand. There is at least a certainty dignity in being the mistress of a prince. But a physician . . .'

'I don't expect you to understand, Maressa,' Angel said stiffly. 'Why have you come? Was it to impress Alexander? Shouldn't you be returning to London to be with your husband?'

'Is that the gratitude I get for riding here?'

Angel bit back a sharp retort. She did not want to be at odds with Maressa. 'No. I appreciate your coming here. I hate this distance between us. I want us to be close again, Maressa.'

'I can't forget how you humiliated me.' Maressa's voice was coated in ice. 'I'm ashamed to have a wanton for a sister.'

Angel hid her pain from Maressa's words behind a flash of anger. 'At least I'm an honest whore. I don't pretend to be something I'm not.'

Maressa strode to the door. Such hatred sparked in her eyes that Angel involuntarily shivered. At a groan from Nathan she ignored Maressa's departure. Touching his brow, she was relieved that his temperature was normal, and his cheeks were no longer ashen. When his eyelids opened she found herself drowning in his vivid blue stare.

'Welcome back to the land of the conscious,' she said lightly. 'You gave me quite a scare. It's a shoddy way to return to a friend.'

He did not speak, but his eyes crinkled at the corners. His stare was so tender that her heart contracted.

'I had forgotten how beautiful you are, Angel,' he said softly.

She rested her palm on his unshaven cheek, 'Sssh, you're still weak. Don't speak. You lost a great deal of blood.'

A spasm of pain clouded his eyes. He closed them briefly and when he opened them again, their expression was bleak. He raised his bandaged hand, his mouth thinning as he stared at it. It was easy to guess his thoughts.

'Your wound will not stop your work,' she said. 'You're still a great physician.'

'I could not tie the simplest bandage now.'

'So you will have to employ an assistant,' she encouraged. 'It's your knowledge which is important.'

A wry smile touched his mouth but it did not reach his eyes. 'You're always so practical, Angel. Who will permit me to examine them? People shy away from deformity.' There was no self-pity in his tone, just bitter resignation.

She shook her head. 'Are you worried that ladies will no longer pursue you? That would be very short-sighted of them.'

'There's been only one woman I've wanted these last years.' His gaze took in every detail of her figure and face, the longing in his voice almost destroying her control.

'Did you ever think of me, Angel?' he asked.

'Every week.'

'Just once a week? That's brutally honest, but not very flattering.'

The intensity of his gaze ploughed through her composure. 'Did I say it was only once a week?' she could not resist teasing.

'More than twice?' he queried.

'Oh, quite possibly so, but I'll not pander to your conceit.'

He grinned, satisfied. 'Same old Angel giving nothing away.'

Maressa burned with indignation as she rode away from the hut. Years of resentment scalded inside her. She had seen the admiration on Alexander's face as Angel had ridden away with Nathan. It had been the last straw. There was a prickling sensation at the base of Maressa's neck and she looked over her shoulder. That feeling had been with her since she had left London, a feeling that someone was watching her.

On her return to Rowan Hall, she discovered the Roundheads again searching the house. Alexander was being restrained by two soldiers while the troop's commander paced up and down the old hall, his wooden peg-leg thudding hollowly on the ochre and black tiles. She summed up the man's narrow-shouldered figure. His slack lips, weak chin and large paunch were evidence of his weakness of spirit.

Jeremy Pollett carried a riding whip and as Maressa approached he struck Alexander across the face, his voice shrill with frustrated anger. 'Answer me, damn you! Where have you been, if not to Worcester?'

Alexander's eyes blazed and a trickle of blood ran down his cheek.

'He was with his mistress,' Maressa cut in, knowing Alexander was too stubborn to lie. 'He's too much of a gentleman to speak of such matters before his wife.'

Pollett swung round to face her, his eyes widening appreciatively as he regarded her figure in the close-fitting riding jacket.

'And who are you, Madam?'

'I'm Mr Rowan's sister.' She looked at the two men holding Alexander's arms. 'Is such treatment necessary? My brother has been ill with the tertian fever and laid low in Chester for a fortnight. He's still weak.'

'Why should Rowan stay silent when his freedom is at stake?'

Maressa shrugged. 'I've never troubled to understand the concepts of honour which govern a man's mind. Perhaps Beth has a shrewish tongue?'

'Take him to the gaol,' Pollett ordered. 'He'll stay there until I'm satisfied with his answers.'

Beth burst into weeping, but Maressa checked her outrage as Alexander's hands were tied and he was pushed out of the house.

'Major Pollett?' She hurried after him. 'Is visiting a mistress now a crime, that you arrest my brother?'

Beneath his wispy moustache Pollett's lips narrowed. 'This family are known Malignants.'

'Not my brother!' She leaned closer, lowering her voice to a whisper. 'You do not look like a man to miscarry justice. Especially when I've just learned that there is a true Malignant in our family. Even now she is concealing a man wounded at Worcester. Angel Rowan has brought nothing but shame and disgrace to our name. Whilst my brother was away, without his knowledge, she has harboured a fugitive.'

'In the house?' Pollett rapped out.

'No. She knew Alexander would never permit it.'

Pollett's eyes narrowed. 'Then where?'

'First release my brother. He is innocent.'

All her life Maressa had coerced men, no one had ever failed to fall beneath her charm. Her manner was confident. The speed of Pollett's movement took her completely by surprise.

His face twisted with hatred as he grabbed her wrist and jerked her arm behind her back. 'Tell me where your sister hides, or I'll break your arm.'

He increased the pressure, making Maressa cry out in agony. Her shoulder felt on fire and tears stung her eyes. Too late, she realised the depth of Pollett's hatred for her family.

'Tell me,' he snarled. The pressure on her shoulder brought her to her knees in agony. 'Or I'll have your brother hanged from the nearest tree. Perhaps that will loosen your tongue!'

'I'll tell you. The pain . . . my arm, please . . .' The leverage was lessened slightly, but his grip remained firm. 'There's a woodcutter's hut in the next valley,' Maressa sobbed. 'They are there. But Alexander please, let him go free.'

Pollett released her with such violence that she fell flat on the floor. The Major's eyes blazed with triumph. 'Just think yourself fortunate I don't throw all of you in gaol.' Grabbing Maressa's hair, he hauled her head back. 'If you've lied to me I'll be back. And it will be the worse for you.'

Beth ran to her side. 'Maressa, what did you say to that man to make him so angry? I thought he'd break your arm.'

Maressa stood up and, still trembling, shook out the creases in her skirt. 'I was pleading Alex's innocence. The man is a monster.'

'They have nothing against Alex,' Beth reasoned. 'Though if they discover Colonel Carver on the estate I fear the consequences for us all.'

Maressa closed her eyes, unable to stop the shudder which gripped her body. She had underestimated Pollett, but to cover her betrayal she spoke sharply. 'Angel is to blame for anything which befalls her. We could have hidden the Colonel in a cellar or somewhere. She had to take it into her head to play the heroine. How like her to think of no one but herself. Pollett is no fool. He'll have every blade of grass searched if he thinks there's a rebel in this valley.'

'Then we must warn Angel.'

'And lead Pollett directly to them?' Maressa countered. 'He's bound to leave a man to watch the house.'

Beth gripped Maressa's hands. 'What are we to do?'

'I don't know. But there must be something.' Maressa hid a satisfied smile. Beth had no idea that she had betrayed her sister.

The interior of the woodcutter's hut was gloomy. The tiny window let in little light and the sky outside was black and overcast. A single candle gave off a feeble light as Angel prepared the evening meal. Lifting the cauldron from the fire, she spooned thick potage into wooden bowls and took them to where Nathan sat on the bed. She put the bowls on the floor.

'First take your medicine.'

She uncorked a phial and measured out several drops on to a spoon and lifted it to his mouth. He took it docilely enough until the bitter herbs burned his tongue. With a cough, he screwed his eyes shut and shuddered.

'I taught you better than to poison your patients,' he gasped.

'And I've heard it said that physicians make the worst patients.'

'You're a hard woman, Angel. Don't I get even a little sympathy?'

The teasing in his voice did not conceal his constant pain, and to take his mind off his injury, she asked, 'What made you return to England and risk so much, Nathan? The last I heard of you was when I visited Rome. I'd missed you by a sennight.'

He studied the toe of his boot for a long moment before lifting his gaze to hold hers. 'There was unfinished business I needed to attend to in Venice. It took me weeks to trace Sanchia. She had become the concubine of a wealthy Florentine and moved to that city. When she was unfaithful to him he threw her out. I found her in a convent hospital. I'd never have recognised her. She had smallpox. Her face was ravaged by the disease and she was close to death. I wanted to be free of her, Angel. I never expected to feel pity for the wretched creature. At least the money I gave the nuns ensured that her last days were more comfortable.'

'You treated her with more kindness than she deserved, but I would not have expected less from you.'

'I'm finally a free man.'

Angel laughed. 'Marriage hardly shackled you, Nathan.'

The yearning in his eyes smote her. 'I never thought it was possible to miss a woman as much as I have missed you these last years. God knows, I've done everything in my power to forget you. It was impossible.' He lifted his uninjured hand to touch her face.

She rested her cheek in his palm. 'I missed you too. All the travel, the new and exciting sights, even the plays were not the same without you. Were they wasted years? The playhouses are still closed. With King Charles defeated, his cause must surely be crushed. There's no place for me in England. Yet I've no further wish to travel. I want England to be my home. Must I then deny the stories in my head – banish my dreams?'

'Whatever dreams you have you'll achieve,' said Nathan. 'The future is always uncertain. Today is what matters. And today we are together again.'

They smiled into each other's eyes. Nathan's uninjured hand sought hers, their fingers entwined. No words were necessary. No length of parting could dim the desire which irrevocably bound them together. A rush of emotion overwhelmed her and she saw it answered in the depths of his eyes.

As she opened her mouth to speak there were shouts outside the hut – a jangle of harness and stamp of horses' hooves. Before she could reach for the musket the door burst open, and the hut was filled with Roundheads.

Angel was grabbed by two soldiers and her arms wrenched behind her back. Nathan, still weak from loss of blood, was hauled to his feet.

'This one's wounded. He was obviously at Worcester,' a soldier grunted and slammed his fist into Nathan's gut.

Angel cried out, 'For pity's sake! He's too weak to fight you.'

'Silence the wench.' The order was shouted from the doorway.

Angel was slapped twice across the face and she tasted blood in her mouth from her cut lip. As her head came up a man hobbled into the hut. Her eyes went to his wooden leg and slowly lifted to encounter Pollett's hate-twisted features. Her hopes were blasted, this man would show them no mercy.

'Tie them up,' Pollett shouted. 'They will repent of their Royalist sympathies in gaol before they hang!'

Chapter Seventeen

A month in prison had dulled Angel's rebellion. Her cell was tiny and without light, the straw rat-infested and foul. She had been stripped to her shift for Pollett's first sadistic questioning and her clothes had never been returned to her. She was half-starved and half-frozen, her mind numbed with misery. She did not even know where she was being held, except that it was in England. Nathan and Alex had been taken south, whilst she had been locked in gaol in some strange town.

Night and day merged into one, broken only by the torment of frequent questioning. Pollett was determined to prove that she had given aid to the fleeing Charles Stuart and knew his hiding place. Every denial earned her a beating with a birch rod from Pollett. When she still did not break, she had been left alone for the last three days without food.

At the sound of bolts being drawn back, Angel tensed and pushed herself up from the cold damp floor. She bit her lip to stop her teeth chattering, loath to show any sign of weakness. She swayed dizzily to her feet, gathering the soiled linen of her shift around her thighs, desperate to hide her shame. Her flux had started several hours ago and she had no bindings to pad its flow. The gripping stomach cramps she could bear, but the thought of this man seeing her bloodied was too degrading.

The flaring of a pitch torch sent her scurrying into a shadowed corner. Squinting painfully at the unaccustomed brightness, she raised a hand to shield her eyes from the glare.

'God, the wench stinks,' Pollett jeered, holding a nosegay close to his face. 'And the foul creature bleeds. At least the world will be spared another Royalist bastard. She can't go

427

to trial looking like that. Get Mother Brewer from the bawdy-house to see she's washed, fed and made presentable. The church elders must not have their sensibilities offended.' Pollett laughed maliciously. 'Your lover will rot in London's prison for months. Like as not, he'll be hanged before you.'

Angel fought aside her fears for Nathan. Maressa had come to see her once, to tell her that Alex had managed to escape and had fled to France. Nathan was still imprisoned.

Pollett grabbed Angel's chin. His fingers pinched her flesh, and he forced her to stare into his cruel eyes.

'Still defiant? You won't remain so proud. First you'll be put in the pillory. I've known women leave their wits behind after too many knocks on the head. Then of course there'll be the whipping through the town – a hundred or more lashes you'll get that day. And what will your sentence be? Hanging? Or do you think they'll burn you as a traitress?'

Angel ignored his taunts, knowing he was trying to frighten her. She kept her stare defiant and controlled the need to scratch at her armpit, where lice and fleas feasted upon her flesh. His face was contemptuous as he took in her filthy matted hair and figure.

'I vowed to see your family broken for crippling me. Your pride will be smashed, as your grandmother smashed my kneecap. The fines are due on Rowan Hall, and if they aren't met that will be the end of your precious family home.'

Thank God she had her annuity from Alex which was with a Chester goldsmith. She'd told Maressa to get Beth to use it to save the Hall. She held Pollett's stare unflinching. 'I have faith in English justice.'

'So you say now. Wait until you've experienced it.'

Laughing maliciously he left the cell, taking the light with him. Alone again, Angel sagged against the wall, trembling with fury. Alexander was an exile and she was to face public humiliation, possibly death, because of Pollett's spite. Yet he was the murderer. He had shot Mark Rowan in cold blood. Her head came up. At her trial her voice would be heard. She would denounce Pollett, and if there was any justice in England, Gabriellen and Mark would finally be revenged.

Maressa came into town to witness Angel's trial. With her hood low over her face she watched the proceedings from the upper gallery of the courtroom. When her sister was brought into the panelled chamber, her hands and feet shackled, she felt a moment of triumph. Angel wore an ill-fitting loose gown which emphasised her slimness and height. Her black hair was matted and worn indecently loose, as brazen as any farthing strumpet. Yet Angel showed no shame. Boldly she outfaced her accusers, her head tilted proudly. Her green eyes were contemptuous as she listened to Pollett's lies. Her stance reminded Maressa of their father and her triumph curdled. How could she have betrayed her sister? Llewelyn would never have forgiven her for so unnatural an act.

Then she heard Angel's voice rise above the clamour of the spectators. It rang out clear as a church bell as she turned the accusation back upon Jeremy Pollett.

'If in the eyes of the law I've done wrong, then I accept I must be punished,' Angel declared. 'As all criminals must be punished – especially those who have committed murder. I denounce Major Jeremy Pollett as a murderer. He ordered the death of my grandparents Mark and Gabriellen Rowan, in cold blood. As justice will be passed upon me this day, I demand that justice be done to my grandparents' killer.'

A stunned hush fell over the gathering. Then all at once everyone began to shout. The noise was deafening. Justice Ryecroft banged on his bench, his thin face with its wart-stippled chin turning purple with rage.

'Silence!' he demanded. 'Or I'll have this court cleared. It's not for a prisoner to denounce their own accuser.'

'Even when that crime is murder?' Angel asked. 'I call upon English justice. Mark Rowan was a respected landowner and horse-breeder, once in the confidence of our late Queen, Elizabeth Tudor. He was unarmed when he was shot. A man of four score years, who all his life had lived in honour.'

Uproar again broke out, and Justice Ryecroft nodded to the steward of the court who fired his pistol into the air. The clamour lulled to a low muttering. The grey-haired judge sucked in upon almost toothless gums and leaned forward on the bench, his colourless eyes piercing as they stared at Angel. 'You say Mark Rowan was your grandfather? That Major Pollett had him shot in cold blood?'

'I was there and I saw it all. As did several witnesses.'

The Justice shook his head. 'Mark Rowan was an exceptional man. I knew him well. I heard of his death some years ago, but not the circumstances.'

'Mark Rowan was unarmed,' Angel repeated. 'Pollett ordered him shot when he tried to prevent his stallion from being stolen.'

Again the crowd began to shout.

'The woman's a Royalist! A hoyden!' one woman screamed. 'She's lying to save her hide.'

'I knew Mark Rowan. He were a good man.' A man in a leather apron with the muscular arms of a blacksmith waved an angry fist in the air.

Pollett was white-faced and visibly shaking. 'I did my duty as an officer of the Parliamentary army. I lost my leg in the service of my country,' he blustered, trying to win the sympathy of the crowd.

'If Rowan were murdered,' a well-dressed merchant announced, 'then justice must be done.'

'Rowan was a malcontent!' Pollett shouted. 'He was a traitor!'

'Mark Rowan was a God-fearing man.' An elderly alderman in a fur-trimmed robe and old-fashioned velvet cap added his voice to the cries for justice. 'He was revered and respected. Whereas . . .' He allowed his gaze to fix contemptuously upon the officer. 'In the troubles Pollett's troop gained a name for savagery and looting. Didn't he have a boy whipped to get his mother to reveal where the family silver was hidden? The boy died under the lash. And a young maid – not a whore, but a respectable merchant's daughter – was raped and left half dead in the churchyard where Pollett's men had dragged her for their sport. There have been other cases of his brutality. If Rowan was murdered then his butcher must face trial.'

A farmer with cropped brown hair and a greasy leather jerkin stood up to speak.

'Aye, Pollett has long believed himself above the law. Twice he raided my livestock to feed his troop. I got not a penny. Took my chickens and cows. Two of my children died one winter because the poor mites had no food. They'd have lived if he'd left us just one of the grain sacks. All we had was turnips, and they half-rotten.'

Justice Ryecroft banged the bench again, and several soldiers marched in, their halberds pointed at the crowd. In the confusion Pollett tried to run out.

'Arrest Major Pollett,' Ryecroft ordered.

Soldiers surrounded the Major and dragged him, protesting, from the court. When the hubbub finally subsided, Justice Ryecroft again addressed Angel.

'There are still the crimes to consider for which you are accused. You harboured a rebel – a traitor to the Government.'

'I tended a wounded man who was also my friend.' Angel remained unrepentant. 'Who amongst us could call ourselves a Christian and desert a friend in dire need? During the conflict I was Colonel Carver's assistant. He is a gifted physician – a rarity amongst his kind. In his hospital we treated the wounded of both armies. Colonel Carver never turned away a patient, Cavalier or Parliamentarian. And I'd not let any man bleed to death for want of his wounds being tended.'

'We're not here to pass judgement upon Colonel Carver, but upon your own conduct. Were you not Carver's mistress during your time in Oxford?'

'I was not. I was his assistant.'

'And during this time you dressed as a man and unashamedly paraded yourself in that guise.'

'I dressed as a man to save my reputation. Only camp followers were allowed to tend the wounded. I saved many lives.'

A shocked gasp went through the crowd.

'Were you at this time Prince Rupert's whore?'

'Whilst in Oxford I tended the wounded,' Angel evaded.

'That was not my question. Were you the whore of the Devil Prince? Remember you are under oath.'

Angel remained silent. She was not ashamed of her affair but she did not want notoriety.

'Your silence condemns you.' Justice Ryecroft regarded her with thin-lipped disdain. 'Your conduct is that of a wanton. Your intent may not have been treasonable in harbouring a rebel, but you have shown no shame. Wantonness is a crime before God and as such must be punished. I sentence you to two days in the pillory, whereby you may repent of your sins and see the godlessness of your ways.'

431

Maressa sat back, satisfied that Angel would pay for the shame she had brought upon their family. Yet her satisfaction was marred by the reluctant pride she felt for her sister. To denounce Pollett had taken courage. What would Angel care about spending time in the pillory if she lived to see Pollett hanged and Mark and Gabriellen avenged?

Even in her shame Angel had managed to find glory. Jealousy swamped Maressa again. She pulled her hood lower over her face and watched Angel being led from the courtroom by two guards. Maressa stood up and pushed through the crowd, determined not to miss the spectacle of her sister's disgrace.

A fine drizzle added to Angel's discomfort. The wooden clamps of the pillory were at shoulder-height, her head pushed through a central hole and her wrists shackled on either side, at a level with her ears. The pain was excruciating. She had been locked in the pillory for an hour. At first insults and rotten vegetables had been pelted at her, but when news of her speech against Pollett spread the abuse died away.

Angel still had no idea where she had been brought. It was a small town without a defensive wall. The market-square where the pillory and stocks were set up was partially filled with livestock pens containing poultry, cattle, sheep and pigs. To one side of the pillory was an old stone gateway, which had once belonged to a monastery before the Reformation. Just visible through its arch was a squat Norman church with a low battlemented tower. Opposite the pillory was a thatched timber-framed ale house, bordered by thatched wattle and daub houses. The court house stood behind her, its overhanging upper storey supported by six wooden pillars. The building doubled as the Corn Exchange and Town Hall. From the thin spirals of smoke rising sluggishly from tall Tudor chimneys, Angel guessed there to be fifty or sixty residences within the town.

After her initial surveillance, Angel kept her stare fixed on her bare feet on the wooden platform. In an effort to shut out the pain she concentrated on how she could find the witnesses to speak against Pollett. Popinjay was the obvious choice, but she had no idea where the pedlar was. The only man she knew who was capable of tracking the pedlar down was Thomas and his network of spies linked through the criminal fraternity. That was if Thomas had escaped arrest after fighting at Worcester. Knowing Thomas she suspected that he had.

The drizzle penetrated her sodden clothing and Angel's feet and hands began to turn mauve with cold. Her teeth chattered and as her hair dripped down her back, she began to shiver.

By midday the drizzle had stopped and the crowd gathered around Angel again. A group of apprentices began jeering at her misery. Gradually she became aware of a cloaked figure pushing through the people surrounding her. A wide-brimmed hat hid his features, yet there was something familiar about him which caught Angel's attention. With a swift lunge the man grabbed hold of a woman and snatched off her hood.

'Behold another Rowan!' he shouted.

Angel was shocked to see Maressa struggling in the man's grip.

'Behold Maressa Rowan,' he proclaimed. 'Once – Lady Maressa Mortimer. Adulteress. Arsonist. Murderess. Poisoner and bigamist.'

Maressa struggled wildly in the madman's arms trying to break free. Something in his voice penetrated her initial fear and it turned to ice-cold horror. The voice was that of Henry Mortimer. The voice of a ghost.

She twisted to stare up into glacial blue eyes. One hand was around her throat and the other forced one of her arms up behind her back.

'Call the constable. I want this woman arrested. In London she's wanted for the murder of Lord Northcliffe. She also tried to poison her husband.'

The commotion had brought several aldermen from their meeting in the court house, Justice Ryecroft among them.

'You, sir!' The Justice stabbed his cane towards Henry Mortimer. 'Explain yourself.'

Maressa was dragged through the crowd. 'This woman is my wife,' Henry shouted. 'She tried to poison me. She murdered Lord Northcliffe with his own dagger and then burnt down our house to destroy the evidence. I was wounded within it and left to die.'

Justice Ryecroft looked shocked. 'These are serious crimes, sir. Where did they take place?'

433

'In London.' Henry released his hold on Maressa's neck and pulled off one of his gloves. As he held up his hand a gasp went through the crowd. The flesh was twisted and scarred. 'I got these wounds trying to escape the fire. Murder and poisoning are foul crimes. I've spent years hunting my bigamous wife down. She remarried a month after she thought she had killed me, and became the concubine of the leader of a gang of thieves and cut-throats. For the last seven years she has lived in one of the most notorious bordellos in London.'

The crowd which earlier had turned upon Angel now bayed for Maressa's blood. Fear choked the breath in her lungs and her head began to swirl. Henry was alive? It was not possible. He knew she had killed Northcliffe. And this talk of poison? Did he mean Hazel's potions? And bigamy . . . ? Dear God, she had lived in sin for seven years with Thomas. Thomasine and Richard were bastards. Another greater fear drenched her in a cold sweat: she had no claim to Thomas's fortune. All she had endured and worked for was for nothing.

In desperation she stared around for a means of escape. All she saw were faces, eyes staring, malignant and outraged; their mouths were gaping red holes as they chanted for her arrest. Faces swirled like dancers around a maypole, their expressions blurring as the violent pounding of her heart reverberated through her head. She was being swept inside the court room to the gaol. Then terror mazed her senses and she fainted.

Henry Mortimer let Maressa's unconscious figure crumple to the floor. For seven years he had waited for this moment, and he intended to savour every second of it.

'Lady Mortimer must be put under guard and escorted to London to face trial for the murder of Lord Northcliffe,' he demanded.

Justice Ryecroft was seated behind a large desk and signalled for his scrivener to write down the charges. 'First Angel Rowan accuses Major Pollett of murdering her grandparents and now you drag a woman out of the crowd, accusing her of murder, poisoning and arson – serious crimes which cannot be acted upon without proof.'

Henry thrust his scarred hands at Ryecroft. 'Are these not proof enough? I've others on my back.'

'They prove you have been burned in a fire,' the older man countered. 'Not that this woman is your wife nor that she murdered Lord Northcliffe.'

'In London she will be identified as Lady Mortimer. Why did she go into hiding if she was not guilty?'

Ryecroft studied the woman who lay unconscious on the floor, her beautiful face framed in a halo of blonde hair. It was an angelic beauty which stirred even his cynical heart. When she moaned and her eyelids flickered, he nodded to a guard to lift her on to a chair.

'This woman does not look capable of such wickedness,' he said.

Mortimer laughed, its mirthless sound like a dagger chipping into ice. 'Was Lucifer not once a beautiful angel? Until he fell from God's grace? That creature is a fallen angel in every sense. She's a bigamous whore – her beauty hides a demon's heart. For months I was bewitched by her evil, unable to perform as a man should towards his wife. Some days I was so ill I had no strength to rise from my bed.'

'How did she murder Lord Northcliffe?' Ryecroft asked. He studied Mortimer's face. There were lines of dissipation carved around the man's mouth, and a chilling arrogance in his blue eyes. He knew Mortimer's type: insufferably conceited, proud to the point of vengeance.

Ryecroft added, 'Your wife is delicately built. Some years ago I was the magistrate at the Sessions held close to Northcliffe's estate. Two women once servants in his house were accused of vagrancy. They were both unmarried and pregnant. Each said Northcliffe raped them. It was also rumoured that the suicide of a young stableboy in his employ was because of his master's sodomy. Northcliffe was a degenerate of the worst order. He was also powerfully built. He could have forced himself into your wife's chamber intent upon rape.'

'Northcliffe was our dinner guest on the night of the fire. My wife had been flirting with him all evening. I was suddenly taken ill with stomach pains and went to my bed. Later, I realised that my wine had been drugged. It had happened before and I'd been ill for days. I remember little of what happened that night, but something woke me. Flames were coming from her bedchamber and I staggered

435

through a barrier of fire to escape. My clothes ignited. Only by rolling on the dew-covered grass did I save my life. It was several months before I recovered from my ordeal. I've been searching for that murderous bitch ever since.' He flung an accusing arm at Maressa. 'If she's innocent why did she not answer the Justices' summons when Northcliffe's death was investigated? When I was strong enough I began my own investigations. A waterman remembered picking up two women from the river steps close to Mortimer House that night. He took them to Blackfriars and they mentioned Nell Lovegood's bordello. That place is owned by her cousin, a rogue embroiled with the dealings of the criminal under-world. I suspected that her cousin was her lover for some months before the fire.'

'It's all lies.' Maressa put a hand to her temple, her eyes large and pleading as she gazed up at Ryecroft.

The elderly man regarded her sourly. 'That will be for a jury to decide. You'll be taken from here to the gaol and transported to London for your trial, Lady Mortimer.'

Angel was stunned to recognise Henry Mortimer suddenly resurrected from the dead and accusing Maressa of such horrific crimes. Maressa had refused to speak of the night of the fire and Angel knew how vindictive Henry could be. But what had made him hold his peace for seven years and strike at Maressa now?

Angel's discomfort was great, but tomorrow she would be freed from the pillory. Not only must she now see that Pollett was brought to justice, but she must ensure that Thomas knew of Maressa's arrest. It dawned on her that Thomas must know Henry Mortimer was still alive. For him to have guarded that secret meant he must care for Maressa. Surely he would not abandon her now . . .

As soon as Angel was released she would go to London. She would save Maressa and bring Pollett to justice . . . And Nathan was in London too. Not least of her problems was to also find a means of securing his release. She had lived without him too long to sit back and allow Fate to part them now.

Thomas Angel walked into Nell Lovegood's and was immediately accosted by Nell herself.

'Thank God you're back, Tom.' Her face was white with fever. 'You're in danger of losing everything. Fat Jake's used your absence to make himself Upright Man in your district. He's hired a dozen henchmen as his bodyguards, and told everyone you were killed at Worcester.'

Thomas was not unduly surprised. Big Jake had been his father's second-in-command for years. At five and forty he resented taking orders from a younger man. Big Jake was one of the most dangerous men Thomas knew and there were many within the fraternity who were in awe of him. Thomas was not one of them. Big Jake had to be dealt with and at once.

Thomas stayed long enough to change his travel-stained clothes and revive his strength with a hasty meal. While he ate, word was sent to a score of his most trusted men.

Thomas sent two men ahead to deal with the lookouts posted outside the warehouse, where the fraternity's daily meetings took place. The warehouse was in the heart of Thomas's domain, where no constable dared venture. Thomas led the way through the dark labyrinth of streets. He knew every rat-infested hovel, every hiding place and escape route. An Upright Man was King in his domain and Thomas had spent his childhood at Laurence's side learning its secrets. The warehouse was on a darkened corner. A two-storey building of wooden weather boards, it stood detached, separate from the terraces of tall gabled inns, bawdyhouses and shabby warren of tenements. All the property in this quarter was owned by Thomas and each one of its four hundred inhabitants was answerable to his good will. Generations of his ancestors had accumulated the property and with it the bawds, their pimps, beggars and pseudo-cripples, and every type of known thief and scoundrel who inhabited it. Every bawd owed him a cut of her earnings, and if any thief took his plunder elsewhere, he'd be floating in the Thames before the day's end.

Thomas ruled supreme. Like any lord of the manor, he dealt justice to those who petitioned him about disputes. Thomas had known the risks of Big Jake's defection when he joined the King. And so did Big Jake. After tonight only one of them would be alive.

Thomas's men had already entered the warehouse and he stood for a moment in the doorway. Several wooden chandeliers, larger than cartwheels, hung from the rafters, each holding a dozen candles. The room was only half-full – a sign that many of Thomas's loyal vassals had stayed away. The majority here tonight were the beggars, cripples and bawds, the weakest inhabitants of his district. Only the hard-bitten thieves and cut-throats had defied Big Jake.

The air was thick with the fug of tobacco smoke and the stench of unwashed bodies. Thomas's nostrils flared in disgust at the odour of stale urine where the men had relieved themselves in a corner, too lazy to stagger outside – something Thomas had never allowed. Two ancient pickpockets were urinating at the moment. A toothless bawd jeered. 'That's the only action your puny tools will get tonight.'

'Least I ain't rotting with the pox like you, you old hag.'

Angry shouts broke out as three men holding fighting cocks with spurred talons, baited each other. Fiddle and pipe music battled to be heard above the din of voices. Bawds with breasts exposed and cheeks flushed from ale, danced country jigs, their skirts lifted to their knees. A subdued queue of petty thieves, clasping their spoils of the day, shuffled forward to receive Big Jake's payment. Young pickpockets wrestled or lay on the floor trying to look up the swirling skirts of the dancing bawds. Men seated on upturned barrels argued over a turn of a card, or squatted in circles wagering upon a throw of the dice. Ribald invitations were mixed with jeers. Old scores were settled often breaking out into fights.

Thomas nodded to his men who had spread out to cover the hall, each with a brace of pistols in their hands. His eyes narrowed as he stared at the dais where Big Jake and a scrivener were collecting the day's plunder. On each side of Big Jake stood two armed guards. At his feet sat a snarling white bull-terrier, one eye and ear missing, gouged from its bull-baiting. It was a vicious brute and had maimed several men who had tried to attack its master. There were piles of coins on the bench and behind it, silverware, pewter, household goods and clothing. Stolen jewels and money pouches were stashed in two deep chests. Even though the accomplished thieves had stayed away, there was over two hundred pounds' worth of goods in the warehouse.

With a flamboyant gesture Thomas threw off his cloak, tossing it to a startled catamite who should have been at work in the bawdy house next door. The boy's carmined lips quivered in alarm at recognising the Upright Man.

'Make yourself useful, Jamie-boy, by looking after my cloak,' Thomas cooed. 'And I may just forget you should be working tonight.'

Thomas had dressed deliberately in scarlet and gold to draw attention to himself. A gold-embossed baldric hung across his chest and its sword clanked against his hip as he sauntered into the midst of the revellers. Two pistols were thrust into the gold sash about his waist and a dagger hilt showed above the deep cuff of his boot.

The fiddler's bow scraped a jarring note on the strings and fell silent. The dancers froze, their laughter draining away to gasps of alarm. A hoot of laughter broke out from a black-haired bawd whose forehead was branded with a W for whore and who had lost one ear, hacked off as a punishment for thieving. Thomas recognised her as Bandy Moll, Big Jake's wife. She had been deserted by him when her face was disfigured by the French pox. In her youth Moll been trained as an acrobat until her height and huge breasts had ruined her balance. For several years she had been a great attraction at Nell Lovegood's. Bandy Moll was double jointed and there were positions she could twist her body into which could leave a man ruptured for life, or bring him to an ecstasy unparalleled. No woman worked at Nell's past the age of three and twenty. Moll was so popular Laurence had kept her on for another four years, until she married Big Jake. Last winter she had become so peppered with the pox, she'd taken to begging to avoid starvation.

Moll waved a long clay pipe in her hand, jabbing it towards Big Jake. 'Didn't the big man threaten to turn me into the gutter just now for only earning him a shilling? Yet there has always been food here for those who have served Tom Angel. Looks like your days of glory are past, Big Jake. You'll be food for the carrion by morning.'

All eyes were on Thomas, the people parting as he approached them, his passage to the dais unmolested. The two bodyguards behind Jake raised their weapons, but before they could fire, found themselves surrounded by Thomas's men. Big Jake rose from his chair like a cornered bear. He was huge, thickset and hirsute. His once-brown hair and bushy beard were streaked with grey, but his large body was all muscle. Big Jake could still take on all comers and win in any wrestling match. At his side, Inky the old scrivener scampered away, his thin, stoop-shouldered frame shaking with fright.

'Just doin' me job, Mr Angel,' he whined. 'Kept the records proper. Ready fer yer inspection.'

'My quarrel is not with you, Inky,' Thomas answered without even glancing in his direction.

The bull-terrier growled, rising to its feet, its yellowed fangs bared at Tom. Big Jake's ruddy colour had receded, but there was nothing subservient or repentant in his stance. He scanned the room, growing pale when he saw pistols held against the heads of his men.

'Just bin looking after yer interests, Angel. Rumour had it you were dead.'

'How unfortunate for you that I'm not.'

The bull-terrier bunched its body and hurled itself at Thomas's throat. A shot rang out and as Thomas side-stepped, the dog lay dead at his feet.

'Put Jake in chains,' Thomas commanded.

It took seven men to bring Big Jake down. Four of those had black eyes and bloodied lips and one ended up nursing a broken arm before Jake was secured in chains.

'Suspend him upside down from the ceiling beam for now,' Thomas rapped out. 'Then summon everyone here at midnight. They must witness how I deal with any who would usurp my authority.'

He nodded for Jake's henchmen to be brought forward. There were ten of them. All big men, with mean faces and cruel eyes.

'I doubt they won many friends amongst the fraternity,' Tom snorted. 'Vicious, ugly bastards the lot of them.'

Bandy Moll stood on a barrel and shouted, 'Whoresons, they've killed at least five of us who tried to defy them. They took what women they wanted, raping any who refused. Beat them bloody. Give the whoresons a taste of their own medicine I say.'

There was a chorus of approval.

Thomas nodded. 'Each one will run the gauntlet at midnight. Any with a grudge or who has been abused by them

440

may stand in the line with a cudgel.'

His judgement was swift, the only way to control the villains he ruled. 'Big Jake's punishment must fit his crimes as governed by the rules of the fraternity. His hands shall be struck off for stealing from me. His tongue torn out for ordering the brutality against my vassals. His privy member cut off for permitting the rape of the women under my protection and, lastly, his treacherous heart will be fed to the dogs.'

Thomas played to their bloodlust, knowing that had Jake known of his return to London, a similar fate would have been his. 'Tomorrow night will be a banquet. An ox will be roasted. I want the bakeries scoured for their finest delicacies, the vintners told to deliver a dozen wine vats. No expense will be spared.'

'Long live Thomas Angel!' A cheer filled the warehouse. 'Long may he prosper and us with 'im!'

Thomas was hoisted up on to two men's shoulders and carried triumphantly around the room. He was the undisputed master of his kingdom once more.

The icy rain was relentless, driving like needles, whipped by the east wind. The two riders were soaked to the flesh. Their sodden cloaks flapping like weighted sails behind them, they did not slacken their gruelling pace. The Heath was a favoured haunt of highwaymen, but only the most desperate thief would venture out on such an evening.

Angel's legs were numb with cold and she was close to exhaustion after the three-day ride. Willpower alone kept her in the saddle. She was dressed in man's clothing and Owain the groom was her companion. Angel believed that Maressa regretting the rift between them had wanted to help her. Now she must save Maressa.

The skyline of London, some miles distant, was lost behind the curtain of rain. Suddenly, a lone masked figure rode across their path, his pistol levelled at their heads.

'Hold or I fire!' he shouted above the wind. 'Hand over your money.'

As Angel reined in, her temper snapped. She was soaked, hungry and aching. She had been arrested, beaten, starved, frightened half to death and subjected to the ridicule of the pillory. She was also near out of her mind with worry about Alexander, Nathan and Maressa.

The strong wind swirling fallen leaves about their figures was making the highwayman's horse nervous. The rider before her was slightly built, but at the moment Angel would have taken on Lucifer himself.

'I damned well won't,' she shouted, and rode straight at the highwayman's skittish mount. At the same time she brought her riding whip down across the man's cheek.

Caught unawares he gave an unmanly yelp, and his frightened horse reared, unseating the rider with remarkable ease. He lay sprawled on the ground, his cloak blown over his face, his arms waving like windmills to escape the blanketing cloth. When he surfaced, Angel's sword-tip was an inch from his throat. To her astonishment the eyes behind the mask blinked rapidly against the tears which filled his eyes.

With a flash of her sword Angel severed the strings of the mask. When it fell away she saw the robber was a beardless youth of fifteen. His short fair hair was a riot of tight curls, reminding her of Firkin.

'Are you sick of life, lad?' she said, forgetting to disguise her voice.

'But you're a woman,' he groaned. 'Brought to grief by a wench. Won't never live this down. The gallows will be an easy end compared to the mockery I'll now face.'

'Lord, lad, I'd not send you to the gallows. Though a lesson or two in horsemanship would not go amiss.' Angel's anger subsided. 'What possessed you to ride the Heath? There's more to being a High Toby than riding a prancer with a pistol in your hand. Get up. As if you weren't wet enough, you're sitting in a puddle.'

With a scowl he rose to his feet, his face red with embarrassment.

'Why have you taken to the life of a High Toby?' she persisted.

'Didn't have no choice,' the boy said. 'Pa died at Naseby. Ma couldn't pay the rent and we were turned out. She were eight months gone with child . . . died giving birth in a ditch. I was eight. Thieving's all I know.' He cocked his head to one side and grinned. 'But there's big money to be had, here on the Heath.'

'And certain death on the gallows,' Angel said. 'Was this your first attempt?'

When he nodded woefully, she asked, 'What's your name?'

'Nicholas Grey. But most call me Hapless.' He bent his knees and pulled his soaked muddy breeches away from his thighs. 'Hapless, on account of if that were the only puddle 'tween here and Oxford I'd fall in it.'

'If you're set upon a life of crime, I've a cousin who's an Upright Man in London. He'll ensure that you're trained properly.'

'Why should you help me?'

'Because you remind me of someone.'

Angel kicked her mare into a canter, unwilling to say more, but her heart was full as she remembered her young brother, killed in battle. An hour later, she was huddled before a roaring fire in Nell Lovegood's and Hapless had been sent into the kitchens. When Thomas joined her Angel threw herself into his arms and poured out her news.

Thomas's expression was murderous. 'I knew Mortimer was alive. That's why I tried to stop Maressa leaving here. His spies must have followed her to Wales. Get some rest, Angel. I'll see to everything. Thank God, she'll be tried in London. I've some influence at Newgate.'

'I also need to contact Popinjay,' Angel said, rising stiffly to her feet. 'I won't rest until Pollett hangs for murdering Gabriellen and Mark. Then there's Nathan, too. I must see him. He's a prisoner somewhere in London.'

'I'll make enquiries.' Thomas hugged her, then strode out.

Maressa took heart at being tried in London. Thomas had influential friends there. Men who could not risk losing his goodwill.

The journey to London was a nightmare. Hazel had also been arrested, and the women had no privacy. Even the necessary calls of nature were watched over by a grinning guard. On the first night Hazel became hysterical.

'Fool!' Maressa slapped her maid's face. 'Act guilty and we'll both be burnt at the stake. I shall deny everything except that Northcliffe tried to rape me. A candle was knocked over in the scuffle, and he was too drunk to escape. As to Henry's accusation of poisoning, speak only of simple potions for fevers and colds. Admit to no further knowledge of herbs. Understand?'

'What if I'm put to the question?' Hazel gulped back her sobs.

'Keep your wits about you and say nothing to incriminate yourself,' Maressa warned. 'Thomas will save us. Be strong, Hazel. I doubt Henry will prove a reliable witness. How come he's not lived openly these last years? He has his own secrets. Thomas will discover them and discredit him.'

Gradually the strain of imprisonment began to take its toll on Maressa. Fear kept her awake at nights. To cope with the degradation she withdrew behind a shield of hauteur, forcing herself to shut out the squalor and humiliation. But nothing could control her terror as she was led into Newgate. She had heard too many tales of the depravity and cruelty which the inmates inflicted on each other. Bullies reigned here, stealing the clothes and food from the weak. On arrival, Maressa was leered at by the gaolers, her body mauled as she was herded with several other prisoners into the gate-ward. Across the yard the clamour of rattling chains and the pitiful cries of the suffering inmates assailed her ears.

The horrific tales of Newgate had not prepared her for the reality. Repelled, Maressa watched as each prisoner was summoned before a corpulent prison officer. The warder's bald pate was ringed by a circle of greasy grey hair, and his crooked nose and squinting pale eyes enfolded in pouches of flesh gave him a brutal expression. The warder laboriously copied out each person's crimes in a book. Then he demanded payment for the privilege of lighter shackles, giving each prisoner the choice of paying 'garnish' for better accommodation. Extra money was demanded for food or a bed; most expensive of all was for a private cell. The price of every privilege was extortionate. Maressa could only pay for a cell for Hazel and herself for a week on the Commons side, which held the female ward.

Her spirits sagged as she regarded her companions. Most looked as though they had been dragged from the gutter, unwashed, ragged and foul-mouthed in their abuse. They were an unsavoury assortment: sly-eyed forgers and sharpers; swaggering bawds and cheeky-faced pickpockets; morose bankrupts and debtors, defiant thieves, and brash scoundrels of every order. One of these was the auburn-haired Red Roland, a highwayman dressed in gold velvet who demanded the best accommodation. He winked at Maressa as he was escorted to the door.

'This ain't the place for a lady, for all they name you murderess,' he grinned. 'Be my doxy. I'll keep you in comfort until I ride the three-legged mare over Tyburn Hill.'

His gallows humour shocked her. She turned away from Red Roland, her voice thick with disgust. 'I'm a married woman, Sir.'

'Aye, twice wed and never a widow, with a brood of bastards.' He hooted with laughter. 'After a night fighting to stop your fine clothes being stripped from your body, you'll find Red Roland's bed is the closest you'll get to heaven in this midden.'

The coarse-featured gaoler escorting Red Roland guffawed. 'She'll 'ave ter take 'er turn, I reckon. This is the best trugging house in the city. Don't know what thrill you High Tobies give the ladies. There's women of quality pay up to a pound in garnish to visit your cells, all eager to kick their heels at the ceiling.'

Maressa watched despairingly as two debtors and a young girl cutpurse were dragged off to the Hole, the poorest quarter of the prison, where prisoners relied upon charity for their food and slept wherever they could find a space on the cramped floor.

'Maressa Mortimer!' the gaoler grunted.

Maressa started at the name she had not used for several years. Fear turned her stomach sour. What if Thomas abandoned her? Legs trembling, she stood before the warder. His gaze roamed over her figure, assessing the value of her clothing, the five rings adorning her fingers and the diamond and pearl earrings.

He hawked and spat into the rushes around his table. 'There ain't many murderesses can afford to pay for lighter shackles. For the price of those jewels you can 'ave a single cell and regular meals.'

'But what of my maid?' Maressa protested. 'Must we be separated?'

'You mean your accomplice,' the warder snarled. 'She'll be lodged in the Hole if she ain't got the means.'

445

Hazel cried out, 'My lady, don't abandon me!'

Maressa stared from Hazel to the warder. She removed all her jewellery and flung it on to the table. 'Does that cover the cost? You're the one who should be awaiting trial for extortion and roguery.'

His eyes narrowed and another gaoler cracked a whip, cutting into Maressa's back. 'Any more insolence and it will be fifty lashes,' he cackled.

Her back stinging from the whip, Maressa kept silent while they were taken into a second room and the heavy iron shackles were removed and lighter ones put on. Still Maressa stumbled as the chains bit cruelly into her ankles. Together with Hazel, she followed a gaoler into a yard where a ragged collection of prisoners exercised. Fog shrouded the prison, and as they approached a door on the far side of the yard, she saw two couples leaning against the wall of one of the buildings. Both women had their skirts hoisted to their armpits. The men, one with his breeches round his ankles, were plunging into them, their buttocks heaving, whilst a group of bearded prisoners yelled encouragement. A couple of spectators rubbed their swollen groins, demanding that their turn was next.

Maressa had witnessed such scenes often enough at Nell's, but in the brothel there had always been an atmosphere of merriment. This was one of bleak desperation – sex as a brief respite from day-long misery.

Maressa pressed a corner of her cloak to her nose and mouth as they entered the gloomy building. Little light penetrated the warren of corridors, and the air was thick from the smoking wall cressets. Maressa gagged at the foul stench. An open sewer smelt sweeter than the air of Newgate. Somewhere behind these walls, she knew, the executioner boiled the heads of traitors before they were set on pikes on London Bridge. The stink made her eyes water and her breath catch in her throat. If this was the elite quarter, only God knew how the wretches endured in the poorest Ward.

Holding their skirts high above the mildewed litter on the stairs and hearing rats squeaking in dark corners, the two women followed the guard up two flights of stairs. At last he stood back to allow them to enter a small cell. The unglazed barred window let in a dim light which did not reach the floor. The guard handed Maressa a candle and she held it aloft. As its feeble light spread across the bare flagstoned floor and green-slimed walls Maressa was filled with despair. There was a single bed with a stained straw mattress.

'There are no blankets and where will my maid sleep?'

'This ain't no hostelry. You provide your own bedding. To 'ave another bed in 'ere will cost yer three shillings a night.'

Maressa nodded and counted out the shillings from her diminishing hoard and continued to look round. In one corner was an uncovered wooden slops pail. Cobwebs draped the walls and ceiling and several huge spiders and cockroaches ran across the floor as the candlelight fell upon them. She stifled a scream. Her skin broke out in a sweat. She could not abide spiders. The thought of one of them running across her flesh at night made her skin crawl.

'There must be some mistake. I paid for the finest quarters.'

The guard sneered. 'These are the best. Doors are locked at nightfall. Until then the prisoners can do as they please. There's a taproom on the lower level.' He was gone before Maressa could question him further.

She put the candle on the floor and sank down on to the bed, her head dropping into her hands as the hopelessness of her situation overcame her.

'My lady, don't despair,' Hazel said. 'Trust in Master Thomas.'

'Now that's sound advice.' A stranger's voice came from the doorway.

Maressa looked up as a short, foppish man strutted into the cell. She recognised him as a frequent visitor to Nell's gaming tables.

He bowed to her. 'I'm Hugh Spenser, or Huge Spender as Tom likes to call me. He had me arrested for debt, to ensure that I could protect you.' He laughed at her puzzled expression. 'Tom pays for all my privileges. Once your trial is over and you're free my creditors will be paid. I fear it's not what you're used to. But I'm here to help you in any way I can.'

Maressa nodded, touched by Thomas's foresight and generosity. He had not abandoned her. She managed a weak smile. 'Would you think me very foolish, if I asked you to get the spiders removed from this cell?'

Since the death of Charles the First, London had been the scene of continual disturbances from Royalists. Now, after the battle of Worcester, the prisons were overflowing. Nathan had been lodged in the Horse Guards, a new guardhouse close by the Banqueting House where the martyred King had been beheaded.

It was Angel's third visit to him, and she was heavily muffled against the November cold and continual fog which lay over London.

'Good day, Mistress Rowan,' a young fresh-faced soldier greeted her. He was warming his hands over a brazier outside the guardhouse gate. He inspected the basket of food she carried, to check there were no hidden weapons. 'Colonel Carver will be pleased to see you.'

Angel entered the stone building, passing several Royalist prisoners sauntering at their ease through the corridors. The atmosphere was relaxed, and some prisoners were even allowed to visit their families, if they lived in London, providing they returned to the guardhouse at night.

'Colonel Carver is not in his cell.' A Cavalier stopped Angel in the doorway. 'He's in the infirmary giving advice to Dr Yardley. Several prisoners have been taken ill.'

Angel glanced into Nathan's cell. It was clean and tidy. His desk was laden with books, quills and papers, and kindling and logs lay ready in the fireplace. On another stand was a washing bowl and a shaving mirror hung on a peg. It was as comfortable as any inn lodging. Angel placed her basket on the bed. Amongst the food and wine provided by Nell Lovegood, there were candles, two books which Nathan had requested, a leather-bound book for a scribe to write up Nathan's notes and a sheaf of writing paper. Though Nathan had been given the use of a scribe, he was persevering in writing with his left hand.

Angel went up to the infirmary on the next floor to find children were playing in the corridor. Their mothers in plain dresses of black, brown or grey with their hair hidden under linen caps gossiped as they waited in a straggling line. There were several soldiers queuing for medical attention. One man had a bandaged eye, another's arm was in a sling; two were coughing, their noses streaming from colds.

'Reckon Colonel Carver's a mite too busy to see you, Mistress Rowan,' a prisoner on crutches called to her. 'Just saved my leg, he has. The man's a wonder. Dr Yardley was all for amputating. I broke it last night falling down the stairs.'

He looked beyond Angel to the line of patients. 'Word has spread of Dr Carver's skill. Last week he cured a soldier's child of the croup – saved the shaver's life he did. Then there were old Will's wife and his five children all smitten with the spotted fever. Carver told Will exactly what to do. They all survived. He even saved Captain Morris one of the guards here, when the man thought he was dying of fish poisoning.' The soldier laughed. 'You should have heard the Colonel when he heard that Captain Morris was being purged, fasted and bled.'

Angel smiled. 'I can imagine. He has little patience with quacks.'

When she entered the dormitory set aside for the sick, Nathan was standing over a bed, his wounded hand in a black silk sling. As she watched he lifted the patient's eyelid and then looked into his open mouth. Next to him stood Dr Yardley. Angel was surprised at his youthful appearance. He had a shock of brown hair which stuck out beneath a black physician's cap, the type Nathan had never worn. Dr Yardley was full-bearded, tall and thin. She guessed he wore both the beard and the cap to give greater maturity to his boyish face. He was listening intently to Nathan's diagnosis.

Nathan turned, as though aware of her presence. It was often like that between them. Some indefinable alchemy made them acutely aware of each other. He smiled at her and continued to summarise the patient's treatment before excusing himself. His gaze caressed her as his hands could not in public and Angel ached to be crushed into his arms.

'I've come at a bad time. You're busy.'

'Yardley can deal with these patients.'

She shook her head. Nathan had regained the sparkle in his eyes which had been lost since his hand was crippled. 'It's you they come to see. Don't disappoint them. I've been hearing of the marvels you have performed.'

'Just simple advice and breaking through superstition and ignorance.'

'I'll not take you from your patients. I'll wait until you finish.'

'Perhaps I cannot wait,' he teased. His gaze fastened upon her lips. The intensity of the longing in his stare, dried her mouth and she ran the tip of her tongue over her lips.

He groaned softly and whispered, 'I want to make love to you so much.'

'If only that were possible.' Her own need was reflected in her eyes, and Nathan raised her hand to his lips.

'I'll be done here in half an hour,' he said huskily.

She walked over to the window, loath to leave his presence. She loved to watch him at work, to see the way he soothed a patient's fears, the gentleness with which he touched a painful swelling or examined an open wound. As the half hour dragged into an hour and then two, he moved from one patient to another, frequently glancing across at her. She did not notice the time, nor begrudge him the chance to continue his work. Every patient cured was proof that he remained one of England's finest physicians, despite his crippling wound. When the last of the patients had left, Dr Yardley began to discuss with Nathan the efficacy of administering mandrake to a patient to kill the pain when surgery was needed, and she controlled a smile at Nathan's obvious exasperation.

'Later I'll discuss its merits and drawbacks in detail. Mandrake is highly dangerous. It could cause a patient to fall into a dead sleep and render their body insensible,' Nathan said, putting a hand on Dr Yardley's shoulder. 'Come to me later. I have John Woodall's book on amputation which you will find enlightening. But now my visitor has been kept waiting long enough.'

Dr Yardley blushed, his manner awkward with embarrassment. He was never at ease in the company of women. He was a studious man who had been brought up strictly by a Puritan widow. There was a holy air about him and in another age he would no doubt have taken his vows as a monk. Angel doubted that celibacy would ever have been a problem for him.

That was not the case with Nathan or herself. Her body

ached for his touch. Her nights were haunted by the memories of his lovemaking. There had been no opportunity for such intimacy since their reunion in Wales. Neither would there be while Nathan remained in a Puritan-governed prison.

The moment they entered Nathan's cell, he slid his injured hand from the sling and held her close. The passion in his kiss stole her breath and her senses. Angel clung to him, drowning in the heat of his body. He kissed her hair and then his mouth was upon her throat. Her head lolled back, desire igniting like a powder keg.

Nathan lifted his head to stare deep into her eyes, then at her lips, swollen from the passion of his kiss. He looked towards the open door and sighed. Nathan's privileges did not extend to being awarded the intimacy of an hour in private with his mistress.

'Do you love me, Angel?'

She raised a dark brow. 'When did you ever have anything but contempt for love?'

'I need to know.' His voice was strained.

'You must know that I do.'

'You never say so.'

'I'd not embarrass you with sentiments you cannot return.'

'Do you truly think me so heartless?'

His expression was so pained that she spread her hands across his cheeks and lifted her lips to kiss him deeply.

'Rather than lose you I've learned to accept what we have,' she added softly.

'You deserve better.'

The tautness of his voice alarmed her. Fear clutched at her heart. 'Are you telling me it's over between us?' She stepped away from him, struggling to hide her pain.

He looked startled. 'Good God, no! What I'm making such a pig's ear of saying is that it's impossible not to love you.' The admission was torn from him. 'So often I nearly abandoned my studies abroad to come and find you. Now we're together we're forced to act like brother and sister.'

'Abstinence never was your strong point,' she quipped.

He tensed and turned aside to rest his uninjured hand on the wall. 'I'm a cripple now and no use to anyone.'

Angrily, she pulled him round to face her. 'Don't ever

speak that way. Look how the patients flock to you! Even with only one hand you're a better physician than any other in England.'

He pulled off the leather gauntlet with its two padded fingers which covered his wound, and thrust his hand towards her. 'Could any woman bear to have her body pawed by that hideous mutilation?'

Though healed, the wound was puckered and swollen with unsightly scars, the two stumps of fingers twisted and useless. Without hesitating, Angel took his wrist and pressed his palm against her breast. 'Nothing about you is hideous, my love. And don't think that just because you're feeling sorry for yourself I'm going to elaborate on what a loyal, handsome, courageous, amusing, passionate lover and unforgettable person you are.'

His expression cleared and with a laugh he kissed her, his hands caressing her breasts until she gasped with pleasure. Hearing a guard's keys jangling in the corridor Angel drew back. Her eyes had the unfocused look of a woman lost in the throes of sensual pleasure. Her voice was ragged. 'If you weren't so against the lunacy of love and marriage, or so recently free from its constraints . . . I'd ask you to marry me, Nathan.'

'And if I thought I could give you the life you deserved . . .' He broke off abruptly and ended lamely, 'You deserve better than a cripple.'

'Is that an acceptance?' she pursued.

Nathan studied her in silence, his expression guarded. 'No.'

Angel felt her knees give way, but she recovered quickly, blinked rapidly, and turned away to hide her pain.

'When will you learn to do as convention demands.' Nathan put his hand on her shoulder. 'It's for me to do the asking.' He turned her round, and took her hand. 'I decried love because I blamed it for a youthful infatuation which I thought had ruined my life.' He knelt, looking up at her with adoration in his eyes. 'I love you as only a man who once decried the folly of love can love – wholeheartedly and without reserve. Without you my life is incomplete. You are my future. Will you do me the honour of becoming my wife, Angel?'

452

'Yes!' Her cry was ecstatic. 'Oh, yes. Yes. Yes.'

He caught her in his arms and spun her round and round, their laughter drawing the attention of several grinning Cavaliers.

Chapter Eighteen

Marriage plans were relegated to the back of Angel's mind as the Michaelmas Quarter Sessions approached. Both Maressa in London and Major Pollett in Chester would be on trial, and it would be impossible for Angel to attend both. Without her evidence, Pollett would not hang; Thomas promised to save Maressa and Hazel.

When she visited Nathan at Horse Guards on the day before she left for Chester she was anxious. 'There's been no word from Popinjay.'

Nathan held her in his arms. 'Your evidence will condemn Pollett and others will come forward. He was a weak man who used brutality to gain authority. He leaves a legacy of rape, torture and plunder – excessive even in a country torn by war. Such a man deserves to die.'

'I'll be gone for weeks. For I must visit Wales to see how Beth is coping now that Alex is in exile.'

'Remember, your cousin Davvyd promised to visit her once a week and settle any problems.' Nathan began to kiss her hair and face, his voice growing husky. 'You cannot be everywhere and do everything for your family. You take on too much.'

She returned his kiss. 'I'll miss you.'

'By the time you return, I may have been granted parole during the day. Captain Morris has agreed to speak on my behalf, although I must swear not to offer my sword to any further Royalist cause.' He looked at his mutilated hand. 'That's no hardship since I'd be useless in a fight. My work is most important, and I can't help the sick locked in here.' He tipped up her chin with his left hand. 'I want us to be married in the spring.'

'On parole you must still return here every night and I

must spend time at Rowan Hall. The horses meant so much to Mark and Alex.'

'I know.' Nathan did not argue. 'I never expected our marriage to be without its problems. Whilst in Wales do not neglect your plays. That talent is also a legacy from your family.'

Angel slid her arms around his neck and kissed him. Nathan drew a ragged breath and regretfully put her from him, his glance moving to the open door. 'Don't tempt me from my noble path. I want nothing more than to slam shut that door and make you mine, but I love and respect you too much to let you become the butt of guardroom ribaldry. Spring cannot come soon enough for me.'

Angel returned to Nell Lovegood's to find a visitor waiting for her in Thomas's study. When she entered, she saw a man asleep at the desk, his grey head buried in his arms. As the door clicked shut, the figure moved with startling speed. His head shot up and a pistol appeared from nowhere and was pointed at her.

'Good God, Angel, you gave me a turn.'

Popinjay had changed almost beyond recognition. His thick grey hair was cut to his ears and brushed back from his forehead. His gaunt cheeks had filled out and he had grown a narrow beard and moustache. The beard was a dark brown in contrast to his grey hair and it completely changed his appearance. The travelling pedlar had turned into a wealthy merchant.

'I'm sorry if I frightened you,' he apologised with a laugh. 'Old habits died hard.'

She crossed the room and kissed his cheek. 'I knew you'd not fail me.' Beneath his long full-skirted coat Popinjay wore a poppy-red waistcoat, and she smiled. His thin figure had fleshed out and she was so relieved to see him she could not resist teasing. 'First you ape the popinjay, then the sparrow of your name. Now it's Robin Redbreast.'

'Would you rather I became the black crow or raven in Puritan garb?'

'It wouldn't become you.' She became serious. His eyes were reddened from lack of sleep and his cheeks pinched from fatigue. 'You must be tired. Have you eaten?'

'Thomas saw to my needs. When do we leave for Chester?

456

Snow is in the air, and the journey will be arduous.'

'Tomorrow. But first tell me of yourself: what have you been doing these last years?'

He spread his hands dismissing any importance in his life. 'Roamed the Continent for a time. Scraped together enough money to start up as a furrier in Bristol and opened another shop here in London in Gracious Street. I travel between the two which provides cover for my visits to The Hague and St Germain. I missed the fight at Worcester. When I was in Scotland His Majesty sent me to The Hague with a letter for his sister, the Princess Mary. I was delayed by storms. Then I spent some weeks in the Low Countries and only reached Dover last week. There word reached me that Thomas Angel had need of me. Thomas has told me everything. Pollett will not escape justice.'

'Is there any risk to yourself, Popinjay?'

He smiled at the use of his old name. 'Please call me John. It's as John Sparrow, furrier and friend of your family that I'll give evidence. Popinjay has a price on his head. Pollett had no idea of my identity.'

'It's good that you have prospered. Too many Royalists have lost everything.'

'Your family has suffered as much as any,' Popinjay replied. 'I met Alex in Calais before I sailed. He had heard of Pollett's arrest from another exile and wanted to return to support you.' At Angel's frightened gasp, Popinjay shook his head. 'I dissuaded him. He intends to visit your aunt in the Loire Valley. He wants Beth and the children to join him, and for you to have the Rowan Estate if it escapes sequestration.'

'I could never be more than a caretaker for Alex. One day this madness will end. If there's any justice, the King will come into his own again and Alex will return.'

'And you will have your plays performed upon the London stage.'

'Are they just dreams, John? Hopeless dreams?'

'Without dreams we achieve nothing. Keep faith.'

There was a tap on the study door and Hapless entered.

'Mr Angel said you were leaving for Chester come morning, Mistress Rowan.' He broke off, disconcerted at finding Popinjay present.

457

'That's right,' Angel answered. 'This is John Sparrow. He'll be giving evidence against Major Pollett.' She turned to Popinjay. 'This is Nicholas Grey, a would-be High Toby. But he's rather too accident-prone for his own health. He's also known as Hapless.'

'I don't want to be a High Toby no more, Mistress Rowan. Mr Angel said you wrote plays. I want to be an actor. I always used to sneak into the playhouses when I was a lad. Never missed a performance if I could help it. You wouldn't be wanting a servant, would you? I'd be your groom, look after the horses – act as your bodyguard. I'd give anything to be an actor.'

'Can you read, Hapless?'

He shook his head.

'Are you willing to learn?'

'To be an actor I'll do anything.'

'It could be years before the playhouses re-open. I can't afford to pay you much in wages, but I'll gladly teach you to act and to read and write.'

Popinjay coughed. 'Angel, your heart is too big for your purse. How many more lost causes must you espouse?'

Nicholas looked stricken and Angel smiled at him. 'Hapless is not a lost cause. I rather think he's a redeemed one.'

Beth Rowan wondered if she would ever get used to the constant Welsh rain. Did it never stop? She shook out the sopping leather cloak which afforded little protection on the walk from the house to the stables of Rowan Hall. All the mares had been brought inside for the winter which meant an extra expense of hay and oats to keep them fed and warm. There had been a mysterious fire last week in the barn which held the straw bedding. It had not spread, but it had been a harrowing experience for Beth, and she realised how little she knew about horses: Cousin Davvyd's visits helped, but she missed Alexander desperately. If only Angel could have been here to help her. Beth had been stunned by the misfortunes which had befallen her family in quick succession. Yet out of all the heartache and anxiety had come one joy. She was expecting Alexander's fifth child in June. It was her greatest comfort, but it was also her hardest trial. Since the first month she had been feeling ill, unable to keep any food down. She was constantly tired and her ankles had swollen to twice their normal size.

She forced herself to perform her household duties. The Dunnocks could not do everything. Perhaps it was a mixed blessing that Isaac Dunnock had arrived on the estate two nights after the fire. Her first reaction had been to turn him away, but Prudence, who had not seen her son for seven years, pleaded with Beth to allow him to stay. Elijah swore that Isaac had learned his lesson. In the end Beth had relented.

His acceptance was sullen though, and there was a glitter in his eye which made her uneasy. At five-and-twenty, Isaac was a heavily built man, his narrow brow and bushy ginger eyebrows giving him a truculent expression. From his broken nose and the scars about his face he was obviously given to brawling.

'Elijah!' she had called after his father. 'At the first sign of trouble Isaac leaves.'

The day after Angel, Popinjay and Hapless left London it began to snow. It was falling so heavily they could not see more than a few feet ahead. They were on a lonely stretch of road and there was no welcoming light in sight to give them shelter. Hapless began to sneeze. Angel looked across at his figure hunched over his mare's neck and sighed. She should have realised that he was no horseman after the episode on the heath. Three times he had fallen off his mare. Once into a holly bush.

It was obvious Hapless was suffering, but he did not complain. He had a stubborn courage which Angel admired. The snow lay deep and the countryside was muffled in an eerie silence. In another hour it would be dark. They had to find shelter for the night or freeze to death.

She peered through the curtain of snow. 'Is that a light?'

'Wishful thinking,' Popinjay answered. 'There's only common land on that side of the road.'

Angel suspected that John Sparrow's eyes were not as keen as hers. She stared harder. 'It is a light.'

'Then it will be vagabonds or the like. They'll rob us blind,' Hapless said morosely.

'Not necessarily,' Popinjay suggested. 'If that's common

land it could be a community of Diggers. They may give us shelter. God knows the wretches would be grateful to share our provisions.'

'Diggers?' Hapless snorted in disbelief. 'What kind of people are they?'

'Families who have lost their homes,' Popinjay explained. 'They band together and believe in common ownership not in private property. I've heard of several groups in Buckinghamshire, Bedfordshire and Gloucester. With so many men crippled in the fighting and unable to meet their rents more people become homeless. By joining such a community is the only way they can survive.'

'They are little better than vagabonds, then,' Hapless groaned.

'Vagabonds never stay in one place for long. Diggers got their name because they squat on the common land and plant crops. Only after extreme harassment from local residents and the Justices do they move on. Then usually not until blood has been spilt. They fight for the land they've taken because they've nowhere else to go.'

'Will they give us shelter?' Angel asked.

'First we must convince them that we mean no harm,' Popinjay replied.

As they rode slowly between the row of wooden huts, every door and window shutter remained closed. Only a glimmer of a feeble rushlight could be seen through a knot-hole in the wood.

'We are travellers caught in the snowstorm,' Popinjay shouted. 'We've food to offer to any who'll give us shelter for the night.'

Silence greeted his words.

'Please, we mean you no harm,' Angel added. 'There are but three of us. Do the laws of hospitality not apply amongst your community? All we ask is some shelter and that you share our food.'

A door opened a crack and a bearded face peered out. 'We have reason to be wary of strangers. But you can put your horses in the cow-byre behind the house. It's empty. Our cattle was stolen last week and two of our men were killed trying to stop them. It will give you shelter.'

Reaching into the bag hanging from her saddle Angel held

460

out a loaf, a large wedge of cheese and a dozen saffron cakes wrapped in linen.

'Even a byre is a welcome haven in this weather,' she said. 'Please take this food.'

The door opened and the man stepped out. His face was battered from a recent beating, no doubt trying to save the cattle. A young girl ran out to stand snivelling beside her father, her face pinched with hunger. As she held out her hand to take the loaf from Angel she saw it was blistered from a painful scald burn.

'I have a salve which will ease your daughter's pain.' Angel rummaged in another saddlebag and held out a small pot.

The man wavered before accepting it. Then he said gruffly, 'Once you've seen to your horses, come into the dwelling. You'll have to sleep on the floor but you'll be warmer by the fire.'

The grudging hospitality did not thaw all evening. The single-roomed hut was smoky from the feeble fire, but at least it was warm. The floor was covered in rushes which from their fresh, tangy scent had been recently laid. The single rushlight, which gave off a poor light, showed three cooking pots, an earthen jug and some wooden bowls on a shelf. The family bed where everyone slept was against a wall, heaped with articles of unworn clothing for extra warmth. There was a small wooden bench which served as a table and two three-legged stools. One of these was offered to Angel to sit upon. The three children ranging from four to eleven squatted on the floor their eyes riveted on the cheese and bread their mother was cutting into slices.

Though clean the hut smelt unpleasantly of damp clothes, onions and animals. A pig was tethered in one corner and two chickens clucked in a wooden cage.

Their wet cloaks were taken and several ragged petticoats with sodden hems were snatched off a line of twine hanging near the fire and the cloaks spread over it to dry. The family of Diggers remained distrustful. The wife was stooped and her face lined and Angel was shocked to learn she was only ten years older than herself and had buried seven children. The three surviving were thin and under-sized, their faces grey with dirt. They fell upon the bread and cheese, tearing at it with their fingers.

461

Appalled at their poverty Angel gave them the rest of their provisions of bread, cooked beef and a spiced sausage. Though her own stomach rumbled with hunger she ate sparingly, aware that the family had little to get them through the winter.

When questioned it was the father who grudgingly answered. Most of Angel's attempts at conversation were ignored and it was Popinjay who finally drew their story from them. They had lost their home, when soldiers looted their farm and set fire to the house. It was the same for others in their community – all were homeless and received no help from the parish. Refusing to become vagabonds they tried to support themselves by feeding their cattle on the common and planting a few crops. They were despised by the local villagers. Five times in three years they had been forced to move off common land after their crops had been trampled and shelters burnt down. They had been here long enough to replace their tents with wooden huts but were persecuted by the villagers.

When it became obvious that the family intended to retire for the night, Angel stood up and reached for her cloak, bracing herself to face the snow and relieve herself outside before retiring for the night. To her surprise the woman came with her, speaking her first words of the evening.

'Ground's treacherous. Wouldn't want you to twist an ankle. Not after your kindness. That salve has given Sal the first ease from her pain for three days.'

Having said her piece the woman did not speak again. On her return to the hut a space had been cleared on the floor before the fire. Popinjay and Hapless were already wrapped in their cloaks preparing to sleep.

Despite the discomfort of the hard floor, Angel fell asleep at once. She was awakened in the middle of the night by an unholy squealing and a yell from Hapless. Sitting upright she peered across the room. Popinjay had also sat up and was laughing softly. From the dim light of the glowing embers, Angel saw that the pig had broken free of its tether and was rooting about under Hapless's blanket. It stood with legs planted over him, his snout nugging hard against Hapless's chest.

'Get off!' Hapless groaned, pushing ineffectually at the huge pig who grunted louder.

'Have you hidden some food in your jerkin?' Popinjay chuckled. 'The pig can smell it. Give it to him and he'll leave you in peace.'

Hapless mumbled a curse and pulled a saffron cake from out of his jerkin and threw it on the ground by his feet. The pig leapt on it like a dog on a bone. Grunting contentedly it wandered back to its corner and flopped down.

'Why did it pick on me?' Hapless muttered as he wriggled closer to the fire. 'I thought it was some hell-fiend come to devour me in my sleep.'

'Go to sleep, Hapless,' Popinjay said in drowsy amusement.

'Sleep? I doubt I'll ever sleep again after a scare like that.'

Sir Henry Mortimer could not relax. He snapped at his manservant when the fool burnt his neck applying the curling irons to Henry's blond hair. Dismissing the servant, Henry studied his reflection in the mirror on the table. Not for him the Puritan crop, or sober garb. He was dressed in scarlet banded with blue velvet and gold trimming. His eyes narrowed as he flicked the cascade of lace which covered his scarred hands. Seven years had faded those scars, but not the hatred which burned in his soul. Tomorrow Maressa came to trial, and his evidence would send her to her execution. The penalty for husband murder was burning.

He stood up and laughed as he buckled on his sword. Seven years he had waited. The tendons in his throat corded as he remembered the fire which had almost killed him. The ungrateful bitch had only to open her legs to Northcliffe for one night. She'd spread them fast enough for Thomas Angel.

Henry had not realised how devious his wife was until he regained consciousness in her smoke-filled bedchamber. He had crawled to the door and seen Maressa touching the candle to the tapestry on the staircase, then run to the back of the house. The only way out had been through the wall of flame. Unfastening his doublet, he pulled it over his head and stumbled down the burning staircase. The heat was intense, scorching his skin. Breaking through the flames he hurried coughing to the front door. The flames licked at his heels and snaked around his head. For precious seconds he fumbled with the heavy bolts. He could smell his long hair singed by the flames. As he pulled the door open there was a wafting of cold air on his sweating face. Then there was a roar of engulfing heat behind him and he was propelled forward by the blast on to the lawn at the front of the house.

The next he knew he was being tended by a stout, middle-aged woman who never left his bedside, and kept calling him 'Ben' and 'husband'. Her name was Meg Nicolls. Though her face was fleshy she was still an attractive woman with reddish brown hair which she wore loose to her hips. As she spoonfed him, her vast bosom strained over the top of her gaping bodice. Each morning she insisted she bathe his fevered body and her hands lingered upon his flesh. She was hungry for sex and starved of passion, but Henry had been incapable of anything in those first months. Often he would awake from a nightmare and discover his head laid against her bare breasts, his lips fastened against her nipple, taking comfort as he suckled like a child.

Under her care his strength slowly returned, and throughout the months of his recovery Henry pretended that he was Ben Nicolls. It was a convenient way of avoiding the creditors, to whom he owed hundreds of pounds.

Meg told him he had been found on the lawn of Mortimer House in the Strand by a linkman who recognised him as her missing husband. She told him Ben Nicolls had been pressed into the navy three years ago.

It had not taken him long to realise that Meg, a few years older than himself, was an extremely wealthy woman. Apparently, Ben Nicolls was her third husband. Pretending to be Meg's husband had served Henry well, and he had bided his time, waiting. He had grown a beard and trimmed his long hair to aid his disguise, quickly adapting to his new role. Meg spoke of his life as clerk to her second husband, a moneylender. When he died Meg continued the business. Her acumen had amassed a fortune when many others were made destitute by the war. The only drawback to his life had been Meg's possessive streak. She refused to let him out of her sight. Once when he suggested going out to a tavern, she hit him with a poker.

'I made you what you are, Ben Nicolls!' she screamed. 'You owe everything to me. Last time you went out at night you were pressed into the navy.'

As Henry recovered his strength he had begun to resent Meg and his assumed identity. Then it occurred to him that, as Ben Nicolls, he stood to inherit a fortune should an accident befall Meg.

A month later Meg plunged down the stairs, breaking her neck. She was laid to rest by a grieving husband who then sold the house and demanded all payment on the loans given by Meg Nicolls. He employed two men to search for Maressa. By the time he had Meg Nicolls's fortune in his hands Henry knew that Maressa had married Thomas Angel. Thomas was a dangerous man to cross. More disquieting was the information that Thomas had men looking for him.

Henry decided that his revenge on Maressa could wait. A cousin of Meg's who had expected to inherit her money was beginning to ask awkward questions about her death. It was time for him to go on an extended tour of the Continent and enjoy his new-found wealth. He returned from a life of debauchery in Italy when information led him to believe the time was right to exact revenge. His plans were carefully laid. Presenting himself to an old friend, Sir Cecil Verduyn, he poured out the story that his life had been a blank to him for seven years, until he had awoken one morning in Rome. Verduyn believed him, and so did his only child, the plain heiress to Verduyn's large fortune, his sixteen-year-old daughter. Henry had already seduced her and intended that once Maressa's death freed him, he would marry the wench. His future and comfort were assured.

Henry laughed now. The jury could not fail to be moved by his story. He had rehearsed it well. Tomorrow he would play the wronged husband – the victim of Maressa's greed. But tonight he was restless. He needed entertainment. Where better to relax and celebrate his triumph tomorrow than in the arms of his latest mistress?

Leaving his room in the inn, Henry called for a sedan-chair. Two bearers, heavily muffled against the freezing fog, materialised out of the grey mist and set down the chair. As Henry settled back on the seat, he irritably brushed off the flakes of soot which had fallen on his clothing from the city chimneys. He closed his eyes and contemplated her eager welcome. Mentally, he stripped the clothes from her figure. Tonight he'd make her scream with ecstasy. His loins stirred as in his imagination he could feel her velvet heat enclosing him, the rhythm of her heels drumming against his back as he drove into her. The image was so fierce he groaned aloud.

With a start he realised that the chair had been set down, and began to whistle in anticipation of the pleasure which awaited him. He stepped out of the sedan, his hand in his pocket to withdraw a coin for payment. A fist slammed into his gut and the pain doubled him over. He gasped and a second blow to his windpipe brought him choking to his knees.

Dimly he was aware that this was not the street where his mistress lived. It was a foul reeking back-alley. He was being robbed and would be lucky to escape with his life.

'Here, take my purse! Take the diamond pin at my neck,' he pleaded. 'My rings . . . anything . . . Spare me, I beg you.' Another boot slammed into his kidneys and he felt the cold steel of a dagger pressed against his throat. 'Spare me,' Henry begged. 'I'm a wealthy man. I can pay you a ransom.'

The response was a kick in the groin. 'That's for raping Angel Rowan.'

The familiar voice emptied Henry's bladder with fear. Excruciating pain shot upwards from his testicles, his mind a red haze of agony. Another kick jerked his body into a ball, sending the tears streaming from his eyes.

'That was for the perversions you forced upon Maressa.' A hand clawed at Henry's hair and yanked his head up. Thomas Angel's face was inches away. An accomplice held a torch above his head and Henry's death was written in Thomas's silver eyes.

'Did you really think I'd let Maressa die for Northcliffe's murder? I've ensured the guilt will be yours.' The dagger pricked Henry's throat. 'Already your signature has been forged on the necessary papers and your goldsmith released your fortune to me an hour ago.'

Thomas squatted over Mortimer. 'A diary of all your crimes has been planted amongst your possessions at the inn. In it you confess how you murdered Northcliffe because of your debts and set fire to Mortimer House to destroy the evidence. It explains how you planned the murder of your wife and son that night. Then it describes how you impersonated Meg Nicolls' husband. How you pushed her down the stairs and killed her for her money. No judge will bring Maressa to trial once they've read that diary. Your death tonight will be taken for a robbery, since only fools venture into this quarter after dark.'

A dagger flashed in the torchlight. Henry Mortimer felt the searing pain as it entered the side of his neck, ripping and tearing. Fire burst into his skull and blood gushed into his mouth. As his eyes began to glaze he stared up at his killer, silhouetted by orange torchlight. As the blackness of death closed in, the dark silhouette rose in stature, the flames of the torch rising behind him. Horns protruded from the figure's head and Henry saw the swish of a pointed tail. Satan had come to claim his own.

Maressa awoke in her cell, her flesh prickling at the chittering of the rats squabbling over scraps of food. Her candle had burnt away and she pushed a fresh one into the sconce and struck a tinder to light it. She hated the dark with its scurrying animal noises, the snores and wails of the prisoners. The light from the candle sent the creatures back into their holes and she breathed easier.

A pink glimmer of dawn was visible through the tiny barred window of her cell. Today was her trial. Fear swirled around her in bone-chilling waves. Thomas had promised that she would be freed. Desperately, she clung to that hope and struggled to be calm. She would never have survived her imprisonment had it not been for him. Only his reputation had saved her from the usual indignities endured by other female prisoners. She was never molested by guards or male prisoners. Even the women who would beat another senseless for her clothes, or food, never dared to accost her. Absently she scratched her armpit, even with her clean clothes the lice and fleas tormented her body. At least with Hazel's potions they had both escaped the gaol-fever which killed several prisoners every day. Each morning a death cart daily carried its load to a commoner's grave as the poor succumbed to fever, starvation, cold or brutality.

Unable to sleep, she pressed a hand across her eyes as the scamperings began again. Even Thomas could not stop the spiders, cockroaches and rats invading her cell, and her nights were filled with terror. There was a tickling across her fingers. With a shriek she sat up, flailing her hand frantically to get rid of the huge spider crawling across her flesh. She leapt from the bed and cringed, sobbing, in a corner.

Hazel quickly killed the spider with her foot. 'It's all right. It's dead,' she soothed. 'Come back to bed. You'll need your strength for the trial.'

Maressa bowed her head and dragged her trembling hands through her hair. 'I can't sleep. I can't breathe. I can't bear being shut up like an animal. The walls press in on me. There's no air.' She panted like a cornered doe, drawing gulping breaths into her lungs until she felt light-headed. From the first night the door had been locked, she had felt a fear of confined spaces which rivalled her terror of spiders. She despised her terrors, but found it impossible to conquer them.

Hazel held out a phial of perfumed oil. She had already built up the fire against the cold. 'Let me rub your body with oils. It will help to calm you.'

Maressa undressed by the fire and lay naked on her stomach on the bed. The cell was so small the fire warmed it pleasantly. Few cells had such luxury and Thomas had paid highly for her to be so privileged. She reached out a hand. 'Is there any wine left, Hazel?'

Hazel drained a flagon into a goblet. It only half-filled the cup. Knowing her mistress was close to hysterics, she measured a few drops of poppy juice from a tiny phial into the goblet, and handed it to Maressa.

Maressa drank and stretched with a sigh. Hazel stared adoringly at her mistress, and, tipping the perfumed oil into her hands, began to massage Maressa's neck. Her love for her mistress flowed through her body and into her fingertips. Her thumbs traced the indent of her spine, spreading out in a slow sensuous fan across her ribs, then down to her waist. Maressa sighed and rolled her shoulders.

'Lower, Hazel.'

The wine was making Maressa's senses blur, blocking out all that was frightening in the prison. Hazel's hands glided over her flesh, soothing away fears and the terrors of the dark.

'There's magic in your hands,' Maressa murmured. 'I can feel the stiffness and aches leaving my body.'

Hazel stared at the golden flesh as she straddled the narrow pallet to lean forward and gently stroke her fingers along

468

Maressa's spine. Her own shift hampered her movements and impatiently she tore it off. When she leaned forward her small pointed breasts brushed Maressa's warm skin and the glow within her intensified as Maressa sighed contentedly.

Pouring more oil on to her hands Hazel curled them around delicate shoulders, then slowly back down to the narrow waist. She could feel the tension leaving the beautiful body. Maressa lay relaxed and pliant. Hazel paused, needing to combat the heat which was spreading through her own loins at the feel of her mistress's body beneath her hands. Since the sailor had raped her, all those years ago, Hazel despised all men. The thought of their touch made her physically sick. How could any woman stand those hairy bodies pressed against their own softness? Or those callused hands, groping and pinching.

'Don't stop,' Maressa urged.

Hazel poured more oil on to her hands and ran them in lazy circles over Maressa's back, like a leaf floating in an unseen spiral of air slowly but inexorably downward. The delicious tingling again spread through her loins, and her heart pounded until its rhythm hammered in her brain. Hazel forced her breathing to remain even as her hands moved over Maressa's figure in the way she had seen the whores caress each other at Nell Lovegood's. Women who were world-weary of the hurried, unfulfilled couplings of their profession. Every touch was designed to relax and then rouse to slow and sensual rapture. Hazel had often watched, fascinated; now, as she practised her new arts, she bit her lips to contain a cry of pleasure as her fingers moved over the warm, responding flesh. A sensuous heat expanded through her body as she caressed Maressa's hips. When Maressa sighed, and moved languorously beneath her touch, sweat broke out on Hazel's skin, and her breathing grew painful.

Maressa surrendered to pleasure. The wine had relaxed her into a dream-like trance. The horrors of Newgate faded, her body glowed with warmth, and in her mind she lay on silken cushions, her flesh caressed by the sun's heat. Adoring slaves, praising her beauty, awaited in shadows to tend her every need. Reverent hands trailed jewels over her recumbent figure; clothing her in fine chains set with rubies, diamonds and sapphires. Like a second skin they spread down over her hips and lay glistening along her inner thighs. Her body pulsated to the touch of the sun-warmed jewels which caressed her flesh, sliding between her parted legs.

Hazel's teeth drew blood from her lips as she bit back her gasps. Then her hands froze. A faint chink of the gaoler's keys came from the corridor. The cells were being opened for the day. Hastily, she dragged on her shift and gown and shook Maressa by the shoulder.

'The guard comes. You must dress quickly.'

Maressa was abruptly jerked from her reverie, and the dream faded. The silken cushions became the coarse straw-filled mattress, the sun's warmth the flames of a log fire. The mantle of jewels was . . . she frowned. She didn't know what that was, just that her body felt peaceful and at ease. The fears which had unnerved her had somehow been dispelled and she could face her trial with dignity and calm.

She was still only half-dressed when the keys rattled in the lock. The door was thrown open with such ferocity that it banged against the wall, and Maressa cried out, fearing something dreadful was about to happen.

'You're free, my darling! Free!' Thomas captured her in his arms, spinning her round and round. 'Mortimer is dead.'

'Put me down, Thomas,' Maressa said as she recovered her breath. 'You're making me dizzy.'

Thomas stooped to kiss her and whispered, 'I will explain everything later. I've come to take you home.'

Christmas without Alexander at Rowan Hall was miserable for Beth, but for the children's sake she hid her heartache. Boughs of holly and ivy had been cut to decorate the old hall and the yule log burned brightly in the grate. The snow had stopped that morning but it lay six inches on the ground. Sledges had been dragged from the hayloft and the children had spent the morning sliding down the nearest hill, and the afternoon skating on the frozen river. Drained by her pregnancy, Beth stayed inside, working in the kitchen.

The children tumbled into the kitchen, shaking the snow off their clothing and hair after a snow fight. They stamped their boots, their laughter infectious as they stripped off their mufflers revealing bright red faces and fingers mauve with the cold. Beth sat on the wooden settle by the fire gently massaging their fingers back to warmth.

'Go and change your wet clothes,' she ordered. 'The skittles have been set up in the Long Gallery and there's time for you to play Shove-penny before we eat.'

'When do we get our presents?' Thomasine fluffed out her mass of golden curls and smiled sweetly at Beth. She was like Maressa and just as grasping. Unlike her mother she had yet to learn to hide her avarice.

'After we have eaten,' Beth replied. 'There's a goose, quince pies and marchpane.'

Beth watched the children run out of the kitchen to change their wet clothes and exchanged a smile with Prudence, but as she made to follow the children Isaac Dunnock barred her way.

'Thou condemns thy children to hell-fire with thy frivolity.' His pale eyes blazed with fanaticism. 'Christmas is a heathen rite.'

'If you do not approve you may leave the estate,' Beth said sharply. 'Keep to the servants' quarters and your piety will not be offended by the sound of children's laughter.'

'The Lord sees all. Repent of thy sins—'

'Isaac, that's enough!' Elijah appeared behind his son and pushed him aside. 'Thou knows the conditions upon which thou art allowed to stay here. Mistress Rowan is a good Christian. There are logs to be brought in from the woodpile. Attend to thy work.'

Isaac's lips whitened but he held his peace and with a scornful glance at Beth he went back outside.

Elijah brushed a hand through his thinning russet hair. His freckled face was strained with worry. 'I apologise for my son, Mistress Rowan.'

'I've no wish to offend your principles, Elijah,' Beth answered. 'But there will be singing and music this evening. If it offends Isaac then he is welcome to spend the night in one of the outlying huts.'

'Art thou banishing him, Mistress Rowan?'

Beth shook her head, for she knew that Prudence doted on her eldest son.

'Christmas is the time for good will towards all men, but Isaac must be more tolerant of my ways, or leave. I'll not be lectured by a servant in my home.'

471

Beth went to the music room where the harpsichord and other instruments were laid out ready for the children to play. Winters in Wales were spent singing around the fire and, proud of his Welsh blood, Alexander had always encouraged it. Defiance made her sit at the harpsichord and begin to play. Not carols, but merry country dances and occasionally a slow love ballad, as her thought dwelt upon her husband, so far from home.

Three hours later, with the meal eaten, the presents opened and the excited children finally gone to their beds, Beth returned to the harpsichord. Her heart ached for Alexander, and it transferred to the haunting melody of her music. She lost track of the length of time she played, until the coolness of the room made her shiver. The fire had burnt low and the candles were down to their last inch. She rose tiredly to her feet. The wind was howling down the chimney and she hugged her arms around her. Then, lowering her hand, she caressed the swelling of her stomach. As she did so the baby quickened – a feeling like the flutter of butterfly wings. She gasped with delight. Her other babies had quickened weeks before this and she had been alarmed that not all was well with this one.

'Alex, my darling. Where are you?' Her voice was low and passionate. 'How can I bear another night without your arms around me? To feel your kisses and the heat of your body. I want you, Alex. I want you so much.'

'The whore condemns herself.' Isaac's voice flayed her from the door. 'It's not thy husband thou wants, it's any man. I saw how thou used to follow him like a bitch on heat at Oakfield Manor. Thou weren't married to him then.'

'How dare you speak to me that way?' Beth rounded on him.

'I speak the Lord's accusation.' Isaac's face was flushed and spittle sprayed from his mouth. 'Whore! Jezebel! Corrupter of innocents!'

He advanced towards her, his hands clenching and unclenching. Beth backed away, frightened, but she was brought up short by the harpsichord at her back.

'I am mistress here. You are a servant. Go to your quarters.'

Abruptly his manner changed. He was no longer aggressive

but sullen, and she could smell the ale on his breath. 'Don't look at me like I was the devil,' he whined. 'I'd lead thou to righteousness, Beth.'

'It is Mistress Rowan to you. Get out!'

His face twisted. 'Thou art a wanton. Repent, sinner!' His massive hands reached for her.

Beth screamed. A hand clamped on to her shoulder. Terrified she jerked away. The silk of her gown ripped in his fingers and tore down to her waist. His eyes glazed as they fastened upon the whiteness of her breast. Isaac swallowed and his face tensed with naked desire.

'No, Isaac!' she screamed, covering her breast with her hands. 'Get out!'

He reached for her. His wet mouth was upon her throat, forcing her head back on to the harpsichord. Frantically, she fought him, but his weight was crushing her.

Huge, callused hands squeezed her breasts.

'Jezebel! Thou tempts a man beyond reason,' he groaned. 'Rowan is never coming back. He's a rebel.'

'No!' Her shrill cry echoed around the room. Beth clawed at his face, but his strength overpowered her. His knee jammed between her legs as he fumbled to lift her skirts.

As she twisted and kicked to be free of him, her spine felt on the point of snapping. Yet her greatest fear was for the safety of her baby. Already her strength was failing. Her head wrenched from side to side to evade his mouth. 'No! No! I beg you, stop!'

His fingers were on the bare flesh of her thighs above her gartered hose. He was mouthing obscenities and cursing the layers of petticoats which hampered his hands. Beth began to sob in terror, knowing that she was powerless to stop him. Then all at once the weight was lifted from her. There was the sound of a fist striking flesh.

Trembling, she pushed herself upright. Elijah struck his son a second blow which sent him reeling across the room. There was blood on Isaac's mouth and one of his eyes was shut and beginning to swell.

'No, Pa,' he blubbered. 'I didn't mean no harm. Just giving her what she wanted.'

'Vile lecher!' Elijah raged. 'Thou disgusts me. Thou art no son of mine.'

He punched him a third time, and Isaac howled as blood

spurted from his broken nose. Relief at her escape turned to shock as Beth saw Elijah lashing into his son. The Quaker was a man of non-violence. She had never even heard him raise his voice in anger before.

'Stop it!' she ordered. 'Just make him leave.'

Isaac ducked another blow from his father and in so doing, tripped over a footstool. He toppled towards the fireplace. There was a thud as his head hit the marble surround and he fell to the floor. He did not move. Beth stared at the sprawled figure. As Elijah bent over his son, an agonised groan was torn from him.

'Is he dead?' Beth asked.

Elijah nodded and stood up. His shoulders sagged and his face was ashen. Beth burst into tears.

''Tis the Lord's justice for his sins,' Elijah said, brokenly. 'May He forgive me mine.'

'It was an accident, Elijah,' Beth began, but the Quaker's expression halted her words.

'Isaac was an extremist. He used violence to get his way,' Elijah declared. 'There are growing numbers in our sect who teach that all violence is wrong. It is our way to turn the other cheek. But after all thou has done for us, how could I let him . . .'

'You acted out of honour,' Beth reassured him. 'How else could you have stopped him?'

He hung his head, her words giving him no comfort. 'Go to bed, Mistress Rowan. I'll deal with this. 'Tis best there's no scandal. With thy leave I will bury him by our rites in the valley. I'd rather Prudence didn't know of this. She worshipped Isaac. I'll tell her that we quarrelled and he left.'

As Beth left the music room she heard Elijah begin to pray for Isaac's soul. Before she had time to undress she heard raised voices from downstairs and went to investigate. On the landing, she recognised Prudence's distraught voice.

'How could thee have quarrelled with Isaac?' The woman was beside herself with rage. 'It's freezing out there. What kind of father art thou to send thy son away in such weather? You go after Isaac and bring him back, or I'll never forgive thee, Eli.' Prudence burst into hysterical weeping and an outer door slammed.

Beth retreated to her chamber, and opened the shutter

across her window to stare down at the snow-carpeted land. A lantern glowed yellow in the darkness and she saw Elijah's silhouette, stooped over as he trudged through the thick snow carrying his son's corpse over his shoulder. Beth watched until the yellow speck had faded into the distance, and as she closed the shutter she saw that it had begun to snow again.

The Michaelmas Assizes at Chester had been packed, despite the roads made almost impassable with snow. Pollett's trial had lasted three days. Apart from the evidence which Popinjay and Angel had given, a dozen other people had accused Pollett of atrocities. Mark and Gabriellen's murders caused the greatest horror and Angel had not realised how respected her grandparents had been.

Pollett was condemned to hang the following week.

On the day of the hanging the snow was beginning to thaw. Angel was finishing breakfast in her room when there was a knock at her door and Popinjay entered.

'We will have to leave now if you want to see the execution.'

She shook her head. 'I've seen too many deaths already. The cart carrying Pollett from the gaol goes past the window. I just want to see his face as he passes.'

There was a loud clatter outside the door and a muttered curse. Popinjay opened the door to see Hapless holding a tray, the ale mug upturned over the chicken legs they had ordered. He was hopping on one foot, the other held up as he tried to shake off a wooden pail. Angel stifled her laughter at the boy's glum expression. Popinjay rescued the tray from Hapless, who hopped into the room and sat on the floor to wrestle with the pail.

'What idiot left that water-bucket on the balcony? Damn it, I could have crippled myself!'

'You should look where you're going.' Popinjay gripped the bucket and yanked it off Hapless's foot, bringing his boot with it. Popinjay laid the bucket aside and, picking up the lad's foot, gently twisted it from side to side. 'No bones broken.'

'But just look at that bruise!' Hapless said.

As Popinjay bent over the foot once more, Angel

intercepted a tender look between the two men which surprised her.

An hour later the mood in the room was sombre as they watched Pollett pass below the window. The jeering of the crowd told them the cart was coming long before it appeared. Pollett trembled with fear and had to be supported by a guard. He was sobbing, blabbering his innocence, and pleading for mercy. Angel turned away disgusted.

'Because of that spineless vermin, Gabriellen and Mark were killed.' She broke down, unable to stop the sobs which juddered through her body.

Popinjay put an arm around her. 'Cry all you need. God knows you've been through enough these last years and borne it bravely.'

'But I'm not brave,' Angel sobbed. 'I miss Father and Gabriellen and Mark so much. The man I love is a prisoner and we don't even know if they will allow us to wed in the spring.'

'Of course you'll wed Colonel Carver,' Popinjay soothed, his hand stroking her black curls. 'This week you honoured your vow to your grandparents. Their murderer has been brought to justice. And Colonel Carver will not always be a prisoner. You promised to rear the Rowan horses for your brother and there are always your plays. Do you still write?'

'When I can. But only comedies – there's too much tragedy in England to write about it as well.'

'Apart from love, laughter is the greatest gift you can give a person.'

Angel took his hand. 'Thank you, Popinjay. I couldn't have got through these last days without you. I'll miss you when you return to your business. When do you leave?'

'You'll not get rid of me that easily. I'll escort you to Rowan Hall. If Hapless here drew a pistol to protect you against a robber he'd likely shoot off his own foot.'

There was a grunt from Hapless. 'Thanks for the confidence in me.' His pique would have carried more weight if he was not still nursing his bruised ankle.

Two days later they entered the Vale of Clwyd. Once across the ford they could see Rowan Hall ahead. Spirals of smoke rose from two of its chimneys, a welcome sight to the chilled and weary traveller.

Angel could see Owain by the far paddocks, a rifle slung over his shoulder and three dogs with him, setting off to hunt. Owain waved and awaited their approach. The dogs had run off on the scent of a rabbit. Moments later they began to bark excitedly, but it was not the bark of a hound on the scent of an animal. It was eerie. Angel's skin prickled. Something was wrong.

She turned her mare towards the wood. Popinjay spurred his steed ahead of her, and was out of the saddle and running towards the barking dogs. When Angel whistled and called the dogs by name, they ran to greet her, tails wagging in pleasure. Popinjay was bent over a dark mound and he staggered as he stood up.

'Stay back, Angel.' His voice was bleak. 'It's Elijah Dunnock. I think the other man is his son. Looks like the son was injured and Elijah was carrying him back to the house. They must have frozen to death.'

Chapter Nineteen

'How can I comfort Prudence?' Beth wrung her hands as she sat with Angel in the winter parlour. 'She blames herself for Isaac and Elijah's deaths, yet the truth would be even harder for her to bear.'

'You've done all you can,' Angel consoled. 'Prudence knows she has a home here. She believes that Elijah was bringing Isaac back, that they were reconciled. Eventually she'll take comfort in that.'

Beth twisted the wedding band on her finger. 'I'm useless with the horses, and they're so important to Alex. Now he wants me to join him in France, but I feel too ill to travel.'

'The stud is prospering. We have another ten mares in foal,' she said, seeking to cheer her.

Angel had never seen Beth look so ill. Her complexion was the colour of dough and she had no energy. She had confided in Angel that the baby did not move much and she feared that all was not well.

'Alex will return,' Angel went on firmly. 'Parliament will grant a pardon to the exiles, I'm sure of it.' But she did not believe her own words. 'Once the baby comes you can join Alex in France. You know I'll look after the estate. I'm staying until the mares have all foaled, and I'll return again in time for your lying-in.'

Beth's amber eyes remained troubled. 'My place is to safeguard Alex's home. Your place is with Nathan in London. I know what it's like to be apart from the man you love.'

'Nathan understands how much Rowan Hall and the horses mean to me,' Angel said, putting a comforting arm around Beth's shoulders.

Several of the children burst into the room at that moment all speaking at once.

479

'As it's raining again, Aunt Angel,' Julian spoke out, 'will you tell us a story?'

'Have you done the work set by your tutor?' Angel asked. The children's tutor was a retired cleric who lived in a cottage on the estate. They pulled faces and began to make excuses.

'I'll tell you a story when your schoolwork is completed.'

'Aunt Angel we always learn so much from your stories,' Marcus said widening his brown eyes. 'Your tales of knights and battles are better than a history lesson.'

Angel found it hard to resist Marcus, he had inherited Alexander's charm as well as his looks.

'Very well, but not a story. It looks like we're in for a week of rain. We'll write a play about an event in history. You'll decide which. You will act in it. We'll raid the attics for the costumes.'

As the children clambered up the stairs to the schoolroom to complete their lessons, Popinjay sauntered into the parlour. He was carrying his saddle roll.

Angel went to him. 'I'll miss you,' she said sadly. 'You've been such a support to us this last week.'

Popinjay raised her hand to his lips. 'We shall meet again at your wedding. I'd not miss that. Have you seen Hapless?'

'He's in the kitchen with Owain. They're cleaning the tackle.'

As she spoke there was a crash from the kitchen and a scream of laughter from Ruth. Angel and Popinjay arrived in time to see Hapless sprawled on the floor, a heavy cart-horse's halter around his feet and his arms entangled in a mass of bridles and reins. His frantic efforts to free himself only made things worse, and Popinjay went to help Hapless to extricate himself.

'I came to ask you to keep an eye on the womenfolk and protect them,' Popinjay said with a laugh. 'But it looks like you need protection from yourself.'

Prudence appeared at Angel's side. 'I see Hapless had another mishap! He'll miss Mr Sparrow when he leaves. They've been like father and son this past week.'

Angel had mixed with too many actors, to know that it was not as a father figure that Hapless saw Popinjay. The boy idolised him. He sat at Popinjay's feet for hours while the older man spoke of his adventures during the years of conflict. As for Popinjay, he was too circumspect to reveal how he regarded Hapless's devotion. It was obvious he was fond of the lad, but on their journey to Wales Popinjay had regularly taken a tavern wench to his room at night. And yet there was nothing paternal in the affection in Popinjay's eyes as he put a hand on Hapless's shoulder. To give the two men a moment of privacy, Angel found jobs for Owain and Ruth outside. Taking Prudence aside, she confided her fears about Beth's health.

'She does look ill,' Prudence agreed. 'A sickly pregnancy usually means a sickly child.'

'I know you'll take good care of her. I'll return before the baby is born. It means a lot to her that I'm here.'

Angel returned to London at the end of March, when ten foals had been born to continue the Rowan strain. From the previous year's stock she took four geldings and two mares to sell in the capital. One colt, named Glendower after the first of the Rowan stallions, had been kept aside and Angel had high hopes that he possessed all the qualities to eventually succeed Caradoc as the Rowan stallion. Once it was known that the Rowan strain was still being bred the horses sold at good prices, and she received several orders for future sales. The money was sent back to Wales to pay the fines on the estate. Providing their crops did not fail the money would support the family and servants throughout the year. From her own annuity Angel sent money to her brother in France, telling him it was from the horse sales.

Free at last to pursue her own goals, Angel rode through the London streets. The atmosphere in the capital was oppressive. Carefree laughter had disappeared. Tumblers, morris dancers and minstrels were no longer allowed to perform in the streets. Above her, the overcast sky could just be glimpsed above the high, leaning gables, tall chimneys and church spires. Each alleyway carried its own pungent smell: mouth-watering pies and bread, exotic spices, soap from the laundries, malt and ale from the breweries, the rancid tallow from the candlemakers and, equally unpleasant, the mixed stench of offal, fish, tanning leather and slaughter-houses. Above the noise of knife-grinders and hammering of carpenters, coopers and blacksmiths, rose the jeers and rivalry of the 'prentices and cries of the street-sellers. Most appalling and sobering of all were the beggars, some hideously scarred by the weeping sores of the French pox. Women's faces were disfigured from burns when their long skirts caught fire as they tended their cooking pots. On every street corner there were cripples, some deformed from birth, but most mutilated by the war, with eyes blinded or limbs severed by cannon shot. Children wailed – the homeless, starving orphans, ragged and pinch-faced, their eyes bleak with misery. Those who survived to their teens were sly-faced pickpockets or sneak-thieves destined for an early death on the gallows. Drunkards lay senseless in the gutter or started fights. Hollowed-eyed prostitutes flaunted their fading charms and jeered obscenely when their advances were rejected.

Having dispensed with all her small coins to the beggars, Angel stared straight ahead as she rode through the crowded streets, depressed by so much misery. Ahead was the main thoroughfare of Cheapside. Even in this vast market, the song of caged linnets was drowned by ranting preachers berating their congregation for their sins. Everywhere was so drab. No one wore bright colours or smiled now. The Puritan yoke had stifled England. Angel passed St Paul's Cathedral with its square central turret and rode up Ludgate Hill into Fleet Street. Here she turned into an alley and was almost deafened by the sound of tinware being pounded. Another alleyway gave her a glimpse of the river, its waterway as crowded as the streets. Wherries were massed like ants around the high-rigged sailing vessels moored at the wharves, or ferrying cargo and passengers to and fro.

When at last Angel arrived at the red-brick four-storey building of Nell Lovegood's, the weariness and despair from the recent sights left her. Here, at least, she would find a warm welcome.

Maressa looked at the gilded French clock on the table and hid her exasperation. With Thomas away on business, she had invited a guest, intending to seduce him. She had dressed with care. Her gold hair was arranged to fall sensually about her shoulders. Her oyster silk gown was cut revealingly low, and her full breasts enticingly displayed. Her guest's welcoming appraisal had encouraged her that he would easily fall prey to her charm. His reputation as a womaniser assured her of success.

Yet it had not proved as easy as she expected. She had flattered him, listened to him with rapt attention and encouraged him to speak of his work. Throughout, her smile remained beguiling. Sitting close to him she leaned forward so that his gaze would be drawn to her breasts and the seductive perfume specially blended by Hazel would tease his senses. Though his gaze admired her beauty, he had made no move to kiss her. Piqued, she began to wonder whether his vaunted reputation had not been exaggerated.

This was the first time that Nathan had been alone with Maressa. He had been delighted when she sent a message for him to attend her, saying she had news of Angel. Most days he was now free to leave his prison, providing he returned before nightfall. He had not expected Angel's sister to openly flirt with him. He had been faithful to Angel since their reunion, but denying his body for so many months now began to pay its toll.

No man could not be moved by Maressa's beauty. Hair like woven gold, a figure to rival Venus, she was all temptation. He was conscious of the musical resonance of her voice, its tone changing to a beckoning warmth as she encouraged him to speak of his work. When she leaned closer her low-cut gown displayed her breasts: high, firm, tempting a man to bury his head in their curves. Her hands were never still as she talked. They were upon the curve of her hips or thighs, provocatively outlining their contours. Her restless fingers would move to her breasts delicately skimming their fullness, her forefinger briefly touching the deep cleavage from which it was becoming increasingly difficult to withhold his gaze. Her perfume engulfed his senses. When she spoke and parted her lips in that self-assured smile of invitation, Nathan's throat dried. His blood pumped rapidly through his body.

When her knee brushed against his, his control almost cracked. He stood up, every muscle tense. As he moved away, he caught the glitter in her eyes, a glitter which belied the soft feminine allure. It was not attraction he saw in those amber depths, but cold-hearted calculation, and it acted like iced water on his heated blood.

He wandered over to a Rubens painting and commented upon it.

'Thomas bought it recently,' Maressa replied, the irritation obvious in her voice. 'It came from Whitehall Palace. The treasures there are being sold.'

A waft of sultry perfume warned him that she had come to stand beside him, and he moved away to study the next painting. It was of Maressa and two of her children – a boy of about three and a baby. The likeness to Maressa was outstanding, even down to that cold-eyed glitter in the otherwise perfect face. He smiled as he saw the signature. It had been painted by Angel.

'I should have guessed,' he said with a laugh. 'Angel has remarkable talent as an artist.'

Maressa did not want to be reminded of her sister, nor of her qualities. Nathan studied the next painting. It was Thomas astride a Rowan horse, again by Angel.

It was then that she heard a woman's laugh, an unmistakable laugh. Glancing at Nathan she saw that he was too absorbed in studying the portrait to have heard it. At the sound of hurrying footsteps on the stairs, Maressa said quickly, 'Would you like more wine, Colonel Carver?'

Whilst reaching for the silver flagon, she stumbled and fell against him. She was caught in his arms as she heard the footsteps approach the door. Wrapping her arms around his neck she kissed him hard on the mouth.

Angel froze in the doorway. Maressa was locked in Nathan's arms in the midst of a passionate kiss. Then she saw that Nathan's eyes were open and his expression incredulous. Maressa looked towards the door and with a gasp of dismay stepped back from Nathan.

'Angel!' she said, flustered. 'What must you think?'

Nathan looked aghast, his eyes narrowing with anger as he regarded Maressa's playacting. Angel knew he was too much of a gentleman to defend himself at her sister's expense. Maressa was paying her back for all the times Thomas had shown his affection for her.

'What would you like me to think, Maressa?' she challenged, but her gaze was on Nathan. She walked towards him, her eyes shining with love. 'Did you trip, Sister? I trust Nathan.'

She moved into his arms, decorum permitting only the briefest of kisses whilst Maressa remained in the room. Even so, the light touch of his lips was enough to set her body afire. Nathan's arms slid possessively to her waist, and the desire in his eyes scorched her soul.

Angel could feel her sister's resentment that her ploy to seduce Nathan had failed. 'Maressa,' she said, 'how thoughtful of you to invite Nathan here to await my arrival. There would have been no privacy for us at Horse Guards.'

'It was the least I could do.' Maressa forced warmth into her voice. 'After all you have done for me in the past.'

The double-edge to these words was not lost on Angel, and it saddened her.

'In my joy at seeing Nathan, I neglect you.' Angel kissed her sister's cheek. 'Your imprisonment must have been hell. Henry was never worthy of you, Maressa, and you deserve all the happiness you have with Thomas.'

Maressa stiffly suffered Angel's embrace. 'I'll leave you and Nathan alone, since he must return to his cell by four.'

As she left them she was simmering with rage that Angel had not been duped. Her thoughts of Thomas were no less charitable. She was grateful for all he had done to free her from Newgate, but gratitude was not enough to keep her bound to him.

Their marriage was invalid. She was still beautiful and her figure had not been marred by childbirth. There would be no more babies. Ambition burned in her. During her years as the contessa singing in the saloon many noblemen had propositioned her to become their mistress. Several had even offered her marriage. Tied to Thomas she had been forced to refuse.

Life was different now. She had no intention of squandering her beauty at Nell Lovegood's. Thomas would never settle out of London. His position as an Upright Man demanded his presence here, and he was too much of a rogue to give up the excitement and power of that life. Maressa had her own ambitions to fulfil. She wanted wealth and position. When she married again, it would be to a man who could give her both. Next time she would aim higher than a landless baronet.

* * *

The moment the door closed behind Maressa, Nathan caught Angel in his arms and kissed her. Breathless and trembling with desire they broke apart, and Nathan gazed into her eyes.

'We marry at the end of the week,' he said hoarsely. 'It's all arranged. I cannot wait any longer to make you truly mine.'

Angel gazed at him with a sensuous smile. She spread her hands over his chest, feeling the powerful rhythm of his heart. Her voice was husky and breathless. 'My love, here we can be alone.'

She moved so that her body was pressed against him. His hands slid down the curve of her neck, his lips warm and demanding against the pulse at her throat. With a soft groan his palms cupped her breasts, and at his touch, passion spiralled through Angel. Her kiss was ardent before she broke away and, taking his hand, drew him to the door. Outside, Maressa was pacing the corridor.

'That was brief,' she said, surprised. 'There's much we must discuss.'

'Later, Maressa,' Angel replied, leading Nathan to her room at the back of the house. 'Nathan and I also have much to discuss, but I intend to speak with my body not with words.'

Maressa could not control her shock. 'Can't you wait until you're married?'

'Most definitely not. We've waited for this moment for over four years.'

Maressa closed her eyes and shuddered. 'Really, Angel, Father would expect better of you.'

'Father was never a hypocrite. Only you, Maressa, could remain shocked, after living in a bordello for several years.'

'I was married to Thomas. Or believed myself to be. And he certainly never touched me before the ceremony.'

'Poor Tom!' Angel said to Nathan as she shut her bed-chamber door behind them. Leaning against it, she devoured him with her gaze. 'Four years! I was mad to let you go to The Hague alone.'

'You had a dream to follow, as I had mine.' Nathan's kisses stopped her words. 'Are you going to talk all afternoon, or do you intend to show me how much you've missed me?'

486

'Actions speak more potently than words,' Angel murmured, her fingers already at work on the buttons of his doublet.

'From a playwright I shall expect you to honour that promise with imagination and verve.'

'If I disappoint you, there's still time for you to cancel the wedding.' The last of her garments fell to her ankles. Provocatively, she lifted her arms and, removing the pins from her hair, shook out the raven tresses, sending them tumbling over her shoulders and breasts.

'You couldn't disappoint me, Angel.' He led her to the bed. 'And I warn you now I shall be expecting an encore.'

Maressa was planning her own future. For the moment she was still financially dependent upon Thomas. Though she had decided not to remarry him, she was annoyed that he had not asked her. At least he had the decency not to expect to resume his place in her bed. But that he seldom sought her company unaccountably added to her frustration. She could feel her hold on Thomas slipping and she did not like it.

An hour later when Thomas returned she followed him to his study. He looked up from writing in a ledger.

'My dear, what an unexpected pleasure.' He sat back in his chair.

'I see you so rarely these days, Thomas.'

He raised a blond eyebrow. 'I wasn't aware that you wished my company.'

There was a hardness to his voice which made Maressa uneasy. Was his use for her at an end, now that he had his son? She forced a smile. 'I would speak to you about our children. They cannot remain indefinitely in Wales. Neither is it suitable that they live here when they are older. I want a house in a respectable area.'

'You ask for much.' His gaze moved over her figure. 'And give little in return.'

'I've given you two children!' Her temper flashed white-hot. 'Is that not beyond price? You demanded a son of me, I did not fail in the bargain. You may wish Richard to inherit this ungodly empire, but what of Thomasine? Do you intend her to take over from Nell Lovegood, or would you prefer she makes a grand marriage? She'll not achieve that if her name is linked with this house.'

'Of course I want the best for Thomasine, but there's scandal attached to both our names. She's better off living in Wales with Beth.'

'You would pass Thomasine off as Alexander and Beth's child!' Maressa was appalled.

'I'll do whatever it takes to secure her future.'

'She's my daughter.'

'And this is the first concern I've seen you show for her.' Thomas stood up, his stance menacing. 'You've no love for Thomasine. You've resented her since birth, because it meant you had to endure my advances until you conceived another child. You're an unnatural mother and an unnatural wife.'

'I never refused you.'

'Neither did you give anything of yourself.'

Maressa staggered back. There was cruelty in his merciless stare. 'You can't mean to cast me off like a common whore? I'm the mother of your children.'

'That's all that saves you,' he pronounced darkly. 'You can have your house, Maressa. And an income until you find either a protector or sell yourself again in marriage. I'll also provide for Julian's education. After that, he must make his own way in the world.'

'But you have made a fortune in gold through Henry's death.'

'So I did.' He stood close to her, his gaze mocking. 'But I never give anything away without a service being rendered in return.' When he ran his forefinger along her cheek, Maressa flinched. 'Your body no longer interests me, Maressa. But the contessa has always been a good attraction for Nell's. Continue to sing here and you'll live in comfort. Who knows? As the contessa you might even snare yourself a wealthy husband.' His hand moved from her cheek to grip her throat. 'We know too much of each other, do we not?' The warning chilled her. 'I rule supreme in this district and you know how I deal with treachery. You may no longer be my wife, but you remain my property until I decree otherwise.'

Maressa nodded, too frightened to speak. This side of Thomas terrified her. She had been a fool to antagonise him.

Two weeks later Maressa moved to a grand house in St Martin's Lane. A cook, a coachman, two footmen and two maids besides Hazel were engaged. Here she could live as a wealthy widow, and her neighbours would be kept ignorant of her double life as the contessa at Nell Lovegood's.

Nathan and Angel were married in the porch of St Ethelburga's Church. In the rafters overhead two doves cooed as they began their mating dance. Nathan smiled and gazing into Angel's eyes, he repeated his vows in an assured voice. When it was her turn to speak her vows, she found her heart so full of love that it choked her. To her horror, the words would not form. Nathan waited, his blue eyes burning like the heart of a flame, and Angel cleared her throat, reciting the vows firmly.

After they had gone into the church to receive their blessing, wellwishers crowded around them. The wedding party was small. Apart from Thomas and Maressa there were only Popinjay, Hapless, Nell Lovegood and some of the other women from the house whom Angel had befriended. None of Nathan's sisters were present. Two had been widowed during the war and remarried Parliamentarians who had no wish to align their families with Royalists. The third had died of smallpox while Nathan was in Venice.

'A kiss. A kiss!' Thomas demanded as the bride and groom walked back into the sunshine. 'Not like you, Carver, to be so remiss. Kiss your wife, so we can all take our turn.'

When Nathan took Angel into his arms, kissing her with a passion which left her breathless, there were whistles of appreciation from Thomas and Popinjay.

'Od's-blood man, I said kiss her, not devour her!' Thomas laughed. He nudged Nathan aside. 'My turn now.' Not for Thomas, a discreet peck upon the cheek. Embracing her, he planted a long open-mouthed kiss on her lips, and he was grinning when he released her. 'Damn it all, Nate,' he said. 'But if I don't envy you this night.'

There was a harsh intake of breath from Maressa, but the others cheered, taking the jest in the good-natured manner it was intended.

'Does the bride get all the kisses?' Maressa asked with false sweetness. 'Ladies, we neglect the groom.'

Nathan grinned and bowed his cheek to his sister-in-law, but, rising on tiptoe, Maressa kissed him as deeply as Thomas had kissed Angel. Angel saw her cousin stiffen at Maressa's conduct and was relieved when Nell Lovegood and her women circled Nathan loudly, all claiming their kisses and bustling him from one to the other.

Popinjay kissed Angel on both cheeks. 'I wish you happy, my dear. You deserve it. Dr Carver is a fortunate man.'

'The fortune is all mine,' Angel replied.

She turned to Hapless who was standing awkwardly, holding his hat in his hand. He shuffled his feet, then coughed and darted forward to place a swift peck upon her cheek.

'A happy life, Mistress Carver,' he stammered, his face scarlet. As he turned away his sword tangled with his leg and he tripped. He was saved from falling only by Popinjay catching hold of him.

'Are you all right, Hapless?' Popinjay's voice was the gentlest Angel had ever heard it. Hapless was often at Popinjay's house and Angel was surprised when he insisted upon returning with her to Wales in early summer.

Before they left the churchyard Angel laid her nosegay of flowers on the grave of her great-grandfather, Esmond Angel. She gazed at the headstone. Would she ever achieve her dream of having her plays performed upon the English stage? Certainly, it would never happen until the Puritan government was brought down. And now there were rumours that Oliver Cromwell was being pressed to accept the role of Lord Protector. The man who had contributed to the King's downfall was about to become absolute ruler of England.

Thomas had insisted that the wedding feast be at Nell's, but it was to be a family celebration. Thomas respected their need to curtail the bawdry of the nuptials. With Nathan forced to return to Horse Guards before dark on his parole the couple were given the privacy they needed.

Laying in the fold of her husband's arm, Angel was dismayed to see the light fading from the sky. Leaning on her elbow she smiled down at him. 'Would that I could make time stand still for this one day.'

He brushed aside the ebony curtain of her hair and gently pulled her head down to receive his kiss. 'We have a lifetime to be together. But were I to spend every moment with you it would never be long enough.'

He knelt and began to kiss her, starting from her toes, taking each one into his mouth. 'I want to taste and know every part of you,' he said between kisses.

Angel laughed softly. 'We're married now – you don't have to resort to outrageous flattery.' The timbre of her voice became husky as his mouth travelled higher, over her ankles, calves and thighs.

'No flattery, my love,' he avowed. When the heat of his breath skimmed the sensitive flesh of her inner thighs she moaned in pleasure.

He lifted his head, desire blazing in his eyes. 'My prison is more loathsome than ever for it keeps me from your side. I hadn't realised that love could be a living death when we are apart.'

'Damn your gaolers to hellfire for taking you from me,' she groaned as he kissed her stomach, waist and then captured her breast.

'I love you, Angel.'

Her need for him was a hunger beyond sanity. She writhed in a sensuous fire, consumed by its flames as the sun dipped behind the rooftops. Time was deserting them. Their sighs of ecstasy were muffled by ardent kisses, encapsulating both their immediate pleasure and the torture of the parting to come.

'I love you so much,' Angel murmured. 'No woman has the right to feel such joy this side of paradise.'

Paradise for Angel lasted eight weeks. She had taken rooms in a house overlooking St James's Park. Her time with Nathan was limited since he would never neglect his duties to the sick, and so she spent her time sketching the characters she saw around her, knowing that in the future many of them would find themselves in her plays. She even began a new comedy, refusing to believe that Puritan rule would continue forever.

All too soon it was time for her to return to Wales. Maressa's farewell had been warmer than her greeting, and she pressed gifts into Angel's hands for her children. Maressa had refused to make the long journey to Wales to see them, but Thomas joined Hapless to escort her. He was bringing Julian back to London to study at St Paul's School. Angel had expected Thomas and her sister to remarry, but her cousin shrugged the subject aside, while Maressa smiled in a way which had made Angel uneasy. The only one who seemed to be close to her was Hazel.

With Thomas for company and in high spirits the ride to Wales was a pleasant one. Angel suspected that he had been responsible for Henry's death. The Underworld which he governed showed no mercy. Fear and respect kept him their leader. She had never witnessed that cold-blooded side of his character. To her he was always charming. A proven friend when needed.

They had reached the paddocks of the Rowan estate, and Angel's practised eye studied the chestnut foals grazing there. The sound of dogs barking and children playing in the orchard drew her gaze, and seeing her nieces and nephews playing hoodman-blind and romping with the dogs, brought a sharp pain to her heart. She was five-and-twenty, no longer a young woman. Was she fated to be barren? Since her marriage she was obsessed with the thought of bearing Nathan's child. Nathan had kissed her fears of barrenness aside.

'It is you I want. If we cannot have children it is God's will. Nothing will change how I feel for you.' But she had sensed that he had spoken to reassure her.

Angel knew she had been fortunate in her life, and she could not shake off the cynicism that no one had everything they wished for. No one's life was truly perfect. Everything had its price.

She pushed the thought from her mind. Rowan Hall was weaving its magic upon her and she could not be gloomy. She stared at the high gables, the tall chimneys, the mullioned windows surrounded by ivy, and the mellow stonework, gilded in the afternoon sunshine. Impatient to be reunited with Beth, she urged her mare to a canter. When no one came out to greet them as they clattered into the courtyard she became uneasy. Something was wrong. She hurried into the house, to meet Prudence Dunnock, carrying a water pitcher down the stairs.

'It's Beth, isn't it?' Angel said, seeing her stricken expression. 'What's happened?'

'Her pains started two days ago.' Prudence wrung her hands, and her eyes filled with tears. 'The waters broke at the start. A dry birth is always dangerous. Doubly so when 'tis twins and the first babe is in breech. Mistress Rowan is very weak.'

Angel raced up the stairs. On entering the lying-in chamber she was pulled up short by the stench of sweat, candlewax and fear. The shutters were closed and two candles lit the scene in a dim amber light. Beth was hunched over the birthing-stool, groaning and sobbing, her eyes shut against her agony. Her face was the colour of sour curds, her long hair hung in straggles down her back and was plastered to her scalp by sweat. The stout figure of Mother Giffard bent over Beth, her hand under the stool and nightgown as she examined the labouring woman. Beth's scream split the air, sending icy shudders through Angel.

'Help me! Dear God, help me!' Beth's body arched, her distended abdomen straining. Her face was contorted as the contraction knifed her, but even her screams no longer had strength. Beth's fingers clutched at her stomach as though she would pluck out the babies and put an end to her torment.

'Jesu have mercy on me,' she panted as the contraction subsided. 'I can't bear this any more. Let me die – just let me die!'

'Beth, don't speak that way.' Angel pulled off her cloak and knelt at her side. She put an arm around Beth's weeping figure. 'Be strong.'

Beth opened her eyes. They were sunken, purpled by hours of agony, and the pupils dilated with fear. 'I'm going to die, Angel. The other birthings were never like this. Why won't my baby be born?'

'It will be soon. Now rest. Save your strength.'

'She must walk to aid the birth,' Mother Giffard declared.

'I can't,' Beth wailed. 'Just let me be.'

Angel was alarmed to see Beth so exhausted. 'Has she been given honey for strength? What herbs has she taken to ease the pain?'

'Do you think I don't know my work?' Mother Giffard snarled. She picked up a large pitcher of ale and filled a tankard, gulping the contents down. She belched loudly and smacked her lips in satisfaction. 'I've done everything. Look you, there's a knife beneath the stool to cut her pain. There's a reliquary containing a tear of Our Lady around her neck. That's saved many a mother, so don't go saying it's Papist nonsense and has no place in a Protestant house. Everything's been done, short of taking the grappling hook and tearing the babe from the womb. And I swear that's all that's left. Might save the other twin that way, you see. The poor lass can't take much more.'

Appalled, Angel stared at the midwife. 'That's barbaric!'

Blackened teeth were bared in outrage. 'I don't take no interference at a birthing.'

At another groan from Beth, Mother Giffard bent again to examine her. The woman began to chant in Welsh as she lifted the nightgown, and the fleshy claw was streaked with grime and her nails lined with dirt. Angel slapped the woman's hand away. The thought of that filthy hand touching Beth made her cringe.

'God-a-mercy, woman, have you come straight from the cow-byre? Don't you ever wash your hands? No one knows what causes the childbed fever. Surely if a wound can be poisoned by being inflicted with a dirty sword, then pushing filthy hands into a mother's womb could lead to infection!'

'I've delivered nigh on a hundred babies. Childbed fever is part of the birthing. There's no more than a score of my mothers died from it.'

Angel's patience snapped. She seized the woman by the shoulders and pushed her protesting from the room. 'Get out! You'll not kill Beth. Prudence, send for another midwife. One that's sober and clean.'

'There's only Gwyneth,' Prudence answered. 'She's not very experienced, though.'

'Send for her. In the meantime we'll do what we can for Beth.' She turned to Mother Giffard who was muttering curses in the doorway. 'Tell me what I must watch for and I'll still pay your fee.'

'Go to hell with that poor wretch in there. You think yourself so clever? Then you deal with the breech, my fine lady. Look you, only a meat hook can save the mother and possibly the other child.'

Fear for Beth made Angel's temper erupt. 'I'll not believe that!' She gripped the midwife and began to shake her. 'Tell me!'

'Pay me first.'

Angel dug four silver coins from her purse and held them

494

out. They were snatched from her hand and spat upon before being dropped into the midwife's bodice.

'Say your prayers, fine lady. Nothing to be done, you see, but wait and pray. I've tried to turn the child and it wouldn't budge. No room in the womb with twins, you see. Likely all three will be dead come morning.'

'That won't happen,' Angel vowed.

She returned to the lying-in chamber to find Beth crouched forward, vomiting on to the floor. The stench in the room was unbearable. Angel held Beth until she sank back weakly into her arms. The poor girl began to shiver between her labour pains, and her breathing came in fractured gasps. The cramped position on the birthing-stool looked more like an added torture than an aid to the delivery.

Knowing little of birthing procedures, apart from attending the mares when they foaled, Angel still felt that such torment was not right. Were not the mares first made comfortable in clean straw?

'Can you stand, Beth?' she said with sudden decision. 'Let's get you back to the bed. There at least you can rest between your pains.'

'God bless you for coming, Angel. I need your strength.'

Angel virtually carried Beth to the bed. When another pain tore through her, she gripped her hand, speaking words of encouragement. 'Take heart, Beth. I'll give you something for the pain.'

Her arm was clutched in Beth's bruising grasp as the next pain struck. 'Help me, Angel.' Her eyes were wild with fear. 'God have mercy on me. This is my judgement for Isaac's death.'

Angel was relieved that Prudence was not in the room. 'Nonsense. That harridan of a midwife has been sent away. Another will be here soon. I have some notes dictated to me by a London midwife at Nathan's suggestion.' She squeezed Beth's hand. 'It will be all right. The potions will ease your pain. Soon you'll be holding your twins.'

During the next half hour Angel left Beth's side whenever the pains abated. She pulled open the shutters to let fresh air into the room. On studying her notes, a herbal bath of warm water was prepared, containing hollyhock, bettony, mugwort, camomile and parsley. Beth was helped into this

495

and washed down, and her hair tied back in a plait. Spasms shook her body and twice the nausea returned. Angel fed her with honey to sustain her strength. Then, dressed in a clean shift, Beth was propped up on the bed.

'I do feel better,' Beth said weakly. Her lips were bloodied from biting them to hold back her screams. 'But the children. They mustn't hear my screams. Gag me, Angel.'

Beth jerked rigid as the next pain attacked, and she bit down upon the kerchief which Angel had placed between her teeth.

Without the notes she had copied in London Angel could not have coped. Word had been received from Gwyneth that she was at another delivery, but would come as soon as she could. She had advised them to send for the physician in Llangollen, and Hapless had ridden to summon him. This was a complicated birth, and Beth needed an experienced midwife. Feeling her own panic welling up, Angel fought to stay calm.

Placing a cool lavender-scented compress on Beth's brow, Angel studied her notes. 'I must try and turn the babe, but not like Mother Giffard. I've a compound of duck's grease, oil of almond, comfrey, rosemary and ground quince. It will help the passage of the babe into the world.' As she spoke she smeared the ungent on to her hands. 'Raise your knees, Beth.'

The grease was smothered between Beth's legs and very gently Angel's eased her fingers inside the mother. Her other hand rested on the swollen abdomen. Beth stiffened and Angel steeled herself against the pain she knew she must inflict. When tending the mares she had turned several foals without qualms. This was very different.

'I'm sorry, Beth,' she gasped. 'The baby must be turned. I can feel its bottom. Be brave. Now here's a foot. Easy, Beth. Take deep breaths.' Slowly Angel felt the baby respond to the pressure of her hand. Sweat ran down her arms, her back and between her breasts. Her lungs were bursting as she held her breath as she worked. A glance at Beth's face showed it running with sweat, her eyes rolling back into her head, her lips bloodless. Angel kept her other hand on Beth's stomach and at the next contraction she felt the muscle straining under her hand like a taut ball. It was impossible to turn the baby with its twin still in the womb. But now she could feel both its tiny feet and, her heart battering against her chest, she took them between her fingers and eased them down through the birth channel.

With the next pain she prayed the baby would be born. It wasn't. She looked at Prudence. 'Do you think I should pull the baby from the womb?'

Prudence shook her head. 'I've heard tales of terrible deformities that way. Leave it to nature. It is God's will. This is Eve's burden.'

Angel bit back her irritation. She did not believe in superstition or religious doctrine in such matters. It was not rational. But she bowed to Prudence's experience. The thought of maybe mutilating Alexander's child filled her with dread.

The sun disappeared behind the hills and the candles were relit. With each pain Beth grew weaker. An owl hooted in a tree and she again arched up, grunting and twisting in her travail. Angel lifted the sheet which modestly covered her sister-in-law and to her relief she saw the baby's legs begin to slide into the world. With thundering heart, Angel took hold of the infant and very carefully eased it towards her. Beth was panting, her eyes rolling back in her head with the pain. There was a tearing of flesh then Beth fainted as the baby slid on to the mattress, covered in blood and mucus. Prudence cut and tied the cord and lifted the first-born aside. It looked too tiny to have caused so much suffering, and one glance showed Angel that it was not breathing.

'Make sure there's no mucus in its mouth,' she ordered Prudence. 'I know foals can die if it's not removed.'

Leaving Prudence to deal with the first baby, she turned her attention back to Beth. The next pain following hard on the last brought Beth back to consciousness with a scream.

'No more! Please, no more. Give me peace.'

Angel saw the head of the twin appear. 'The second baby's coming, Beth. Be strong.'

Behind her she heard three sharp slaps and turning, saw Prudence holding the baby upside down. The tiny figure shuddered, gasped and gave a feeble cry.

'God be praised,' Prudence sobbed with joy. 'It lives! You have another girl, Mistress Rowan.'

'Do you hear that, Beth?' Angel smiled encouragement. 'A bonny baby daughter.'

Beth was too weak to acknowledge the words. Her body twisted in another spasm and the second baby slipped from between her legs. It was even smaller than the first, but had a cap of black hair. Its tiny hands shuddered as it met the cold air and its face screwed up. Its cry was surprisingly lusty for one so frail. Angel laughed with relief. This one would be a fighter.

The door opened and Gwyneth appeared, her voice breathless with apology. 'Couldn't get here before. First child it were and a drawn-out birth. Oh, but it looks like I'm not needed. Twins! How wonderful.'

Angel wrapped the second girl in a linen towel then bathed it and settled the twins in the cradle whilst Gwyneth tended to Beth when both afterbirths came away. Angel saw the midwife frown as she studied the second afterbirth. Beth was deathly pale and then, to Angel's horror, she saw blood soaking through her linen shift.

'Gwyneth, what's happened?'

'Not all the afterbirth has come away. Lift her legs. She's bleeding.' Gwyneth began to massage Beth's stomach.

There was blood everywhere – the sheets were scarlet. Gwyneth called for linen clouts and packed these close into Beth's body until the flow of blood appeared to stop. An hour later it started again. Beth was unconscious before they had halted its flow. Angel worked with Gwyneth, both of them laying on tepid compresses to try and cool the raging heat of her still swollen body.

'I need the flayed skin of a sheep and a hare to put on to her belly,' Gwyneth demanded. 'That will stop the onset of fever.'

'Aye, it worked for a woman in Oxfordshire,' Prudence agreed.

Angel had no such faith. Where was the physician? Surely he should have arrived before now. As the moon passed across the sky and the first glimmer of dawn appeared on the horizon, Beth returned to consciousness, but was very weak. Despite the stomach massaging and all Gwyneth's care the bleeding began again. This time it would not stop. By mid-morning it had begun to seep through the feather mattress on to the floor. Despite the heat of the sunny June day, Beth was shivering with cold one moment, afire with fever the next.

'Alex, Alex,' she murmured her husband's name over and over again.

It was evening before the physician arrived. He immediately advised that leeches should be placed on the swollen abdomen. Angel's flesh crawled at the sight of the thin black bodies which fastened their mouths to Beth's stomach. When they were fat and engorged salt was sprinkled on them to get them to release their hold. Still Beth's fever raged. By midnight the physician was shaking his head in defeat. Beth lay still, pale as linen except for two circles of red, like sealing wax, on her cheeks. Her breathing was ragged and when Angel touched a cup of honeyed wine to her lips she caught the smell of her foul breath. A few drops of the liquid seeped between her lips and Beth swallowed. Her eyes flickered and opened. For the first time in hours they were lucid.

'Alex. Tell him I love him.'

'Don't speak. Save your breath.'

Beth's lids flickered then opened once more. 'Babies?'

'Two beautiful daughters.' Angel nodded for Prudence to bring the twins closer. 'Have you thought of names?'

'Emmy . . . for Firkin your brother. And Alisaundre for my Alex.'

A tear ran down Beth's cheek and her frail hand lifted from the sheet towards the twins. Prudence stepped forward and laid them on the bed beside their mother. Both were sleeping soundly, wrapped in their swaddling bands. Beth touched the dark hair of the nearest child. 'Alisaundre,' she whispered. Then her hand lay still. Angel stared at Beth, watching with horror as the light faded behind her eyes. She was dead.

Angel bowed her head against her grief. Prudence began to sob. 'Oh, poor mites, poor, motherless mites. Who will look after them now? And their father in exile.'

'I will raise them as though they were my own,' Angel vowed as she closed Beth's eyelids. By her words she knew that she condemned herself to a life in Wales. She must continue to safeguard Alexander's children's inheritance, and to do that she must be parted from Nathan for weeks at a time.

She moved towards the twins who had both woken up. She reached out to take Emmy's finger. She was the firstborn. The baby did not respond to her touch. She touched Alisaundre's hand and immediately the baby clutched at it, holding it fast. Despite her grief Angel smiled. How long would it be before Alexander saw his twins?

She raised a fist in frustration. Just wait until the King came into his own again, then all would be different. She never doubted the certainty of that. And yet, as soon as the thought was formed she wished it unspoken. Hadn't she tempted Fate enough?

First she had willed there to be a way for her to fight for her King . . .

The murder of Gabriellen and Mark had led to that.

Then just yesterday she had passionately wished for a baby. Now Beth's death had made her guardian of the twins and four older children.

What was it Gabriellen had once said? 'Be careful what you wish for – you may get it. But at a cost.'

If the King came into his own again, would then another tragedy face her?

Chapter Twenty

London, 1660
In the spring of 1660, excitement spread like a heathfire through London. Angel caught it, her heart racing with expectation. At last the dreary shackles of the Protectorate were over. Charles Stuart was returning to England to take his throne.

There had been many false hopes in recent years, most notably in the autumn of 1658, when the Royalists had celebrated the death of Oliver Cromwell. A secret body of supporters – the 'Sealed Knot', whose members included Thomas and Nathan – planned a rising. It collapsed about them in disorganisation when feelings for the English Republic remained strong. The succession of the ineffective Richard Cromwell, now derided as Tumbledown Dick, had lasted less than two years. He had been dismissed by the Long Parliament, and General Monck was now working to reinstate the monarchy.

The turbulence of the last years seemed to be over. Angel had managed to keep the Rowan estate in Wales intact. The horses remained popular and the breeding stock flourished. Her own work with the horses and her guardianship to Alexander's children meant that Angel spent half the year in Wales. After a five-year parole Nathan had been released from Horse Guards, but his work amongst the sick meant he could not live on an isolated estate. He rented a house in Chester, enabling Angel to visit him more often. Perhaps that was why they remained so deeply in love. Every reunion was like a honeymoon. And Nathan's letters were so passionate, Angel wondered they did not melt the seal.

Though she missed him when they were apart, she did not miss the wildness and adventure of her earlier life; improving the Rowan strain was a fulfilling task. The stallion Glendower rivalled his predecessors, and time sped on wings for Angel. Apart from the horses there was her painting and her writing to absorb her days and also the children.

Alexander's sons, Marcus, aged sixteen, Bryan, thirteen, and ten-year-old Wyn were usually away at University and Grammar school. None of them had shown much interest in horse-breeding. Marcus was interested in architecture, taking after Llewelyn, and Bryan wanted to be a scientist. Angel had lost count of the number of times minor explosions and foul-smelling concoctions came from Mark Rowan's old laboratory when Bryan was at the Hall. And as for Lizbet . . . At fourteen Lizbet was a beautiful young woman whose life was filled by her love of the horses. In the last year she had begun to train the yearlings on halter and leading-rein, and the results had been amazing.

But it was the twins, Alisaundre and Emmy, who clutched most firmly at Angel's heart. At eight, Alisaundre was everything Angel would have wished for in her own daughter. She was an intelligent, black-eyed, raven-haired firebrand with all the passionate blood of her Celtic forefathers. She was a little mother to Emmy, watching over her twin like a guardian angel. Outwardly, the twins were identical until you looked closely into Emmy's eyes. Like Alisaundre's, they sparkled – not with mischief and high spirits, but with serenity, trust and a heartbreaking void of anything other than simple understanding. Emmy would never be as other children. Her protracted birth had rendered her a simpleton. Nathan had consulted with other physicians, but could give Angel no comfort. Many such children did not live to adulthood, and it was unlikely that she would ever attain more wit than a five-year-old.

Yet in her own way Emmy was happy and everyone adored her. Today, however, Angel was more nervous than usual about Emmy's behaviour. For the first time in nine years Alexander was coming home.

Angel walked through the hall, checking that everything was in order and exactly as her brother remembered it. The furniture gleamed with beeswax, and arrangements of flowers covered the dressers which had once held the family silver – all sold to pay the fines imposed upon Royalist estates during the Protectorate.

Outside, the paddocks were full of horses. Twenty-five breeding mares and seventeen colts and fillies, their ginger coats with the distinctive white blazes and stockings groomed until they shone. They would form a guard of honour on Alexander's approach to the Hall. In a separate paddock, away from the mares, Glendower patrolled his fence.

At that moment the dogs began to bark, announcing that riders approached. Smoothing her ebony ringlets, Angel rang a handbell to summon the servants to line up in the courtyard and welcome their master home. She was too impatient to wait in the doorway. Disregarding the dignity expected of a matron of three-and-thirty summers, she ran down to the first paddock. Her heart was thundering as she saw Alexander urge his horse to a canter. He outstreaked his three companions and whipping his beaver hat from his head let out a loud whoop and vaulted to the ground before his horse had skidded to a stop. Then Angel was clasped in his arms, and his lips were against her cheek as he swung her round.

'Dusty, I despaired of ever seeing you again.' His voice was tight with emotion. He put her down and stared into her eyes. 'As I despaired of ever seeing my home again. Thank God you've not changed. Still the same old Dusty, running like a hoyden to meet her aged brother.'

She was held tight against him again and when she drew back to look up into his face, she saw that his gaze was upon the paddocks.

'My debt to you is immense,' he said tautly.

'Speak not of debts. I've missed you so much. Tell me you're here and that I'm not dreaming. Let me pinch you, then I will know you are real.' She tweaked his arm and he winced and rubbed it.

'Aren't you supposed to pinch yourself, not me?'

She laughed, feeling as young and carefree as a child again. 'I know, but how many times did you play that trick on me at Chichester?'

He laughed. 'So I did.'

His companions were drawing closer but Angel could already see Alisaundre, wearing her best scarlet dress, hopping impatiently on one foot. Angel hooked her arm through her brother's and drew him towards the children and the servants waiting to greet him. He embraced Lizbet first, then Bryan, Wyn and Marcus, home on leave from their studies.

Alexander hesitated as he saw Alisaundre gripping Emmy's hand, encouraging her to greet their father.

'Come on, Emmy, 'tis Papa. Say hello to Papa.'

Alexander's frigid expression drained the colour from Angel's face. He looked stunned as he stared at the twins. 'They are the image of Beth. Take them out of my sight, Angel. They robbed her of life.' His voice was a hoarse whisper. 'I loved her so much. Take them away.'

'Alex, it will break their hearts. They never knew their mother – don't deny them a father too.'

She felt a shudder go through him. For a moment she thought he would ignore her plea, then he walked stiffly and unsmiling to the twins. 'Do you know who I am?'

Alisaundre threw herself against him, her arms locked about his legs as she passionately declared, 'You are our Papa!'

Still Alexander did not respond. Angel could not believe he could be so cold towards his children. Emmy's large eyes were studying Alexander intently.

'Papa, big,' she said simply.

Angel became aware of tears streaming down her face. Emmy never spoke directly to anyone, she always whispered to Alisaundre who spoke for her.

'Papa,' Emmy repeated slowly. Her expression full of trust, she held out her arms for him to lift her up.

A choking sound came from Alex. He knelt and drew first Emmy into his arms, then Alisaundre. When he spoke, his voice was unsteady. 'We have a lot of years to make up for, my daughters.'

There was a discreet cough from behind them and Alexander looked up. When Angel followed his gaze she saw that one of her brother's companions was a woman. Then, belatedly, she recognised her cousin Rhys and his son Seth. They tipped their hats to Angel.

''Tis wonders you've done here, cousin,' Rhys said. 'There's wonderful to see so many fine horses. Now we must leave you. It's a surprise my Blodwen will have this night. Not expecting me for another month, you see. We met Alex in Bruges when we were without funds. He generously paid our passage to Bristol.'

'Then I'll not ask you to stay, if you're eager to return to your family. But a special celebration must be planned for us all soon.'

'God bless you, cousin,' Rhys bowed and wheeled his horse.

Angel turned her attention to the woman. She had not been introduced and she made no attempt to follow the departing men. Embarrassment and unhappiness was evident on her plain, round face, and her portly figure was encased in a saffron riding-dress which accentuated her sallow complexion. She kept her head bowed, but from beneath the peak of her hat Angel saw that her hair was as pale as moonlight.

'Alex,' Angel said, 'you've not introduced your guest.'

He did not trouble to look over his shoulder. 'No guest, Angel. That's Thérèse. She speaks no English, only Flemish. She's my wife.'

'*Wife!*' Angel voiced her astonishment. Alexander was treating the woman worse than a servant.

Alexander set Emmy on the ground and released Alisaundre. 'Take your sister inside. The other children had better go in too. I need to speak with your aunt, but I won't be long.' He turned to Angel, taking her arm and drawing her away out of earshot of the servants. 'Thérèse is my wife. Unfortunately. She can have a room in the West Tower. The less I see of her the better.'

'But why did you marry her if you have so little regard for her?' Angel was appalled at her brother's callousness.

'A drunken indiscretion when I had lost faith in ever seeing my home again,' he said with bitterness. 'I had rooms next door to her father's saddlery. It was after that failed rising two years ago. I'd been drunk for ten days. When I sobered up I found myself married to Thérèse. I had a dim recollection of feeling sorry for her and even sorrier for myself. Her father demanded that I learn his business as he had no son to carry on his trade. Him, I consigned to the devil, but Thérèse, I'm stuck with.'

'She's your wife and deserves your respect, Alex.' Another glance at Thérèse, who was struggling against tears, fuelled Angel's anger. She looked scarcely older than Lizbet. 'How old is she? Sixteen? You were the one who was drunk. Did you seduce her?'

505

He shrugged. 'I've no recall of what happened. Though I remember that before this mismatch I felt sorry for her and stopped to speak with her on occasion. Her father was a brute. He constantly beat her, and one night he tried to rape her. It wasn't the first time. He'd been abusing her since she was twelve and always beat her into submission. This night she got away. Terrified, she ran naked into the street. Her father barred the door so she could not return. I was in my cups, returning to my rooms from the tavern, and I suppose I took pity on her. The next morning the constables burst into my room with her father. She had cried herself to sleep in my arms and that's how they found us. Her father demanded we marry. I was still drunk and stayed that way for three days. By the time I sobered up I had gained a wife. I haven't touched strong drink since. Nor her.'

'I don't blame you for drinking to forget your misery, but don't you think the poor woman has suffered enough? She was as much a victim as you were. I cannot believe you could be so callous.'

His mouth beneath his narrow black moustache thinned to an angry line. 'God's wounds! After all I've been through, you lecture me. By this marriage I've betrayed Beth . . . tarnished our love.'

'Do you think Beth would have wanted you to live alone? She would want you to give her children the chance to live a normal life with a mother to love them. Emmy needs special care.' Angel looked at her new sister-in-law. Thérèse was watching Alexander and from her gaze, it was obvious that she adored him. 'Would you replace a selfish, tyrannical father by a selfish tyrannical husband? And you are being selfish! Don't shame Thérèse before the servants and your children. She has a kind, honest face. Give her the chance and she will be a good mother to your children, I am sure. Treat her kindly, Alex. You may even discover that you did not get such a hollow bargain.'

'Ever the playwright, Dusty. Seeing romance in every chance encounter.'

'It's better than being a sour cynic. I could teach Thérèse English.'

'Do what you like,' Alex said gruffly. 'Just don't expect me to fall in love with the wench.'

Angel smiled at Thérèse, who responded with pitiful eagerness. She had a lovely smile. Angel had learnt a little Flemish in her travels and now she welcomed Alexander's bride in her own language. 'Welcome to your new home, Thérèse. I am Angel, Alex's sister. I hope we will be friends.'

The nervous smile spread to a radiance which lit up the sallow face and brought a sparkle to her green-and-gold-flecked eyes. Beautiful eyes, Angel saw as Thérèse raised her pale blonde lashes. And now that her mouth was not turned down in misery, its shape was a perfect Cupid's bow, a mouth which many men would find very kissable.

Angel spoke softly to Alex. 'If the servants see that you have no respect for Thérèse her life will be miserable here.'

For an instant his dark eyes sparked with anger and the sardonic lines deepened about his mouth and brow. Exile had changed Alexander, as she knew it must have changed many once carefree men.

Then his expression altered and he smiled wrily and put his hand on her shoulder. 'Thérèse does not deserve to be shamed. I'm as much to blame for the marriage as she is. We'll have adjoining chambers – that should stop the servants' gossip.' He turned to Thérèse, who was gathering her skirts to dismount. 'Your pardon, my dear,' he said in English for the benefit of the servants. 'I neglect you in the joy of being reunited with my family.' He repeated his words in Flemish and, putting his hands about her waist, he lifted her to the ground. She came no higher than his chest and looked more vulnerable than ever beside Alexander's tall figure. 'This is your new home. I will introduce you to the servants.'

Again the radiance of Thérèse's smile heartened Angel. She could not believe that Alexander had become so hardened after his years abroad. Exile was like a malevolent humour festering inside a man, destroying hope, faith, even self-respect. But all humours of the flesh and soul could be treated, and though the healing process might be slow, time was the greatest healer. A sparkle of devilment flickered inside Angel, as her brother's challenge echoed in her ears. How wonderful it would be to make her cynical brother fall in love with his new wife.

When Maressa heard that King Charles was to return to

England, she flew to the nearest mirror and scrutinised her face. There were faint lines about her eyes which a dusting of powder did not quite conceal. She had waited for years for the King's return and now it had arrived, she was a haggard old crone of five-and-thirty. Her wail brought Hazel to her side.

'What ails you, my lady?'

Maressa pointed at her face. 'This! I'm positively raddled with age.'

'My lady, you're more beautiful now than you were a decade ago,' Hazel consoled. 'Last month four men begged you to marry them. Were they not devastated when you refused?'

'They were commoners – little people of no importance. Two of them were tradesmen.'

'A wealthy gem merchant and a goldsmith are hardly tradesmen, my lady.'

'One was a baronet with a balding pate, and the other a callow youth scarce out of breeches.'

'That youth was twenty and heir to Lord Featherston.'

'Heir to a crumbling castle! The family are impoverished.'

Hazel touched her mistress's cheek. 'Your skin is flawless, and how many women have such lovely hair? You still have the figure of a young woman.'

Maressa pouted and turning from side to side considered her reflection in the looking-glass. Her breasts, pushed high by the whalebone corset, were as firm as ever.

'My lady, a discreet lifting of your skirts to show your ankles would have the King himself enslaved by your beauty,' Hazel added.

A satisfied smile spread across Maressa's lips, and her topaz eyes glittered with ambition. 'Do you really think so?'

'How could any man resist you?'

Again Maressa surveyed her image, running her hands over the full curves of her breasts and breathing in to enhance the smallness of her waist. With a triumphant laugh, she spun round.

'Hazel, summon the most accomplished dressmaker and milliner. I want hats which will flatter, and which shade the sunlight that makes a woman look so haggard. More subtle lighting will be arranged within this house for when I entertain my guests. Thomas has been generous with his allowance since our separation. I want new liveries for my two footmen and servants.' She frowned in the midst of her jubilation and stamped her foot. 'It is too cruel that the scandal attached to Sir Henry's death prevents me from using his title and taking my rightful place at Court.'

'There are many places to rub shoulders with the nobility other than the Court,' Hazel suggested. 'Will they not stroll in the park? The theatres will soon be reopened and with your beautiful voice . . .'

'The theatres . . .' Maressa interrupted, her eyes bright with calculation. 'Angel is always saying that when the King returns women will appear on the stage. But then it is an unsavoury profession. I'd not cheapen myself.'

'You could play upon Sir Henry's notoriety,' Hazel suggested. 'That a noblewoman should be reduced to such straitened circumstances as to support herself by performing on the stage will make you famous. Once they hear you sing, dukes and earls will be clamouring for your favours. You will come to the notice of the King. Mistress Carver will write a part for you in one of her plays and your success will be assured.'

'I've no wish to be beholden to my sister,' Maressa snapped. She flicked open her fan and waved it agitatedly. 'Angel has even turned my children against me. All they ever talk about is their time in Wales with her. Just because she's barren, she does not have to steal my children's love.'

'Your children adore you,' Hazel said hastily. She could see the angry colour rising on her mistress's cheeks. Maressa was capable of working herself into a fury within minutes, ripping and tearing at her clothes and smashing ornaments in her frustration. The bouts were becoming more violent in recent years. Maressa hated her sister. Hated her because she saw her as a rival to the affection of her family. Every storm of temper ended in Maressa being brought to her knees in sobbing agony with the headache.

'My lady, please you must not upset yourself. Let me prepare a tisane for you. You will give yourself a headache.'

'It is because of *her* that I suffer so,' Maressa continued to rage. 'Papa . . . Alex . . . Henry . . . Thomas. She stole their love from me. That hoyden could wrap Papa around her little finger; he never saw her for the wanton she was. Neither could Alex. It was to me my brother should have turned for companionship and advice. Aren't we the closest in age? She only got into those wild scrapes and said such outrageous things so that people would notice her. Then there was Henry . . .' Maressa shuddered. 'She betrayed me with my own husband. That was unforgivable. Not content with doing it once, she had to have Thomas as well. Now it's my children. She has turned them all against me.'

Hazel did not comment. Maressa had sent the children to Wales because she did not want to trouble herself with them. Her mistress could not even bear to look upon Thomasine, who was now sixteen. How could Maressa pass herself off as a woman in her mid-twenties when a sixteen-year-old daughter proved the lie. Also, Thomasine was beautiful. Maressa had never been able to tolerate rivals, so Thomasine had grown up in Wales. As for Julian, he cared for no one but himself. He had his father's good looks and at twenty-five would inherit Sir Henry's baronetcy, an empty title with no income or lands to support it. Nineteen now, he was already a degenerate. After he had been sent down from Oxford for his wild behaviour, Thomas had sent him to the Continent, telling him to find a wealthy wife. Thomas was no longer prepared to support such a wastrel. Richard, at fourteen, the youngest of Maressa's children, had inherited the wildness of the Angel blood. He could not look at something he wanted without stealing it. Thomas doted on him. The boy attended St Paul's School here in London, and his father spent every weekend initiating him into the rites and knowledge of the Underworld. Maressa was content to forget the boy's existence.

Maressa lay down on her bed and closed her eyes to blot out the pain building in her temples. She turned her mind to the future. Images filled her head. Noblemen would flock to pay court to her. She would be the toast of the stage. Even the King himself would fall beneath the spell of her voice. In the last eight years she had played every man like a puppet to which she jerked the strings.

Many men had showered her with jewels, a few she had permitted a kiss or a coy caress. None of them had been to her bed. Living without a man had not troubled Maressa. She received all the devotion from them she needed at Nell's, without the necessity of having to endure their lecherous fumblings. She prided herself that she had kept herself pure amidst the depravity of the bordello. Now she moved restlessly on the bed. The tension in her shoulders and neck could only be soothed by Hazel's special oils and massage.

'Bring the oil, Hazel,' she ordered. 'Make me forget my ungrateful offspring.'

There was magic in Hazel's touch. Exotic perfumed oil filled Maressa's senses until she floated on a cloud of languor, and she could drift into a hazy half-world of reality. Tender, adoring hands skimmed over her tense muscles, their sensuous massage bringing longed-for peace.

Maressa rolled on to her back and was vaguely surprised to find that she wore only her chemise, and that it was draped across her hips. Hazel's skill was so refined she had not noticed her garments being removed. She sat up, unconscious of her nudity in her maid's presence.

'I don't know how I'd manage without you, Hazel.' She walked naked across the room to her jewel casket and took out an agate and amethyst cross. 'I want you to have this as a token of my gratitude. I know you're not religious, but from this Sunday we shall attend the service at St Paul's twice daily. Soon the exiled Royalists will return to London. I must earn a reputation of purity if I am to create the right effect upon the stage and snare a wealthy nobleman as my husband. Do you not agree?'

The twenty-ninth of May, in the year of 1660, was a day of rejoicing for every Royalist. On his thirtieth birthday, Charles II was making a triumphant procession through London. It was as though his exile had never been. If there was a man or woman amongst the citizens who mourned the passing of the Protectorate, they kept their opinions to themselves. Even the 'prentices, notorious for their disruptions and riots, clung to railings or squatted on rooftops to cheer, their mood made more effusive by a quantity of wine flowing from the street's conduits.

London had shed its dour Puritan cloak to don one of glittering splendour. The sky was a cloudless blue and the sun gilded the lattice windows and reflected off brass weather-vanes and shop signs. Every window, sign, balcony and archway was draped with tapestries, rich hangings and garlands of greenery or spring flowers, and brightly coloured flags and pennons fluttered from the rooftops.

Along the route from Southwark to Whitehall, local trained bands of militia were lined up to control the populace. These men had once secured the capital against Charles I and many would have lined the route of that King's walk to the scaffold. Today they were on duty to safeguard Charles II from the enthusiastic welcome of his people.

By mid-afternoon Angel, Maressa, Thérèse and all the children, were crowded into the three large windows of Popinjay's London house which overlooked Cheapside where the King was to pass. Popinjay, together with Thomas, Alex and Nathan, rode in the procession to London. They had ridden out yesterday to join the King as he made his way from Dover.

To entertain the waiting crowds before the procession approached tumblers, jugglers and minstrels moved along the street. Each was accompanied by a child or companion who held out a cap for pennies to be dropped into. Morris men danced in their hobby horse costumes; strolling players after years of banishment dusted off their costumes and performed their favourite soliloquies, clowns leapt and did impromptu jigs, banging tabors or blowing recorders. Flower-sellers did a brisk trade too. Gallants gave them to their sweethearts, and women purchased flowers to be strewn on to the ground before the Cavaliers. Tightrope-walkers teetered high above the street. Choirs sang at crossroads, and from every church the bells rang out. Bawds and beggars rubbed shoulders with wealthy citizens. The beggars had been the first to arrive that morning, ensuring that they had the best places to cry for alms. Thomas had long ago explained to Angel the hierarchy of the Underworld and the tricks used to gull unsuspecting victims. To pass the time Angel began to point them out to Thérèse, so she would be forewarned against their antics.

'See there is a Dummerer,' Angel said, pointing to a ragged man who waved his arm about frantically. 'He's pretending to be mute and deaf. Now that woman who is shouting at a pedlar and tearing at her clothes . . .'

'But she is a mad creature,' Thérèse declared. 'She should be pitied.'

Angel smiled. 'That Bess o' Bedlam is a good actress. She apes the inmates of Bedlam, London's Hospital for the insane. Don't be taken in by her performance, or the others. Many of the beggars have self-inflicted wounds. Though since the war London is full of soldiers who lost limbs in the fighting. It is not always easy to tell the true unfortunates from the pseudo-cripples. The pretend ones have long practised their poses to distort a limb for sympathy. They usually display ugly weeping sores. Those wounds are rubbed weekly with ratsbane to ensure they never heal. Many beggars die young from such poisons.'

Angel scanned the crowd to pick out a counterfeit crank to show to Thérèse. 'Look at the man in the brown jerkin and red cap.'

As she spoke the man began to roll his eyes back into his head. He threw himself down on to the ground and the sliver of soap previously placed in his mouth began to foam and froth from his lips as his body spasmodically writhed. Several people close by backed away. A ragged woman stood over the counterfeit crank, her grimy hands held out in pleading. 'Alms, good people. How can I support my poor son taken by the falling sickness? Alms. Have mercy, good people. Alms!'

Thérèse's eyes were wide with shock. 'We have much the same in Bruges, I think. Many times I give them money. They're not truly afflicted, you say?'

'Keep your eyes on the man on the ground and watch,' Angel advised. As soon as a group of jugglers diverted the crowd, the ragged woman kicked the man and, making a remarkable recovery, the counterfeit-crank sped off through the crowd to find a new place to perform.

Thérèse shook her head in disbelief. 'It's wicked to pretend such illness. How do you know who is really afflicted?' Her attention was caught by a man on stilts walking in a long swirling cloak. Hidden by the cloak was a dwarf who popped his head from between the stilts to make faces at the crowd. It was a comical act, one of many such performances to keep the crowd from becoming bored as the sun climbed higher in the sky.

At last the first of the thousands of Cavaliers who had fought for Charles I appeared. Bugles and trumpets sounded and drums beat the rhythm of the march as foot soldiers passed, their pikes and muskets clasped proudly against their shoulders. Horses pranced, their hooves clattering on the cobblestones. Cavaliers dressed in newly purchased finery rode by on beautifully groomed horses. They waved at the cheering crowds. Many who only a few weeks ago had been living in squalor now found their credit high, for the King would reward all who had loyally served him and his late father.

Yet to Angel's eyes, many of the young men looked world-weary before their time. Their bellies might be full but a hunger remained in their eyes. They resolved never to be poor again, never to be denied even the simplest pleasure. In exile to forget their troubles they had turned to debauchery. It was a legacy they brought with them on their return to England. And none would frown upon them for it. The grim Puritan rule had been an onerous one.

Angel put her arm around Lizbet's waist as her niece threw a rose to a handsome Cavalier, who bowed to her as he passed beneath their window. Catching it, he lifted it in salute to her.

'I wonder who he is?' Lizbet sighed.

'There will be many handsome Cavaliers in our streets now,' Angel said. 'Don't throw your heart away on the first one you meet.'

Angel leaned back against the stone pillar of the window, realising the procession would take hours to pass by. She could see it stretching far back to where it had crossed the river by London Bridge. There was as much activity within the crowd as there was in the procession. Pedlars continued to shout their wares. A hat-seller, wearing a dozen beige and black beaver hats with coloured feathers, one on top of the other on his head, rang his handbell, his voice drowned by other street-vendors.

'Hot spicy capon!'

'Ribbons! Coloured ribbons to wave at your King!'

'Marchpane crowns! Come buy my marchpane crowns!'

The street-sellers pushed through the crowd and trade was brisk. Pot-boys from nearby taverns ran backwards and forwards with tankards of ale and platters of bread and meat to refresh the spectators. Pickings were high for the nimble

514

fingers relieving spectators of their purses, jewels or handkerchieves. Lechers used the press of the crowd to sidle past young maids, peering into the bodices of their low-cut gowns, their fingers brushing against breast and thigh. Gallants strutted in their finery, bowing or blowing kisses to any beautiful woman. Infants cried, frightened by the crowds and the noise. Scuffles broke out as people jostled for better positions. Assignations were made. Once prim sober-clad wives, now dressed in reds and golds, were not averse to making cuckolds of their dull husbands.

Soon the flowers and sweet herbs strewn on to the cobbles were trampled to a pulp by the passage of boots and hooves. Women and children threw flower petals from the windows, covering the cavalcade in a perfumed and colourful shower.

'A health unto His Majesty' was the constant cheer. And still the procession seemed endless. Aldermen paraded their gold chains, dignitaries from the City's Guilds were richly costumed, standard bearers at their sides carrying banners emblazoned with their liveries.

A flock of pigeons disturbed from their rooftop roosts circled overhead, and one unfortunate Cavalier at least was splattered by their droppings.

'A sign of good luck, me fine lords,' chimed out a cheeky barrow urchin, selling nosegays of wild flowers.

The gentleman scowled unappreciatively at the urchin's humour. He was brushing his sleeve to rid it of its foul slime, and not paying attention to the road. Suddenly a dog ran out of a doorway, giving chase to a tabby cat which darted straight between his horse's hooves. The horse shied, and knocked the flower-boy off his feet. His barrow overturned, spilling the nosegays on the ground to be crushed under hooves and feet. Angel cried out fearful lest the urchin himself met a similar fate. Then she saw Hapless dart out of the house and haul the lad to safety.

'Ger orf!' the urchin shouted. 'Got ter save me flowers. Pa will 'ave me 'ide if I lose me takings.'

Hapless and the urchin grabbed for a few posies, but it was too dangerous. When Angel saw Hapless slip on a stream of urine splaying on to the street from a passing stallion she called out, 'Hapless, bring the lad to me. I'll buy the flowers you've rescued and pay him for what was ruined.'

The boy was paid and Angel took up two of the undamaged nosegays, smelling them as she returned to the window.

'I shall throw one to Nathan.'

Lizbet and Thomasine also picked up some flowers, and, giggling, chose which handsome Cavalier to throw them to.

'Sister, must you encourage the children to act like hoydens?' Maressa said from the far window, where she had placed herself at the best advantage to see and be seen by any rider glancing up.

'I am as I am, Maressa,' Angel returned, with a wink at Lizbet. 'I'm too old to change now.'

Thomasine giggled, her eyes wide and adoring upon her aunt.

'Thomasine, come and stand next to me,' Maressa snapped. 'I will not have you making a spectacle of yourself.'

At that moment a great roar like summer thunder rippled through the crowd.

'The King comes!' Thomasine cried, leaning far out of the window in her excitement.

Maressa pulled her daughter back inside the room. 'Behave like a young gentlewoman or I will send you from the room.'

Thomasine stood meek and subdued, but Angel was not fooled by that demure pose; her niece's eyes were sparkling with devilment.

Trumpets blasted a fanfare and Angel leaned expectantly out of the window. There, in the very centre of the street, rode the tall figure of Charles II. A few paces behind were his brothers James, Duke of York, and Henry, Duke of Gloucester. Further behind them came General Monck, whose machinations had brought a bloodless restoration to the monarchy.

But Angel's attention was focused on the King. It was twelve years since she had parted from him in the tavern outside Paris, and she had not seen him since. Her heart surged into a frantic beat. He was as tall as she remembered, his slender physique regal and commanding without arrogance. A mane of thick black hair curled to his shoulders and he raised a jewelled gloved hand to acknowledge the acclaim of his people. The handsome youth she remembered had changed. Cynicism had scored his face and hardened his swarthy features, yet his presence still held its own magic.

516

His open smile captured the hearts of the people and if his hooded eyes still held a trace of their old disillusion, it was not apparent in his manner.

'Long live the King!' The deafening cry rose from the streets. 'Long live the King!'

He was almost beneath their window. Years ago, when they were lovers, Angel had spoken of his entry into London and how the people would welcome him. She had said that everything was possible. Now that her words had come true, she wanted desperately to share just a moment of it with him. Not that he would remember, of course . . .

'*Vive Le Roi*!' she shouted, knowing only a foreign tongue would penetrate the English voices below her. '*Tout est possible!*'

The dark hooded eyes lifted and held her gaze. Holding a nosegay to her lips she kissed it and tossed it towards him. He caught it in one hand and a light in his eyes flared with remembrance. His head dipped in brief acknowledgement and the warmth of his smile encompassed her.

'*Tout est possible*,' he repeated and laughed. 'Indeed, everything is possible.'

Heads swivelled to stare up at the window which had drawn their King's attention, but Angel saw none of them, only the smile in the eyes of her sovereign. He had not forgotten her.

'I have never been so shamed,' Maressa blurted out. 'The whole of London will know you were his whore.'

'I'm not ashamed of it. I'm not ashamed of anything I've done.' Angel's irritation at her sister's hypocrisy flowed from her. 'Can you say the same for yourself, Maressa?' As she turned away, Angel could almost feel her sister's antagonism from across the room. She shrugged it off. Today was too important to be spoilt by petty jealousy.

For another half hour Angel scanned every face in the procession, anxious to miss none of her friends. The first to ride by was Popinjay, dressed in peacock green satin, slashed with purple and edged with gold braid. His long grey hair was pomaded and curled into waves around his shoulders, a small beard and moustache, so popular in many of Van Dyck's portraits, gave distinction to his long narrow face. In the next body of cavalry rode Alexander and Nathan, and tears of pride blurred Angel's vision as they came abreast of the window, both looking up to wave. Angel tossed her nosegay to Nathan and he caught it with a grin. The adoration in his eyes made her catch her breath. Even from a distance he could make all her senses come alive. Her pulse catapulted and her hands went out towards him, unable to contain the need to draw him close. Seeing her involuntary movement, Nathan's eyes darkened to indigo, and his lashes came down to conceal his own flaring desire.

'Tonight, my darling,' he mouthed.

Angel suppressed a sigh of longing. The sexual rapport between them was like a river, swollen and turbulent with spring tides, ready at any second to overflow its banks. A look – a touch – sometimes even a shared thought communicated between them – was all it took to ignite their passion. Marriage had not dimmed its blaze, nor familiarity dulled its heat. Mentally, Angel ticked off the desolate hours before the procession and celebrations were over and Nathan could return to her. Then there would be no more long partings. Nathan wanted to tend the sick in London. Thérèse adored Alexander's children and Angel was no longer needed in Wales.

Aware that Thérèse was still clutching her own nosegay, Angel nudged her and nodded for her to throw it to Alexander. For a moment the Flemish girl hesitated, then she launched it into the air. Alexander was looking at Angel, not his wife, and as the posy struck his chest he snatched it instinctively. Puzzled, he turned his gaze upon Thérèse, and to Angel's delight, his eyes widened in surprise. He kept his gaze upon his wife as the procession carried them along Cheapside, and kept turning his head in disbelief.

Angel put an arm around her sister-in-law's shoulders. Thérèse's radiant smile must disarm the stoniest of hearts. It was two weeks since Alexander had seen her, for he had been busy with the spring horse sales and financial and legal matters. During that fortnight Angel had shown Thérèse how to apply powder and carmine to her face, to hide the sallowness of her complexion and enhance the beauty of her mouth. Thérèse's hair was thick and its pale silvery-blonde colour exceptional. It had been restyled into soft curls and ringlets. With several new gowns of flattering colours added to her wardrobe and encouraged by Angel not to nibble at sweet-meats, Thérèse had been transformed from a plain unhappy woman, to one who, though not a beauty, was attractive. Now her lovely eyes were sparkling with happiness at her husband's appraisal.

Aware that the procession would take another hour at least to pass the window, Angel watched it more distractedly. One figure was noticeably absent from the parade. From Alexander she had learned that Prince Rupert was pursuing a vagrant life in Germany, visiting his sisters, and carrying out alarming experiments with gunpowder. Knowing the Prince as she did, she guessed that he was still grieving for the death of his younger brother Prince Maurice. The two brothers had always been close. The younger prince's ship had been sunk during a hurricane whilst they were sailing to the West Indies where all the English Islands had fallen under Parliamentary control. What a voyage that had been! Rupert had emerged as the Grand Pirate, sailing first to the Mediterranean and harrying the Parliament fleet sent to destroy him. Capturing what prizes of war they could, they turned their back on Europe and continued to the Azores and down along the coast of Africa then across to the West Indies. Thirty prizes of war were captured in all from 1650 to 1653 which had greatly boosted Charles II's exchequer during his years as an exile. On his return Rupert had taken to wandering Europe, pursuing his military career in the Austrian army.

It was almost midnight before Nathan escaped the endless ceremonies and returned to his wife. When he entered the house which doubled as a temporary surgery for his patients and a laboratory for his experiments he was struck by the crampedness of the living quarters. Tomorrow he would look for larger premises, with grounds where he could found a hospital and isolate the more contagious diseases which spread through the city. He was convinced that the only way to stop the virulent spread of smallpox, typhus and the plague was by isolating the infection. By studying how his patients reacted to treatment he hoped to find both the means of curing the diseases and halting its spread. But the hospital must be far enough away from the house so that Angel was not put at risk.

He bounded up the stairs to the bedchamber. Upon entering the room, his heart twisted to see the candle-stub still burning by the side of the wooden tester bed. The ruby velvet hangings were open, for the night was warm with a hint of thunder in the air. Angel had fallen asleep, a book still clutched in her hand. He placed his cloak and the bundle he was carrying on the foot of the bed, before sitting on the edge of the mattress and kissing her. She murmured and her arms drowsily circled his neck. As his kiss deepened her lips parted and she moaned softly with pleasure. Then with a squeal she pushed him from her. From beneath Nathan's arm, wriggled a small liver and white fur ball, its pink tongue lapping at Angel's cheek as it snuggled between them.

'What the . . . ?' Angel gasped. Then she laughed and clasped the spaniel pup to her breast, burying her face into his wriggling body. 'Where did you come from?'

Nathan's smile was as warm as hers. 'Her name is Bella. She's a gift from His Majesty.'

Angel scanned her husband's face to see whether he was offended. He knew she had been Charles's mistress. His smile did not waver. 'His Majesty spoke of you with affection, much to the annoyance of Barbara Palmer, his favourite paramour. From the look on her lovely face, I would say you've made an enemy, Angel.'

'But I've never met the woman!'

'Barbara Palmer holds the King in her hand. They met in Breda. Her husband had joined the Royalists who swarmed about the King once it was known that his restoration was assured. She's a proud beauty – a member of the powerful Villiers family. But there's little sweetness in her nature.'

'Then I feel sorry for her husband. I doubt there's a woman alive who is capable of making Charles Stuart faithful to her.' The ancient tester bed creaked as she came up on to her knees and the sheet slid from her naked figure as she put her arms around his neck. 'I was infatuated with Charles, and with Rupert too, but you're the only man I have ever truly loved. I was such a fool to take so long to admit it.'

He stopped her speech with a kiss and lowered her on to the mattress. Indignant at being ignored, the puppy whimpered and, fastening his teeth into the lace at Nathan's wrist, began to tug at it. Angel and Nathan broke apart, laughing.

'King's gift or not,' Nathan said, snatching the puppy to

his chest and standing up. 'She sleeps in the kitchen tonight with the other dogs.' He paused by the door. 'Bella was not the only favour . . . if you can call this jealous bundle of fluff a favour! His Majesty spoke of a promise to you. Next month he wishes one of your plays performed at Court and he requests that you take the leading role.'

Whilst Nathan carried Bella to the kitchen, Angel leapt out of bed. Too distraught even to cover her nakedness with a robe, she darted to the coffer containing her plays. Her mind raced in panic as she began to sort through the leather-bound copies.

Nathan paused by the door to watch his wife. Her black hair tumbled in disarray down her back and as she pulled papers from the chest his eyes were drawn to her breasts, moving sensuously as she worked. Nathan felt his body respond with a passion which never ceased to amaze him. Nine years they had been wed. It was the unpredictability of moments like this which held him captivated. In those nine years no other woman had tempted his fidelity to Angel.

'A month is no time at all,' she wailed as she pushed a shaking hand through her hair. 'What play is suitable? Who will act in it? There are no costumes. How can I possibly . . . ?'

His hands slid over her shoulders and along her arms to take her hands and raise her to her feet. 'Whatever must be done you will do superbly. His Majesty does not expect a grand production. You must have kept in contact with some of the players in recent years. I did hear that Fortemaine and du Luc are back in England.'

'They will not work for a woman. They made that obvious in France.'

'In France you had not been asked to perform before His Majesty. Fortemaine and du Luc are too vain to refuse.'

'They are good actors, but temperamental. Thomas will help me to locate others. Nothing misses his network of spies in the city.'

'Then the problem is solved.' Nathan's arms tightened around her. 'Now I've been parted from my wife for three whole nights.' He rested his hands against her breasts and felt them grow firm, the quickening beat of her heart throbbing against his palm.

He lifted her up and her legs encircled his waist as he

carried her to the bed. Stripping off his clothes, he pulled her beneath him. The perfumed heat of her body filled his senses. Mind and soul and desire became a raging tempest unrivalled in its power. Later, Nathan stared down at Angel, his head propped on to his hand.

'Now that Alex is settled in Wales, let there be no more partings,' he murmured. 'There have been too many wasted nights between us, too many hours of loving sacrificed for duty.'

'There'll be no more partings,' Angel vowed. 'For the rest of my life I want to devote all my spare time to you.'

Nathan raised his scarred eyebrow. 'Spare time, Madam?' he said with a low growl. 'Do you put me in second place to your plays and ambition, now that the King has commanded a performance?'

'How can you think that?' she answered, horrified that he should believe such ill of her. 'Nathan, I swear I but meant—' She broke off as she saw his eyes glitter in the candlelight.

Before Angel guessed his intention, her arms were caught in his hands. With a grin, he pulled them over her head, arching her body so that her breasts grazed the rough hairs on his chest.

'It's time you learned submission to your husband and master.'

Holding her wrists in one hand, he began to tickle her with the other. Angel wriggled frantically, her legs drumming against the mattress to escape.

'Stop it, Nathan.' She was laughing, gasping for air. 'You know I can't bear it. No! Please, Nathan. Stop, please.' He was merciless. Tears of laughter ran down her cheeks. 'Oh, stop, I beg you,' she pleaded.

'Am I your master?'

'No man is my master.'

'In your marriage vows you promised to obey. Your husband is your master.'

'I also promised to love and honour you,' she gasped between helpless laughter. 'But I vow if you don't stop this minute I'll floor you. And your honourable rump will be as bruised as your dignity.'

'Threats, wife!' He increased his assault until Angel was laughing so hard she could scarcely get her breath.

Wriggling to the edge of the bed she managed to sit up. Her gasps of protest halted. Both of them were breathing heavily and her gaze was inviting as their bodies touched, rekindling desire. Her tongue traced the tip of his ear and when she felt the tremor of his response, she nipped his lobe. The surprise of her attack loosened his hold. Like quicksilver she slid from the bed and, with the flat of her hand, playfully whacked his buttocks.

'You damned vixen! Just wait till I get hold of you.' He was laughing as he leapt off the bed in pursuit.

His fingers brushed her shoulders, but, determined not to be caught, she jumped on to the bed to escape his clutches. Nathan dived at her, catching her around the waist and bringing them both down on the mattress. The bed shuddered and there was a protesting crack, as two of the legs collapsed. In a tangle of sheets and pillows Nathan and Angel slid on to the floor. Nathan landed on one of the rowels of his spurred boots and let out a yell.

Angel sat up bruised from rolling on to the hilt of his discarded sword. Nathan cursed as he dragged the boot from under him and flung it across the room. It hit the corner of a painting by Angel of the Rowan horses. The force knocked it off its peg and it fell on to a coffer beneath which one of the household cats had fallen asleep. Amidst angry spitting and hissing, the terrified animal shot across the room and leapt into Nathan's arms.

At the look of astonishment on her husband's face, Angel collapsed back on the floor and curled up with laughter.

'I'm glad you find the incident so amusing, my dear,' Nathan said drily. 'We must now sleep on the floor until the bed can be mended. One of my favourite paintings has a cracked frame. Worse still, I've suffered an injury from that damned spur which will make sitting uncomfortable for some days. And you find it amusing. And it's all because of your stubbornness.'

'My stubbornness!'

He put the cat aside who ran off under a chair. 'Well, if you'd acted like any normal wife and bowed to the submission of my will, none of this would have happened.' His teasing tone belied the sternness of his words. 'And I wouldn't have known more pleasure and laughter than I ever

523

thought possible. Don't you ever dare change.'

Angel lay back on the scattered covers and lifted her arms to embrace him. 'Kiss me, my darling, and I will show you how submissive I can be.'

'Have you no shame?'

'Where you are concerned, none at all.'

'Thank heavens for that.'

In the shambles of their half-wrecked bedchamber their laughter mingled again, soon to be silenced by the deepening fulfilment of their lovemaking.

Four days later, Angel was busy copying out the last of the parts for the rehearsal which would start tomorrow. She had spent the morning with Thomas Killigrew, whom she had met amongst the King's entourage at St Germain, and who had now been appointed a Groom of the Bedchamber. Killigrew had been a popular playwright before the Civil War, the most famous of his plays being *The Parson's Wedding*, which Angel had seen three times. The King had sent Killigrew to help Angel assemble a cast of players and produce her play.

At first the playwright was wary. Angel knew he was testing her knowledge of the intricacies involved in staging a play. His piercing blue eyes shone in an aristocratic face framed by white hair and a neat pointed beard. She answered his questions easily, telling him of the innovations she had seen for scenery in Italy and Spain. Within an hour she had won him over. There was no question of taking the play into a theatre after the Court performance. During the Protectorate 'The Globe' had been turned into tenements and the other playhouses were unusable after eighteen years of neglect. It was decided that the play would be performed in the Banqueting House at Whitehall.

Angel was hesitant. 'Will the King be reminded that it was from that place his father had stepped out on to the scaffold?'

Killigrew was encouraging. 'What better way to chase those demons from His Majesty's mind than with a comedy? And what better setting could we have, with the great ceiling there painted by Rubens?'

Angel was convinced and listened to all Killigrew's advice. On his second visit Killigrew was accompanied by Charles

Hart, whom Angel had met several times before. He had risked his freedom during the Protectorate to perform plays in private houses or inn yards.

Hart bowed over her hand, his stentorian voice filling the room. 'Angel, it has been too long. What possessed you to moulder away in Wales for so many years? London was dour enough in Commonwealth times without also being denied your wit and beauty.'

Angel smiled at his flamboyant manner so favoured by actors to set them above ordinary men. Then Hart was no ordinary actor. He was the grand-nephew of William Shakespeare, the eldest son of the great bard's sister Joan. Their mutual link with the Elizabethan stage had formed a fond acquaintanceship.

'So what's this play you've written?' Hart demanded. 'Something risqué, I trust, to appeal to His Majesty.'

'I'm aware of His Majesty's taste.' Angel smiled. 'It's one I wrote several years ago which I have recently adapted. *Everything is Possible* is the title.' She did not explain that she had renamed the play as a private jest for the benefit of the King. She went on, 'It was a comedy about three couples whose love affairs are entangled. Each character wishes their affair with the other to remain a secret. All goes smoothly until the female lead appears. She is dressed as a man, hiding from her family who would marry her to an aging lecher. The three women each decide to seduce the newcomer, who becomes hard-pressed to escape their advances and maintain her disguise. When she meets Sir Gaylord – which is the lead whom we are honoured that you will play, Charles – she falls in love with him and returns to her women's finery to seduce him.'

Hart laughed. 'So at last I get to hold you in my arms without risking your husband challenging me to a duel. How delightful to have a real woman as one's lover on stage, and not be forced to endure the embrace of a beardless youth.'

'Just ensure you do not step beyond the proprieties,' Angel warned him. 'Besides, in the play your character spurns the heroine.'

The actor put a hand to his heart, his expression stricken. 'And I had such hopes. Not that I'd risk facing your sword,' he returned. 'I've not forgotten you can wield a sword as well as any man. Wasn't Prince Rupert your instructor – and if rumour is true in more than swordsmanship? There's speculation why His Majesty should honour you of all our playwrights for this first play to be performed at his Court.'

Hart turned to Killigrew and raised an enquiring brow. 'Wasn't Mistress Carver in France at the same time as the Prince of Wales? He was supposed to be paying court to the Grand Mademoiselle, but wasn't he rather remiss in his duty? Rumours thrived that the Prince had given his heart elsewhere.'

'I was Queen Henrietta's Vice-chamberlain, not her son's keeper.' Killigrew evaded the question, and by so doing won Angel's gratitude. She did not want acclaim for her plays because she had been Charles Stuart's mistress.

'Speculation has always followed my family history,' Angel parried.

'Not least your great-grandfather, Esmond Angel. Such amazing stories I've heard of that rogue – and his daughter Gabriellen,' Hart countered. 'But back to the play. How many characters are involved and how is the drama resolved?'

'Eight main characters, and divers small parts which can be doubled up with two or three stage-hands playing the servants. When your character spurns the heroine, two other men pursue her. The complicated circle of infatuation and secrecy leads from one comic scene of near discovery to another, building to the climax which is risqué enough to appeal to His Majesty.'

'And does the heroine win her love?' Hart persisted.

'In the play, she does.'

Hart gave a satisfied smile, his bold gaze signalling his interest in making her his mistress. It was not the first time Hart had propositioned Angel. He was a handsome man, with great charm and wit, but Angel wanted no lover but Nathan.

She picked up Hart's copied part. 'You may read the play for yourselves.' She gave another copy to Killigrew for his opinion.

Several times both men laughed out loud as they read it. They were interrupted by a third actor being ushered into their presence, and Killigrew hurried to the newcomer's side.

'Mistress Carver, may I present Michael Mohun.'

Mohun bowed over Angel's hand. 'I am acquainted with Mistress Carver. We met in Oxford when I was wounded in a skirmish.'

'Yes, I remember. You were a Major, were you not?'

'Indeed, and I was privileged to be present for your performance of *A Widow Went a-Wooing*. You were superb. It was some time later that I learned Dusty Rowan was in fact Major Rowan's sister, not his brother. Your talents as an actress were remarkable. No one saw through your disguise.'

Shortly after Mohun's arrival du Luc and Fortemaine were announced. They were appalled to learn that the play had been written by Angel.

'It is an outrage.' du Luc preened his brown moustache. 'I cannot believe this honour goes to a woman.'

'A very talented woman,' Hart said sharply.

Thomas Killigrew said, 'You have a reputation on the Continent for being difficult, du Luc. There are other actors who would be honoured to perform in Mistress Carver's play. However, Mistress Carver assures me that both you and Fortemaine will be right for the parts, which is why I have agreed to this interview.' He handed the Frenchmen their copied parts, of a straight-laced, acerbic-witted Puritan who is debauched during the play, and a boisterous, Falstaff-like valet who completely steals the second act.

The two men were mollified by Killigrew's presence, but remained wary of Angel. Their years on the Continent had not curbed their prejudices, but, fortunately, both Fortemaine and du Luc were unable to refuse the honour of performing before the King of England.

Occupied by his Court duties, Killigrew left much of the preparation work to Angel. He saw Hapless perform a faultless soliloquy and agreed that he must be part of the company. With only the minor roles to cast, Killigrew left that task to Angel, whilst he arranged for the carpenter to start work on the special effects.

Hapless flushed and full of enthusiasm returned one evening from a night of carousing in a tavern with two young boys, both eager to apprentice themselves to an acting troupe. Unfortunately, Angel could give them no guarantee for the future. The play was a one-off. Until all the theatres reopened actors' lives must remain uncertain. Besides, she had no wish

527

to be a player-manager, with all the responsibilities that held. To write and to perform occasionally was enough.

When Angel saw the boys' disappointment, she relented, and employed them on the understanding that it was just for the one play. They were each given a minor part which required two costume changes, and told that their duties included that of general stage-hands.

Once word spread that Angel was producing a play for the Court, and that she was taking the female lead, two young women approached her. Jocey Field was the mistress of a musician whom Angel had engaged the previous day. She was a pretty, vivacious woman of seventeen with a pleasant singing voice. She was tall with large breasts and a mass of bright red hair. Knowing that the King would enjoy seeing other women in the play, Angel hired her. Jocey had brought along her friend Esther, whose lover had just abandoned her. A year younger than Jocey, Esther was as pretty and delicate as her friend was strapping. Her hair was the colour of polished oak, and together they made a striking partnership. Desperate to avoid a life of prostitution, Esther begged Angel for a chance to be an actress. Since she had a natural aptitude and had followed Angel's guidance easily when delivering her lines, she too was accepted into the expanding troupe.

They needed only two more actors for the lesser roles and the company would be complete. Fortemaine assured Angel that he knew the very men, and to keep the actor's good will, she agreed to see them that night. Yet as she rubbed the plume of her quill pen against her cheek she was aware that the play still lacked something. She was puzzling on this when the maid announced Maressa.

Angel put down her pen and came to her feet. 'Maressa, what a surprise! It is not often that you visit me.'

'I heard that you are to perform before the King,' her sister said without preamble. 'And that you have employed two actresses, one an indifferent singer. Why was I not asked? As the contessa I was proclaimed the Nightingale of London.'

'You've always had such strong views about the stage as an unsuitable profession for women,' Angel said, bewildered by her sister's change of mind. 'You appeared masked as the contessa keeping your identity a secret.'

528

'Indeed, I did when performing in Nell's. Do you think I wanted everyone to associate me with that place? But to appear at Court before the King is not shameful.'

'It's still a play, Maressa, not a musical soirée. You have always despised actors as a lowly, uncouth breed.'

Maressa slapped the fan she carried in her palm as she paced the chamber, her agitation obvious. 'Is it not in my blood?'

Angel bent her head to conceal her smile. Never before had she heard Maressa acknowledge her links with Esmond Angel. Maressa had a magnificent voice, and was exactly what the play needed. But what Maressa's motives were in wishing to join their troupe, Angel could only speculate.

Chapter Twenty-One

Three weeks of rehearsals were not long enough for the less experienced players. On the morning of the Court performance there was a full dress rehearsal within the Banqueting House, where a temporary stage had been erected. Pandemonium reigned. Jocey couldn't stop giggling. She reduced Esther and the 'prentices to helpless laughter.

'Go outside until you can control yourselves,' Angel ordered, and shamefaced but still giggling, they shuffled out.

Du Luc let out a scream of fury. 'My costume does not fit!' He paraded before the other actors, straining to pull the edges of his doublet together. 'That seamstress is an incompetent fool.'

'There's nothing wrong with my work.' The seamstress, a redoubtable woman from Whitechapel rounded on him. 'If you weren't such a glutton, the costume would fit. You've put on an inch around your fat gut since I measured you.'

'Me? Fat?' du Luc screeched. 'I've a splendid figure. You're too addled with drink to read your own measure.'

'That's enough,' Angel interceded. 'Clearly, du Luc's costume does not fit. Can you alter it in time, Mistress Atkins?'

The seamstress nodded sullenly. 'There were nothing wrong with my measurements.'

Angel handed the doublet to the seamstress. 'There has been delay enough. Start the rehearsal.'

Ten minutes later Maressa began to scream hysterically. The golden chariot she was in, which was being lowered from the heavens as she sang her first song, had jammed in mid-descent. The carpenter found a ladder and Charles Hart climbed up to help Maressa down. She was weeping and sobbing in distress.

'I'm not getting back in there!'

'There's nothing wrong with the chariot mechanism that a little grease does not cure,' Angel declared.

'I refuse to endanger my life in that contraption,' Maressa flared.

'The chariot is the most sensational effect in the play. Everyone's eyes will be upon you. You will steal the scene.'

Maressa fidgeted with her fan. Then Charles Hart took her hand. 'My dear, we cannot cut the chariot from the scene. If you will not play the role, then Jocey must take the part. Since your particular charms are too refined for the comedy roles, Esther must take those. Her part is a minor one, and your talents would be wasted in it.'

'You would replace me with Jocey?' Maressa stormed across the stage. 'She cannot sing as well as I. Just get rid of the chariot. I will walk on stage.'

Charles Hart shrugged. 'The chariot stays. The choice is yours.'

Maressa turned to Angel. 'Tell him the chariot will not be used.'

'Charles is right.' Angel lowered her voice. 'I thought you wanted to steal the scene, Maressa? You are like a goddess descending from the heavens in the chariot. Every man in the room will fall in love with you.'

Maressa was breathing heavily, but Angel's words achieved the desired effect. 'Very well, I shall do it,' she announced grandly. 'And I hope the sacrifice I am making for this company is appreciated.'

Fortemaine laughed sarcastically. 'I am sure you will not let a single one of us forget. Every day there is some new tantrum from you. But what else can one expect from a woman.'

'Continue the rehearsal,' Angel ordered before Maressa could lose her temper and waste more time.

Now that Maressa had conceded, Charles Hart put his arm around her waist and praised her courage. He would never jeopardise the play, but his interest in making Maressa his mistress was obvious to see.

The players resumed their places. Within minutes Angel was holding her head in despair. Hapless had tripped in the swordfight with Michael Mohun and banged his nose. It bled all over his costume, completely ruining it. Following that,

Bart Herne was supposed to swing down out of a tree on a rope, but he lost his grip and landed on Fortemaine's shoulders, knocking him to the floor. Furious, Fortemaine slapped Herne's face and demanded a duel. Herne retaliated by striking Fortemaine on the chin and a fight broke out.

Charles Hart left Maressa's side to placate the actors. Aware that Maressa was watching him, he returned to her, casually rearranging the curls of the blond wig which flowed in full curls over his shoulders and was tied with black ribbon into love-locks.

At last the rehearsal progrssed smoothly, with Angel only occasionally having to prompt the players. As female lead, she was on the stage for most of the performance, which gave confidence to the inexperienced players. At the end of the first act, Hapless appeared carrying a lit torch for the night scene. Angel wondered briefly why he had bothered to light it for a rehearsal and was about to tell him to douse it when he turned to say something to Mohun. He was walking backwards and did not see Hart until he collided with him. There was a flare of orange as the flame touched the curls of the wig and sped up the side of Hart's face.

With a scream of warning Hapless thrust the burning torch at Mohun then snatched the wig from the startled actor's head, before it burnt him, threw it on the stage and stamped on it to put out the flames.

Hart's outraged yell echoed to the ceiling. 'Clod! Addle-pated cow-turd!' He clipped Hapless about the ears and swooped down to rescue his wig. When he held it up between his fingers, it resembled a scorched fleece. 'Look what you've done! Just look what you've done! You useless son of a poxed whore!'

Appalled, Hapless backed away. He worshipped Hart, but with each insult Hart hurled at him, Angel saw the boy's admiration turn to loathing. As Hart continued his invective, Hapless stumbled against a scenery cloth and became entangled in it. It was pulled from its hangings and fell over du Luc and Fortemaine. Their muffled cries put the 'prentices into hysterics again. Jocey and Esther, who had been shown nothing but disdain from the two actors, jeered as the men pushed and kicked under the curtain in their frantic efforts to be free.

Both heads emerged together, their bodies still wrapped in the backcloth. Disembodied they looked like the heads stuck on poles over London Bridge, amongst which in recent weeks was Oliver Cromwell's after his body had been exhumed on the King's orders and his head displayed as a traitor. It was one of the few acts of vengeance Charles II had committed and after the martyred end of his father, Angel did not blame him.

The image on the stage was dispelled when du Luc finally struggled free. His immaculately curled hair stuck out like a startled hen's, and his face was puce with fury. As for Fortemaine, his black make-up around his eyes was smeared across his ashen cheeks, so that he looked like some ghostly apparition instead of the blustering, boisterous character of his role.

Angel quickly intervened. 'Herne, Mohun, help those two to their feet. Bart, take Mr Hart's wig to the wigmaker and insist that it is repaired by noon. If it cannot be done then the wigmaker must call here and I will purchase a new wig for Mr Hart.'

'Dear lady, there is no need for such . . .' Hart began.

'Hapless is my servant. I'll not have dissent amongst the actors. This afternoon's performance is too important. I'm happy to replace your wig, Charles.' She shook her head at Hapless, warning him to be more careful.

In dismay she looked at the shambles around her. Disaster loomed. Her heart thundered at the prospect of failure. How could they be ready in time? She rounded on the players, fear spurring her to anger.

'I've never seen such a display of incompetence! A herd of geese could give more entertainment.'

'What do you expect when a woman takes charge,' du Luc sneered. 'Where's Killigrew?'

'Damned women have no place in the playhouse,' Fortemaine scoffed, the colour returning to his cheeks.

'If that is your opinion, sir,' Charles Hart interrupted, 'then you have no place in this play. His Majesty requested that Mistress Carver performs the lead. Or do you fear she outshines you?'

Fortemaine teetered forward on his high-heeled shoes. 'A woman outshine me? Impossible. To the devil with this play, sir. It's a paltry inconsequence and unworthy of my talent.'

Sweeping back his long hair, he strode off the stage and picked up his cloak. 'To the devil with you all.'

Without Fortemaine the play could not be performed. His role was too important to be cut and there was no one to replace him at such short notice. Angel swallowed her pride and ran after him.

'Gentlemen, the setbacks of this morning have overset us all. Let us be calm. Fortemaine, to desert us now is nothing less than an insult to His Majesty who has commanded our performance. You will never perform in England again.'

'You threaten me?' Fortemaine flared.

'Mistress Carver is right.' Thomas Killigrew appeared looking harassed. 'I cannot be everywhere and do everything. The King has commanded a play. Fortemaine, take your place on stage.' He subjected each player to a judgemental glare. 'Now, gentlemen and ladies, if you have finished your childish tantrums, please proceed.' He drew Angel aside. 'You did well to try and diffuse the situation, but players like Fortemaine will never accept advice from a woman.'

'The King has honoured me in allowing my play to be the first one performed in his reign,' said Angel. 'I don't want to disappoint him.'

'You won't,' Killigrew assured her. 'Better the mishaps now than later.'

Angel nodded. 'Surely nothing else can go wrong?'

It did. Esther was halfway through her dance when the hem of her skirt got caught on a nail sticking out of the scenery. As she pirouetted across the stage, her skirts and petticoats were jerked up to her waist exposing her in all her naked glory to the delighted gaze of several courtiers who had strolled into the Hall.

Harry Killigrew, the rake-hell son of Sir Thomas, leapt up on to the stage and laughingly released Esther's skirts, fondling the actress in the process. After a perfunctory protest Esther clearly began to enjoy the courtier's attentions.

'Esther!' Angel called. 'Stop encouraging Mr Killigrew.'

Angel had met Harry Killigrew at St Germain when he had been a companion of the Prince of Wales. He had been wild and reckless then, and accused by Queen Henrietta's staid advisers of leading the Prince of Wales into a life of debauchery.

With a sigh, Esther pushed Harry Killigrew away, but he

did not relinquish her until he had kissed her and made an assignation for later. Somehow they got through the scenes and Thomas Killigrew called a break, ordering them to return two hours before the performance began.

Reassembled, and with the King's throne now placed in the centre of the front row of seats, the actors were short-tempered with nerves.

Sir Thomas Killigrew was engrossed in the final testing of the special effects. Because of the openness of the Banqueting Hall rather than an enclosed stage, most resembled those used in Masques and were wheeled forward from behind erected screens.

Jocey and Esther were shaking with nerves, and Angel reassured them. The 'prentices, Dick Oldham and Bart Herne, strutted proudly about the stage in their costumes. Charles Hart was relentlessly pursuing Maressa. To Angel's surprise, Maressa encouraged him. Maressa's part had been specially written to include four solo songs, and Hart had insisted that her role was expanded. At his suggestion, she was given another twenty lines. These included a romantic pursuit by Hart, allowing him to kiss her.

As Hazel helped her mistress into her costume, Charles Hart leaned against the wall, watching. Maressa serenely accepted his adoration as her due.

'Come now, sweetheart,' Charles Hart said as Hazel finished fastening the gown. 'A kiss to bring us good fortune this day.'

Maressa put her fan to her lips. 'Shame on you, sir. Would you ruin my good name?'

'Dear lady, I would be the making of your reputation.' He grinned. 'As an actress, of course.'

Angel knew Maressa could handle Hart. She could keep him fawning over her whilst she got what she wanted from him and gave nothing in return. Not so Esther Beckton. Harry Killigrew had returned and was kissing the actress ardently. Esther was eagerly responding, and in that moment Angel had an insight into the future of many actresses. The profession would attract women from the lower classes as a means to escape poverty and an uncertain life on the streets. They would use their wit and beauty to win a protector who could keep them in comfort until their beauty faded. She

536

was exasperated by Esther's conduct. The actress was still not sure of all her lines and should be studying them, not encouraging Killigrew.

'Mr Killigrew, will you kindly stop molesting my actresses?' she said tartly. 'Esther needs to study her lines. Would you have His Majesty's entertainment spoilt because you cannot keep your hands out of his players' skirts?'

Harry Killigrew trailed his hand across Esther's breast as he gave her a final kiss, then, with a challenging smile, approached Angel. As he attempted to pull her into his arms she slapped his wrist aside, her glare so icy that he took a step back.

'I don't care who you make advances to in private, but I don't want my actresses' work interfered with.'

'You never used to be so strait-laced, Angel,' he returned, taking no offence at her manner. 'I'm delighted His Majesty is following the French custom and allowing women on the stage. Though all they're good for is showing their legs and giving us a show of their bosoms.'

'When a man's wit is governed by his cock and not his brain, then we can expect no better from him. All I ask, Mr Killigrew, is that you wait until after the play before you accost the actresses.' She turned on her heel and left him gaping in astonishment.

For the next half hour, Angel placated nerves, boosted selfdoubters, encouraged, praised and pampered. The players were hidden from the audience by the scenery backcloth, and from the other side of the cloth, gathering voices alerted Angel that the hall was filling. Sir Thomas Killigrew checked his pocket-watch.

'Is everyone ready?'

There was a murmur of assent.

'Then as soon as His Majesty arrives and gives the signal we will begin,' Killigrew commanded.

The professional players composed themselves for their entrance, while the 'prentices went suddenly pale, their eyes starting with horror. Jocey began to tremble and Esther burst into tears.

Angel hurried to the two women. 'There's nothing to fear. This is a private performance. The Court will adore you. Be brave. Remember, you are the vanguard of all women who will follow you on to the stage. Show the Court that women have a place in the playhouses, and when the theatres re-open we shall be amongst their players.'

'But His Majesty is out there,' Esther groaned. 'I can't remember a single line.'

'You will remember everything the minute you step on the stage. No man appreciates a pretty woman more than King Charles. He will be delighted with your dancing.'

'Maressa has a sweeter voice than I,' wailed Jocey, 'and she's so beautiful and she never forgets her lines.'

'But you are a natural comedienne, Jocey. Twice this morning when one of the men forgot their lines you extem-porised and got the play back on to its path. You have a natural wit and the playgoers will love you for it.'

Angel glanced at Maressa, who looked ravishing in a cloth of gold gown. Aware of her sister's limitations as an actress, Angel had been cautious with her lines, but to satisfy Maressa, left her on stage for most of the scenes. The actors were taking it in turns to peer through the backdrop curtain, except for the two 'prentices who were reciting their few lines to each other.

Assured that everything had been checked, Angel neverthe-less began to re-check everything again in her mind. Deep in thought, she started violently as an arm scooped round her waist and a kiss was pressed to her throat. Her protest changed to a soft laugh as Nathan spun her round.

'I thought I'd never get here,' he apologised. 'There were two cases of plague admitted to the hospital this morning. At least there have been few cases this year, so hopefully, we will be spared a major outbreak. I don't want you visiting the sick while we have plague victims there.'

So that was why Nathan smelt so strongly of soap. When-ever he attended such patients he always bathed before join-ing her.

'I'm glad you're here.' She took his hand and squeezed it. 'The rehearsal this morning was a shambles, and I'm sure everything will go wrong. If I fail today, they may never perform a play by a woman again.'

'Your play is a masterpiece of wit. The Court will love it and they will adore you. I'm proud of you, Angel. This is what you have worked for. Enjoy your success.'

A fanfare announced the arrival of the King and a hush fell upon the gathered courtiers. Nathan kissed her swiftly and with a wink of encouragement took his seat on the side of the stage. Killigrew hovered by the curtain, awaiting the signal for the play to begin.

When he nodded to the musicians seated behind another screen, they began to play softly. Charles Hart strode on to the stage and spoke the opening lines. The music died but the audience continued talking amongst themselves as the other actors joined Hart. When Angel appeared for the first time she was applauded, but the murmuring in the audience persisted, plunging Jocey and Esther into a panic. Angel ignored it as did all the professional actors, and gradually the comedy of the play drew the audience's laughter and several comments of appreciation. When Maressa's chariot was lowered, the musicians played louder to cover the creaking of the windlass. The chariot halted six feet above the stage, Maressa began to sing. At once all conversation stopped. A woman's tart comment was hissed into silence.

'A beauty to match her voice,' a young nobleman cried as the song ended. 'Sing on, sweet linnet.'

The chariot was lowered to the stage and Maressa stepped out. 'A goddess! Did you ever see such beauty?' The young nobleman was clearly enamoured of Maressa and continued to praise her.

'St Aubryn is smitten, I declare,' Harry Killigrew announced to a round of laughter from the younger noblemen present.

As the play unfolded Angel scanned the crowd. The King was smiling at her, but beside him sat an auburn-haired woman whose expression was far from amused. Her beauty was sensual. It could only be Barbara Palmer, the King's paramour. In the row behind them, Angel saw the young Earl of St Aubryn. He was unable to take his eyes off Maressa. For all his jewelled doublet and thick chestnut lovelocks, the wispy moustache on his upper lip added little maturity to his nineteen years. Apparently St Aubryn had inherited his earldom at the age of ten, after his father had been killed at Worcester. His estates included three castles and four manor houses. The Countess, his mother, had died last winter and St Aubryn had barely seen her decently interred before he left for the Continent to swear fealty to King Charles.

To Angel's surprise, she saw that Maressa was deliberately encouraging the young earl. Her most passionate lines were addressed to him, even though two of her songs were delivered from the front of the stage and the invitation in them had been all for the King.

The bawdy laughter proclaimed the play's success. From the outset, it was clear that the audience cared little for eloquent dialogue. It was the innuendo and ribald overtones which caught their interest. And it was not just the gallants who lecherously eyed the women. The ladies fluttered their eyelashes and pouted their lips behind their fans, admiring Hart's, Mohun's and Hapless's handsome looks.

They cheered loudest when the faithless wife fled half-clad to escape discovery. They roared when the dancing showed the women's shapely calves, and they hooted at the moral blandishments of Fortemaine as the Puritan, and cheered when he was seduced. In the sword-fight scenes the cows' blood spurting from hidden pigs' bladders won loud approval. A soliloquy on the vices of the city's fleshpots had them leaning forward in their seats and slapping their legs with laughter. But a scene which had only superb acting and brilliant repartee to carry it forward soon had them yawning. Angel watched these reactions and made careful notes for future amendments to her plays.

The applause at the end rang sweetly in Angel's ears. There had been no mishaps during the performance and the King was smiling his approval. When His Majesty rose from his throne, leaving a disgruntled Barbara Palmer unattended, he beckoned to the players. They filed from the stage down the side steps and stood in line as the King approached. He spoke first to Thomas Killigrew.

'A marvellous performance, Tom. It's time the playhouses were reopened.'

'I fear they are in need of repair, Your Majesty,' Killigrew answered.

'Then the matter must be put in hand without delay. This afternoon's entertainment must be made available to all my subjects. I would discuss with you the subject of Royal Patents for two companies: The King's Company, which I hope you will manage . . . I had thought to award Sir William D'Avenant the responsibility of a second company. He thumbed his nose at the Government often enough during the Commonwealth and risked imprisonment by putting on several plays. His opera *The Siege of Rhodes* was a great success. He even managed to convince the authorities that opera was but a revival of an ancient art of Greece and Rome and therefore was not prosecuted.'

'I am honoured to accept, Your Majesty. D'Avenant is indeed a worthy choice.' Killigrew bowed.

The King put a hand on Killigrew's shoulder. 'The Royal Patents will be drawn up and if needs must new playhouses will be built.'

He moved on to speak briefly to Charles Hart and Michael Mohun. To du Luc and Fortemaine he politely nodded but did not speak. When presented to each of the women the King raised their hands to his lips. Maressa, he praised lavishly, but as he gazed into her face, Angel saw that his interest wavered. Despite Maressa's artful cosmetics, she could no longer pass for a woman in her early twenties. Perhaps, as a connoisseur of women, Charles had seen through her superficial beauty to the hard shell beneath.

Angel glanced at Barbara Palmer, who was surrounded by gallants. Though she laughed and flirted with them, her brittle stare watched every movement of the King. That her lovely eyes would spark such venom shocked Angel. Could the King not see through Mrs Palmer's sensuality to the virago underneath?

Maressa stiffened with affront as the King passed on after praising her voice. When he lifted Angel's hand to his mouth, his lips lingered upon her fingers and his smile was warm with remembered intimacies.

'Your talent has surpassed itself. Never have I enjoyed a play more.' He continued to hold her hand as he spoke. 'Will you take the female lead in Killigrew's company?'

'It would be a great honour to have Your Majesty as a patron. But I've decided not to be a player. Though I will continue to write.'

'And I shall insist that Killigrew puts on every one of your plays.' He smiled into her eyes. '*Everything is Possible*. I am glad you chose that title for today's play. I haven't forgotten your kindness to me in those dark days.'

'It was not kindness.'

His smile broadened. 'No, you were always honest. My position makes me cynical. 'Odsfish, have I not an ugly face?'

'To me, you were the most handsome prince in Christendom, saving your cousin Prince Rupert.'

Charles threw back his head and laughed with such gusto that every head turned to watch them. 'Madam, your honesty has a barb in its tail, but I would not change it.' He took a ruby ring from his little finger and pressed it into her hand. 'It is a small enough token for all that I owe you. You made those months in France bearable.'

'They were happy days for me, Your Majesty. That you remembered your promise and I am the first woman to have her play officially acknowledged and performed means a great deal to me.'

The King looked over her shoulder and lifted a black brow. 'Ah, here comes your husband. I've heard nothing but praise for the cures he has worked among the sick.'

'He's a dedicated physician.'

'And from the sparkle in your eyes, you love him.' He wagged a teasing finger. 'A husband and wife in love, you'll cause a scandal. 'Odsfish, I hope it won't become a fashion at Court.'

'Ah, but then Your Majesty has yet to marry,' Angel rejoined.

'One of the burdens of state I must eventually fulfil.' He turned as Nathan joined them. 'Angel seems to thrive upon marriage. I have never seen her more beautiful. You're a lucky man, Carver.'

'No luckier than I, Your Majesty.' Angel's voice was low and vibrant with passion as she smiled at her husband.

The King held up his hands in mock alarm. 'Too much domestic bliss can sour a man's stomach. But it pleases me to see you both happy. I much enjoyed your wife's play, Carver. I expect to enjoy many more from her pen. Your own achievements have not escaped me. I would appoint you as one of the Royal Physicians.'

Nathan bowed. 'Your servant, Sire.' He kept his head lowered as the King walked away, to be immediately surrounded by courtiers.

Angel put a hand lovingly on Nathan's arm. 'Are you not pleased at the King so honouring you?'

He sighed. 'My work is mostly with the poor. I've no wish to be at the Court's beck and call.'

'His Majesty is hale and hearty. God willing, he will remain so. He knows that you are no lackey. You're the foremost expert in contagious diseases. The smallpox and plague are no respecters of rank. He honours both your loyalty to his cause and your eminence as a physician. A court stipend is necessary for the upkeep of your hospital, since the poor rarely pay you for your services. Oh, Nathan, today we have both received the highest accolade of our chosen professions! But most important to me, now we have time to be together.'

He chuckled. 'Angel, I know that look. Temptress, I cannot resist it. If we were alone now I would—'

Angel's eyes danced with answering devilment. 'Then why are we still loitering here?'

Tom Angel paced the study of Westcombe Manor. He had purchased the estate on the borders of Hampshire and Sussex eight years ago to provide a suitable home from which to launch Thomasine into society. His daughter was now sixteen, and it was time that her marriage was arranged. The estate was far enough from London for his family history not to be common gossip. Here he was known as Thomas D'Angell, the original family name from the twelfth century. The first Thomas D'Angell had been a Knight bachelor and a robber baron in the time of King John. Though Thomas's descent was on the wrong side of the blanket, he still carried noble blood in his veins. The most notorious of his ancestors, 'Wildboar Tom Angel', had fallen in love with a nun and abducted her from a local priory and forced her to marry him. The nun had been a distant cousin of the powerful Percy family, Lords of Northumberland. Thomasine also inherited that ancient blood and he would provide his daughter with a dowry worthy of a princess.

Thomas had selected James Lauceston, Viscount Lymeton and heir to the Earl of Harwood, as a suitable husband for Thomasine. Harwood Hall adjoined Westcombe and during the last few years Harwood had become steadily indebted to Thomas. The aging earl would have gambled himself into bankruptcy had Thomas not deferred the payment to his loans. He would agree to the marriage between his heir and Thomasine to save the family estate. If not, Thomas would bankrupt him and the family would lose everything.

Thomas planned his move carefully, and had not scrupled to use Maressa in his schemes. During the last three years, whilst Thomasine had been studying at a Ladies' Academy in Tunbridge Wells, he had ensured that Maressa was always present at Westcombe whenever their daughter returned home. Thomas had insisted on Maressa's compliance if she wanted to keep the generous allowance he gave her. Knowing that Maressa could not afford to lose his support she grudgingly did as she was told.

Thomas paused before the study window, his mouth set in a grim line. The vast parkland with its herd of roe deer grazing between the trees blurred as he dwelt on long-awaited revenge. He was still angry with Maressa for refusing to continue in her role as the contessa at Nell's. Since she had joined The King's Company of players, she had become more difficult to control. Several noblemen were amongst her admirers. The contessa had been popular at Nell's, attracting a good class of customer. Now that more actresses performed on the stage, and were only too willing to sell their charms to the highest protector, trade at Nell's was diminishing rapidly. And with it the hold Thomas had over the clients who frequented it. The theatres were bad for Thomas Angel's business. Worse, they were under royal patronage and as such he had no control over their revenues or employees, as he had done with the old playhouses. Yet if Maressa thought she could dictate terms to him, she was about to learn her mistake.

Over the years, necessity and ambition had forged an unusual bond between Maressa and himself. He knew that she had set out to use him when Mortimer died, and still the marriage had suited him. It had given him the son he needed to inherit Laurence's wealth and a daughter he adored. At the moment Maressa danced to his tune because that was what he wanted. The day would come when he would exact his revenge for all the times she had rejected his advances. She was the only woman to get close to his affections, and her rejection had angered him. He never forgot an insult, and Maressa had given him the greatest insult of all – to his manhood.

He could hear her in the saloon above him now, her voice rising as she criticised the servants for the inefficient running of the house. There was to be a masked ball at the Manor that evening. Maressa was the perfect hostess. To establish a respectable background for Thomasine, he had insisted that Maressa attend Westcombe in the guise of his sister. She was introduced as the respectable widow of Sir Humphrey Canning, killed at Naseby. He explained the absence of a wife by saying that she had died during an outbreak of plague.

Unfortunately for Thomas's plan, Viscount Lymeton was not eager for the match. Harwood was reluctant to press his son, who at nineteen, he felt was still too young to marry. Thomas had begun to suspect that Harwood was scheming for a match with a noble family, and new tactics were needed to bring Harwood to heel.

He rang a handbell to summon a footman.

'Ask Lady Canning to attend me,' he ordered.

Maressa arrived, looking displeased at such a summons. 'Your servants are a disgrace,' she complained. 'The silver has not been polished since I was here a month ago and there's a rent in the bedhangings in my chamber.'

'I didn't ask you here to discuss the servants,' Thomas silenced her. 'At the ball this evening I want you to use your charms on Harwood to ensure the match between Thomasine and Viscount Lymeton.'

'You know I can't stand Harwood,' Maressa snapped. 'He makes my flesh crawl. He looks like a bloated toad with those bulbous eyes and fleshy jowls. He's ugly, fat and bandy.'

'If he was a blond Adonis I doubt he'd move your heart. You don't like men, Maressa. Though you're not averse to accepting jewels from them. You regard me as a means to settle your dressmaker's bills. Talking of which, the last one came to four hundred pounds. It's still unpaid.'

The unspoken threat made Maressa grow pale. 'If I get Harwood to agree to this match will you pay the bill?'

'Don't I always, when you do as you're commanded?'

She glowered at him. 'Very well.'

Thomas laughed. 'Who knows?' The old boy may even

offer for you. You've always fancied a grand title.'

Maressa itched to strike the grin from his face, but she did not dare. Thomas was too dangerous a man to cross. 'Harwood is not the only earl available,' she said defiantly.

'So it's St Aubryn you're after?'

'And why not? He's besotted enough. This last month he's been at every performance of mine.'

'But you've not bedded him yet, have you?'

Maressa flinched at the amusement in Thomas's tone. She quelled her unease. 'There's been no man in my bed since our marriage was annulled.'

'Is that anything to boast of?'

'I value virtue, even if you do not.'

'Virtue won't win you St Aubryn. Though it might appeal to Harwood's jaded palate.'

'I'd rather sell myself to the devil.'

'You've already done that, my dear.' Thomas spoke without humour. 'When you threw your lot in with me.'

'Fresh 'errings!' a child's voice rang out. 'Lovely 'errings. Come buy me lovely 'errings.'

Angel stopped to buy some of Nathan's favourite fish. The red-haired child was about ten or eleven and had a pretty face beneath the layer of dirt. There was such impish laughter in her eyes, that Angel could not resist giving her an extra penny.

'Bless yer, lady. 'Ere, ain't yer the one that writes them plays? And that's yer sister, the actress Maressa Mortimer. She 'ad a crowd of gallants round 'er when I saw 'er leaving the theatre in Vere Street last week.'

Maressa held a nosegay to her face impatiently. 'Angel, must you stop and talk to every street urchin? Killigrew is waiting for the copied parts and you know I like to arrive early to prepare for my performance.'

The red-haired girl pulled a face at Maressa's back. 'She ain't as pretty when there's no men around to simper to. Got a sour mouth. And she don't look so young as she did when I were selling oranges the other week in the pit.'

'You're Nell, aren't you?' Angel said, smiling. 'And weren't you doing a dance outside the theatre and having pennies thrown at you.'

The girl beamed at her. 'That was me – Nelly Gwynne!'

'Perhaps one day, Nelly, you'll find yourself dancing on the stage.'

Nelly rolled her eyes ecstatically. 'D'yer reckon?' She struck a haughty pose, fluttering her eyelashes as though she was enticing a gallant.

'Yes, Nelly, I reckon you will do very well on the stage in a few years.' Angel threw her another penny before rejoining her sister.

'Really, Angel! I wish you would not encourage those urchins. I suppose it's because you've never had children of your own.'

The barb stung Angel, for her only regret was that she was barren. She desperately wanted Nathan's child. She brushed the regret aside. Nathan had assured her that it was still possible she would conceive. But she was now four-and-thirty. In the year since the Restoration, she had stayed in London, the passion she shared with her husband undiminished. Yet still there was no child.

Maressa swept into the theatre which was a converted tennis court in Vere Street. A grand theatre was to be built for the King's Company in Drury Lane but the work on it had only just started. Now that the King and the Court regularly visited the play, it was unthinkable to expose His Majesty to the rough element of the weather. The new playhouses unlike the open air round O of Gabriellen's day were to be roofed and decorated in a manner befitting the presence of a King. When Maressa entered the tiring room, she was annoyed to discover so many actresses. Since the Restoration women seemed to be crawling out of the woodwork to appear on the stage. Few had any talent. All bosoms, high-kicks and low morals, was how Maressa viewed them. An actress needed little talent to be popular, providing she showed off her body and could sing in tune.

Although Maressa remained the undisputed nightingale of the King's Company, she was aware that Sir Thomas Killigrew wanted her out of the company. She would never admit that she owed her employment to Angel's plays which had parts specially written to enhance Maressa's limited accomplishments. Once, when she was a half hour late for a rehearsal, Killigrew had actually cut her from the day's performance. She had been outraged. With so many younger actresses eager to steal her roles, Maressa had pleaded the headache and apologised to Killigrew. She took care never to be late again.

Gradually, however, a year on the boards had begun to lose its charm. Maressa had not realised until she lost his patronage how much Thomas had supported her extravagant lifestyle over the years. On an actress's pay she could not afford to cross him. So far, her cousin had continued to pay her bills in return for her compliance to his orders. The old Earl of Harwood had been easy to captivate, but he was becoming too ardent and still he would not agree to the betrothal between his son and Thomasine. Last weekend the Earl had cornered Maressa in the garden maze. Overcome with lust, he had pushed her against the hedge and begun to hoist her skirts to her waist. His strength had frightened her, and his slavering kisses were nauseating. Her cries of protest had brought Thomas to her rescue. He had begun to whistle as he entered the maze, giving Harwood time to step back and for Maressa to adjust her gown.

'Dear Lady Canning, I crave your pardon,' Harwood groaned before Thomas came upon them. 'Your beauty haunts me. Let me come to you tonight.'

'I could not so dishonour my husband's memory,' she said, forcing herself to remain cool and polite. 'The wine and the hot sun must have overcome you, my lord. This time I'll not mention your conduct to my brother.'

Maressa shuddered at the memory. Harwood was a problem, and now Thomas was pressuring her to take up residence at Westcombe. In the summer Thomasine would leave her Ladies' Academy and must be suitably chaperoned until she married. That did not suit Maressa at all. But unless St Aubryn proposed, Thomas held the purse-strings and so she would have to obey him.

Her future would be assured if she wed St Aubryn. A moment of fear clutched at Maressa's stomach. Was she losing her charms? Although she admitted to being no more than five-and-twenty, her birthday last month had taken her into her seven-and-thirtieth year. Her beauty was her greatest weapon. What if it was fading? Hart and Mohun no longer even tried to seduce her. Many of the courtiers who forced their attentions upon her in the tiring room were older men, seasoned roués intent on seduction and not marriage. Even the propositions to set her up as a mistress were becoming fewer.

Maressa peered into her tiring room mirror. The creams which Hazel nightly applied to her face and body did seem to be keeping age at bay, and the stage lights were flattering. Her body was still firm, her full breasts rounded. She had always taken care of her teeth and sucked a cinnamon lozenge to sweeten her breath. She frowned at her reflection. Those tiny lines around her eyes were becoming more difficult to conceal.

How much longer would she even be able to keep her place at the playhouse? It had been a year now and still she had not snared the Earl of St Aubryn into marriage. She had done everything but sleep with him. And she held back on that as his ultimate reward for her marriage lines. It had worked for Anne Boleyn and Henry VIII. Why not Maressa Angel and Harry St Aubryn? Her eyes narrowed. She'd get Hazel to prepare another love-philtre for when he dined with her this evening.

'I see the nightingale has arrived,' one actress sniggered. 'More like an old rook. I heard the other day she's thirty if she's a day. Peg-leg Dobbs swore she used to be wed to Tom Angel, him as owns Nell Lovegood's trugging house. Gave him a daughter, said Peg-leg, and the girl's ripe to be wed.'

The second actress eyed Maressa sourly. 'That'll make her nearer forty. But give the old vixen her due. She don't look it.'

'Haughty cow,' the first actress added. 'Always thinks she's so pure. Just 'cause she's kept St Aubryn panting after her. She gives us more obliging actresses a bad name.'

Maressa felt anger burning through her. She'd have Hazel make up a special mix of comfits to be sent to that actress. The woman was always boasting of the gifts bestowed on her by admirers. When she had scoffed her way through Maressa's gift, liberally doctored with cassia fistula, she'd be squatting over the privy-stool for two days in agony. The woman was no better than a shilling-whore. She'd spread her legs for anyone.

Maressa knew she must keep her reputation intact if she

was to marry a great nobleman. The need was becoming an obsession with her. Unlike most of the women, she did not encourage men to attend her in the tiring room. Not for her to permit them the liberty of stolen kisses, loosening the laces of her bodice or fastening a garter. Her thoughts returned to St Aubryn. Tonight he would be brought to heel.

Few of the actresses acknowledged Maressa's arrival, but as soon as Angel appeared, they rushed to surround her, all talking at once.

'Have you brought the new play?'

'How many lines have I got?'

'Who's the unlucky one who gets to be kissed by du Luc? It's like kissing a lizard with his tightly shut lips. I vow I felt him shudder the last time I tried to force my tongue into his mouth.'

There was a burst of laughter at du Luc's expense. Maressa turned on her heel, fanning herself with her copied part. Her sister's popularity irked her. She was annoyed to discover that there were only two songs for her to sing in the new play, and out of the six women only one other had fewer lines than herself.

She stormed back outside. 'Angel, I need to speak with you.'

Angel sighed, guessing that Maressa had seen the cuts in her part. How could she tell her sister that Killigrew was tiring of her tantrums. He had not even wanted her in this play.

'I'll be with you a moment, Maressa,' she said. 'First I must give Sir Thomas Killigrew the other parts.'

She left the tiring room to walk on to the stage. Killigrew and Charles Hart were seated in the front row of the tier of boxes opposite the stage, discussing the adjustment of the scenery. The tennis-court theatre copied the layout of those in France and Italy. The roof protected the players and groundlings from the weather, so performances never had to be cancelled because of high winds or rain. A further innovation had been added. The King had his own special box. Four tiers of galleried boxes surrounded the three sides of the stage, and above the stage was built a proscenium arch. The scenery was set behind this arch and the actors played under the blaze of two immense chandeliers and the row of

550

candles set within a low barrier at the front of the stage. Beneath the raised structure the musicians had a small cubicle and were hidden from the view of the playgoers.

The galleried boxes were fitted with cushioned seats to accommodate the nobles and wealthy residents of the city. The pit was lined with benches where the 'prentices, fops, and bawds sat. They were rowdy – laughing and joking amongst themselves and were the first to jeer or hiss a bad actor off the stage. The nut-sellers and fruit-sellers roamed freely amongst the groundlings, calling out their wares. High in the top of the building was a narrow gallery where the servants accompanying their masters could also watch the performance.

Even empty, the theatre held a unique atmosphere. The laughter and shouted calls, whistles and applause seemed to echo around the walls. There lingered the musky smell of overcrowded bodies, exotic perfume, make-up, orange peel and candlewax. The stage conjured up ghostly images of warrior kings, ill-starred lovers and defiant maidens.

'Mistress Carver,' Sir Thomas said warmly. 'You have the new play, *Lady of Misrule*. Hart tells me it is your best yet.'

'Charles is kind enough to say that every play I produce surpasses my previous work. I hope you find it adequate, Sir Thomas.'

'You've never disappointed me. 'Tis your fifth play we have presented? As usual, His Majesty has sent word he will attend Wednesday's performance. He requested that you and Dr Carver join him.'

'We will be honoured.'

Angel turned to find Maressa glaring at her from the wings. She scowled as Angel approached. 'If the King is to attend I should have been given a third song.'

Angel shrugged. 'Killigrew insisted on just two for you. But you are on stage throughout the second and third acts.'

'With no more than twenty lines to say in all.'

'Three of them are the wittiest in the play! When has a shortage of lines stopped any actress from becoming the most sought-after woman in the tiring room?'

'The playhouse is little better than Nell Lovegood's for all the assignations which take place here,' Maressa flared. 'The way Gabriellen spoke of the life I thought it would be more glamorous and exciting. Instead, it's exhausting! The tiring house is overcrowded and some possession of mine is always going missing. The costumes are often tawdry. Some of them are positively indecent.'

'Do we not create illusions of valour and splendour? The excitement is in the thrumming in our ears, as our heartbeats quicken to the sound of applause. We create our own world with our speeches. It is in our blood and our life's breath. Obviously it is not in yours.'

'Should I be proud of my Angel blood?' Maressa fluttered her fan, her bosom heaving in disdain. 'Rogues to the core, each and every one of them. Even Gabriellen was not so innocent.'

'And are you, Maressa?' Angel said, lifting a dark brow.

'I've always tried to lead a respectable life.' She snapped her fan shut and flounced back to the tiring room. There she called to Hazel to lay out her costume and then accused an actress of stealing her perfume.

Angel sighed, turning as she heard a footstep behind her.

'Maressa will have to go,' Sir Thomas said heavily. 'I know she's your sister, but her tantrums are upsetting the other actresses. I've decided to give her part to Peg Hughes.'

Angel nodded. 'Could you not let her appear in the first two performances? It's important to Maressa not to lose face, and everyone knows the part was written for her. The King is not coming until Wednesday, Peg could take over then.'

Killigrew considered her words. 'Very well, since it's you who ask. I'll give Maressa a warning to behave or she will be dismissed on the spot. If I give in to one, the other actresses will take advantage. Too many of them have gained the attention of important noblemen and give themselves false airs.' He turned away as a man of medium height and dark hair approached. 'Ah, here is Mr Pepys! He asked to attend a rehearsal. He will be delighted to meet you, Angel. I hope you do not mind.'

Angel smiled at Samuel Pepys, who was often at the play. He asked her several questions about the inspiration behind her plays and characters, and explained the form of shorthand writing he had devised, which he used for his own amusement when keeping a daily journal. He was a charming man with an eye for the pretty actresses she noticed.

The rehearsal had its usual problems: du Luc demanded more lines; Fortemaine declared the actresses were too busy waving to their lovers waiting behind the scenery and missed their cues. Two of the special effects would not work. Hapless managed to cut his hand in the mock sword fight. Poor Hapless, Angel thought as she bandaged his wound. He hungered to play the great roles immortalised by Charles Hart, but he was so accident prone he remained the company's comedian. Angel had already started to write a special comedy to give Hapless the major role he craved.

Throughout the rehearsal she copied any extemporised line which added lustre to the play, but the theatre was uncomfortably stuffy that morning and she began to feel unwell. They had taken a short break when she heard a familiar laugh and was delighted to see Alexander striding towards her.

She jumped to her feet. The sudden movement made her dizzy and she clutched the back of her chair for support, but quickly recovered herself as she was clasped in her brother's arms.

'Alex! I didn't expect you for another fortnight. Is Thérèse with you?'

'I had to deliver six horses in the south, so I thought I'd spend a day or two in London before returning to Wales. Thérèse is looking after Emmy. She's very poorly.'

'Is it serious?'

Alex looked worried. 'I'm afraid it is. She's been listless all summer. She has the lung fever . . . just like Firkin.'

'I'm so sorry, Alex. She's a darling girl.'

'With care she could live for some years yet. You remember how long Firkin fought it.' He sighed. 'But there's no use dwelling on it. Marcus and Bryan are in London.' He brightened. 'They're with Thomas at present. He's taken them to see the lions in the Tower.'

'I dare say that will please Bryan who's only fourteen, but what of Marcus? Are you sure Tom won't initiate him into the delights of Nell's?'

'I took the lad there myself on my last visit,' Alexander said flippantly.

Angel did not judge her brother. She knew he often visited Nell's when he was in London and that on his last visit he had been very taken with Esther Beckton. He turned to watch the actress now. She had seen him enter the theatre and was hovering to catch his attention.

'How is Thérèse?' Angel asked, saddened that Thérèse had failed to capture Alexander's heart.

'She's well. There's a child due next Candlemas.'

'I'm pleased, Alex. She loves children. Are you happy together?'

'We rub along well enough,' he said dismissively.

'But you don't love her?'

'I still love Beth.' He looked over to where Esther was standing. When he turned back to Angel, his eyes were sombre. 'Don't think I didn't see what you were doing last summer. You transformed Thérèse. She's a good wife and more confident. For that I'm grateful.'

'Then I will not keep you from Esther any longer.'

'You knew?'

'It's impossible to keep a liaison secret in the theatre.' She put her hand to her head as the stage began to swim before her eyes.

'Angel, are you ill?' Alexander demanded, taking her shoulders.

'It has passed,' she said weakly. 'It must be the heat. It's very stuffy in here.'

'I'll take you home.'

She shook her head. 'No. Go to Esther. I'll be fine once I get outside. But you could call me a hackney.'

Alexander took Angel outside, but the fresh air did not clear her head and for a moment her knees buckled. Alexander hailed a carriage and helped her inside. As she settled back on the seat she put a hand to her mouth.

'Perhaps it's something I ate. I feel so queasy.'

Alexander looked at his sister and grinned. 'Thérèse will not be the only new mother, come Candlemas. Go home and rest.'

Angel's eyes widened. 'But I'm not—' She stared incredulously at her brother. 'Oh, Alex, do you think I could be with child?'

'You ask me that when you're married to a physician!' He laughed. 'You do have the same dreamy look in your eyes I saw so often in Beth's. And faintness and sickness are the first signs.'

554

To his astonishment, tears coursed down Angel's cheeks. 'I'll call on a midwife and check before I tell Nathan. I had thought I was barren.'

The opening of *Lady of Misrule* was a success. After the warning from Killigrew, Maressa put her heart into her performance, and her voice had never sounded sweeter. A dozen courtiers flocked around her in the tiring room afterwards, clamouring for a keepsake to cherish, importuning her to dine with them. One foppish lord offered her a grand house in Lincoln's Inn and an allowance of one thousand a year if she would become his mistress.

'My lord, you insult me,' she had declared in a voice intended to carry to St Aubryn. 'I do not barter my favours. Who has led you to believe that I, a respectable widow, would sell myself like a whore? You have a wife, do you not, your Lordship? Let her comfort you, as is her duty.'

The arrogant Duke of Buckingham had been with St Aubryn and she saw him wink at the Earl. Maressa did not like Buckingham. He was a rake of the worst order. Fortunately, St Aubryn was so besotted with her, he had not strayed. But Maressa knew the weakness of men, and knew better than to count on constancy when a man's blood was lustful.

She was uneasy at Killigrew's warning and she suspected that he thought her too old for her parts. He was always trying to push Peg Hughes forward. She would show Killigrew that she did not need him. St Aubryn dined with her tonight. Hazel had her instructions. The food would be laced with aphrodisiacs and the wine drugged with a love potion; St Aubryn would be unable to resist her. Tonight she would seduce him and tomorrow she would be his betrothed. She had taken the precaution of making Thomas an accomplice, albeit an unwitting one. For she had asked him to come to the house to discuss Thomasine's future at ten that evening.

As she entered the saloon on the second floor of her house, she saw the adjoining door to the bedchamber was open, and both rooms intimately lit. Hazel had arranged the lighting so that it flattered Maressa wherever she sat. St Aubryn hiccoughed and staggered slightly as he entered the room behind her. Being drunk would aid her to compromise him. She'd had enough of the playhouse. She would have a new role as the Countess of St Aubryn.

'My lord, will you help yourself to brandy?' She gestured to the silver flagon. 'Then you can talk to me while I change. This gown is so heavy that I find it difficult to breathe.'

She rang for Hazel to attend her and kept talking to St Aubryn over her shoulder as her maid unfastened the lacings at her back. St Aubryn lounged at ease in a scarlet velvet upholstered chair, his gaze admiring as he watched the gown slide from Maressa's shoulders. Putting a hand to her breasts to keep the gown in place, she moved behind the Chinese painted screen in the corner of the room. Hazel removed the French corset and held out a peach satin robe for her mistress, then left the room. Tying the wide sash so that it cinched in her waist, Maressa came from behind the screen to smile at St Aubryn. For all his youth, the Earl was a handsome man, with long curling brown hair and heavy-lidded grey eyes – although the lips beneath his narrow moustache had a tendency to pout rather sullenly when he did not get his way.

Her smile enticing, she placed a hand on his shoulder and leaned forward, allowing him to glimpse the fullness of her breasts. Immediately his eyes darkened with desire. St Aubryn was just a youth, she reassured herself. It would be easy to manipulate him.

'Shall we eat, my lord?'

Her hand was caught as she was pulled down on to his lap. She did not resist when his fingers caressed her hip, and moved up to touch her breast. She waited until she heard his breathing quicken, then with a sigh pulled back from him.

'You are too bold, my lord. And too handsome. Would you dishonour me?'

'You are so beautiful, Maressa,' St Aubryn said with a reverence which heartened her. 'I respect you, but I'm tormented with love for you.'

She rose from his lap and went to the table. When he came to stand behind her she allowed her robe to slip down over one shoulder and arm. His lips pressed against her neck and, sighing, she turned in his arms to receive his kiss. A tremor passed through her as he squeezed her breasts and

556

she forced herself to overcome her repugnance at his rough handling. Let him think she was trembling with desire.

'I'm but a weak woman,' she said breathlessly. 'I must guard my honour.'

'I would guard your honour with my life, fair Maressa,' he said huskily. 'Where is the dishonour in loving when that love is returned?'

His face was buried in her hair and his hands became bolder. When they probed between her thighs she flinched and pushed him away. But her hips were gripped and pressed against the hard evidence of his arousal.

'Feel how I need you, Maressa. I am mad with desire.'

She swallowed against her rising fear. She must keep control of the situation. She glanced at the clock. It was only nine-thirty. Twisting from his hold, she put a shaking hand to her temple. 'My lord, you will be my undoing. Please, let us eat. I am ravenous.'

'My hunger is all for you, dear lady.'

She slipped away from him and removed the silver covers from the food. 'Would you have me faint away with hunger?'

He drew in his breath sharply like the hiss of a snake, but when she turned a questioning look upon him, his expression was suitably chastened.

'You beauty overwhelms me. I crave your pardon if I have offended.'

She reclined on a daybed, draping her robe over her legs as she nodded for him to take the chair at her side. Aware that his gaze was on her hands, her fingers trailed across her hips and up to her breasts. He was flushed with desire for her. When he poured two goblets of wine, she took the cup and raised her hand for him to kiss. In the large Venetian mirror over the fireplace she saw her reflection. She looked beautiful and seductive. Throughout the meal she flirted with St Aubryn, praising his restraint, his solicitation of her welfare. He responded with lavish compliments upon her beauty and her charms.

'Can you doubt my undying devotion?' he demanded.

She chose a choice cut of spiced capon and held it to his lips. He drew it slowly into his mouth, his lips caressing the tips of her fingers. She smiled as she wiped a thin trickle of ginger sauce from the corner of his mouth. She sucked the juice from her finger and ran the tip of her tongue over her lips, watching his fascinated reaction. With an impassioned groan he left his chair to kneel at her side, and cover her hands with kisses. Then his mouth was against her throat, his hands easing back her shoulders, his kisses growing more demanding as they moved to the swell of her breasts.

'This is wrong, my lord,' she protested breathlessly.

'I am dying for love of you. How can my loving you be wrong? I cannot live without you. I am yours forever.'

'As I would be yours, but . . .' Her robe was caught beneath his thigh and as she moved it parted, showing her stockings held in place at the knee by scarlet garters.

The sight inflamed him. 'If you love me, you will not deny me.' His voice became belligerent. 'You are heartless.'

'Do not say that,' she said, distraught. 'I believe in honour and virtue.'

'You are heartless,' he repeated, his face ugly with thwarted desire.

Fearful that she had overplayed her role, Maressa reached for him. 'You are the one who is cruel. You toy with my affections.' In desperation, she clutched at his wrist and drew his palm to her breast. 'Do not call me heartless. I am weak for love of you. Feel how my heart pounds. It beats in anguish that my passion will make you despise me.' Maressa moved so that her leg brushed his thigh and her breast rubbed against his arm. 'Perhaps you should leave.'

He kissed her with a fierce passion, his voice rough against her ear. 'I cannot live without you.'

Still the proposal was not spoken. She bit back her frustration and glanced over his shoulder to the clock on the mantelpiece. It was five minutes to ten. Let Thomas not be late. If he caught St Aubryn making love to her, he would insist that her honour was saved by marriage. Thomas would see the advantages behind the match, especially for Thomasine. Thomas would not fail her. He would play the outraged cousin.

She gasped as St Aubryn parted her robe. When he eased her breasts free of her chemise to kiss their peaks she moaned softly, 'My lord, you overwhelm me. I am lost.' He began to tear at his clothing. His sword belt and jacket was on the floor, his diamond-buckled shoes kicked impatiently across the room. His hands were rough upon her tender flesh, squeezing and kneading with no finesse. She controlled her disgust, steeling herself to submit to the growing intimacy of his caresses. His tongue invaded her mouth, almost making her gag. He was fumbling with his breeches, pushing them down to his knees with one hand whilst the other probed between her thighs.

The clock chimed the hour. Where was Thomas? She feigned passion, but the roughness of St Aubryn's lovemaking nauseated her. He was panting, his member pushing against her thigh as he lifted her hips to enter her. She bit back a cry. She had not intended that it should go this far. Where the devil was Thomas? St Aubryn thrust inside her and her body went rigid. The pain was intense. She was not ready for him. Her dry flesh tore as he hammered into her, uncaring of her agony. She forced herself to submit, to make the necessary responses, to make him believe that he was giving her pleasure. Her eyes were open and staring as his body jerked in a frenzy. The mirror showed his pale pumping buttocks above her, his shirt plastered to his back with sweat and his satin breeches looped behind his knees. It was an obscene tableau. It took all her willpower not to push him off her with a scream of disgust. With a grunt of triumph and a last shuddering thrust, he slumped over her.

The door burst open and Thomas strode in, his expression one of astonishment. Maressa screamed and covered herself as she pushed at St Aubryn's half-naked figure.

'My reputation is destroyed! Oh, the shame of it. I trust you will honour your obligation, my lord, and marry me without delay.'

St Aubryn stood up and unhurriedly pulled up his breeches and fastened them. Throwing her a look of undisguised contempt, he gave a snort of laughter. 'Marry an actress? I grant you this was a fine performance, Madam. And you kept me dangling long enough for it. Though in truth a little more passion during our coupling would have been more gratifying.'

He turned to Thomas. To Maressa's dismay, her cousin said nothing.

'Are you in on this, Angel?' St Aubryn demanded.

Thomas held up his hands in denial. 'Would I risk

annoying one of my best customers at Nell's? My cousin asked me to call at ten. On a matter of some urgency, she insisted.'

'The urgency of ensnaring an earl in wedlock, no doubt.' St Aubryn's tone was nasty.

Maressa covered herself with her robe and stood up with as much dignity as she could muster. She was shaken by St Aubryn's manner and hurt that Thomas had betrayed her trust. How could he not defend her virtue?

St Aubryn laughed at her horrified expression. 'Your trickery has failed, Madam! Do you think I'd take a fortune huntress for my wife? And one old enough to be my mother.'

Maressa gasped and staggered back, but St Aubryn was merciless. 'I had a wager with Buckingham that I could get beneath your skirts. He said you were hanging out for marriage. It was Buckingham who suggested I play the innocent, declaring it was the only way I'd ever gain entrance to your frigid portal. He was right. I suppose I'll have to declare the wager a draw.'

'You filthy, degenerate swine!' Maressa found her voice at last. 'You mean, all these months of you playing the lovesick youth was just for a wager? You never cared for me?'

'I prefer to sport with younger game. But you were a challenge. To win the notorious Lady Maressa Mortimer, when she has refused all other advances on her virtue – now there's a story to boast of. Though I can see why Sir Henry waited seven years to surface after his suspected death. You're a cold fish to make love to.'

'You wouldn't be so callous as to speak of tonight? I'll be a laughing stock.'

'And what would I have been, had I been the gullible youth you believed? It's no more than you deserve. Next time you fancy yourself a countess, pick an old dotard. He might be gulled by your tricks.'

He jammed his hat on his head, gave a mocking bow to Maressa and grinned at Thomas. 'See you at Nell's later. Buckingham said you've a couple of new wenches. I'll have them both tonight – together.'

When the Earl had strolled from the room, Maressa broke down. Covering her face in her hands she sobbed out her anger and humiliation.

'I marvel at you, Maressa,' Thomas said without sympathy. 'It astounds me how innocent you can still be.'

'Go on, mock me! I have taken pride in my virtue. Now St Aubryn will tarnish my good name. I'll never be able to hold my head up in London again. Why didn't you warn me that the man was a reprobate?'

'You didn't ask.'

Maressa screamed and, grabbing at a silver candlestick, launched it at Thomas's head. He ducked and it hit the wall behind him.

'Temper, my dear. Having lost St Aubryn, can you afford to smash up your home? I've heard that Killigrew wants shot of you. I'm giving you until the end of the month to get Viscount Lymeton to propose to Thomasine or your bills will not be settled. Your face is your fortune, Maressa. How long will it remain so in the squalor of a debtor's prison?'

Chapter Twenty-Two

Matthew Carver came into the world on the same day as his mother's sixth play was performed before His Majesty and his new Queen, Catherine of Braganza. The King sent Angel a bracelet of pearls and amethysts. Nathan had just extended his hospital to hold forty beds, and his book, *Remedies and Treatments of Infectious Diseases*, had been highly acclaimed by the College of Physicians.

Angel was holding her son in her arms when Nathan was allowed in to see them. Royal physician he might be, but the midwife had no time for men in the lying-in chamber and had promptly banished him from the room.

Stooping over the bed to kiss his wife, he asked, 'How are you, my dear? I have never seen you look more beautiful.'

'That's because you have never seen me holding our son before. Isn't he wonderful?'

There was an unnaturally bright glitter in Nathan's eyes as he took Matthew into his arms, and he had difficulty swallowing. 'I never realised that a child could make you feel like this,' he said hoarsely.

'It's frightening, isn't it?' Angel was serious. 'I want so much for him. At the moment my life is perfect. But does anyone get everything they want in life? I've not seen it happen without pain and suffering. I'm frightened, Nathan. Do you think we have too much happiness?'

Nathan laughed softly and put his son back into her arms. 'The trials of childbirth have made you morbid. What we have, we have worked and striven for. Have we not paid for our happiness by all those years of duty, hard work and uncertainty? And haven't you, more than most, shaped your own destiny?'

'I'm being foolish, aren't I?'

'No, my darling. They're the natural fears of new-found motherhood.'

Angel nodded in agreement, but when Nathan left to return to the hospital her fears returned. Why could she not put them from her mind? Why could she not shake the certainty that no one ever achieved complete happiness in life. That everything must be paid for.

Maressa, in self-exile at Westcombe, knew well that nothing in life came without payment. The scandal of St Aubryn and the actress Lady Maressa Mortimer had been the talk of London for a month, branding her a fortune-huntress. It had revived the old scandals of the fire, Northcliffe's death and Henry's murder. She had fled to Westcombe, too ashamed to live in London. She would make a new life for herself there, as the widowed Lady Maressa Canning.

She must have been insane to put her trust in Thomas. Thomasine had been married to Viscount Lymeton for three months and was now touring Europe on her honeymoon. Her use to Thomas at an end, he had informed Maressa that she must leave Westcombe at the end of the month and find someone else to protect her, since she had made no attempts to seek a means of supporting herself. He was no longer prepared to pay her bills or indulge her extravagances.

She was furious with him. After all she had done and suffered because of him. She was the mother of his children. She ran up an endless list of what she considered to be all her perfections. Thomas had appreciated none of them. He had never forgiven her for denying him her bed. How dare he treat her like some light-of-love? From the outset he had tricked her, degraded her into believing that she was his legal wife. Then, when he could have righted the wrong, he made no atonement for using her like a whore. Maressa conveniently forgot how she had used Thomas, or that she had been relieved to find herself no longer bound in marriage to him.

She blamed him for her misfortune. All she had ever wanted in life was to be respected and admired, to be a pillar of society. Thomas had destroyed that.

Needing to assess her resources she had sold the house in London for a good price and invested the money with a goldsmith. She had been pleasantly surprised to discover that, because Thomas had paid for everything in the last five years, she had accrued a substantial fortune. There were also the dozens of jewels heaped on her by her admirers over the years. That money would be her dowry; her fine clothes and jewels, the lure to make a wealthy and respectable match. In another two years she would be forty, and the thought filled her with dread.

She was still considering the problem when Hazel appeared, looking flushed. 'My lady, the Earl of Harwood is here.'

Maressa scowled and waved a dismissive hand. 'Tell him I cannot receive visitors. I have the headache.'

'But, my lady, he's not alone! He's accompanied by the Archduke Frederick von Heissel.'

Maressa's eyes lit up with interest.

'A handsome man, my lady, for all he's foreign,' Hazel stated, knowing her mistress's obsession with the nobility. 'From the little conversation I overheard between them, he is recently widowed.'

'How old would you say he is?' Maressa asked.

'About Mr Angel's age – early fifties. But, like your cousin, he could pass for a dozen years younger.'

Maressa was still in her petticoats. 'I will wear the sapphire satin with the silver lace trimming. I must look my best. I shall wear the two diamond bracelets and the smallest of my three diamond necklaces. I must not appear a pauper, but it would never do to look overdressed.'

A half hour later, Maressa glided into the saloon, apologising for the delay. 'My dear Harwood, I was in the middle of dressing. How appalling of me to have kept you waiting for so long.'

Harwood took her hand possessively. 'I could forgive you anything when you look so radiant. May I present His Highness, the Archduke Frederick von Heissel.'

Maressa had become increasingly short-sighted in recent years, and she saw a slim man of medium height move away from examining the portraits of her family, all painted by Angel.

Von Heissel stepped forward and bowed over her hand. He had the self-assurance of a man born to command, and now that he was close, Maressa could see that his long curled hair, the colour of burnished oak, was a periwig. When he raised his head his velvet brown eyes were admiring as he regarded her. There were pouches beneath his heavy-lidded eyes but they did not detract from his handsome looks. His mouth was wide and thin-lipped, and he smiled, revealing white teeth with a gap between the front two which gave him a rakish air. He was dressed impeccably in the latest fashion and from his interest in the paintings, Maressa felt sure he was a man of culture.

'Lady Canning, I've heard nothing but praise for your beauty and charm from Lord Harwood. Yet I find he does not do you justice. Your beauty is incomparable.'

Harwood was glowering at them. If von Heissel was a friend of the Earl it would not do to antagonise Harwood. At least, not until she had captivated the Archduke. And captivate him she was determined to do.

She smiled at Harwood. 'I should be cross with your Lordship. You have neglected me this last fortnight.'

She turned to von Heissel. 'Have you been long in England?'

'A few weeks. After my wife died last autumn, giving birth to my second son, I found I could no longer stay in Vienna. There were too many memories. I had received many invitations to visit England and renew my acquaintanceship with the Royalists who shared my exile. I, too, have lost my homeland in the Catholic wars against the Protestant duchies.'

His words pleased Maressa. Here was the titled husband she sought. With two sons he would not expect an heir from her. Unfortunately, too many exiles were penniless, though from his looks he did not appear to be a pauper. With a gesture designed to appear impulsive, Maressa touched his arm.

'Your Highness has my condolences for your tragic loss,' she murmured softly.

'Whilst you are in England we must ensure that your stay is a pleasant one. A pity my dear niece is still on honeymoon, and that Lord Harwood has no hostess to entertain you with a ball or musical evening. Such entertainment would have brightened your visit.'

566

'The remedy is simple,' von Heissel said smoothly. 'As the aunt of his son's wife you are the perfect hostess for such an occasion. What do you say, Harwood?' He turned to the Earl, who frowned. 'But I importune. I had not meant to stay more than a day or so. How inconsiderate of me to expect—'

'Not at all. I'm in your debt. It was considerate of you to bring my son's letter and divert your journey from London.' Harwood turned to Maressa. 'Von Heissel met James and Thomasine in Paris. Three months wed and Thomasine is already with child. A musical evening would indeed be entertaining. Though, were I to ask Lady Maressa to be my hostess, I fear speculation might arise that there was an understanding between us.'

'Oh, there is always speculation, my lord,' Maressa parried with a smile. 'We are family now. Am I not also an old friend and neighbour? I would be happy to be your hostess for the evening.'

He bowed to her. 'I shall send the invitations out for Thursday. Perhaps Lady Maressa will honour us by singing?'

Von Heissel lifted her hand to his lips. 'I look forward to renewing our acquaintance.'

'If you are not otherwise engaged, perhaps you could call one afternoon? I miss my niece, and it would be a kindness to hear news of her.'

'It would be no kindness, but a pleasure, Lady Canning.'

When he did not call the following day Maressa was distraught. She had dressed with particular care to impress him, and by mid-afternoon she was pacing the long gallery in mounting agitation. At four the following afternoon he still had not visited and her nerves were frayed. By the evening impotent anger ground through her. He was not coming. To release her frustration she went to the music room and sat at the harpsichord. At first she toyed with the notes, then her pent-up anger burst, and she played with passion, her voice vibrant as she sang of love's betrayal. She surrendered to the passion of her fury, unaware that tears of frustration sparkled on her cheeks.

The song ended and, exhausted by the storm of her emotions, she bowed her head. Applause came from behind her and she swung round, alarmed. Von Heissel stood outside the casement window which opened on to the terrace. Maressa's hand flew to her throat.

'I thought I was alone.'

'I did not mean to startle you. I was taking the air in Harwood's garden when I heard you singing. Forgive me, but I was irresistibly drawn. I walked across the fields and over the bridge which separates your land, and took the liberty of walking through the gardens. I did not want you to stop. I've never heard such heartfelt passion in a voice. Were you thinking of your late husband as you sang?'

She lowered her eyes demurely. 'There are times when my loneliness is almost too much to bear,' she said quietly, relieved he had so interpreted her song.

He came into the room. 'Such a beautiful woman should never be alone. And you will have thought I had abandoned you.' He remained standing stiffly by the window. 'I had to stay away. My mind has been in turmoil since our meeting. I cannot stop thinking about you. Is it madness that after one meeting I feel for you such a regard, such overwhelming affection? And now having heard you sing tonight—' he broke off. 'I fear I am lost. I am bewitched by your beauty.'

Maressa rose from her stool and went to him, placing a hand upon his arm. Her heart beat rapidly with excitement. 'I am honoured by your regard. I have thought much of you. I was quite downcast when you did not call.'

'Can I hope that you return my affection?'

She crossed to the fireplace, knowing that she presented a pretty picture in her lilac satin gown with her hair piled high in ringlets and studded with diamond stars. 'I hardly know you. I must ask you not to speak so passionately. I'm a respectable matron. I cherish my husband's memory too dearly to bring shame to his name. I am but a Baron's wife and you are an Archduke. I will summon my maid to sit with us.' She rang the handbell and was relieved to see that he was not annoyed that she maintained the proprieties.

'I may possess a grand title but my duchy is small,' von Heissel said, 'and is at present overrun by a usurper. My family barely escaped with our lives. We were lucky that the baggage train holding the treasury was not stolen by brigands. Until I can raise an army I have settled in Vienna.'

Maressa noted that his treasury had remained intact. From

Angel and Alexander she had heard much of the splendours of Vienna. It sounded like a city where one could live in grandeur and contentment.

At Hazel's arrival, Maressa gestured for her maid to sit by the window. 'You will remain here, Hazel. Archduke Frederick and I will take the air on the terrace. The evening is quite warm.'

They reached the end of the moonlit terrace before von Heissel spoke again. 'Have I offended you, Lady Canning? I should not have spoken as I did.'

'I'm not offended, unless you intended to continue your impassioned speech by a proposition of an unacceptable nature.'

'Many women would not regard being my mistress as dishonourable.'

'Then I am sure that in London you will find many to accommodate you.' She turned away with a swish of her skirts and waving her fan rapidly, she stared out over the terrace wall. A full minute passed and he made no move to come to her. Her nerves stretched taut. Had she overplayed her hand?

Then his hands were upon her bare shoulders and she felt his warm breath against her neck. She held her breath, waiting for him to speak. He did not. His hands dropped from her shoulders as he said, 'I bid you good night, Lady Canning.'

There was the sound of his footsteps across the terrace and then silence as he walked over the grass. Maressa stood rigid with disbelief. She had expected him to plead, even to take her forcefully in his arms to kiss her. He had done nothing. Seething, she turned and watched him stride across the gardens towards the bridge.

She twisted the fan in her hands until it snapped. She had completely misjudged the situation. What if he left for London before Harwood's reception tomorrow evening? Had she just thrown away her chance to fulfil her wildest dreams?

Hazel's special headache potion and soothing massage with the perfumed oils eased Maressa's tension, but it took several drops of poppy juice before she fell asleep that night. Then the nightmares began. She was old and ugly and no one loved her. Henry's ghost jeered at her misfortune, and

569

Thomas stood before her. She crawled to him begging for help, but he remained just out of reach. Deserted by family and friends, she lay shivering in the gutter. Respectable matrons reviled her. Their abusive shouts filled her head. She was back in Newgate chained to the wall, and this time there was no one to protect her from its horrors. Somewhere a lunatic who should have been in Bedlam was screaming. With a start Maressa came awake. She was bathed in sweat, and Hazel was shaking her. It was she who screamed, not the Bedlamite.

'My lady, you were riding the night mare,' Hazel said.

Maressa threw her arms around her maid. 'I was abandoned, reviled! They called me names! Everyone turned against me!'

'It was just a dream.' Hazel sat on the bed and smoothed Maressa's hair. 'You're loved and admired.'

'Von Heissel walked off. He's my last chance, Hazel! I wanted to show Thomas that I could make a grand match, because he laughed at me over the St Aubryn affair. I want to be an Archduchess.'

'You have all day to prepare for the reception tonight.'

'But what if he leaves for London beforehand?'

'He won't. He was truly smitten. Now stop crying, or I'll never be able to repair the damage to your face.'

'You will give me a love philtre to put into his wine?'

'He will not need it.'

'I must be certain. Don't fail me, Hazel.'

'If it makes you feel easier, I will prepare one. You are so lovely, no man could resist you.'

'But I'm old, Hazel! Thomasine is about to make me a grandmother. Oh, I can't bear it. A grandmother! It's too awful.' She flung herself down on the bed, working herself into a fury as she thumped the pillows and drummed her heels on the mattress.

Hazel poured several drops of amber liquid from a small phial into some wine for Maressa to drink. The potion was a strong one and she did not like to use it often. But her mistress's rages were becoming wilder. If Maressa was not calmed quickly, she would be ill with one of the fevers brought on by the violence of her anger.

'Drink this, my lady.' Hazel held out the potion. When

Maressa showed no sign of halting her tantrum she spoke sharply. 'Very well, act like a spoilt child. A fit of the mother will not get you an Archduke. It will only ruin your looks even quicker.'

Maressa became still and turned a blotchy face with swollen eyes upon her maid. 'How can you be so cruel, Hazel? After all I have done for you.'

Hazel's knuckles whitened as she held the goblet. What about all I've done for you? Hazel mentally fumed. It's my potions have kept your beauty. My loving hands which have brought you relaxation and eased your pain. As quickly as her rebellion flared, it was doused by the misery in Maressa's eyes. Hazel had spent nearly twenty years in devoted service to her mistress. She would give her life for her, if necessary.

'I've asked the footmen to bring up the bath. Have you decided on what dress you will wear? And your jewels. You must wear your finest diamonds.'

As she spoke Maressa's mouth lost its petulant droop and the life returned to her amber eyes. 'I shall wear the ruby silk gown over a petticoat of cloth of silver. My jewels will be my finest rubies and diamonds. I will show Archduke Frederick that I'm no pauper.'

'Is it wise to display so much wealth?'

'I must prove I'm his equal in wealth, if not in title.'

Maressa took the potion handed to her by Hazel, her eyes calculating as she contemplated von Heissel's seduction. He was a mature and cultured man. He was vulnerable after the death of his wife and susceptible to a beautiful woman's charms.

When Maressa's carriage drew to a halt outside the steps of Lord Harwood's mansion at five o'clock, she was calm and composed. In her pocket was the love-philtre, which she would slip into von Heissel's wine.

Harwood came out on to the steps to greet her and lead her into the Grand Saloon. Archduke Frederick put aside the book he was reading at her entrance, his gaze admiring. Maressa sank into a respectful curtsy. Before she could rise he took her hand and assisted her. That he showed no anger at the way she had rejected his proposal restored Maressa's confidence that she could win him.

In her role of hostess she went to the wine flagon and

571

poured three glasses. She handed one glass to Harwood. Another, into which she had surreptitiously poured the love-philtre, she gave to von Heissel. 'Let us drink to this evening and its success.'

'I would drink first to our beautiful hostess.' Von Heissel spoke with such warmth that Maressa's pulse leapt with expectancy. Perhaps she had not needed the love-philtre. A man did not look at a woman with such devotion unless he was falling in love with her.

Von Heissel stood by Maressa's side as Harwood introduced him to each guest as they arrived. Overhearing the Archduke's compliments to her Harwood's manner grew tense and disapproving. Von Heissel forestalled Harwood from leading Maressa into the music room by offering her his own arm, then he stood attentively behind her as she began to play the harpsichord. Her first song was a lilting ballad, followed by a love-song. Maressa gazed at the Archduke when she sang the poignant and tender words. Applause greeted the end of the song and a demand from several men for another. Von Heissel took Maressa's hand and raised her to her feet.

'Lady Canning must be tired,' he said. 'Perhaps she will play for us again later. But now we have adequate musicians to entertain us, whilst our hostess recovers her breath.'

Harwood was glowering at them and von Heissel dropped his voice to a whisper. 'I must speak with you alone.'

'It is not possible.'

'Meet me in the gardens when the refreshments are served.'

'But I shall be missed! What you ask is most improper.'

'Do not deny me, Lady Maressa.' His dark stare was ardent. 'I cannot remain here after tomorrow.'

Her heart missed a beat. 'You would leave so soon?'

'Harwood has told me that he wishes to marry you. It would be impossible for me to stay.'

'But I've no wish to wed Lord Harwood,' she blurted out.

'Then we must talk. Meet me in the gardens – by the sundial.'

He escorted her to a seat beside Lord Harwood as the musicians struck up their first tune. The music blurred, its sweet harmony lost on Maressa. All she could hear was the rapid drumming of her heart. As the guests began to file into the dining saloon for refreshments, Maressa waited until she saw that Harwood was occupied with Squire Bracegirdle in a discussion about cattle-stealing in the area. Quickly she stepped through an open casement widow into the gardens. The sundial was in the walled garden and secluded from the house.

'Lady Maressa, you came.' Archduke Frederick was awaiting her. 'I feared I had displeased you yesterday and that you would refuse my request.'

'I wonder if I'm wise to come. The sundial is far from the house. I would not have you think . . .'

'Your virtue is beyond question. I've been in torment all day.' Her hands were taken in an impassioned clasp. 'My country is being governed by a usurper and it could be years before I regain my throne. My greatest chance of success is a marriage to a strong power. It would be political suicide for me to marry where my heart bids.'

Disappointment speared her so acutely that Maressa turned away. She put a hand to her mouth, not trusting herself to speak.

'My emissaries are already at the Courts of Europe, working secretly towards such a marriage,' he went on ruthlessly. 'My visit to England was to win King Charles's support, but my advisers have informed me that he is reluctant to openly support my claim. He feels his own Restoration is too recent. I will not humble myself before his Court. Instead I return to Vienna. There I will establish a rival Court to the Usurper, but each move must be planned with care.'

'I understand little of politics, Your Highness,' Maressa managed to force out through her disappointment.

'I have put this badly.' He took her elbow and turned her to face him. 'It was not of politics I wished to speak, but to ask you to be my wife. Yet there is a condition. Our marriage must remain secret for a time. I cannot alienate any foreign power. They must believe I am still free to wed. I want you to come away with me tomorrow. There is a chaplain outside Winchester who has agreed to marry us.'

'I'm overwhelmed. This is so unexpected.' A twinge of suspicion made her ask, 'But can we be legally wed so soon?'

'Wealth can procure many things. The marriage will be legal. I love you, Maressa.' He drew her close. 'I will not

573

lose you. My kingdom is a small one, but I would lay it at your feet. In a year, perhaps two, you will be sharing my throne. You will be the Archduchess, the most revered, beautiful and accomplished consort in all Europe.'

Maressa put a hand to her temple. He spoke with such force and command she could not help but be swayed. She could not believe her good fortune. A nagging doubt rose up to blight her happiness. Could she trust him? And what did she really know of him? She didn't like the speed with which events were happening.

Von Heissel gripped her shoulders, his anguished face silvered by the moonlight. 'Tell me you're not a Catholic. I could never marry a Catholic for then I'd never be accepted as ruler of my duchy.'

'I am not a Catholic,' Maressa answered.

His hold on her arms gentled and he searched her face as though he sensed her doubts. 'Do you doubt that I love you? I know it has happened so fast. If I did not have to leave England it would be different. I could woo you properly and prove my devotion.'

His low persuasive voice cut through her doubts. These were the words she craved to hear. Why should she hesitate because the marriage was to be a secret for a few months? She did not want a grand wedding, anyway. Too many people knew her true identity. Better to marry him quickly before he learned that Lady Maressa Canning was the notorious Lady Maressa Mortimer.

She shrugged aside her doubts. His story of exile was not unique, and European politics were complex. Protestants were constantly at war with their Catholic neighbours, small kingdoms were often overrun. And yet caution urged her to go carefully. This man was about to turn her world upside down, and she knew nothing about him.

'I must have your answer,' he said impatiently. 'There are plans to be made before we leave tomorrow.'

It was a command not a request delivered with the full force of his royalty. When she looked into his eyes she saw the adoration she desired. It was madness to accept. But life was a gamble. Even if he never gained his kingdom, she would still be an Archduchess.

'Does this secrecy also include my family?' she asked.

'I fear so, since they are not here for you to consult. I can trust no messenger with such news. Later you can write to them from Vienna.'

Her hesitation was momentary. In that instant, the Angel blood – the blood of gamblers and opportunists – rose to stifle caution. 'My maid will, of course, accompany us,' she insisted.

'Does that mean you accept?'

'Yes.'

He drew her close and she lifted her face for him to kiss. The touch of his mouth was tender upon hers, his kiss all she expected from a cultured nobleman, with none of the base urgency of common passion.

'My carriage will be at the end of Westcombe Drive an hour before dawn. I have hired two outriders for our journey, so you need not fear that a highwayman will steal your jewels. We must return to the guests now.' He kissed her and murmured, 'Until an hour before dawn tomorrow, my love.'

Hazel hid her misgivings as she packed her mistress's clothes and jewels. She had unsuccessfully tried to reason with Maressa. Seeing the light of excitement which had long been absent from her mistress's eyes, Hazel hoped that her doubts about the Archduke were wrong. There was something about his manner she did not trust. And what did they know of him . . . ?

Maressa was too excited to sleep. Long before the first cock crowed, two bleary-eyed footmen were carrying her trunks to the end of the drive. She told them that she was journeying to Bath to take the waters in the company of Archduke Frederick. Against von Heissel's instructions she had left a message for Thomas, telling him of her intended marriage. It was unlikely that he would visit Westcombe until Thomasine had returned from her honeymoon.

Her eyes narrowed as she remembered Thomas's laughter at St Aubryn's betrayal. She had revelled in informing Thomas that she was to be an Archduchess. Thomas had derided her too often for her coldness towards men. It added to her triumph that he would now have to admit that her beauty remained unrivalled, and that she had risen to emi-nence by her wit and charm. To have got the better of

Thomas Angel was as satisfying as having won von Heissel as her husband.

The church in which Maressa spoke her vows was bleak and delapidated. It had suffered under the Protectorate, and the stained-glass windows were smashed. One had been replaced with plain glass, the others were boarded up against the weather. The altar held a single silver cross, which leaned tipsily to one side. The rood screen had been smashed, its splintered framework protruding from each wall. The colourful murals depicting scenes from the Bible had been white-washed over as idolatrous images. The air still smelt of horse excrement where the church had been used as a stable by the local Puritan militia.

Maressa lifted the hem of her travelling dress off the filthy floor. Overhead, starlings and martins squabbled as they nested in the rafters, flying in and out through a large hole in the roof. Unperturbed by the presence of the wedding party, a mouse perched on the lectern, cleaning itself. Maressa was stunned. She had not expected a grand wedding, but this was degrading.

'My darling, I apologise for the sorry state of the church.' Von Heissel voiced his dismay.

'We cannot be married in here,' Maressa groaned.

'It's the only way to save your reputation,' he insisted. 'It would not be right for us to spend two nights on the road to Dover unwed. Surely, it's the ceremony which is important – not the place. I promise I shall make all this up to you. Once I rule in my country, there will be a second grand ceremony, where we will repeat our vows before the cathedral in the Royal Square before my palace.'

Her hand was taken and she was drawn towards the altar. A chill was settling over her heart, and only the ardour in the Archduke's eyes stopped her from fleeing. The priest wore a grubby surplice, stained with wine from the sacrament. His thick grey hair sprouted out around his head like a gorse bush, and every word he spoke was accompanied by a spray of spittle. Maressa's gaze was drawn to the crooked cross whilst von Heissel repeated his vows. Her foreboding grew and she began to feel sick. She felt trapped. How could she have agreed to this madness?

She was aware of an uncomfortable silence in the church.

The priest cleared his throat. Von Heissel was staring at her, waiting for her to say her vows. Panic filled her. Her mouth opened and no words came. She couldn't do it! She couldn't marry in a hovel which passed as a church. Then her hand was squeezed by von Heissel, his gaze so adoring that her confidence returned. Within her grasp was marriage to one of the royal houses of Europe. She could not throw that away. In a firm voice she spoke her vows. There was a touch of warm gold as a ring was slipped on to her finger and a chaste kiss brushed her lips before von Heissel handed a pouch of coins to the priest.

In a daze Maressa was led outside. After the darkness of the church, her eyes stabbed against the sun's brightness. Her husband's arm was possessive about her waist as he propelled her towards the carriage. Even the sunshine could not dispel that feeling of foreboding. She should be elated not fearful. She was the Archduchess Maressa von Heissel of – With shock she realised that she did not even know the name of her husband's country. She opened her mouth to form the question, and found von Heissel ordering Hazel to travel on top with the coachman.

'A husband and wife should be alone,' he said, as Maressa settled herself on the velvet upholstered seat.

She was surprised when he pulled the leather blinds into place over each door and window. She submitted passively to his kiss, but was shocked when he began to pull at her bodice. He laughed aside her protests. His eyes were glazed. Adoration was replaced by naked, urgent lust.

'Have you never had it in a moving carriage before? A delightful experience, my dear.'

To her disgust, he freed her breasts, then with a skill clearly achieved by long practice, he dragged her skirts to her hips and threw his weight forward so that she was trapped beneath him on the seat. The courtly sophistication had vanished. He took her in a manner more debased and insatiable than Henry or Thomas had ever subjected her to. Maressa submitted with gritted teeth. Tears of misery scalded behind tightly shut eyes as she endured his violation. The carriage swayed towards Dover, carrying her forward into another nightmare marriage.

* * *

577

The jovial atmosphere of the Carver household on this late summer's evening was typical. Angel was one of the most popular hostesses in London. Earlier, a dozen players had filled the room. They had all left, and only Popinjay had stayed to enjoy a quieter moment of conversation. Popinjay had prospered with the Restoration, and was now a wealthy merchant, with two ships to his name and several warehouses in various cities. He was talking of his planned voyage to Venice, to expand his furrier's business and import silks and brocades from the East. Hapless, who had left Angel's employ to join the King's Company, sat at Popinjay's feet. Hapless had become an accomplished actor and he was dissatisfied that only two patents had been granted for new theatres. It meant that competition was fierce for the leading roles. Any actor not with the King's or the Duke's players was destined to stroll the highways, scraping what living they could in country fairs.

Angel watched Nathan lounging on the window-seat, a long clay pipe in his hand. Silver had begun to thread through his dark blond hair. He spent hours each day in his hospital, writing up his notes on the diseases and cures he studied. He was one of the most respected physicians in England.

As for her own work, her plays grew in popularity and she always took care to create special parts for any actresses favoured by His Majesty.

There was a spate of barking from Bella and the other household dogs, and a loud knock was heard at the outer door.

Angel looked at her husband. 'I hope it's not for you, Nathan. You were up at four this morning, tending a small-pox patient.'

'Popinjay will keep you company if I must go out,' Nathan said with an affectionate smile.

'It's not the same,' Angel responded, knowing that Popinjay would take no offence.

Nathan laughed. 'I'm glad to hear it!'

A commanding voice carried to them from the hallway and, before the maid could announce their visitor, the door opened. A tall figure in a wide-brimmed hat ducked his head to avoid knocking it on the low lintel. Dark hair fell forward, curtaining his face and a plain black cloak covered him to the floor. As the man straightened the cloak fell away and there was the glint of a diamond garter star against a gold satin jacket. Everyone present sprang to their feet and Angel sank into a deep curtsy.

'Your Majesty, this is a great honour for our home,' she said as the King raised her to her feet.

Charles smiled, but he looked tired and the lines of melancholy were deep about his eyes. 'It is an informal visit. I was returning to Whitehall and had a mind for congenial conversation.'

It was the second time the King had visited them late in the evening, and unannounced. Angel guessed that Barbara Palmer was dictating terms to the King again. His favourite was fast becoming a virago, throwing tantrums when an actress was taken to the King for a night of pleasure. If rumour was true, Barbara Palmer was carrying the King's child, but everyone knew that he was not the only lover to visit her chambers. Whilst the King enjoyed the earthy pleasures of the actresses, his favourite took coachmen and grooms into her bed. Angel picked up a Spanish guitar and handed it to Popinjay.

'Would you like me to sing for you, Sire? I fear my voice is not as true as Maressa's.'

The King sat and Angel winked at the merchant as he struck up the notes of a bawdy ditty. She sang two songs and the King slowly relaxed and enjoyed the lively wit and banter of their conversation. Later he asked to see Nathan's laboratory and spent a further hour with him, discussing experiments. When they returned to the parlour, the King drew Popinjay to one side.

'It is fortuitous that you are here, Mr Sparrow, for I've not forgotten your services to my father. Have you ships bound for Holland?'

Angel contained her surprise. Instead of giving up his spying, Popinjay had actually extended it. His ships and warehouses and his contacts in every capital in Europe were the perfect cover for a network of spies. Realising that the King would prefer to be alone with Popinjay, she gestured for Nathan and Hapless to follow her from the room.

After the King had left the house, Popinjay announced that he was taking ship to Holland and might be out of

579

England for some time. Hapless was just helping Popinjay on with his cloak, when there was another rap on the outer door. Angel sighed. Nathan was looking weary and would have retired an hour ago had it not been for the King's visit. To their astonishment, Thomas Angel burst into the room. His scarlet cloak was splattered with mud and his long hair was dishevelled.

'Your sister's done it this time,' he said without preamble. 'She's got herself married to one of the most notorious rakehells ever come to England from Europe. The fool fell for his grand title – Archduke von Heissel. The man's a blackguard. He's married her for her money, hoping to keep the wedding a secret. No doubt he intended to squander her fortune then ditch her penniless on the streets. I've stopped that game. I've sent word to every Court in Europe of the marriage.'

'Calm yourself, Tom. It can't be that bad. Maressa knows how to look after herself.' Angel was surprised to see Thomas so upset. 'Maressa was obsessed with the idea of marrying a nobleman. She must be delighted to be an Archduchess. Your conduct over the St Aubryn affair did not help her. For a while I feared for her sanity. One minute she was raging and pacing the floor until she ran up a fever, then she would collapse and spend days just staring blankly at the wall. Doesn't she deserve a little happiness with her Archduke?'

'Archrogue more like!' Thomas ground out savagely. 'He's already transferred all the money from the sale of the London house out of the country. Didn't she learn anything from me? She's so vain all she could see was his damn title.'

'Was that so bad, Tom? Perhaps von Heissel can give her the lifestyle she craves.'

'I doubt that. At the rate he spends, her money won't last the year.' Thomas went to the table and poured himself a large brandy. 'Von Heissel's last wife died in mysterious circumstances. There was talk of poisoning, though it was hushed up and explained as childbed fever. She was a wealthy heiress. I doubt he informed Maressa that his duchy is forever lost to him. The family are unfit to rule. Franz Johann, von Heissel's father, was a drunkard and a sodomite. He murdered his wife when he caught her in bed with a footman.

580

Frederick's uncle, Wilhelm, was elected to the throne, and the people adore him.'

'Poor Maressa,' Angel said sadly. 'This will break her heart.'

'Don't worry, coz. Maressa hasn't got a heart to break.'

Angel glared at Thomas, but the withering comment she was about to deliver was never uttered. Deep lines of remorse were etched in his face, and there was a vulnerability about him which she had never seen before. Did he still love Maressa? The tragedy was she believed Maressa did love Thomas. Or loved him as much as she could love anyone other than herself.

Chapter Twenty-Three

Four years of disillusioned marriage had hardened Maressa. She was an Archduchess without a country. Frederick took her all over Europe and one capital was beginning to look very like another. Frederick had been furious when news of their marriage had reached Europe. Now their money was almost gone. At least Frederick had not pawned her jewels, though Maressa suspected that he often used them as collateral against loans, which was why they kept moving from country to country, to escape creditors.

There had been many shocks to overcome in her marriage, not least that Frederick had known all along that she was Maressa Mortimer. Frederick had married her for her money, and because she was beautiful enough to attract wealthy admirers. These he fleeced in the gambling dens they frequented. Her life was little different from the years with Thomas. All her husbands had been the same type of man. Too late, she realised that only Thomas had truly cared for her, and she had killed his love by banishing him from her bed.

Wherever Frederick went he was treated as royalty. But pandering to the sycophants who surrounded her husband bored Maressa. She hated her life. They had arrived in Holland a month ago, in mid-September. Frederick was already becoming restless. Red crosses had begun to appear on the doors of several houses in the port and in the last week he had begun to speak of taking ship to the Americas and starting a new life there in one of the colonies. Horrified at the prospect, Maressa argued with him. His mood had turned ugly and he'd beaten her into silence. What frightened her most was that he enjoyed hitting her. He did it often, and with little provocation.

To dull her misery Maressa had begun to drink heavily. Within weeks of their wedding Frederick was unfaithful to her, and a stream of mistresses had followed their progress across Europe. Without Hazel, she did not know how she could have endured her life. Her title of Archduchess was nothing but a sham, and all her grand dreams had been crushed like eggshells. Yet she was too proud to return to England and admit her mistake. She would not give Thomas the satisfaction of laughing at her again.

That night Maressa refused to accompany her husband to a gambling house, and retired early. The vast quantity of wine she had drunk to forget her unhappiness made her fall into a heavy sleep. In the middle of the night strange noises penetrated her befuddled mind. She heard Frederick talking. Then the bed moved and she groaned as his hand sought her breasts. With a murmur of discontent she pushed it away, her eyes too heavy to open.

'So beautiful and always so cold,' Frederick whispered in a slurred, excited voice. 'But not tonight. Not tonight.'

Maressa was too drunk to protest as her nightrail was pulled from her body. She hoped he would get it over with quickly. But tonight his lovemaking was different. The light caresses were gentle, seductive as silk, making her body relax then tingle and glow, until she was floating in a half-world governed by a sensuality she had only glimpsed with Thomas. The wine made it impossible to rouse herself to full wakefulness and it was easier to succumb to the pleasure of her responding body. A sigh was drawn from her, and her body moved sensuously as skilled hands played over her stomach and thighs.

Feelings built within her that were so powerful she cried out. She did not try to analyse Frederick's new tenderness, and was unwilling to break the spell by opening her eyes. The wine had weighted her eyelids and it was easier to keep them closed. The disembodied caresses fulfilled her illusions of her body being worshipped for its perfection. The feeling grew, the softness of his hair tantalised her as he moved to kiss her between her thighs. She began to writhe in growing pleasure. Passion awakened dormant senses. When his kisses seemed to be upon her breasts and her womanhood at the same time, the sensation was so exquisite that she did not

584

question the absurdity of such a notion. Soft hands and warm lips skimmed over her. Even the smell of Frederick was more exciting than usual.

Maressa drifted in the soporific world of sensuality, her eyes tightly closed against the image of her husband. She did not want her pleasure ruined by seeing him straining over her. Time and time again the wondrous joy exploded through her body. Time and time again she reached a fever pitch of yearning and then found release which left her panting and gasping. Her voice was hoarse from her moans, until gradually the wine-induced mist receded, and she became aware of other movements within the bed, other voices, other sighs of pleasure.

The wine distorted her vision. She rolled over and in the light of a candle there seemed to be three figures on her husband's side of the bed.

'Frederick!' she murmured drowsily. 'Douse the candle.' The three figures disentangled. On each side of her husband sat a courtesan.

'My God, Frederick!' Maressa gasped, the wine still clouding her mind. 'What debauchery is this?'

The three figures laughed and then they were all reaching towards her. Her screams were stopped by kisses. Those hands which had earlier brought her such joy were remorseless in their quest to rekindle her passion, and her winesodden brain betrayed her. She had no willpower to resist the desire which enflamed her body. Every concept of her morality was disgarded, laid waste by the force of her passion. A breast and hard nipple moved tantalisingly above her lips. She reached up, succumbing to the need to take it into her mouth. She was no longer the goddess being venerated, but the willing supplicant, tasting the forbidden pleasure of ardent female love.

Daylight stabbed through Maressa's eyelashes, and her head throbbed as consciousness returned. The air was stale with sweat and the covers wrapped tightly around her body were heavy. She opened her eyes, and immediately shut them again. It was not the covers which were wrapped around her but two female forms. Frederick lay sprawled and snoring across the bare legs of one of the courtesans.

Nausea rose to her throat. It had not been some demonic nightmare induced by the wine. It had been reality, the final degradation. Since childhood she had craved respectability. No longer could she deceive herself. The Angel blood which she had spent a lifetime suppressing had triumphed at last. The only sexual pleasure she had ever experienced had been given to her by women. Horror sent fingers of fever clutching at Maressa's skull, and she began to scream, unable to stop.

Hazel ran into her mistress's bedchamber and froze in the doorway. Two naked women and von Heissel lay entwined. Maressa, also naked, was sitting upright in bed, her knees drawn up to her chest. Her blonde hair was in wild disarray, her eyes wide and staring, as she rocked backwards and forward. Most frightening of all was the gaping mouth from which now silent, but soul-wrenching screams were emerging.

The maid was galvanised into action. She took up Maressa's robe and wrapped it around her mistress's body. It was easy to guess what had happened, and Hazel felt a stab of jealousy. She had known how well Maressa's body could respond to a woman's gentle hand. The massages she performed each week were proof of that. But Hazel had never overstepped her role of servant. And despite her own cravings for a caress to be returned, she had known that Maressa, who believed herself so morally pure, could never accept her true sexuality.

Her subservience deserted the maid and she ran round to the far side of the bed and shook the man awake.

'What the devil—' he snapped, wincing as he held a shaking hand to his head.

Hazel had no sympathy. 'You stupid fool!' she raged. 'Look what you've done. You've destroyed her.'

'What are you on about, wench?' Von Heissel pushed Hazel aside and swung his legs from the bed with a groan.

'You drunken sot,' Hazel continued to rage. 'Get these strumpets out of here!'

She slapped the women's bodies in her anger and they woke with a scream. The red-haired one was the first to notice Maressa, and she scrambled back in fear.

'Mother of God!' She crossed herself at the sight of the deranged woman.

586

Hazel slapped her face. 'You filthy slut. You defiled her. You destroyed all that was good in her. Get out! Get out, all of you!'

She rounded on von Heissel who was staring at his wife, his lips quivering with terror. 'The woman is mad. Stark mad.'

'What did you expect? You debauched whoreson!' Hazel shouted.

He turned on Hazel and struck her so hard that she was knocked several paces across the floor and lay stunned. The two women had scrambled from the bed to hunt for their discarded clothes, while Maressa continued her pitiful rocking, her mouth opening and shutting in soundless torment.

'For God's sake do something for her,' von Heissel snarled. 'Give her a potion to make her sleep or something.'

Hazel scrambled to her feet and hurried to her mistress. She gathered her into her arms, cradling her as she would a child. Maressa struck the maid's hands away, her mouth forming the silent words, 'No, no, no!' This was a trauma beyond Hazel's help. She had to get a physician to tend her mistress. The two women left the bedchamber and von Heissel disappeared into his dressing-chamber and Hazel heard him shouting for his valet. She ran out into the street to the nearest physician's house, but there was no answer. After a while, a neighbour stuck a head out of her upstairs window.

'He's gone,' she shouted. 'As have most of his kind. They're as scared of the plague as the rest of us.'

'Plague!' Hazel queried. 'There's only a small outbreak in the port.'

'Depends what area you live in. In the poorer quarter there's scarce a door without a red cross on it. I'm leaving today, and if you're wise you'll do the same.'

Hazel backed away from the house. She'd not realised the plague was spreading so fast. She had to get Maressa away. If she drugged her mistress, von Heissel could get her into the carriage and away from the port to safety.

When she returned to the house, she found the front-door open and no sign of any servants. Fearful, she ran upstairs, but Maressa had not moved from her position on the bed. For once, Hazel's first concern was not for her mistress.

The room was disordered. Clothes were scattered over the bedchamber. Hazel ran to the coffer where Maressa kept her jewel casket. The casket had gone. She whirled to stare at the toilette table. It was empty of jewels and everything of value. Panic seizing her, she ran to von Heissel's dressing-room. His things were gone. He'd abandoned Maressa, taken everything of value and left them penniless.

'Bastard!' Hazel raged. Her mind tumbled over a confusion of thoughts. Once it was known that von Heissel had fled, the creditors would flock here like vultures picking the carcass clean. She ran to her own room to snatch up her bag of herbs. She had to get Maressa dressed and in a fit state to travel.

An hour later Maressa was propped on a chair beside the bed. Hazel had just returned from selling three of her mistress's expensive gowns for a fraction of their original cost, but at least she had enough money to take a ship back to England.

Hooking Maressa's arm over her shoulder, she managed to get her down the stairs and into the hired carriage. The coachman backed away at their approach.

'She's sick. I can't have her in my coach.'

'It's not the plague, if that's what you think.'

'I've heard that before. I'm not risking my life. Find another coach.'

'She's not sick of the plague. Look in her eyes, man. The poor creature has lost her wits. She's been abandoned by her husband. Just take me to the harbour. Here's double the fare.' Hazel held out several coins to tempt him. 'She's English, and needs to be with her family to recover.'

The coachman scratched his scalp and eyed Maressa narrowly. Finally, he nodded.

At the harbour Hazel had to pay the coachman more money so that Maressa could remain in the coach whilst she searched for a vessel to take them to England. Fear of the plague made the captains wave her away. When she returned to the coach she found it had gone. Maressa was sitting woefully on her coffer, rocking backwards and forwards. Several sailors were mocking her. The seamen had begun to circle Maressa and Hazel sensed menace in their manner. They wanted better sport. They began to tweak at her cloak with their dirty fingers. When one squeezed her breast, Maressa leapt to her feet and fled along the quay. Hazel took after her, fearing that her mistress might throw herself into the river and drown. Hazel was gaining on Maressa, but she could see the edge of the quay dangerously close.

'Stop her! For the love of God, stop her!' she screamed out in English.

A tall man standing at the rail of a ship began to run down the gangway, pushing aside a seaman who got in his way. He stood in Maressa's path, and, catching hold of her shoulders, pulled her to a halt. Hazel could see Maressa's open mouth issuing its silent screams. The man struck Maressa twice across the face, and she slumped like a puppet whose strings had been cut. To her astonishment she recognised Angel Carver's friend, John Sparrow.

'Mr Sparrow, what good fortune to find you here! We're in desperate need of a passage to England.'

'I could not believe my eyes when I recognised this demented creature as Maressa Angel. What has occurred to make her so distraught?'

'Betrayal, sir. Bitter betrayal and abandonment by her husband.' Hazel was sobbing from shock. 'Please, we must return to England. Is that your vessel? Will you give us passage?'

'Come aboard and tell me everything,' Popinjay said, leading the way towards his ship, *The Sea Snake*.

It was the season for storms and it was December before *The Sea Snake* finally docked in London. Throughout the voyage Maressa had been heavily sedated. As they stepped on to the quay customs men surrounded them.

'Where have you sailed from?'

'Holland,' Popinjay answered.

'And your cargo?'

'Furs.'

'They cannot be unloaded. There's plague in Holland. A ship docked some weeks ago with silks. The goods were taken to a warehouse in Long Acre, and the plague has broken out there. You carry plague goods. I cannot permit them to be unloaded.'

'I carry no plague goods,' Popinjay argued. 'Neither are

589

any of my crew or passengers infected with the distemper. Also I have news to be delivered to the Admiralty concerning the Dutch Fleet.'

'You may go about your business,' the officer said primly. 'But the ship will be moored in the Channel and your seamen examined. Two sailors on a ship from Holland yesterday fell dead of the plague before they docked.'

Listening to the officer, Hazel felt a stab of fear. Suddenly, there was a scream, and Hazel saw Maressa surrounded by young men. They had emerged from one of the quayside taverns, and their swaying figures showed their drunken state. One of them lurched at Maressa, flicking back the hood of her cloak.

'She's a beauty. How much for a good time, wench?'

Another staggered to take Maressa in his arms. 'I saw her first. You can take your turn.'

Maressa's eyes rolled in terror. Before Hazel could call out for help, Maressa had taken to her heels in a panic-stricken run towards the busy streets.

Hazel shouted to Popinjay, then took off after her mistress. But as she ran, her foot caught in a rope, tripping her. By the time she scrambled to her knees, Maressa had disappeared from sight. They searched for an hour, calling her name. It did not seem possible that she could have disappeared without trace, yet no one remembered seeing her, and eventually they had to give up their search when darkness fell.

Chapter Twenty-Four

London was a city of tears. By May 1665, Death was riding triumphant through the streets, His great scythe overhanging the gabled houses. Since the first cases last December, the plague had begun its inexorable spread. At first the colder weather stemmed its flow, but in February red crosses with the words 'God Have Mercy on Us' had appeared on many doors. Behind shuttered windows mourners wailed, while the dying, mad from the torment of the plague boils, screamed or howled like animals in their agony. Every house where there was infection had a watchman posted outside to prevent the inhabitants leaving and spreading the distemper.

Funeral processions were an hourly occurrence, the tolling parish bells rarely silent. The number of deaths rose steadily, and panic stalked the streets, fear stark upon haggard faces. By April, people were beginning to leave the city in droves. They queued for hours outside the Mayor's office for Certificates of Health.

Nathan Carver noticed the increased hysteria and the red crosses with a heavy heart. He had been summoned to address the College of Physicians as to the best means of halting the outbreak. As he walked the streets, he grew angry at the many signs showing Mother Shipton or Merlin's head. They proclaimed the business of the soothsayers and astrologers, whose trade was prospering as citizens sought any means to save their families.

'Poor misguided fools!' Nathan said beneath his breath, as he saw yet another servant with an amulet pinned to his breast. This one was a piece of paper with the word 'abracadabra' written in the shape of a pyramid. Others parted with their money for the magical sliver of a unicorn's horn, which in reality was nothing more than the shavings of a ram's horn. The ignorance and superstition of the people astounded Nathan. Fear made them clutch at hope.

Behind him strode a servant, distributing Nathan's printed pamphlet on the precautions to take against the disease. He despised the apothecaries who stole his advice, reprinting it and adding their own remedies which they sold, charging a shilling for the pamphlet. He had brought three such apothecaries before the Justices already, and each had spent a morning in the pillory.

He passed a church which was so overcrowded that the congregation spilled into the churchyard, kneeling in prayer, beseeching God's intervention to end the plague. Over the sound of their prayers carried the shouts of fanatical preachers.

'Forty days and London shall be destroyed. Forty nights of suffering for the children of Gomorrah!'

One Rantist preacher naked but for his drawers punched the air with his fist as he cried out, 'Repent, ye sinners! Have mercy, oh great and vengeful God.'

Nathan's progress through the streets was slow. The roads were jammed with baggage carts piled with possessions, often children and the elderly perched high on the top. Already there was a shortage of horses. People, bent almost double by the weight of their bundles on their back, shuffled through the crowds. Crying children were dragged along as they held their mother's skirts. Tempers were short and fights frequent. Those fleeing were jeered at by those who had no choice but to stay. Drunken seamen staggered in the streets, cursing that their ships were moored in mid-Channel. They had to shift for themselves and the seamen were not the only unemployed. More trades ground to a halt with each passing day. The looms of the ribbon-weavers and the hammers of the pewterers and coopers were stilled. The workshops of carpenters, masons and furniture-makers fell silent. Skilled workers were laid off, 'prentices and servants turned out of their masters' houses. Reduced to vagabonds overnight, they broke into deserted houses for shelter, and by day they begged in the streets.

Nathan had never felt so helpless. The hospital in the grounds of his house took no plague cases, but when the plague deaths had begun to rise in March he had rented a large barn outside the city walls and converted it into a pest house. Even its grounds were filled with tents housing those smitten with the distemper, but he took in only those with the plague buboes which appeared in the neck, arm or groin. They at least had a chance for survival. The less fortunate were the ones who were suddenly struck by the plague tokens – the black gangrenous spots of mortified flesh the size of a silver penny and hard as horn. None so afflicted survived.

A half hour later he stood before the most eminent physicians in London. He was shocked to discover that a great number of them had already fled the capital.

'Learned gentlemen, our efforts to rid the city of the pestilence have failed. We must take more stringent measures.' He saw that several of the younger physicians were taking notes. 'Gentlemen, I am not here to debate whether the distemper is spread by poisons in the air, transmitted by the sweat or the breath of the afflicted, or carried by creatures too small for the human eye. In my years abroad little success was achieved by enclosing whole families within a house once the first member is smitten. The afflicted must be quarantined, but let them be attended by a nurse whilst the rest of the family are examined. Those free of the tokens may be allowed to take up a separate residence. There are enough houses emptied by the people fleeing. Too often, the hale are shut in with the infected and entire families frequently perish.'

There was an outbreak of argument. Nathan allowed it to quieten before he continued, 'I believe that the distemper is spread by fleas. Every corpse examined had flea bites upon it. Every cat and dog within the city must be slaughtered and ratsbane put down to control the vermin. Extra ratcatchers should be employed to ensure that the carcasses are burned.'

One old gentleman shook his head. 'The city's resources are stretched to the limit. We already pay for the nurses, watchmen and the searchers who examine every corpse to discover whether it was the plague which killed them.'

'The place is teeming with feral cats scavenging in alleyways,' another man muttered.

'It will be a grisly job, but a necessary one,' Nathan insisted.

'You tell us nothing that will help.' The first man waved his hand in dismissal. 'What of the cures?'

'There is no miracle cure, gentlemen. Those smitten with the black plague tokens are beyond help. As to those with the buboes . . . I can state a case I heard of in Italy. There was a man in Florence driven insane from the pain of the swellings. He broke out of his house and ran naked through the streets. In his dementia he jumped into the River Arno and swam across, and on the far side he continued running through the streets. People were too frightened to go near him. Eventually, he plunged back into the river and swam back and returned to his home. The violence of his exercise had burst the buboes and the poison drained freely from them. He lived. I can only surmise that the cold waters of the river doused his fever to less dangerous levels. In my own treatment I've found that by exercising the muscles around the swellings and applying them with poultices to draw the poison the buboes ripen and burst. All those so treated have survived. If the bubo does not burst the patient dies.'

'Is there nothing which will prevent the infection?' someone demanded.

Nathan shrugged. 'Many swear that Venice treacle is as good a physic as any, if taken every day as a preventative. Also a daily intake of garlic. I myself take it and I have been tending plague victims since January.'

'What else is there?' A younger physician leaned forward in his seat, eager to learn all he could.

'The use of plague-pans. It is a simple device like the warming-pan which heats our beds in winter. The warming-pan can be adapted. All it needs is for the lid to be pierced with holes. Hot coals are placed inside and over these should be burned rosin, pitch and brimstone. These pans should be placed throughout the house. The smoke clears the air of poisons and discourages the fleas.'

'Back on that old tack again, Carver,' one white-bearded physician sneered. 'In my day tobacco smoke was a good remedy, and there was none of this talk of fleas. Good God, man, there's not a week goes by when we aren't bitten by the creatures! Can't be avoided. They thrive in dirty rushes and on household pets. You can see them leaping on most of the 'prentices serving in the shops. So why do we get years when there's no plague? Fleas are God's affliction to the slovenly.'

Again argument broke out and continued for another half hour. Nathan lost his patience and walked out. He had too many sick patients to tend to waste time with physicians too pig-headed to seek enlightenment.

Outside in the street a thin, bald-headed man was wringing his hands in distraction. He approached Nathan. 'Are you a physician, sir?'

'I am.'

'Then you must help me. Four of my children lie sick of the plague in Cripplegate.'

Nathan wavered. It would take him a half hour to get to the house and another three-quarters of an hour to return to the hospital. He had already been away for most of the morning and some of the cases were at a critical stage.

'I regret, sir, I can do nothing. I've patients elsewhere in dire need of attention. Even my pest house is full. Have they plague boils or the black tokens on their breasts?'

'All have the swelling in the groin.'

Nathan took one of his pamphlets from his servant and gave it to the man. 'Read this and follow the instructions,' he said. 'The buboes must burst if your family are to live, but take care that none of the poison enters your own bloodstream. The wounds must be cleansed and left open to drain. Also apply to the Sheriff for a nurse to be allotted to your family. But watch over her. Not all nurses are reliable, many are thieves.'

As Nathan walked away, he pondered the question of the nurses. As the plague spread it was harder to get the women properly vetted. Desperation drove many to the gruesome work, and frequently they died within a day or so of their patients expiring. They were employed from the workforces made destitute by frightened masters whose workshops had closed. The poor wretches preferred to risk catching the plague than face the certain death of starvation on the streets.

Nathan turned off the main street which was crowded with people making for the city gate. In the narrow alleys he was appalled by the number of men and women squatting in doorways, hands outstretched.

'Alms, good sir,' a sallow-faced man begged. 'My family hasn't eaten for three days. I'm a cordwainer skilled for twenty years, but my master closed his workshop. There's no work. How can I live?'

It was not easy to ignore such plight. These people were the responsibility of the parish. Though the city gave some money to support Nathan's hospital and pest house, his own income was steadily drained in keeping it going. He had none to spare.

To arrive at the pest house he had to walk past the rows of tents lining the field around it. He spoke to the more lucid patients and listened to the reports of his helpers and nurses before moving into the converted barn, where the worst cases were lodged. A man lying on a truckle bed was screaming with pain. His wife, who was tending him, had tears coursing down her cheeks. There were patches of sweat on her gown as she bent over her husband, circling his arms and then his legs in the way Nathan had taught her, to assist the plague boil to harden and burst.

She turned her face to him as Nathan paused to watch and nod approval. Her husband was gagged to stem his cries of agony.

'It breaks my heart to put him through this torture, Dr Carver,' she sobbed.

'I know, Mistress Cooper, but there is no other way.' He studied the buboes on the man's neck and under his arm. 'Keep applying the poultices and give him plenty of the herb cordial. It will dull the pain. Continue to move the arm and his neck for another hour. If the bubo has not burst by then I'll lance it. But his pain will be all the more dreadful if I have to resort to such measure.'

He continued along the row of beds, his expression worried as he stared down at a ten-year-old boy. The child's face was red with fever and he shouted in his delirium. So violent had the boy become that he had been tied to his bed to stop him harming himself. His bubo should have burst this morning and it hadn't. The boy's breath was foul. A bad sign. When Nathan lifted the sheet covering the body, he saw the rash of small red spots on his stomach. Very few survived when those spots appeared.

'Nurse!' he ordered. 'Bring me the knife and bowl.'

Nathan took up the knife with its long sharp blade. Bending over the boy, he waited until the nurse had lifted the thin arm, to expose the scarlet swelling in the armpit. It had grown to the size of an apple. The boy was gagged to stifle his scream, then, with a quick slash, Nathan drew the knife across it. The boy's body jerked, his muffled scream still capable of making Nathan's stomach turn cold. Bracing himself to inflict yet more pain, he squeezed the swelling with a specially-designed long-handled tool. The foul-smelling poison gushed out, the stench making both Nathan and the nurse gag.

'Clean up the wound,' Nathan ordered as he stepped back, 'and keep his fever down with tepid compresses.'

Demented cries came from the next room, warning him that another patient, crazed by the agony of his swellings, had broken free of his bonds. Nathan appeared on the scene just as one of his heavy-built helpers laid the man out with a blow to his jaw. As the patient was lifted back on to his bed Nathan saw the bubo in his neck had broken.

After dealing with a dozen more critical cases Nathan listened to his assistant's morning report. Three of his sixty patients had died, including a woman in labour. The baby had been born with the plague tokens and had died within the hour.

It was late that afternoon when Nathan returned to his house on the outskirts of Holborn. Before entering it he went into a small outhouse, where a brazier constantly burned. Throwing more coals and a handful of pungent herbs on to the fire, he stood for several minutes in the smoke. All his servants, helpers and family followed the same procedure when returning from the street and, so far, no one had been afflicted.

Upon entering the parlour, he saw Angel spoon-feeding a small child who looked as if he had been freshly bathed. 'So you have decided on this madcap scheme to start an orphanage?'

'There are so many, Nathan, and some are tiny infants left to wander the streets crying. But I'll only take those who show no sign of the distemper. The house next door is vacant. Widow Grout asked me to look after it whilst she is at her brother's house in Surrey. I'll house the children there to start with and then, when they have been quarantined for a month and remain free of the distemper, I will move them to another house.'

'You miss young Matthew, don't you? Do you regret not going to Wales when Alexander took our son back with him?'

'No. Thérèse will care for Matthew as she does her own. I'd rather he was safe. Also Bella, poor dog. At least she will be spared the general slaughter of pets. We've had too many partings, my love. I know you will never abandon the sick when they most have need of you. There's so much misery and suffering, and I want to do what I can to alleviate it. This orphanage has become important to me.'

Hearing the passion in her voice, he felt the familiar tightness of pride and love swell his heart. 'Age has made you respectable, Angel. But will you have time to write your plays?'

'My plays will support the orphanage. As for being respectable . . . Maressa was always the respectable one, not I.' Her voice was heavy. 'It's been six months, and still no word of her. How could she have run off like that?'

'Maressa's mind was unbalanced. She was capable of anything.'

'It's the not knowing which is so hard,' Angel sighed.

'Then you must have faith,' Nathan said gently. 'Maressa is a survivor.'

The woman kneeling by the river's edge, beating her weekly wash on the stones, would never have been recognised by anyone who had known her a year ago. Her pale gold hair was now completely white and she was thin and gaunt. Her proud figure was stooped with fatigue, her hands reddened and callused from hours of back-breaking work – cleaning, cooking and caring for Rob Hervey and his six children. They called her Mary and she seemed vaguely comfortable answering to that name. She had no other identity. Her past was a blank.

Her memory began upon waking in a straw pallet in an attic in Knightrider Street close to the river. Rob had told her that he found her clinging to a large stone angel in the churchyard of St Mary Magdalen in Old Fish Street, her body burning with a fever. Shrinking away from Rob in terror she had run away. Exhaustion made her collapse within a few yards, and Rob had brought her to his house and ordered his housekeeper to care for her. When she recovered she remembered nothing of her past. Rob insisted they wed. Alone, penniless and afraid, she agreed.

She did not like her husband, he was coarse and squat and unattractive. She liked his children even less. After the marriage Rob dismissed his housekeeper and she had become a slave to the family. She had no friends. Rob guarded her jealously and kept her shut in the house. A maid did all the shopping.

Life had become relentless drudgery. She was up before first light and in bed as soon as darkness fell. Rob did not believe in wasting his hard-earned money on unnecessary extravagances such as candles or rushlights. She did the work required of her and at night lay rigid while her husband fumbled beneath her nightclothes. She straightened now and rubbed her aching back. A jab inside her stomach made her frown. She looked down at her swollen abdomen where the child kicked within. She felt no emotion. There was only work and more work. It had become worse since Rob had shut up his chandler's shop in May, dismissed the maid and moved his family on to a wherry to live. They had sailed up river to escape the plague. A sail rigged over a wooden frame gave them protection against the weather. They moored by marshland, and within days other crafts had joined them and a tented village sprang up in the drier part of the marsh.

She sighed. Vague remembrances of a life of comfort and ease tugged at the corners of her mind. Or were they just dreams . . . like the vision of the demon-angel who haunted her sleep. A golden guardian angel one moment, vengeful, unremitting and unforgiving the next. This morning she had woken in a cold sweat after the dream, a name still echoing through her brain. Thomas . . . Thomas was the angel. Thomas was the devil. And she was . . . But the veil remained firmly in place, blocking memory.

Thomas Angel groaned as he dropped his aching head into his hands. The ledger on his desk with its scrawled lines of figures blurred before his eyes.

"Odsblood but I'm getting too old for this life,' he

muttered to himself. Today was his fiftieth birthday and he was hungover and feeling sorry for himself. His back was aching and there was an itch and a discharge to his genitals which warned that he must undergo another painful treatment for the pox. 'Curse that whore, Sarah!' She was new to Nell's. The trollop was imaginative, his aching back was proof of that, but if she was poxed she'd have to be suspended from work until she was cured.

He reapplied himself to the figures in the ledger. Trade was brisk, despite the plague. A shrewd rumour spread by him that fornication was a sworn remedy against the pestilence meant that men were paying four times the normal rate. He increased the women's cut of the profits and the freeflowing drink throughout the day ensured that the whores forgot their fears of contagion. As a result, Nell's flourished . . . as did the other side of Tom's empire. Empty houses made easy pickings to rob. A bribe to the constables made them look the other way. In the last four months Thomas had accumulated more wealth than in the last eight years.

He sat back in his chair and laughed. He did not fear the plague. Didn't the devil look after his own? That's what his father used to say. His laughter aggravated the stabbing pains behind his eyes and wincing he fell silent. He never used to get hangovers. It must be his age. He snorted in disgust. He still felt the same as he did twenty years ago. Although his hair had turned white and receded slightly from his brow, it remained thick and waved to his shoulders. He carried little spare flesh on his body and from his easy conquests he was obviously still attractive to women. Thomas was content with his life.

Or was he? The hangover was making him more reflective than usual. He had been an Upright Man for so long the excitement had long since paled. His son Richard had been trained and was eager to take over the leadership. But at twenty the lad was too young. The boy's impatience delighted Thomas, but only the most ruthless kept their leadership of the Underworld. Richard had run his first man through when he was fifteen, when challenged by an older bully of a villain. In three or four years Richard would be ready to take over from him.

Yet every man had his weakness. After nearly twenty years of wrestling with his, Thomas wondered if he would ever be free of Maressa's ghost. When he learned that she had disappeared he had ordered his men to scour the city for information, but nothing had come to light. And now with the outbreak of the plague, Thomas presumed that she was dead. No other woman had affected him like Maressa; she was the only woman he could not master . . . but she was the weakness he could not afford. An Upright Man had to stand alone, his emotions encased in steel. A loud knock on the door broke through his reverie.

'Who is it?' he said sharply, in no mood to be disturbed.

'Mortimer.'

Thomas's temper simmered. Sir Julian Mortimer was a leech on the backside of mankind. He was a reminder of Henry Mortimer and of Maressa – of many things that he preferred to forget. Sir Julian Mortimer had inherited all his mother's cunning and his father's debauchery. To clear his own gambling debts, Mortimer brought young noblemen to Nell's where they squandered their fortunes and increased Thomas's wealth. For the moment Thomas tolerated Mortimer, since their arrangement was mutually beneficial, but he did not like the man.

'What is it you want, Mortimer – another loan?' Thomas eyed him stonily.

'More of an investment, cousin-stepfather.'

Thomas felt his stomach churn with dislike. Whenever Mortimer claimed any form of kinship it was always followed by a request for money. Thomas sat back in his chair, waiting for him to continue.

'I need funds to entice old Lord Delgannon into giving me the hand of his daughter Lady Celia in marriage. She's his only child and, though the title will go to his nephew, the estate remains hers. Lady Celia will be worth sixty thousand a year when the old boy dies.'

There was an edge of excitement in Mortimer's tone which told Thomas that he was holding something back. Mortimer was a handsome man and a degenerate. This girl must be special to him.

'Have you met the Lady Celia?' Thomas probed.

'Twice last season. Her father guards her like a hawk.

She's a ravishing creature,' he sighed. 'She's only fifteen and innocent. If it's possible, she's even more lovely than Mama.'

Thomas put his fingers against his lips. Mortimer was smitten with the girl, and from the intonation of his voice her innocence was as important to him as her money. Interesting.

'And what would be the return on my investment?'

'Ten per cent of her income once we are wed.'

'Forty per cent.'

'That's robbery.' Mortimer glared at Thomas down his long arrogant nose. 'Twenty per cent.'

'Thirty.' Thomas picked up his quill and bent over his ledger. 'Close the door when you leave, Mortimer. Let me know when you're leaving London to pay court to the wench.'

'That's just it. Lady Celia will have nothing to do with me. I rashly forced my attentions on her and the stupid virgin was terrified. I was hoping that you could get Thomasine to invite her to Harwood Hall. You could put in a word for me. It's worth twenty thousand a year to you.'

Thomas considered for a moment. The money was a temptation, but it was not the reason he was interested. It was the thought of duping Lord Delgannon. Thomas remembered a score that went back twenty-seven years when Delgannon had stolen a favourite mistress of his. So far Thomas had waited to get his revenge upon Delgannon for taking property Thomas considered his. It was some years since Delgannon was last in London. A seizure shortly after the Restoration had robbed him of health. A plan began to form in his mind. It appealed to his jaded appetite and would offer him the excitement which had been sadly lacking recently. He bit back a wicked laugh. There was no man more protective of his daughter's virtue than a roué.

'I shall see what I can do. But I'll not have Thomasine involved. Delgannon's estate is in Buckinghamshire and I shall pay him a visit. The broken coach axle ruse should work well.'

Throughout the hot summer Angel threw herself into her work at the orphanage. Saving these children when over a thousand people died in each parish every week gave her a sense of purpose which not even her success as a playwright

602

had achieved. Thirty healthy children, ranging from six months to eight years old, lived in the orphanage established in a large house outside the city walls, in a plague-free area. She still used the Widow Grout's house to quarantine new arrivals and another dozen children were housed there now. Those who became infected were admitted to the hospital if the swellings developed, and those with the black plague tokens were nursed in a converted stables until they died. So far, only six of the orphans had died.

Angel had been nursing Susie in Widow Grout's all morning. The two-year-old admitted three days ago had been fretful all morning, and she had just been sick. Putting the child to bed, Angel felt her beginning to burn with fever. There were no plague tokens on her body, and Angel hoped the girl was suffering from some childhood ailment.

The day was hot and the house stuffy. Picking up a wicker shopping basket Angel decided that the household purchases could not be put off any longer. The Mayor had forbidden provisions to be brought into the city, lest the farmers and carriers spread the infection to the surrounding villages. Stalls had been set up, therefore, outside the walls at Whitechapel and Spitalfields. Fortunately, because of the large number of patients needing food within the hospital and pest house, Nathan had fresh meat regularly delivered to the pest house gate, and then it was dispersed by servants to the hospital, orphanage and to their own house. Fresh vegetables were distributed in the same way and a barn had been turned into a warehouse, where grain and malt were stored and servants employed to make adequate bread and beer. A milk cart arrived daily and two dairy-maids made butter and cheese. Any remaining milk was sent to the orphanages for the children to drink. The outlay was gradually draining Nathan and Angel's resources and without funds from the capital's charities the pest house and orphanage could not have supported so many hungry inmates.

When the Queen had learned of Angel's orphanage she sent one thousand pounds for its upkeep. Catherine of Braganza remained barren, and Angel knew she must suffer cruelly at the King's infidelities and the host of bastards he fathered.

Today Angel had to buy spices and a large quantity of soap for the laundresses. Hazel, who had come to work in the orphanage, scoured the fields and open spaces for many of the herbs she needed for her potions and unguents. Even so, there were times when shopping had to be done in the London streets. Precautions were taken to avoid the contagion. The shops which remained open kept a brazier burning, as instructed by Nathan's leaflet. Money was placed into a bowl filled with vinegar and most customers preferred to purchase exact quantities for their coins rather than accept change. Usually a servant bought the shopping, but Angel had needed a fresh supply of paper for her writing and had used the last of her quills. These she always liked to select for herself.

Her purchases made, Angel turned for home. The headache which had been with her on waking was getting worse and her back began to stab with pain from the weight of her basket. The streets were eerie in their near-desertion. Grass grew between the cobbles and wild flowers and dandelions took root along the walls of the houses. There were no wagons in the streets, and only the occasional pedlar. People who ventured abroad did so furtively, never stopping to chatter in groups. The taverns were not short of customers, as people sought forgetfulness in drink. Most houses were shuttered now. Others had their doors swinging open on broken hinges and the glass panes broken. Looting was unavoidable with so many houses left empty, their owners dead from the plague or fled from the city. Those caught plundering were whipped, but it was difficult to keep law and order. Daily, the constables and churchwardens were growing fewer in number and there were no soldiers, for the army had been disbanded before the Restoration. It was impossible to raise the trained bands. Even if the drums were beaten to call them up, the citizens were too frightened to answer the summons.

A window above her was flung open and a naked man scrambled on to the sill and perched there. The watchman on guard by the front door with its large red cross sat down on the step, seeking shade from the hot August sun. There was an upturned ale pitcher on the step beside him and his eyes were beginning to droop. At the man's shout he jerked awake, looking up in horror at the window.

'Damn you! Get back inside!'

The naked man crouched, his eyes rolling wildly. From where she stood, Angel could see a bubo in his neck the size of an orange, taut and swollen with pus. Inside the house a woman was shouting and crying. Then the man jumped. There was a sickening thud and Angel turned her head away from the sight of the grey mess of his brains spilling from his split skull. The watchman swore and ran down the street, calling for a handcart to have the body removed. Death carts were only permitted in the streets after dark now. Funerals were no longer allowed in daylight, and the tolling bells had been silenced.

Nausea rose in Angel's throat and she stumbled. The heat had drained her energy and the sun was making her head ache unbearably. She shifted the weight of her basket and rested a hand on one of the wooden posts set into the cobbles outside a tavern.

A sharp blast on a horn made her look up as a raker turned into the street. He paused some feet away, resting on the handle of his long rake as he took a leather bottle from inside his grimy jerkin. Removing the yellow kerchief tied around his lower face he drank deeply. His hair was wild and matted and, as he scratched at his bushy beard, he crushed a louse between his fingers before continuing with his work, to clear the debris in the streets. Unwilling for her skirts to be dirtied by the mound of rotting vegetables, fouled rushes, broken glass, horse dung and general household rubbish he was gathering up, Angel moved away.

The heat was making it difficult to breathe. Twice, Angel stopped to overcome a wave of dizziness. She had not eaten this morning and her stomach cramped. The thought of food made her feel queasy. At the end of the street she stopped again, her legs aching, and a sharp pain piercing her side. The headache worsened and her vision was blurred. Then her foot caught against an unseen object, and she pitched forward, grazing her cheek against the wall of a house.

'Look where yer bloody goin'!' A face emerged from a bundle of rags in a doorway. 'Can't a poor sod even die in peace?'

Angel stared down at the bloated, red-faced figure of a watercarrier. Like many people in their ignorance and fear he wore a dead toad around his neck to ward off the plague.

His yoke was still around his shoulders but its buckets had spilled into the gutter. His jerkin and shirt were open to the waist and the black tokens were clear on his chest. Angel staggered away and crossed the street to a church. A notice saying 'Pulpit to be sold' was pinned to the door. Obviously the preacher had fled, leaving his flock without the comfort of absolution or prayer. A hand reached out from the open door, and through the crack Angel saw a well-dressed servant dragging herself into the sunlight.

'Pray for me, lady,' the woman begged. 'Repent now. Don't delay like I did. Lord have mercy on me for I die unshriven.'

As the woman collapsed, painfully gasping her last few breaths, Angel walked on. The city smelt of death, putrefaction and fear. Angel's movements became slower, every step sapping her energy. Her bodice stuck to her shoulders and back in the scorching heat. In the short distance she had walked from the church she felt as if she had run for miles. The stench of fear closed in upon her with sickening clarity. It filled her nostrils and mouth, turning her blood sour and her breath rancid. There was a tightness under her arms, and the pain in her back was building . . . her head seemed about to split in two. Suddenly, she bent double, vomiting bile over some cowslips growing in the gutter.

She summoned her willpower to keep upright. Two streets away was her home. Each step was a concentrated effort of will. The sun was sinking behind the high gables as she approached her red-brick house. Caution stopped her entering by the front door. Holding on to the wall, she groped her way to the side entrance. Tears of frustration pricked her eyes as her fingers fumbled with the latch. She had no strength left. The gate opened and she collapsed on to the flagstones of the garden path. The pain in her arm and groin sent scarlet streaks of agony through her mind, and she bit her lip to stop herself screaming out.

Dimly she heard a maidservant shriek, then Nathan was running towards her. She managed to sit up, putting out a hand to stop him. 'No, my love. Stay back. 'Tis the plague.'

Nathan stooped to lift her up into his arms. 'Dear God, could You not have spared her?' His voice shook and his tears splashed down on to his wife's closed lids.

* * *

The old ruses were always the best ones, Thomas reflected, as he sat in Delgannon Manor a week later. Lord Delgannon squinted short-sightedly and did not recognise him. He introduced himself as Baron Thomas D'Angell. To complete his disguise, he affected a slow country drawl, very different from his normal commanding way of speaking. He had fashioned a sling from a lace collar for his left arm, saying that his shoulder had been wrenched from its socket when his carriage overturned.

Thomas leaned heavily on his walking-cane as Delgannon regarded him with open suspicion. 'I hate to impose upon your generosity, your Lordship,' he continued. 'Truth is, the carriage broke its axle and it will take two days to repair.' He winced and with his free hand cradled his ribcage. 'I think I've cracked a couple of ribs. I'd be indebted to you if I could rest an hour or two. Perhaps your housekeeper has a posset which will ease the pain. The ride on the carriage horse here has quite . . .'

'Sit yourself down, Sir Thomas,' Delgannon said, rather ungraciously. 'I won't hear of you travelling further today.'

Thomas smiled. The laws of hospitality rarely failed in such circumstances.

'You've seen no cases of plague?' Delgannon demanded. There was a film of sweat on his forehead and his brown periwig had tilted at a slightly odd angle.

'No cases at all, though the news which last reached me from London spoke of thousands dying each week. A dreadful visitation. I never go to the ungodly city.' Thomas studied Delgannon. The man had changed. Now there was a prim sternness about his mouth. Thomas had heard of seizures that could strip a man of his virility. Often, such men became pious and condemning.

Delgannon nodded, apparently satisfied. 'Are you travelling far?'

'To my cousin's estate in Lancashire. Last month he suffered a hunting accident and broke his back. The poor man will never walk again. His son is also my heir, since I was never blessed with children of my own. Have you children, Delgannon?'

The man's wrinkled face softened. 'A daughter, Celia. A dear child. I cannot bear the thought of her marrying. A young husband is bound to keep her from my side and expose her to the loose morals of the Court.'

'You are fortunate to be so blessed. Have you not considered that an older man might suit her better? A man who does not hang upon the favour of the Court? A man wise enough to understand a father's need to be cherished by his only child?'

'I have considered it, but I can deny Celia nothing. During my last illness I promised I'd not force her to wed any man not of her choosing. I merely ask that his blood must be as noble as our own, with an income to match.'

'As is right and proper,' Thomas agreed.

'I'm tiring you, Sir Thomas. A maid will show you to your room. You're welcome to stay until you're fully recovered. We get little company here.'

Over the evening meal Thomas met Celia, and was astounded by her likeness to Maressa. No wonder Julian was smitten. Thomas's own heart began to beat harder as he contemplated the revenge he would take upon Delgannon and which would also demonstrate his superiority over Sir Julian Mortimer.

Thomas worked to a meticulous plan. Towards Delgannon, he was entertaining and respectful. After the meal, Celia excused herself from the room and Thomas was enjoying his port when Delgannon peered across at him and rapped out, 'Thomas D'Angell? Is it an old name?'

Instantly on the alert, Thomas remained relaxed in his chair. 'The first Baron D'Angell belonged to the Court of King John.'

Delgannon grunted and moved a candelabra, so that the light fell more brightly on Thomas's features. 'No relation to a Thomas Angel of London, are you?'

Thomas's palms broke out into a sweat but he was too practised at deception to show his unease. 'I've no relations in London that I know of. The D'Angells are plain country squires.'

The strains from a Spanish guitar could be heard at that moment and Celia's sweet voice carried to them as she began to sing a ballad in another room.

'The Lady Celia has a beautiful voice.' Thomas changed the subject. 'I fear I've kept you from her company.'

'We will join her.' Delgannon rose shakily to his feet, his

gait unsteady as he moved to the door.

Over the next few days Thomas dispelled any suspicions Delgannon might have about himself, and began to win Celia's confidence. To this end, he used subtle flattery, his manner always circumspect and deferential. She responded with trusting faith. It was clear she doted upon her aging father, and he was aware of her growing interest in himself. He schooled himself to patience. On the fourth day, whilst they were strolling in the gardens, he pressed a kiss upon her hand.

'These last days have been an unexpected pleasure,' he said. 'It was worth a cracked rib or two to find myself in such charming company.'

'You flatter us.' Her violet eyes sparkled, showing him she was not averse to his attentions.

He was astute enough not to force his hand. First he must win her trust.

Three days later everything was in readiness. His coach was hidden in a nearby coppice. The weather was fair and all he needed was to persuade Celia to accompany him on a morning ride.

'But, Sir Thomas, surely your ribs are still too sore for such exercise?'

He laughed. 'I'm not used to so much inactivity. A gentle canter across the hills will do me no harm. I suffered far worse during the Battle of Worcester. I rode for three days with two bullets in my body, one in my leg and another in my side. I must leave in a day or two and should build up my strength. Will you accompany me, Lady Celia? Is that not an old castle ruin on yonder hill? You could tell me of its history while we ride.'

An hour later, a heavily drugged Celia lay with her head in his lap as they sped along the road back to London. As they travelled, Thomas revised his plans. Celia was the innocent party here, and her beauty had moved him. His revenge on Delgannon and Mortimer would be equally rewarding if he married the wench, and that way he would also inherit the Delgannon fortune on the old man's death.

Thomas leaned his head back on the leather upholstery, his grin devilish. His hero had always been his namesake, Wildboar Tom Angel, the most notorious of his ancestors.

Had he not abducted and married an heiress? Any one of several preachers in London would wed Thomas without further questions, he knew enough of their visits to Nell's to defrock them all. But first Celia must be compromised. Once ravaged, she would be so shamed that she would willingly wed him to save her honour.

Thomas could not restrain a deep rumble of laughter. At that moment the carriage lurched sickeningly as it hit a pothole in the road. Thomas was about to yell abuse at the coachman when the carriage tipped at a precarious angle and, to his horror, he heard the alarming crack of splitting wood. This time the carriage wheel had splintered in a real accident.

Clambering from the overturned carriage Thomas pulled Celia to safety and laid her unconscious form on the road. Several yards behind the carriage lay the bloodied figure of the dead coachman. Thomas cursed roundly. Just when everything was going so well.

They were only seven miles from Delgannon Manor, and in another hour Delgannon would be growing concerned at the absence of his daughter. The countryside would be alerted and the horses they had tethered in the coppice discovered. The carriage had passed several farm carts on its rapid journey south. Someone was bound to talk to Delgannon's men. With Celia drugged, they could not get far on carriage horses and Thomas dared not risk stopping at an inn. He had to get back to London, but that was a four-day ride. The drug would keep Celia unconscious for another two hours. They'd have to travel as far as they could, keeping off the main highway as much as possible. But an unconscious woman would soon arouse suspicion. He'd have to risk taking cover in a wood. To keep his control over Celia, he'd ravish her before they continued their journey. By the second day she would be willing to pass herself off as his wife. By then he would have purchased saddles for the horses.

Confident that he would succeed, Thomas unharnessed the horses from the carriage. Then, holding Celia before him on one horse, he tied the reins of the second mount to his own and they set off through the woods. They travelled for two hours, until Celia showed signs of regaining consciousness. Thomas saw a charcoal burner's hut ahead. To his relief it was deserted. Dismounting, he led the horses inside, away from prying eyes, then carried Celia up to the loft of the single-roomed hut. Thomas had never needed to use force on a woman and was reluctant to do so now. Celia was still drowsy as he began to kiss her, murmuring encouraging endearments as he did so. To his surprise, her mouth opened beneath his and there was little innocence in the fervour of her answering kisses. Her response roused his desire to such a pitch that he was incapable of reason. Her legs parted at the slightest pressure from his knee, and when he entered her, he was too inflamed with passion to notice that she was not a virgin. He groaned as his seed was spent within her whilst her hips continued to move until she cried out, reaching her climax.

'Oh, Sam! Sam, my darling, my love. You came back.'

Thomas jerked upright. Her eyes were half-closed and glazed with the last effects of the drug. He sat back on his heels. Her petticoats were pushed to her waist and he stared at the swelling of her stomach. Celia was four months gone with child! His astonishment was so acute that he let out a harsh bark of laughter.

The woman's eyes opened wide. As she recognised him and how she had betrayed herself, she rolled on to her side and burst into tears. Thomas stood up and stared out of the grimy window. He had not expected this setback. It took some moments for his anger to cool.

'Who is Sam?' he demanded coldly. 'Your lover, obviously. I suppose he seduced you, then abandoned you?'

Celia sniffed and sat up, tears streaming down her cheeks. She nodded.

'Who was he?' he rapped out.

'One of the King's Life Guards. I met him whilst visiting my aunt at Greenwich last Easter. Papa had taken a chill and Aunt Joan was fussing over him. I was bored until I met Sam. He said he'd wed me. I only lay with him once, and he told me it was impossible to get pregnant the first time, but I never saw him again. The Court moved to Richmond and then to Oxford.' She burst into fresh weeping. 'And now you've used me. I thought you were kind and might wed me. Papa will kill me when he learns I'm a whore.'

'I need to think this out.' Thomas was still hoping to retrieve something from the wreckage of his plans. From

Celia's response, it was obvious she had made love more than once. He had no intention of wedding her and bringing up someone else's bastard. The sound of her weeping pierced the armour which he thought enclosed his heart. If only she was not so like Maressa.

She sobbed. 'Papa will disown me. I've dishonoured him. He thought me so virtuous. Now I'll be left to starve on the streets.'

'Come to London with me.' Thomas saw a way of salvaging something from this mess. Mortimer knew nothing of her pregnancy. He'd get them married within a week of their arrival in London. Delgannon would accept that his daughter had married a baron and Thomas would get his twenty thousand a year from Mortimer, as agreed. He rubbed his hands. Mortimer would not get the sweet virgin he anticipated, better still – he'd be forced to acknowledge another man's bastard as his own!

'I've a plan to save your reputation. We will talk of it in London.'

'But you will not marry me,' she said forlornly.

'No. But you will be wed, and to a suitable husband.' For an instant, Thomas contemplated abandoning her. He had an uncomfortable feeling in his gut. A sixth sense warned of danger. The girl was trouble. As he looked into the face which was so like Maressa's he felt himself weakening. It angered him. Weakness was not something he could afford. Yet Celia was too like Maressa, the only woman he had ever loved. And she was looking at him with such trust that something noble stirred within him. Surely a man was allowed one weakness in his life? he reasoned grimly.

In a moment free from delirium Angel stared into Nathan's worried face. 'Your work is at the hospital.'

'I've brought you to the pest house. See, your bed is in my study. I'm sleeping on the truckle bed beside you. I'll not leave you, Angel.'

She stared about her, taking in her surroundings. Her voice was weak when she asked, 'The children? Are any of the children infected?'

'The children are fine. You mustn't fret. Save your strength.' He took her hand and held it tightly. He could

612

not tell her that Susie had died of the plague two hours after Angel had left the house. Unless he was called to deal with a patient, he allowed no one but himself to tend his wife.

It was her fourth day with the distemper upon her and in her pain and delirium Angel was often violent, thrashing her body wildly as the buboes swelled larger. Sometimes she would sit upright, her eyes wide and staring and shout incoherently. The sound of his voice calmed her at once. Her fever raged on. Her body was drenched in perspiration, the cords in her neck strained, and her lips bled as she bit into them in agony. As a physician, Nathan had learned to detach himself from the suffering of his patient. Loving Angel made that impossible. Her screams were like knives cutting into his heart.

In her fever she threw off the blankets piled over her and pushed away the heated bricks wrapped in towels which were packed all around her body. Every half-hour he forced her to drink liquid, and every two hours he painstakingly spoon-fed her meat-broth, milk and honey possets or wine-caudles. Few of these stayed in her stomach for long, and the room was heavy with the stench of sweat and vomit. To freshen it, a plague-pan filled with aromatic herbs burned by the side of the bed.

When Nathan removed the bread and mustard dressing over the swelling in her groin, he saw that it had grown to the size of a plum but was still soft and far from ready to burst. He had already given Angel a dose of the willowbark and herbs brewed by Hazel to deaden the pain. Steeling himself against the agony he knew he must inflict, he tied leather straps across her body to hold her down. Bending her knee out to the side, he began to move it up and down. She screamed as the pain became unbearable.

'No! No! Leave me to die. Let me die in peace.'

He closed his ears to her screams before his resolve weakened. He was drenched in sweat from the high-banked coal fire which blazed in the grate. At last Angel slumped into unconsciousness, her face twitching with spasms of pain as he continued to manipulate her leg, then moved on to perform the same process with her arm, where another bubo was becoming hard and yellow with poison. Fearfully, he checked her body for the bluish plague spots which would appear shortly before death if the buboes did not burst. There was no sign of them, thank God.

The room was stiflingly hot and Nathan shrugged off his own growing exhaustion and forced himself to eat. Everything tasted like ashes and he had no appetite. The dishes pushed aside, he changed his shirt, first examining his own body for signs of the plague tokens. Then, calling for a nurse to sit with Angel, he went to check on his other patients. He stepped carefully over the patients lying on the straw palliasses on the floor and was saddened to recognise that yet another of his nurses had succumbed to the distemper. He looked around the long room and saw only five women tending the thirty patients. He must report to the parish officers that more nurses were needed – not that he had much hope of getting them. He walked out of the ward, standing aside as two bearers carried out a corpse wrapped in a sheet.

'Did the buboes not break?' Nathan asked.

'No, doctor.' Another helper leaned against the doorpost, his voice strained with exhaustion. 'The poor wretch died under the knife when I tried to lance it.' He wiped a hand across his stubbled chin. 'Another was found hanging by his bedsheet from the rafters of the storehouse. No one saw him get out of the ward. We can't have eyes everywhere. Two more helpers were smitten this morning, Dr Carver.'

'How many patients appear to be recovering?'

The man brightened. 'Another twenty have been moved to the recuperation building today. There were seven deaths last night, including the suicide.'

'And therein lies another problem. I shall speak to the parish about arranging for some houses and nurses to be made available for those past their first week of convalescence. They still need special care and are too weak to cook and tend for themselves. Most patients need at least a month before they can leave their beds for any length of time, and we need the beds for the new cases.'

Nathan moved on to another ward. Everywhere he heard the cries and moans of the suffering. In this ward two women were miscarrying, their suffering the greater as they fought both the rigours of the plague and childbirth. A woman with some skills of midwifery had been assigned to them.

His rounds completed Nathan returned to Angel's bedside.

Horrified, he found the nurse asleep on her chair. Angel had thrown off the bedclothes and somehow found the strength to rise from the bed. She lay prone and shivering on the floor.

'Wake up, you useless bawd!' Nathan shouted at the nurse. 'Get out of here. Report to the steward for what money is owed to you, then leave.'

'You can't turn me off. I were sent by the parish. All this pulling the poor sods about ain't helpin' them none. Why not jus' let the poor bleeders die in peace?'

'And die they would,' Nathan fumed as he lifted Angel in his arms and carried her back to the bed. 'Get out before I call the constable! I suppose the pickings aren't rich enough for you here. There's no helpless victims for you to rob of their valuables. Get out!'

The nurse shambled out. Nathan cursed her and her kind. It was becoming harder to get trustworthy nurses, though he knew that some came here knowing that if they fell ill they would at least be cared for.

Settling Angel back in the bed, he examined her. Her fever was higher than ever. Both buboes were hard but had not burst yet. If they drained inwardly she would die from their poison. Strapping her securely to the bed, he reached for the thin-bladed knife and heated it in the fire. When he withdrew it he paused over the distended swelling in her groin. It would have been easier to plunge the knife into his own heart than to inflict this further torture on his weakened wife. God willing, she would not die from the shock of the pain.

Nathan drew the blade across the yellow-headed swelling. Angel's body jerked, arching up and straining against the leather straps. Her scream was deafening. The foul-smelling poison erupted in a great gush and he wiped the bulk of the gore away with a linen rag, leaving the gaping wound to drain, then braced himself to cut into the bubo in her armpit. As the blade pierced the swelling, Angel's eyes opened, bulging from their sockets, their expression manic and terrible enough to rival the Medusa. Nathan felt as if he had been turned into stone. He couldn't find the strength to make her suffer any more. Only the pain of her fingernails digging into his flesh through his shirt sleeve and drawing blood, broke the mesmeric spell of those shocking, hell-visioned eyes.

The blade twisted and slashed. Angel fell back, her body bucking like a maddened stallion. Then she became absolutely still. Nathan could not see her breathing. Frightened, he put a hand to the pulse at her neck. A weak beat was just discernible. Taking her hand, he willed her to fight the disease with all her strength.

'Fight it, Angel. You're over the worst. My love, you must fight it. How can I live without you?' The words were repeated like a litany, over and over, until the room was deeply shadowed and Nathan dozed.

As his head fell forward on to his chest, he woke with a start, his back and arms stiff from his cramped position. Easing his fingers from Angel's clasp, he studied his wife. Her face was thin and her lips bloodless. Through the thin cotton of her chemise her collar-bone stuck out and her ribs showed through her wasted flesh. Her arm was flung back over her head revealing the gaping wound, wide enough for a child to put their fist in. A thin trickle of poison was still draining from it. Unwilling to disturb her while she slept, he decided the wounds could be left for a short while before a healing poultice was placed over them. There were still patches of feverish colour on her cheeks and Nathan dipped a linen cloth in some tepid water and laid it across her brow.

Rising stiffly, he stretched and walked to the window. An early evening haze shimmered over the golden thatch of the hospital buildings. A solitary blackbird trilled out its song from a nearby tree. Listening to it, Nathan realised how little birdsong there was in the capital now. With the shortage of food, the birds had fallen prey to the catapults of the starving.

From the entrance gate across the yard, the bell rang for admittance and he saw a piebald horse pulling the death cart outside. He detested the inhumanity of the conveyance, but with so many hundreds dying every day, the coffins had long been used up and even the churchyards were full. It was an ignoble end, to be dragged in a winding-sheet on to the cart and piled high like so much discarded refuse. War and his profession had hardened Nathan against most horrors of death, but the death carts and the plague pits turned even his stomach.

When the deaths had begun to overtake the city, and the first plague pits had been dug, he had wandered over to one of them one evening. It was a sight which still haunted his dreams. The immense pits were forty feet long, sixteen feet wide and twenty feet deep. Around their perimeters were circles of candles, illuminating the gruesome sight in all its horror. The one he had seen was three-quarters full, the bodies tumbled carelessly down on top of one another. Many of the corpses were naked, robbed even of their linen winding-sheets by either the nurses, watchmen or bearers.

Nathan had resolved that Angel would never suffer that fate. He had purchased two coffins and they were hidden in the cellar of the hospital. The preacher of their parish church had been paid a huge sum for a small plot of land and the promise that if either or both of them were taken, they were to be decently buried.

Refusing to dwell upon such morbid thoughts Nathan turned back to study Angel. His heart jerked into renewed life. Angel's eyes were open and clear of delirium and she was watching him.

Angel had come awake in the dimly lit room and first noticed the crimson sunset lighting the sky through the window. Her arm and legs still throbbed but the pain was now tolerable. When her gaze fell upon the dark silhouette of her husband outlined against the window, she wanted to call out to him. Her lips moved but her voice was so weak it was no more than a whispering breath. Nathan turned and the sunset revealed the joy in his haggard handsome face as he saw that she was conscious. Again she moved her lips. The hoarse croak bore no resemblance to the words of love she wanted to pour out.

'Don't try to speak. You're very weak.' He knelt beside her and lifted a goblet of mead to her lips.

The cool liquid made her feel stronger and she smiled weakly. 'You saved my life.' Then her gaze dropped to his arm, and her eyes widened as she saw the scarlet blood on his sleeve. 'You're hurt.'

Nathan looked down in surprise. Though his arm throbbed from the cuts her nails had gouged, he had been unaware of it until now.

'A battle wound of love.' He smiled.

'I did that?'

'You suffered far more at my hand.' His voice broke into

husky laughter. 'And you should have heard your language when I was exercising your arm and leg to get the buboes to form. It would have made the roughest seaman blush.'

'What did I say?'

'My parentage has never been so slandered, nor in such colourful detail. As for the threats you made to parts of my anatomy, and what you would do with them when you had sliced them into a hundred pieces with my surgical knife . . . Quite frankly, my dear, I was shocked. The devil himself could not have devised greater tortures than those you threatened to subject me to.'

'Nathan, you exaggerate.'

'Angel, in delirium you have an original and most unladylike turn of phrase. And if you hadn't been so close to death, I would have been thoroughly entertained.'

She blushed such a fiery red he thought her fever had returned. 'Did anyone else hear me?'

She was so mortified that he could not help laughing. 'No, and if they did, they would be used to it by now. Delirium has that effect on many of the patients. Remind me to tell you what one of the preachers intended to do to a whole group of choirboys whilst he was raving.'

'That proves you are teasing.' Angel summoned a smile.

He pushed a black tendril of hair away from her brow and to his relief felt her head almost cool to his touch. 'My love, you gave me such a scare.'

'How so? I had faith in you.' She paused, labouring for breath, but was determined to say what was on her mind. 'Are you not the best physician in all England? I never doubted you would save me.'

Her faith touched him as profoundly as her love. It overwhelmed him. Against all the preventive measures which he insisted were maintained, he held her against him and kissed her tenderly. She tried to lift a hand to touch his face but it fell back weakly on the pillow. Taking it up, he kissed her palm, his voice hoarse with emotion.

'Now we begin the long convalescence. It will be a week before I'll permit you to leave your bed and then only for an hour.'

'Nonsense. I shall be up in a day and back working in the orphanage in a week. Can I return to our house tomorrow?

How fortunate I purchased paper and quills, for I might as well use the time to start another play.' She tried to push herself up on one elbow and failed. She scowled in frustration. 'Perhaps the day after tomorrow I will start the play. I've never felt so weak. And I don't like it.'

Nathan stood up and struggled to control his exasperation. 'Mistress Carver, for once in your life you'll do exactly as you're told. And don't give me that injured look. You always were too stubborn for your own good.'

The bright sunlight reflected off the white stonework of the Tower of London three miles away. Thomas and Celia were forced to skirt around another turnpike set up on the road. The local villagers wanted no strangers in their community who might spread the plague. Thomas cursed the delay. All day he had been on edge, sensing approaching danger. They had been on the road for four days – long enough for Delgannon to have them pursued. Celia had been complaining of stomach pains all day which had slowed their progress. Thomas had hoped to reach Nell's before nightfall, but now accepted that it would take them another night.

Ahead was an open heath which gave little cover from pursuers, and Thomas felt his unease grow. It had to be crossed to reach London. Annoyed at his qualms, he pushed them aside. Though his original plan had misfired, once Celia was wed to Mortimer he would still have his revenge upon the two men. First they must reach London – and safety. All his life he had stayed just one step ahead of the law. Even during his short spells in the Marshalsea and Counter prisons, bribery and influence had soon gained his release.

Why did he need to risk his freedom now by settling old scores? He was the most successful of the Upright Men, and his business ventures had made him immensely wealthy. Pride had made him risk all in this last ruse. Pride and the madcap idea to emulate Wildboar Tom Angel's most infamous exploit. What he had chosen to disregard was that 'Wildboar' had ended his days swinging from a gallows.

Caution made Thomas look back and scan the track. It was deserted except for an old woman bent double as she returned to the village, a bundle of faggots strapped to her back.

He kicked his mount to a canter. It was too hot to risk a

gallop after the horse had travelled so far, but he wanted to cross the heath as quickly as possible. They were halfway across when prickles of alarm crept down his spine. Swivelling in the saddle he saw a half-dozen riders steadily gaining ground on them.

'Keep up with me, Celia,' he shouted as he raked the gelding's sides.

'Tom, I can't,' Celia wailed. 'I'm in pain. I think I'm miscarrying.'

Thomas cursed his ill-fate at this new setback. A glance behind showed that the riders would overtake them long before they reached cover.

Drawing the saddle pistol from its holster, he shouted at Celia, 'There's no point in both of us being taken! Just keep going. Once in London head towards St Paul's and Fleet Street. Go to Nell Lovegood's and tell them I sent you. If I'm taken alive it will be Newgate for me. Nell will know what to do and who to contact.'

With that, he swung his leg over the saddle pommel and leapt to the ground. He rolled as his body hit the grass and with the instincts of a predator came up on his feet, his pistols at the ready. Taking aim, he fired at the approaching riders. Two men fell, the others bore down on him, their faces crazed with bloodlust. Stuffing both pistols into the sash at his waist, Thomas drew his sword. Odds of four to one did not trouble him. In his twenties he had taken on twice that many and emerged the victor. But, thirty years on, his reflexes were slower. Three of the riders circled him, the other went galloping after Celia. If the girl got through to Nell's there was a chance for him. There was a pistol shot and through a gap in the circling riders Thomas saw the carriage gelding go down and Celia was pitched through the air.

Then he had time only for his own plight. The horses with their stamping hooves were menacingly close, but the riders kept just out of reach of his blade. He ran forward and jabbed one in the thigh. At that moment all hell broke loose. The riders jeered. Thomas could smell the stench of their unwashed bodies and the sweat from the lathered horses. He lunged at a rider, but did not see the kick aimed at his head from the man behind him.

Red stars exploded through his brain as he reeled from the

blow. He staggered and fell to one knee. The grass swooped and receded before his eyes. He tried to push himself upright, but another kick slashed his cheek open with its spur.

'Delgannon says not to kill 'im,' a gruff voice ordered. 'There's extra in it for us if Delgannon gets to see his neck stretched on Tyburn Hill.'

Thomas's skull felt like an erupting volcano; flames of pain were blasting through it. He swayed to his knees, his face a bloodied mask. He didn't see the blow which laid him out cold, or the kicks slamming into his ribs and stomach as a man dismounted to vent his fury and grief for the brother Thomas had just shot dead.

'That's enough.' The leader dragged the man away, but felt no mercy as he regarded Thomas's battered, bloodied figure. 'Put 'im on the horse.'

The leader rode over to where his companion was kneeling by the woman. Her neck was broken and there was a great deal of blood seeping on to her skirts from between her legs. 'Take her up, but we will get her cleaned up before Delgannon is sent her body. Ain't no point in the old man knowing she aborted of a bastard. Might make him cut that hundred pounds reward he offered us for capturing Thomas Angel.'

In the fortnight which followed Angel's recovery, everyone declared that she was the worst patient they had ever encountered. She was constantly found out of bed, and three times fell in an exhausted heap. Once it happened at the top of the stairs and she narrowly missed tumbling down their length. When she was allowed up, she insisted on paper and pens being brought to her. Then her temper threatened to bring on a return of the fever when she found that trying to concentrate for longer than two minutes at a time was impossible.

Angel hated the inactivity forced on her by her husband. She refused to admit that walking more than twenty steps tired her and struggled to stay awake when every hour fatigue made her eye-lids droop.

At the end of August Nathan returned from the hospital to find her struggling to harness a Rowan mare. For the first time in weeks he had felt a lightening of his spirits. For the second week running the plague figures posted on bills in each parish had begun to drop. He believed the worst of it had passed, but had not realised how bone weary he was until now. Seeing Angel behaving so foolhardily made his temper finally snap.

'What the devil are you about, woman?'

'I'm going to the orphanage. They haven't enough staff.'

He snatched the bridle out of her hands and flung it violently across the cobbled yard. 'Haven't you the sense you were born with? You're not strong enough to walk let alone ride a horse.'

'I won't be treated like a spun sugar confection which will break at the least pressure.'

'No. You're a selfish, stubborn jade. The servants have run themselves ragged keeping an eye on you so you don't do anything foolish. They're worn out and frightened that they might be the next plague victim. You're just making their lives more difficult.'

With that he spun on his heel and marched out into the street.

'Nathan!' Angel shouted after him, appalled at his words. She had never seen him like that . . . And he had spoken the truth. She had meant to help the servants by continuing her work. Now she saw that she had placed yet another burden upon them by her stubbornness.

Hating to part from him with heated words between them, she hurried to the garden gate. As she stepped into the street she saw Nathan about to turn the corner. For a moment he staggered under the fury of his pace and put a hand on the wall to steady himself. Then he continued and disappeared from sight.

She wanted to run after him, but her legs were too weak and shaky. What a pig-headed fool she'd been. Nathan had come home for a welcome respite from his duties at the hospital and she had driven him away.

For the next hour she could not settle. Her quarrel with Nathan was eating into her and a desperate need grew in her to go to him and apologise. At first she fought against it knowing he would be angered that she had disobeyed his wishes. But the feeling persisted and twice in the next hour she had the strongest sensation that Nathan was calling to her. The second time she did not hesitate. Something was wrong.

'Hazel, have the carriage made ready,' she ordered, swallowing against the growing panic which was threatening to overwhelm her. 'I must get to the hospital.'

'But Dr Carver says . . .'

'Never mind what he says, he needs me.' Her stricken look sent Hazel running from the room.

Deep shadows were cast across the hospital courtyard by the late afternoon sun and as Angel stepped from the carriage a chill pierced her body. She staggered at its intensity and her heart hammered so painfully she thought it would suffocate her.

Hazel took her arm. 'Lean on me, mistress. You should never have come.'

'Nathan, I must see Nathan,' Angel gasped, unable to shake the crushing sense of foreboding.

Drawing upon her last reserves of strength, Angel leaned on Hazel as they entered. Her panic grew with each step. There was a feeling of oppression where there should have been ease and light.

A male assistant came out of one of the wards, his face haggard with exhaustion. At seeing Angel he looked distraught. 'Mrs Carver, I hadn't expected you so soon. You had better come this way.'

Angel pushed Hazel away and followed him to Nathan's study. He opened the door and the first person Angel saw was the preacher. Wide-eyed she stared beyond him to the body laid out on the desk, a candle at its head and feet.

'Nathan. No. Not Nathan!' Sobbing she staggered towards her husband but as she would have flung herself across him the preacher caught her and held her back.

'It was mercifully swift,' he said quietly. 'He collapsed shortly after returning here. The tokens were already on his body. He did not suffer. He died without gaining consciousness.'

'Oh God. No!' Angel cried. 'Not Nathan. Not my love,' her voice rose to a shriek. 'No. He can't be dead! He can't be!'

Angel's legs buckled and close to swooning she sank down on to a chair. The preacher spoke to her but his words were an unintelligible drone. Stunned she stared at Nathan's body and began to shake her head, tears drenching her cheeks. A bee beat itself against the window pane trying to get out. Its

623

angry buzzing grew louder and louder in Angel's ears until reality exploded and she let out a strangled sob.

'Why Nathan? He had saved so many. Why didn't I die and he live? There's no God to allow such injustice.' There was madness in Angel's eyes.

'Hush, Mrs Carver, you must not say that,' the preacher remonstrated gently.

'We parted in anger.' Angel's fingers clutched at her heart, tearing the silk of her gown as though she was trying to tear out the agony which threatened to destroy her sanity. 'That's the worst of it. I loved him more than life itself. How could I have driven him away? He was sick by then. I could have saved him.'

'No one lives long once the plague tokens appear,' Hazel said. 'You know that, mistress. The master loved you. You only quarrelled because he was tired and ill. He didn't mean his harsh words.'

Angel stood up and fell to her knees by her husband's side. 'Oh my love, forgive me.'

Hazel was frightened. She had never seen Angel lose control before. But then she had never known two people so much in love as Nathan and Angel. It had been apparent in a hundred ways every day, in the way they looked at each other and smiled absently when apart, and in the way they seemed to communicate without speaking, so often anticipating each other's needs.

'After all Nathan had done,' Angel sobbed, her body trembling violently with shock. 'He saved so many lives. If he had to get the plague why didn't he develop the buboes so that he could be saved by the treatment he had devised? Oh, my darling, how can I bear life without you?'

There was a discreet cough by the door and two men came in with a stretcher. Angel stared at them as they made to lift Nathan on to it.

'What are you doing?' she demanded.

'Death cart is outside, Mistress Carver,' one man answered, visibly upset.

'No. The death cart will not have him,' Angel stood up and placed herself between her husband and the bearers. 'He will not be buried in a plague pit.'

'My child, there is no choice,' the preacher intervened. 'It is the law.'

'Not the plague pits.' Angel's eyes were wild with grief. 'It was the only thing he dreaded if the plague took his life. There is a coffin . . . Our parish preacher promised Nathan he could be buried decently in our church. He deserves that at least for all the lives he has saved.'

The preacher nodded agreement. 'It will be done as you wish, Mistress Carver. But it must be done at once.'

The funeral took place in the dead of night. Throughout the service Angel's mind and senses were numbed with grief. On her return to the house she sat on the window seat of the parlour and Hazel pressed a brandy goblet into her mistress's shaking hands.

'You've got to be strong, Mistress, or you'll make yourself ill again. The master would not have wanted that. And what of the children in the orphanage? You have to be strong for their sakes.'

Angel leaned her head back against the window her voice cracked with pain. 'I will be strong, Hazel. But not today. Leave me. I want to grieve for Nathan.'

Alone in the room Angel stared at her husband's favourite chair by the hearth. Next to it was his clay pipe and the china pot which held his tobacco. 'Oh, Nathan . . . why you? Why did we part in anger? Forgive me, my love.'

Grief gripped her heart in iron claws. With her eyes screwed shut she mourned the only man she would ever love. Slowly the room began to fill with the musky tang of sandalwood and a mixture of balm, leather, tobacco smoke and subtle scent which was uniquely Nathan's own. Her eyes opened. Her hands reached out towards his chair and for a brief moment the ravages of grief left her face. Nathan was there. His smile bathed her in the glow of his love as he watched her. An aura of tranquillity was in the light surrounding his shadowy figure. He winked at her and his hand was raised in farewell.

Angel took a step forward, but already the vision was fading.

'Stay, my love – my heart!' she pleaded.

The vision was gone and only the faint lingering tang of sandalwood remained. The oak chair was empty but a feeling of peace pervaded her being. Nathan had said his farewell and left her with the afterglow of his love which transcended their separate worlds and would never leave her.

Chapter Twenty-Five

Without Popinjay's support Angel did not know how she could have coped during the following winter.

Ironically, after Nathan's death the plague had finally abated. The pest house was closed and the hospital buildings sold, for Angel needed the money to support her orphanage. Now she faced the trauma of Thomas's trial.

She had not learned of his arrest until September, and that was through Popinjay's searching. The merchant had also told her that there was plague at Nell Lovegood's. One of the women and two customers had died and when Richard Angel had tried to smuggle the bodies out he had been seen by a neighbour and was reported to the authorities. The house was closed within the hour, incarcerating not only the women, but a score of customers. Within a fortnight every single one of them was dead, including Richard Angel.

On her visit to Thomas in Newgate, Angel had been the one to tell him the news. The blustering rogue had shrivelled before her eyes. Richard's death took all the fight out of him. Popinjay had warned Angel that several criminals were coming forward to give evidence against her cousin. A new Upright Man had taken over Thomas's territory and his enemies, jealous of his wealth and success, wanted to see him hanged.

Though it grieved Angel to admit it, Thomas deserved to die. She had attended his trial at the Sessions House and had been appalled at the charges and accusations against him. She had not realised that he controlled so many crimes, including theft of every description, extortion, blackmail, abduction, protection and fencing of stolen goods – even selling goods back to their original owners after his men had stolen them. She lost count of the murders accredited to his orders, and the mutilations he apparently ordered to maintain his rule as an Upright Man had horrified her. This was a side of her cousin she had never known. She was aware that he was ruthless, but had never suspected that he was evil. To Angel, Thomas had been a cousin to turn to in her time of need. He had never failed her. When the death sentence was passed on him, despite his crimes, she could not desert him.

Always stubborn, Thomas had remained silent throughout his trial. Many of his accusers had been dragged out of prison and promised a pardon if they gave evidence against him. When he was asked to turn evidence against his associates he said nothing. He neither refuted the evidence against his crimes nor pleaded guilty. If only he had pleaded guilty it would have saved him from his gruesome fate. His manner of execution was to be *peine forte et dure* – pressing to death by heavy weights. A strong man could take two or three days to die in this way, some lasted even longer. It was the penalty inflicted on any defendant who refused to plead guilty when charged of a capital offence. But it meant that his property could not be confiscated, and Thomas was prepared to face torture if it secured his fortune for Thomasine. That haughty minx had repaid her father by publicly disowning him. After the scandal broke, her treachery was repaid by Viscount Lymeton banishing her to his estates in Ireland. He had since applied to Parliament for a divorce.

The day before Thomas's sentence was to be carried out, Angel dressed with care. Her black gown was of watered silk with a low, scooped neckline. To alleviate the severity of it she wore a deep lace collar which fell in a dozen points from its neckline to her waist. She wore the low neckline to show the black angel patch which covered the scar on her shoulder. Around her waist she looped the rope of pearls given to her by Prince Rupert when she had been his mistress. Beside her wedding band, her only ring was the one given to her by the King, and she also wore the bracelet given to her by Charles on the birth of Matthew. Popinjay was waiting at the door to escort her to Whitehall. He held out a black velvet cloak lined with white satin and settled it over her shoulders.

'This is madness, Angel,' he said. 'Are you sure you want to go through with it?'

628

'I'll not let Tom die in that horrible manner without trying to save him.'

An hour later their carriage rolled through the King Street Gate of Whitehall Palace. They passed the old tiltyard and Banqueting House before reaching the main courtyard. Popinjay was informed by a liveried footman that the King was at leisure on the Bowling Green. Taking Angel's arm, Popinjay led her through the maze of buildings of the Privy Gallery and into the Privy Garden. As they approached the bowling green beyond, Angel was dismayed to see so many courtiers in attendance. It was a chill morning and she had not expected the King to be exercising so vigorously, although she knew he was a keen sportsman and regularly played tennis.

The women were muffled in furs and the men paced briskly up and down to keep warm. Charles Stuart's tall figure was easy to discern. He was chatting to Barbara Palmer, now the Countess of Castlemaine since her cuckolded husband had been given an Irish earldom. She was still the King's favourite, though she vied for her place now amongst a regiment of others. These included King Louis of France's spy, Louise de Kéroualle, Duchess of Portsmouth; Hortense Mancine, Duchess of Mazarin; various actresses and the still chaste Frances Stuart who had declined the King's fervent suit for many years. It was said that Charles never discarded a mistress, even when he ceased to frequent her bed. Would the King be so charitable towards a woman he had loved nearly twenty years ago?

To save her cousin, Angel had swallowed her pride to come here. She stood apart from the milling courtiers as the King turned to walk back to the Privy Garden. She was counting on him acknowledging her and prayed he would not ignore her plea.

While she waited for the King to approach, Angel scanned the courtiers, disappointed but not surprised to see no sign of Prince Rupert. Since he had taken charge of the English Fleet last spring, to fight the Dutch, he had been laid low with illness. He had not returned to England until the King's coronation and Angel had seen him only once since then, when she had been walking in St James's Park one Sunday with Nathan. Surrounded by his dogs, the Prince had stopped to talk to them for half an hour. She had been saddened to see that his robust health which had accompanied him through the years of battles had deserted him. He mentioned a constant headache from the old head wound and she knew Nathan had treated him several times for a Tertian fever which returned from time to time and was a legacy from his long years at sea. Two years ago, the Prince had begun an affair with Francesca Bard and she had recently borne him a son, Dudley. The affair had surprised Angel for at the time the Duchess of Richmond was a widow for the second time. Since Rupert had been so in love with the Duchess during the Civil War Angel had expected him to marry his early love. It was not long after the Duchess of Richmond took a third husband that Rupert ended his affair with Francesca.

Angel broke off her contemplation as she saw that the King had recognised her. His expression was not welcoming, and icy fingers clutched at her stomach. Would he ignore her? Curtly excusing himself to Lady Castlemaine, he beckoned Angel to approach him.

She sank into a deep curtsy and he gestured for her to rise. Her heart thumped wildly and her breathing was restricted.

'You would not be at Whitehall without a reason,' he said grimly. 'I have the greatest regard for you, Mistress Carver. I hope you will ask nothing of me which would go against my conscience and England's laws.'

'I do not ask for England's laws to be flouted. I ask for Your Majesty's clemency as to the manner of my cousin's execution.'

'The case has rocked London with its scandal and infamy. I'm surprised you even own Thomas Angel as your kin.' His expression remained unrelenting.

'For his crimes against humanity Tom Angel deserves to die,' she said heavily. 'But when I was accused of harbouring Royalists after Your Majesty's defeat at Worcester Tom did not desert me. I need not remind Your Majesty that Tom fought in that battle too. He has never failed me in my time of need. You are his only hope.' Seeing the look of displeasure on the King's face at being reminded of past obligations, she hurried on, 'Like all felons, Tom must pay for his crimes. The clemency I ask is that his death is not by *peine forte et dure*. He won't plead guilty because he blames himself that Viscount Lymeton is divorcing his daughter. He fears she will be penniless if his goods are confiscated. It's the only way he can provide for her security. Sire, Thomasine Angel is innocent. This scandal and divorce is shame enough. Must she also suffer?'

'I understand the daughter has denounced her father and wants nothing to do with him.'

'The more reason for me to stand by Thomas. I'd never desert a friend or a member of my family in need.' Fearful that the King would not relent, Angel knelt on the cold ground. 'Sire, I'll not embarrass you by begging. This is the only way I can repay my debt to Tom. Only you can grant him clemency in the manner of his death.'

She had not realised that tears were streaming down her cheeks until the King stooped and gently wiped them away. 'Rise, Angel. You still refuse to ask for anything for yourself, always for others. I grant you this request: Thomas Angel will be hanged one week from today. It will be the first of the executions since the plague broke out last July, so there'll be a goodly crowd to cheer the rogue on his final journey.'

'Thank you, Your Majesty.'

At last the King was smiling, though it was touched with cynicism. 'But Thomas Angel must still forfeit some of his wealth – his death does not repay his debt to society. You're struggling against ruin to support the orphanage you established. Its rent alone must cost you dearly.'

'I am managing, Your Majesty.'

'You never could resist a hopeless cause, could you?' he smiled tenderly. 'You always were generous with your money. I have not forgotten. The property which has been in your family for generations will be given to you. Highly as the bordello was esteemed, it's time a more beneficial use was put to its premises. Nell Lovegood's is no more. In its place will be the Angel Orphanage and a quarter of your cousin's wealth from his ill-gotten gains will be set aside in trust to pay for its upkeep. His daughter will have another quarter, more than adequate to provide for her future. The rest will be given to the city authorities to be dispersed amongst various charities. Does that satisfy you?'

'It's more than I dared hope. Thank you, Your Majesty.'

'To see you smile again, Angel, is reward enough. I know you still mourn Nathan. A tragic loss, and the city owes him a great debt for the lives he saved.' He turned to leave, then paused and came back. 'With all these good works you are now performing I trust your playwriting does not suffer? One of your comedies is just what we need to lighten our spirits in the aftermath of the pestilence. I'd be displeased if our most talented woman playwright abandoned the theatre. Respectability is an onerous yoke, Angel. You're too beautiful and talented to don its sobering mantle.'

The condemned hold in Newgate prison must be one of the bleakest places on God's earth, Thomas Angel reflected, fighting against rising despair. Lady Luck had finally deserted him. What demon had possessed him to emulate his namesake Wildboar Tom Angel and thereby be brought to the same ignominious fate?

He shuddered. At least he had escaped being crushed to death. He had been haunted by nightmares at facing that gruesome end. He passed a hand across his stubbled cheek and his throat worked against a surging agony within his breast. Thomasine's repudiation of him had been a cruel blow. As hard to face as his son's death, and much harder to come to terms with than the hanging he must face in a few hours' time.

Thomas turned his thoughts from his daughter. Thomasine's rejection was not unexpected. She was like Maressa: beautiful, but calculating and heartless. And where was Maressa now? Hazel had said that her mind had been unhinged over an incident in Holland. Thomas could guess the cause! Maressa had discovered her true sexuality – that knowledge would have destroyed her. She had been so proud of her high moral principles. He smothered his regrets about Maressa. He had loved her, but he had failed her. The pain of loving her returned and he willed himself to fix his last thoughts upon happier things.

He grinned into the gloom of the single candle as his thoughts turned to Angel. Pacing the floor as far as his manacles would permit, his sudden crack of laughter made a foraging rat dart for cover under the mildewing rushes on the floor.

'God bless you, Angel!' he said aloud. 'I should have

known you'd not desert me. No matter I've been named the greatest rogue to blight London in a century. Having your name linked with mine will make you infamous as a playwright – the theatres will be packed to see your plays. They may come expecting a salacious comedy, and they'll not leave disappointed. Your wit is the sharpest I've heard performed.'

There was a rattle of keys and the door creaked open. The turnkey remained outside the ring of feeble light. 'Visitor to see you. Another woman. Reckon you've got more sisters and cousins than any man alive. This must make two dozen who've visited you.'

Thomas sighed. He was tired of being a showpiece for rich merchants' wives, and courtiers who were titillated by visiting his cell. Even the haughty Lady Castlemaine had come in disguise – twice. She had been one of the many women whose favours he had not rejected. The woman was as depraved as any of Nell's Lovegood's whores and amazingly imaginative – no wonder she had remained the King's favourite for so long.

Thomas had known that, with Celia Delgannon's death, no amount of bribery would allow him to escape the scaffold. Yet he refused to be morbid. Women and wine could be bought aplenty in Newgate and until last week he had entertained lavishly in the taproom. Now he was in the condemned hold and placed in chains.

With only two hours before his execution Thomas was in no mood for female company. The dampness of the cell had stiffened his joints and they ached intolerably. And he suspected one of the court ladies had left behind more than the lingering fragrance of her perfume. The itch and stabbing pain in his groin was an unpleasant legacy from such dalliances. He was about to tell the turnkey to send the woman away when a black-cloaked figure stepped into the cell. With a sob she threw herself across the intervening space and wrapped her arms around him.

'I had to come and say farewell, Tom. Rogue that you always were, I love you dearly.'

'Angel, I'd rather you did not remember me here in this stinking hold.' His arms tightened around her and he was unable to stop his body trembling. 'Go, before you unman me. Remember me as I was.'

'That's why I'm here.' She blinked against her tears and

held out a bundle wrapped in linen. 'Do you think I'd allow Thomas Angel, Arch-Rogue, Upright Man and King of the Underworld to go to the scaffold looking like a bedraggled pauper? I've brought you fresh clothes and intend to trim your hair and shave you before you meet your public.'

He peeled away the linen wrapping and stared down at the cream brocade jacket lavishly decorated in gold braid. There were also clean underclothes, a silk shirt with expensive lace at its wrists, plus cream silk hose and black shoes with a large gold satin rosette on each toe.

'I shall go to my execution dressed as a king. But the extravagance of it all, Angel! You know the hangman gets my clothes as his payment.'

'Then such riches should ensure that he does not bungle his work. It's been arranged that you'll be on a horse when the time comes.' Angel dropped her gaze from his.

Thomas hugged her again, overcome with affection. It could take a man up to half an hour to strangle slowly to death if he was hoisted by the noose over the heads of the crowds. But on horseback, the swift fall and jerk usually broke a man's neck, and death was instantaneous. For the unfortunate ones who gasped and kicked out their last tortuous breath, spectators added to the sport by swinging and dragging on the hanged man's legs. The thought of such an end had nauseated Thomas, but Angel had spared him that. Dressed in such finery he would die with dignity. He would give the crowd the spectacle they desired. This was one devil who would go laughing and jesting to his death.

Thomas Angel did not disappoint the public. As he was driven through the crowded streets on a tumbrel, he waved to all the beautiful women. From a large pouch of coins he scattered largesse to the urchins and beggars who ran behind.

'Murderer! Thief!' The jeers were hurled at him. 'Devil's spawn!'

Thomas acknowledged each insult with an exaggerated bow. His coffin was in the front of the tumbrel and in defiance he rested a foot on it as he called out compliments to the ladies. The brandy Angel had brought him had taken the edge from his fear and he rode the tumbrel as though it was a gilded carriage. The people who had thronged the route to get a last look at Thomas Angel would see him not as a cringing broken felon, but as a lord of his domain, holding court.

The white lace at his wrist was snowy in the pale February sunlight. His white hair had been trimmed and fell in thick waves to his shoulders. Angel, attempting a feeble joke, had said that he still looked like a marauding Viking, though an extremely well-dressed one. Throughout his last journey his smile was dazzling, charming all who beheld him.

'Don't look a hardened murderer, does he?' A man spoke from the crowd.

His companion sniggered. 'Believe it. Tom Angel would murder a man one minute and jump into bed with his victim's wife the next.'

Thomas heard the comment and shouted, 'Only if she was beautiful!'

He maintained the façade of carefree nonchalance. Only when he leant forward to blow a kiss at a comely wench did they glimpse the bleakness in his eyes. One woman swooned as he bowed to her. The matron next to her let out a scream, 'I see a demon on Tom Angel's shoulder! He's waiting to drag his soul to hell!'

Thomas forced himself to laugh. Surely hell was where he was heading. And no one lining the route doubted it. When the chaplain accompanying the tumbrel began to chant a prayer, Thomas flung back his head and sang a bawdy song that carried to the far reaches of the crowd. He did not stop singing until the tumbrel drew up to the three-cornered gallows on Tyburn Hill. Here the crowd numbered five hundred or more, and amongst them the pickpockets and cutpurses were busy at work. Shrugging aside the driver's help, Thomas leapt nimbly to the ground, despite his manacled wrists.

The chaplain turned to help him, his pale eyes glittering with malice. 'Repent, sinner! The hour of judgement is upon you. Black heathen that you are, may the Good Lord have mercy on your soul.'

The wind had stiffened, ruffling the lace collar at Thomas's throat. It was not just its chill which sent a shiver through his body, but he wanted no one to think he quaked in fear. 'I hope you're wrapped up well against the February air, my friends. I alone here go to a much hotter place this day.' A horse was led towards him. It was a chestnut, inferior to any of the Rowan breed. 'Am I expected to ride on that broken-down nag?' he jeered.

'It will carry you as far as you need to go,' a rough voice shouted from the front of the crowd.

Thomas hauled himself on to the back of the horse and drew a deep breath to still the smothering pounding of his heart. The hemp of the noose scraped against his clean-shaven jaw as it was positioned around his neck.

'Do you repent?' The chaplain raised the cross which hung on his chest.

'I repent of all the women I never lived long enough to tumble. I repent of all the adventures I will never again experience.' His voice carried across the crowd. His defiance was a brave attempt to still the quivering beat of his heart and the nausea churning in his stomach. His face muscles twitched. It felt as though he was prising open the jaws of a mantrap as he forced a cocky grin. Somehow he managed to raise an unshaking hand to wave to a wench in the crowd. When the hangman approached with a hood for his head he waved it aside. A clamouring broke out amongst the throng but one woman's voice, shriller than all the rest, carried back to him.

'Dear God, no! Thomas! No!'

He turned. Below him, battling her way to the front of the crowd, was Maressa. Her lovely face was streaked with tears. And he saw with shock that her hair was silvery-white. The luscious curves of her figure had disappeared, and her drab brown linen dress hung loose on her gaunt figure. She reached out a hand towards him. 'Thomas! Don't leave me, Thomas.'

'He ain't goin' nowhere,' a sneering voice yelled from the crowd, ''cepting to hell.'

'Maressa, go to Angel! She'll take care of you,' Thomas shouted. The crushing pain in his chest at being unable to save her now was a dozen times worse than suffering the *peine forte et dure*.

He gazed into her amber eyes, large and wild. In the fourteen months since Maressa had disappeared she had changed drastically. Most harrowing of all was the dementia which was stark in her dilated eyes. He scanned the crowd for someone to help her, but he had asked Angel to stay away. Behind him, Thomas could hear the chaplain muttering a prayer. He did not have much time. His concern for Maressa stilled the nausea which had threatened to unman him. He had to save her! Was there no one he could turn to for help? His frantic search picked out Popinjay's tall figure, standing with his head bowed to one side of the scaffold.

'Maressa!' he shouted. 'She's—' The words were cut off as the horse he was astride was slapped on the rump and bolted forward. Thomas was yanked backwards and upwards. Hemp scorched his neck. Then he began to perceive every detail in slow motion as the weight of his body dragged downwards on the choking tightness.

'Thomas!' he heard Maressa scream.

His mouth was open but his tongue, forced forward to protrude between his teeth, blocked the words he wanted to say. Red flashes burst like fireworks through his skull, pressure building, hemp gnawing, choking. The last sound he heard was like a whip cracking as his neck snapped.

Maressa stopped in mid-scream. Her mouth stayed open, but no sound came from it. Yet the screaming went on in her head. She saw the face she had recognised from her past, turning purple and ugly. His eyes bulged and his tongue lolled from his mouth. Putting her hands to her ears to stop the sound of her screaming, she turned and hurled her way through the crowd. The wildness in her eyes opened a path for her. A man reached out to stop her, but she evaded him, looking through him as though he was a stranger.

Rob Hervey was puzzled at the change which had come over his wife. He had brought her to the hanging as a treat. She had been looking pale and ill of late, and a hanging was always good entertainment. He had forgotten that his wife could act strangely at times. Indeed, today was one of the rare days he thought much about her at all. She was there to clean his house and look after his children and serve his bodily needs. He began to push his way through the crowds after her, but soon lost sight of her amongst the vast numbers.

Popinjay had jerked up his head at the sound of Thomas Angel's desperate shout. Surprise at the name Thomas had shouted made him follow the direction of the condemned man's fixed gaze. At the same time the hangman had whacked the horse on its rump. A cheer had gone up from the crowd and Thomas was jerked above their heads. At first Popinjay did not recognise Angel's sister, then he saw the madness in her eyes and the way she fled into the crowd.

Taller than most men, he had no trouble in pursuing Maressa at first. But then the crowd began surging forward to get a closer look at Tom Angel's body and he lost precious minutes pushing through them. When he saw her again she was far ahead of him. He cursed his shortage of breath. He was too old for a wild chase through the maze of city streets. The woman seemed to be flying on wings, driven by her dementia. When he rounded the first corner Maressa was nowhere in sight. He slumped against the timber framework of a tenement house and drew gulps of air into his tortured lungs. At least he knew she was alive. If he had to search every house in the city he'd find her, and return her to Angel's care.

After an hour Thomas Angel's body was taken down from the gallows and laid in state at an inn in St Giles. For two days people filed past it, paying a penny to see the most notorious of England's rogues. The following day he was laid to rest in St Ethelburga's churchyard, close to the graves of Esmond and Laurence Angel. The inscription on his tombstone read . . .

> *Here lies Thomas Angel of infamous fame,*
> *Devil by nature, Angel by name,*
> *Rogue of high order – illustrious thief,*
> *His blackguard adventures brought many to grief,*
> *Women adored him, men cursed his acclaim,*
> *Tyburn's swift justice ended his game.*

Weeks of searching turned into months and Maressa Angel seemed to have disappeared from London. Popinjay kept his vow and, using his network of spies, continued to have the city scoured. No one was more shocked than himself when he finally learned the woman's fate. He was loath to tell Angel, fearing to place yet another burden upon her shoulders.

In the year since Nathan's death, Angel had hidden her pain behind a steel-coated heart. Occasionally at the end of a long day he would glimpse her sadness, evident in the drooping of proud shoulders, in an escaping sigh or the lethargy in her eyes. To the outside world she remained witty and carefree. She still ran the orphanage, raising funds for its support as a general would organise a military campaign. Two more of her plays had been performed by the King's Players. They were acclaimed as the wittiest of the age, but Popinjay saw behind the barbed wit to the cynicism beneath. Angel would never find peace until her sister's fate was known. And how would Angel take the news he must now give her?

The last week in August was stiflingly hot. The London streets were malodorous with accumulated filth. Horse dung was trampled to dust under foot, offal from the slaughter-houses ran into the kennels along the centre of the streets, adding to the overwhelming stench of unwashed humanity. Angel held a nosegay of gillyflowers to her face as she and Popinjay approached the ancient priory in Bishopsgate. It was bordered by two open sewers. Here the stench was overpowering and clouds of flies hovered over the stinking sewage. At the door they waited in line behind several court-iers and their ladies, who had come for an afternoon's enter-tainment. Behind her mask Angel eyed them with cold disdain. How could anyone take pleasure from the suffering of the patients within St Mary of Bethlehem's hospital?

Popinjay paid their admission fee and taking Angel's arm led her into the grim interior of Bedlam lunatic asylum. The noise was deafening. There were screechings, roarings and howlings to rival the beasts of the jungle. Chains clattered and hideous profanities were hurled at the visitors by the gibbering wretches. Many of them were chained to their beds. Some crouched in their own excrement, swaying from side to side. Others stood with their faces against the wall, unmoving. The guards patrolled, cracking whips indis-criminately.

Angel was sickened by the sights. Many of the unfortunates were clothed in scanty rags, their ribs and bones showing through grey flesh. Their heads were shaved or their hair matted with knots and straw. Some of them had visible bald patches where either the patients, or the guards, had pulled out great chunks of their hair during a fit of dementia. A man knelt on all fours beating his head against the floor and when his face lifted, it was a mask of blood.

'I can't believe Maressa is here,' Angel said, pulling back from the sight of a woman hoisting her skirts to her waist and waggling her bare bottom at the laughing gallants as they sauntered past.

'It may not be Maressa,' Popinjay explained. 'The poor creature gave no name but "Duchess". It's the only word she speaks. That's why it took so long for my men to track her here.' He looked with concern into Angel's troubled gaze. 'Prepare yourself. If it is Maressa, you will find her much changed.' He paused outside the door of a single cell, his voice gruff as he went on, 'They keep her apart from the others because she can be violent.'

There was the sound of grunting from within as Popinjay pushed open the door. For a moment Angel was transfixed with horror. The room was gloomy, lit only by a tiny window high in the wall, but there was light enough to reveal the appalling scene. A naked woman, her eyes wide and staring with terror and her mouth open in a silent scream, lay on mildewed straw. Above her were the fat, heaving buttocks of a warder. Twig-thin fingers were extended above the woman's head, gripping the chain which clamped her wrists to the wall. Two more gaolers held her legs spread-eagled to aid their companion's rape.

'How dare you abuse her so!' Angel screamed, bringing down the ivory handle of her fan on to the warder's exposed buttocks. 'Bastard! Is that how you cure your patients?'

'That or the whip,' a bearded man holding one of the woman's legs said, stepping back. 'Keeps the loonies quiet.'

The man on top of the woman grunted as he reached his climax. Rolling to his feet he did not even trouble to turn his back as he adjusted his breeches. He smirked at Popinjay. 'Come to see the Grand Duchess 'ave yer? Likes to think she's royalty, she does. A bloke who 'ad 'er last week reckoned she used to be on the stage. He said the King had taken a fancy to 'er. Perhaps that's where she gets her grand notions. Ain't so proud now, is she? A shilling'll give yer entrance where the King took his ease.'

'Open yer legs, whore.' The warder turned to the woman who lay motionless, her eyes tightly shut. 'Open them, I say. Bloke 'ere wants ter dip 'is wick in yer loony's silken purse. Spread 'em, whore.'

'Duchess,' the woman said in a crackling voice. 'Archduchess!'

'Spread 'em, Duchess. That will cost him two shillings, to 'ave a loony duchess.' The warder laughed.

'Get out of here.' Popinjay sprang forward and grabbed the man by the throat.

The other two ruffians pounced on him and within seconds he was overpowered. When one lifted his foot to kick Popinjay in the groin, Angel shouted in outrage.

'Stop it! He has a warrant from the Mayor. He is to search this hellpit for an inmate. Lay a hand on him and you'll be arrested for assault!'

At once the three men drew back, their expressions cruel. One carried a wire whip which he cracked against the floor as they backed through the door.

'Hasn't this woman any clothing?' Angel called after them.

'Wot she need clothes for? Highest earning whore in 'ere, she is.'

Angel edged closer to the wooden bed and stared in disbelief at the white-haired woman. Despite the warder calling her the duchess, Angel could not believe that this was Maressa. She had already seen a man who believed he was Moses and a woman who screamed obscenities and declared she was Good Queen Bess. The woman on the bed was nothing like her sister. Her body was skeletal, and the sunken cheeks and swollen, cut lips and eyelids were those of a stranger. Angel turned away. Whoever the Duchess was it was not Maressa.

'We'll have some clothes sent to her,' Angel said heavily. 'And I shall report the way she's been used as a whore by those brutes to the city authorities.'

'Water! Water for the Archduchess!'

Angel saw a leather water jug and horn cup on the floor by the bed. Filling the cup, she held it to the woman's mouth. Amber eyes, slanted like a cat's, stared up at Angel, and shock made her spill the water over the woman's breast. A transformation came over the figure on the bed. She reared up, her lips curled back in a snarl. Foam flecked the corners of her mouth as she strained against the chains, snapping like a wild dog at Angel's hand. Angel jerked back to avoid the vicious bite, her legs shaking as she stared down at the snarling crazed figure of her sister.

'It is Maressa! We must get her out of here,' Angel gasped.

'That's not so easy once they've been committed.' Popinjay looked shaken. 'You sure it's your sister?'

'Positive.'

Popinjay sighed. 'I'll speak with the Head Keeper.'

A half hour later they left Bedlam without Maressa. Angel was shaking with anger.

'Damn the arrogance of the man. How can he keep her in such torment? I'll take care of her. I can make her well again.'

'It won't be that easy,' Popinjay reasoned. 'You heard what he said. Even the clergy believe the afflicted are stricken by the hand of God. Once committed, the inmates of Bedlam are kept restrained until God calls them to His mercy, or to their wits again.'

'Pish to that!' Angel flared. 'I'm not leaving her there. I'm going to the Mayor and then to the King if I have to.'

'But you know nothing of treating the insane.'

'I know enough not to keep a human being chained like a bear at the baiting, or whip it into submission. I'll take her to Rowan Hall. All she ever wanted was to be loved and admired. Alexander and I can give her that in plenty. There she'll recover.'

Once outside the grim building, Angel sat in the carriage hired by Popinjay and tears flowed down her cheeks. 'What if I cannot save her wits? What if she stays that way?'

'She will recover in time. When have you ever failed?' Popinjay said gently.

She shook her head. 'I fail all the time, my friend. I've made so many mistakes. Maressa hates me, and I'm to blame.'

Popinjay took his friend into his arms and rested his chin on top of her head. 'Maressa has always been jealous of you. You can't help that. You've survived so much – the terrors of war, plague, betrayal and persecution. Even Nathan's death. Not once has your spirit been broken.'

'Then I've never felt despair before. I do now. My faith in mankind is destroyed.'

'You're worn out from worry. You work for hours at the orphanage then spend half the night writing your plays. No one can keep up such a pace and not break under the strain.'

'But I have to work so hard.' Her voice shook with emotion. 'I daren't give myself time to think. To think about the bleakness of a future without Nathan . . . I miss him so much. The success of the orphanage is as important as my plays—' She broke off, unable to continue. A shudder passed through her body and she drew a deep, quivering breath. Forcing a shaky laugh, she said, 'Only fools dwell upon what might have been. I have my memories. And such memories . . . Fourteen years we were married, every one of them happy. And I have my son. In my heart Nathan still lives and that love gives me the strength to carry on. What is a few years without him on this earth when we will soon be together for all eternity? I have that faith, my dear friend. Life goes on. I do not regard my life as over because I no longer have at my side the only man I will ever love.'

Releasing Maressa from Bedlam was harder than Angel could have believed. Even the King could do nothing to interfere with the welfare of the insane. Angel paid ten pounds to the Keeper of the asylum to have Maressa well clothed and fed and for her chains to be lightened. She also demanded that her sister be kept apart from the other lunatics, and that the guards did not molest her. She then set about haranguing the city Justices for her sister's release.

Angel forced herself to make regular visits to Maressa, but her sister gave no sign of recognising her. If she went too close, the vacant look left her eyes to be replaced by a manic light. Years of festering jealousy had eaten away at her. It was not until Angel took Hazel on one of her visits that Maressa lost the wildness in her eyes. When Hazel spoke softly to her, Maressa allowed her to put an arm about her shoulders, and silent tears streamed down her haggard face.

The physician in charge stood in the doorway, watching. He nodded to Angel. He was a short barrel-chested man with a hooked nose, and a periwig too large for his small face. There was dispassion in his expression when he studied the

643

lunatics. He had hardened his heart against their suffering, resigned that nothing could be done for them that was not in God's mercy to provide.

'Never seen the Duchess so peaceful. This woman is a relative, perhaps?'

'She was her maid for twenty years and has always been devoted to my sister.'

The physician nodded. 'You say she's Maressa Mortimer – the nightingale of the playhouse some years ago.'

'She is.'

'I heard her sing once. A beautiful voice. She was beautiful. Never would have recognised that old hag as the same woman.'

'With good food, love and kindness,' Angel said firmly, 'Maressa will be beautiful and sane again.'

'Wife of Nathan Carver, aren't you?' the physician persisted.

'Yes.'

'Good man, Carver. Tragedy, his death. Started an orphanage, didn't you?'

'Yes.' Angel was fast losing patience with the man's interrogation.

The physician nodded sagely and looked back at Maressa, who now lay with her head in Hazel's lap. He cleared his throat. 'You spoke of taking your sister to live at the family estate in Wales. Would the maid accompany her?'

'Certainly. If anyone can restore my sister's wits it will be Hazel.'

'Your sister don't take kindly to you, Mistress Carver.'

'No. We're not as close as sisters should be. But we are family. Wales will provide the peace she needs to recover. My brother will ensure that.'

Angel looked at the adoration on Hazel's tear-streaked face. That was the love Maressa needed to help her recover. The love that no man could give her. Maressa was not a pauper either. Weeks of wrangling with the lawyers over Thomas's estate had brought to light a large sum of money at a goldsmith's in Richard Angel's name. With Richard dead, that money had reverted to his mother, Maressa. Once free from the asylum Maressa could live an independent life, in the luxury she desired.

Hazel looked over Maressa's head to Angel and the physician. 'Can I stay here with her? I can give her the care she needs. She's quiet now. I know she has to be better before she's released from here, but I can make her well.'

'Perhaps you can,' the physician replied. 'Would you agree to allow the maid to stay here, Mistress Carver?'

'I'll do anything to help my sister.'

'Then I suggest you return in a week. That will be the third of September. If there's an improvement in your sister's behaviour I'll reconsider the matter then.'

Angel slept little that week, lying awake for hours worrying about her sister. Once out of Bedlam, she was convinced that Maressa would recover her wits. She thumped her pillow in frustration. It was the early hours of Sunday 2nd September – one day before Maressa would be safely in her care. Hazel's last report had said that Maressa was greatly improved, and Angel did not doubt that she would be released on the morrow.

It was still dark as Angel stirred restlessly in her bed. She sat up and stared towards the window which was open to catch any breeze in this stiflingly hot summer. She frowned. There was an unnatural orange glow in the sky. During the week she had seen a comet blazing a fiery trail across the sky. Angel was not normally superstitious, but at the time she had recalled that a slow-moving comet had appeared before the outbreak of the plague, and she had been unable to stop a shiver of foreboding.

Rising from her bed, she went to the window. Towards the river near London Bridge a fire had broken out. It appeared to be a large one, for the flames had risen high in the sky, devouring the wooden houses dangerously dry after the long hot summer. Fortunately, it looked as if it was close to the waterworks on London Bridge, where the waterwheels drove a pump raising water from the river. It was then pumped through lead pipes over the tower of St Magnus's Church and along the wooden conduit pipes that ran up Fish Hill Street and Gracious Street. That was where the fire was brightest. No doubt it would all be under control by morning.

Fire was a constant threat in the narrow streets of timber-built houses, warehouses and large market halls. Over sixty years ago, during the reign of King James, a law had been passed that all buildings must be built of brick or stone. Such materials were expensive and in the poorer quarters the law had been ignored. Some of the houses did not even have slates or tiles on their roofs and any fire spread rapidly through the dry thatches. Last year King Charles had ordered the Mayor to imprison anyone who built a new house of timber, but still the law was disregarded.

Angel watched the fire for some minutes. Every now and then a flame billowed high into the sky as another roof caved in. The fire was close to the river which was lined with warehouses crammed with tar, canvas, brandy, oils, sea coal, fabrics and many more other volatile and highly flammable goods. Every inn and stableyard, of which there were many in that area, were filled with hay and straw, for the livestock. An easterly breeze made her hug her arms about her body. The first refreshing wind in days had chosen an ill moment to spring up.

Still Angel felt no undue alarm when she awoke the next morning to discover the fire still burning brightly. After breaking her fast she retired to Nathan's study to work for three hours on her latest play before visiting the orphanage. When one of the maids brought her a mid-morning tray of wine and cinnamon cakes, the woman was bursting with news of the fire after returning from market.

'I never did see such a blaze! Upwards of three hundred houses have burned and several churches. St Magnus's was gutted and with it the water pipes; the lead of the conduits melted. Also the waterworks have been destroyed and now some of the houses at the end of the bridge are alight. But they say the rest of the bridge is safe. It's terrible to see, Mistress Carver. Terrible! People running from their burning homes carrying what goods they can. The river's filled with wherries overloaded with people and their possessions. Some say people have jumped off the bridge to drown themselves after they lost their homes or businesses.'

'What's being done to halt it?' Angel asked, perturbed by this further tragedy to strike the city.

'Little that I could see. People are too busy trying to save what they can. No one thought it would get out of control like it has. When the Mayor was roused from his bed early this morning and he saw the burning buildings in Pudding Lane, he declared that a woman could piss it out.'

'I dare say he's now regretting his remark. Do they know what caused the fire?' Angel asked.

'It broke out in the King's bakery in Pudding Lane. The family had to escape across the roof, but one maidservant was too terrified to follow them, and she perished in the blaze. You should go see it, Mistress Carver. The flames are gobbling up the warehouses along the river front and the heat . . . I've never seen the like of it. Be something to tell my grandchildren.'

Angel put aside her quill and stood up. 'I'll take a boat to see the damage. Mr Sparrow has warehouses in that area and his house is close by in Cheapside. I would know he's safe.'

Out on the river Angel stared ahead at the great pall of black smoke rising over the city. It was beginning to blot out the sun. Wind fanned the bloody jaws of the flames as they devoured steeples and towers. Even from the river, the roar of the inferno and the thundering crash of falling walls was deafening. Everywhere women and children screamed. Was this how Sodom looked on the day of its destruction? Whole streets were in flames. As she watched there was an upsurge of flames and with a dragon-like roar several houses linked together tumbled like playing cards.

Barges filled with cargo moored at the wharves were on fire. Small craft loaded with furniture and people bobbed precariously in the turbulent waters close to the bridge. The air was heavy with the smell of burning tar, tallow from the candlemakers, and malt from the breweries. The smell of roast meats was overpowering from the butchers, slaughter-houses and stables where not all the livestock escaped. Several people with their hair or clothes on fire leapt into the Thames and were rescued by lightermen. Both of Popinjay's warehouses by the river were ablaze, and as Angel's wherry came closer, she saw the tall figure of her friend signalling for a boatman.

She ordered the ferryman to take Popinjay on board and when several other desperate people tried to come with him, the small craft rocked precariously. A large woman slammed her elbow into Angel's chest as she struggled to find a seat.

'We can take no more,' the ferryman yelled, pushing off from the steps.

Two men began fighting and both fell into the river. One swam towards the wherry as it edged further from the bank, but the ferryman whacked him across the shoulders as he gripped the craft's side, almost upsetting everyone into the water.

'There ain't no room. Would you drown us all?' he shouted.

Angel was squashed up against the wherry's sides, as Popinjay sat down beside her. His clothing was thick with soot and in several places his velvet jacket was burnt. His white hair was singed and frizzled around his ears and his face streaked with smoke and sweat.

'I'm sorry, John,' she said, coughing against a gust of dense smoke. 'Have you lost everything?'

'Less than most poor wretches,' he answered wearily. 'I've still my warehouses in Bristol, Plymouth and Dover. I'm going on to Whitehall. The King must be told of the extent of the fire. Something must be done. There's panic and confusion everywhere. All the wells are low in water after the summer drought. Houses should be blown up to stop the spread of the fire. But no one wants to risk it. They all fear being made responsible for the cost of rebuilding. But this fire will not burn itself out until all London is consumed. The wind is spreading it and there's no chance of rain.'

Angel feared he was right. Even here in the middle of the river the heat from the fire scorched their faces. Angel scanned the blackened, frightened faces in the small craft. A preacher clutched a few pieces of church plate. A woman hugged a parrot cage to her breast and a broken Venetian glass vase. Another, naked except for her shift, carried a set of ivory-backed hairbrushes and a worthless tin kettle. It was odd the possessions people grabbed in a panic. The river was choked with vessels. Bundles of clothing and small coffers dropped in people's flights floated amongst the water craft. On top of one box, a terrified kitten mewled in its fear, but the current was too swift and the kitten too far away for Angel to attempt to save it. There were also a great many blackened bodies of pigeons in the water. The birds, loath to leave their roosts, hovered until their wing feathers burnt and they fell from the sky.

'John, do you think the orphanage will be safe? Should I move the children?'

Her friend scanned the burning skyline before answering. 'The wind is veering . . . The flames are still a couple of streets away from St Paul's. Though if they reach the Tower where the gunpowder is stored . . . ? Could be we'll all be blown to Kingdom-come. Keep the children where they are for the moment.'

Before Angel alighted she made Popinjay promise to return to her house later. It was safer than his in Cheapside which was in the path of the flames.

'I can't promise, Angel. If there's firefighting to be done, I must do what I can.'

When Angel attended church that Sunday she was surprised at the mass of people filling the building. In the fields just visible from her house, tents were springing up like mushrooms as people fled from the fire to safety outside the city walls.

It was impossible to sleep that night. The red glowing sky was brighter than midday. Popinjay did not come to the house, and as Angel looked out on the city from an attic window she saw that flames had spread the length of the vast thoroughfare of Cheapside. The roof of the great cathedral of St Paul's was alight. She could not help worrying about the children, but the orphanage was outside the city walls and there was a vast expanse of fields between them. The orphanage roofs were of thatch, and in the stiff wind sparks soared like flaming arrows starting small fires. There had briefly been a stable on fire across the river at Southwark, where the wind had carried burning brands. But, as Angel watched, it was brought quickly under control. For the moment she judged the orphanage safe, but she ordered all the fire buckets brought up from the cellar and filled with water from the well. The menservants were ordered to stand guard and douse any windblown sparks that might land on the building.

Precautions taken, Angel ordered three mares saddled, and prepared to ride through the fields on the north side of the city walls to reach Bedlam. Today Maressa was due to be released, and the fire in the city was not going to stop that.

Popinjay could feel his skin scorching from the inferno's

heat. His body ached from the torture of overused muscles, as he used long firehooks to pull down smouldering thatch. Men around him doused it with water or beat out the flames with wet sacking. Nearby, unrecognisable from the blackened grime which covered his fine clothes, worked the King. In another part of the city laboured James, Duke of York, and the sixteen-year-old Duke of Monmouth, the King's oldest illegitimate son. Though Popinjay ached in every limb, he could not flag when his sovereign worked so tirelessly.

He had reached Whitehall some time after Samuel Pepys had already warned the King of the fire's progress. But he had been amongst the first sent back with orders to get the gunpowder from the Tower and blow up whole streets in a bid to form a fire-break. That had been hours ago. Now most of the great landmarks of the city were gone: the Royal Exchange with its elegant shops, wealthy merchants' halls and many of the ancient churches. Even St Paul's was now a gutted shell. The lead had melted from its roof and its crashing masonry had sent pieces of stone shooting out like deadly firecrackers into the streets below, injuring several firefighters.

To look up at the sky was to look into hell's kitchen, furnace-hot and skin blistering. Popinjay worked on. Frequently he jumped out of the way of falling chimney-stacks. He strained his arms hauling water buckets. His voice was raw from yelling warnings as rows of houses were ready to be blown up. He carried injured children to safety and calmed screaming mothers. His eyes streaming from the smoke he held back a frenzied father whose child was still within a burning house, with no hope of rescue. He skinned his elbows and knees clambering over piles of broken furniture thrown from windows and missing the wagons which would have taken them away from the flames. Everywhere were burst sacks and boxes as people tried to save their goods from the fire, and the firefighters were impeded by the press of baggage carts leaving the city. They also faced the danger of being trampled by cattle and horses freed from their stalls, the animals stampeding in their panic.

Throughout, Popinjay hardened his heart against the cries of the wounded – some from burns, others from broken limbs as they fell from a roof or jumped from an upper window to escape the flames. The wails of the homeless was pitiful. The sacking and pillage of emptied houses by brigands was lamentable. At seeing a thief emerging with a sack of stolen goods from the house of one of his friends, Popinjay laid him out cold with his fist.

Molten lead ran along the central kennels in many streets and the cobbles were so hot no man could walk along them. Occasionally a charred body was found – the old or crippled, knocked down by the rush of panicking citizens. Everywhere was the crash of falling masonry and wooden beams, and the occasional clang of a church bell ringing its own death-knell as it toppled to the ground.

Finally beaten by exhaustion, Popinjay swayed. He wiped his sweating brow on his sleeve and staggered back from the raging wall of flame. His strength was gone. If he did not rest, his weary body would also be swallowed up by the fire. Stumbling to the nearest water-steps he joined the slow-moving queue of people shouting for 'Oars' – the cry to summon a boatman. Few boats were available and as the fire progressed along the waterfront people scrambled from one set of water-steps on to the next. Finally aboard a craft, Popinjay sagged down in its helm. His head rolled back and he stared for a long moment up at the sky. Yellow and black smoke covered it like a canopy and when a glimmer of sky could be seen he was startled to see by its blueness that it was daylight. He levered himself up and stared back at the burning capital. The fire raged as virulently as ever. Mounds of smoking rubble covered vast areas where timbered houses had once stood, and only a few stone skeletons of church towers and blackened brick walls remained standing.

It took a day of arguing to gain Maressa's release. There was a slyness in the manner of the Head Keeper which warned Angel that something other than Maressa's state of mind was keeping her a prisoner here. Angel remained adamant that her sister was well enough to leave. She argued. She threatened. She pleaded. Nothing moved the man in whose fate Maressa's future lay. When the King's name was mentioned in connection with freeing Maressa, he began to waver. Finally, a bribe opened the man's mouth. He was being paid by a lawyer to keep Maressa here. Another bribe gave her

651

the lawyer's name, and further payment, guaranteed to satisfy his greed, ensured Maressa's release.

In the week since Angel had last seen her sister Hazel had performed little short of a miracle. A special brew of herbs had calmed the wildness in Maressa's eyes and carefully applied cosmetics hid the worst ravages to her beauty. In a blonde, fashionably coiffeured wig and an olive green satin gown, Maressa looked almost her old self. Her illness had given her an aloofness which was regal, but the sparkle had gone from her amber eyes. That sparkle would return one day, Angel vowed.

With the fire still raging, Angel decided not to leave London in case the orphanage was affected. When she reached her house in Lincoln's Inn Fields she found Popinjay slumped over the table asleep.

On the Tuesday morning the fire still burned and Angel's concern for the orphanage mounted. It had leapt the city walls, and even the Fleet River had not stopped its hungry passage. Now Whitehall and Lincoln's Inn lay directly in its path. The smoke blew in choking gusts across the open fields, sparks like fireflies settling on thatch and grass. The militia was marched into the city from Hertfordshire, Middlesex and Kent and fire posts were established to try and keep the fire at bay. By the evening it seemed that nothing would stop the conflagration. An arc of flame lit the sky from the Temple in the west to Smithfields and St Giles Cripplegate in the north. It was only halted from reaching the Tower in the east by blowing up the nearby buildings.

Angel gathered the children into the courtyard, each with a bundle of clothing to carry. The road to the west was packed with baggage carts and fleeing people. No one had dreamed it could reach such proportions. London was a blazing funeral pyre, cleansed at last of centuries of accumulated filth and gloomy fetid alleyways. It was a pile of blackened rubble, unrecognisable, gutted, a few church towers standing like skeletal fingers pointing heavenwards in accusation of their destruction. St Paul's – its glass windows shattered, the roof gone and the walls perilously close to collapse – stood like a blinded queen, stripped naked and exposed before her subjects, awaiting the final blow from the headsman's axe before a new soul could be reborn.

Angel looked anxiously at Maressa sitting on a wall. Her sister's stare was vacant as she watched the burning capital. Hazel stood behind her, a comforting hand on her mistress's shoulder. What if Maressa suddenly took it into her head to run again? How could Angel go after her when she had nearly sixty children to organise?

As she watched she saw Maressa take Hazel's hand and hold it tightly, and breathed a sigh of relief. Hazel was Maressa's anchor, more binding than any chain. Then, while Angel began to count the children to ensure all were present, the wind died down. She paused. From this distance the roar of the flames was like thunder, yet the blaze had lost its fierceness and the flames seemed to be receding.

'Go back to your beds, children,' she ordered. 'The danger is past. The fire is no longer advancing.'

It was another week before Angel, Popinjay, Maressa, and Hazel set out for Wales. It had taken another three days before all the flames had been doused and the city still smouldered in places. The fire had been visible sixty miles from London. Already people were returning. Like ants, they clambered over the still-hot rubble and began carting the debris from the streets. Temporary market-stalls were set up outside the walls and the citizens resumed their business. It was reported that thirteen thousand houses, nearly ninety churches and fifty or more great company halls had been destroyed, but surprisingly there had been very few deaths.

There was even a cheerful atmosphere as the people worked. The stalwart Londoners who had survived the ravages of the plague last year were too resilient to have their spirits broken by the fire. Already, they were speaking of the grand new capital which would be built. The old London with its filthy streets and disease was no more. This was a time of rebirth and fresh hope. These dreams were echoed in Angel's heart as she set off for Wales.

Chapter Twenty-Six

London, 1667
It was Angel's fortieth birthday and, though it was supposed to be a secret, she knew that the family planned a surprise celebration for her. There were abrupt lulls in conversation whenever she entered a room. When her nieces and nephews turned up unexpectedly in London their eyes were alight with mischief. Alexander insisted he was here to sell horses and at first she had believed him. Then the suppressed air of conspiracy began. Angel, unwilling to disappoint her family, acted as though she noticed nothing.

Since her latest play, *A Knave Bedazzled*, was to have its first performance this afternoon she assumed her surprise celebration would be awaiting her at the house when she returned. When Hazel urged that she put on her best gown of ruby velvet she did not demur. Alexander had taken Maressa out earlier in the carriage and they would later attend the performance. A year in Wales had restored Maressa's wits and vivacity, but there was still a shadow lurking in the depths of her eyes which dismayed Angel. She was still not as close to her sister as she would have wished. Perhaps they never would be in total harmony. Maressa clearly resented Angel's success as a playwright.

Popinjay had traced the lawyer who had been paying to keep Maressa in Bedlam. From him they learned that the Archduke Frederick had died in a duel in France. His uncle's family, ashamed of Maressa's past, was paying to keep her out of the world's eye. Since then a settlement had been made which returned most of Maressa's money squandered by Frederick during their marriage. Together with the money she had inherited from her son, Maressa was a wealthy woman now. Yet with each passing week it became more obvious to Angel that Maressa wanted more than comfort. Even the adulation lavished on her by her family was no longer enough to satisfy her. Hunger for admiration and praise had been her sister's downfall, but how was it possible to stifle such a need?

Pushing her fears aside, Angel went to the nursery before leaving for the theatre. Matthew was playing with his cousins. At four, he was a bright boy with an enquiring mind, already able to read and do simple sums. He was a happy child, caring and affectionate to others. But there was a dare-devilment in his nature and a teasing light in his eyes which was so like Nathan it often made Angel catch her breath. Matthew was playing with Alisaundre, building a house out of wooden blocks for Emmy to knock down. Emmy was pale and in the last year was often listless from her illness. She looked up as Angel entered and held out her arms for a cuddle. As Angel embraced her she smiled at Alisaundre. The child had all Beth's practicality and sweetness. Thérèse's three girls were watched over by their nurse. They were all mild-tempered like their mother with none of the wild streak inherited from their father. Had the devil's brood finally been tamed?

No, never tamed, but perhaps tempered. Alexander's three eldest children, Marcus, Lizbet and Bryan were all married. Marcus was an architect and Bryan a lawyer. Lizbet lived at Rowan Hall with her husband, and since they were both devoted to continuing the Rowan strain it had been agreed by the family that she would inherit the Hall. Wyn, the youngest of Alexander and Beth's sons, was studying science at Oxford. Of Maressa's surviving children, Sir Julian Mortimer was one of the Duke of Monmouth's companions at court. He was married to a plain but wealthy heiress and content with his dissolute life. Thomasine had escaped from her banishment in Ireland while Viscount Lymeton awaited his divorce. She had gone to Paris and, knowing of Angel's life there, had introduced herself to Molière. Angel's old friend was now a famous playwright and frequently his players entertained King Louis. Thomasine was accepted as an actress in his company and it was rumoured that she was the mistress of a French count. The scandal had been the talk of London. Maressa had been appalled at her daughter's conduct, but Angel had smiled at the news. Thomasine had all the ambition and wildness of her Angel blood.

Fortune had smiled on the family since the fire. Apart from Maressa's recovery, Alexander had been knighted for his loyalty to the Royalist cause. Since the Restoration, Alexander had been petitioning for the return of Oakfield Manor from Douglas Fairburn. Unfortunately, Fairburn had seen the Restoration coming and had adroitly supported it after the death of Oliver Cromwell. Nevertheless, His Majesty had insisted that Fairburn pay Alexander recompense for the estate, and a generous sum had been awarded. To increase the status of the family six Rowan horses graced the royal stables, ensuring the popularity of the strain.

Later, as Angel drove to the Cockpit in her carriage, she stared up at the mass of scaffolding around the newly rising buildings. Everywhere was the clamour of hammers and shouts from the masons. The new churches, many designed by Christopher Wren, were beginning to rise from the ashes. Houses and grand company halls were all built in brick and stone to safeguard against further fires again laying waste to the capital. The street-sellers cheerfully cried their wares, and though the streets were still filled with beggars, there was generally a brighter air of expectancy and hope.

She arrived at the theatre shortly before the performance was to begin, and as soon as she entered the building she was aware of suppressed excitement. There had been a press of people outside the entrance, but ten minutes before the play was to begin Angel stood in the wings, dismayed to see that though the pit and upper gallery were full, the lower galleries remained empty.

Shoulders slumping, she turned to see Nell Gwynne eyeing her with merriment. The young girl who used to sell herrings outside Drury Lane had first appeared on the stage eighteen months ago. In *A Knave Bedazzled* Angel had written a small comedy part especially for her.

'Looks like you'll not be having your first comedy role before much of an audience, Nell. Maybe I'm not so popular nowadays.'

'Yer plays be the best there is, Mistress Carver. Why, I wouldn't be surprised if the King didn't show up – it being yer birthday an' all.'

'And what would His Majesty know of a humble play-wright's birthday?' Angel laughed, her disappointment fading in the wake of Nell's cheery smile.

'Well, you ain't jes' any playwright. The King loved you once, so I heard. Wot was it like, Mistress Carver, being loved by a King?'

'I wouldn't know, Nell. He was only a prince then.'

'That was before he met Lucy Walters and she gave him his son Monmouth, wasn't it?' Nell persisted. 'But she didn't treat him right. She were like that haughty bitch Castlemaine. You'd think the mistress of a king would be a kinder person.'

Angel laughed, despite the impropriety of Nell's questions. It was not kindness which kept Barbara Palmer, Countess of Castlemaine, his favourite for so many years, it was sensuality.

'If ever I'm lucky enough to attract the King's eye,' Nell said, her eyes glowing, 'I wouldn't flaunt me airs and graces. I'd love him as a man deserves to be loved.'

'Then I hope you win the King's favour. Indeed, I think you'd make him happy.'

Several actresses joined Angel in the wings to peer into the theatre and were disgruntled at seeing the Royal Box empty.

'Peg, it don't look like your love-sick Prince is coming,' an actress giggled. 'Guess I've lost me bet that Prince Rupert won't be carrying you off with him tonight. Can't understand what you see in the old warhorse. He's still handsome enough in a dark, brooding sort of way, but he's got such a prickly temper. Reckon Buckingham was jesting when he said the Prince was taken with you. Never known royalty backwards in coming forwards when a pretty woman takes their eye.'

'His Highness is not like the King or his brother,' a low sultry voice answered, 'or indeed most of the nobles who visit the tiring room.'

Angel turned to regard the blushing Peg Hughes, and her curiosity was pricked. Peg was a pretty actress, and one of the first to perform on the stage after the Restoration. She had been in only three of Angel's plays and today she was taking the lead.

She was a vivacious young woman, talented and full of high-spirits, and Angel liked her. She had thought that Peg was the mistress of Sir Charles Sedley. But if Rupert was interested . . . ? A spark of devilment rose in Angel's breast. She had not seen Rupert for months, and then only for a brief talk when they met by chance, riding through St James's Park. Then he had looked strained and pale after defeating the Dutch in a sea battle. It had surprised her that he had never married, and she suspected that he never would now. There were times when Rupert took himself and life too seriously. He needed a mistress as warm-hearted and vivacious as Peg. And the way the young actress was blushing proved that she was not immune to the Prince.

From the theatre an unexpected cheer went up. Angel's heart raced with excitement as the King, the Duke of York, Prince Rupert, Monmouth and a score of noblemen and ladies took their places. So many courtiers filed into the boxes that many of the men were forced to stand to make room for the ladies.

The musicians struck up and the stage manager called the players to their places. Throughout the performance Angel remained in the wings, her throat working against a lump of emotion at the laughter coming from the Royal Box. At one time the King was forced to hold his side and twice she saw him dab at his eyes, so great was his merriment. Whenever Peg Hughes came on stage, Angel saw Prince Rupert lean forward in his seat, his interest in the actress apparent.

As the play ended to tumultuous applause and the players took their bows the musicians struck up an unscheduled tune. It was the ballad which Maressa had made famous before she left the stage. Then, to Angel's astonishment, Maressa's sweet voice filled the playhouse from high in the heavens. From above the players' heads a golden chariot was being lowered – and Maressa was sitting inside. Her beauty restored, she was radiant in a gown of silver tissue and diamonds sparkled in her blonde wig.

A hush fell over the audience as the song rose to its crescendo. When it finished Maressa stepped from the chariot and came towards Angel, to draw her out of the wings. To see Maressa vibrant and glowing with excitement again was the best birthday present Angel could have had.

'Today is Angel Carver's birthday.' Maressa drew her sister to the front of the stage as she spoke. 'This play, her finest yet, is staged in her honour. Let us all raise a cheer for

Angel. Her talent has made everyone here forget the cares of state, or the struggle of survival. A salute to Angel Carver, the leading woman playwright of our age!'

The cheers were deafening and the applause so loud that Angel could not speak for the joy choking her throat.

'Speech!' someone from the pit cried. The shout was taken up and echoed by a hundred voices around the theatre.

Angel, smiling, put her fingers to her cheeks and felt the wetness of happy tears.

'I think for the first time in my life I'm at a loss for words,' she said at last, her voice quivering.

There was a loud crack of laughter from both Prince Rupert and the King. With a typical flamboyant and courtly gesture, Charles Stuart leaned forward and tossed her a gold jewel-studded pomander. She caught it and lifted it to her face to smell its perfume.

'*Tout est possible*, Angel. Everything is possible,' the King declared. 'May this birthday be both memorable and merry for you.'

'It will be the most memorable ever,' she laughed, sinking into a deep curtsy with applause and cheers ringing in her ears.

In the tiring room Angel was surrounded by laughing wellwishers. Every actor and actress had a small gift for her, and when Peg Hughes pressed a phial of her favourite perfume into her hand, Angel kissed the girl's cheek with great affection.

'I need no gift from you, Peg. You were superb in the role of the seductress. One would almost think you were trying to seduce someone in the audience from the way you put such feeling into the role.'

Peg blushed and the colour in her cheeks deepened as she looked towards the doorway. The King had just entered with Prince Rupert, who was holding a wriggling white spaniel puppy.

Angel was still clutching the jewelled pomander given to her by the King and again she spread her skirts to curtsy. Her hand was instantly taken and she was raised up to look into the King's dark smiling face.

His voice was slow and intimate. 'Don't ever stop writing your plays. I cannot remember when I last laughed so hard.

Though I wonder if it's not perilously close to treason to give your King a pain in his side from too much laughter.'

Rupert added his voice. 'Laughter is said to be a gift from the gods. What else would you expect from the pen of an Angel?'

Angel smiled at them both, warmed by the compliments of her two royal lovers. 'My name has been linked more with the devil than with God.'

The King winked. 'Ah, but then, my dear, fallen angels are always the most interesting ones.' Without ceremony he stooped to kiss her cheek, giving her hand an affectionate squeeze before joining an impatiently scowling Lady Castlemaine. Briefly, Angel saw Nell Gwynne pouting at the King's departure. Then with an impudent flick of her skirts she set out to charm another nobleman.

'You'll get your turn, Nelly Gwynne,' Angel said beneath her breath. 'Charles Stuart will not remain blind to your mischievous charm for long.'

Rupert remained at her side and she smiled at the struggling puppy in his arms. 'He reminds me of Boy,' she remarked. 'Just his white colouring.'

Rupert smiled and held out the spaniel. 'A birthday present for you. I heard that Bella had died recently. His name is Blanco. May he comfort you as you once comforted a disconsolate prince.'

Angel took the puppy, laughing as it licked her face. 'I shall treasure his companionship as I treasured the company of his master.'

For a moment their eyes held, each with pleasant memories of their affair. Rupert favoured her with a smile, and stayed at her side, strangely ill at ease in the company of the actors. When she saw his attention was drawn to Peg Hughes who was surrounded by several noblemen, Angel called to a maid to hold Blanco. She, who had never feared to act boldly, linked her arm through Rupert's and, as she drew him into a secluded corner, called out, 'A word, Peg, if you please.'

She kept her arm through Rupert's, though she felt him tense at the forwardness of her action. When Peg joined them, her expression glowing with pleasure, Angel released his arm.

'Your Highness, Mistress Hughes. Mistress Hughes, His

Highness Prince Rupert of the Rhine, Count Palatine, Duke of Cumberland, Earl of . . .' She laughed. 'I've forgotten the rest of his titles. I'm sure he will be happy to dispense with formality . . .' Her voice trailed off as she saw that neither of them were paying much attention. Their gazes were caught in the age-old way of newly discovered lovers, and without another word Angel left them alone. It was the start of an affair that was to last twenty years until Rupert's death.

Angel was embraced by Popinjay. 'The play will be another great success for you, Angel. The public adore you. Not to mention a prince or two.'

'I have been fortunate in my friends – especially you. You've never failed me, Popinjay.' She laughed. 'I'm sorry, John. I really should stop calling you that.'

'Don't you dare. It keeps me young, and reminds me of the adventures of long ago – and talking of popinjays.' He picked up a huge object draped in scarlet silk. 'Happy Birthday, Angel.'

When she drew the silk cloth aside she saw a red and blue popinjay in a cage. She laughed softly. 'A pale replica to my own dear popinjay, but a wonderfully thoughtful gift.'

'Just so you don't forget me.' His expression sobered. 'I'm sailing to Venice again. I may not be back for a year.'

'Isn't it time you let the grass settle under your feet? You're not as young as you were.'

'I'd rather die at sea than snug in my bed, and I miss the intrigue of old. There's still a big world out there – I want to explore it.'

'And when you return you will tell me all about it?'

'You will be the first I call upon, as always, my dear friend.'

Hapless, now famous for his comedy roles, presented Angel with an ivory sailing ship as he joined Popinjay at her side. At thirty, he was a handsome, self-confident man, dressed in the height of fashion with a long, fair, curling wig.

'I'm leaving the stage, Angel,' he announced. 'Thanks to the wonderful parts you have created for me I've been able to save enough money to become John's partner. I'm to be a respectable merchant now.'

'I wish you well. Do you sail with John?'

Hapless looked abashed. 'Sadly no. I'm a poor sailor. I'm

looking after the warehouses whilst he's at sea.'

'Will you miss the stage, Hapless?'

There was a sparkle in his eye. 'Likely so, but it's a hard life and not a very profitable one unless you attract the eye of the King. Alas, he has no fancy for his own sex. I'll make my fortune quicker in trade.'

Alexander interrupted and drew Angel aside. 'This is the first chance I've had to speak with you all day. Didn't I always say you'd be a famous playwright? Gabriellen would have been proud of you.'

'No less than she and Mark would be of you.' She gazed adoringly into her brother's eyes. His hair was streaked with grey and the long wet Welsh winters had eaten into his bones so that now he leaned heavily on a walking-cane. 'The Rowan horses continue to be the finest in the land,' she went on. 'We have both made our mark, Sir Alexander Rowan.'

He turned to look at Maressa and sighed. 'She doesn't give up. I'll give our sister that.'

Angel followed his gaze and was surprised to see her flirting with a grey-haired man no taller than her shoulder, and in his eyes was the adoration Angel had seen so many times before. When the man moved away Maressa joined them.

'Another heart you've stolen, Maressa,' Alexander teased. 'What do you do with them all?'

'He's an earl,' Maressa said wistfully. 'Owns two castles and four manor houses and is one of the King's advisers. He spends most of his time at Court. That's always the life I've craved.'

'Haven't you had your fill of noblemen?' Angel saw that the light of battle was back in her sister's amber eyes. 'Maressa, don't even think on it,' she said, hastily. 'You don't even like men.'

'But he's old.' Maressa's voice was low and conspiratorial. 'And wealthy. He doesn't want someone to warm his bed. He has two fine strapping sons and four grandsons already. He wants a wife to bring happiness to his declining years. A woman with charm and beauty.'

Angel sighed. 'Maressa, do you never stop your scheming?'

'I'm an Angel, sister. Thomas taught me that. Take life in both hands and live it to the full. That's what you did. Why should I settle for less? But what of you, Angel?

There're three or four noblemen here you could marry.'

'I'll not marry again. Though that does not mean I may not take an occasional lover. I have the orphanage and my writing to fulfil my life. For two centuries since the time of our ancestor Wildboar Tom Angel, our name Angel has been infamous. No matter how far we fall, we will always rise and defeat our oppressors. Has that not always been so?'